Mis-fits Anonymous

◈

Mr. E

NEWMAN SPRINGS PUBLISHING
320 Broad Street
Red Bank, NJ 07701

First originally published by Newman Springs Publishing 2019

ISBN 978-1-64096-850-9 (Paperback)
ISBN 978-1-64096-851-6 (Digital)

Printed in the United States of America

Dedicated to Bob Newhart, whose comedic spirit has been a tremendous inspiration to the creation of this book.

Prologue

DR. PENDLETON STARED ABSENTLY THROUGH the plate glass window, observing the late afternoon sun struggle to assert itself against a mass of unthreatening yet abundant clouds. The neutral sky was a deep blue, one of the last true vestiges of summer to be seen as autumn slowly moved in to take its place. It was September.

Below this seasonal battle, the murky outline of the city disrupted the otherwise watercolor-like effect of the sky, its unceasing brown smudge of pollution more like that created by a smearing crayon. The contrast served to convert Dr. Pendleton's quietude back into a more attentive stance as he realized that he was being addressed by the gentleman across the desk from him.

"I...I beg your pardon," he stammered slightly.

Dr. Whittaker also glanced toward the window, looking out at the city's skyline thoughtfully. "Yes, these offices do afford a remarkable view, don't they?" he mused with appreciation, before once more focusing on Dr. Pendleton. "I was saying that I was curious as to where you might hold your meeting," he repeated, his bold and yet mellow voice enunciating almost musically.

Blinking, Dr. Pendleton appeared to be considering the question and then nodded suddenly, seeming to remember what they had been discussing.

"Oh...Yes, I...I've gone ahead and rented a space... It's, uh... an old union hall. So, of course, it will come with, uh...chairs and such...," he explained haltingly. "The owner assured me that it would more than suffice for what I had in mind. In fact, I've gone ahead and paid for six weeks in advance, for its use..."

He nodded with confidence he did not feel, glancing at Dr. Whittaker as if for confirmation that this was a good idea, having been describing it while directing his gaze anywhere but toward his listener.

Dr. Whittaker merely leaned back, the sumptuous chair in which he sat assimilating so well with his bearing and form that it might well have been custom-made for him. Usually, when they met, they sat in a pair of wing chairs situated to one side of the office. Today, however, Dr. Pendleton preferred having the desk between them, finding that the formality it created gave their meeting a renewed sense of purpose and professionalism, even though the seating arrangement was most likely of little priority to Dr. Whittaker. In fact, it struck Dr. Pendleton that the gentleman opposite him could exact an air of distinction wherever he sat or stood, for that matter. With his graying, precisely trimmed Van Dyke beard and neatly swept-back tufts of nearly white hair, his scholarly eyes peering unwaveringly over the gold-rimmed, half-moon reading glasses perched regally on his narrow Roman nose, Dr. Lionel Whittaker emanated an auspiciously elegant and intellectual persona, one that somehow enabled him to "resemble" his profession.

Dr. Pendleton, however, over ten years younger but nevertheless solidly in the middle-aged bracket, seemed to be everything that Dr. Whittaker was not. He was short, neither stocky nor slender, merely just...there. He had a round, clean-shaven face; lifelessly receding brown hair; and larger, rather clunky, reading glasses, plastic, which while magnifying script for him simultaneously enlarged the drooping crevices beneath each of his small, blinking eyes. Even their smiles differed—Dr. Whittaker's was loose and free, quick to spread widely and reveal gleaming white teeth, while Dr. Pendleton's was fleeting and nervous, a bland expression between a small nose and weak chin. He fought the urge to sigh.

"It can certainly be prudent to pay one's rent in advance," Dr. Whittaker returned at length, withdrawing a beautifully carved pipe from a vest pocket.

Dr. Pendleton stared at the pipe, distracted as he watched the older man begin to fill it with an aromatic tobacco from a small pouch he withdrew from his other vest pocket, his long narrow fingers moving deftly, not spilling so much as a fiber. He lit it, inhaling and leaning even further into the recesses of the chair, blowing the smoke discreetly to one side and offering a profile view of his dignified frame.

As the pervasive yet fragrant pipe smoke filled the office, Dr. Pendleton could only look on in silent contemplation, his eyes drifting to Dr. Whittaker's attire. He was dressed in a conservative gray suit with a white vest, a burgundy necktie angled neatly from a narrow, stylish collar, its half-Windsor knot held in place by a dapper collar bar. Each article was neatly pressed and free of wrinkles, dust, and lint, not even a stray hair lay upon his sloping shoulders.

The Charles Pendleton look, by contrast, seemed to be brown—a light-brown sports coat and dark brown slacks and a tan dress shirt and rumpled knit tie, also brown, arranged in a hasty four-in-hand knot. (He had never been able to remember how to tie it in any other way.)

On his feet, he wore stodgy brown slip-on penny loafers. He glanced down at them, knowing that, although the monumental desk obstructed his view, somewhere beyond it lurked Dr. Whittaker's tapered, gleaming cordovan wing tips. His face creased in a meek grimace, a particularly glum expression on his round visage. He blinked once or twice, sensing a bit of depression asserting itself.

Dr. Whittaker had turned his attention back to Dr. Pendleton, clearing his throat swiftly. "Have you set up a date and time for your first meeting?" he inquired casually, his trim, swirling eyebrows lifting toward the other doctor as he continued to smoke his pipe.

Dr. Pendleton's grimace vanished as he sat up in his own uncomfortable chair, gesturing loosely with his hands. "Oh yes, definitely," he replied, clearing his own throat and managing a smile, feeling a hint of confidence. "Uh…It's going to be about a week and a half from now, uh, Tuesday evening, at around seven o'clock. That way, it will give everyone time to have their dinner and…well, whatever all they might need to take care of beforehand," he added, nodding for emphasis.

His own smile flourishing, Dr. Whittaker nodded back at him, holding the bowl of his pipe poised between thumb and forefinger.

"Good foresight," he concurred approvingly.

Beaming slightly, Dr. Pendleton nodded once more, his gaze then falling upon Dr. Whittaker's long, trimmed, almost aristocratically nubile fingers, and then lowering to his own squat, pudgy, rather commonplace hands. He bunched them together in his lap.

"And how are you planning to inform people of the meeting?" Dr. Whittaker asked only seconds later, perhaps hoping to avoid another lengthy respite in their conversation.

Looking up from his hands, somewhat startled, Dr. Pendleton blinked rapidly. "Oh well, I've…I've decided to utilize a…direct approach, as it were…," he explained, his voice wavering diffidently. "I'm going to make use of…flyers…paper advertisements…pinned up in various prominent locations…" He paused, attempting to exact an air of assertion, struggling to sit up in his overwhelming chair and becoming even further engulfed.

Dr. Whittaker nodded once, his eyebrows lifting encouragingly, bidding Dr. Pendleton to continue.

His confidence resurfacing slightly, Dr. Pendleton eagerly grasped the neatly folded document he had set to one side of the desk, quickly unfolding it, speaking all the while. "Yes…you see… contrary to the, uh, the attendance of most sessions of this type… I'm not planning on having a lot of people show up. I didn't put an ad in the paper or organize some kind of radio or TV commercial. Well, I don't really have the money for either… But you see…I don't actually want too large a turnout, uh, because I feel it would, uh…compromise the individual attention…" He paused, inhaling deeply, having spoken his explanation very briefly, as if it were a timed response. He held up the flyer, which was a slightly off-center photocopy of large, block letters, hand-printed on a sheet of vividly bright green paper.

Dr. Whittaker accepted it, glancing over it briefly and passing it back, withdrawing his pipe from his mouth. "That should more than suffice to inform people of your meeting," he stated meaningfully.

Dr. Pendleton's dry little smile bloomed outrightly at this remark, lasting for several seconds as he hastily continued his description.

"I had one hundred of these flyers printed on this color of paper. The girl at the copy store said that a lot of advertisements are made with it…because it sort of…you know, grabs people's attention."

He nodded in vigorous approval of the notion. "Yes, it was either, uh…'neon green' or 'violent violet'…which was, uh, more of a…dark purple color…I chose the green because it was brighter, more cheerful." He read over the flyer, appearing genuinely pleased with himself.

Nodding his majestic head slowly, Dr. Whittaker laid his hands upon the arms of his chair. "Yes, I agree. It is a very arresting shade of green. I'm certain that it will capture the attention of everyone who sees it," he declared encouragingly, leaning forward slightly in the seat.

This action, subtle that it was, served to unnerve Dr. Pendleton, his smile diminishing pensively. He stole a glance at his wristwatch, abruptly clearing his throat and speaking quickly as he began to refold the bright-green flyer.

"Of course"—he went on, his tone more subdued—"I am hoping for a sizable enough turnout at the same time…I mean I…I certainly hope that at least…a few people will be interested in attending."

He gazed across the desk at Dr. Whittaker, who was staring silently right back at him. "I do not doubt that several people will be interested in attending your meeting," he remarked at length, gripping his pipe as if it were a highly delicate item. "Even if, perchance, they do not come to the initial session, you will still have five weeks in which to organize another." He inserted the pipe between his slender lips and puffed quietly, exhaling with the ease of a person spending a quiet evening in a conservatory.

Dr. Pendleton attempted another smile, only managing to summon up his grimace. "Of course," he nodded as agreeably as he could, not going on to mention that, obviously, the five successive weeks were supposed to be devoted to follow-up meetings, respectively, from the first one so that a semblance of progression could be had. This was only if it all went according to his plans.

He looked at his watch more openly, clearing his throat all over again and grasping the edge of the mammoth desk in a conclusive motion.

"Well, I'd probably better call it a day… I have a lot of last-minute preparations to consider," he announced, climbing hesitantly to his feet.

Dr. Whittaker regarded him in momentary surprise, glancing over at the ornate clock on the wall and then nodding, taking the hint and rising slowly from his chair, instantly dwarfing the other doctor.

"To be sure," he stated briskly, removing his eyeglasses and placing them in a neatly hinged protective case, Dr. Pendleton taking off his own glasses, slipping them into their nondescript, stubby, leatherette case.

"I too should be on my way," Dr. Whittaker concurred easily. "Traffic and all."

"I'll walk down with you," Dr. Pendleton proposed, forcing a smile as Dr. Whittaker grasped a thick, seemingly varnished black briefcase, its combination locks and latches gold-plated. He then stooped to retrieve his own paper case, a battered leather attaché case; even its zipper was brown. "Let me get the door for you."

The office locked behind them, the two doctors headed down the mostly empty corridor, pausing before the elevator. Dr. Whittaker carried a long, expertly tailored topcoat, a stylishly gray fedora tilted atop his head. Dr. Pendleton had donned a plain tan raincoat, a compact, squat trilby hat pressed squarely on his head.

The elevator was occupied by various others who also had offices in the building, and the two joined in the customary hushed silence that accompanied the closing of the doors. In the spacious lobby, amid the reverberations of footsteps upon slick marble, Dr. Whittaker broke the spell, folding a woolen scarf around his neck and slipping into his top coat, smiling confidently at the smaller man.

"Well, I look forward to hearing about the outcome of your meeting, Dr. Pendleton," he declared pleasantly, extending a hand that Dr. Pendleton hastened to shake. "I imagine that it will be quite successful."

"Thank you, Dr. Whittaker," nodded Dr. Pendleton, looking rather grave, almost ashen. He then forced another smile at a sudden recollection. "And, uh, good luck to you too at your seminar, and, uh, lecturing tour next week."

They bade each other farewell, Dr. Pendleton carefully buttoning his coat and then turning up its collar, stepping out into the chilly twilight air. The sun had lost the battle overhead, the gray clouds accumulating in abundance, bringing with them a subtle but increasingly prominent wind.

He moved quickly along the crowded sidewalk, his hand clutching securely at his attaché case, which contained ninety-nine neon-green flyers, identical to the one folded in his jacket pocket.

He caught sight of Dr. Whittaker's spry form as he slipped regally into the back of a taxi cab and was whisked away, his own steps purposeful and determined as he made his way back to his bus stop.

Chapter 1

CHRISTOPHER GALVESTON CLOMPED GLOOMILY ALONG West Darcy Boulevard, his battle-scarred skateboard tucked loosely under one arm, his gaze fixed upon the stained sidewalk. Ordinarily, his lanky frame would be barreling down the streets of the somewhat run-down neighborhood, the spiky plumes of his green Mohawk slicing through the air like a shark's fin, his slender form steadily balanced atop his deck, his long legs braced, occasionally pumping with as much might as his painfully snug jeans would permit, his raggedy T-shirt and worn military overcoat bedecked with pins, buttons, and patches, flapping wildly with the wind resistance as he coasted along, lost in his thoughts.

Tonight, however, while just as introspective, he did not feel like riding; and his huge, cumbersome combat boots, scuffed beyond polishing, plodded heavily against the cement with each step. Like most kids nearing nineteen, he did not know where he was going, in general; but that night, he definitely knew where he was not going. However, not content with moping around in his room, he had opted to wander the streets for a while.

So far, his decision had only contributed to his depression, and he was gradually beginning to regret going out at all. Yet Saturday night was hardly a time for a punk rocker as fierce as he appeared to be to sit at home and do nothing. It was much better to get out and walk around and do nothing, he reflected darkly. *Nothing but feel worse than he did in the first place.*

Already, a taxi driver had yelled at him, calling him a dirty punk when he had absently stepped off the curb in front of his cab. The older couple trundling the shopping cart between them had also not helped in elevating his mood, as, when he had paused to let them

13

pass, smiling politely, the dual glare he was served in return had made his Mohawk bristle, his adolescent features crestfallen when they brushed past, their mumbled exchange inaudible, save for, "Yes, the filthy hoodlum."

Further dejected, he had pressed onward, unable to comprehend why people were so hateful. Naturally, it occurred to him that punk rockers, on average, not only were not supposed to be bothered by such interaction but also were supposed to invite it. Such was part of the whole concept, wasn't it?

This reflection only discouraged him all the more so to such a degree that he decided to go home. His bus stop was just ahead, and there was a chance that she had called while he was gone.

That, he knew, was a laugh. It had already been one-full week since they had last spoken.

This line of thinking was sidetracked by the sight of a young girl at the bus stop, casually dressed as if in defiance of the cold, a few text books clutched beneath one arm. The bus, he could see, was just then two blocks away, dispensing passengers in front of a grocery store; and the girl was attempting to balance the books while digging in her purse for bus fare.

As Chris drew nearer, the largest book slid out of her grasp and tumbled to the pavement in a flurry of pages, and he hastened forward to assist her, without really considering the consequences until he was scooping it up to hand to her. Not that there should be any consequences of such an act, beyond simple gratitude, but he had come to know better, appearing as he did. It wasn't his intention to intimidate the girl; in fact, he doubted if he could. It was an intriguing thought, he considered, until he recalled his last exchange with his girlfriend, realizing that repelling girls was something at which he seemed to excel.

The careening approach of the bus diverted these thoughts, as he quickly stood up and handed the book to the girl. "Um, here you go."

The girl glanced up from the book to regard him in surprise and then with a puzzled amusement that was far from intimidated. "Uh, thanks," she told him, hesitantly smiling as she looked him up and down.

Blushing deeply, Chris shifted awkwardly, attempting to slide his hands into his jeans pockets in a nonchalant manner and then dropping them loosely to his sides when they would not fit.

"Um, no problem," he mumbled, trying to quash the embarrassment that the girl's bewildered but thankful appraisal incited in him, summoning up a limp smile as he cocked his head meekly to one side.

"Hey!" a virtual growl assaulted him as a burly policeman came bustling past, enclosed in a thick woolen coat with dual-brass buttons.

"You, tweaker, you bothering this girl?"

Chris turned to gesture to the girl only to find that she was already boarding the bus, his mouth clamping shut in frustration, falling open again when the policeman actually gave him a poke with his nightstick.

"You better be movin' along, punk. There's no loitering on my street," he declared in an almost comically officious tone, then prodding at Chris's skateboard. "No skating, either," he added, lumbering importantly away, his jaw outthrust challengingly.

Chris gaped after him, awed at the injustices that were being heaped upon him that day. He felt like chasing after the cop and telling him that he couldn't move along, because he had also been waiting for the bus—the bus that even now was pulling away from the curb, he noted in muted, hangdog defeat.

He sat down heavily on the bus bench, blinking quietly at a disheveled old man digging in the wire trash receptacle attached to the sign pole of the bus stop and then cringing when the aged vagrant glowered back, his whisker-enshrouded features puckering in disgust as he moved crossly away, the creaking wheels of his shopping cart serenading a rasping diatribe about "worthless, rotten, lousy punk kids."

Chris watched him shuffle away, almost feeling the childish urge to cry. He could not believe the day—the week—no, the *life*, he was having. If God Almighty were to lean down out of the heavens and spit on him right then, he would scarcely be surprised, the notion sparking enough of the latent anger in him to propel him up off the bench, inducing him to turn and kick savagely at the brick wall of the old warehouse behind the bus stop. The motion felt good, and he repeated it, then glancing quickly about to make sure no one had seen him and then sighing self-depreciatively at his own inhibitions.

There was a dust-coated window set in the wall; and in the glow of a streetlight, he saw his reflection, his attention diverted to it as he surveyed himself, all the while wondering again why people were so mean.

As always, he was unable to engage these thoughts without contemplating why he, in turn, was so nice. This constant conundrum made little sense to him, while the image he beheld in the grimy window, ironically, did.

In spite of the pronounced contradiction that he knew he embodied, what he saw in his reflection was incredibly, vividly real to him. His clothing, his hair, his lifestyle—this was not an act, not some exercise in playing dress up. He may have been a late bloomer, but the day that he had cut his hair and dyed it and donned his rag-tag clothes, the feeling that he invoked in himself was as free and as natural as being born. He had truly felt as if he had discovered a piece of himself that he had then been able to release with the force of a spirit leaving a body. The hair and the clothing, of course, were only accessories, as were the piercings and tats that would surely come later, once his family was more willing to embrace this "phase he was going through."

To him, of course, this was not a phase, something to be out-grown. He was a punk rocker, and while the hair and clothes were mainly superficial, they were important passkeys to the punk rock underworld that this city fostered and that he very much wanted to join.

Attitude, however, was also a tremendous factor in the punk equation, and it was this integral aspect that imbued him with such doubt and misgivings. It was not enough merely to look the part, even if such was sufficient to convince the majority of people he encountered to judge by how he was treated. In fact, the only ones who were not intimidated by his appearance were other punk rockers, though not because they saw him as one of their own, but because they doubted his authenticity, altogether.

Hence, scorned on both sides, he had nowhere to turn, save within himself, wherein he would agonize over and second-guess his choices, his feelings, and, generally, his existence.

He did so now, staring at his reflection, his downtrodden thoughts once more alighting on the place where he was *not* going that night, conjuring up images of where he had been exactly one week prior—the same place.

He had been so excited when Candy had told him about their—about *her*—invitation to the party. Since high school, neither of them saw many of their friends; he didn't, anyway, and they rarely went to parties. An opportunity to meet new people had seemed wonderful, particularly when he had learned it was to be a punk party. When they had arrived at the dinghy, dark apartment to find it filled with punks screaming and inadvertently smashing furniture in the living room, which had become an improvised mosh pit, he had honestly thought that he was in his element. Prior to the party, Chris had felt fairly accomplished in his relatively new ascension to manhood. His original awkwardness with his burgeoning punk identity, while still prominent, had at least been balanced by a sense of maturity, and his once profound lack of experience had been eased by several concerts and even a few raves.

Nevertheless, the truth was that, when compared with most of those older, meaner, wilder punks, he was still a novice; and within seconds, his self-assertiveness had shriveled. Everyone there had been so much more hardcore and genuinely fatalistically punked out than he was that his discomfort became virtual fear, and he felt like an imposter as he stood there gaping.

The smoking, snorting, and drinking of all manner of pleasure-enhancing diversions had been rampant; and many of the punks had been eager to share with them, Chris feeling even more of a hopeless fool each time he politely declined. He was dead certain that he would not be so opposed to experimenting if he did not have a young and cynical cousin who was a paramedic and who, for years, had inundated him with gruesome horror stories, all of which were ascribed to some addictive substance. This indelible impression had left him not merely traumatized but with a veritable mental block, one that he could not seem to dispel.

Candy, on the other hand, did not possess any such inhibitions; in fact, she did not seem to have any reservations of any kind, which was curious, in as much as Candy was not a punk rocker, by any means. While she applied all of the social labels to others, she avoided attaching any to herself, thereby retaining a free range of exploration, in every sense of the notion. In the nearly six months they had been together, she had insisted from the start that they must have an open relationship, one based upon a very liberal understanding; and he, of course, had consented, his feelings for her making him agreeable to anything.

As such, she loved the mayhem into which they had wandered, mingling with muscle-bound headbangers and gutter punks engaged in a game of drunken Twister, with enviable ease, carrying herself as if she had nothing to prove, as if, indeed, far from it, everyone else had something to prove to her. Chris had watched her in awe, fleetingly trying to take pride in the knowledge that she was with him, the attempt clouded by the fact that no one would guess this from the way they were—and were not—interacting.

Naturally, Candy had leapt at the chance to sample anything that was afforded to her, coaxing Chris to join her, scoffing at his abstinence, eventually growing angry, then insulting, and opting to ignore him altogether. It was not the first time that this had happened.

Hurt and feeling even more displaced, he had sought refuge in the only revelry that was not foreign to him, the makeshift dance floor. Plunging into the mosh pit, he had worked out most of his aggressions, losing himself in the frenzied punk free for all; and those frustrations that he did not exorcise on his own were pummeled out of him by the thrashing, amoeba-like throng that engulfed him. The music had been excellent, combining standards with more recent songs, and he had soon found himself daring to believe that he was having fun, that he belonged.

This welcome notion seemed to be on the verge of being consummated, when Candy, much more mellow now, approached him during a slower interlude and began dancing with him, Chris's heart having leapt at the opportunity, because he loved to dance, all the more so with his girlfriend, taking pleasure in their time together, as it was usually their only mutual ground in social settings.

All had been going well, and the night had seemed salvageable; he had soothed her volatile temper by dancing with her, knowing how thoroughly she loved being the center of attention. He knew that this desire was actually what had drawn her to him in the first place, but he didn't mind; it seemed to work, and he had rationalized it into seeming like an abstract way in which she approved of his appearance.

As it happened, even in their buzzed delirium, the other punks had paused in their stomping to stare at them as Chris's moves became more unconventional and complex. Hence, they were also watching when he accidentally trampled on her foot with his wide combat boot.

Enraged, she had launched into a drunken tirade, calling him, in effect, a clumsy, stupid, cowardly, boring fool, though her exact words were much more severe, incorporating terminology that was fatal to the reputation of anyone in the punk rock scene. *"Lame-assed, limp-dicked, not even livin'-on-the-edge, Straightedge, shit-for-brains..."*

His cheeks burned now at the recollection of his just standing there, gaping at her, cringing in his usual haplessness at the livid gleam in her eyes as she glared at him through the disarrayed strands of her hair, and that had not even been the end of it.

Like it or not, he had been introduced at the party by his punk rock name, a designation that Candy had dreamed up and that he, of course, had automatically accepted. "Stud Stomper," while not espe-cially creative, was not totally uncool sounding. It was, in retrospect, much more pleasing to the ear than what he could only guess was to be his new form of address.

In sneering recognition of his cumbersome feet, massive boots, and all-around clumsiness, Candy had dubbed him "clodhopper" then and there to the uproarious approval of the other punks, who, apparently familiar with this term, began to chant it derisively, Candy instantly ducking this negative attention and joining their ranks, leaving him alone in his ignorance to bear this obviously insulting recitation, the mere sound of the word seeming to embody what he suspected it meant, giving him an unsettling insight into just how appropriate it most likely was. Where Candy had heard such an outdated expression, he could not guess; he had been forced to look it up in a dictionary when he finally got home that night, his speculation confirmed when he read its definition.

Fitting as it may have been, it was not as if he could not dance; far from it, in fact, he could dance very well. Least ways, he thought so. It was simply that it depended upon the situation and the music—the environment. He knew this, intimately well; but, of course, Candy did not. She did not—could not—understand that other part of his personality that he had shared with so few people. He closed his eyes. It did not matter.

He had left the party shortly thereafter, alone; she had refused to go with him and had since returned none of his telephone calls. Knowing full well where she was at that exact moment did not help, for she was where he could not be—at that apartment, at virtually the same party. It was not really even that he wanted to go there, but it was where she was, after all, and it was where all of the punks were, and it was difficult to withstand the idea that he was missing something or even just the childish yet poignantly real sense of being left out, altogether.

Reopening his eyes, he continued to examine his reflection with a veritable self-loathing. That party, that mosh pit, had been the closest he had ever come to feeling like a part of that group and was probably the closest he ever would come, judging by how it had ended for him.

Swallowing self-consciously, he made a fierce scowl, forcing his lower lip outward and then curling it horribly, baring his teeth, intensely studying the image that glowered back, wishing that he could at least appear to possess the confidence and attitude that would fortify such an expression. Tough. Mean. Invincible. Fearless. Why couldn't he manage such basic traits without making such a fool of himself?

As he watched his visage slowly untwist itself and meld back into his regular, pitiably earnest expression, his doubts soared, always on-hand to supply the usual answer, his ears and cheeks smoldering as his thoughts once again reverberated with the discordant chanting of the drunken punks, calling him what he was, by name. His reflection seemed to corroborate this assessment, the ferocity of his Mohawk and studded apparel deflating, leaving him with the sense that he was staring at little more than a colorfully spiked clown.

He sighed and then slumped in dejected rejection, feeling stupid, confused, and alone, his unhappiness tugging restlessly at his heart.

When at last he looked up again, he was sidetracked from further self-ridicule by the image of someone on the other side of the street, pausing and fussing with something in front of a telephone pole. Blinking, he watched the figure's reflection for a moment, then turning in time to see him brace something against the pole with one hand and attempt to apply something else to it with the other hand, dropping this second item and stooping to retrieve it, and then standing upright and staring at the first item, which had somehow stayed attached to the pole.

The figure, short and huddled, applied something from the second item anyway, then moving quickly up the street and around the corner. His curiosity aroused in spite of his somber mood, Chris waited until the figure was gone and then crossed the street to investigate.

The item affixed to the pole was, as he had guessed, a flyer, just out of the glow of the nearest streetlight, Chris having to ignite his Zippo lighter to read it; he did not smoke, but carried a Zippo simply because it was a regulation punk accessory. Examining the flyer by its steady flame, he found that it had been pinned up with a few erratically placed thumbtacks, but was more securely fused to the pole by the sticky black tar, which seems to ooze from all telephone poles.

The flyer was nothing more than an advertisement for an anonymous peer-counseling group, for people who might be having trouble adapting to life, in general. Snorting smugly at its homespun, generic wording and uncreative design and then grimacing self-consciously as he realized that it was the same shade of green as his Mohawk, he reflected bitterly that the punk rock thing to do would be to rip the flyer down and toss it into the street, and he was just about to do so when his mind was crossed with an image of the ungainly shadow and his fumbling efforts to post the flyer, a twinge of guilt scorching him.

He then gasped when the flame from his Zippo licked the bottom of the flyer, and he was thus forced to snatch it down, waving it frantically to extinguish it, afraid the tar would catch fire and ignite the entire telephone pole.

This averted, he sheepishly went about reattaching the flyer with the thumbtacks, only to rip it down all over again when he lowered his arm.

Baffled, he realized that his fingers were now coated with the tar, and the flyer was stuck to his hand like bubble gum. Furious with himself, he tried to pull it loose with his free hand and ended up tearing it in half, just as his bus came sailing forth, hurtling toward his stop.

Now clawing at it, he managed to remove it and, unable to bring himself to litter, had stuffed both wadded-up halves into his coat pocket and then raced across the street, cutting directly in front of the bus, the driver lashing into a barrage of verbal abuse as he scooped up his skateboard and tried to extract bus fare from his jeans without getting his hand stuck in his pocket, succeeding, although the fare, itself, stuck to his hand, the driver angrily waving him past, Chris slinking in shame to the back of the bus, headed for the rearmost seats, because that was where tough punks sat on a bus.

*****

"Bon appetite, Mr. Mc— Sir," the waiter smiled obsequiously, bowing his head sharply and scooting away, his expression almost maddened.

Mr. McClintock pleasantly returned the smile, nodding courteously and then surveying the extensive serving of food before him—chicken cordon bleu, asparagus tips in Béarnaise sauce, and delicately scalloped potatoes. The small sterling silver bowl of sherbet, which had preceded it, was still untouched, the meal having arrived seemingly only seconds after he had placed the order for it.

The Bistro d'Paris was by far one of the city's more upscale restaurants, lavishly decorated, with billowing curtains and lacquered partitions creating private dining alcoves for its similarly embellished tables. Its elite staff of waiters were clad in formal wear; the maître d' wore tails; the busboys were never seen. All of them undoubtedly knew who he was and why he was there; upon his arrival, the master chef was the first to be made aware of his presence.

Having taken a moment to scrutinize the atmosphere with a discreet glance, he had found that he could not look in any single direction without seeing at least a half-dozen fleur-de-lis and was grateful for the diversion that the meal presented to him. As he glanced over it now, inhaling its aroma with great pleasure, he both felt and heard his stomach rumble imploringly; and he self-consciously glanced about, hoping that no one had overheard.

As much as he longed to delve into the main course, he was forced to observe decorum, instead shifting in the rather confining booth and reaching for the sherbet, knocking his dessert spoon to the floor, and hearing it clatter down beneath the table.

"Drat!" he murmured, knowing he could not possibly hope to retrieve it; the mere act of squeezing in behind his table had left him breathless. His jowls bulged as he tried to peer past his wide, sloping midsection, sighing quietly as his stomach growled more emphatically, inducing him to grab up a salad fork and employ it instead, manipulating the tines so that almost no trace of the sherbet remained in the little bowl when he set it aside.

His palette cleansed for the sake of etiquette, he now clasped his pudgy hands together and focused gladly on the main course for one tantalizing moment before fingering a more substantial fork and an ornate knife, wading into the chicken, his plump nose sniffing gently at the scintillating aroma, his stomach churning sharply at this delay. Grimacing, he quickly tasted a small portion, his features metamorphosing into a look of pure delight, as the pungent flavors mingled within his mouth, seeming to dance upon his tongue.

"Ah," he exhaled, enraptured, having to restrain himself from tearing into the entrée and shoveling it into his mouth, staying the urge and taking only a slightly larger bite.

The flaky breading, the spiced smokiness of the ham, the succulence of the chicken, and the sharp bite of the cheese, all swimming in the creamy sauce, were virtually overpowering. He attempted to exact a small, discerning frown, his thick eyebrows set judgmentally, his mind focusing upon the critique and evaluation of this repast; but as he glanced around at the secluded privacy of his alcove, he relinquished his stance and virtually stuffed another helping into his mouth, chewing fervently. "Oh my," he breathed euphorically. "Oh, that is really very, very good."

His entire course was thusly devoured in short order, the potatoes and asparagus little more than distractions, his table setting devoid of every morsel and droplet when he was abruptly finished.

It seeming to dawn on him that his meal was concluded, he cleared his throat officiously, sipped discreetly from a tall glass of white wine, dabbed at his lips with a linen napkin, and then surveyed his crumb-free surroundings in satisfaction. He then shifted uncomfortably and removed a fountain pen and a little booklet from within the folds of his jacket.

"Bistro d'Paris," he murmured, jotting quickly. "Exquisite atmosphere, attentive staff, and"—he paused, glancing contritely at his empty plate—"superlative cuisine."

With some difficulty, he replaced these items to his pocket, musing quietly that, of course, the portions were much too small, when the waiter suddenly rematerialized.

"Ah, Mr. Mc— Sir! Ah, have you finished?" he inquired, rather needlessly, eyeing the spotless tableware with one pencil-thin eyebrow uplifted, his hands clasped almost ghoulishly before him, his smile even more maniacally unctuous than previously.

Startled, Mr. McClintock smiled floridly, laying his thick hands upon the tabletop and attempting to scoot out from behind the booth with as much dignity as he could muster.

"Yes, in fact, I am," he replied, the waiter stepping swiftly aside to give him plenty of room. "If I may, I will take my check now," he requested, beaming cordially at the waiter, his massive girth now balanced with his tall frame.

"Of course, sir," the waiter complied, extending to him a small leather folder, almost as if in shame. "I do hope you enjoyed your meal, sir?" he asked, smiling nervously at him, his head tilted at an awkwardly servile angle.

Mr. McClintock's small, pursed mouth offered a polite smile, the thin, neatly trimmed mustache positioned beneath his rounded nose twitching slightly.

"Oh yes," he assured the waiter, adjusting his lapels briskly. "I found it to be most satisfactory."

The waiter's quivering dis-ease dissolved into a visible relief as he bowed stiffly. "Ah, thank you, sir."

Nodding cordially, he strolled to the front of the bistro, eventually finding his way through the labyrinth of dining sections, locating the maître d' standing, sentry-like, behind his podium.

"I trust you found our cuisine…sufficient?" he surmised, loftily peering at Mr. McClintock as he processed the credit card for his expense account.

Mr. McClintock nodded deeply, his small reserved smile still in place. "Oh yes, indeed, I did."

The maître d' considered this and, apparently finding his response to be sufficient as well, returned the credit card with an aloof smile of his own.

"I am pleased to hear that, sir."

Nodding again, Mr. McClintock stepped out of the cool foyer of the restaurant, instantly finding himself in the explosively sunny afternoon of the city, his small, sensitive eyes blinking rapidly as he headed up the street, still smiling pleasantly at the thought of his lunch.

Exhaling contentedly, he proceeded at a leisurely pace, his posture and gait unusual for so large a man; he walked perfectly upright, the full bulk of his person thrust forward, his ambling steps neither sauntering nor shuffling as they bore his immense proportions, instead swift and almost nimble, deliberate, but light. His clothing, conservative and neat, fit him with perfect abundance, his flowing jacket enfolding his top half, and his wide trousers engulfing his lower, his lapels centrally buttoned over his thick necktie.

He was meticulous about his attire, fastidiously maintaining a presentability that stereotypes insisted was unfeasible for overweight people; he was determined that his build must never seem untidy or constrictive, not out of vanity, but from an ardent desire to meet the degree of refined formality that his occupation required.

Pausing at an intersection, he glanced carefully in all directions before easing himself off the curb and bobbing quickly across the street, his tremendous frame bouncing cumbersomely with the increased velocity.

Reaching the other side, he breathed deeply, dabbing at his forehead and thinning hairline with a handkerchief, an almost dainty, if needless, action for, in defiance of another stereotype, he did not seem to perspire very much, although he still went through all the motions of looking as fresh and clean as he could, again, due to his trepidation at being regarded as slovenly or unkempt.

His focus was diverted from his course by a full-scale reflection of himself in a storefront window; and he hesitated, regarding his image pensively, for, in spite of all of his efforts, his principle area of concern seemed even more copious; and he flushed slightly at the usual angst that accompanied such scrutiny.

As the years had gone by and his weight had increased, he had gradually begun to consider the unsettling idea that should he ever become too noticeably heavy, he might lose a great deal of prestige, if not his occupation altogether. It was for this reason that he had commenced taking such a painstaking interest in his overall appearance.

Swallowing dryly, he unbuttoned his jacket and gave his trousers an unnecessary hoist, for they abundantly encompassed his lower belly, dividing his girth neatly in half. He only wore suspenders, a salesclerk at the Big and Tall store having instilled in him a fear of belts, warning him that belts had a way of slipping beneath the bulk and hugging the hips, forcing the stomach to overflow in bouncing prominence. Better, he had been advised that he wear his pants high and wide and look like Humpty Dumpty than permit them to ride low so that he resembled an ostrich wearing an embroidery hoop around his waist. Slightly offended by the clerk's candor, he had been even more alarmed by it, especially when he had next worked up the nerve to inquire about a man's corset and had been informed that they did not come in his size.

Grimacing at the recollection, he noted that his pants were neatly in place, his shirt properly tucked in, and his jacket unwrinkled and spotless. All was as it should be, and the real cause of his uncertainty once again presented itself, beyond any hope of argument.

Of course, he reflected, rebuttoning his jacket and moving briskly away; he had only just eaten lunch. This rather flimsy logic did little to cheer him, particularly in lieu of the fact that he was still hungry.

His spirited pace slowed a bit, but he forced himself to focus upon the task at hand, enjoying a trace of enthusiasm as he drew near the elaborate facade of another establishment, comparing its discreet golden placard with a notation in his booklet.

Felini's Fine Italian Dining. Such would be tomorrow's subject of review, he noted with growing anticipation. Mr. McClintock often liked to locate the prospective restaurants ahead of time, instead of relying on street maps or last-minute directions from cabbies, since punctuality was essential in matters of fine dining.

His eagerness was dampened again when he once more saw his reflection, this time depicted in the tinted window of the restaurant's wide door, and he quickly turned away as if fleeing a phantom, his mind nonetheless embracing the usual worries as he headed up the street. He knew, very well, that his being so very much overweight was not actually the problem, not really; yet when he even briefly considered the true source of his trouble, he just as quickly dismissed it, for to acknowledge the idea would contradict almost everything in which he believed and held dear. It was an exasperating situation, one which he customarily dealt with by putting out of his mind altogether.

It was an easy-enough feat to accomplish, for, as he paused to wait for a traffic light to change, his delicate nostrils balking slightly at the odors drifting from a nearby trash receptacle, his averted gaze took in the place of business arranged on that corner, a small, cramped diner entitled simply "Lou's Café."

Mr. McClintock paused, staring past his reflection in the café's hazy window, oblivious of the rather seedy clientele slumped before the counter, focusing instead upon what they were eating. Hamburgers appeared to be Lou's specialty. His stomach rumbled sleepily within him.

Swallowing, he glanced at the traffic light, considering that he really ought to be getting back to the newspaper building. A quick look at his watch informed him that he still had plenty of time. His stomach rumbled again, wide awake now.

Of course, Lou's Café was not on his list of restaurants to review. Then again, neither were any of the other restaurants in which he had spontaneously dined at moments like this one.

Naturally, Lou's Café did not appear in the slightest to be an exercise in fine dining. Yet, again, neither had any of the other improvised stopovers; many of them had been even less promising in terms of looks; and as a fair and impartial food reviewer, he knew not to discriminate against any place because of its outer appearance or location; and, besides, he had always eaten at these spur-of-the-moment intervals in an unofficial capacity, anyway, in between visits to actual, legitimate prospects.

That, however, was all the more reason to keep on walking, his consistent internal struggle argued; he should realistically only eat in the restaurants that he was reviewing.

Blinking suddenly, he was struck with an idea that, incredibly, in all of these years of identical crossroads of conscience, had some-how never before occurred to him. It was so simplistically obvious that he would have chastised himself for his long-over-due percep-tion were it not for the fact that he was too impressed with its stag-gering potential.

His mind thus clearly made up, he dismissed the surge of out-rage arising from his suppressed counter thoughts and strode boldly toward the café, his eyebrows uplifted righteously.

Greeted by the buzz of an electric fan and a few houseflies, his entry was met with blank appraisal by the few grizzled customers, a middle-aged man clad in a grease-smeared apron, T-shirt, and trousers, his paper hat and hair likewise saturated, peering at him from over the newspaper he had been reading alongside the blackened grill.

"What'll it be, Mac?" he asked, his tone the measure of apathy that could only belong to Lou, himself.

Surveying a row of narrow booths, Mr. McClintock opted for one of the counter stools, precariously balancing his immense proportions on it by laying his wide hands upon the streaked Formica before him.

"Well," he replied congenially, looking with unbiased anticipation at the cluttered cooking area in which Lou stood. "I don't know. In fact...what might you recommend?"

Lou regarded him with a deadpan lack of enthusiasm. "Well, I might recommend a hamburger."

Mr. McClintock's indefatigable smile only grew larger. "Ah! A hamburger, yes. Then, that is what I shall have," he declared heartily, his stomach heralding its approval, causing him to blush in mild embarrassment.

Staring at him momentarily, Lou then put aside the newspaper and took up a gristle-encrusted spatula. Mr. McClintock watched him set to work, clearing his throat and speaking conversationally.

"How long have you been the proprietor of this diner, may I ask?" he inquired politely.

Lou's eyes narrowed suspiciously. "You from the Health Department?" he demanded.

"Oh no," Mr. McClintock assured him apologetically. "No, I was merely curious, having never dined here before," he explained earnestly.

"You don't say?" Lou remarked at length, his indifference partially restored as he focused on his cooking. "I been here seventeen years."

"Ah," nodded Mr. McClintock, deciding to refrain from further conversation, the ensuing silence punctuated by his growling stomach to such a degree that he was both eager and relieved when a plate was rather unceremoniously placed before him.

"Your hamburger," Lou announced, then managing a leering smile. "Sir."

Rubbing his hands together with the same zeal he had experienced only a short while ago at the Bistro d'Paris, he quickly removed a napkin from a thumb-printed dispenser, placing it on his expansive lap and then leaning forward and savoring the aroma of the undercooked, hastily compiled meal—a greasy hamburger with limp lettuce and tomato, coupled with a handful of French fries. Lou had returned to his paper but was clearly watching his newest patron, as were most of the other diners. Quite aware of this, Mr. McClintock inhaled and then commenced his review.

"Well, in appearance and aroma, alone, this entrée is particularly appealing," he stated boldly.

Lou's eyebrows lifted ever so slightly. "That a fact?" he asked, looking inscrutably at the portly gourmand.

"Oh, most definitely," Mr. McClintock confirmed, nodding energetically. "One has only to examine the basic components. We have the hamburger, carefully balanced with the French fries, leaving no unsightly gaps on the actual plate. Nutritionally, of course, the basic food groups are represented. And, moreover, the piquant of the condiment will no doubt be subtly enhanced by the sesame seeds on the bun."

He smiled enthusiastically at Lou, who conjured up a sour smile in return.

"Yeah, well, the sesame seeds was my idea," he informed him in stilted politeness. "Seems we're all out of parsley, so I thought we better spruce up the buns, ya know."

"An excellent substitution," Mr. McClintock proclaimed almost solemnly. "In fact, I might tell you that, statistically, in so far as garnishes go, people are more inclined to eat the sesame seeds and leave the parsley untouched."

Lou stared at him. "You're puttin' me on," he said at last.

"Of course, in addition to appearance and presentation, which, I might add, was rendered with great expedition and a hospitable smile, one must always reserve judgment for the quintessential test of the entrée—its flavor," Mr. McClintock went on with great finality.

Nodding slowly, Lou apparently concurred. "Oh yeah, by all means, please do."

With pronounced expectation, Mr. McClintock gently fingered the hamburger, taking a very small bite. The burger was underdone, its juices had saturated the bun and diluted the catsup; these factors all converged to define Mr. McClintock's inescapable assessment.

"Delicious!" he proclaimed, taking a substantially larger bite. "Quite delicious."

As Lou and the other diners looked on, Mr. McClintock ingested the burger and fries with amazing velocity, seemingly dabbing at his mouth with his napkin only seconds later, withdrawing his booklet and pen, and beaming over at Lou with immense satisfaction.

"Well, permit me to thank you for a delightful repast," he stated cheerfully, then beginning to jot in the booklet with swift flourishes of the pen. "Lou's Café, excellent cuisine, hospitably staffed, a reputable clientele, and a charming atmosphere, resplendent with an... urban ambiance!"

He replaced the booklet and pen, carefully lowering himself off the stool, all eyes on him in blank disbelief as he nodded once more to Lou. "You shall receive an excellent review, sir."

Blinking, Lou wordlessly rang up the bill, continuing to gape at him.

"Ah, and quite affordable, as well," Mr. McClintock noted, removing his wallet and paying for his second lunch and then glancing at his watch. Now, he really should be getting back.

Leaving Lou and his speechless diners with an amiable farewell, he loped up the street, sighting a telephone booth and hastening toward it, reflecting that now he at least felt reasonably full. His mind began to cloud with misgivings over the spontaneous rationale of his actions; and he sought to justify them with the idea that he was, in a way, obliged to review as many restaurants as possible. Surely, productivity and efficiency were qualities well-worth pursuing.

Nevertheless, his handkerchief was out and wiping subconsciously at his brow as he approached the telephone booth, finding to his dismay that he could not quite fit inside of it, forced instead to lean into it and grasp the receiver, punching in the digits with his fountain pen.

As he waited for the taxi dispatcher to answer, his eyes fell upon the flyer scotch-taped to the glass panel of the booth, its unappetizing shade of green catching his attention. *A peer-counseling group, promising, among other focal points, to address matters of will power and the like? Hardly anything new.* He had even considered such channels before, either to lose weight or to concentrate on his more trying weakness, but had never actively looked into such a process. He simply could not imagine discussing such personal issues with other people.

He placed an order for a taxi cab and then turned to glance about for a shady spot in which to wait, his gaze instead alighting upon something else entirely. His nostrils flicked and his mustache twitched. His stomach rumbled faintly.

He blinked in disbelief. His stomach rumbled more adamantly.

Gulping, he dabbed at his dry forehead and then sighed in defeat. Moving away from the telephone booth, he then surrendered to the opposite end of his internal battle as well, pausing to retrieve the flyer from the booth and rereading it and then carefully folding it within his jacket.

This action, noncommittal as it was, made him feel slightly better; and his head uplifted and his mood upbeat, he strolled lightly forward, nodding affably as he began to speak.

"Good afternoon, sir! I could not help but notice the buffet-like style in which you have arranged your condiments, a virtual invitation to the creativity of your patrons that, when coupled with the bold colors of your umbrella and general, al fresco ensemble, convey a very definite stimulant to the average appetite."

The hotdog vendor stared at him, inducing him to flush slightly.

"In short...one foot long, please," he requested briskly, his diminished smile becoming radiant as he savored the anticipation.

*****

Vivean Talbott stood before the vending machine, poised with her purse, staring hesitantly from the bright blue package of Sudsies and the flaming red box of Soapy-Os, uncertain as to which laundry detergent might yield the best results. She continued to deliberate, for the considerable mess that had incapacitated her own washing machine—as well as most of her wardrobe—would require an especially potent cleanser to reverse it.

She glanced around the Laundromat, finding it empty save for a pair of older ladies seated across the room and a burly man in a soiled T-shirt, lounging against a sorting table nearby, absorbed in the action film blaring forth from the television mounted high in the corner of the room.

"Excuse me, sir?" she addressed him timidly, her voice light and introverted.

The man's eyes slid away from the screen to settle upon her. "Yeah?"

Wilting a bit at his tone, she pointed meekly toward the vending machine. "Can you tell me which detergent is better…'Sudsies' or 'Soapy-Os'?" she asked with a feeble smile.

The man stared at her and then shifted upright. "Well, now, I wouldn't know that, lady," he replied coarsely, rubbing at his unshaven jaw and then reaching for a battered box of detergent on the table. "Ya' see, I only use 'Fresh-as-Spring' on *my* laundry." He held up the box with the grinning flourish of a television commercial.

Nodding gratefully, she thanked him and hastened back to the vending machine, before blinking at it uncertainly and then moving reluctantly back toward the man.

"I'm sorry to bother you again," she apologized, wincing as he once more interrupted his viewing to deal her a surly look. "This vending machine is out of 'Fresh-as-Spring,'" she explained hastily. "If you had to decide between 'Sudsies' or 'Soapy-Os,' which would you choose?"

His mouth twisting into a sneering smile, the man shrugged his wide shoulders. "Well, now, in that case, I would most likely have to go with the bargain brand," he responded sweetly.

Attentively considering this, she nodded rapidly, thanking him once more and then scurrying back to the machine with this advice, discovering that neither choice was the "bargain brand," inasmuch as they both cost precisely the same.

Her hopeful expression crumpling with a perplexed sigh, she wondered why she had not thought to bring her own detergent from home; it then occurred to her that it could well have been that soap that had caused the problem.

At this point, she really had no way of knowing. When one of her colleagues had heard of her forthcoming promotion, she had insisted on giving her a congratulations gift, even though the advancement had not become official yet. It was—it *had been*—a beautiful cardigan sweater, forest green; its instructions directed that it should be washed once before wearing to eliminate any imperfections in the fibers by causing the garment to constrict, thereby ensuring a snug, conforming fit. It was a personalized fitting that she would never be able to exact from it, however, because in one wash cycle, its dye had bled all over her other clothing, rendering them a bizarre, mottled green; and a loose thread had wound around the washer's agitator, dismantling the entire sweater and creating the appearance of a giant spool of yarn in the center of her washing machine.

Now, she not only was left with the task of running all over town to find an identical sweater, for the sake of her friend's feelings, but also had to have her washer serviced and, moreover, had to attempt to remove the dye from her other clothes as best she could.

She was not a woman given to aggravation, her mellow, accepting personality unsuited for anger or exasperation, but it was an incredibly trying situation. It had been such a lovely thought; but, then again, the promotion had yet to be finalized; and a congratulatory gift was premature, even if it did seem inevitable that she would be moving up the career ladder.

This notion was enough to make her shudder as she stood before the vending machine, the idea of advancing still somehow foreign to her, although, logically, it had been in the making for quite a while now. "It was only a matter of time," her colleagues had told her cheerfully. "You should be proud you've come so far so quickly."

Yet pride and excitement and even a sense of fulfillment were all still quite far removed, and, instead, only a swiftly mounting trepidation was consuming her. She patted absently at her hair in the vague reflection of the machine, noting that it seemed to be standing on end these days. Her shy, dark-brown features, usually so quick to smile, had been anxious and troubled the past few weeks, these traits, themselves, making her even more nervous, because she was simply unaccustomed to feeling this way, having long since attained a life-style of balanced equanimity and quiet contentment.

Such an achievement was scarcely in keeping with the life of any public defender, particularly after fifteen years in court, yet she had managed to uphold such a buoyant frame of mind in spite of the grim and oftentimes tragic reality of her work. It was most likely due in part to her easygoing nature, but could also be ascribed to the fact that, unlike so many of her colleagues, she had never given into the burnout that eventually consumed so many practitioners of the legal profession, transforming eager, idealistic law school graduates into jaded, cynical, and many times embittered people, no longer bent on changing an unchangeable world and inwardly having lost faith in any concept of the prevalence of justice.

Somehow, despite the arduous and demanding role she had to play, even in lieu of the fact that it was, by and large, unrewarding, thankless work, she had maintained her original ideals of doing as much good as she was able and of basically helping people as best she could. Her detractors labeled her a hopelessly bleeding heart do-gooder, and even her closest colleagues considered her a soft touch, yet still she persevered unhardened and open-minded, eager to see the positive side in people and reluctant to condemn.

After fifteen years of such, she had actually reached a point at which she thought she was happy or, at least, content and, to some degree, safe. Now, however, all of that seemed to be on the verge of changing in an almost unimaginable way.

An explosion jarred her thoughts sharply, her eyes darting up to the action film overhead, her nerves jangled enough to bring her focus back upon the vending machine. She found herself employing a trick that she had developed as a girl, deciding between the two detergents alphabetically, inserting a few coins, and then staring at the very small box of Soapy-Os that the machine yielded. She wondered briefly if it would be enough, then brightening when she reflected that, if not, she could come back and get the other brand as well.

Compromises were highly valued by Vivean Talbott; they made her profession—indeed, her entire life—so much easier.

Leastwise, they had up until now. Sighing again, her angst out of place on her spritely, eternally girlish features, she turned to contemplate the row of washing machines, trying to recall which one contained her laundry. Lifting up a few lids, she finally located the rumpled, tangled mass of potentially ruined clothes and poured the little box of soap over it, then coaxing the machine to accept a wrinkled dollar bill into its slot, holding her breath as the washer emitted a few internal groans and then began to fill with water, prompting her quickly to lower the lid.

Not especially interested in the action film, she did not know how to change the channel on the television, not that she could reach it anyway, and could only guess what the burly man would say if she were to turn it to another station. Hence, she found herself with nothing to do, trapped in Quicky Laundry for at least two hours. She had been in such a hurry to leave her apartment with her garbage bag of leaking clothes that she had forgotten her book, a collection of mystery stories that she had only just begun to read, but which had already captured her fascination.

Perhaps in some abstract reflection of her work, it was her favorite genre of both literature and the cinema. She loved a good who-dunnit detective story or a crime drama, even the more graphic television programs that were now so popular. Even after so many years in court and so much exposure to the raw and the indecent, she was still capable of being made squeamish in the privacy of her living room, as well as gratified when the innocent were vindicated and justice was carried. But her favorite would always be the typical murder mystery, replete with sleuths and clues, be it a case pursued by Sherlock Holmes, Miss Marple, or Nancy Drew. Somehow, the righteous always seemed to prevail in those stories, just as she had tried so diligently to have happen in court. It had never been easy, and she had not always succeeded, but her best efforts had often been rewarded with leniency for her clients, and all of her endeavors and principles had certainly not gone unnoticed. *No, indeed, they certainly hadn't*, she thought uneasily.

Left with her worrisome thoughts to harass her, she crossed the length of the Laundromat to sit in the row of plastic chairs arranged against the wall, settling her petite form into place, her little feet scarcely reaching the floor. While not particularly elegant, she was pretty in a quiet sort of way, not quite tall enough to be sophisticated and not quite trim enough to be fashionable. She had always been small and attractive in an in-between sort of way. Smoothing at the skirt of her two-piece gray wool suit, she began to tug absently at the imitation pearl necklace that she wore to augment the simple broach centered in the collar of her silken blouse, having to stop herself, for she had once sent an entire strand of pearls cascading over the floor of a courtroom from the habit. She folded her hands in her lap and tried to resist the urge to swing her dress pumps to and fro beneath the chair. She was, after all, not twelve any more, in spite of her youthful appearance.

Wanting very much to divert her thoughts from the stressful contemplation of her career, she glanced at a few sun-bleached magazines, not really wishing to read about fly-fishing or soccer, and then peered at a section of week-old newspaper, eventually digging distractedly in her purse, if for no other reason than to keep from fidgeting. It then occurred to her that it amounted to the same.

She also realized that, on and off, she had become aware of the conversation between the two older women who were seated nearby. Not intending to eavesdrop, she had caught enough of the exchange to be sidetracked by it; and, as she continued to rummage through her purse, pretending to look for an imaginary stick of gum, she found herself listening in growing curiosity.

"But it was justified, Pearl," the larger of the two women was saying, unruly wisps of her graying hair standing out from the frames of her narrow eyeglasses, bordering her rather sour face. She was dressed in navy blue polyester, while the smaller woman, Pearl, wore a pink turtleneck sweater and dark slacks, her auburn hair a mass of curls around a birdlike face, her eyeglasses attached to a gold chain looped around her spindly neck. Both women were folding laundry, transferring it from the Laundromat's wire carts into their own plastic baskets, the movements of their twiglike fingers deft and mechanical.

"It may've been wrong, but Rodney was right to do it," the larger woman insisted.

"For three months?" Pearl rasped in disbelief. "Esther, a three-month affair is a lot different from a two-week fling, you know."

"Yes, but I'm not talking about the time that it took," Esther countered emphatically. "I'm talking about the actual act of being unfaithful in marriage."

"Well, in any case, they're getting a divorce," Pearl concluded bluntly, whipping a dishtowel out of the cart and forcing its edges together. "They can actually manage to see eye to eye on that!"

"Yeah?" Esther laughed mannishly. "Now, all they have to do is figure out who gets what, and it'll be a cold day in hell if they can agree on who gets anything from that marriage! Community property, my heinie!"

Pearl nodded wisely. "Ya can't split a house in two. It'll be for the judge to decide who gets that, because Lord knows neither of them'll be willing to give it up."

They fell silent for a moment, their discreet listener continuing to fumble with her purse and eventually setting it aside, picking up the old newspaper, and peering at it with feigned interest, having completely given into eavesdropping on the conversation now, intrigued by the scenario the two women had outlined and curious about the details. Knowing gossips as she did, she was correct in assuming that they were not finished with the topic.

"Well, she started it," Esther pointed out at length. "Rodney was a good husband to Dorris, and she went off and had that fling with Bill—*Bill*, of all people! If there's any justice, she won't get a dime, not even alimony."

"I know, but Rodney didn't have to go after Jane, though," Pearl returned shrewdly. "That just turned the whole thing into a soap opera. Even if he's telling the truth and didn't do it out of spite, he couldn't possibly have just 'fallen in love with her' at the *exact* same time that his wife was on the prowl! That's a pretty damn big coincidence, doncha' think?"

"So, you're saying they're both to blame and neither one deserves nothing at all?" Esther posed flatly, pulling savagely at several static-clung socks. "Maybe so, but that's not how it works. Somebody's gonna win, somebody's gonna lose."

Frowning slightly, Vivean Talbott reflected on that idea, having battled that kind of mentality for so long in court. She had thankfully been spared much fall out from divorce cases and such, but had experienced enough to know that even these kinds of cases could be handled with compromise if one could only succeed in appealing to the feelings and emotions that existed prior to all the trouble.

Even though the couple went separate ways when it was all over, it could still be with peace of mind and closure, as well as a fairly balanced settlement.

"Yes, no judge is gonna look light on the case when Bill puts that daughter of his on the stand," Pearl concurred, beginning to separate a tangle of blue jeans.

Kids. When there were kids involved, they could end up suffering the most. She stared sadly at the newspaper, her small mouth tautening slightly. They made the attempt at a compromise an absolute essential, not merely in terms of visiting rights and child support and the legalities of the issue, but mainly for their own feelings of security and worth in the eyes of both parents.

"Ho-ho, you said it there," Esther squawked, shaking her head. "No matter what she says, Rodney's gonna look bad, and Bill and Dorris are gonna come out smellin' like roses."

When, however, some parents used their children as pawns to play against one another in divorce proceedings, even the most compassionate attorney found it difficult to maintain sympathy for both sides in the quest for an all-encompassing compromise. Her frown deepening, she began to wonder if "Bill and Dorris" warranted such consideration.

"You're right there," Pearl shot back, denim snapping in her hands. "The kick in the head is that, of course, she's on Rodney's side, but everything she says to defend him'll only make him look worse and worse, and Bill and Dorris know it! Bill's using her to get back at Rodney for what he did."

No, sometimes a compromise was not possible. Sometimes, one side was definitely more in the right than the other, and justice had to be dealt accordingly. Bill and Dorris were obviously undeserving of such leniency, even if Rodney had a simultaneous affair with this Jane person; Bill's eagerness to use his own daughter's testimony to further his gain clearly displayed that. No, if she were the judge… she actually nodded behind the newspaper, pleased with herself for the swift, concise pseudoruling she had inwardly made; even the too-nice, wishy-washy public defender could be tough, decisive, and prosecutorial, if needs be.

"Yeah, it's a circus, all right," Esther continued warily, pausing in her folding. "Do you know when the whole divorce proceedings are going to court?"

Pearl shrugged. "I guess sometime after Rodney's arraignment," she surmised.

Vivean Talbott blinked behind the newspaper.

Esther sighed. "This whole mess would be a lot simpler if Jane wasn't still living at home with Bill."

"This whole mess would be a lot simpler if Jane wasn't still a minor!" Pearl stated definitively.

Both women clucked their tongues and shook their heads, focusing once more on their laundry as the small, younger woman nearby gaped blankly at her newspaper. Jane *was* Bill's daughter?

Bewildered, she put the newspaper aside and climbed out of the plastic chair, moving quietly across the chipped linoleum, her fleeting confidence in her sense of judgment vanquished as she tried to dismiss the feeling that she had just freed the wrong guy.

Obviously, her little vicarious exercise in blind justice had been thwarted by not having been given all of the details, but this fact was of little consolation to her already firmly entrenched misgivings, and she felt trapped, unable to go backward and reluctant to go forward. She simply could not make up her mind as to what she was going to do.

Her pensive gaze fell upon a bulletin board arranged alongside the vending machine, and she began to peruse its various ads, reading about a litter of free puppies, a motor scooter for sale, a room for rent ad coupled with an extensive, descriptive list of people who need not apply, and a flyer promoting an upcoming peer-counseling group meeting, offering an open forum for discussing issues of self-confidence and personal assertiveness. The flyer's jarring shade of green reminded her of her ruined laundry as she fingered it, accidentally dislodging it when a severe harrumphing sounded behind her, and she spun around to see the burly man smiling at her, pointing one thick finger.

Following its indication, she gasped when she next took in the ring of dense, soapy foam beginning to seep out from under the lid of her washer, the sudsy froth as green as the flyer. Hastening over to it, she gingerly tugged it open, disengaging the wash cycle and staring forlornly at the verdant mess that gurgled forth from her laundry, spilling over onto the floor. One tiny hand flew to her mouth as she gaped over at the burly man.

"I don't know what could have caused that!" she declared in dismay. "Some...some kind of chemical reaction?" Wincing at the absurdity, she began to glance in panic all around the Laundromat. "What is the manager going to say when he sees this?" she fretted.

The burly man rested one elbow on a nearby machine, still smiling jeeringly at her. "Oh, he'll probably say something like 'Hello there, I *am* the manager,'" he informed her, lumbering over to her side and surveying the damage, the small woman staring up at him in embarrassed shock.

"He'd probably ask you if you knew that Soapy-Os are super-concentrated and are only s'pose to be used in our Jumbo Machines," he continued, his voice liltingly surly. "He'll probably go on to ask if you had to pick one, which would you choose, checkbook or credit card?"

He paused, leaning down to leer sweetly at the mortified little woman. "Or do you prefer the bargain brand?" He paused. "Cash."

Smiling weakly, she began to dig through her purse in meek resignation.

*****

"All right, now I would like for you to execute a left turn at this next intersection," Mr. Crimpton instructed, reluctantly taking his eyes off the road in order to glance at the course outlined on his clipboard. He looked up again as they turned past a gas station, his features narrowing a bit behind his wire-rimmed glasses as he focused on the lightly perspiring kid next to him.

"Um, how was that, sir?" the kid, freckle-faced, plump, and nervous, asked, his eyes pivoting from one mirror to another but avoiding Mr. Crimpton's.

"That was fine…" He flipped over the route sheet to see what this one was called. "Billy, just fine, although, in future, when I request for you to make a left turn, it would be for the best if you didn't turn right," he explained pointedly.

Billy did gape over at him now, Mr. Crimpton bracing himself and pointing out the upcoming traffic signal, the kid gasping slightly and braking harshly. They both jolted forward, then sitting there awkwardly, watching a woman wheel a stroller past them.

"Um, sorry, sir," Billy offered contritely. "I'm just a little nervous."

Mr. Crimpton reopened his eyes, giving him a look. *He* was nervous?

"Why don't you take us around the block so we can get back on course?" he suggested by way of distracting his forthcoming head-ache. It was early today.

Nodding quickly, Billy checked all of his mirrors, hesitantly sig-naled, and brought the car around the corner, then carefully turning once more to circle the block. He was not doing all that poorly, and although Mr. Crimpton knew better than to let down his guard, he was at least able to appreciate the idea of letting down his guard. It was better than nothing.

They proceeded uneventfully enough, until a garbage truck began backing into the street, quite slowly, Billy nevertheless taken off guard enough to jerk the wheel, dipping the little Datsun toward oncoming traffic, a horn blast spooking him back into his lane with a burst of acceleration, the kid nearly rear-ending a Volvo and avoiding it by dodging into a parking space, not quite colliding with another parked car, but slamming into the curb violently enough to rupture the car's prematurely bald tire.

Letting a few moments pass, Mr. Crimpton gradually reopened his eyes and unclenched his teeth, turning to face the meekly shrinking kid, who still clung hopefully to the wheel.

"Um, do I get points off for that?" he asked anxiously, Mr. Crimpton removing his glasses to pinch the bridge of his nose, forcing his hands to manipulate a pen as he made three pronounced strokes on the now useless route, filling the entire page with the letter "F."

Billy peered at it, crestfallen. "Aw, man, not again," he murmured, his round features sinking in disappointment. "My mom's gonna kill me."

Mr. Crimpton's own features twisted as he entertained that notion.

Sighing, Billy moved to open his door, shrugging sheepishly at him. "Um, I'm gonna go call her so she can come pick us up and take you back to the DMV," he said morosely, then gesturing with a thumb. "Plus, I gotta go get that hubcap."

Mr. Crimpton's face moving into a sneer, it contorted painfully when the kid flung open his door and almost lost it, a fierce horn blast imbuing him with last-second caution as he paused and then heaved himself out of the car, hitching up his jeans and then hunkering away.

Sitting in the tensed silence that the still car now afforded him, Mr. Crimpton replaced his glasses but closed his eyes, resting his elbows on the dashboard and cupping his forehead in his hands.

He had come back too soon. He could have had an entire extra week of sick leave. But no, he had opted to return, having thought, having actually believed, that it would be for the better. After all, the full week that he did take off to recover had been spent virtually climbing the walls of his cramped apartment, too much in dread of going back to work to be able to relax. Cooped up there with nothing to look at but inane television and his aquarium, he had ended up pacing and chain-smoking the whole time. So he had returned to work, thinking that there must be some truth to the notion of facing adversity and throwing oneself right back into the ring. He had gone back, expecting to confront his problems and had then been appalled when, indeed, he had ended up doing just that, finding that now they had somehow compounded to be much worse.

Lifting his head to blink through the Datsun's chipped windshield, he recalled yet again how much the interior of a car reminded him of an aquarium. He had purchased his a few years ago when a coworker had attested to how tranquil and soothing it was to sit and watch hers. In fact, she had informed the office forthrightly; she found that she watched it more than she did her television set. So he had gone out and bought a sizable tank and a number of colorful fish and had set it all up, waiting hopefully for the magic to happen. True, it was more captivating than anything on television, but, then, so was staring at the wall, and he had found the entire enterprise to be minimally diverting, although, if nothing else, a genuine hassle. Yes, he would give her that much; it was definitely a pain to maintain.

In the interim, he had begun to reflect upon the phenomenon of how each driving test seemed like a ride in a massive aquarium on wheels, in which he and his alternating contestants sailed around the city, safe within the climate-controlled, hushed inner sanctum that a car's interior and frame and shock absorption could create, just flowing along as if in pressurized slow motion until they encountered any manner of obstacle and then the aquarium promptly and neatly erupted, exploding and imploding simultaneously in a fuel-injected tidal wave of sparks and flames. Almost twenty years with the DMV had rendered him a highly strung individual; he had always been nervous, even as a child; but this constant, tensed uneasiness had evolved until he was no longer merely a nervous case, but was now a nervous wreck. The accident, naturally, had not helped.

One accident, in nearly two decades of stringently constrained anxiety, he'd had only one major accident in all of that time; and yet, just as the statistics insisted, one was all that it took; and the fact that everyone was able to walk away from it, while yielding a multitude of compliments and slaps on the back, as well as pointed remarks about how lucky he was, did not succeed in reassuring or, moreover, reasserting his shattered nerves.

He closed his eyes and lowered his head again, feeling the tension extend tautly past his sinuses and up into his temples. Why had he left his cigarettes back at the office? They were not really supposed to smoke while out on the driving tests; but, then, they were not supposed to go slamming into curbs and incurring blowouts either. He rested his haggard face in his hands and permitted his narrow shoulders to go slack.

That day had started out promisingly enough. The kid had been his first driver that sunny morning, as they headed out in the showroom-perfect Buick, so nice and clean—even the fresh plastic smell was intact.

The kid had been well-dressed and polite, a sheep dog's mane of blond hair framing a studious face, his eyes serious behind his glasses. He had executed all of the instructions given to him with virtually flawless compliance, and they had proceeded along the set route without delay. The course was different each time, but the progression was always the same; they began in a residential area, worked their way up into a business district, and then headed out for the ultimate proving ground, the freeway.

Most kids—and even a lot of adults—did not often make it that far; Billy, for example, he thought caustically. But that kid, that day, had brought them onto that eight-lane expanse of prospective terror with such smooth confidence that even in his usually stricken frame of mind, Mr. Crimpton had been induced to relax a bit and even engage in conversation with the kid, something that no driving examiner ever encouraged, Mr. Crimpton certainly no exception.

However, this kid's level-headed maturity had put him at ease, especially when even the topics he broached were related specifically to driving. What, for instance, was in those squat, round, jumbo Tupperware-like containers that were arranged at various junctions and exits along the freeway? Mr. Crimpton explained that they were absorption buffers intended to diminish vehicular impact in the event of a collision and that they were usually filled with either sand or water or, as in the case of newer versions, some sort of thick gel deemed to be even more effective.

The kid had nodded comprehendingly, noting when they next passed a cluster of them that their arrangement was similar to that of ninepins set up in a bowling alley lane. This comparison had not sat very well with Mr. Crimpton's nerves, a comment like that being unexpected from a kid like that—or so he thought at the time. Now, it was an obvious omen of what was to come; but, on that morning, he could not have guessed that the kid would take an opportunity to test his theory.

It was, nonetheless, still an accident, though, for neither of them could have foreseen the speed demon who had come racing up from behind, apparently late for some engagement and vastly discontent to find himself behind a driver who was actually observing the speed limit.

Unable to pass, he had bore down on them, tailgating and blaring his horn, startling the heretofore unflappable kid, who reflexively sped up, pulling right into the blind spot of an adjacent semitruck just as it was lumbering to change lanes, diagonally cutting off their path and plunging the kid into a frozen-panic attack, Mr. Crimpton becoming just as rigid as the stately Buick plowed up onto a median and buried itself in the triangular arrangement of buffers, the thick gray cylinders bursting open, their lids sailing, saucerlike in all directions as the car was, indeed, brought to a careening halt. Had they been bowling, it would have counted as a strike, and the only other silver lining in evidence when the aquarium shattered that day was that the sand and the gel were runners up, for the verdict was ice-cold water, so much sweeping into the fractured car that it obscured the compromising if coincidental fact that Mr. Crimpton had wet himself upon impact.

Sitting there, staring into the ethereal white of his airbag, he had wondered if he had transcended into the heavenly firmament, the sound of the sirens hardly angelic as he began to regain what remnants of his senses he still possessed. When the paramedics came and retrieved his body from the car, he let them do all the work, allowing them to place his stiffly-braced form on the gurney, his clipboard still clutched in his hands. So this was what rigor mortis felt—or didn't feel like. As they took him away, his destination either the hospital, a mental institution, or a mortuary, he didn't know which, his speechless, failing cognizance was able to register one final observation before they sedated him and all was at peace with the world—that little sheep dog was up and walking around, angrily berating everyone, including Mr. Crimpton, for the accident, assiduously taking notes for his parent's insurance company.

A fierce burst of recollection brought Mr. Crimpton upright again, his eyes blinking severely as he glared about the car. Even the thought of the accident made his hair stand on end. That had scarcely been two months ago; what was he doing back out here driving around with these lunatics? People as nervous as he was did not generally pursue death wishes, did they? It was certainly not job loyalty; he had been burned out almost ten years ago and by now outrightly hated what he was doing for a living. Was it complacency then? If so, how was it possible to be so complacent and on the edge of a nervous collapse simultaneously?

Sighing bitterly, he squinted at the windshield, noticing the flyer that had not been there a few moments ago. Glowering at it, he would have dismissed it altogether—it wasn't his windshield, after all—but he was confused about it having been placed there without him having heard anything. Were his lapses into catatonic catnaps of mind-splintering contemplation of the all-too-certain uncertainties of his future becoming so profound that they disenfranchised him from the whole world one blackout at a time? And if so, was that good or bad?

Reluctantly, he climbed out of the car, seeing other flyer-bedecked windshields, but no indication of who had been distributing them. He slipped it out from under the wiper blade and peered at it, wincing at its color, the shade of green that only a used-car salesman would wear. Expecting a series of coupons for pizza takeout or the announcement of the opening of a new dry-cleaning store, when he read what the flyer instead entailed, a sardonic smile very nearly crept onto his thin features. A self-help group, with an emphasis on relieving work-related stress? Now, that was a good one. Anything for a buck, he surmised, as "free" as the flyer otherwise indicated. If it really was a voluntary service, then it would surely be that much more of a joke.

In spite of what this leaflet obviously was, he despised litter and instead absently affixed it to his clipboard, seeing the clear-cut grade he had marked on the route earlier and grimacing in disgust, then glancing up as Billy came bounding back toward him, wide-eyed and out of breath, his bulky form resting against the Datsun, a hub cap in one hand.

"Well, Billy?" Mr. Crimpton asked in his most clipped voice.

Flushing, Billy hitched up his jeans, his apple-cheeked face even redder as he puffed and shook his head. "My mom says she won't come and get us," he exhaled concisely.

Mr. Crimpton stared at him, frowning quiveringly. "*What?*"

Billy continued to shake his head. "She says I gotta fix the tire," he explained, looking at Mr. Crimpton imploringly. "Can you show me how?"

Clutching his forehead, Mr. Crimpton was unable to respond at first, glancing about in all directions, seeking out the nearest bus stop.

*****

Vanessa studied her face in the mirror, allowing her eyes to travel over each curve and angle of her young but striking features, grateful for the bright lighting of the theater's restroom. She paused and added a bit more eye shadow, then a bit more rouge, and a bit more eyeliner and then simply added more of everything. She could not merely look the part; she had to *be* the part; and, to her mind, it required a lot of makeup; leastwise, that was what she always had been led to believe. The fact that she was young for the role also contributed to the need for these touch-ups, especially the lipstick. She tensed her lips and applied another coat of ruby red, drawing them together expertly and then surveying the result in satisfaction. Her hair, she knew, windblown and unruly, was fine as it was, conveying a look of dark, shampooed abandon, clean but wild.

Pulling her bag up off the floor, she rested it on the counter, digging through the jumble of clothes and then deciding that her blouse was fine. It was white and flowing, giving her a maiden-like appearance. She did want to change skirts, though, having brought along three for her escape to the city—one brown, one black, and one red—all clustered together with her other belongings in the battered old canvas military bag.

She had been living out of that bag for two weeks now, since her arrival there. It contained all of her favorite possessions, few though they were, but nothing that was superfluous or trivial, and she prided herself on having packed so well. She had not exactly been in a hurry that last night, although she had been in a rush, for all of her seventeen years prior, to get out of Portertown as soon as was humanly possible. Kids who grew up in small towns very often came to resent their rural upbringing and long for a more contemporary situation, Vanessa differing from them only in that she outrightly loathed Portertown, as well as most of its inhabitants, including and especially those self-same commiserating kids.

Early on and certainly by the age of ten, she had exhibited a discontent with her far-removed environs, displaying it in a precocious but impressive personality that leaned toward the theatrical; she was often praised as being highly creative and endowed with the talents that would greatly complement a pursuit of the dramatic arts. Her parents had been flattered by these remarks from teachers and other parents, but had passively resisted inspiring their daughter's dreams, because, of course, she was a small-town girl living among small-town folks; and the reality of this environment spoke for itself.

When the train wreck took her parents from her at that age, she had been forced to go and live with her uncle, a decent-enough grump who, unfortunately, was also a drunk. Twenty years in the Army had garnered him his pension, just enough to keep the rent paid on his trailer space and to keep him in bologna and beer.

He was good to his niece and actually gave up his own room in the cramped old Airstream for her, sleeping either on the couch or in his recliner, which was where he spent the bulk of his time anyway, the television his snowy window to the world, through which he watched everyone succeed but himself.

"Ya can't win, darlin'," he would tell her, several times a day in the seven years she lived with him, even though he played the lottery fanatically and watched the results each week religiously. "Ya just can't win."

She was grateful for his generosity; but appreciation was something that she simply could not summon forth, the image of her parent's grave still branded in her young mind, as it would forever be, since the day her uncle had taken her little hand in his grubby bear-paw and led her mutely away from the graveyard. She could not have known then what was in store for her, for a little girl could not be expected to know that, where as she had previously been stamped as lower-class poor folk, she was now, straight-up white trailer trash, a designation that her schoolmates did not hesitate to point out to her.

In the nightmare years of early adolescence that followed, her life alternated between an ongoing, no-holds-barred prize fight and a cold war, smoldering grudge match, high school the ultimate battle ground, each day, literally, every single day proving to be a challenge to her stretched-taut perseverance. Yet she accepted the challenge; as a survivor, she had little choice. She fiercely cast aside her stereotyped stigma, rebelling against preconceived notions by doing passably well in school, but even more so when she was on her own time. She worked any odd job she could find, saving money and building up an impressive wardrobe, its sole purpose to disguise the shame of the birthright that she desperately tried to scrub away each night in her uncle's foul, mold-plastered drizzling shower.

Always clean and presentable, she managed to penetrate the upper strata of elitism in the small town, small-minded school. Classes were a secondary inconvenience to the real purpose that the school served, that being as an opportunity to elevate herself from her lowly beginnings, as she was made to see them, up to a level of respectability, wherein she could at least break even and be treated as an equal. It was a difficult illusion to maintain, for she could never have any friends over to her squalid residence, instead stoically braving bad weather and mile-long walks on back roads to meet them halfway at the movies or the mall or any other typical hangout spot. She had had some truly good friends, some silly and pretentious, not phony, no more than she was, anyway, for she had the good sense to fool everyone but herself, never once losing sight of who she was and what she had been traumatized into thinking she was, instead, holding onto that ugly notion, if only to use it as an impetus to thrust herself further and further away from that perceived truth.

Whereas she could never have friends over to her uncle's trailer, for, although she rabidly attacked its clutter and soiled dinginess, he and his habits simply could not be contained, she oftentimes visited her friends in their homes, modest, domestic examples though they were, their sharp contrast with her own situation always enough to keep her in awe of what it was like to have a family in a regular house, eating dinner, and talking like normal, regular people. She enjoyed these commonplace aspects of her various visits and sleepovers and such, by far more than the actual girlish private time she spent with her friends, during which, as the years passed and their interests evolved, she was a silent participant in their increasingly intense confidences.

At first, she was envious of all that they were beginning to experience, and then, she had begun to take a vicarious pleasure in the exploits in which they all at once seemed to be involved, eventually watching in confusion and then anger as these exploits became hopeless entanglements, all of which revolved around a never-ending constant.

Her formative years had rendered her brash and brazen, and, small-town peer pressure being of an even more wicked variety than the urban sort, she had partaken in more than a fair share of diversions, always ending up disenchanted when the spell broke and she was still who, what, and where she was, disgusted with the reverent significance that the other kids placed on what, to her, were dead-end forms of recreation. The only pseudoadult pursuit, however, was that same never-ending constant; and she witnessed firsthand time and again the disastrous consequences that, in the hands of the school's clique of hormone-stricken boys (this group constituting, in her estimation, the real trash of the region), the soap opera procession of empty and meaningless interactions was unleashed. She had been close, many, many times to becoming embroiled in such affairs herself; but it was, ironically enough, her background that prevented her from being ensnared. Because her delving into these actions would go hand in hand with what everyone's perception of what her shallow, ignorant, slatternly, easy upbringing *must* have been, she knew that, were she to indulge, she would instantly validate every rumor ever whispered about her; and her struggle to obscure her true circumstances would be over. In the face of such defeat, she would never have been able to revive her dreams of escaping and would have surrendered to her clear-cut predestination. To give up, however, was something she just could not do.

Circumstances did little to augment her stand; in fact, it was challenged more vehemently with each year that went by. Even in her senior year, she was hounded by social, economic, and private obstacles, each determined to break her. She doggedly maintained, though, that final year of school; and the rewards of such tenacity were nearly hers to claim in, again, a vicarious sense, when the night finally came on which her uncle compared his lottery ticket with the Ping-Pong balls on his television screen, choking on his beer when the match was made. He had squealed and sputtered in disbelief, Vanessa rushing to his side, not even knowing why he was suddenly so delirious; and she had stood there, daring to share in his joy, watching as the shock of finally seeing his ship come in overwhelmed him, the dire realization of what was happing to him apparent on his gradually pained face as he looked piteously up at her, shaking his head in stunned confusion, murmuring. "Ya just can't win, darlin'," his last words before his heart attack quietly swept him away.

Her life changed, irreversibly so, from that moment onward, although, initially, all she had to do was just stand there and observe. The Army promptly reclaimed their own, and the Lottery Commission was very understanding; the ticket had been his, he was dead, she was underage, and that was that. She had been right there to see them rip the ticket into pieces, stamping it "Null and Void" evidently not good enough.

The tears never came; they were too enmeshed in shock, further waylaid by the State, which likewise deemed her underage, insisting that she go to a foster home. She had been smart enough to see that coming, though; and that last night in the grungy Airstream, she had slowly, methodically, packed her bag, gathered together the money she had managed to tuck away over the years, and had then walked out the door and kept on walking.

The smelly greyhound took her far away from it all, and she never looked back. Landing in the city with only her bag and her ambitions, undaunted by the ridiculous naivety of her dreams, she had instantly set about shedding her small-town stigma.

Her brutally turbulent school years and a steady diet of television dreck had hardened her against what was to come, but, although she was much better prepared than most and the city could not eat her alive, she was a novice, just the same, and it showed.

The Hotel Rochester, a once stately, now sleazy fleabag, had been the first seemingly affordable accommodations she had encountered, the openly hostile desk clerk lewdly sizing her up and down as she had inquired about weekly rates, his beady eyes drawn to her money as she counted it, the price then quadrupling as he informed her that some new policy insisted on monthly rent, instead. Seeing her incredulousness and interpreting her thoughts, he went on to point out that she would not find a better deal anywhere around there, unless she wanted to bed down in a homeless shelter.

Reluctantly, she had paid the exorbitant price, knowing full well that she was being had, reflecting as she climbed the dank stairwell that the bad news was that she was now virtually broke, but that the good news was that she had at least bought herself a roof over her head—with no questions asked—for an entire month. A rundown roof, naturally, she discerned, as she peered around at the room, a faded relic of hostelry, complete with a stubborn, creaking death trap of a Murphy bed. It had hot and cold water, though, and the cockroaches were not immense. What was more, it was her own space, solidly, singly, her very own space.

With a full month to seek out employment, she had wasted no time in plunging into a routine of job applications and interviews, always keeping her eyes open for any theatrical pursuits or venues. She devoured the classified ads and casting calls, but her age and inexperience coupled with her questionably transitional address and minimal knowledge of the city handicapped her in both respects. After a lean, hungry week, she was not about to entertain the idea that she had made a mistake, for there was absolutely no going back. She did not have to ponder the conundrum about being unable to go home again. There was no home to which she could return.

What she did not realize was that she obviously would have to adjust her sights and change her approach to the situation. Fighting off doubt and depression with a conviction in her aspirations and a now desperate determination to succeed, if only for spite, she had forced herself to concentrate and brainstorm, at length, dwelling upon and then rationalizing her priorities. By the end of the second week of Top Ramen and PBJ, she definitely had a plan of attack. Nothing would stand in the way of her goal of becoming an actress, because, apart from that goal, she had nothing else.

Her perseverance ever the guideline, now scarcely a week later, she stood before the mirror in the theater, only a few minutes away from what would be the biggest, most demanding performance of her life. She opted for the red skirt, scooting into a stall to put it on, smoothing over her new pantyhose, and slipping on her plain but carefully cleaned-up heels. Stepping back toward the counter, she surveyed herself in the mirror once more, impressed with her reflection. The semienjoyable escape of high school drama classes had taught her well not only in the art of acting but also in the mechanics of stage presence and appearance.

Removing the flimsy little purse from her canvas bag, she then stashed the bag securely under the counter, wedging it between a pipe and the wall.

She looped the purse over one shoulder and opened it, yanking out the flyer she had snatched off a transistor box earlier that week. Rereading the notes she had scrawled on its blank reverse, she paused, taking a moment to glance at the actual import of the brochure, skimming over the description of peer counseling for people finding themselves at a difficult crossroads in life.

"Lame," she concluded, stuffing the puke-green flyer back into her purse.

Emerging from the theater's restroom, she strode confidently through the lobby, ignoring the posters for coming attractions that flanked the walls, as well as the concessions stands, and, for that matter, the hunger she felt as she exited the theater into the cool night air, pausing under the brilliant lighting of the marquee and then moving up the sidewalk to a bus stop.

It took an investment of nearly two dollars in change and three bus rides, each one appreciably warm, before she reached her destination, stepping out into the chill and wishing her blouse was more substantial or at least not so thin. She had a jacket, of course, but wearing it tonight would most likely defeat the purpose of her intentions. All her life, she had been dodging stereotypes; and the past few years, she had defied conformity; and while the routine of the starry-eyed country girl who went to the big city to be a movie star and wound up out in the cold, on the streets, was so laughably identical to her circumstances, the one point that differentiated herself from the myriad lost dreamers who had come before her was quite simple, in as much as they were all *themselves* and she was *herself*, and she was going to make it. She was going to win. Period. She would succeed as an actress, because, as an actress, she could be—or do—anything at all. The only requirements were resolve and a suspension of reality.

With this in mind, she found the intersection she had discreetly asked about earlier and then, after scoping out any competition, commenced a leisurely stroll up and down the sidewalk.

*****

His pace swift in spite of his years, his posture rigid and poised, Father Gilchrist approached the wide, sloping steps of St. Leonard's, his gait unslowed as he walked right past, rounding the corner and heading up the sidewalk alongside the spike-tipped wrought iron fence that encircled the churchyard. His tall figure unmistakable in a black homburg hat and raincoat, traditional outdoor apparel for a priest of his age and seniority, he was obliged to return the greetings of the few people he had passed along the way with a brisk nod and smile, the latter vanishing as he passed through the side gate and entered the church through the rear entrance that connected it to the rectory.

He had long since discovered that, by using this route, he was least likely to encounter any of his parishioners along the way back from his various outings. Moreover, if he had timed it right, as Father Gilchrist took great pains to do, he would be able to avoid any of his church colleagues as well.

Pausing in the dark vestibule, he hung up his hat and coat, standing still and listening, his wizened, pale features focused upon the linoleum, his snow white hair neatly combed back in a way that might complement his frosty eyebrows and rather distinguished features, were it not for the perpetual frown that he wore. He was clad in a black suit with a traditional clergical collar and front, avidly disliking the modern black shirts and their plastic white tabs, the priest's version of the clip-on tie, he had once informed a group of novices, who persisted in wearing them anyway.

Perceiving not a sound, he nodded in satisfaction and moved to the entryway table, scanning over the day's mail and irritably scooping it up, carrying it down the corridor, passing through the appreciably empty kitchen, noting that Mrs. Tucker must still be out grocery shopping, purchasing whatever she needed to prepare the travesty that would pass for dinner.

He strode into the small, cluttered office that housed St. Leonard's administrational needs, his frown intensifying as he set the mail on the old rolltop desk and sniffed sharply. The usual stale air of the musty office was strangely pervaded with a clearly foreign odor, saccharine and offensive. He glared about, noticing a few spindly flowers arranged in a narrow vase atop a filing cabinet, alongside a photograph of Mrs. Henley, the secretary for St. Leonard's for nineteen years, up until the cancer had claimed her last spring.

His gaze rested on her lopsided, salty smile, his features hardening even more so than usual as he thought of her—the short, sassy woman who took no guff and had run the office with clockwork ease. She had been beloved. His pouch-like lips puckered severely and then relaxed as he inhaled perfunctorily and pulled the flowers out of the vase, turning to yank open the window alongside the desk and tossing them outside. She had been loved, and now she was gone, and she needed the stench of fresh flowers about as much as he did. Pausing, he then grasped the flower vase and dropped it out the window as well, lest anyone attempt to repeat the affront. He then slammed the window closed and turned the photograph face down, seating himself at the desk and briskly delving into the mail. Since Mrs. Henley had been irreplaceable, he had not looked into hiring a new secretary, in spite of the protests his refusal evoked, instead handling the office work himself. He too could achieve clockwork efficiency.

The electric bill—no need to pay that; they had plenty of candles in the vestry after all.

The water bill—same thing. They could set out a rain barrel, for all he cared. The heavens shall open up and the droplets shall fall.

The gas bill—Mrs. Tucker's cooking gave them gas enough, as it was. What was more, without gas, her stove would not function, and she would hence be unable to cook, so much the better.

The telephone bill—ah, final Shutoff notice, no less! He scarcely glanced at it, had never even opened it before. The beauty of the telephone bill going unpaid was that if you left the phone off the hook as often as he made it a point to do, it really didn't matter if there was a dial tone or not.

The final piece of mail was enclosed in an impressive envelope with an embossed seal signifying that it was a special document from the Archdiocese. One eyebrow lifting skeptically, Father Gilchrist deigned to open it.

It proved to be an invitation to a class reunion, from the Archbishop himself, the enclosed list containing countless names that Father Gilchrist recalled all the way back to parochial school, its formally rendered calligraphy requesting an RSVP.

Scowling, Father Gilchrist folded up the invitation. I'll give you an RSVP all right, he glowered, placing all the contents neatly back into the envelope and resealing it. Hadn't he seen enough of those dunderheads back when they were all studying for the priesthood?

Seizing a fountain pen, he drew an arrow upon the envelope, pointing it toward his name and then writing in swirling formal script, *Not at this address. Return to sender.*

Nodding sharply, he surveyed his handiwork and then, inspired, wrote the same on all the bills, gathering them all together and standing up. Now, it was in the hands of the mailman, he thought briskly, then frowning as he discerned an even more expedient way of dealing with these irritants, dropping them all in the wastepaper can.

His office work thus completed, he was about to depart when his eye caught the dry-erase whiteboard hung alongside the door, on which had been arranged the weekly agenda. He noticed that in the four o'clock hour, he was scheduled to be taking confession, all week long. His face darkening, he was about to correct this obvious inaccuracy when a knock at the side entrance penetrated his anger, and he crossly replaced the eraser to its tray, stalking out of the office. Ordinarily, he would ignore someone knocking at the door, but today, he was just in the mood.

Pulling open the door, he glared down at a short, gawky boy who clutched a small package. "Um, special delivery for Sister Angelica," he said hesitantly.

Father Gilchrist's features pinched distastefully. "Do I look like Sister Angelica to you?" he snapped back, startling the kid. "She's next door at St. Leonard's Hospital, no doubt in the nursery, crooning to her brood!"

The kid took a step back but held his ground. "Well, can't I just leave it with you?"

"Well, what is it?" demanded the old priest severely. Knowing Sister Angelica, it was probably a time bomb. Lord knew he had contemplated sending her one more than once.

His jaw dropping slightly, the kid shrugged. "How should I know?" he retorted, looking down at the package. "It's from some music store on the south side."

Father Gilchrist grimaced in aggravation. Guitar strings, no doubt. The tireless girl went through guitar strings the way a hangman went through rope.

"Oh, very well!" he grated, reluctantly accepting the package. "It's a pity you didn't bring it COD. I could have used a good laugh," he added, thus instantly settling any question of a tip.

The kid shook his head. "Man, I thought you guys were supposed to be nice and friendly and all that!" he declared bluntly. "What the hell's your problem?"

Father Gilchrist rose to his full height. "I have no time for rhetorical questions!" he snapped enigmatically. "Be on your way, you impertinent churl, or I'll conjure up a storm and have you struck by lightning!"

With that, he slammed the door, staring sourly at the package in his hands, tempted to place it with the other mail that had arrived that day, instead dropping it on the side table and then striding briskly back into the office to the schedule board.

Now then, where were we? He glared at the arrangement of the agenda, seizing the eraser again. He recognized the handwriting as that of the only other priest at St. Leonard's, the young and progressive and eager and quite unwanted protégé imposed upon him by the Archdiocese. Almost forty years younger, fresh from Notre Dame and aglow with new ideas and concepts and an unfailing enthusiasm that was unbearably upbeat, he had come to St. Leonard's almost a year ago and had been enthusing ever since.

"Hello, you must be Father Alistair!" he had proclaimed upon their first meeting, extending an energetic handshake. "I'm Father Ralph!"

Father Gilchrist's indignation at being addressed by his first name had been outweighed by his disbelief over that of his new associate.

Father Ralph? Now there was a distinguished appellation! Not as impressive as, say, Father Hank or Father Chuck, but still quite commanding.

Well, Father Ralph, since you are so Gung-Ho about your new tour of duty, I will take you out of the trenches and put you where the real heat is. He erased the four o'clock column for both of them, patiently, pointedly reversing what had been written so that now, Father Ralph would be appearing in the confessional booth and *he* would be making the rounds at the hospital next door, a much less-taxing responsibility, especially when, as was the case with Father Gilchrist, he had no intention of doing any such thing.

Brushing his hands together, he glanced at his wristwatch, seeing only his wrist and blinking. *Damnation!* Naturally, he could only have left it in one place, having purchased it for just that reason. His jaw set in the bitterest consternation, he stalked down the corridor and paused before the door that would lead into the church, opening off to one side of the altar in a thankfully discreet alcove. He slowly turned its ancient knob, drawing the door open and peering past it, much relieved when he beheld that the church pews were empty, the only person in evidence a small woman meditating before a lit votive candle at one of the stations of the cross near the front entrance. Moving with pronounced stealth and surprising vigor, he darted past the chancel and made his way toward the opposite wall.

As old as it was, St. Leonard's Parish still retained most of its original beauty, its stained glass and statuary rendered in the classical styles, all intact and lending to the smoky, incense-infused hush, which was the hallowed essence of any House of Worship, all of these simple but majestic qualities having long since gone unnoticed by Father Gilchrist over the years, no more visible to him now as he hastened over to the varnished austerity of the confessional booth.

Even in his haste, he was obliged to slow down as he approached it, lest there might actually be a penitent inside of it, waiting to vent. It was still well within the four o'clock hour after all; and Father Gilchrist was, in fact, the one scheduled to be on hand for the task that day, which, of course, was why he had gone out in the first place. And what a mistake that had been, he now reflected crossly. That had been one of the worst films he had ever seen, and upon its conclusion, he had steadfastly demanded—and received—a refund.

Still in all, a box office flop was preferable to the pitfalls of the confessional, and he studied the innocuous-looking box as if it might contain a booby trap. Glancing over at the lone woman, he gratefully noted that she was still deep in meditation, her lips moving silently, her gray features intensely focused.

No doubt praying for a new pastor, he deduced dryly, turning to focus upon the penitent's side of the booth, then gingerly pulling open its gleaming door.

It was empty—of sinners, anyway. He scowled at the few pieces of litter, which some imbecile had left inside, obliged to bend down and scoop them up. A candy wrapper and a hideous green flyer, both of which he shoved in his jacket pocket before turning toward his side of the booth. Why people couldn't leave anything sensible, like money, was beyond him. Over the years, that had been the one item he had yet to find, although in all other respects, the confessional had been a veritable lost and found, save for once when a drunken derelict had mistaken the booth for a port a potty. Oh, the relief of unburdening one's soul!

Glowering horribly at the recollection, he pulled open the adjacent door, not even leaning inside, able to see the luminescent watch face hanging from the nail he had unceremoniously affixed to the interior some time ago. He snatched the watch away from it and slid it onto his wrist, wondering how he could have forgotten to retrieve it at the close of yesterday's bull session. One prominent reason presented itself, but he abruptly dismissed the idea as he turned to flee the scene, almost crashing into the short meditator as she smiled up at him.

"Oh, hello, Father," she whispered happily. "Will you be taking confession now?"

Somehow managing a chilling smile, Father Gilchrist wordlessly reached past her and pulled open the penitent's door, holding it open for her in forced gallantry as the woman scurried eagerly inside, the old priest staring up at the vaulted ceiling and distinctly mouthing the words, "Why hast thou forsaken me?"

*****

Later that evening, having skipped dinner, Father Gilchrist had taken refuge in his quarters at the top floor of the rectory, where he knew, for the most part, he would be undisturbed.

As he prepared to retire for the night, he crossed to the room's only window, glaring out at the streetlight below before firmly closing the frayed curtains, trying to recall why he had opened them at all. In the thirty-odd years he had been pastor of St. Leonard's, he had been a privileged constant in the gradual decline and disintegration of the neighborhood and its parish. The altar had given him a bird's-eye view of the sweeping changes that had decimated a once-thriving congregation, the original parishioners having died off unprogenitated or moved away altogether, in either event, going unreplenished. The dismal, funereal throng that huddled in those vacuous pews now resembled not so much a church roster as a group of refugees from a fallout shelter.

Yet he seemed to be the only one aware of this encroaching, stagnant decay, which he had witnessed over all the years. Father Ralph was too busy, out saving the world with some charity event or social function, and his eyes were too young and untrained to see the wreckage.

It was sometimes amazing to him that the Archdiocese maintained their charter at all, though the reason was not long in the guessing. It lay next door, in St. Leonard's Hospital; now, there was the real moneymaker. It was a very small facility, but in its twelve years of existence, it had been a staple, in the medical community anyway. The church was just part and parcel with it—Gothic window dressing.

That, however, was *not* why Father Gilchrist regarded the hospital with such unabiding loathing. It was not even Sister Angelica's first floor daycare nursery school and all of its suffocating promise, which engendered such wrath. It was the staggering death toll that those corridors represented to him, the hundreds, literally hundreds of ghosts whom he had to face whenever he ventured down its icily sterile halls. All of the friends and colleagues he had ever even remotely cared about had passed through those doors, never to return.

Well, Mrs. Henley had been the last. He had scarcely set foot in the place since her passing and rigidly avoided having anything to do with it. Its languishing occupants did not want to see him anymore than he wanted to see them. He had long since faced the fact that he was viewed as some sort of ghoulish embodiment of the Grim Reaper, delightedly working his beads in the shadows and waiting by their bedsides to steal their souls. To be inundated with the unchanging finality that awaited every person in the end was bad enough; to be directly associated with it was intolerable.

Hence, he scarcely even made the pretense of making the rounds there any longer, a fact that went neither unnoticed nor unappreciated by the senior nurse, an officious bulldozer of a woman, behind whose back he had never once referred to as Nurse Wretched, preferring to address her as such face to face. Nor was his cheerful disposition missed by the chief physician, a snooty, baronial wasp whom Father Gilchrist had long since dubbed Dr. Blue Blood. He had once informed Father Gilchrist that his services were not, in fact, missed at all, since he had "the bedside manner of a mortician," an assessment that Father Gilchrist heartily endorsed, since, he had replied, the funeral home was where most of their patients ended up anyway.

No, he did not miss making the rounds and took pride in the fact that he was not missed either. That suited him just fine, he reflected, as he changed into his pajamas, too tired to run a bath. Ready for bed, his scowl fell upon the rubbish he had found in the confessional, having emptied his jacket pockets onto his bureau top. He read over the flyer briefly before tossing it and the wrapper into the trash. *A self-help group for people feeling out of sorts with the world?*

He bitterly turned back his bedcovers and removed his slippers. *Self-help, indeed*, he scoffed. In a world in which all anyone did anymore was to help themselves to whatever they could get, the flyer's promises seemed quite apropos. *Give and then take and then take back what you gave in the first place, that was the order of the day, wasn't it? The Survivor's Guide to Salvation, in three easy steps.*

Scowling, he climbed into bed, switching off the bedside lamp and thrusting his head against the pillow, pulling the covers up over his shoulders, and rolling abruptly over onto one side, turning his back to the faint light that shone in through the thread-bare curtains, hazily penetrating the darkness of his room.

Chapter 2

"YOU GOT THE BATHROOM IN front, storage in the back, table in the corner, and a whole mess a' foldin' chairs," the woman explained concisely, gesturing widely, the keys to the union hall rattling in her hand.

Dr. Pendleton had paused in his polite nodding, his gaze continuing to slip to the worn concrete floor as the owner pointed out the various amenities. The majority of it was covered in a heavy layer of sawdust, save for the center, which had been cleared enough to reveal the chalk outline of a human form.

"You got full run a' the place, seein' as how you've paid up so much in advance," the owner continued, smiling at him crookedly. She was a sturdy woman, with a florid, wide face, her curly, blonde hair partially covered by a naval watch cap. One eye was obscured by a black eye patch, the other twinkling in a shrewd, all-knowing way. She wore a massive peacoat over mostly denim clothes, her feet ensconced in thick mariner's boots. Dr. Pendleton had found it difficult to focus on her one eye and impolite to regard her eye patch and had then been distracted from looking at her at all, once he had glanced down at his penny loafers and noticed what was underfoot.

"Come and go as ya' please. Nobody to bother ya'. Electricity up and runnin' obviously. Otherwise, I'd be talkin' to ya' in the dark," she laughed boisterously.

His automatic nodding resuscitated, Dr. Pendleton cleared his throat, shifting his grip on his attaché case. "Uh, thank you, Mrs. Simms," he replied, cautiously glancing around at the rest of the murky union hall.

It was an older building, tucked between even older structures, in a less-than-upscale neighborhood, its walls coated with chipped plaster, its rafters exposed. It was drafty and rather dank smelling, and there were occasional rustling noises, which he had yet to identify, lurking in the shadows. Lacking windows, the walls had been arranged with faded union posters, which might have gone all the way back to the Great Depression. He cleared his throat. Or earlier.

"Well, if there's nothing else then, Doctor, I'll be off," the owner, Mrs. Simms, announced congenially, gesticulating with an upturned thumb. "My boys and me are fixin' to ship out for a week or three. Gonna' go trollin' for crabs."

Blinking, Dr. Pendleton attempted to meet her gaze again, flushing as he took note of the chalk outline once more, feeling slightly obliged to ask.

"Uh, I was curious, Mrs. Simms," he began, immediately modifying the question when the woman's eyebrows lifted dauntingly. "Who…who leased your building before I inquired about it?"

Mrs. Simms' singular eye sparkled. "It was the Longshoreman's Union, of course!" she replied forthrightly. "Had all of their pow-wows, weddin's, birthdays, and bar mitzvahs here. And a rowdy, drunken, hell-raisin' lot they are. I can promise you that!" She nodded vigorously, stepping in closer to him. "And I ought to know. I was their shop steward for twenty years!"

She emitted a bellowing laugh, roughly clapping the doctor on the shoulder, still guffawing as he winced and accepted the ring of keys she extended to him.

"I'll be off, now, Doctor. Have a good time doin' whatever t'is you'll be up to here!" She paused, eyeing him curiously. "What is it you're plannin' on doin' here, Doc, if you'll pardon my askin'?"

Shifting, Dr. Pendleton shrugged with strained casualness. "Uh, well, I plan to use the space for a meeting, uh, for a peer-counseling, self-help group," he began, prepared to warm up to the subject. "As a psychologist—"

"Aha! A psychologist!" exclaimed Mrs. Simms in discovery. "Oh, so you're not a sawbones. You're one of them headshrinkers! Well, I'll be! Never did put much stock in all that malarkey, but it's for certain there's a passel a' screwballs out there could benefit from a dose! Well, cool beans, Doc, you have yourself a time!" she declared, sauntering toward the door and turning to give him another twinkling glance. "And if you've any friends interested in leasin' other places, you tell 'em Gertie Simms is their gal, damn straight! I'll be at sea for a spell, but back in port soon's the beer runs out!"

With another veritable cackle, she left Dr. Pendleton to contemplate the hall he had rented sight unseen over the telephone, trying to envision it after a bit of basic cleaning and rearrangement. He tried, for several minutes, in fact, idly clutching his attaché case and the key ring, turning in slow circles, and eventually ceasing the attempt.

It would suffice because it had to suffice; it was not as if the meetings would be centered around interior decorating. He did want for the participants to be marginally comfortable, of course, and had a few ideas as to how to begin to achieve that—at least for the first few sessions. After that, if all went well, he was certain that the essence of the meetings would transcend their actual environment, because they would actively be focusing upon the issues before them. He considered that idea briefly, reflecting that, in that light, having plain, unremarkable surroundings could be advantageous, in as much as there would be little to distract them from their discussion.

This notion impressed him slightly, and he resolved to remember to mention it to Dr. Whittaker when next he saw him, curious if the older doctor had ever had a similar situation. Feeling somewhat positive, he looked about a bit more, this time seeing the potential of the place as he began to walk toward its front entrance, deciding that he should, nonetheless, do something about the floor.

Peering closely at the set of keys as he paused outside of the union hall, he tested the various locks, his attaché case situated between his feet. He still had a number of flyers to distribute, having learned a few of the more prominent dos and don'ts on his first night, mainly don'ts. Thumbtacks were not especially efficient; staplers worked very well unless dropped in the street and run over by a cement mixer. Scotch tape did well only on glass. Bulletin boards were helpful. Car windshields were not the best approach; he had only covered about five of those before looking up from a Volkswagen to see the driver of a Rolls-Royce approach his car and remove the flyer, holding it up and smiling over at him as he shredded it to pieces and drove away.

From that point forward, he had confined himself to community places with more success, or less interference. It had been taxing work, which he had hoped his enthusiasm for the project would fuel and which quickly had become too much to handle all at once.

Hence, he had paced himself and allowed at least for a few days, and now, he was down to perhaps a couple dozen or so. He stooped and selected one from his attaché case, carefully thumbtacking *and* scotch-taping it to the front door of the hall, focusing on it briefly.

This would be the place. Getting the word out had not been easy, but he knew that it would be worth it in the long run. It had to be.

*****

Later that week, Mr. Crimpton happened to be in the employee break room to hear an interoffice rumor, another occupational hazard that he did his best to avoid, this particular hearsay being something that he would have been especially anxious to shun, since it had a dread-inspiring authenticity to it.

Time flies, none other than Mrs. Aquariums herself observed as she mentioned the forthcoming employee review, which they would all have to undergo, with special emphasis on the driving test examiners. It stood to reason, of course, that, periodically, the efficacy of these people should be assessed to determine that their abilities, instincts, alertness, and sanity were all still on average in keeping with the basic job parameters.

With a shudder, Mr. Crimpton had recalled how his last review had gone; the car had nearly ended up in a ditch. The only reason he had passed at all was that it had been conducted by an examiner with whom he once closely worked, and he had given him a good rating only out of friendship. It would be highly unlikely to receive that sort of deference again, since that examiner had finally opted for retirement—*lucky bastard*. What was worse was that test had been administered long before the accident, when his nerves were only just half shot. God only knew how he could hope to pass any such review the way he was now.

It was such a ridiculous routine anyway, he had inwardly raged, as he listened to his coworkers babble about how inconvenient it would be, on company time. Why did his own skills as a driver have to be tested when his job was to sit in the passenger seat and observe? What difference did it make if he were a Sunday driver or a stock-car racer behind the wheel? What did any of that have to do with what his actual job was?

Naturally, he knew the procedural platitudes that such questions would receive in response; this was the DMV after all. Its office workers were reviled for a reason, although Mr. Crimpton's own dislike for them was mostly out of jealousy—an air-conditioned stationary aquarium, even if filled with sharks, killer whales, stingrays, and other such species of the general public, wherein the only wheels with which one had to be concerned were attached to a chair. Divine. Utopian. These people had it made, and they didn't even know it.

The unwelcome news was punctuated by the fact that the reviews would commence within the next month. Already, he could feel the walls closing in as he choked down some aspirin with the sludge-like coffee. There was nothing he could say or do to prevent it, since so much as discussing his inhibitions with a coworker would be tantamount to making an announcement over the PA system, and once they smelled blood, it would be all over for him. That left him just a few weeks of harrowing, chain-smoking worry to prepare for this vehicular crucible—or, more realistically, enough time to buy a policy, name a beneficiary, and then purchase a burial plot. Instead of a headstone, they could set up an engine block, the hood ornament standing as a testament to his life's work and to his last ride, which he would no doubt be obliged to oversee, if only in spirit, to make sure that the procession of cars following his hearse had all turned on their headlights.

*****

Vanessa's first night of her improvised career had been unsuccessful and yet had yielded results. She had walked up and down that street for over three grueling hours, swallowing her mounting, almost immutable, shame by adopting a virtually marching pace, eventually calming down and reviewing the dozens of rationalizing, logical points of what she had made up her mind to do. It was necessary, it was a job, it would provide money, and it was not real.

That was the main point—it was not real.

Her pacing had expanded to incorporate two more blocks and would have extended further had she not, at length, encountered other prospective sellers, receiving from them an ear-scorching and humiliating diatribe, which had sent her racing back to her previous stretch of sidewalk. Bold as she was, street smart as she had become, she was not about to encroach upon anyone else's territory, particularly not on that of obviously veteran merchants.

Their screeching censure had so cowed her that she at first clung to the shadows and doorways of the miserable few yards of cracked, stained concrete, shying fearfully away from anyone's approach, the foot traffic appreciably minimal, the noise of the city nevertheless roaring against her braced and inwardly petrified senses. Her knees began to quiver with each step, the cold joining with her increasing misgivings, doubt and humility clouding her thoughts as she began to question how it was possible that she could even be thinking of doing this, even as that first car rolled up and paused, idling ominously alongside of her.

Heart pounding, she had tentatively approached it, peering into its open window at the driver, a youngish man with a lewdly suggestive grin, everything about him, even the casual dangle of his hand as he leaned against the wheel conveying his intention as he gazed expectantly up at her.

"You into the whole group thing?" he asked, invitingly blunt, Vanessa only then realizing that he was not alone in the car.

Seated in the rear were two girls, one perhaps in her early twenties and the other, for all of her makeup and poised sophistication, clearly younger even than Vanessa. Her own age obviously perceived as the perfect complement between these other two, she had glanced back at the waiting driver and summoned up a curt smile.

"No," she had replied concisely, giving him a precise nod.

He had shrugged in utter nonchalance. "Too bad," he returned easily, driving away.

Watching him go, she blinked in mild surprise, knowing that she had made the right decision, but unsure as to why. That clearly would have been easy money, and it could even have offered the incentive of safety in numbers. Yet, she had passed on it.

Confused and rapidly trying to discern if she should be furiously lambasting herself, her introspect was diverted by the approach of the second car. A bit more emboldened, she had leaned over to peer into it, her gaze settling on her uncle.

Startled, she realized, of course, that the man only looked like her deceased relative, looked and smelled like him; she noticed, catching a whiff of the virtual fumes that were emanating from him as he peered hopefully at her, his pudgy features soused and plaintive, an open can of beer clutched in one thick hand.

Staring back, she opened her mouth, and the words came out before she could contemplate how instinctually perfect they were. "Can you give me a ride uptown, mister? I'm s'pose to meet my boyfriend, and I'm already a half-hour late."

She had watched as the man's face sank in utter dejection, slowly shaking his head, almost expecting him to say, "Ya' just can't win," as he quietly pulled away.

The third car marked the turning point, Vanessa noticing it only after it had passed her at least three times. The driver appeared to be circling the block, and she began to wonder if maybe he were lost. Either that or very highly particular she had reflected, trying to determine if that was good or bad when, upon the fourth revolution, he pulled up alongside of her and leaned awkwardly toward the passenger window to speak to her.

A few minutes later, she was seated in the car, silently studying him as they both commenced to circle the block. He was middle-aged, thin, and nondescript, his eyes darting owlishly behind his glasses, his voice dry and nervous. His obvious agitation actually helped to put Vanessa at ease as she realized with almost flippant surprise that this was *his* first time in the market, this insight giving her considerable confidence as she awaited his heretofore unstated expectations. They eventually pulled into a parking space and merely sat there, Vanessa simply watching him as he continued to grip the wheel and stare through the windshield out into the dark.

At length, the silence became strained, and she had begun to wonder if he were actually waiting for her; was she supposed to start seducing him without any directions, or was it all on him to call the shots?

She didn't know; how the hell should she know? Was this guy a psycho or something? Why were they just sitting there?

As she regarded his profile, taking in his pensive, frozen expression, his moist, transfixed gaze, the answer began to dawn on her. Even if it hadn't, the ring on his white-knuckled finger and the child's car seat in the rear were indication enough; and it was no surprise when, at last, swallowing harshly, he continued to avoid her gaze as he spoke. "I can't do this," he murmured, mainly to himself. "What am I doing here?"

Staring at him, Vanessa had felt a surge of remorse and could only combat it with the sudden anger that likewise filled her heart. She attempted to direct it at him, as a reaction to his having obviously been wasting her time, but knew that such was not at all the case.

Swallowing quietly herself, she had tried to think of something, anything, to say, wanting to scream at him and yet also comfort him and something else besides. She felt the impending desire to confide in him, the thought instantly rejected as she shifted in her seat and moved to push open the door, for the transaction was clearly not going to happen.

"Wait!" he had called out, the desperation in his voice startling her as she turned to stare uncertainly at him, unable to believe that he had changed his mind, and knowing that it wouldn't matter if he had, because *this was it for her.*

He had fumbled with his wallet and handed her a crisp twenty-dollar bill, at last meeting her eyes. "Sorry about…"

He broke off, shaking his head. "You just…take that and go and…and get yourself something to eat…or something…"

Hesitantly accepting it, she had forced herself to adopt the most dispassionate tone she could, as she said, "Sure thing, mister, whatever you say…"

Closing the car door, she waited for him to drive away, watching as he just sat there, hands locked on the steering wheel, motionlessly staring, until she finally turned and walked away herself, briskly putting the money in her purse and focusing upon how far she could stretch that, knowing she could make it last quite a ways. She tried to take heart in this notion, proud of her practicality, and she also attempted to draw enthusiasm from the fact that she had not actually done anything at all for the money.

In that sense, the night had been a complete success; yet, if she hadn't done anything, she was to ponder as she walked back to the bus stop, why did she feel so bad? She was smart enough to have foreseen being made to feel used by the end of the night, but she never would have guessed that, even after having done nothing at all, she would instead feel like she had betrayed the trust of everyone who had ever loved her.

*****

In spite of Father Gilchrist's pointed machinations, he was obliged to take the confessional duties one day that week, Father Ralph having explained that he had a prior commitment, some sort of jogging marathon to raise money for who knew which earthshakingly vital charity. Although it was only one day, it was one day too many, and Father Gilchrist's carefully polished foul mood was even more acidic than usual by the time he had heard the final bout of whispered misdeeds. Bitterly hanging up his stole and remembering to retrieve his wristwatch, he climbed out of the booth, wincing as he stretched his aching knees, muttering crossly.

Jogging marathon, indeed. Important work to be rendered, and he was out carousing at some recreational event. Such irresponsible and flagrantly selfish behavior was inexcusable. He had himself intended to go and see a Greta Garbo film that afternoon, and now, his plans were utterly ruined.

This was no surprise, he reflected sourly, closing the door to the booth. It was quite typical and, therefore, no longer relevant. All he had to do now was get past Mrs. Tucker and her shrewish insistence that he partake of her dubious endeavors and then ascend to his quarters where he could read the last rites for this miserable day and then lie down and die for the night, all in all, an excellent notion, because, frankly, he Vanted to be A-lone.

Hence, he was predictably overjoyed when he heard footsteps and turned to see a short young man dressed in the conservative attire of the church approaching him, his prematurely grave features solemn yet somehow bureaucratically pompous. As he drew nearer, Father Gilchrist could see the small pin arranged on his lapel, which confirmed his impression.

"Father Alistair?" he stated promptly, extending his hand from a few paces away. "How do you do, sir? I'm Deacon Richard. I was sent by the Archdiocese."

Father Gilchrist's eyebrows lifted, his indignation sidetracked. *Deacon Richard? Sure, and why not? And I'm Father Dyke Van Dick.*

"I'm afraid 'Father Alistair' isn't here," he instead replied airily. "He's off on a special mission, raising funds to buy platform shoes for the Pygmy tribes of New Guinea. Perhaps I can assist you? My name is Father Gilchrist."

Deacon Richard regarded him hesitantly and then smiled in taut comprehension. "Oh yes, of course," he replied, swiftly nodding. "Father Gilchrist. May I have a word with you, please?"

"Is it in the nature of a confession?" Father Gilchrist inquired in mock interest. "I've never heard a Deacon before. This ought to be good. Shall we step into my shoebox?"

Emitting a dry, short laugh, the sound similar to that of a camera shutter, Deacon Richard shook his head. "No, Father Gilchrist, nothing quite like that." He gestured toward one of the pews, then clasping his hands before himself. "Sit down, won't you?" he requested, his tone cordial but expectant.

Pursing his lips, Father Gilchrist reluctantly seated himself, prepared to make the appearance of listening to the Deacon while letting his mind wander. Whatever he was about to be told, he had heard it all before, ad nauseam; only the names had been changed to prolong the annoyance.

"Father Gilchrist"—Deacon Richard began, sitting down alongside of him—"I have a matter of some delicacy to broach with you. It had not been my intention simply to drop by and discuss it quite so…informally. Naturally, I would have preferred to have made an appointment to see you, but I seem to have had repeated difficulty in getting through to your parish on the telephone…"

Father Gilchrist considered this, mutely nonchalant.

"In any event, I hope you won't take any offense if I speak to you candidly on this issue…," Deacon Richard continued, his tone still flatly anticipatory.

"Oh, by all means, be as candid as you like. I won't take exception," Father Gilchrist assured him robustly. "After all, you and I go such a long ways back."

Deacon Richard cleared his throat, a clipped, constricted action. "Yes, well, to come directly to the point, the Archdiocese has received several…well, let us say that it has come to the attention of the Archdiocese that there is a strong indication of some sort of… perhaps personal problem that, private though it may be, is inadvertently affecting the administration of church duties here at St. Leonard's…" He crossed his legs in the semblance of a casual pose. "I have been dispatched by the Archdiocese to inquire if, perhaps, there is any troublesome matter causing you undue stress or that is, in some other way, inhibiting your role as pastor of this congregation."

Father Gilchrist gave Deacon Richard a sideways look. He certainly liked the word "Archdiocese," didn't he?

"Well, now that you mention it, there are a few concerns that have been preying on my mind lately," he replied forthrightly. "I think that this entire building could do with a new coat of paint. Something pastel, I fancy, and perhaps some new drapes. Apart from that, though, everything is peachy keen."

Managing a brittle smile, Deacon Richard uncrossed his legs. "Father Gilchrist," he said at length, the smile gone. "I assure you, I am quite serious."

Frowning irritably, Father Gilchrist waved a dismissive hand. "As am I," he returned sharply. "Undue stress is a fact of life when endured by a priest and pastor. I should think that the—who was it sent you again—no matter, whoever it was, I would hasten to wager that they are quite aware of this, and paradoxically so, inasmuch as this perfunctory and patently offensive inquest is yet one more contributing factor to this burdensome load of 'troublesome matters'!"

Deacon Richard considered this impassively, finally nodding. "Father Gilchrist, I can appreciate that you may not wish to discuss whatever it is that has so upset you in recent months—"

"Oh well, excellent! In that case, good day!" Father Gilchrist rose to his feet.

Remaining seated, Deacon Richard gazed immovably up at him. "However," he continued meaningfully. "I must inform you that the Archdiocese is gravely concerned about your ability to continue to perform the basic responsibilities incumbent upon a pastor. They view your station, age, and seniority with the highest regard and, as such, are all the more determined that you be given the proper support required to deal with whatever challenges you may be facing in your personal life."

Father Gilchrist, having not resumed his seat, now towered above the Deacon, his dour features becoming a mottled red, his unfailing sarcasm almost displaced by his sudden anger.

"If they view my 'station, age, and seniority' with such awe, then why did they send you over here to question my competence? Every priest and nun who has ever recited a rosary has an indescribably onerous cross to bear. And when you have been submerged in this societal war zone for as long as my 'station, age, and seniority' can attest, the mere fact that you are still passably coherent is more than sufficient evidence that you can hold your own and still maintain the flock. And the only 'support' that your blessed Archdiocese could possibly give to me to assist in my duties would be something along the lines of an electric cattle prod!"

As the last sizzling echo of this assessment died out in the empty church, Deacon Richard now actually crossed his legs again. "Father Gilchrist," he spoke quietly and concisely. "The Archdiocese feels that it would be in the best interest of the church, of your parish, and, most importantly, of your own well-being if you were to seek out some manner of professional counseling to assist in easing your stress and anxiety. They feel that—"

"Professional counseling?" Father Gilchrist repeated, now laughing acerbically at the sheer absurdity of the notion. "A clergyman undergo therapy? Is it possible that you are serious?"

Deacon Richard stared up at him. "Professional counseling," he reaffirmed somberly. "They feel that—"

His incredulous mirth vanquished, Father Gilchrist leaned down slightly to glare at the younger man. "Do you mean to suggest that an ordained priest, an individual who himself is an institution of counsel and advice, should actually undertake the counseling services of some secular guru, thereby effectively undermining the very foundation of the priesthood as a bastion of self-perpetuating wisdom and insight?" he retorted, having begun in hushed vehemence and ending in a snarling shout.

Undaunted, Deacon Richard sat, motionless. "That is precisely what I mean to suggest, Father Gilchrist," he replied evenly, reaching into his jacket and withdrawing an envelope not unlike that which the elder priest had thrown away earlier that week. "To that end, I have here a signed and sealed directive from the Archdiocese detailing their expectation that you should do just that."

He placed the envelope in Father Gilchrist's hand, gradually standing up himself, pausing when the older man did not open it, merely gaping at it in rage.

"It is from the Office of His Excellency, himself, with whom, I believe, you are closely acquainted," he added, with a conversational smile that was also politely pointed.

Father Gilchrist's fury was diverted as he glanced up at the Deacon, his own smile pure vinegar. "Oh why, yes, of course!" he proclaimed with thunderous enthusiasm. "He and I go all the way back to parochial school!" He nodded in maddened nostalgia. "Tell me, is 'His Excellency' still flunking algebra?"

Deacon Richard's smile froze as he stepped out into the aisle. "I was asked to convey the best wishes of His Excellency to you, on your ability to…sort out whatever difficulties you are currently battling," he stated summarily, then regarding the priest steadily.

"I might add that the Archdiocese is so confident in your compliance in this matter that they are quite certain that there will be no need for you to substantiate the fact that you will have since undergone this…therapeutic route, even though, should the matter arise, you will undoubtedly be able to do so." His smile flickered once more.

Father Gilchrist's eyebrows lifted in severe comprehension. "Oh! Oh, I see!" he returned, nodding insightfully. "You mean in case I *claim* to be attending counseling sessions and instead go off on my usual sprees to the local opium dens and bordellos?"

The smile slid into a smirk. "Indeed, Father Gilchrist," he concurred quietly.

"Well, it is still out of the question," Father Gilchrist declared, officiously brisk. "I cannot possibly abandon my duties here to attend to this fool's errand. I simply have too much work and no time to devote to such folly."

Deacon Richard gestured lightly, his voice reassuringly smug. "I have no doubt that Father Ralph will be only too happy to cover for you."

"Ah!" Father Gilchrist nodded again, lifting up the envelope as his features collapsed challengingly. "And suppose, Deacon Richard, that I refuse to cooperate with this absurd, debasing, and indefensibly unnecessary charade?" he demanded, deftly ripping the unopened envelope in half and then quartering it for good measure.

Deacon Richard regarded the shredded letter impassively, his eyes lifting to meet those of the elder priest. "As I say, Father Gilchrist, it is not a request. It is a directive." He nodded shortly. "Good evening, Father Gilchrist."

Watching him withdraw in stunned outrage, Father Gilchrist swallowed his wrath if only to have the last word. "Oh yes, by all means, *Deacon* Richard, a jolly good evening to you, sir, and to Reiner, Carl, as well!"

He glanced about for the nearest lit votive candle with which to burn the offensive letter on the spot, instead finding himself unable to move from where he stood, his chronically sour face twisting into the most frighteningly, biliously stringent expression it had ever assumed in all of his nearly seven decades of life.

*****

Days off tended to be scarce in the legal profession, making Labor Day the perfect interval for doing nothing especially industrious. As she sat on her sofa in her modest apartment, distractedly watching the television, Counselor Vivian Talbott was still coming to terms with the fact that she would never again be addressed in such a way.

It was official now; like it or not, the swearing-in ceremony, such as it was, had taken place the day after she had been approached with her confirmation. She felt an inner shudder at the solemnity, the finality of what had actually been a perfunctory and rather informal procedure. It had entailed all of the pomp and circumstance of being issued a new library card and yet had felt like the reading of her death warrant.

She pressed the remote control buttons, trying to decide between Judge Judy or Perry Mason, eventually opting for the latter, partly because it was her favorite and partly because its somber, film-noir simplicity was less nerve-jarring. Usually, she would be excited by the rare opportunity of being home on a weekday, for there was an entire lineup of law-oriented programs aired; and while some were less outrageous than others, they could all be engaging—or, at least, entertaining.

Today, however, while she could easily anticipate staying on the sofa indefinitely, she could not concentrate on the television's offerings, her thoughts congested with images of what lay in store for her, of this vast change in her career path, which she had apparently worked so hard to achieve.

Try as she might, she could not seem to remember setting such a goal for herself. It seemed to have been outlined for her by the legal structure and then had become a reality. Certainly, she had applied, had gone through all of the motions, and had done so because it had been expected of her; but between the interminable slowness of legal bureaucracy and her own doubts that anything could possibly come of it, she had almost forgotten that the whole process had even been initiated.

And now it was real. She felt like a person whose name her friends had secretly entered into a sweepstakes and who had actually, inexplicably, won, except that the prize was a trip down the Amazon, and she didn't want to go.

An insistent mewling intercepted her thoughts, and she turned to blink at one of her three cats who was standing in the entryway of her kitchen, yowling anxiously. Frowning skeptically, she stood up and ventured into the kitchen, finding, of course, that the three food dishes were all plentifully stocked—with dry food. Nonetheless, now that the attention had been successfully captured, the cat began a plaintive chorus of begging, the other two scrambling forth from wherever they had been secluded, knowing what was coming and joining in the effort.

Her lips pursed knowingly, she placed her hands on her hips, nodding and then relenting in frustration. "All right, all right, if only for some peace and quiet!"

She turned to the row of cupboards and retrieved a small can of wet food, using a spoon to place a dollop of Feisty Feline in the respective dishes of Oliver, Wendell, and Holmes.

Standing upright and watching them devour the preferred selection as if famished, she had to smile, heading back into the living room in time to catch a commercial advertising at virtual light speed the miraculous services of some ambulance-chasing law firm.

Her smile gone, she switched the station back to Judge Judy, watching a young college student slowly disintegrate before the bench as the ruling was screeched at him. Staring as if mesmerized, she listened to the harsh but logical swiftness of the decree, marveling over the woman's decisiveness.

They were all like that, the TV judges; their interpretations of the law were always so concise, their deliberations so flawlessly delivered.

All of them, from Judge Joe Brown to Judge Mills Lane, from Texas Justice to Superior Court; if one stripped away the Hollywood glitz and focused upon the actual legal aspects of the programs, the parameters by which these judges fundamentally had to preside and which she, as a public defender, knew were authentic, they could be fascinating shows; and the dynamic between the litigants and these people who were both appointed judges and television personalities was always intense. Naturally, this type of programming was heartily disparaged by her colleagues, and she would never have shared with them her interest in watching them, content to keep the vicelike pleasure to herself.

Today, however, even these courtroom histrionics could not downplay her worries; and she began to dwell, yet again, upon the velocity with which this was all happening; and, moreover, the dwindling amount of time between the present and her actual "day in court."

She tried to focus upon not focusing at all, taking up the remote control as Judge Judy came to a close, tuning out the protests of her three cats as they petitioned her for seconds, attempting to decide whether to watch *Matlock* or reruns of *The People's Court*. Previously, she would always have gone with the crime-solving attorney over the small-claims court forum of Judge Wapner. Now, however, Judge Vivean Talbott found that she could not make up her mind.

*****

Mr. McClintock checked the scale again, wincing at the figure that it registered. It could not possibly be inaccurate; the scale was practically brand new. It was an upright model that he had purchased (discreetly via mail order), once he could no longer see past his own girth to read the dial of his previous floor model.

According to its precision measurement, the tally was up by five more pounds, an increment that seemed small, but that he knew very well, when converted into inches and centimeters spoke, no *held* volumes.

Gulping, he stepped down off the scale onto the cool tile of his bathroom floor, then moving slowly back into the bedroom of his townhouse.

It was all so frustrating. Even though he knew perfectly well the obvious flaw in the rationale of his brainstorm earlier that week, it had just seemed so logical and accommodating. The very notion of validating all of those intermediary meals that he had previously been guiltily interposing between reviews by turning them into reviews as well had been a godsend idea. Far from guilt-inducing, it had enabled him one more way in which to do his job.

Yet, already, the consequences were asserting themselves. Five pounds up, and this *after* he had just come from the Big and Tall store to upgrade a few pairs of pants, having learned that they did not have the next larger size. He had had to have them let his pants out while he hid in a tiny dressing room, clad only in his copious undergarment, not unlike he was now. He had shed his outer clothes when the scale began to play its tricks, until it became apparent that the weight gain was not textile in nature.

Glancing at his reflection in the floor-length mirror of his closet door, he could not perceive any pronounced difference. Of course, over all, if a whale gained five pounds, that would not be very easy to discern either, he reflected glumly. Yet it was not his reflection that gave him such angst; as again, his weight was really not his problem.

He pulled on his pajamas and bathrobe, thinking with some degree of pleasure about the week behind him. Whereas the restaurants that had been on his list were above average and elite, their portions, as always, had been less than adequate—there! That was a large part of the problem in and of itself. It was no secret that the more upscale the establishment and the more expensive the meal, the smaller and more triflingly superficially insubstantial the portions were. If only they were more generous with their servings, he might well have never gone beyond the triple X category.

It was that salient factor coupled with his own fundamental character flaw that had started all of the trouble—and who was to say that it was a flaw anyway?

Some of the most well-known icons in the culinary realm upheld the notion that enjoyment of fine food was not at all a negative attribute, but was instead a cause to be celebrated. Julia Child had advocated this philosophy; Paul Prudhomme actually embodied it. True, *Yan Can Cook* and the *Frugal Gourmet* were thin; but then, the latter was, after all, on a very tight budget. One of the most respected dignitaries in the field, a gentleman with whom Mr. McClintock heartily empathized and whom he physically resembled, had been the late James Beard, who had said it best, "I love to eat."

Try as he might, Mr. McClintock could see nothing wrong with this very basic philosophy. While he was not indifferent to his health, he was also not overly concerned with dieting. If it were a simple matter of continually enlarging his wardrobe, inch by inch, to maintain his presentability, all the while enjoying his singular pursuit, he would gladly do so.

It was not, of course, that simple. Leastwise, he doubted that it could be. A hollow trepidation in his stomach, this time in tandem with his hunger pangs, seemed to herald this concern, and his pleasant recollection of the week's repasts was thwarted with the contemplation of the potential ramifications of his actions.

The results need not automatically be supposed as disastrous; they could, in fact, prove to be quite positive. His endeavors, while a slight departure from the norm, had been just that, indeed, had been rather creative. Beyond that, moreover, was the comforting idea that his editor had often told him—that most people probably never bothered to read his column anyway.

To think, that, at the time, such a remark had hurt his feelings. Now, however, the idea might possibly work to his advantage.

In any event, he would know soon enough; his reviews had been submitted on time and neatly typed, as usual; only their actual text was a bit divergent from previous renderings. They either would be intercepted by the editor (a doubtful possibility, owing to his assessment of the column, overall) or would be out in the Sunday Edition.

Somehow, he felt that if his words made it out into print, this would be a form of confirmation that he had, indeed, touched upon a journalistically sound approach to his job. Naturally, he knew that this was more dubious rationalization; but if he were proven wrong, he at least had a contingency plan, although how effective that would be was unforeseeable to him. The whole idea seemed a bit unrelated to his concerns and stresses. Nevertheless, it was an option; and, on top of that, there was also that little added incentive promised toward the bottom of the flyer.

His stomach rumbled again, and he glanced at the clock on the nightstand alongside his monumental bed, a thrill of anticipation eclipsing all other thoughts. He had fifteen minutes in which to prepare a late-night snack—this evening some manner of hot fudge sundae, before he could settle down in front of the television set. The Food Network aired episodes of his favorite cooking shows at that hour, and he had taken to watching them prior to retiring for the evening. Unlike most people, he had found that rich, lavish treats before bedtime induced excellent sleep and pleasurable dreams.

*****

Chris sat on the edge of his bed and worked at the laces of his boots, the dull roar of the punk music from his adjacent stereo going unheard, his thoughts elsewhere. Since graduating from high school, he had noticed that the days all seemed like one perpetual weekend, and while he had anticipated that they would, he had also expected this to be a good thing. When the days were as endlessly empty as his were turning out to be, the phenomenon took on a different edge, particularly in terms of the actual weekends. With a girlfriend who had free license to run wild and who was also angry at him, he had found his most recent weekend to be little more than a void.

When he had gotten home that Saturday night, he had returned so early that he took his whole family off guard, and he cursed himself all the more for not having thought to wander around aimlessly for another few hours rather than endure their surprised, teasing reaction to his having come home so soon, remarks that were not ill-intended but that did not make him feel any better.

"Well, well, the 'Wild Thing' returns," his father had called out sardonically from behind his newspaper. "All set to go back in your cage already? And it's not even midnight yet."

"Leave him alone, Phil," his mother had sighed, glancing up from a magazine as Chris reluctantly entered the dimly-lit living room in which his family had converged. "Did you and Candy have fun, honey?"

"Why is her name *Candy*?" one of his brothers had interjected from where they were sprawled, playing on the rug with some of Chris's old toys.

"'Cause she's so sweet!" his other brother declared, following this deduction with a gagging noise that sent both of them into giggling hysterics, Chris flinching in weary aggravation.

"Ha, Rooster! Cock-a-doodle-doo to you!" his grandfather bellowed from the couch, seated next to his grandmother, pointing excitedly at the television set. "You just in time, Kristov!"

"Look! Look! Remember, Liebling?" his grandmother smiled brightly.

Chris glanced toward the set, realizing that he had come back even earlier than he had thought. The *Lawrence Welk Show*, a Saturday night staple adored by his grandparents, tolerated by his mother and father, and ignored by his brothers, was blaring forth from the screen, the stammering maestro announcing the upcoming performers.

"You, come, sit, as before!" his grandfather boomed in his hearty Pennsylvanian Dutch vigor, gesturing with his powerful hands. "Or do you too Rock und Roll, now, eh, to enjoy the good life?"

Flushing, Chris stared at the program, recalling the years he had spent watching its outdated episodes with his grandparents, incited by their rampant enthusiasm, listening to the ensemble of old tunes and big band dance numbers. Shaking his head, he was about to decline when the lineup shifted to a Bohemian piece and the accordionist launched into a dizzying rendition, his fingers whirling deftly over the keys, the pleated bellows pumping widely, sporadically, while a pair of dancers leapt into a polka of almost frantic velocity, stomping and swaying to and fro, the band fortifying the accordionist with a steady, flourishing background as the song rippled insanely forward with almost magical precision, the jagged, jarring chords punctuating the melody with the intensity of thunder.

His mouth agape, he had watched the performance, very nearly coming and sitting down beside his grandparents, as he had not done in a number of years, the abrupt close of the song diverting his attention, causing him to blink and recall all the misery that had comprised that night.

"Come, come, sit down, Liebling," his grandmother had beckoned.

Blushing again, he shook his head. "Uh, no thanks, Grandma. I...I'm tired. I think I'm just gonna go to bed," he responded, turning quickly, but not before seeing her disappointment.

"Chris, are you feeling all right?" his mother called distractedly after him.

"He's fine," his father cut in, eyeing the television with deadpan endurance. "He's just brain-damaged, is all. It's what comes from having a green saw blade stuck in your head."

"Oh, phooey on the rooster, then!" his grandfather called with spirit. "Let him go, mit his green hair and rama-lama-ding-dong! Someday he remembers! Someday he knows!"

"Papa Schmidt, could you, for the love of God, please turn that down?" his father's voice followed him down the hall.

Sitting on his bed now, he felt his ears and cheeks burn as red as they had on Saturday night. He thought of the accordion piece he had seen and wondered what his grandfather would say if he knew that Chris did remember, that he had never really forgotten. His love for punk music had not eclipsed his appreciation for the older music he had grown up hearing; instead, the two genres had collided and then comingled in his mind to agglomerate into a schizophrenically unlikely dichotomy, one which few people would understand—he certainly didn't. None of the punks would. Candy, he knew for certain didn't, couldn't, understand it.

No, he had not forgotten, nor was it likely that he ever would, even if he tried. He just could not separate these two disharmoniously incompatible worlds, nor could he seem to unite them.

He kicked off his boots and then shrugged out of his studded leather vest, pausing to consider how far he should undress. It was very punk rock to sleep in one's clothes, for days on end, if possible. It was not easy to do, however, when one still lived at home with a family that was fanatical about cleanliness. True, his room was his own, its juvenile untidiness his to enjoy, but when he and any potentially lingering odors walked among them, the nagging started. Besides which, he secretly had nothing against being somewhat clean.

He ended up tugging off his T-shirt and reaching to unfasten his jeans, unable to do so as he fingered what served as his belt, a length of chain passed through two belt loops to support a punk accessory commonly known as a "butt flap," a jagged, patched square of leather that hung over the rear in a somewhat tribal likeness to a loincloth, a padlock in the front serving as its buckle. It was a rather stark adornment, but one which he thought, hoped, looked cool.

Biting his lip, he glanced around his room and then crossed through the debris littering his carpet to retrieve his overcoat, pulling his key ring out of a pocket. He found the key to the padlock and set about unlocking it, frowning when the key stuck to his fingers and then sighing when he realized why.

Picking up his coat again, he pulled the tar-smeared halves of the flyer out of its pocket, piecing them together and staring at its message, noticing the date on which the first meeting was to commence.

A peer-counseling group. He imagined sitting down with a bunch of grown-ups, telling them about *his* problems, watching their jaws drop. He snorted derisively; just walking into their meeting would be enough to cause that reaction. The only question was, if their jaws would drop in shock or in unrestrained laughter? Flushing, he put the sticky flyer aside.

Removing his padlock, chain, and butt flap, he was about to inhale and peel off his jeans when he realized that the punk album he was playing had ended. About to reset it, he glanced down at the milk crate of old records next to the stereo, then absently flipping through them, a smile almost touching on his lips as he glanced over the musty, familiar jacket covers.

A good deal of them had been his grandfather's, and he still played them, much more often than anyone would imagine. A few of the others were original punk albums, prized additions to his collection. He already knew what he wanted to see, though, moving toward the rear of the crate and extracting a specific album, gaping at its cover, the mane of his Mohawk poised downward as he balanced it on his knees and stared at it, the utter and profound absurdity of what he was seeing far surpassed by the imagined potential of this fantasy of what if.

In his mind, such things were possible—if only in his mind and here in the safety of his room.

When he finally did lie down to go to sleep, he found his mind drifting from the unlikely album cover to the equally improbable green flyer and all of its promises. Somehow, in the hazy region between his tired, slurring thoughts and inevitable sleep, the ludicrous notion of the one began to lend itself to the laughable potential of the other.

He knew where that street corner was, and the first meeting was set for the very next evening; before long, he was actually contemplating going. It was not like he had anything else to do. Candy had finally called, if only to inform him of her plans for the entire week, all of which pointedly disincluded him. Left with nothing but the limited prospects of riding around on his skateboard and endlessly browsing at various record stores, he was faced with an indefinite period of time to fill until she was ready to acknowledge him once more. This, the famed summer vacation of them all, appeared to have no end in sight, and its days promised to be empty and aimless.

There was no reason why he couldn't go to this meeting, even though there was no reason why he should go or, at least, he reflected automatically, no reason that he could possibly share with anyone.

Still, though, there was always the possibility that it could be interesting. His dwindling consciousness focused once more on the shadowy figure that had appeared in the night to post that flyer on the telephone pole and then hurry mysteriously away.

An anonymous peer-counseling group? It could be very interesting; it could end up being really cool. In fact, who knew? It might even turn out to be just like *Fight Club*.

Chapter 3

DR. PENDLETON PAUSED TO SHUFFLE through his keys, bypassing those for the union hall and fingering the key to the trunk of his car. Although he had taken to making use of public transportation the last year or so, he did find occasion to drive now and then and had wanted to arrive in plenty of time to prepare for the first meeting that evening. He pulled open the trunk, removing a hastily packed cardboard box, balancing it against the rear bumper as he slammed the trunk closed, and then heading briskly through the alley to the back entrance of the hall.

He set the box on a table in the back corner, then pausing and anxiously surveying the room, wishing that it were not so gloomy. He had turned on all of its overhead fixtures, but the murkiness still prevailed.

Dismissing the matter for a moment, he turned to the box, carefully lifting out the coffee maker he had purchased earlier from a St. Vincent De Paul, having dropped his own on his way out of his office earlier. He placed it on the table, grasping its glass server and hurrying toward the front of the hall, bypassing the chalk outline, and stepping into the bathroom, discovering that it was more of a janitor's closet equipped with a toilet. The lighting was even poorer in there, he noted, as he peered at the industrial sink and gingerly rotated its spigot handle, concluding that the dimness was probably for the better, as it would obscure the less than tidy condition of the room. The squawking, shuddering release of the air in the pipe induced him to let the water run for a full minute before he filled the server and bustled back to the coffee maker, plugging it in and setting it up to commence brewing, watching uneasily as it belched and began to churn sluggishly.

Glancing at his watch, he hurriedly arranged sugar, instant creamer, and a package of Styrofoam cups alongside the growling coffee maker, next darting toward the folding chairs, setting up several in a makeshift circle, the center of which prompted him to race back to the bathroom and grab a broom, using it to sweep a layer of sawdust over the chalk outline as best he could.

Pausing to catch his breath, he gazed around the room, taking in his efforts, blinking uncertainly at the walls. He had also been planning on bringing a few of his credentials from his office to hang alongside the union posters, but had been sidetracked by having to clean up the pieces of his broken coffee maker. It then dawned on him that he did not know how he might oversee the meeting, having not come across a podium or the like as he had unfolded the chairs.

His eyes fell upon something comparable, if only geometrically, and after a few moments of reluctant hesitation, he dragged a wooden packing crate over to the circle of chairs, upending it and creating an improvised rostrum.

He next removed a fresh batch of flyers from his attaché case, placing them alongside the coffee maker in hopes of encouraging any of this evening's participants to get the word out for future meetings, thereby possibly enlarging the group and also saving himself a bit of legwork.

Setting his attaché case beside the packing crate, he withdrew a clipboard, several pieces of blank paper, and a small bundle of index cards, donning his glasses and quickly thumbing through them, making sure they were in order. Having not heard the front door open, he was all the more startled when his perusal of his notes was sidetracked by the sound of someone stumbling against one of the chairs.

Spinning around, he blanched upon seeing the tall, lean punk rocker standing there, balancing a backpack and a skateboard in his hands as he repositioned the chair he had bumped into, smiling apologetically.

Momentarily speechless, Dr. Pendleton hastily cleared his throat, intending to explain that this was a meeting place for peer-counseling group sessions that anyone at all was welcome to attend, in hopes that this individual would realize that he was clearly in the wrong place and leave, instead managing to stammer, "Uh, can I help you?"

Blushing deeply, Chris continued fidgeting. "Um, I'm here for the, um, the anonymous self-help group?" he explained haltingly.

Dr. Pendleton had been shifting himself, wondering if he would have to call the police, then blinking in puzzlement. "The self-help group?" he repeated, gazing more closely at the flushed awkward visage of what was actually just a young kid—a rather colorfully exclamatory kid, but a kid just the same. "The anonymous peer-counseling group?" he asked, as it dawned on him that this person was actually there to attend the meeting.

Chris nodded vigorously, as did his Mohawk, Dr. Pendleton blinking at both of them and then glancing toward the door as a short woman stepped shyly into the room with mouselike movements, very gradually making her way around the chairs and then abruptly sitting down in one of them, clutching her purse tautly, and shooting both Chris and the doctor a nervous smile before focusing intently on the floor. Dr. Pendleton was about to address her, but paused when her lack of surprise at Chris's appearance in turn surprised him.

A narrow, bespectacled man next came into the hall, his robotic steps almost like scissor strokes, as if he were compelling his legs to take him some place he did not really wish to go.

As Dr. Pendleton glanced toward him, Chris took the opportunity to stow his things beneath the table and then duck into a seat near the makeshift podium, planting his cumbersome boots, effecting as inconspicuous and innocuous a pose as he could.

Gaping over at Chris anyway, Dr. Pendleton started as his attention was diverted to the sheer enormity of the next person's entrance, the excessively stout man using both of the hall's double doors as he moved carefully into their midst, smiling benignly as he gracefully lowered himself onto one of the folding chairs, the doctor watching nervously, worried that it might just go right on unfolding. He returned the enormous man's smile as best as he could, glancing cordially at the others and then at his watch, attempting to gauge when he should start the meeting, finding himself pondering *if* he should start the meeting.

*****

Vanessa glanced over her shoulder even as she continued running, a difficult task in heels. She had lost sight of the purple Lincoln, but that did not automatically mean that its driver had lost sight of her. Between explosive gasps for air, she was still able to balance her fear with a pronounced anger.

Everything had been going so well—meaning not totally screwed-up. In the few days since she had been handed that twenty for doing nothing at all, she had a streak of ongoing good fortune in the same way—money for nothing.

In between walking the street, she had just begun to perfect a technique of alternate hustling. If she wasn't portraying the small-town girl asking for directions and hinting at her dire straits (all of which was true), she was straight-up asking for help, a buck some spare change, anything, explaining that she needed it (which she did).

Her entire sense of inner resolve, having come so close to crumbling that first night, was vastly reasserted now. She felt more than adequately prepared to take on whatever the streets had to offer, her luck alone refortifying her determination. She had staunchly repressed the stinging notion of hurting those few people who had loved her, because they were all gone now, having, in effect, been the ones to betray her love, leaving her on her own to do whatever it took to survive—to win.

Yes, money for nothing. She still had not so much as kissed anyone, continuing to give in at the last second to some inner reservation about the prospective john or, in some cases, not at the last second, but before she had even been approached. The carload of frat boys had been a prime example.

Just looking at their matching concupiscent smiles had rankled her prejudiced loathing, invoking all sorts of images of her earlier years, so many so that when one lewdly asked her how much she would charge to blow all six of them, she had replied that she would do it for free, offering them the "dickless discount," since there was obviously nothing to blow.

Her response and their obscene enraged reaction had felt good, but she still had been forced to consider the fact that, as a prostitute, she really wasn't getting anywhere nor would she if she continued rebuking her potential clientele.

Nonetheless, it had seemed that if the days could continue to be as cleanly prosperous as today had been, she might not end up having to go that route, *had seemed* as such, of course, until about a half an hour ago.

By his very appearance, she had instinctually thought he was a john; naturally, she had responded cautiously to his question of how much, telling him evasively that it depended upon what he wanted.

That reply had apparently been enough to confirm to *him* that she was, indeed, walking that corner; and the split second in which she wondered if he were an undercover vice squad cop was followed by the realization that he was, instead, a pimp—a very angry pimp, who demanded to know how it was that she thought she could embark on some little freelance hustling enterprise on *his* turf.

Terrified, she had stood her ground as he offered her a job in his outfit by explaining to her that she basically already was working for him just by being there. When she had declined, he had moved to grab her, and she had put her knee to work, turning and running away, only to have him leap into the Lincoln and pursue her with a murderous vengeance, his shouted threats assailing her ears savagely.

She had jumped aboard a crosstown bus, grateful to find that even in her panic, her luck was holding. Her hotel was on the east side, which was why she had taken great pains to get those directions to the south side, having had the foresight not to set about establishing her new career path anywhere near home base, just in case.

Her mind reeled in almost delirious gratitude at her precaution, and she took additional satisfaction in the fact that this bus was headed to the west side, foreign ground on which she could lose the demon who even now she could see was doggedly tailing the bus, after which she could make it safely back to the east side, and then...

She closed her eyes and sighed. *One disaster at a time, please.*

When the Lincoln got trapped at a red light, she had yanked at the cord and bolted off the bus at the next stop, darting down an alley way and racing to the next intersection, careening diagonally across it, and charging past a bus bench, ducking breathlessly into a doorway, hands braced against her bare knees. As she inhaled profusely, she noted from the bus stop sign that the very bus she had just ditched should be rumbling past any minute now, after which, if he still thought she was onboard, the pimp would also pass by, and she would know she was safe.

As an eternity of seconds elapsed with no sign of either vehicle, she swallowed in confusion, trying to will her heart to slow as she slid herself upright against the door, not quite daring to peer out beyond its frame. Instead, her eyes fell upon the slight form of the person occupying the bus bench; from where she had crouched, she hadn't noticed that anyone was sitting there at all.

"Psst!" she hissed urgently, her desperation overriding the ridiculousness of her actions. "Psst! Do you see the bus coming? Do you see anyone?"

When the person made no response, she cupped her mouth, her anger beginning to sizzle into her voice as she grated more loudly. "Hey! Are you deaf? Do you see anyone coming, like in a bright purple pimpmobile?"

With exasperating slowness, the person turned to regard her, then actually standing and moving around the bench to approach her. As Vanessa's mouth fell open in bewilderment, she gaped at the elderly woman, stooped and frail, clad in powdery gray apparel that she could only relate to reruns of *Leave It to Beaver*, her pillbox hat, thick wooly coat, and tiny Mary Jane pumps eons out of fashion, her gleaming black purse clutched in childlike gloved hands.

Her eyes widening, Vanessa met the milky, vague gaze of the woman as she trundled forward, smiling lightly, her expression somewhat "spaced" from the much younger person's perspective. As she surveyed the woman's doddering progress in mounting alarm, afraid that she might draw attention to her hiding place and wind up caught in the middle of her territorial dispute with the enraged procurer, she backed against the door, her shoulder encountering the rustle of paper.

Turning, she found herself facing a familiar shade of green, her eyes darting over the unimpressive flyer that she now recalled reading earlier that week. Blinking in disbelief, she realized that this was the building in which the flyer's promised meeting was to take place, astounded because in her pell-mell race for its doorway, she had sized up the structure and had figured it was condemned.

The old woman had drawn up alongside of her, peering fleetingly at the flyer as she reached for the doorknob. "I had forgotten there was an after-hours meeting scheduled for today," she stated in a slight voice, high and warbled with age.

Watching in amazement, Vanessa stared as the doorknob turned and the old woman hobbled inside, then grasping the knob herself, glancing once more at the ominously quiet street, and then deftly ripping down the telltale flyer, without which the building would once again look uninhabited. Delighting in her further good luck, she vanished within the union hall as well, taking the first seat she saw and commencing to be invisible.

Dr. Pendleton looked up at these two late arrivals, eyeing his watch again, smiling quietly whenever anyone happened to look his way, the utter void of conversation made deafening by the shuffling of boots, purses, chairs, and the occasional cough or throat clearing. He fingered his knit tie, following the elderly woman with his gaze until she had settled into a seat nearby, fearful that she might slip, in spite of the fact that her toddling feet never seemed to leave the floor.

His attention was startled to the forefront as a spectral figure suddenly stomped into their midst, an imposing man in black who stood in the entrance way and appeared to be assessing his surroundings with one searching glare before marching around the circle of chairs and rather brusquely slamming himself down into one of them, eventually removing his hat and placing it on the chair beside him, folding his arms over his chest, his raincoat still buttoned up to its collar as he dourly scrutinized the room.

Viewing the hall with an outrage that balanced between fury and laughter, Father Gilchrist clenched his teeth in resentment.

So this was it. The final degradation. Forced to sit in a group confessional with the likes of these individuals. He had long suspected that purgatory awaited him, yet somehow had assumed that he would not find himself there until after he had actually died. He inhaled astringently through his nose as he peered acerbically at the others, feeling like a captive audience in a carnival sideshow. And, oh, what a carnival it was—a postapocalyptic, lightning-struck delinquent, a diminutive ditz with something apparently spellbinding in her purse, a hypertense neurotic seemingly two steps from a rubber room, a Junior Miss Femme-Fatale Beauty School Drop-Out and, unless he missed his guess, Oliver Hardy, himself. And, lo and behold, just right of center stage, it was Lillian Gish, resurrected for one final scene in the limelight. Oh, they were in for quite a floorshow, on that he could rely.

His appraisal lingered disdainfully upon Chris as he surveyed the boy's chain and padlock ensemble—no doubt some form of neo-punk chastity belt. The dear boy must be saving himself for some she-creature who was out crusading from rave to rave. How perfectly romantic.

He glanced past the others as Mr. McClintock discreetly stood up and aligned a second chair with his first, dapperly grasping his trouser legs as he settled himself down upon both of them, beaming at the increased comfort.

Ah, just in time to catch the balancing act, the aged priest reflected dryly. *Little wonder that the floor was layered with sawdust, befitting as it was to a three-ring circus.*

Having surveyed the freaks, clowns, and elephants, he began to ferret out the ringmaster of this singular arena, his acidic gaze settling upon the shifty little man behind the crate who was coughing into one hand like a barker prepared to launch into his spiel, his bland round countenance and lackluster appearance promising all the intellectual sharpness and exciting inspired charisma of Charlie Brown.

Father Gilchrist closed his eyes. Why in God's name did he have to be here?

Forcing a smile, Dr. Pendleton put aside his clipboard, planting his feet behind the upended packing crate. He gazed swiftly around the room, from person to person, drawing little encouragement from their expressions. Maintaining his smile as best he could, he cleared his throat and discreetly focused on his note cards, drawing a bit of encouragement from his innate excitement at commencing the long-anticipated meeting.

"Uh, good evening, everyone," he greeted them, abruptly clearing his throat again when his voice cracked with a hollow almost preadolescent tremor. He stole a glance at the topmost card, flushing slightly, realizing that he needed his glasses to make out his cramped writing.

His forced smile now sheepishly genuine, he nodded apologetically to the frozen-featured crowd, which was motionlessly observing him. Clearing his throat yet once more to buy himself some time, he reached for his glasses, his elbow jarring the crate, his note cards slipping neatly into a chasm between two of its boards, like a ballot into a voting box.

Gasping slightly, unsure of how he might gracefully retrieve them, or even retrieve them at all, he grimaced and directed his focus at the assemblage, blundering forward as spontaneously as he could, his hands fidgeting nervously, in search of a confident pose.

"I would like to welcome all of you to our very first meeting"—he told them sincerely—"and to thank you for taking the time to attend."

As he spoke, he took in each of the audience, silently tallying seven. *Not an unimpressive turnout,* he allowed himself to reflect. *Surely, Dr. Whittaker would agree.* Of course, the older doctor's therapeutic sessions were more in the nature of seminars, their attendance filling an auditorium. Still, in all, it was helpful to see the circle of chairs reasonably filled and with such a diverse crowd too.

His initial excitement arose again as he considered this, as diversity was interesting, especially if it was commingled with adversity. He paused, realizing that this notion was rather an elegant one; he would have to remember to write that down.

"My name is Dr. Pendleton, uh, Charles Pendleton, and I am a trained psychologist," he continued, his nervousness slightly abated. "Although, for the purposes of our meeting, I would like for you to think of me as a counselor, a confidante, and a friend."

He paused, allowing this notion to sink in, a little of his confidence waning as he perceived the mixed yet overall dubious reaction to his statement. The kid with the Mohawk smiled lightly, giving him a bit of reassurance. He smiled back, wondering briefly if this kid was a Native American. The pale, bespectacled man seated near him met his gaze with an unshifting look of consternation, as if perplexed by the very concept, while the short woman between them withdrew a legal pad and a pen from her purse and appeared to be taking notes.

"Of course, that may seem both presumptuous and premature," he hastened onward, starting slightly when it seemed that the rather sour-faced old man in black actually snorted derisively. Somewhat taken aback, he cleared his throat and continued unsteadily. "I know—we, all of us—know that, first and foremost, an atmosphere of mutual trust and respect must be attained."

That was pretty good, he thought, wincing when the girl toward the rear actually rolled her eyes, inserting a piece of gum in her mouth and beginning to chomp mechanically. His glance slipped from her to the elephantine man off to one side, who was still settling his girth as quietly as he could, his features a florid red.

"Uh…," he paused, losing his train of thought, his eyes darting to the vacantly smiling old lady who sat near the dour old man. Hadn't he seen her sitting on the bus bench out in front of the building?

"Uh…," he fought to bring his introduction back into focus, gesturing lamely as he habitually cleared his throat. "Uh, and…that can of course be attained…or, at least, uh, initiated by a general introduction of ourselves to each other…"

When only silence prevailed, he clasped his hands together and then gestured again, in what he hoped was an inviting way.

"Uh, and so, who would like to get the ball rolling?"

Smiling anxiously, he glanced from face to face, his eyes flashing desperately when no one so much as shifted. Somehow summoning forth a bit of assertion, he nodded pleasantly toward the older man.

"Uh, how about you, sir?" he asked cordially.

Father Gilchrist gave him his best scowl. "I see no reason why I should have to be the one to go first," he snapped sourly, almost peevishly.

Startled, Dr. Pendleton almost replied that it was only natural, in deference to his obvious seniority of age, but thought better of it, and was spared the chance to make such a mistake when Father Gilchrist continued.

"Anyway, why should any of us introduce ourselves at all if it is the purpose of this function to remain anonymous?" he challenged sharply.

Blinking, Dr. Pendleton paused uncertainly. "Uh, well, the purpose of our meetings is more along the lines of discussing our respective lives and such," he explained haltingly. "The anomimit— uh, the amoninit...uh, the amomymity..."

He stopped as the older man pursed his lips acerbically. "Uh, the *anonymity*"—he managed breathlessly—"of our meetings will apply, of course, to the outside world. We cannot really expect to get to know each other in here and yet remain anonymous at the same time, now can we?"

Laughing wheezily, he shrank at the old man's unamused disdain, as well as the humorless almost sympathetic glances he was getting from the others. "Uh...as I say, we...and I really do wish to stress this"—he plunged onward, drawing strength from his own earnestness—"our discussions here in this room will be treated with the utmost respect and confidentiality. The anonymity factor is a very traditional and fundamental guarantee of our ability to share private details about our lives and problems and feelings, not at all unlike that observed by people in Alcoholics Anonymous or Narcotics Anonymous or Overeaters Anonymous..."

Mr. McClintock blanched and then blushed.

Cringing, Dr. Pendleton fought to stay on track. "And, so, uh, yes, we will likewise be observing this very important, very reassuring practice..." He paused, latching onto a detail that thankfully had just occurred to him. "And, of course, in keeping with that anonymity, we may all feel free to use only our first names." He nodded encouragingly to the old man.

Father Gilchrist sniffed. "No one addresses me by my first name," he informed the air in front of him rhetorically.

Dr. Pendleton blinked rapidly, wishing he had not chosen to commence with this very difficult man. "I...see," he replied weakly, swallowing and trying to rally his strength. "Well, what may we call you then?" he finally asked, deciding not to push the issue.

"I can think of a few things," the girl in the back volunteered dryly, cracking her gum. Beside her, the enormous man chortled or coughed or perhaps used one action to disguise the other. Dr. Pendleton gulped in shock.

Bristling in outrage, Father Gilchrist shot a searing look at the stubbornly undaunted girl, defying his own intentions and swiftly unbuttoning the top of his raincoat, pulling it open to reveal the clergical collar underneath.

"You may call me *Father* Gilchrist," he sizzled, the girl's resolve actually wilting slightly as she beheld his attire. He turned his withering gaze toward the doctor again, folding his arms once more, a look of acrimonious triumph in his eyes.

Slack-jawed, Dr. Pendleton struggled to find his voice, nodding quickly and assuagingly. "Ah, yes, I see. Uh, Father Gilchrist, uh... welcome..."

The priest ignoring him, he cleared his throat and nodded again, removing a handkerchief and wiping at his brow.

"Well, uh, now that we've, uh, gotten the ball rolling," he stated with weak cheerfulness. "Uh, why don't we move onto the next person?" he proposed, noting that this would be the little old lady, who did not appear to be following anything being said.

"My name is Stanley F. Crimpton," the pale, nervous man sidetracked them all by abruptly standing up and announcing. "And I work for the Department of Motor Vehicles."

Dr. Pendleton stared at him as he almost robotically sat back down and resumed his tensed, pensive stance.

"Uh, welcome, Mr....uh, Stanley," he nodded, unsure of how to comment upon this man's anything *but* anonymous introduction without discouraging him or any of the others.

He was diverted from addressing this when his glance slipped from Mr. Crimpton to the petite woman beside him, who was still taking copious notes. Not certain if one should really be doing so in an anonymous setting, wondering if he should say something, he was distracted all over again when the woman suddenly looked up, smiling demurely.

"Oh! Hello, everyone. My name is Vivean Talbott, and I'm a judge at the District Courthouse, across from City Hall," she declared congenially, before shyly averting her gaze and apparently making a note of this.

"Uh," Dr. Pendleton began to acknowledge, blinking hesitantly.

The girl in the back abruptly got to her feet, tugging at the bottom of her short skirt and glancing at the profile of Father Gilchrist and then up at Dr. Pendleton, seeming indecisive for a split second before obstinately speaking up.

"My name's Vanessa Fox"—she stated assertively, then adding with a touch of defiance—"and I'm a freelance prostitute."

Her focus having flashed back to the priest's profile, she was then flanked by competing distractions as Dr. Pendleton's eyebrows nearly collided with his receded hairline and Mr. McClintock coughed harshly beside her, his main chin dipping into his other two as he fought to regain composure.

Dr. Pendleton, somewhat slack-jawed, gladly focused on the beet-red man, who, as if taking a cue, heaved himself to his feet, gasping for breath, producing his own handkerchief and dabbing it against his throat.

"Uh, my name is Percival McClintock," he wheezed, pressing one large hand almost old-womanishly against his massive chest. "I, uh, am a food and restaurant reviewer for the *Global Tribune*, for which I write a weekly column." He managed to nod politely to whomever happened to be listening before settling himself back down onto his chairs, overtly avoiding the gaze of the nearby girl.

"Uh," Dr. Pendleton tried to begin again. *Welcome, Percival? Who named their child Percival in this or even the last century?*

"Welcome," he nodded succinctly, then moving quickly to gesture to the tiny old woman who had scarcely moved since taking her seat.

"And, how about you, ma'am?" he prompted gently.

To his surprise, not only did the old woman glance up at him, but also she reached out and took his hand, standing and moving slowly toward the crate, her vague smile still loosely in place on her sagging lips.

"Yes, of course, Mr. Bergdorf," she told him cordially, her voice pleasant yet tired. "Will everyone be having some?"

Dumbfounded, Dr. Pendleton stole a quick glance at the others, then bending slightly toward the woman. "I'm…sorry?" he told her hesitantly. "Uh, will everyone be having what?"

"Coffee, of course," she replied promptly, smiling and shuffling toward the table where the coffee maker was still gurgling ominously.

Dr. Pendleton stared after her in speechless confusion and then turned back to face the group, his gaze shooting to Chris as he awkwardly got to his feet, his introduction already tumbling out of him, cut short when, upon standing, his butt flap caught a loose screwhead protruding from the chair, causing it to topple backward and fold up on itself as it crashed harshly to the floor.

Mr. Crimpton cringed in horror, one hand clasping at his heart, the other flying to his forehead as he gasped for air. Alongside him, Judge Talbott lifted her pen. "How do you spell 'Gilcrest'?" she asked the priest.

Chris hastily stooped to pick up his chair, knocking over the packing crate in doing so, apologizing in embarrassment all the while, the doctor grimacing helplessly behind him, his attention diverted to the reappearance of his note cards scattered on the floor, presumably having fallen directly through the crate. He gratefully moved to scoop them up, realizing even as he did so that they were now more or less useless.

"I'm really sorry," Chris was saying, his young features a bright crimson. He gestured in hapless clumsiness to the doctor and then gave a flustered look at the either startled or disdainful others.

"Uh, I'm Chris…Christopher Galveston," he murmured glumly, shifting his big feet and tall frame uncomfortably.

"Um…in punk rock circles, they call me 'Stud Stomper,'" he added with a pitifully hopeless glance at them.

When this failed to make a favorable impression, or any impression at all, Chris shrugged self-consciously and next heard himself saying, "But, um, they call me 'Clodhopper' too 'cause I'm kinda clumsy sometimes."

Cheeks burning, his mind reeling as he pondered why he had told them this, he moved to sit down again, just as Dr. Pendleton inadvertently made matters worse by cheerfully, obliviously stating, "Welcome, uh, Clodhopper," the sting of this accentuated by the fact that the loose screw was now missing altogether, causing him to sit down and keep right on going, the chair buckling beneath him, his rump slamming soundly against the floor.

There were a few chuckles at this, Vanessa's scornful laugh the most prominent, burning in Chris's ears, as, sitting there in the sawdust for one dejected, frustrated moment of self-disgust, he grimaced woefully and forced himself to clamber back to his feet under the scathing gaze of Father Gilchrist.

"Uh, careful now," Dr. Pendleton was cautioning with an oily smile, his features somewhat pained. He was, after all, accountable for these chairs.

"Here's your coffee, Mr. Bergdorf," sang the old woman, returning from the side table with a Styrofoam cup, which she deposited into the doctor's hands. "Cream and three sugars, just the way you like it."

Dr. Pendleton blinked from the woman to the coffee, about to raise the question of "Mr. Bergdorf," but even more mystified as to how this woman knew precisely how he took his coffee.

"Uh, thank you…," he told her, hastily putting the coffee atop the crate and moving to her side. "Uh, wouldn't you like to introduce yourself to the group, *Mrs.…?*" he proposed.

The woman turned to take all of them in with her hazy, milky eyes. "Oh yes, of course," she replied agreeably. "My name is Eleanor Spindlewood." She fingered the front of her outdated dress and gave the semblance of a curtsy. "I take shorthand. I'm very good at filing, and I can type forty words a minute."

The others focused upon these vocational assets in bemused silence as Mrs. Spindlewood smiled back at the doctor. "Will that be all, Mr. Bergdorf?"

Clearing his throat, Dr. Pendleton was on the verge of correcting her when he instead returned her smile and nodded, gesturing her toward her seat, his own smile then fading in puzzled uncertainty as he watched her shuffle away, her pumps leaving a pronounced trail in the sawdust. Putting the matter aside, he took in the group once more, stepping up to the crate but taking care not to touch it, for fear of upsetting the cup of coffee. He arranged a chair alongside it and sat down, doing his best to seem casually at ease.

"Well then," he beamed encouragingly, clasping his hands together. "Now that we all know each other, perhaps we can begin our discussion." Pausing, he gazed from person to person. "So, uh, who would like to get the ball rolling?"

Judge Talbott waved to him, wincing apologetically. "How do you spell 'Berkdorf'?"

Dr. Pendleton opened his mouth, Father Gilchrist waylaying his response by stating, "I believe I can suggest an excellent way to commence these proceedings," accentuating this claim with a puckered little smile.

"Oh?" Dr. Pendleton regarded him gratefully, glad that anyone had spoken up and rather impressed that it should be this, so far, uncongenial priest. "By all means, please, uh, Father, feel free to get the ball rolling." He smiled invitingly, then wondering if the cleric was going to propose opening with a word of prayer, fleetingly unsure if such would be good or bad.

Father Gilchrist's smile became even more frosty. "I would suggest that you find some other phrase to employ as an exordium," he declared pedantically. "You have already used this other figure of speech far past the point of cliché."

Balking somewhat, Dr. Pendleton did not know quite how to respond; the semantics were not really what was at issue after all.

A pained expression creased Mr. Crimpton's already weary features as he considered this exchange. A week's worth of deliberating had brought him here, only after he realized that he had no other alternatives save to embrace a nervous breakdown head on. Attending the meeting had seemed more productive or, in any event, less destructive. Now, however, he was beginning to wonder if a breakdown might not actually be preferable.

Nonetheless, he forced himself to give the meeting a chance, having little other choice. Raising his hand, he spoke up reluctantly. "How about, 'Who will be our first contestant?'" he offered half-heartedly, having once upon a time commenced each day of driving tests with those words.

Dr. Pendleton regarded him blankly. "Uh, that's...that's pretty good..."

Managing a minute smile, Mr. Crimpton settled back in his seat. Audience participation had never been one of his strong suits, which was why he had spoken up now and gotten his input out of the way.

Next to him, Judge Talbott, pausing in her note-keeping, thought of an idea of her own, raising her hand and then abruptly lowering it, changing her mind.

The doctor stared uncertainly at her, his mouth slack, as Mr. McClintock gestured from the rear.

"Perhaps, 'Who will be serving our first course?'" he proposed helpfully.

Frowning slightly, Dr. Pendleton slowly nodded. "Uh, yes, I'm sure that would also suffice..." he allowed hesitantly, the entire matter seeming irrelevant to the issues at hand.

Still, though, he realized this discourse could be the preliminary to the establishment of a dialogue; at least, some of them were opening up a bit. He felt renewed enthusiasm as this occurred to him. Perhaps this was after all the perfect way to get the ball...He grimaced, clearing his throat.

Alongside Mr. McClintock, Vanessa was scarcely listening, her gaze having resettled on the sphinxlike profile of Father Gilchrist. She was considering how, to her surprise, far from appearing sanctimoniously offended by her candid statement earlier, he had merely shifted slightly in his seat, his features revealing only an indifferent, unastonished cynicism. She had been certain that her announcement would shock him. Had she been speaking to the minister back in Portertown, he most likely would have slapped her and then dropped dead on the spot. Of course, she had not realized that the old guy was a priest until he flashed that collar; if she had, she most likely would not have made her antagonizing comment earlier. If that were true though, she wondered, her teeth chiding her lower lip, chafing at the waxy layer of lipstick, why had she been all the more willing to rankle him *after* she had learned this?

Her focus moved past the priest and settled on the dufussy punk across from him, who, she realized with an indignant start, had been gaping at her.

She served him a scowl that caused him to shrink and banish his gaze to the floor, his cheeks flushing satisfyingly. She smiled at this accomplishment, considering it a minor victory in an eternal struggle. She had been ogled all her life; if only deflating them could always be that easy.

Nonetheless, she was forced to consider there had been something to his look. Overall, of course, it was nothing new—the same unblinking stare; same boyishly open mouth, dangling vacantly; and same slack-shouldered posture, feet-planted, legs apart. She had seen this naive little boy stance a thousand times, often in men twice this punk's age. Usually, it conveyed ignorance, which, cute though it could be, got old very quickly.

This time, though, there was something in addition to all of the above, something indefinable. It was in his eyes, she realized, thinking of the image he had held right before she had rebuffed him. There was a sort of ashamed innocence in them, made all the more pronounced when he had looked away. It was made even more striking, she perceived gradually, in conjunction—or, rather, in contrast—with his ridiculous appearance. That was little more than a costume, anyone could see that, even the wing nuts in this group, even the screw-up of a doctor could see it. It could not even be called a facade.

No, it was a costume, not unlike her own, she reflected, with a bit of self-reproach. Of course, she knew what she was—and was *not*—hiding and could straight up guess what he was hiding. She knew a loser when she saw one.

"Well, uh, these are excellent suggestions," Dr. Pendleton had been saying with feigned conviction, anxious to channel the dialogue into a more meaningful exchange. "Uh, with that established, uh, why don't we proceed…"

Met by silence, he hurried onward, determined not to drop the ball… He grimaced. "Perhaps if anyone had any questions or comments about our format here tonight?" he proposed coaxingly. "Or about the goal of our meetings…"

There was a momentary lapse, during which Mr. McClintock very hesitantly raised a hand. "I had a question, I suppose," he said doubtfully.

Much encouraged, Dr. Pendleton nodded eagerly. "Uh, yes, Mr.…uh, McClintock?" he replied, triumphant at having remembered the man's name.

Smiling meekly, Mr. McClintock removed the neon-green flyer from his jacket, unfolding it neatly. "It was in reference to a point made on your brochure."

"Ah," Dr. Pendleton affirmed, stooping to retrieve a flyer from his attaché case, donning his glasses, and peering over the page. "Yes, well, of course, these advertisements were very basic in their summation of what we would be doing here. They merely suggest a format, while, of course, it falls to us to develop an agenda truly suited to our own personal needs and ambitions."

He beamed at Mr. McClintock, who smiled weakly back, shifting on his chairs. Pausing, Dr. Pendleton then nodded, glancing from the man to the flyer, waiting a moment or so before taking up the initiative again.

"And so you…had a question, Mr. McClintock?" he hinted encouragingly.

Flushed, Mr. McClintock was forced to proceed, appearing to do so with considerable reluctance. "Oh well, I was merely curious. Your flyer offers a great many features for the meeting's potential, including I believe some mention of…refreshments?" He smiled in hopeful chagrin.

Dr. Pendleton blinked at him. "Uh, I beg your pardon?" he responded, fairly certain that he *had* heard correctly.

Mr. McClintock's jowls were pressed beneath his chins as he attempted to sink into his chairs or perhaps disappear altogether.

However, the faux-pas gambit had been made; why not see it through? After all, the man was clearly looking for a way to break the ice; what better way than to pass around a tray of canapés or pastries or cocktail wienies or even crackers?

"I was merely wondering about the mention of refreshments in your flyer," he prompted with a polite smile, indicating the notation on the page, his stomach rumbling quietly. The nearby girl gave him a sideways look.

Dr. Pendleton's gaze fell to his flyer again. Of all its promised potential, *this* was the one detail that had evoked so much interest?

"Uh, refreshments, yes," he stammered, motioning toward the side table. "Uh, please feel free to help yourself to some coffee."

Mrs. Spindlewood looked up. "Oh, another cup, Mr. Bergdorf?"

"Uh, no, Mrs. Spindlewood. I was speaking to Mr. Percival, uh, to Mr....Uh, no thank you," he assured her, brandishing his cup with a show of appreciation. "I'm still enjoying mine." He took a deep sip and froze. This coffee was black with at least twelve sugars.

"Do you prefer regular or decaffeinated?" Mrs. Spindlewood asked Father Gilchrist.

Mr. McClintock cast a disappointed glance at the sputtering coffee maker, a sinking feeling coming over him. "Is...that the extant of the...comestibles?" he inquired, nonchalantly innocent.

Choking down the swallow of coffee, Dr. Pendleton blushed. It had not occurred to him to bring any snacks to the meeting, a rather large oversight, he chastised himself. Even the lesser-known anonymous groups at least had doughnuts.

"I'm afraid so," he confessed, watching Mr. McClintock's face deflate like a Macy's Day Parade balloon. "However"—he hurried onward, recalling a thought that had struck him earlier that week—"I had considered the possibility that, in future meetings, we might share snacks and such, something perhaps along the lines of a potluck."

A few faces lifted in interest, including that of the food critic. Encouraged, Dr. Pendleton continued with enthusiasm. "In fact, once we are quite comfortable with each other, we might consider alternate meeting spaces. I had actually foreseen something as informal and relaxed as a session held as a picnic in the park."

Mr. McClintock considered this with something akin to anticipation, having not given much thought to future meetings. When his column had appeared, word for word, in the Sunday edition, with neither residual questions nor criticism from anyone, he had almost decided against the need to act upon this "contingency plan." However, his misgivings and customary angst had sought to coerce him, and he had ultimately conceded, if only from the expectations suggested by the flyer. With that enticement now depreciated, the idea of the refreshments that forthcoming sessions might yield seemed doubly promising. Potlucks were a veritable artist's palette of variety and creativity; and, after all, if he were to continue to attend these meetings, it was good to know that he would be getting something out of them.

He beamed up at the doctor. "I think that that sounds like a splendid idea!" he stated approvingly.

"Yes, what a perfectly droll notion," scoffed Father Gilchrist. "I am certain it will be very gay indeed."

Dr. Pendleton nodded and then blinked. *Could he mean... Clearly, he was old enough that, to him, that word would instead mean... Of course, on the other hand...*

Mr. Crimpton stared at the priest with a narrow, bewildered scrutiny, while Judge Talbott's head shot up, jabbing at the air with her pen.

"Uh, yes, Judge...uh, Vivean?" nodded the doctor, still distracted.

Judge Talbott moved to speak and then quickly retracted her hand.

"Oh, it was nothing, really," she giggled nervously. "Never mind."

Gaping at her, Dr. Pendleton then looked toward Chris, who was waving half-confidently. "I think that sounds like fun," he spoke up, a bit bashfully. "In fact, I know a good spot at Teasedale Central. There's even some picnic tables right by the skate park."

The doctor appeared to consider this, as Father Gilchrist leveled Chris with a scorching appraisal. "Teasedale Central Park?" he all but spat. "Oh, won't that be picturesque! We shall spread our picnic cloth in the shade of the train trestle. I shall bring along some communal wine in case we should run low on Ripple."

As Chris wilted in shame, Judge Talbott took a deep breath and forced herself to be assertive, her pen once more jabbing at the air. As comparable as this group was to a courtroom, she was finding herself increasingly out of her element.

"I can make some Rice Krispies Treats!" she heard herself squeak.

Everyone in the room turned to regard her, prompting her to contemplate how she might hide inside her purse. "That is, if everyone likes those...," she managed to add, looking to the doctor for help—or rebuke.

Dr. Pendleton inhaled to reply, Mr. Crimpton shaking his head toward the judge. "I'm sorry, I can't eat those," he mumbled as apologetically as he could. "I'm lactose intolerant."

Judge Talbott nodded sadly as Vanessa sneered from across the room. "There isn't any milk in those!" she told him scornfully.

Mr. Crimpton turned to serve her a severe look that his glasses seemed to punctuate. "There most certainly is, young lady!" he told her sharply. "There has to be. Rice Krispies are never prepared without milk. That's how they were designed! That's how that whole 'Snap, Crackle and Pop' trademark first got patented!"

Vanessa's mouth fell open in a gasp of scathing disbelief, Dr. Pendleton clearing his throat from where he stood, uncertain if he should intervene, for, after all, they were still establishing a dialogue. Sort of.

"I could make some without milk," Judge Talbott was offering in a conciliatory way, as if devastated that she should cause such controversy.

"You can use nondairy creamer as a substitute," observed Mrs. Spindlewood sagely.

Father Gilchrist looked from Vanessa to the old woman, having been mildly impressed with the girl's sauce. Of course, such insolence went hand in hand with the streets, he knew; a tart had to be just that. As for this other, addle-minded soul, he reflected, staring sternly at Mrs. Spindlewood, clearly the woman was senile, no doubt belonged in a hospital. He scowled, considering how such a trait had somehow been missed by their illustrious "doctor." A portent of what they could expect from this cartoonlike charade, he sniffed disdainfully.

"I'm sure we'll be able to iron out all the details as they develop," Dr. Pendleton finally interposed, nodding back to Mr. McClintock. "I hope that settles any concerns about refreshments we'll have in upcoming meetings." He paused, awaiting what he hoped would be confirmation of this. "Mr. McClintock?"

Mr. McClintock had been focused upon an image in his mind's eye, contemplating the mention of the Rice Krispies Treats. Those were really good. Glancing up, he caught the gist of the doctor's words and nodded emphatically.

"Oh yes, absolutely…Thank you," he acknowledged gratefully, his stomach rumbling again. Vanessa shot him an unsympathetic look and cracked her gum.

"Now then," Dr. Pendleton stated briskly, feeling that they had at long last reached the crossroads of the establishment of dialogue, finding that he did not know exactly where to take it from here. One idea presented itself, and although he was reluctant to implement it, he knew he would have to take the chance.

"Does anyone else—" He stopped himself and began again, more forthrightly. "Who else has a question they would like to have considered?" he asked, instead, pleased that he had caught himself. By amending his words, he had negated the scenario in which, very feasibly, no one would offer a question, and they would have another unproductive duration of silence; by asking directly, and in such an exacting way, he had superimposed the idea that some, if not all of them, did, indeed, have questions, leaving them little choice but to ask them. That was what psychology was all about after all—choreographing the conversation in the mind, even while carrying it out verbally. He knew Dr. Whittaker would endorse such a philosophy. It was a question of staying three steps ahead of the other person, precisely like the old checkers analogy.

He was surprised when Father Gilchrist spoke, a bit wary but resolved to listen just the same.

"I have a question"—he stated airily, then adding sharply—"and I assure you, it has nothing to do with tonight's bill of fare, or lack thereof."

Dr. Pendleton frowned and then nodded rapidly. "Oh! Oh good, that's fine," he conceded, smiling gratefully, for he was glad to hear that.

"My question has more to do with basic psychological methodology," the old priest continued, somewhat languidly.

"I see," Dr. Pendleton nodded, his interest incited. Now, it seemed they would get to the more profound aspects of his profession and the real reasons why they were all there that evening. Choreography, he marveled. It really was that simple. "Please continue."

"In the therapeutic field, the doctor–patient session, in the traditional clinical setting, is almost without exception one solid hour in length, is it not?" Father Gilchrist inquired broadly.

"Yes, that is correct," Dr. Pendleton responded promptly, then frowning slightly at the unclear relevance of the question.

"And, in as much as this forum is, generally speaking, an extension of that self-same methodology," Father Gilchrist continued, steepling his fingers and gazing thoughtfully at the ceiling. "Can we conclude that the same chronological duration might also apply?"

Dr. Pendleton blinked uncertainly. "Well, I suppose so—"

"Excellent," Father Gilchrist decreed, startling the doctor as he sat up abruptly in his chair, glancing at his wristwatch. "In that case, we have only twenty-five minutes more of this Freudian kaffeeklatsch to endure!" With that, he folded his arms before himself and focused upon the far wall.

Dr. Pendleton blinked, paused, opened his mouth, shut it, and then almost sighed. He could feel his hopes fading. This was not going quite how he had envisioned it. For all his discouragement and diminished confidence, though, he knew better than to give up—not in front of the group anyway.

"Uh, naturally, the one-hour time frame, while it is traditionally observed, is, for our purposes, only a general framework," he began hesitantly. "Uh, obviously, it is my hope to schedule our meetings in such a way that it will, uh, accommodate everyone's respective routines. I'm certain we'll be able to fine-tune it accordingly as our meetings develop…" He trailed off, his glance falling on his note cards, a belated but better-than-nothing idea arising in his mind, one on which he seized gratefully.

"Uh, earlier this evening, it had been my intention to outline for all of you what I, as a psychologist, had thought would be the suitable expectations that go along with the formation of a peer-counseling therapy group," he began earnestly, feeling a semblance of momentum. "I can see now that that would probably not have been the best idea, because it would clearly be much better if you were to tell me what you all hope to get out of our meetings together. After all, you saw the flyers yourselves, and you all specifically chose to come here tonight. Something about the concept must have seemed impressive or…or potentially helpful, uh… Otherwise, you most likely wouldn't be here now."

He let this sink in, sensing that he did have everyone's attention, if nothing else. "Uh…what's more, I would like for you to consider that I am really just a guide, just an…advisor who wants to provide a space in which to explore all our questions and concerns. The true nature of peer counseling is, of course, to help each other. While it's true that I have the training and background to assist, plus the desire and obligation to help, it's my hope that we will all be able to provide each other with the much more conventional, down-to-earth, everyday life sort of guidance and support that we all need from time to time—myself most definitely included."

He paused again, inhaling deeply as he peered from face to face. "With that said, I think it would be great if we could all open up a bit and tell us all about why we came here tonight."

Another dead silence ensued, during which Dr. Pendleton continued to look from person to person, his gaze slipping past Judge Talbott as she raised her hand. He glanced back to her in time to see her hastily pull it back down again. Perplexed, he focused upon her with uplifted brows until she tentatively lifted it again, meeting his eyes.

"Yes?" he asked gently, watching as the hand darted back to her side.

"Oh, nothing, I just…" She smiled feebly. "It wasn't important."

"Ah," he nodded, trying to efface patience as he glanced away again.

"It's just that I—" she blurted out, startling Mr. Crimpton.

Dr. Pendleton likewise started, focusing on her once more. "Yes?"

Even beyond her makeup and complexion, it was obvious that she was blushing, almost girlishly. "I…can't seem to make up my mind," she told him helplessly, offering a small, meek shrug.

"Oh," nodded Dr. Pendleton, disappointed. "Well, take your time, and when you're ready to share, I'm sure you'll…" He paused, the thought striking him. "Oh!" He looked at her again, Judge Talbott braced hopefully. "You mean you have *trouble* making up your mind."

As she nodded in relief, Dr. Pendleton thrilled over this breakthrough. "Ah, I see, well," he nodded, attempting to downplay it, for fear of making the little woman uncomfortable. "A common problem, I know." He smiled reassuringly at her, then looking at the others. "Does anyone else have difficulty in making decisions now and then?"

There were a few general nods, Mr. Crimpton then raising his hand.

"Ah, you have trouble making decisions too, Mr.…uh…" Dr. Pendleton paused.

Mr. Crimpton shook his head. "No, my problem is my nerves," he declared, somewhat emphatically. "My nerves and how they affect my work."

"I see," nodded Dr. Pendleton, still trying to recall the man's name, wondering why he hadn't been taking notes as well. Not wanting to lose volition, he pressed onward. "Does anyone else have trouble with their nerves?" he asked. "Or, perhaps, nerves in relation to their jobs?"

He glanced toward Father Gilchrist, who refused to meet his gaze and then saw Mr. McClintock raise a plump hand from the rear.

"Yes, Mr. McClintock," he called, trying to keep up the rhythm. "Do you have some problem with your nerves in general or at work?"

"Well, in a way," Mr. McClintock replied. "I'm nervous *about* my work. Not that my work makes me nervous, mind you. In fact, I very much enjoy it. It is more a case of my being afraid I will *lose* my work...by losing my job, that is to say..."

"I see," nodded the doctor, trying to connect all of these diverging angles. "Well, so far, these matters all have...some common ground..."

He noticed Chris squirming slightly in his seat as he watched and listened to the others. Mistaking his actions for an excited impetus to join in, he gestured at the kid, startled when the punk rocker seemed startled himself.

"Uh, how about you, uh, Clodhopper?" he asked, making matters worse.

Chris flushed, gaping around the room even as he sought to avoid attention. "Uh, I dunno," he responded, trying to summon up some decidedly punk indifference, the only thing preventing the others from bursting into laughter being that they probably would not know how to judge how pathetic his attempt was, all save for Vanessa, whose upper lip curled derisively into one corner.

"Oh, come now," Dr. Pendleton coaxed. "There must be some reason why you gave up a night at the Disco-Tech to be here with us old folks."

Chris could not imagine how to respond to this idea, but he knew patronization when he heard it. "I don't really know why I came here tonight," he told him, which, in his mind was half true. "I mean maybe sometimes I think that I've got issues...I know my whole family thinks I should see someone..." That was more or less true, he decided, shrugging his sloping shoulders loosely.

Dr. Pendleton nodded quickly. "I see. They feel like you are getting a bit too wild and...out of hand, so they made you come here?" he proposed conclusively.

That was even less true than anything Chris had said, but the whole idea seemed to personify that which he could not seem to manage himself, and he decided to go along with it.

"Yeah," he drawled in a juvenile tone, some of his bewilderment showing when the doctor appeared to be pleased with the entire exchange, as if he heartily approved of having such a problem child in their midst.

"Yeah, I was getting in all kinds of trouble at school," he warned him, which was true. Three years previously. Scholastically.

"I see. I see," Dr. Pendleton replied, almost cheerfully. He could not believe his luck—a bona fide juvenile delinquent in their group. To think, he had been fooled up until now thinking that this might be a nice, decent kid, when he was, in fact, a raging, angry young punk *pretending* to be a nice boy. There were sure to be nuances and profundities to this kid that would constitute a breakthrough for all of them in time.

His glance next flew to the young girl in the back of the room; here, he realized, was what might be an even more challenging case of youth-oriented problems. When he had recovered from the shock of her unexpected announcement earlier, he had discerned that she might only have been joking, perhaps trying to get a rise out of them. Surely, this girl must still be in school, wherein her problems were most likely that of an overactive imagination.

If, however, she was speaking the truth… He frowned, unsure of the legal ramifications of the issue. If she were, indeed, a prostitute, and perhaps even a minor at that, then his own responsibilities were quite clear. Of course, if she were those things, then what became even clearer was the fact that she needed help, which, in itself, was also a part of his responsibility. The very concept of a group like this was its intention to help people. And it was, after all, anonymous.

"Ah, seventeen minutes," Father Gilchrist announced cheerfully.

Distracted, Dr. Pendleton grimaced and then gestured toward the girl, who had, up until then, been regarding Chris with a pained look.

"And you, uh…Miss," he called, her name eluding him. "Have you been able to reflect on what it is that brought you here tonight?"

Vanessa focused on him, eyebrows arching apathetically.

"Me?" she replied bluntly. "Yeah, sure, I knew since the moment I walked in the door. I was trying to get away from a john who turned out to be the pimp for most of the south side. I ditched him and came in here to lay low, since he told me if he caught me hustling his turf again, he'd come after me like Jack the Ripper."

There was a protracted silence, broken by Mr. McClintock, who paled and regarded her in horror. "How dreadful!"

Vanessa turned to give him a look, finding that she had to smile at the enormous man's sincere concern. "Yeah, ain't it, though?" she said coyly.

Dr. Pendleton, sensing the discomfiture of the others at her very candid response, attempted to put aside his own dis-ease.

"I see," he began slowly, unsure of how to address this issue; beyond its psychology, the situation was somewhat bizarre. "Uh, that is very...unfortunate, uh, Miss..." His mind drew several blanks at once.

"Vanessa," hissed Judge Talbott, motioning to her legal pad.

"Uh, thank you, Judge," he nodded. "That is very unfortunate, Vanessa." He paused again, his thoughts abruptly grinding to a halt. *Judge?*

If this woman was a judge, surely she should have something to say about the matter, shouldn't she? He glanced sideways at her, returning her meek smile weakly. Perhaps she had plenty to say but could not make her mind up to say it, he reflected wistfully, clearing his throat and forcing himself to take charge.

"Uh, Vanessa, if you don't mind my asking, how old—" He broke off, realizing, as he would continue to do for some time to come, the mistake he almost made. If they were truly to help this girl, if it turned out that she did, in fact, want any help from them... choreography.

He harrumphed to obscure what he had been about to say, amending it very carefully. "That is, if you don't mind my asking, uh, are you old enough to be...engaged in those sorts of...activities?"

She gave him a placating smile, because she either recognized the pointed ambiguity of his words or maybe even appreciated it. "Doctor, I'm old enough to be engaged in just about anything the world throws at me," she replied evenly. She could see that her answer, while satisfactory, was still startling to most of them, possibly even the poker-faced old priest. "Sorry if I'm being pretty frank," she offered semigraciously, her gaze settling upon Chris. "But at least I'm being honest," she added forcefully.

Chris's head shot up, his eyes widening when they met hers, for it then became obvious that her words were directed at him. She stared him down for a moment, surprised when he did not look away like before, instead returning the intensity of her look with one that seemed somehow wounded and challenging at the same time, so much so that she felt her own cheeks begin to glow. In the end, she looked away first, effecting a manner of boredom as she turned to the doctor again, although she had to wonder what Chris had been thinking at that moment, annoyed that she had been unable to glare him into submission. She hated even the thought that she had given someone the upper hand, having in the past grown so accustomed to giving everyone the finger instead.

"Uh, well, that's uh…good," Dr. Pendleton was saying, the utter lameness of his words apparent even to him as he spoke them.

Chris had let his gaze slip to the floor, his thoughts darkening. The girl's words had stung him deeply, mainly, he knew, because she was right. She had seen right through him. He must seem little more than a joke to her, and this notion hurt his feelings and bristled what little ego he had managed to hang onto after all this time with Candy. Were all girls destined to make him feel that way? And not just girls, it seemed. He felt unable to make any kind of lasting impression on anyone. He knew that his outrageous appearance was not some juvenile bid for attention; but, at the same time, it did not do very much in the way of speaking up for him; and, in this way, for all of its pseudoferocity, his punk raiment once again had made him feel like a clown. He poked at the sawdust with the bulbous steel toe of his boot, wondering why he had come there at all. What could he possibly have been expecting?

"Thirteen minutes," announced Father Gilchrist punctiliously.

Dr. Pendleton grimaced deeply, gazing in frustration at the older man. What kind of priest behaved even *remotely* like…

"And how about you, Father Gilchrist?" he asked at that point, keeping his voice as pleasant as possible. "What made you decide to join us this evening?"

Father Gilchrist scarcely looked at him, instead focusing mainly on the ceiling. "Not that it is any of your business, but the decision, I can assure you, was not one of my own. It came from what passes as my superiors in the Archdiocese. I was strongly advised to seek out some form of therapeutic, social counseling, for whatever ill-conceived reason. As it happens, some benighted person left that carnival-like leaflet in my confessional. Thinking that one group was as good as another, I opted to try this one." He turned his dour gaze toward the doctor. "Imagine my surprise," he concluded suggestively.

Dr. Pendleton's eyebrows had lifted to some degree as he listened, impressed with the priest's words, for all their acidity. "The Archdiocese?" he repeated. "Really, you mean you are a…a genuine article Catholic priest?"

Father Gilchrist eyed him dryly. "Is the Pope Catholic?" he replied archly.

Blinking, Dr. Pendleton smiled uncertainly, paused, and then hesitantly double-checked his meaning. "You mean…that you *are* Catholic, then?"

The priest glared. "Perhaps I should employ a more remedial cliché," he grated. "To wit, does a bear crap in the woods?"

Blanching, Dr. Pendleton cleared his throat, while Chris looked up from his glum perusal of the floor, some interest restored in his face.

"A Catholic priest, really?" he gaped, leaning forward in his chair. "Have you, like, ever performed an exorcism or anything?"

"Why?" snapped Father Gilchrist. "Are you in as dire need for one as you appear?"

As Chris wilted once more into hangdog submission, Dr. Pendleton hastened to counteract the boy's ill-timed question.

"Well, we're certainly glad that you decided to attend," he declared, smiling earnestly. "It's actually a little ironic that you should be here. After all, your vocation and the function of this group have a great deal in common."

Turning to face the doctor in pained amazement, Father Gilchrist folded his arms challengingly. "In what possible way?" he demanded.

Starting, Dr. Pendleton glanced briefly at the others as if for support, before meeting the priest's scowl. "Uh, well, I mean... not unlike the confessional booth, we've created a private setting in which we can hear each other's troubles, uh, offer each other advice, and know that all that we've shared will be maintained in the strictest of confidence..."

He nodded, somewhat pleased with his impromptu comparison.

The others appeared likewise impressed, even Vanessa, all save for Father Gilchrist, who appeared even more vexed than previously.

"A poetic if wholly obtuse analogy," he responded sharply. "This group and particularly this room cannot possibly be likened to a confessional booth, wherein one man must sit, confined for hour after sweltering hour, listening to an interminable parade of whispering, would-be worshippers confiding any and all manner of misdeeds, some of piddling picayune triviality and others of the most unconscionable vice, and then being expected to offer some form of instamatic resolution, as if the booth were nothing more than a penance-dispensing vending machine! I have often been convinced that the church should resume its sale of indulgences and do away with the confessional altogether!"

Red-faced, Father Gilchrist ended his tirade with a punctuating glare at the cringing doctor, before defiantly taking in all the others as well, perhaps sensing their shock. Indeed, he was being regarded with various looks of astonishment. Mr. Crimpton was frozen-featured; Chris appeared scared. Even Judge Talbott had paled. Vanessa had stopped in midchomp, and Mr. McClintock was distracted from his hunger. With the exception of Mrs. Spindlewood, they all seemed aware that they had just witnessed something that they were not meant to see, yet were perhaps not quite sure what it was. Only Father Gilchrist knew that it was a simple matter of demystification, a realization that the differences between the church and the secular world were not as pronounced as legend would have it. He did not care, however, if he had upset the popular notion, and he abruptly ended the silence with a glance at his watch.

"Ten minutes remaining," he proclaimed robustly.

This almost comical about-face brought Dr. Pendleton's attention back to the forefront, and reflexively clearing his throat, he swiftly sought to resume the pace that they had achieved before it had been derailed.

"Uh, thank you, Father Gilchrist," he nodded briskly, focusing hesitantly on the last person at hand. "Uh, Mrs. Spindlewood, would you like to—"

"Yes, Mr. Bergdorf?" Mrs. Spindlewood looked up from her trancelike repose.

"Uh, would you like to tell us what made you decide to join us tonight?" he asked her, hedging his question with what he thought was a safe guess. "Did someone send you here to be with our group this evening?"

"Yes," Mrs. Spindlewood confirmed, slowly rising to her feet and making her curtsying motion to the group again. "I was sent by the Working Girl Temporary Employment Agency," she told them, in an almost recital-like voice, before settling quietly back into her seat again.

Dr. Pendleton, at a loss of how to respond to this, nodded and smiled haltingly. The other members of the group shifted in their seats, glancing about uncomfortably, as if—as there was—a great deal still to be said. Yet so vast was the void of silence that now descended upon the room, no one seemed willing or even able to break it.

Judge Talbott's focus was on her purse again, from which she had withdrawn a folded sheet of legal paper, on which she had written an entire inventory of thoughts and examples of her indecisiveness. It had been her intention to read it to the group, leastwise, in her daydreams, for she doubted that she would have been able to work up the nerve. Just deciding to attend had taken almost all of her resolve, inspired by the final stretch of limbo before she was to assume the bench of a judge who was working out the last few days before his retirement. Grateful for the reprieve, she had just as quickly found herself faced with the suspense that it also engendered and had been forced to seek out some way of dealing with it. Discovering the flyer she had absently stowed in her purse at Quickie-Laundry, she had opted to explore its potential and had wanted to come prepared.

Now, she was considering just handing it to the doctor before they all left for the night, rather like turning in an essay to a teacher. That would certainly be much easier than speaking it out loud. She was struck by the notion of some sort of written-word therapy, wondering if there existed any form of "Correspondence School Sessions by mail." Short of Dear Abbey, she could not think of any...

Mr. Crimpton was sneaking subtle looks at his own watch, trying to recall how late the busses ran in this part of town. He had entertained the idea of catching a ride with one of the group members once he had met them and now, having done so, had dismissed the notion outrightly. Even if any one of these people had valid driver's licenses—*doubtful*—he was not about to subject himself to any of their vehicular neuroses. As for the doctor, he could not possibly ask him. After only a few minutes on the road, it would become apparent why he was attending a therapy group, and he did not want to risk revealing everything all at once, most likely in hysterics, especially when that particular driver had the legal authority to keep right on driving him to the nearest sanitarium.

Chris continually gawked around the room at the others, surprised when no one seemed anxious to resume the conversation. From his point of view, they were the grown-ups after all. Even at eighteen, legalities aside, he had no problem seeing himself as a kid—not a *little kid*, of course, and definitely not immature, but a kid, just the same. What choice did he have? The only other option was to join *them*, and he could never do that—not that they would take him anyway. So, in a sense, he was trapped, which, in a way, was okay. Even the fiercest punk would run a mile screaming rather than embrace John Q. Adulthood. It was strange, though, especially after the priest's virtual diatribe, for him to see them all so quiet and disjointed and for once left with nothing to say. It was almost scary, for that had never stopped them from talking before, this phenomenon making him feel somewhat similar to them. This abstract sense of belonging only made his anxieties more acute, however; he had once heard a figure of speech that depicted rock-bottom as being the great equalizer.

Vanessa had adopted Father Gilchrist's stance and folded her arms defiantly. What she had hoped would have been several smoke-layered hours of tedium, listening to marital problems and failed childhood dreams had turned into a scarcely one-hour joke. She almost felt sorry for him, for this bland, naive little man who clearly thought he knew what he was doing actually believed that he could make a difference. Of course, matching wits with this bunch was virtually a guaranteed flop, especially that crazy priest. He needed to be by himself in a group of therapists. She watched Dr. Pendleton flounder; but, sympathetic as she was, she had a few problems of her own, like getting all the way back to East Traurig Street without meeting up with that pimp again.

Obviously, she was going to have to catch a ride with one of these losers. Both of the women were out; the old lady was on the bus, and if the black chick really was a judge, then she was not about to ask her. If she really *was* a judge, then how come she hadn't said anything about... She shrugged off the thought. Who knew, who cared, just be grateful for the break, right? So it would have to be one of the guys. Reverend Smiles was out, surprise, surprise, and Fatty and Four-Eyes both looked desperate enough to be johns...

That left only the dorky punk. She actually smiled at how easy that would be. If he had borrowed mom's station wagon, it was all downhill. A few smiles, a few giggles, and she would be at her hotel, slamming the door on his fantasies and, most likely, his hard-on too.

She blew a bubble of anticipation, then rolling her eyes at the sound emanating from off to her one side.

Mr. McClintock shifted his bulk, settling his hands reassuringly across the expanse of his stomach, wishing he could still the audible noises of his cravings. He wondered if the larger one became, the more acoustically echoic one's stomach grew, rather like the sliding scale of dimensions between a closet and a warehouse. He had been assiduously running through his mental directory of late-night restaurants in the area, which he had yet to review. There had to be one at which he could still catch a late dinner.

Dr. Pendleton, still at a loss for words, shifted uneasily alongside the crate, his glance once more falling upon his note cards. He considered turning to them one last time, hesitating as he pondered the efficacy of doing so. It might seem a bit odd if he were to conclude the meeting by reading an introductory speech. His contemplation was distracted when he saw Father Gilchrist move to look at his watch again.

"Well," he spoke up in time to intercept the nerve-wracking countdown. "I suppose it would be all right if we were to adjourn for the—"

He choked in midsentence as the old priest shot to his feet and began rebuttoning his coat, Vanessa standing up and moving into the shadows of the entry way, knowing that she had to time it just right.

"For the evening, since we've made so much progress." Dr. Pendleton continued, his voice rising an octave in desperation as it competed with the shuffling of the other members likewise preparing to leave. He glanced about as if in panic, watching as Father Gilchrist picked up his hat and deciding to try one more time to bridge the obvious gulf surrounding this man.

"Uh, I know that most other anonymous groups have a somewhat indoctrinated, uh, spiritual theme," he declared emphatically. "If it's at all appropriate and you all agree with the idea, we could consider closing out meetings with a...general word of prayer..." He lifted his brows fleetingly, standing up from his chair.

Father Gilchrist placed his hat squarely atop his head, turning to nod to the doctor. "An excellent idea. This group needs all the help it can get. I recommend that you do just that!"

Taken aback, Dr. Pendleton could only stare as the old priest paused to add, "And when no one answers, have no fear. Just leave a message on the machine."

With that, he marched stolidly toward the door, the doctor forcing himself to focus on his last few seconds with the fledgling group. "Well, I look forward to seeing you all again on Friday...," he almost shouted, instantly lowering his voice as he perceived Mrs. Spindlewood standing serenely at his side.

"Uh, yes, Mrs. Spindlewood?" he asked, looking past her and returning Judge Talbott's girlish wave goodbye, a little surprised at her method of departure, disappointed to see Mr. Crimpton leave without any manner of farewell.

"When shall I report back, Mr. Bergdorf?" Mrs. Spindlewood smiled vaguely.

Blinking, Dr. Pendleton focused on her. Hadn't he only just now said…

"On Friday, Mrs. Spindlewood," he clarified, managing to return her smile.

"On Friday?" she repeated, the slightest hint of surprise showing on her powdery, gray features. "Oh, how nice. I haven't had a day off in a month of Sundays."

She turned and tottered away, Dr. Pendleton staring after her in speechless dismay, then glancing about the now empty room, grimacing, and then starting as he saw that Chris was still hovering nearby, his features eager and anxious, in contrast with the grotesquely demonic shadow that his Mohawk and tall build cast on the wall.

*****

Vanessa had made certain to be the first one out the door, intending at least to test the other possibilities as they arose. The night air was a relief from the stuffiness of the hall, although it also served as a reminder that her sanctuary had elapsed.

The streetlights illuminated the few cars that drifted past, the avenue otherwise quiet and deserted. Nevertheless, she moved into the shadows of the front of the buildings to await the others, just as, predictably, Father Gilchrist passed through the doors next, inhaling deeply.

"Got a cigarette?" she asked him, spontaneously, though she did not smoke.

Startled, he spun around to glare at her, his expression, while not softening, shifting to a different sort of severity when he recognized her.

"Streetwalking and smoking, eh?" he surmised, surprising her when he reached within his raincoat and produced a pack. "That is quite a load of vice for such a young woman to bear."

Taking a cigarette, she gestured loosely with it. "You're right," she told him, smiling crookedly. "Guess I'd better give up smoking."

The priest snorted, the closest to a laugh that he could manage, as she then nodded toward him. "Aren't you going to have one?" she asked, as he replaced the pack.

He shook his head, thrusting his hands in his coat pockets, the outline of his hat and frame seeming to tower over her, even though he was not especially tall.

"No, I have long-since quit," he replied shortly, his gaze fixed on the street beyond. "I only carry around a pack as an exercise against temptation. I do not, however, carry a lighter or matches."

"Wow," Vanessa nodded, chewing her gum. "I didn't think you guys had to deal with resisting temptation, except for all of you who end up on the six o'clock news."

It was an offensive thing to say, and she regretted saying it, having not really considered its connotations. She flinched slightly, biting her lip, dumbfounded when she saw that he was smiling.

"You are an impertinent little vixen," he told her crisply, not caring how archaic his words probably seemed.

He paused in regarding her young face, his thoughts freezing, his lips poised to speak. A sermon? A lecture? A reprimand? Avuncular— ha! Grandfatherly advice? What was she expecting; what did she need to hear? Any number of questions and concerns arose in his mind as he looked upon this obviously much too young girl. Where would she go from here? Did she even have any place to stay tonight?

All of this in the space of a heartbeat, and then, the smile was gone. Clearly, it was an instance calling for him to mind his own business. Young as she was, she obviously knew what she was doing, and would tell him just that. That, and probably more, so there was little point in dwelling upon it. She would be fine; after all, finding a place to spend the night was precisely what she did.

"Well, be careful, young lady," he told her, gruffly imperious as he strode away.

Nodding, she waved loosely after him. "See you at the next meeting," she called.

Father Gilchrist glared over his shoulder at her. "That remains to be seen!" he snapped, his voice reverting to its nastier tone as he turned, hunched forward, and stalked off into the night.

Brows uplifted, she watched him go in wonder. *That was one screwed-up old priest*, she reflected, chewing her gum in silence, a thought then occurring to her. *See you at the next meeting?* Why the hell had she said that? There was no way she was coming back here.

She heard the door open again, looking up in time to see Judge Talbott wander outside, but not in time to avoid her. The short woman smiled at her, absently turning left and then reverting to the right and heading past her.

"Good night, Vanessa," she said kindly. "See you on Friday."

"Yeah, see you," Vanessa smiled back. What was she doing? She was beginning to feel like more of a space cadet than that woman clearly was.

The door opened again, Mr. Crimpton appearing, zipping up his Windbreaker as he squinted at the schedule posted at the bus stop. She could see his lips moving as he read it, watching as he retrieved a pack of cigarettes from one pocket. Tucking hers up over one ear, she approached him.

"Gotta cigarette?" she asked, smiling when he jumped at the sound of her voice.

Mr. Crimpton turned to glare at her, hastily jamming a cigarette into his mouth and fumbling with a match. Vanessa watched, amazed at how much his hands quavered.

Taking a deep pull from the cigarette, he seemed to hold it in for an uncommonly long time, before exhaling profusely. His gaze settled on her again. "What did you say?"

She gaped as he inhaled again, almost laughing at his virtually neurotic antics.

"Hey, it's a cigarette, not a joint!" she told him chidingly.

Balking, Mr. Crimpton exhaled in a spasm of coughs, bending over slightly, as if in pain. Vanessa very nearly moved to pat him on the back, then thinking better of it.

"I know that!" he grated irritably, his head snapping to one side as he heard the bus approaching, grumbling bitterly as he searched for his transfer.

"Well, anyway, can you spare a smoke?" she asked again, folding her arms.

He gave her a severe look. "You're too young to be—"

Staring at her, his voice seemed to catch on whatever pronounce-ment he was about to make, the squealing of the bus diverting their attention as it pulled up to the stop, its doors flying open.

Mr. Crimpton was about to jump onboard when, phantasmally, Mrs. Spindlewood appeared, once more clad in her gray outerwear, purse clutched in her hands.

"Good night, Trudy. Good night, Mr. Conklin," she warbled, slowly climbing the steps.

Slack-jawed, Mr. Crimpton glanced from her to Vanessa, then muttering bitterly as he pulled out his cigarettes and slap-patted a single smoke out of it, Vanessa's thank you distracted when he some-how handed her the pack instead of the single and clambered hur-riedly onto the bus, still anxiously trying to find his transfer.

Vanessa watched as the bus pulled away, looking at the pack of cigarettes and then shrugging. *A DMV worker who took the bus*, she reflected wryly. *Now, there goes a winner.* The old lady, though, there was something remarkable about her, almost ghostly. There was also something about her that made Vanessa feel like crying. She seemed too delicate, too frail to be riding around on a bus at night. She was so small and wispy; in an odd way, she seemed almost transparent, as if she might just fade away altogether.

The sound of both doors opening interrupted her thoughts as Mr. McClintock exited the building. He smiled at her as he ambled forward, forever tucking and tugging at his jacket, tie, and collar, handkerchief in hand.

"Are you by any chance headed over to the east side?" she asked, figuring she might as well.

Mr. McClintock moved his girth closer to her, shaking his head apologetically as he needlessly dabbed at his brow. "No, indeed, I am not, Miss. I was headed just around the corner," he explained, glancing up the street. He had failed to recall any restaurants on his list that would have foregone a reservation and accepted him at such short notice, but he was positive that he had seen a Taco Bell two blocks over from the intersection. "I have one more restaurant to sample this evening."

Vanessa let her gaze slip from his plump face to his mountainous build. She could honestly envision him doing just that, sampling and then eating an entire restaurant.

"Oh," she nodded, smiling cheerfully. "Well, bon appetite."

Swiping at his jowls, he looked from the intersection back to her. "Hmmm? Oh yes...Yes!" he beamed, clearly impressed with her choice of words. "Yes, thank you, young lady...I hope to see you at the next meeting."

She cocked her head to one side. "Wouldn't miss it," she told him. *What was the harm?*

Smiling, he turned and lumbered up the street, Vanessa noting both the surprising gracefulness and swiftness with which he was able to walk, once he had hit his pace. Probably an indication of how hungry he was, she thought sardonically, focusing once more on the doors. She had been right; it was going to be poser-punk dork boy after all, lucky him. And lucky her, she sneered, kicking at a piece of litter as she awaited her dufus in shining butt-flap.

*****

As Chris gulped, preparing to apologize for startling the doctor, he realized that he had no specific reason for staying behind. He guessed that he had just not expected to have to leave so soon, not really having any place else to go. Candy was at yet another party, to which he had again been coyly and coldly uninvited. He could not go and hang out with their friends, because their friends were *her* friends, most of whom would be at the party anyway. He had hoped that this meeting would last well into the evening, giving him at least the pretense of having something better to do than sitting at home, which was where he would probably end up now, like it or not. Having planned on getting back after they had all gone to bed, he would probably return to find the entire family in the living room, waiting to ask what he, self-proclaimed party animal, was doing home so early, yet again. If only they knew what havoc he had been wreaking tonight, he thought with some disgust.

He had been hoping there would have been some other kids his own age here, maybe even some punks. Oddly enough, though, he had not felt like an outsider; for the most part, he had seemed to fit in, to a degree. He was still wondering if fitting in comfortably with this particular group was a positive thing, but, at this point, he didn't care. And there had been at least one other kid, even if she had been kind of…really mean.

"Uh, yes…Clodhopper?" Dr. Pendleton asked, gathering up his defunct note cards from atop the crate. "Did you have a…question?"

Wincing, Chris stepped forward. "About that nickname—" he began, one of his boots crashing into the base of the crate, sending it teetering. Gasping, he grabbed at it and the Styrofoam cup, his anxious volition sending half of the tepid coffee flying at the doctor, splashing his jacket and note cards.

As Dr. Pendleton shut his eyes in exhausted resignation, Chris managed to steady the crate, apologizing in painful embarrassment. "I'm sorry, Doctor…I…I'm, like, really sorry!" he insisted, taking the cup and automatically, almost penitently dousing himself with it, some of the spray backlashing on the doctor, who grimaced and blinked as it did.

Bright red, Chris continued to apologize until the doctor reached out and took the cup away from him with one hand, gently patting his arm with the other.

"That's…all right," he assured him, shaking his head dismissively, gesturing to his jacket. "It was brown to begin with."

The sugary sweet coffee dripping from his Mohawk, nose, and chin, Chris just stood there in awkward uncertainty, Dr. Pendleton finally forcing a smile up at him.

"Now then," he said, peeling his note cards apart and shaking them out. "Your question?"

Gaping, Chris then blushed again, tugging and fiddling with various fixtures of his attire. "Oh, um…I dunno," he shrugged, not knowing what to say. He gestured blankly at the room. "You need a hand cleanin' up or anything?"

"Uh, no. No, I think I'll be fine," Dr. Pendleton told him, a bit too quickly.

Sensing this, Chris nodded dejectedly and then turned to retrieve his skateboard and backpack from under the side table, loping quietly toward the entrance, pausing to look over his shoulder.

"I really enjoyed the session, Doctor," he said impulsively. "I… feel like I kinda got a lot out of it."

Dr. Pendleton looked up at him and favored him with a sudden smile. "Well…good, good, I'm glad to hear that," he beamed. "I, uh, got a lot out of it too."

It seemed like a strange thing to say, but it made Chris instantly feel better, his mood then improving all the more so when the doctor added, "See you on Friday."

Swelling with the sense of inclusion and, moreover, belonging, Chris grinned back, waving. "See you, Dr. Berkdorf!"

*****

Hearing the doors open yet again, Vanessa stepped out of the shadows, adopting as appealing a posture as she could, leaning against the bus stop sign, watching as Chris came bungling out of the building, fumbling with his things to prevent the door from slamming, failing to do so as he saw her standing there, his features shifting to his customary gape, the door crashing shut and startling him forward under the streetlight. He continued to fidget with his belongings, her presence there obviously catching him completely off guard.

"Um, hey," he murmured, staring at her uncertainly, forever blushing.

She met his gaze, detecting that same innocence she had seen earlier. Between that and the pseudoferocity that his appearance at least suggested (in this light, anyway), she was surprised to find that he was actually somewhat appealing, in a harmless, cute sort of way. She was about to respond when her eyes fell upon the items that had encumbered his already clumsy movements, taking in and then fixating upon his skateboard. *Skateboard?*

Her perusal shot back up to his face, seeing that he was now smiling shyly, undoubtedly trying to think up something clever to say. *A skateboard.* She almost spat out her gum in furious disgust.

Stupid, immature, poser, wannabe punk wet-dreaming whacked-off skid-marked skateboarding punk-assed dork loser!

What had she been thinking? She gave him a look of utterly malevolent contempt, not even feeling a surge of satisfaction when his smile shrank and he squirmed uncomfortably, dropping his skateboard to the sidewalk and clattering atop it.

"Um, see you next time," he mumbled, striking at the cement with one boot and gliding away.

She watched him go, feeling an almost cartoonlike rage. "Oh yeah, I can hardly wait!" she snarled after him, at least making him cringe as he ratcheted over the cracked pavement, into the night.

Her anger was unexpectantly waylaid when the door opened one more time, Dr. Pendleton appearing, attaché case in one hand, keys in the other. Her hopes were suddenly restored as she realized that she had not even thought of asking him, surprised that she had skipped over such a likely candidate. After all, he obviously didn't live in that dump and had to go home too. What was more, he *had* to have driven there and as such was her best bet, as well as her last chance.

Waiting until he had figured out how to lock the door and then turned to walk up the street, a small, content smile on his round face, she then approached him respectfully. "Uh, Doctor?"

Startled, he whirled around, clutching the attaché case to his chest, his smile gone as he blinked fearfully. Recognizing her, he appeared to relax, if only for a millisecond, before clearing his throat and glancing anxiously to either side of them, backing slightly away from her.

"Oh! Uh, Vanessa...," he stammered, his case still clasped, shield-like, his discomfort palpable. "Uh...waiting for the bus?" he asked hopefully.

"No, Doc, I'm not. I can't spare the change for bus fare," she told him bluntly, ignoring his dis-ease. "I'll be straight with you. I need a ride back to the east side, because I'm scared of what that pimp tried to pull on me earlier. Do you think you can help me out?"

Dr. Pendleton, still scanning the sidewalk around them, seemed to focus on what she was saying. "A ride...to the east side?" he repeated hesitantly. "Uh, well..."

"Please, Doc," she said evenly, stepping closer to him. "I hate to admit it, but I really am scared."

Backing up a bit more, Dr. Pendleton found himself literally against the wall at this point, and he moved to shake his head, ending up nodding instead. "Oh, uh, of course, I...I think I can help you."

Vanessa exhaled in relief. "Great! Thanks, Doc," she told him, gently taking his case from him as a gesture. "Here, I'll get that for you...um, where're you parked?"

"Uh, around the...," Dr. Pendleton moved away from the wall, pulling at his tie and still peering nervously about, grateful that all of the other group members appeared to be gone. "Uh, around the corner."

Giving Vanessa plenty of room, he led her into the alley to a neatly kept plain brown sedan, hastily situating her in the passenger seat, Vanessa smiling quietly at his mouselike antics, watching as he glanced nervously about once more and then climbed behind the wheel, inadvertently blaring the horn.

His nerves jarred, he dropped his keys, having to grope for them as Vanessa stifled a giggle. "Relax, Doc. I only asked you for a lift," she assured him dryly. "I'm not looking to take you for a ride."

Smiling weakly at the well-intended, if candid, attempt to settle his concerns, he started the car, for once not letting it warm up but pulling into the street and concentrating on driving, trying to think of anything to say.

"Mind if we listen to some tunes?" Vanessa asked, Dr. Pendleton nodding encouragingly, glad for the distraction. If they were, for whatever reason, pulled over by the police...

Vanessa instantly changed the radio setting from a fizzle of staticky easy listening to a more contemporary station, raising the volume and lowering her window. She leaned back in her seat, stretching her legs and staring out the windshield, enjoying the cool air on her face and hair. It had been awhile since she had taken a ride, a legitimate ride, in a car.

Dr. Pendleton, clutching the wheel and clearing his throat, raised his voice to be heard over the blaring discordant music, Vanessa lowering it for him.

"I said, uh, where are we going?" he reiterated, his voice unnaturally loud.

"Oh," Vanessa nodded, leaning back in her seat. "To the Rochester Hotel."

The wheel seemed to jerk in Dr. Pendleton's hands, Vanessa sighing quietly.

"I mean I'm going to the Rochester Hotel. It's where I've been staying."

She stared at him as he nodded and relaxed slightly. Ordinarily, such uptight prudishness would annoy even her; yet, somehow, in this man, something about it was actually endearing. Obviously, there was a lot to be said for riding with any man who did not try to shift gears with her thighs, but, beyond being grateful for at least that small but undependable miracle, she found herself liking this bland, squarely modest man. She had not encountered many like him.

Sitting up, she turned in her seat to face him, shrugging casually. "So how did you think the meeting went tonight?" she asked, not really interested, but wanting to talk.

Dr. Pendleton glanced in his rearview mirror and then at her. "Oh, the, uh, meeting?" He sat up himself, his lips poised musingly. "I was…satisfied with it, uh, overall," he confided, his tone becoming slightly conversational. "Naturally, it was only our first, uh, so it was really more of an orientation of sorts. But, uh, yes, I think we're off to a good start…" He nodded over to her, smiling mildly.

She nodded back, seeing how uplifted his features had become as they passed by the light of a gas station. "Yeah, I thought so too," she told him, knowing it was what he wanted or even needed to hear. She could not understand the do-gooder mentality that was so neurotically devoted to helping one's self by helping others. Why wasn't helping one's self good enough? Most people could scarcely do that. She hid her skepticism behind a smile as he glanced over to beam at her remark, not at all wanting to discourage whatever his illusions—or delusions—were.

They arrived at the Rochester sooner than she expected; on foot, it would have taken her hours. Sensing a return of the doctor's uneasiness, she waved openly. "You can let me off wherever," she said, glad when this idea seemed to relax him.

"Oh, uh, all right." He nodded toward the aged hotel as he drew up across the street from it. "That's quite an old structure. I think I read somewhere that it's something of a city landmark."

"It's an armpit," she told him lightly, pushing open her door, grabbing her bag, and placing his attaché case neatly on the seat as she climbed out of the car.

"Thanks for the lift!" she called, smiling boldly as she crossed over to her shabby accommodations, pausing when she heard the doctor addressing her, hastily rolling down his window, his smile weak but warm.

"Uh, you're welcome," he told her, nodding. "See you at the next meeting?"

Vanessa stared back at him, unable to repress a wry grin. "Sure, why not?" she replied, not wanting to disappoint him. "If I can," she added, though, just as a safeguard.

Seeing how much this pleased him, she waved and then, her smile twisting mischievously, exclaimed, "Well, g'night, stud! You sure can show a girl a good time!" laughing as his features froze, his elbow jarring the horn again, startling him out of his shock. Somehow blushing *and* paling, he grimaced and drove away.

Her spirits much uplifted, Vanessa swung her bag loosely and skipped schoolgirlishly up to the stoop of the hotel, pausing to remove the one cigarette from behind her ear, insert it into the nearly full pack from her bag, and then hand the pack over to the semiconscious wino huddled on the second step with his brown bag.

"Here you are, sir," she pronounced regally, then bounding up the steps and into the lobby, flouncing disdainfully past the desk clerk, and sailing up the stairs.

*****

Stopped at a traffic signal, Dr. Pendleton watched a troop of rowdy-looking kids skulk past his car; for all of his discomfiture over this unforeseen excursion across town, and all of its suggestive nuances, and for all of the way in which the evening's meeting had transpired, he found himself smiling quietly. All in all, he reflected, for a complete disaster, their first meeting had not gone too badly.

*****

"Well, I think that you can be pleased with yourself, Dr. Pendleton," Dr. Whittaker told him, when they next met, this time in a small coffee lounge adjacent to the lobby of the office building. He paused in filling his pipe to sip from some kind of latté, one of the lounge's specialties. "Therapy groups can be very difficult to initiate. The first one is almost always the most trying. I—and now you—can attest to that." He dabbed genteelly at his lips with a napkin, glancing over at Dr. Pendleton. "And I fully agree with your assessment. Diversity, it seems, can alleviate adversity."

Dr. Pendleton smiled brightly, sitting up and having a sip of his own coffee, realizing that it had grown lukewarm while he had been recounting the details of the first meeting, glowing with the praise it had elicited.

"I, uh, also came to learn that choreography can also play a large part in getting people to, uh, open up a bit," he decided to mention as well.

Dr. Whittaker's brows lifted as he continued to attend to his pipe. "Oftentimes, I will concur that extracurricular activities can be extremely productive. I recall a colleague of mine who took his group bowling. Dancing, however, and at your first meeting, no less. That was rather a bold step to take, if you'll forgive the pun."

Blinking, Dr. Pendleton cleared his throat. "Uh, well, no, I, uh, I didn't actually mean dancing...," he explained hesitantly. "I guess I meant...orchestration...uh, well, no. What I mean is I *don't* mean anything musical, really..."

Dr. Whittaker gazed expectantly at him; even his noncomprehension was elegant.

"I guess I mean it in a figurative sense...in the way you would map out a conversation ahead of time, uh...sort of to stay a few steps ahead of the other person," he continued quickly, gratefully recalling the checkers analogy.

"Ah, of course," nodded Dr. Whittaker appreciatively. "Anticipating what will come next—not unlike in chess."

"Yes—" Dr. Pendleton blinked and then frowned, then exhaling quietly and glancing at his watch. "Well, uh, I'd better let you go… you mentioned you had a patient to see in about a half an hour?"

"Ah, indeed," Dr. Whittaker nodded, discreetly looking at his own watch. "I suppose we had best curtail our conversation until we can meet again."

Finishing his beverage and still smoking his pipe, he stood up, Dr. Pendleton likewise scrambling to his feet. "I look forward to hearing about your second meeting," he told him, smiling congenially. "If it is even remotely as successful as your first, I am certain that you will go a long way in assisting these people in their lives."

Dr. Pendleton flushed, accepting the older man's tapered handshake. "Thank you, Doctor."

"You're quite welcome, Dr. Pendleton," he replied, reaching for his briefcase, draping his Chesterfield over one arm, walking stick poised. "Well, I had best be off. My next patient's needs require me to visit him in his home. Agoraphobia, you know. While some might deem it a nuisance, I find it quaintly nostalgic to be making house calls in this day and age." He donned his homburg and nodded to Dr. Pendleton. "Until next time."

He watched Dr. Whittaker depart, now even more impressed with the man. He wished that he had patients who required house calls; that would be really neat.

Nudged back into the moment by the waitress as she cleared their table, he then gathered up his own belongings, his thoughts eagerly jumping ahead to the next session.

Chapter 4

THE SECOND MEETING WAS IN many ways similar to the first, the most surprising likeness being that all seven of those who had attended the original showed up for it. No sooner had Dr. Pendleton unlocked the front entrance and activated the coffee machine when Chris came tramping through the door, grinning broadly and somewhat less shyly. He had arrived intentionally early in case the doctor needed any help in readying the place and, after stowing his gear, had conscientiously taken a broom from one corner to do some sweeping, while the doctor returned briefly to his car, his mood heightened by Chris's unexpected desire to be helpful and also by his overall anticipation of the meeting itself. Only contributing to this good spirit was the fact that this time, he had remembered to bring along some refreshments, a large pink box of doughnuts he had picked up from a day-old rack at a bakery on his way over.

Retrieving the box from his car, he arranged it alongside the sputtering coffee maker, even its guttural chugging seeming cheerfully participatory. He had just directed the startled and deeply blushing punk rocker to sweep the sawdust back over the chalk outline when the others began to arrive, curiously enough taking the same seats they had occupied the first time.

"Welcome back. Hello," Dr. Pendleton greeted Judge Talbott and Mr. Crimpton, enjoying the stress on informality that he very much wanted to place on this meeting. "Please help yourself to some doughnuts," he added proudly, just as Mr. McClintock came ambling into sight, his features brightening immediately upon hearing this invitation.

"Welcome back, Father Gilchrist," he beamed, as the priest strode through the door, removing his hat and coat this time, though keeping them with him. "I'm glad that you decided to share another evening with us."

"It was either this or deliver the locker room prayer for a junior league softball team," Father Gilchrist returned sourly. "Whether I made the right decision remains to be seen."

Dr. Pendleton was spared replying as Vanessa bounded into the room, the two marked contrasts to her appearance being her clothing, which, consisting of a casual denim jacket and jeans, was more in keeping with that of a high school student, and her smile, which was bright and quite genuine.

"Hey, Doc," she called, tossing her bag in a chair and approaching him.

"Hello, Vanessa," he responded warmly, somewhat surprised to see her. "I wasn't sure if you'd make it back to see us again."

"Are you kidding?" she scoffed. "It's going to take more than one session to cure someone as screwed-up as me." She peered past him at the side table, then grinning at him. "Oh man, dinner is *served!*"

Flushing, but pleased with her enthusiasm, he turned to watch as she joined the others.

"Oh my, they all look so good. I don't know which one to pick," Judge Talbott was fretting, her fingers alternately dancing above the wide assortment of doughnuts and then retracting in dainty indecision.

"I know precisely what you mean," Mr. McClintock assured her, having solved any such dilemma by selecting nearly one of each kind. Lacking napkins, or better yet, a plate, he had opted to use one of the stack of flyers, the others automatically doing the same.

"Hmmm, I love jelly doughnuts," Chris was declaring happily, his mouth smudged with both jelly and powdered sugar.

"So I see," Vanessa told him flippantly, but not unkindly, Chris blushing and slinking away all the same as she focused on the selection.

Very much pleased with the success of his doughnuts, Dr. Pendleton glanced at his watch and then just as quickly dropped his arm, having also decided that he did not want to impose a time frame upon their meeting. Nevertheless, he hovered near his packing-crate podium, smiling patiently and then looking about as a thought occurred to him.

"Has anyone seen Mrs. Spindlewood?" he inquired. "I would hate to start without her."

Vanessa spun around, nibbling on a bear claw. "I did," she told him, then covering her mouthful with a hand, gesturing with the pastry. "She's sitting on the bus bench out front."

Dr. Pendleton frowned. "That's odd. I wonder why she didn't just come inside."

"Probably entertaining second thoughts," grumbled Father Gilchrist.

"I'll go get her," said Mr. Crimpton, having passed on the doughnuts, his stomach in too much of an upheaval even to bear the sight of food.

He scuffled through the sawdust and stepped out onto the sidewalk to find that Mrs. Spindlewood not only was at the bus stop but also was in the process of climbing aboard a bus.

Puzzled, he hastened forward and gently lay a hand on the fuzzy wool of her overcoat. "Mrs. Spindlewood?"

She turned, gazing vacantly up at him with no sign of recognition, nonetheless saying, "Hello, Mr. Conklin," before continuing to move toward the bus.

"Mrs. Spindlewood, didn't you want to attend the meeting? It's about to start," he told her, raising his voice slightly, glaring up at the bus and waving it along. *What on earth was the matter with this woman?*

Mrs. Spindlewood glanced at him and then the building in one motion, then slowly tottering toward it, Mr. Crimpton sighing and hurrying to get the door for her. Watching her feeble, yet steady progress, he thought of the bus ride he had shared with her on Tuesday.

The entire undertaking had been a bit strange. The bus fare, while reasonably adjusted for Senior Citizens, could not possibly be the fifteen cents that he saw her remove from a worn change purse and drop into the fare box. The driver had either not noticed, felt sorry for her, or not cared, for she walked right on by and took a seat, unlike Mr. Crimpton, who ended up having to pay full fare plus extra for a new transfer.

He had reluctantly taken a seat in the rear, tuning out the other typically deranged passengers and had ridden in a tired reverie, not really noticing her again until she pulled the cord. Glancing up, he had been startled by the stop she had selected—Saxbury Commons, one stop before the end of the line. Even in the dark, he could envision what he knew the stop to be, a virtually abandoned cluster of old warehouses, closed storefronts, and mostly condemned tenement buildings.

Why anyone would get off the bus there, at *any* time, he could not guess; and yet there she went, hobbling down the steps like a ghost.

He had almost gone after her but had refrained; unchivalrous as it would be deemed, he had his own problems with which to contend. The evaluation of the driving test examiners had been confirmed as fact and was now scarcely a few weeks away, and he had already worked himself up into an angst-ridden turmoil over how to pass it—or, if he could, get out of it. So he had let her go, hoping she would be fine.

And, as it turned out, she was, he concluded briskly, closing the door behind them and then tactfully sidestepping her and resuming his seat.

Dr. Pendleton glanced up at their approach, then looking at his watch again. "I suppose we can commence now," he observed, mainly to himself, though Father Gilchrist gazed over at him upon hearing this.

"Oh, there's no need to rush, now, is there?" he asked lightly. "Plenty of time to allow everyone to get settled." He gestured expansively.

Surprised, Dr. Pendleton raised his brows at the clergyman's unexpected change of attitude. "Really? Do you...are you, uh, on less of a...time frame this evening?" he asked. "It's always nice when we don't have to clock watch."

"Oh, I'm on the same time frame, to the second," Father Gilchrist told him flatly. "It is simply that the longer it takes to begin the meeting, the less time we will have to sit here pretending to listen to each other rave."

His enthusiasm wilting, Dr. Pendleton inhaled to respond, side-tracked by Mrs. Spindlewood, who had been busying herself at the side table.

"Good morning, Mr. Bergdorf," she greeted him hazily. "Here's your coffee."

Taking another Styrofoam cup from her, one that appeared to be filled with cream and at most one or two drops of coffee, he smiled hesitantly at her. "Uh, thank you… Good… Good morning."

Father Gilchrist watched this with a sour hint of a smile, until Mrs. Spindlewood next approached him with a maple bar. "Here's your prune Danish, Mr. Dembrough."

"I did not ask—" he began to exclaim, then clamping his mouth into a hard-pressed line of tolerance, taking the pastry with a forced air of appreciation. "Oh, why thank you," he smiled with crocodile kindness.

As the elderly woman folded slowly into her seat and her previous sedentary stance, Dr. Pendleton put his cup aside, clearing his throat.

"Well, I suppose we should begin," he began, smiling brightly. "I'd first like to thank you all for making it back here again. I know for some of you, it wasn't easy to do, but I'm really very glad that you did. I think that we have the makings of an excellent group here, and I look forward to seeing that potential, uh, fulfilled."

He paused, his eyes meeting Vanessa's, the girl smiling encouragingly back.

His good mood reenforced, he beamed at each of them, noting that most of them were busily chomping as they listened. "I'm so glad that you like the doughnuts. I thought that—" He paused, noticing his green flyers being used as napkins. Blinking, he cleared his throat. "Uh, that they'd go well with the, uh, coffee."

"Oh, they are most excellent," Mr. McClintock assured him approvingly, his flyer creased and balanced in one hand, held almost regally like a delicate cup and saucer, at least six doughnuts piled upon it, to counter the apple fritter in his other hand.

"Yeah, these are, like, the best," Chris put in, his mouth partially full as he unbraided a cinnamon twist, eating from each hand, crumbs cascading into his lap.

"Yes, nice and stale," nodded Father Gilchrist cheerfully, one bite taken out of his maple bar, the rest placed discreetly on the chair beside him.

Dr. Pendleton blinked, then starting as Judge Talbott sat up excitedly.

"Oh! I almost forgot!" she exclaimed, pulling a large tote bag up from beneath her seat and delving into it. "I made some Rice Krispies Treats!" She then broke off, glancing hesitantly at Mr. Crimpton. "Oh...are you still lactose intolerant?"

Mr. Crimpton gaped at her, as Dr. Pendleton nodded enthusiastically.

"Well, that was very nice of you, Judge Talbott!" he commended her, stepping around the crate to gesture meaningfully. "It's good to see we're all getting into the spirit of things."

Father Gilchrist swallowed a groan as Judge Talbott stood up, smiling bashfully as she produced a bundle of neatly wrapped squares. "Oh, it was my pleasure, Dr. Berkdorf," she told him self-effacingly. "I really enjoyed making them this morning."

Dr. Pendleton nodded, his smile faltering a bit as he watched her distribute the squares. "Good, good, I—oh, thank you," he nodded again as she gently shoved one at him, clearing his throat and returning to his podium.

"Uh, you know, folks, uh, you can all go ahead and feel free to call me, uh, Dr. Pendleton," he clarified, managing only a hint of irony.

"Oh?" noted Father Gilchrist conversationally. "Was the divorce finalized?"

"Thank you, Odessa," Mrs. Spindlewood told the judge, accepting her treat and clutching it in her little hands and then settling back into her reverie.

"Hmm!" Vanessa declared, immediately unwrapping hers and biting into it, chewing gratefully. "Man, I love these things," she told Judge Talbott, the eager little woman glowing as she scurried back to her seat.

"Now then," Dr. Pendleton stated, placing his treat next to his cup. "We had just begun to share some of the various reasons why we had each come here on Tuesday," he recounted pragmatically, attempting to choreograph or, perhaps, anticipate the direction of their dialogue. "We were off to a really good start, and I'd like to pick up where we left off. If anyone has any questions or comments, please, uh, feel free to speak up and get the ball—"

Flushing slightly, he paused. "Uh, that is, uh…oh! Who, uh, would like to be our first contestant?" He nodded politely to Mr. Crimpton, who stared noncomprehendingly back, Judge Talbott raising her hand with surprising assertiveness.

"Betty Crocker, come on down," murmured Father Gilchrist.

"Yes, Judge Talbott. By all means, you may begin," Dr. Pendleton invited her.

Judge Talbott nodded eagerly. "Yes, I meant to ask this on Tuesday," she explained apologetically. "Do you have a restroom here?"

Dr. Pendleton, poised, blinked. "Uh…yes…uh, it's just to the left of the— Right, uh, to the *right* of the front entrance."

Nodding gratefully, Judge Talbott hastened off in that direction, stepping sideways past Mr. McClintock, who did his best to let her squeeze by before polishing off his last doughnut and focusing with relish on his Rice Krispies Treat.

The last time he had had one was at an all-you-can-eat buffet; they simply were not offered as dessert in most restaurants. He thought briefly about composing a supplemental article about this and then just as quickly dismissed the notion, foreseeing how such an idea would be received by the newspaper's editor. Mr. Moynihan, he had come to learn, after the fact, had, indeed, *not* been favorably impressed with last Sunday's column, which had been disappointing and worrisome, inasmuch as he would no doubt be even less enthused over that which he had submitted earlier that day for the upcoming edition. His meal at Taco Bell on Tuesday evening had been quite enjoyable; in fact, he had it in mind to dine there again after the close of this meeting.

Nearby, Vanessa had just finished her treat and was sitting back and relaxing, allowing the sensation of fullness warm her body with a sort of pleasant numbness. Apart from a Snickers bar she had filched from a convenience store that morning, she had had nothing to eat all day. The doughnuts had been a godsend, but the Rice Krispies Treat, that was in a class of its own. Her mother had made those by the score when she had been little, but she had never grown tired of them. In fact, the very last time she had had one was from one of those batches.

She contemplated that in a tired curiosity, just not in the mood to torture herself with another game of Very Last Times with any of her family. She had been preserving as many of those as she could, denying herself anything that would amount to a First Time Since, feeling guilty whenever she deviated from the continuity. She banished the notion this time around, however, because she had been starving and that Rice Krispies Treat had been the best. *Sorry, Mom.*

"Well, uh," Dr. Pendleton had been stammering, his gaze fidgeting from Chris, who was gnawing at his treat, swiping his hands at his jeans, to Father Gilchrist who was grimly appraising a light fixture, then settling upon Mr. Crimpton. "Uh, Mr. Crimpton, you had been telling us that you experienced occasional nervousness when it came to your job," he recalled encouragingly. "Would you like to tell us a bit more about your situation?"

Mr. Crimpton shifted uncomfortably. "Oh, I thought Judge Talbott was going to go first," he replied evasively.

Dr. Pendleton paused. "Well, yes, but she, uh—"

"Sorry to hold up the meeting," Judge Talbott chirped, hurrying back to join them. Watching her resume her seat, Dr. Pendleton winced as the coffee maker sputtered somewhat scornfully behind him.

"Uh, yes, well, as I was saying, uh, sharing our various concerns and ideas with each other is probably going to be the best way to help each other," he stated purposefully, concentrating on getting back on track. "That's not to say that we all have clear-cut and all-consuming problems, of course. But, well, I am fairly certain that we all have some, uh, issues, which might have been on our minds lately and might like to discuss. Uh, after all, I'm sure that's why we've all come here…"

His glance fell briefly on Mrs. Spindlewood, and he cleared his throat, continuing. "Uh, more or less. But, as I say, uh, discussion has proven, time and again, to be a highly beneficial way to, uh communicate..."

Father Gilchrist gave him a look, not deigning to comment.

Clearing his throat yet again, he opted to take Mr. Crimpton's lead. "Uh, Judge Talbott, for instance, you decided to share with us at our first meeting your occasional difficulty in making up your mind, isn't that right?" he prompted.

"Oh yes," Judge Talbott nodded quickly, exhaling. "Yes, and that was very difficult to do," she confided honestly.

Dr. Pendleton paused. "Sharing was difficult to do?" he confirmed.

"Deciding to share was difficult to do," she clarified unselfconsciously.

Blinking, Dr. Pendleton accepted this. "I see. But the point is, you did share, proving that sharing our problems is productive and also proving that, in doing so, you progressed a little bit in alleviating your own problem of making decisions," he summarized neatly.

Judge Talbott nodded boldly. "Oh yes, and later on, that helped me to make up my mind all over again about the validity of these meetings."

"I see," said Dr. Pendleton, gaining confidence. "And what did you decide?"

Judge Talbott blinked herself. "Well...I decided to come back..."

Father Gilchrist regarded her skeptically. "Forgive me, Your Honor, but for precisely how long have you been a judge?" he inquired, somewhat against his wishes.

"Oh, almost a week and a half now," she responded pleasantly.

"Ah," Father Gilchrist replied. That certainly made up *his* mind.

"Well," Dr. Pendleton began again, drawing a blank but continuing anyway. "I have a few questions I'd like to put to you, about your feelings and experiences regarding this matter, if you'll indulge us. Uh, feedback, you see, whether incoming or outgoing, can be invaluable in considering such personal issues as these."

"Do you know, I completely agree," spoke up Father Gilchrist, a look of inspiration seeming to unpinch his features. "Why, it's rather like the relationship between a question and an answer. Or between speaking and listening. Cause and effect. One could almost say that successful dialogue is contingent upon…people talking!" He folded his arms as if in contemplative awe. "I had no idea that this form of group therapy could be so profound."

Dr. Pendleton nodded enthusiastically. "Oh yes, you've summed it up quite well, Father Gilchrist," he stated emphatically. "Talking is the very essence of dialogue."

Father Gilchrist's features constricted. "You're not getting paid for this, are you?"

"I'd be glad to answer any questions and to share with all of you," Judge Talbott spoke up, glancing around earnestly. "I mean I'll do my best to tell you whatever I can."

She had made up her mind to be as assertive as possible when leaving her office earlier. The entire day had lent to this ambition. She had already known what she was bringing to the meeting, hence preparing the snacks had been straightforward. Once at the court-house, she had been faced with her real decisions of the day; still in a transitional limbo as the outgoing judge finished up his term, she had spent the day picking out a new office and then deciding how best to decorate it. The rest of the workday had been devoted to perusing the latest legal journals, which she assiduously reviewed until she concluded that, in the week or so since her elevation to the bench, the law had not changed much. Realizing this, she then focused upon the next chapter of her mystery novel, deciding to finish the book that afternoon.

She had then had dinner at a cafe on the way to the meeting, her order posing no deliberation, as she simply requested the Special of the Day.

It was Mr. McClintock who addressed her, dabbing at his lips with a handkerchief. "If I may, I have a question for Judge Talbott."

Dr. Pendleton glanced over at him. "Oh yes, by all means, that is really what I had in mind, interactive questions and answers," he pointed out encouragingly. "In that way, because the questions won't continually be posed through me, you'll come to think less of me as a doctor…"

Father Gilchrist raised his eyebrows. "Is such a thing possible?"

"I mean you will come to think of me *less* as a doctor and more as a fellow group member," he amended, flushing at his flub, but incited by the momentum all the same, moving away from the crate and stepping toward the seat between the old priest and Mrs. Spindlewood.

"Oh, I am sorry, I'm afraid this seat is taken," Father Gilchrist informed him as he beheld the almost intact maple bar resting there. "As is this one," he continued, settling his hat and coat upon the chair on his other side.

Grimacing but resolute, he sidestepped this section and sat down near Mr. McClintock, who appeared impressed by this proximity.

"Now, Mr. McClintock, you had a question for Judge Talbott?" he orchestrated confidently, leaning inward as if hanging upon the coming exchange.

"Oh yes, ah, I have," Mr. McClintock nodded, shifting a bit self-consciously. "Judge Talbott, I was curious to know, did you use whole marshmallows in your Rice Krispies Treats or a prepared marshmallow cream?"

His gaze locked on Judge Talbott, Dr. Pendleton gaped back at Mr. McClintock.

"Oh yes, I used whole marshmallows," Judge Talbott nodded swiftly. "I've never heard of using marshmallow cream before."

"No way, really?" Vanessa spoke up in disbelief. "My mom always used marshmallow cream. The recipe's right there on the jar."

"Well…," Judge Talbott frowned, trying to recall. "The only recipe on my jar is for something called 'Fantasy Fudge.'"

"Oh yeah, Fantasy Fudge!" Vanessa exclaimed in recollection. "Ah, man, that was some good shit."

Mr. McClintock flinched beside her, Dr. Pendleton wincing himself.

"Fantasy Fudge?" posed Father Gilchrist. "That puts one more in mind of a brownie recipe."

Chris snickered adolescently across from him, Mr. Crimpton glancing past the oblivious judge at the giggling punk rocker, as if suddenly besieged with a migraine. The juvenile timbre of Chris's mirth drove his thoughts back to the morning he had been trapped in a car earlier that week with a very similar kid. He even had the same hair cut; it had kept raking against the car's ceiling like a whisk broom. The driving test would no doubt have raised Mr. Crimpton's hair, as well, had the little idiot not almost immediately backed into a row of garbage cans, enabling Mr. Crimpton to fail him on the spot. The relief, though fleeting, had been virtually heaven-sent.

Dr. Pendleton, his features now somewhat stayed, listened to the culinary banter continue, wanting to get back on a more substantial path, but uncertain how to close this subject and, once again, not certain if he should. After all, they were now loosening up, becoming a bit more familiar with each other, and he had intended to indoctrinate an air of informality, hadn't he?

Of course, that could all be his rationalizing the fact that he did not know how to balance the informality with a more progressive exchange, having relinquished his guise of overseer by assuming this just-one-of-the-gang position. He was trying to figure out how he might discreetly get back to his podium, wondering what Dr. Whittaker would do in this situation and then realizing, self-chidingly, that Dr. Whittaker would never place himself *in* such a situation.

In the end, his eye had fallen on his own Rice Krispies Treat, untouched atop the packing crate; and, feigning surprise, he had declared, "Oh my, and I haven't even tried mine yet," then launching out of the chair and back to his previous seat, more than ready to resume the fundamentals of their meeting. Poised to do so, he hesitated as he beheld the strangely excited and anticipatory expressions with which most of them were regarding him. It then dawned on him what they were expecting.

Rather sheepishly, he unwrapped the Rice Krispies Treat and took a bite, issuing a routine, "Hmmm," to satisfy them, then having to work at chewing its resilient texture as quickly as he could so that he could speak to refocus the dialogue, his jaws simply not fast enough, for his sampling and approval of the snack only further fueled their conversation.

While very pleased with the enthusiasm she had inadvertently inspired, Judge Talbott was also overwhelmed with its implications. In the past, the recipe had seemed so straightforward; she had never dreamed there could so many deviations. Vanessa's mother had put chocolate chips in hers, from time to time, and Mr. McClintock had suggested garnishing each batch with maraschino cherries, also mentioning that he knew of a restaurant that mixed a second cereal into the Rice Krispies, creating a multicolored effect.

"Fruit Loops, I believe," he had recounted confidently.

Faced with so many options, she knew that if she ever made them again, it would be a much more deliberative process.

In the end, to Dr. Pendleton's initial surprise, it had been Father Gilchrist who had diverted the conversation back to its original consideration, announcing that he had a point to raise, one which was, oh, *ever so slightly* more related to the psychological field.

"As much as I dislike having to admit to a mistake, I must confess that the time frame to which I alluded at our previous meeting was actually in error," he stated forthrightly. "Imposing a one-hour agenda upon it was, in fact, *not* procedurally correct."

Dr. Pendleton opened his mouth to reply, though clueless as to what to say, because he could not, in effect, believe what he was hearing.

"No," continued Father Gilchrist, interlacing his fingers contritely. "It occurred to me later, when I reflected upon my own knowledge of such protocol, that the conventional session is *not* one hour in length." His voice abruptly sizzled. "It is, in fact, only *fifty minutes* in length!"

Dr. Pendleton shrank, Father Gilchrist then anticlimactically glancing at his watch and saying cheerfully, "Hence, instead of twenty more minutes of this, we have only ten." He smiled pleasantly over at the doctor.

Grimacing darkly, Dr. Pendleton then cringed with further chagrin when, as if in some bizarre exercise in the abstract, the others reacted excitedly, looking at their own watches and shifting eagerly in their seats like schoolchildren who had just been told that they could skip their last class.

"You mean we get to get out early today?" Chris actually asked, lifting his lanky form upright out of its gradual slouch, displacing an avalanche of crumbs as he did so.

"Uh...," Dr. Pendleton paused, tongue-tied at what felt like virtual betrayal. Somehow, this situation had become terribly reversed. "Well, it's true that...conventional sessions, uh, as a rule, do adhere to that..."

This concession brought a virtual cheer, most of the members then moving to gather up their belongings, Father Gilchrist folding his coat in his lap.

"Yes, I would have thought a seasoned professional like yourself would have known that," he told the doctor archly. "Ah, nine minutes."

Dr. Pendleton stared at him in frustrated defeat, his grimace profound as he pondered where on earth this priest had been ordained. "I, uh, actually did know that," he said, very dryly. "I...I suppose I just misunderstood..."

"Underwood," Mrs. Spindlewood said suddenly.

Taken off guard, Dr. Pendleton blinked mutely at her. "Uh, excuse me, Mrs. Spindlewood?"

"Underwood," she repeated, turning her head slowly to stare vacantly up at him. "We have extra ribbons for the Underwood in the supply room, Mr. Bergdorf," she informed him. "Would you like for me to go and get a box?"

Shifting slightly, Dr. Pendleton cleared his throat, "Uh, no, no, thank you."

"Do you have any ribbons for my Remington in your supply room?" Father Gilchrist asked her musingly. "If so, I could use a box or two."

"Father Gilchrist, please," Dr. Pendleton interjected, almost scoldingly, then taking in the entire group. "Uh, folks, I, uh... Yes, well, perhaps we can...observe this time frame, uh, for today," he allowed, his annoyance now the source of his strength. "But perhaps for our next meeting, we can all feel free to allow ourselves as much time as we like. I'm perfectly willing to give up as much of my evening as needs be for our meetings."

He paused, glad to have reestablished that the main purpose of the group was for *their* benefit. "Uh, for now, though, I guess we can wind things down a bit…If anyone had anything to add, uh, for today's meeting, we do still have a little time left." He glanced around hopefully.

There was a silence, during which he decided to try one final gambit, an idea that had occurred to him earlier that day, when his mood, he recalled morosely, had been so much better.

"Uh, I had wanted to suggest a thought that I had of a means of getting to know each other all the better, inasmuch as the closer we come to being comfortable with each other, the easier we will find it to discuss even the more complicated and personal aspects of our… well, of anything we want to discuss… Uh, what I had in mind was something along the lines of a…a visual aid," he continued, sensing his audience's interest but uncertainty.

Mr. Crimpton frowned. "Do you mean like an eye chart?"

Dr. Pendleton blinked. "Uh, well, no, I mean that if anyone likes, they might consider bringing in a…personal item from their jobs or homes, something that might be symbolic of yourselves or representative of either your lives or maybe even of the points that have been causing you stress or that you'd like to improve on."

He paused, his throat dry, though not so much so that he intended to drink from the Styrofoam cup. "Uh, it could be anything at all, uh, a photograph album or some souvenir…or, well, basically, anything you'd be comfortable sharing with the rest of us."

Chris raised his hand. "Do you mean like Show 'n Tell?" he suggested helpfully.

Vanessa sneered. *What a baby*, she reflected, even though that was exactly what it was like. Moreover, perhaps because of the utter ridiculousness of the idea being undertaken by grown-ups and the sincerely earnest way that Dr. Pendleton was explaining it, she thought it sounded supremely cool.

Father Gilchrist nodded approvingly. "Tiny Tots Therapy," he posed with stilted relish. "Yes, I think such would be perfectly fitting."

"Well, I, uh…," Dr. Pendleton felt himself floundering again and this time decided to go with the flow. Smiling tightly, he brought his hands together conclusively. "Yes, well, it's something to consider for next time," he declared, nodding with finality. "For now, I suppose we could adjourn."

"Splendid." Father Gilchrist abruptly stood, slipping into his raincoat, the others following his lead, Chris clomping over to the side table for one more doughnut, Mr. McClintock and Vanessa close behind. Dr. Pendleton watched as Mrs. Spindlewood tottered to her feet, the priest having donned his hat by then. "Good night, one and all."

"Good night, Mr. Bergdorf," Mrs. Spindlewood recited, scuffling away.

Dr. Pendleton nodded mildly, startled when Judge Talbott and Mr. Crimpton both came forward to address him, the former beaming and extending her hand, the latter less animated but offering the same gesture.

"Thank you, Dr.…" Judge Talbott glanced at her legal pad. "Pendleton, I really enjoyed our meeting."

"Yes, it was very introspective," Mr. Crimpton added.

Blinking, Dr. Pendleton was obliged to smile, even if in confusion. "Oh, uh, good, I'm glad to hear it."

"I agree," Mr. McClintock paused to express, Vanessa pivoting around him. "It's so nice to have a forum in which to relax and speak one's mind."

"Exactly," nodded the judge, showing surprising assertiveness.

"Uh…good," Dr. Pendleton replied, keeping his bewilderment in check. "I, uh, I hope that next time, we'll be able to…you know, uh, open up even more so…"

They all seemed to agree, Judge Talbott excitedly gathering up her purse and tote bag. "I already can't decide what to make for the next meeting," she confessed. "I know I have a recipe for Chex party mix."

Mr. Crimpton appeared thoughtful. "That's actually pretty tasty stuff."

Chris had found that there were only two doughnuts remaining, a glazed and a filled chocolate one. He had thoughtfully chosen the glazed but had picked up the chocolate as well, turning it to find the little hole in which one could tell what the filling was, therefore holding both when Vanessa approached.

"Hey! Don't be such a pig!" she told him sharply, outraged at what she thought she was seeing. "Who said you could kill the box? Didn't you just hear the Doc saying we should be sharing? Didn't you catch Sesame Street on MTV today?

Stung, Chris turned bright red, even on the shaved sides flanking his Mohawk. "Sorry!" he retorted in embarrassed discomfort. "Here, have whichever one you want!"

"Ha!" Vanessa crowed harshly. "I don't want them after your fingers have been all over them!"

She glowered at him, pleased and disgusted that she had so thoroughly cowed him. "Oh here, give me this one." She grabbed the chocolate one and pushed roughly past him, purposefully hitting him with her bag.

As Chris hung his head, blinking and swallowing quietly, Mr. McClintock peered with similar disenchantment at the now empty pink box. He turned to lumber away, his gaze then falling upon Father Gilchrist's abandoned maple bar. Pausing, he glanced about, then moving closer to it, wondering if he should. It did have a bite taken out of it. Frowning, he then grimaced at his apprehension. What harm could there be? The man was a priest, after all.

Dr. Pendleton turned to disconnect the coffee maker, smiling at Chris, who nodded meekly back, gathering up his skateboard and backpack, mumbling a good night, and plodding quickly away.

A bit surprised at the punk rocker's subdued departure, Dr. Pendleton turned to watch him go, taking in Mr. McClintock as well. "Oh, good night, Mr. McClintock. We'll see you next time."

Mr. McClintock nodded convivially back, managing a garbled farewell, his bulging cheeks obscured with his handkerchief.

His mood somewhat improved, he turned back to the side table, once more pleased with the success of his doughnuts. To think, out of that enormous box, only one lone doughnut was left.

*****

Vanessa was waiting for him again, and while taken off guard once more, Dr. Pendleton made it a point to offer her a lift. They both knew that such was why she had stuck around, but she seemed glad to have him ask, and he was glad for the chance, because it served as an extension of the usefulness that he had hoped to derive from these meetings.

Not bothering with the radio, she had been more in the mood to talk, not so much about herself, and not too pryingly into his personal life, merely in general.

"What made you want to become a psychologist?" she asked him, turned in the seat and staring at his profile. "Aren't you afraid that being around so many whack jobs might be catching?"

Smiling at her candor, he cleared his throat. "Well, believe it or not, it's been speculated that everybody is at least a little bit crazy, facetiously speaking," he told her at length. "If that is even remotely true, then it's up to the less, uh, disturbed people to help those who are, uh, on the opposite end of the scale, as best as they can."

"Well, I'm pretty sure I know which category *I* fit in," she had replied wryly. "Which side of that fence are you on, Doc?" she added teasingly.

They laughed a bit, Dr. Pendleton then asking her more seriously what her impressions of that evening's meeting were, as they drew nearer to her destination.

"Are you kidding?" she chided him. "It was awesome! It went *fine.*"

He watched her skip up the steps of the hotel, considering her response. Though his spirits were much buoyed, he was still concerned with how little of substance was discussed that night. It seemed like they had gotten even less accomplished than in their first meeting. All the same, everyone appeared to have benefited from it, and truth be told, the Rice Krispies Treats had been very good.

*****

"Oh, most certainly refreshments will lend to a more conversant atmosphere," Dr. Whittaker agreed, drawing from his pipe and nodding approvingly. "As for the notion that everyone is just a little bit imbalanced, I might tell you that I not only agree but also I have oftentimes garnered comfort from that idea."

Dr. Pendleton blinked, a bit surprised to hear this, shifting his focus from the spray of the fountain to the older man, the hollow echoes of the voices and footsteps of the other people in the court-yard insufficient to sidetrack him. "Really?" he asked uncertainly, unable to sit comfortably on the bench. "In...in what way?"

Dr. Whittaker exhaled an aromatic cloud and appeared to study it for a moment. "Well, simply put, sometimes the comfort of know-ing that each one of us is ever-so-slightly mad is just enough to keep us functionally sane."

Chapter 5

THE THIRD SESSION, WHILE CHARMING in some respects, was not in effect a charm. The unity that Dr. Pendleton wanted to cultivate in the members was, indeed, in evidence in that each member, unanimously, did not bring in a personal item to share. A further irony existed in as much as each member had a specific item that they could have brought in to share—more or less.

Chris sat, rather broodingly contemplating this as he waited for the meeting to commence. He had made his early arrival, glad to see Dr. Pendleton, and lend a hand in what little preparation there was, but had held off on having any of the fresh batch of doughnuts until the others had helped themselves. Only then had he approached the alluringly colorful assortment, his craving intensifying as he saw a cluster of jelly doughnuts. He had taken only two, using the paper plates that Dr. Pendleton had thought to bring and had just taken a bite of one, a well-earned, scrumptious bite, when Vanessa returned to the table, unhesitatingly refilling her plate.

"So, Wild Child, whad'ja bring in to Show 'n Tell for all of us?" she had asked, smiling coyly over a piece of strudel. "Some hardcore punk music? Think you're gonna whip this place into a mosh pit?" She watched as, this time, Judge Talbott ushered in Mrs. Spindlewood.

Swallowing harshly, Chris, already feeling his cheeks glow, could only think to say, "No."

Vanessa had grinned crookedly, pouring herself some coffee. "I didn't think so. I mean what punk music could you possibly have anyway?"

Confused by the implications of this, Chris had responded by naming off his favorite punk albums, not realizing that Vanessa was not even listening.

"Okay, okay, God, why are you such a pussy wimp?" she charged him in mock exasperation. "It's incredible!"

Chris's mouth had dropped open, and he had flushed bright red—in embarrassment. "I am *not* a pussy wimp!" he protested, his jaw dangling in wounded chagrin.

"Ha!" she countered triumphantly. "That just goes to *show* what a pussy wimp you are!"

She turned away with this convoluted summation, Chris's mouth clamping shut as he tried to think up some kind of a comeback, managing only, "Well, what did you bring for Show 'n Tell then?" gaping after her childishly.

Spinning around, Vanessa gave him a pitying look. "What do you think I brought in?" she stated rhetorically. "Why, my diaphragm, of course."

Chris glared as she flounced away, not even completely sure what she meant by that.

Dr. Pendleton had waited for Mrs. Spindlewood to bring Mr. Bergdorf his coffee, actually tasting it as Judge Talbott passed around little baggies of her Chex party mix, which proved to be as well-received as her previous offering. The coffee, however, was straight black, mainly because it was mostly composed of the grounds. Setting it to one side, he swiftly began the meeting, hoping in doing so to avoid another culinary discussion as well as to subvert one other precedent.

"Good evening, folks. Glad to see all of you again," he smiled congenially. "Uh, before we commence, I had wanted to touch upon the matter of the time frame for our meetings." He forced himself *not* to pause, avoiding Father Gilchrist's gaze. "Uh, while we are engaged in what could be considered an extension of the mental health field, we need not restrict ourselves to its procedures and parameters. In short, bearing in mind that I have amended my schedule in order to free up the entire evening, I wanted to give you the liberty of deciding how lengthy our meetings can run."

Here, he had paused, pleased with his forthright address and its inescapable connotations, albeit, not for very long. "How generous of you!" Father Gilchrist beamed, replacing his hat. "Good night."

Blanching, Dr. Pendleton watched as the priest actually stood up to leave. "Uh, no, Father Gilchrist, that's not quite what I meant," he explained, though he was sure that the man knew this.

Father Gilchrist turned and glared imperiously at him. "What's this?" he demanded in maudlin outrage. "You purport one meaning and then retract it? Hypocrisy is a sin, you know."

Shrinking, Dr. Pendleton grimaced, his mind gladly seizing upon a reply of some import, even if a rather flimsy one. "Well, no, it's just that, if you leave now, you'll miss out on sharing everyone's personal items that we all brought in to…uh, share…," he challenged him weakly.

Regarding him with a look of almost feline disdain, Father Gilchrist strode wordlessly back to his seat, crashed down into it, and quietly placed his hat next to him.

Nodding appreciatively, Dr. Pendleton then focused upon the entire group. "Now then, who would like to go first?" he inquired invitingly.

When the members merely shifted, glancing expectantly at each other, he added in a mock scolding tone, "Oh, come now, we mustn't be shy, not at this stage…" As he waited for someone to volunteer, a disquieting notion then occurred to him. "Uh…did anyone bring… anything?" he asked reluctantly.

The answer was reflected in the blank faces staring back at him, Dr. Pendleton swallowing and then daring to glance over at Father Gilchrist, who glared back with deadpan intensity. Smiling reflexively, he paused, then opting to try one other, rather ludicrous angle.

"Uh…did you bring anything to share, uh, Father Gilchrist?"

Father Gilchrist unscrewed his lips and smiled acidically. "Well, now, let me think," he replied musingly. "I was planning to bring the Holy Grail from the Vatican Lending Library. But lo and behold, it was already checked out."

Vanessa snorted into the napkin she had been using to obscure her grin during this exchange. As much as she wanted Dr. Pendleton to succeed, or, well, think he was succeeding, Father Gilchrist was a riot. She would have sworn that being so mercilessly rotten was against some sort of church law, and even if it was, here was one mean priest who didn't care about going against the grain, and witnessing this was amazing.

She was slowly coming to realize that watching these people was precisely why she kept coming back to these meetings. Since she was able to get there on the bus and avoid the entire south side, she was not especially worried about running into any trouble, yet she held no illusions about her attendance in any way helping her personally. Instead, she found that merely sitting there and observing this bizarre cross section in such an exposed, vulnerable setting was fascinating. In a practical sense, it was an excellent opportunity for character study, a facet of the theatrical arts that she knew would be invaluable to an acting career.

However, and much more significantly, on a personal level, she discovered that it was easy to become transfixed, not so much by what was being said, which more often than not was nothing, but by merely watching their actions, their motions, their faces. It was an activity she had come to appreciate, inconspicuously, for as far back as she could recall—merely looking at people, from off to one side, quietly, uninvasively learning whatever subtleties or nuances they displayed, trying to see into their lives. There was an entire, incredible spectacle unfolding in front of all of them, and she was the only one who could see it.

She watched as Dr. Pendleton smiled and drowned, her gaze shifting, as it often did, to Chris, her expression hardening even as a smirk hinted about her lips. For some reason, she took pleasure in observing him with disdain, deriving an almost sadistic thrill from it. Appraising him now, she scoffed inwardly as he chomped at the jelly doughnuts, spilling flakes of glaze all over his punk attire, perpetually rubbing his jeans with his sticky hands, his mouth and chin lightly dappled with raspberry jelly. *Boys were such pigs*, she scoffed, entertaining the idea of standing and marching boldly across to him and wiping his face with a napkin, babyfying and humiliating him in front of the group. This notion caused her smirk to blossom in contemplation.

"Well, I was going to bring in my gavel," Judge Talbott was saying doubtfully. "But it has this little round piece that's used for striking, and that has to sit on a desktop for it to work, and I remembered that we didn't really have a desk here."

Dr. Pendleton nodded, attempting to appear understanding.

"You could use the table over there," Mr. Crimpton suggested, indicating the side table, which was not really the point.

"Uh, what…might you have brought in, Mr. Crimpton?" Dr. Pendleton asked him.

Frowning, Mr. Crimpton shrugged. "I don't know," he responded, somewhat defensively. "I couldn't very easily have driven a test car in here to show all of you."

Nodding, Dr. Pendleton glanced next to Mr. McClintock, whose attention was still on his doughnuts, his cheeks billowed. Passing over him, he smiled hopefully at Vanessa. "Uh, did you… have something in mind that you might have brought?"

Vanessa raised her eyebrows, gasping in a frozen laugh. "Me? Umm, well, you know, I guess I could have brought in one of my clients, but…" She grit her teeth and clucked her tongue. "He just didn't seem too thrilled with the whole idea. Same thing happened back in school on Career Day." She shook her head.

Dr. Pendleton's head seemed to sink into his shoulders as he cleared his throat and fingered one of his temples.

The others appeared just as disquieted, Vanessa only gazing placidly back, until she caught Chris's expression as he glanced at her. Even though jelly-besmudged, his features revealed a mixture of curiosity and disgust and possibly even pity. Realizing this, she glowered at him in surprised anger, forcing him to look away.

Beside her, Mr. McClintock had finished a cinnamon roll and was wiggling his plump fingers over his remaining doughnuts, considering which would be next. They were a pleasant diversion from the topic at hand, for which he was thankful. It had been his intention to bring in that Sunday's Edition of the newspaper to share his column with them. He had been pleased with it, up until the editor, Mr. Moynihan, had cornered him earlier that day with his own appraisal.

"Taco Bell? Taco Bell?" he had charged, mustache bristling as he waved the newspaper at him, his voice unchecked in spite of the proximity of other staff members. "Is this some kind of ongoing joke? We give you a highly detailed list of upper-crust, jet-set, wining and dining establishments in this city, and what do you do? What discerning source do you turn to for an itinerary? From the looks of it, I'd say the Yellow Pages!"

"Well, I did make it a point to visit the Westfalien Gardens," Mr. McClintock had pointed out anxiously. "And that was at the top of your list."

"Yes, and you devoted all of two sentences to it in your entire column!" Mr. Moynihan shot back.

"Well, yes, but you see, the portions were rather small," he had attempted to explain.

Mr. Moynihan, his finger stabbing the air, mouth poised to explode in response to this logic, was sidetracked by a typesetter who reluctantly told him he was needed elsewhere, Mr. McClintock doing his best to hide his relief.

"What's next, McClintock? A dissertation on Happy Meals? An epicurean exposé on Denny's?" he had grated in departing. "Just get with the program and start grazing in five-star fields or you'll be making observations about Whoppers with a spatula instead of a pen!"

"Mr. McClintock?" Dr. Pendleton repeated. "Did you have an idea as to…what you might have shared?"

Blinking back into the moment, he gave the doctor a flushed smile, shifting in his chairs. "Well, no, to be honest," he fibbed, then nodding sincerely at the judge. "However, I must commend Judge Talbott on her delicious party mix."

Judge Talbott shyly beamed, Dr. Pendleton clearing his throat. "Uh, yes, it is quite good." He glanced quickly around, wary of becoming sidetracked. He bypassed Father Gilchrist, pausing and then deducing that there was no harm in trying. "Uh, Mrs. Spindlewood, did you—"

"Yes, Mr. Bergdorf?" she replied automatically, slowly looking up.

He smiled weakly at her. "Uh, never mind, Mrs. Spindlewood…"

"What about you, Claude?" Judge Talbott asked encouragingly.

Chris, fidgeting absently with his empty plate, gradually looked up, starting when he realized he was being addressed. "Huh?"

"Who's Claude?" Mr. Crimpton frowned, Chris gaping stupidly at both of them.

"He is," Judge Talbott stated, withdrawing her crumpled list from her purse. "You are Claude, right?" she double-checked. "Claude Harper?"

Gawking, Chris then understood what she meant, blushing profoundly as Vanessa began to laugh chidingly from her seat.

"Claude, that seems baptismally apropos," Father Gilchrist submitted. "After all, a clod, by any other name, is still…" He left the thought unfinished.

"Yeah, but that's just his 'street tag,'" Vanessa clarified in a mock tough voice, then abruptly shifting to a twangy, hillbilly drawl. "His real name's Forest, Forest Punk," she confirmed lackadaisically.

Squirming and shrinking in his chair, Chris focused unhappily on the judge. "Um, it's Clodhopper," he told her miserably, never thinking that his unwanted nickname could be reduced to be even more belittling, thereby concisely reducing him all the more.

Dr. Pendleton blinked at the disgruntled punk rocker, having been sure the kid's actual name was Chris. For a delinquent, he was inordinately shy, if he could not even bring himself to correct his own name.

"Well, uh, Claude, how about you?" he asked at length, "Did you have something that you had intended to bring?"

Chris peered gloomily up at him; he had planned to bring in a few of his favorite records and had actually fallen asleep the night before, giddily contemplating the group's reaction. He had imagined bringing in his grandfather's old portable record player so that he could play a few songs for them and explain how these decidedly unpunk songs made his heart sing and made him want to leap and dance and thrash, how a ragtime piece or a spicy tango or, above all, a wild and frantic polka could send him into a head-banging frenzy. He had smiled and blushed, even in the kingdom of his own room, as he lay there sideways, envisioning the group's astonishment as they listened to this staticky, ratchety music belt forth on that rickety old turntable, the looks on their faces in his fantasy awestruck and impressed.

He might even have danced for them—that would give them the visual aid the doctor had mentioned. They would have watched him whirl and pivot and stomp and fly and would have realized, without the embarrassment of him trying to tell them; would have seen for themselves why he was in their group; and would have perceived what his problem was, what deep, disturbing factor made him maladjusted and in need of psychological help. They would have witnessed the paradox of a Wild Child Punk Rocker getting his thrills to blazing concertinas and oompahing tubas, warping the room into a one-punk mosh pit of chaotic, gyrating lunacy, replete with champagne bubbles cascading through the air in a rippling glissando of schizophrenic harmony.

But when he asked them what was wrong with him, why he was screwed-up in such a crazy way, their response would be unanimous—he was *not* screwed-up. There was nothing wrong with a punk rocker getting so worked up over this magical, special music. They would all be smiling and cheering, even Father Gilchrist, and Vanessa would be forced to see that he was actually really cool and would be ashamed of how mistaken she had been and…

Even to a person who did not drink, the morning was sobering, and when the day unwound with its usual tediousness, the fantasy remained just that, and he had come straggling to the meeting, empty-handed and closemouthed, now more than ever certain that he was a freak of nature, too screwed-up even to be *in* a therapy group.

He was spared from having to answer by Father Gilchrist, who, arms still folded, had continued to focus skeptically on Dr. Pendleton. "What an ingenious idea," he proclaimed loftily. "Instead of showing each other what we did *not* bring, we can discuss what we did not bring. Or we can discuss discussing what we did not bring. Or, perhaps, we can simply talk about talking again." His glare became less sour and more angry. "If we are expected to sit here time and again, we should at least be entertaining! One notion might—*just might*—be getting some of these kooks to open up and explain why it is they came here in the first place!"

Dr. Pendleton reddened slightly. "Well, naturally, that is our intention—although, Father Gilchrist, uh, words like 'kook' are usually frowned upon in the professional field… Uh, they're deemed to be, uh, insensitive."

"Oh! Heavens to Betsy!" Father Gilchrist fretted sardonically. "Insensitive? Why, I cringe at the mere word! Hmm, what would be a more clinically appropriate term?"

He appeared to think about it. "How about 'Whackos'?"

Shutting his eyes, Dr. Pendleton stifled a sigh. "Does anyone want to share any particularly specific—"

"No, no!" Father Gilchrist nearly shouted. "Don't ask, *tell!* Do you think I ever sit in my confessional saying, 'Hi, can I help you?' Of course not! I wouldn't be able to get anyone to own up to a jay-walking ticket that way! They go into the booth for a reason, just as these nuts must have some reason to keep traipsing back to this barn night after night!"

Dr. Pendleton now looked slightly angry himself, although he knew that the old priest was right. It was a question of choreography again. Nevertheless, he gripped both sides of the packing crate and solemnly regarded the older man. "Would you like to take my place for a little while, Father Gilchrist?" he asked evenly.

Father Gilchrist narrowed his eyes. "I would sooner commit hara-kiri with a crucifix," he replied direly.

Blanching at such a statement, Dr. Pendleton cleared his throat. "Well, uh, in that case, Father Gilchrist, what brought you here tonight?"

"*Don't begin with me,*" Father Gilchrist groaned. "Start with someone else!"

He rolled his eyes as Dr. Pendleton grimaced in frustration, his gaze scanning over the group and then alighting briefly upon the little baggie of party mix atop his crate.

"Uh, Judge Talbott, you shared with us before that you sometimes have trouble making decisions," he outlined slowly, the petite woman nodding quickly, her smile faltering slightly. "Can you tell us what made you decide to come participate in our group a week ago today?"

Judge Talbott, seeming even smaller than usual, peered about at the others, inhaling and then nodding almost guiltily. "Well, just recently, I was promoted from a public defender to a judgeship. I had applied for the position mainly because it's just a matter of procedure to advance in the judicial system if and when the time comes, but to actually become a judge, at my age, is really…well, it's supposed to be quite an accomplishment."

She paused, appearing to gain some strength when she realized that the others were, indeed, listening to her. "You see, when I was a little girl, I led a rather sheltered life. My parents had both grown up in very hard circumstances, and as a result, although they wanted me to be as strong as I could be, they raised me so overprotectively that I ended up coming out…kind of soft…" She kneaded her hands together, focusing on the floor. "Even though I had such an insulated childhood, I can remember deciding early on that I wanted to pursue a career in law. I know that being black and being a woman can be obstacles to getting things done in this world. But I honestly didn't think of these two qualities as handicaps, because, at the time, I didn't think about them much at all. I was kind of a dreamer, but…I saw the injustices that affected my parents—and many other people too. I've seen discrimination against every kind of person, and I realized that while it's true, justice is supposed to be blind, injustice can also be blind in certain instances. So I went to law school to become a defense attorney, because I could appreciate the fundamentals of the law, the basic rights and wrongs. And this, of course, came into play as a public defender with my clients."

Her features creased thoughtfully as she considered how to illustrate her point. "Every case became a cause to champion…an opportunity to help someone out…to make a bad situation easier for someone."

"It was all very straightforward," she began to fidget with the handle of her purse. "When my appointment to be a judge came through, I had to accept it, and I do feel a sense of accomplishment and all, but I hadn't fully realized how it would…alter the circumstances."

Dr. Pendleton, listening raptly, began to nod. "I think I understand what you mean," he told her earnestly. "As a defense attorney, everything must have seemed quite cut and dried, so to speak, whereas in the position of a judge, you have to assume a stance of impartiality at first and then must rule in favor of one side or the other."

Judge Talbott nodded anxiously. "Yes, and that's why I decided to come to your group. I thought it might help to discuss this with others and maybe get some pointers on assertiveness…although, I have to admit, I've been able to make the transition fairly smoothly so far, in spite of all my trepidations," she added brightly.

"Oh?" Dr. Pendleton lifted his brows. "Really? I'm glad to hear that… How were you able to facilitate that?"

Smiling shyly, Judge Talbott forced herself to put aside her purse, placing her tiny hands in her lap. "Well, as I said, I was very nervous at first. To tell you the truth, the more I dwelled on it, instead of excitement, the only feeling that I had toward becoming a judge was dread."

"Wow," gawked Chris beside her. "Just like the comic book."

Dr. Pendleton blinked at him, as Judge Talbott continued. "Anyway, I'm in a transitional period at the moment, and in order to get established all that much more quickly for when I assume the bench, I've been receiving a number of dockets to review ahead of time."

"At first, I started to examine them, and I started to get over-whelmed with the whole process, even if it was only preparatory. But then, the perfect compromise occurred to me." She seemed to increase in size as she spoke the word. "So I looked over each case very carefully, considered all of the factors and then, after deliberating for a while, passed all the cases along to other judges, making sure that each case went to the judge best qualified in presiding over them."

Nodding encouragingly, Dr. Pendleton paused, frowning. "Uh…"

"Now, I'd like to think that the fortitude that it took to make all of those decisions came from myself, but I know that a lot of the credit goes to my participating in this group," Judge Talbott added, smiling and glancing from face to face. "I'm so glad I made my mind up to come here."

Clearing his throat, Dr. Pendleton attempted to rally his thoughts, just as Mr. Crimpton nodded, sitting up in his chair. "It's funny, I actually know what you mean," he spoke up with uncharacteristic enthusiasm. "I feel the same way. I mean I never thought I'd wind up attending a group like this—or any group, for that matter. But I'm kind of glad I decided to take the plunge."

Shifting slightly, Dr. Pendleton, reluctant to turn his focus away from Judge Talbott at such a crucial point, nonetheless, could not resist considering Mr. Crimpton's unexpected declaration. "Uh, I'm glad—we're all glad—that you, uh, that the both of you..." He paused. "We're all glad that...we all decided to attend these meetings...uh, with all of us..."

He nodded conclusively, cringing a bit at Father Gilchrist's expression as Mr. Crimpton continued. "Being a driving examiner is...well, the best way I can describe it is like being in hell," he explained, mostly to the floor, his features becoming drawn. "I mean you're always given the impression that hell's a place where you end up having to do the same thing over and over again as punishment. And that's what it's like being a driving examiner. Every day, there's a line of people waiting to take their driving test, and no matter how many you administer, there are still more. And you have to keep doing it, over and over, and each driver is worse than the last one. But you have to keep doing it, again and again, because that's your job, and your job is...hell."

He paused, glancing up at Father Gilchrist. "Uh, sorry, Reverend, if that analogy was presumptuous or anything. I didn't mean any disrespect."

Father Gilchrist smiled sourly. "Not to worry, my son. Such contemplations are made every day. Why, I, myself often ponder what the netherworld might entail." He looked pointedly around the room and then nodded, as if confirming something to himself.

Grimacing, Dr. Pendleton focused on Mr. Crimpton, even though he *had* been talking to Judge Talbott. "Well, surely, Mr. Crimpton, uh, as repetitious as the scenario undoubtedly is, I would imagine that one saving grace is that they cannot all be unsafe drivers. Some of them must be better than others."

"No," Mr. Crimpton told him with blank matter-of-factness. "No, they're all bad. That may seem like an exaggeration, but it's not. They're all bad in different ways, I'll grant you, but it all amounts to the same—ancient senior citizens who have no business driving anymore, pushy suits who act like they're doing *me* the favor by taking the test, yuppies who force me to squeeze into their tiny foreign trendsetters, mindless little adolescent punks who think they're playing a damned video game..." Pausing, he glanced somewhat apologetically over at Chris. "No offense, uh, Claude."

"Oh, none taken," Vanessa answered for him, nodding reassuringly.

As Chris flushed, Dr. Pendleton cleared his throat. "Uh...but you were saying that you've found that attending our meetings has helped you in some minor way to...cope with the stress of your job?" he hinted hopefully.

Mr. Crimpton nodded slowly. "Yes, it's good to be able to sit down for a while and relax and not have to think," he replied candidly.

"Exactly," Judge Talbott concurred.

Frowning, Dr. Pendleton appeared to be in pain as he pressed onward. "Well, yes, that's...really good. Uh, but what I mean is if your attendance here has helped you to cope with your job...you know, uh, while you're actually at work."

Staring uncertainly back, Mr. Crimpton gradually shrugged. "Well, earlier today, when I was struck in a traffic jam, in a Volkswagen, I was able to look forward to coming here tonight, if that's what you mean," he offered.

"Oh I was too," Judge Talbott put in. "I've been looking forward to it all day."

"Me too," Chris nodded earnestly up at Dr. Pendleton.

"So was I," Vanessa spoke up, smiling brightly. "These meetings are like the highlights of my week. And as for assertiveness and all that in the workplace, I've been feeling the same exact way," she said boldly.

Dr. Pendleton blinked. "Really? How have you—" He paused, considering if he really ought to pursue this. "Uh, that's good... I suppose, uh... How has that been going...for you?" he finally asked euphemistically.

Vanessa hesitated in midchomp of her gum, a thought occurring to her, a wild caprice that, if it worked, would be unsurprising and, if it didn't, well, what the hell? Either way, it would be fun. Settling her gaze directly toward the doctor, but watching peripherally, she sat up slightly in her chair.

"Well, take earlier tonight. I was with this guy who was really interested in having me perform a hummer for him," she stated simplistically.

She observed most of them frown in confusion. But right on cue, she saw Chris jolt slightly, his face turning red as his head pivoted sharply, and he gawked over at her, shifting in his seat.

Having been braced, Dr. Pendleton blinked uncertainly. He had been expecting something a little more... Of course, he wasn't entirely sure what... "Uh, I see," he responded, then cocking his head to one side. "To perform a...hummer." He paused. "Is that some sort of a song?"

Seeing Chris wince, Vanessa smiled sweetly at the doctor. "Well, yes, I guess you could call it that," she nodded agreeably. "It's definitely a style of oral recitation."

Chris began to squirm in his seat, as Dr. Pendleton nodded, hesitated, blinked, and then paused. He could have sworn he had overheard her mentioning her diaphragm earlier, but he had assumed that she had *not* been speaking about singing. He cleared his throat. "I see...and were you able to perform this, uh, hummer?"

Vanessa, struggling to keep a straight face, could only nod, as Mr. Crimpton shook his head impatiently. "No, no, I think what she means is that she performed a song *in* a Hummer," he corrected Dr. Pendleton, then scowling. "God, how I hate riding in those things."

Distracted, Dr. Pendleton seemed at a loss, Vanessa gesturing carelessly, able to focus directly on Chris now, as the punk rocker was avoiding everyone's gaze, preoccupied with adjusting his position, actually crossing one lanky, steel-toed leg over the other in an especially unpunk way.

"Um, it went okay, but since I like to sing in harmony, I suggested a song that was popular back in the sixties," Vanessa continued conversationally, her eyes locked on Chris. "1969, in fact. Instead of a solo, it's more of a duet."

Chris sat up in his chair again and abruptly uncrossed his legs, leaning forward in his seat and then tugging at some of the tighter folds in his constrictively unyielding jeans, his cheeks a fiery hue, his jaw tensed.

Dr. Pendleton nodded, somewhat impressed. He then paused, frowned again, and finally shrugged his eyebrows acceptingly. "I see, and so it all went well then, I take it?" he surmised, gazing at her expectantly with the others.

Vanessa shrugged herself. "Yeah, I guess. I mean look at it this way—I got something out of it for a change," she emphasized dryly, rolling her eyes and then continuing. "And, as for him, he had no complaints. And, even if he did, he wasn't really in a position to say much of anything, now was he?"

She folded her arms concisely, as Chris squirmed so sharply in his seat that he spilled his bag of party mix on the floor, stooping over clumsily as all eyes turned to him. Beet red in the face, neck, and scalp, he began to snatch up the pieces, stuffing them back into the baggie, along with a good deal of sawdust.

"I'm sorry, Judge Talbott," he told her almost tearfully, his voice strained.

Judge Talbott smiled kindly, motioning dismissively. "Oh, that's okay, Claude," she assured him, reaching for her tote bag. "Don't worry about it."

"Yeah, Clod," Vanessa called sweetly. "*Those* things happen *all* the time."

Chris stole a frozen glance at her, a flicker of insight in his eyes, just as quickly looking away.

Dr. Pendleton frowned down at him with mild irritation. Why was the boy so clumsy? He tried to think of how he could segue the conversation back to Judge Talbott's situation just as Mrs. Spindlewood unexpectedly came back to life.

"Oh dear," she remarked vaguely, tottering to her feet. "I'll go get Mr. Henderson."

Blinking, Dr. Pendleton tried to remember which one of them was "Mr. Henderson." "Uh, you're going to get who, Mrs. Spindlewood?"

She stared hazily at him. "Mr. Henderson, Mr. Bergdorf, the custodian."

As she shuffled off toward the entrance, Judge Talbott was extending another bag of the party mix toward Chris. "Here, Claude, I brought along an extra," she told him placatingly. "You shouldn't eat that after it's been on the floor."

In truth, Chris hadn't intended to, but he shook his head allayingly at her, scooping up a handful and putting it in his mouth. "Um, it's okay, Judge," he told her, chomping on the party mix and sawdust enthusiastically, demonstrating how good it was. "Punk rockers eat food off the floor all the time." He moved to grab another handful, accidentally pulverizing most of it beneath one cumbersome boot, the judge nodding, impressed at such a hardcore exhibition.

Mr. McClintock was gazing hopefully at that extra bag, his own having long since been exhausted, his focus diverted when Mrs. Spindlewood returned from her errand. She scuffled past him, Dr. Pendleton looking up in confusion when he saw that she was not alone. A raggedy sleeve caught in her feeble grasp, she was leading a harassed-looking, unkempt man toward him, the latter glancing about in inebriated bewilderment, his eyes eventually settling upon the doctor.

"Here's Mr. Henderson, Mr. Bergdorf," Mrs. Spindlewood announced.

"Wassa big idea, Bergdorf?" the man demanded, leaning unsteadily on the crate. "I's tryin' to take a leak our front there an' this ol' broad says I gotta come in an' an' an'...sssweep the floor!"

Dr. Pendleton shut his eyes against the man's pervasively drunken breath, Chris rushing to get the broom. He returned with it, bristle's skyward, hesitantly uncertain if he should give it to this man or use it himself.

The intoxicated man shifted his gaze toward the punk rocker, focusing with bleary-eyed cogitation. "Which one's the broom?" he finally asked.

Blushing, Chris cringed as the man emitted a horrific cackle and punched him jovially in the arm. "Jus' kiddin', Geronimo," he exclaimed, grabbing the broom and then swiping at the floor with it in the manner of someone raking a lawn, displacing a cloud of sawdust up into the air and exposing the chalk outline on the floor.

As Mr. McClintock instantly produced a handkerchief to shield his breathing, Mr. Crimpton stared at it in horror. "Good God, what the hell is that?" he demanded of Dr. Pendleton.

Father Gilchrist pursed his lips. "Clearly, the result of Dr. Pendleton's success with a previous therapy group," he observed sagely.

Dr. Pendleton stepped quickly around his crate and firmly took the broom away from the man. "Uh, thank you, Mr....uh, Henderson. That'll be fine," he said abruptly, standing back to let the man pass.

"You sure?" he asked unsteadily. "I didn't do such a good job."

"No, no, it was fine," Dr. Pendleton insisted. "Why...why don't you go and clean something down the street?" he suggested with finality.

The man smiled craftily. "Okeydokey, chief," he nodded, holding out a grimy hand. "How's about a little payola for another bottle a' cleanin' fluid? Seein's how I did such a good job?"

Pausing speechlessly, Dr. Pendleton grimaced and then hastily fumbled with his wallet, extracting a single and handing it to the man.

He took it appreciatively, saluted the doctor, and began to stagger toward the entrance. "Say g'night, Gracie," he slurred to them, then stopping in his tracks and turning to face them with a look of befuddled curiosity. "Hey, what're all you folks doin' sittin' in the dark here for anyway? Tryin' to call up a ghost?"

"Yes," Father Gilchrist told him. "We've conjured up a ninety-proof spirit."

"Uh, this is a meeting of an anonymous self-help group," Dr. Pendleton informed him reluctantly, afraid that the man might want to join.

Far from it, the man stood upright in slow-witted concentration. "An anonymous group?" he echoed, then snickering in delight, having to steady himself. He exacted a pose of sincere forthrightness, clasping his hands before himself. "Well, my name is Tim, an' I ain't been sober in seven years!"

He cackled even more hideously, turning and shambling toward the entrance. "Ahhh, ya' buncha drunks! S'cuse me there, Fats!"

Stumbling past Mr. McClintock, he reeled to the door and out into the night.

There was a dead silence, the members glancing about awkwardly, Dr. Pendleton blinking and then seeming to notice the broom in his hands, which he deftly used to sweep sawdust and party mix back over the chalk outline, then stopping as he realized that, at this point, it was not really necessary.

Putting the broom aside, he returned to the podium, clearing his throat. "Sorry for the, uh, interruption," he offered sheepishly.

Most of the members gestured assuagingly, Mr. Crimpton shaking his head. "Don't worry about it, Doctor. I had a guy show up for a test like that once."

Dr. Pendleton glanced at him in surprise. "Really? That must have been awful."

"Oh no, not at all," Mr. Crimpton replied. "I failed him, had him park the car, and then I read the newspaper while he sobered up. Killed two hours, at least."

His brow furrowing, Dr. Pendleton picked up a pen, fingering it lightly. "Uh...now, where had we left off before we were...well, before..."

"We were talking about singing," Judge Talbott volunteered.

"Singing?" he repeated uncertainly, his gaze falling on Vanessa, his memory then jogged. "Oh yes, you..." He paused, clearing his throat again.

"A perfect segue for a song request," Father Gilchrist declared, glancing at his watch. "How about 'We'll Meet Again'?"

Dr. Pendleton moved to object, Mrs. Spindlewood suddenly smiling.

"Oh, that's a nice song," she beamed.

"Splendid!" Father Gilchrist pronounced, rising to his feet and slipping into his coat. "In that case, let it be our closing hymn."

As the others began to shift, not unlike his control over the situation, Dr. Pendleton held up a hand, raising his voice. "Now, just a minute folks," he called, grateful when he was given a degree of their attention. "Now, we can adjourn if you'd like, but…Well, let me ask, are we all very certain that there's nothing more to be said?" He paused expectantly.

When there was no response, Father Gilchrist actually shrugged at him. "Do you know any good Catholic jokes?" he asked, reaching for his hat.

Startled, Dr. Pendleton shook his head. "Uh, no…"

The old priest shrugged again. "Well, in that case, good night."

As the group once more disintegrated in a chorus of thank yous and good nights, Dr. Pendleton watched them go, now more convinced than ever that they were getting very little accomplished and, in fact, might even be progressing steadily backward.

Vanessa had stationed herself outside of the building once again, inhaling deeply in the cool night air, as she watched the others depart, a slight smile twisting on her face as Father Gilchrist emerged. The aged priest paused in the doorway to button his coat, only then seeing her standing there.

Smiling mirthlessly himself, he spoke the words before he could reconsider saying them.

"How's tricks?" he asked, shocked at his own flippancy and instantly hoping she was too young to understand, her own response paradoxically eluding his age.

"Trix? Trix are for kids," she shrugged, her smile growing.

Father Gilchrist snorted, taking in her youthfulness and almost shaking his head. "Apparently so," he conceded wearily, then nodding brusquely. "Well, good night, Miss."

She nodded casually back. "Vaya Con Dios."

He glowered back at her. "Don't be a smart ass!" he growled, stalking away.

Giving a sort of a gasp of a laugh, Vanessa stared after his departing figure in wonder. She could never have guessed that a priest could be such a wing nut.

The door opened, and Chris exited, Vanessa moving to block his way.

"What's your hurry, Sex Pistol?" she asked him cheerfully, smiling at his discomfiture, seeing him blush even in the dimness of the entryway. "You always show up early like a good little teacher's pet. Why don't you ever stay late too?"

Chris shifted his lanky frame, avoiding her gaze. "I dunno," he said, almost inaudibly, adjusting his grip on his skateboard and awkwardly stepping around her. "What for?" he shrugged, edging toward the sidewalk.

"What do you mean what for?" she exclaimed, following him challengingly. "You should stick around to talk a little more. That's what for!"

His Mohawk silhouetted by the streetlight, he glanced back at her. "Why?" he asked evenly. "Just so you can make fun of me and be mean to me some more?"

Vanessa's mouth fell open. "Oh my god, Chris, you are such a baby!" she nearly shrieked, shaking her head and gesturing in virtual despair. "I mean look at you! You're supposed to be a tough, mean, ass-kicking, party animal punk! You're watching *Romper Stomper*, but you're acting like Romper Room! If you're gonna sport that shit, then fuckin' walk the walk already! Christ, you're supposed to be Sid, not Nancy!"

Chris's jaw tightened as he stared somberly down at her. "I am tough," he told her quietly. "I'm as tough as I need to be."

Vanessa laughed scornfully. "Oh yeah?" she countered. "And what have you done that makes you such a tough guy, huh? What makes you so damned tough?"

He dropped his skateboard to the pavement and mounted it, looking at her one more time. "Just getting stuck with being me," he said flatly, turning and coasting away.

Silenced for a moment, Vanessa watched him go, surprised and lightly stung by his response. Just as quickly, though, she regained her composure enough to yell after him. "Oh! Oh yeah, right! Yeah, well, join the club, pal!" she crowed. "You think you're alone in that, you're crazy!"

She watched him lope further away and added in spirited anger, "At least you gotta nice ass, though!" folding her arms and grinning judiciously after him, positive that she saw him flinch.

*****

Her ride back with Dr. Pendleton was very quiet. He seemed deep in his thoughts, and she was definitely preoccupied with her own. Nonetheless, when it seemed that he was focused on the streets and other cars, she found herself giving into her practice and studying his profile. People appeared at their most vulnerable when you watched them lost in thought, so exposed and real. He had such a kind face, always slightly worried about something—probably something he could never hope to fix. As they drew nearer the hotel, she suddenly wanted to tell him the truth, about her nonjob, about her aspirations, everything. She very nearly did. Instead, she thanked him, returned his good night, and quickly climbed up the front steps.

*****

"You mustn't become discouraged, Dr. Pendleton," Dr. Whittaker reiterated, his elegant fingers gesturing above the desk. "Group therapy can take much longer to progress than the standard one-on-one approach, which, if I recall, is the only form of session you have previously employed in your practice. The group approach is a whole new experience for you as well as the members. Why, the initial development of basic rapport can take at least a month alone."

"Yes, I realize that," Dr. Pendleton agreed, nodding halfheartedly. "It's just difficult to balance the clinical, professional guidelines with the informal, conversational environment, which is essential for getting people to open up a bit. Sometimes, the topics and…phraseology are a little…extreme…"

Dr. Whittaker actually smiled at this. "Ah, yes, what was it you had mentioned?" he asked, pressing one index finger to his lips. "'Whacko'? Was that the expression? I haven't heard that one in quite some time…" His smile broadened as he then moved his hand almost dismissively. "Well, certainly, Dr. Pendleton, such terms are, indeed, frowned upon in the vocational sense. But, in the auspices of group therapy, I hardly think they need be avoided altogether."

Shifting in the sumptuous easy chair, Dr. Pendleton blinked. That had not been the sort of extreme that he meant, but he was sufficiently surprised enough by the doctor's statement to be side-tracked. "Really?"

Reaching for his pipe, Dr. Whittaker nodded easily. "Oh indeed. In fact, the occasional use of such vernacular can aid, very much, in establishing the relaxed—and confident—rapport on which the success of group therapy or, indeed, any form of mental health assistance depends."

Dr. Pendleton considered this, feeling a hint of confidence himself.

Chapter 6

"WELCOME BACK. GOOD TO SEE you all again," he greeted them at their fourth meeting, forcing himself to relax and be patient in spite of the excitement he felt over the few specific points he intended to cover that evening. He waited for them to get situated, smiling and avoiding the floor with his gaze. When Chris had arrived even earlier than usual, this time waiting out in front of the building when he had rounded the corner, he had put the eager boy to work at removing the chalk outline, Chris gratefully applying himself to the task with a broom, scrub brush, pail, and cleanser. He had succeeded in cleaning up the outline, as he proudly displayed to Dr. Pendleton so that, indeed, not a trace of chalk could be seen, inasmuch as the entire outline was now superimposed with the scrub marks of the brush and cleanser.

He had thanked him anyway, not wanting to discourage the kid; it was rare to find a juvenile delinquent so willing to be helpful. He had then turned to focus on arranging another batch of dough- nuts, finding Mrs. Spindlewood attending to them, the coffee maker already percolating laboriously. Smiling doubtfully, he had thanked her, as well, leaving her to it as he prepared to commence the meeting.

While Chris had been vigorously reenforcing the outline, the doctor had moved the chairs closer together, hoping that such a maneuver might aid in creating an even more intimate interaction. Now, as he watched Mr. McClintock knock over a few in his attempts to enter the circle, he was given to second thoughts.

Mr. Crimpton was visibly in a better mood; as intolerable as his day had been, it was another Friday, and while he would no doubt spend the weekend in dread of Monday, he could at least do so in his easy chair. He had even helped himself to a doughnut after escorting Mrs. Spindlewood inside. This time, the old woman had been mounting the steps of the bus just as he was climbing off it. Seeming to recognize him, she had automatically gone along with him, prompting him to wonder not only why she went to the meetings but also if she was even aware that she was attending them.

He had put the matter aside as he nodded to Judge Talbott, who likewise seemed in good spirits, her own smile especially bright.

Vanessa, on the contrary, was in a negative frame of mind when she arrived, dumping her bag on the floor, climbing up and over the back of her chair and then crashing down into it, folding her arms, and fiercely chomping her gum. In addition to her overall problems, she had come to hate the weekends. Obviously, with no job and no prospects and nothing to do short of coming to this comedy club, all of her days were very much the same—listlessly empty and boring.

However, she still possessed enough of her high school's regimentation to continue to regard the weekends as two free days specifically allocated for fun. Since they now were anything but pleasurable, she felt like they were completely wasted. At first unwilling to admit it to herself, she was forced to acknowledge that she really did miss just hanging out with people her own age, talking, laughing, whatever. The pseudoadult world into which she had thrust herself was just not much fun. She wanted so badly to spend some time with other kids, but could not, for her situation would not permit it, and so she was left to feel like a total loser, all the more so on the weekends.

She sought out Chris, her spirits lifting a bit when she located him, sprawled in his chair, jelly doughnut in hand. She focused on elevating her mood at his expense, just by staring witheringly at him, but found herself rather jealously wondering what he was going to do with his weekend, the speculation hurting her, making her feel worse.

Chris was, in fact, contemplating his weekend, for once with a fair degree of excitement. His girlfriend had finally decided to acknowledge him again, having received an invitation to a wedding reception of one of her friends from school, and she had decided to include him in her plans to attend. He had heard from her so little in the past two weeks that, while the idea of spending time together at a party with still more people whom he did not know was not very appealing, he was willing to take what he could get, even knowing that Candy most likely wanted him to accompany her in order to show him off to this new circle. She had done it before, enjoying the shock value that his appearance evoked in people, boistering his feeling that such was the only way in which she approved of his lifestyle. At first, he had been proud of her exposition of him, for it somehow seemed to validate the authenticity of what he was, helping to dispel his own doubts. Gradually, though, he had grown to feel more like a prop of some kind; and his shyness would surface, his clumsiness would take over, and she would regret bringing him along at all.

Between that and their open relationship practice, he had been invited to fewer parties with her, and while he felt left out and anxious about what she was up to, he did not miss how miserable the parties made him feel. However, he was excited about going this time; her friend was apparently from one of the Balkan states, which could only mean that the music that they would have at the reception would most likely be traditional Bohemian wedding music. Through no fault of his own, they would be forced to dance to it, whether she liked it or not; and, for once, he could cut loose as a punk rocker to the music he truly loved so much.

Father Gilchrist arrived last, his sour features even more pinched than usual as he made his way into the circle. He had spent half of the bus ride there listening to a woman who had insisted on unburdening herself on him, up until she discovered that he was a priest. She had then accused him of *not* being a rabbi, very much affronted by his perceived deception.

When he had attempted to mollify her by ignoring her from behind a newspaper discarded on one of the seats, despite the fact that it was printed in Chinese, another passenger of that same ethnicity began to chatter at him in his native tongue, excited that he should encounter an Anglo-Saxon who was clearly fluent in his language.

In the end, he had gestured decisively at the newspaper and then pointed insistently at the woman, the Chinese man nodding in delight and then moving to address the startled woman with rapid enthusiasm as the priest got off the bus. All of that, he reflected bitterly, returning Dr. Pendleton's smile with a profound sneer, just to come to this place.

Judge Talbott had busied herself passing out a batch of thickly frosted cupcakes, her face animated, her manner almost giddy. She was quite excited over the events of the day and could scarcely wait to share her good news. As Chris gratefully accepted a cupcake and began to lick somewhat childishly at the chocolate frosting in a way that made Dr. Pendleton wince, he smilingly received his own, his brows lifting at the judge's girlishly giggling demeanor.

"Here's your coffee, Mr. Bergdorf," Mrs. Spindlewood interrupted his contemplation as she placed a cup atop the case and shuffled away, Dr. Pendleton thanking her and then peering reluctantly at the cup, frowning and looking even closer, realizing that it was a cup of hot water.

He glanced over at the coffee maker, seeing the filter off to one side, the coffee maker diligently brewing nothing.

Mr. McClintock had nodded to Vanessa as he lowered himself onto his chairs, enjoying the neatly tucked-in, smoothly streamlined sensation he had been feeling all day. He made no attempt to adjust his waistline, for there was no need, as he buttoned his jacket over his sloping frame, pleased with the unrumpled, wrinkle-free tidiness that he seemed to embody. It had been a productive, indeed, serendipitous few days; and he was in a jovial mood, all the more so when Judge Talbott offered him a cupcake and, to his surprise, Mrs. Spindlewood came tottering over to him with a paper plate bearing an éclair. "Here's your cherry turnover, Mr. Rasmussen," she announced hazily.

Accepting it appreciatively, he looked from one hand to the other, marveling over how well this day had been treating him.

"I can tell from some of your faces that you have some interesting updates to share with all of us," Dr. Pendleton stated at last, smiling at each of them up until he met Father Gilchrist's hostile glare. "I, uh, know we're all looking forward to..." He paused, blinking at Chris, distracted by a splotch of chocolate on the oblivious kid's nose. "Uh, looking forward to sharing these stories, uh, but, before we do…"

He paused again, assuming a semblance of a relaxed stance alongside his podium, leaning one elbow casually against it. "Before we do, I would like to tell all of you something first."

Sensing that he had their attention and knowing how quickly it could be lost, he came directly to the point. "Simply speaking"—he told them confidently—"it's okay to be a little crazy."

He smiled around the room, clearing his throat when he perceived their uncertainty. "What I mean is, uh, in spite of the immense gravity that is placed on the…soundness of mental health, it is perfectly normal, uh, colloquially speaking, uh to…'go a little nuts' sometimes, just as, in the conversational sense, it is quite acceptable to use casual and even slang expressions to illustrate this." Knowing that he held their focus now, he quickly peered at a prepared note card, the print sufficiently large enough to be read at a glance.

"Hence, whether your job is *driving* you crazy," he proclaimed, his smile quavering as if to stifle a giggle as he gazed at Mr. Crimpton, who appeared dumbfounded.

"Or if you are as sober as a judge," he moved on to Judge Talbott, who put her hands to her mouth in embarrassed delight, encouraging the doctor.

"If people think that you're really *far out*," he nodded to Chris, the punk rocker blushing on cue, Dr. Pendleton then smiling back at Vanessa. "Or crazy like a fox," he stated, then wondering if that had been a bit too ribald.

Vanessa's brows shot upward as she stopped chomping. *God, this man was a trip.*

"Uh, whether your eggs are a little bit scrambled," he continued, beaming at Mr. McClintock, who smiled politely, noncomprehendingly back.

"Or if you, uh, have…bats in your belfry," he nodded to Father Gilchrist, whose visage was homicidally pained.

Clearing his throat, he glanced next at Mrs. Spindlewood, his smile faltering as he discreetly skipped over her.

"Uh, my point is that, no matter how one might phrase it, expressing anomalous feelings—feelings that we all encounter, every day, uh, in such a colorful way—can actually serve as an outlet for, uh, pent-up aggressions," he concluded hastily, resurrecting his smile as he nodded self-deprecatingly. "The same certainly applies to me as well. I'm just like all of you too whether I'm in a completely rational, levelheaded frame of mind or whether I'm, uh…" He paused, squinting at the note card and then having to pick it up to recall the phrase, "Or whether I'm off my meds and jonesing for my Prozac."

The intense silence was shattered as Vanessa's laugh cracked sharply through the room, startling the older, bewildered members, who stared at her uncertainly as she leaned back in her seat and cackled. Only Chris joined her in this reaction, the punk rocker subduing his own outburst behind one sticky hand, his long legs bouncing up and down upon the worn tips of his combat boots as he snorted gleefully.

Flushing, Dr. Pendleton put aside the card, clearing his throat. "I, uh…I heard a kid say that on the bus once," he explained to the others, not needing to add that he was also not entirely clear as to its meaning.

Father Gilchrist folded his arms and glared, ignoring the kids' laughter. "I could have sworn that you presumed to chastise me at our last excuse of a meeting for employing those self-same, supposedly nonclinical phrases," he charged acerbically, his gaze boring into that of the doctor.

"Uh, well now, yes, uh, that was my point," Dr. Pendleton clarified, gesturing self-effacingly. "I reflected on it and realized that I should not have, in essence, uh, censored you, particularly in a setting where you're all encouraged to freely speak your minds. So, uh, yes, you should definitely feel comfortable using such figures of speech, uh, if they help you to express yourself."

Lifting one eyebrow, Father Gilchrist regarded him judiciously. "I take it then that you no longer repudiate my usage of the word 'kook'?"

Dr. Pendleton blinked, shaking his head. "Uh, no, not at all," he replied simply.

"Or 'whacko'?" Father Gilchrist challenged.

Dr. Pendleton shifted a bit. "No, uh, that's fine too."

Pursing his lips, Father Gilchrist nodded, then abruptly asking, "What about 'psycho' or 'bonkers' or 'fruitcake'?"

Grimacing, Dr. Pendleton paused. "Well—"

"What about 'crackpot' or 'crank'? How about *Looney Tunes?*"

"Uh…"

"How about 'nutsoid'?"

"All right, Father Gilchrist," Dr. Pendleton interjected, his tone weary but sharp. "However you choose to express yourself is up to you. All I would suggest is that you might consider the sensitivity of the phrase you use."

Father Gilchrist sat back in his chair, folding his arms irritably. "Well, in that case, what's the point?"

Vanessa had continued to laugh during this exchange, suppressing her reaction with the sleeve of her jacket. Her bad mood was now shattered. This group was unreal. She focused on Dr. Pendleton, nearly shaking her head in speechless affection.

"At any rate," the doctor stated, moving back beside the crate, his posture slightly deflated. "Uh…we were going to share some of our updates with each other." He gestured to Judge Talbott, managing a thin smile, the woman's obvious excitement encouraging him slightly. "Uh, Judge Talbott, you seem anxious to tell us something," he surmised. "I take it you have some good news?"

"Oh yes, I do," she affirmed vigorously, forcing herself to put her purse aside, pressing her hands into the lap of her skirt. "At our last meeting, I was explaining how I had been passing along cases to other judges whom I deemed more qualified in order to keep my own docket clear," she outlined carefully.

Dr. Pendleton nodded slowly. "Oh, uh, yes, I was hoping that we would have the opportunity to touch on that again," he said hesitantly.

"Well, naturally, I can't keep doing that indefinitely," the judge continued earnestly. "After a while, someone would be bound to question it."

Blinking, Dr. Pendleton regarded her with impressed interest. "Really, you, uh, came to the conclusion on your own that your... method of coping with decision-making or...otherwise, uh, might not be the most suitable way of handling things?" he returned hopefully.

Judge Talbott had been, after all, the first member of the group to open up to the rest of them, and her progress was of considerable concern to him, particularly when contrasted with her problems. Her marked inability to make simple choices had become all the more apparent in the meantime, as she continually shied away from any deviations in the safety of her patterns and routines. Even her wardrobe conveyed this reluctance toward change; so far, every outfit she had worn to the meetings had been some off-shade of green.

The judge was nodding. "Yes, I did, and the realization hit me when I remembered that I still had a large accumulation of leave time available to me from before, when I was a public defender," she explained enthusiastically.

Nodding, Dr. Pendleton frowned. "Uh, I'm not sure I understand."

Judge Talbott beamed. "I decided to take my leave time now!" she declared happily. "Four weeks of paid vacation!"

As Dr. Pendleton stared haplessly at her, Father Gilchrist glared. "In September?"

"Now, I'll be able to relax a bit and not have to worry about making any major decisions for a while," the judge continued practically. "Just deciding to go ahead and do this took a day and a half. I can really do with the break."

Speechless, Dr. Pendleton swallowed quietly, Father Gilchrist mumbling something about tax dollars *not* at work.

"Taking another leave of absence," Mr. Crimpton interposed suddenly, mainly to himself. "I never thought of that. That is not a bad idea."

Wincing, Dr. Pendleton struggled to find his voice. "What was that, Mr. Crimpton?"

The nervous driving examiner hunched forward in his chair, his eyes straining behind his glasses, as if he were deep in contemplation. "I mean I have done other things, like that time with that drunk," he went on matter-of-factly, glancing at the others. "If it's a day when we're overstaffed, for instance, I'll make it a point to be in the men's room when they're looking for an examiner. Or I'll sometimes purposefully station myself in the simulator room and initiate a test sequence so that we can't be interrupted and they'll have to hunt down some other sap. The simulator room is like being trapped in one colossal, nerve-shattering pinball machine, but it's *still* better than being out in real traffic, believe me. And this is coming from someone who *hates* dealing with those goddamned things!" He paused, glancing over at the priest. "Uh, sorry about that, Reverend."

Father Gilchrist shrugged indifferently. "Don't be," he replied. "I'm sure that even God hates those goddamned things."

Poised to interject, Dr. Pendleton grimaced in distraction, Mr. Crimpton heedlessly continuing. "Even when I do end up out on a driving test, I've got ways of salvaging the day. I've intentionally caused the car to run out of gas miles away from the DMV, and that's not easy to do," he confided gravely, nodding from face to face. "One time, I caused a student to back up into a row of those tollbooth tire spikes. That used up half a day, right there!"

Frowning in grudging curiosity, Dr. Pendleton cleared his throat. "Uh…didn't you end up being accountable for the damage?"

Mr. Crimpton glanced blankly up at him. "What? Oh no, no, I just blamed it on the student," he replied placidly, then taking in the startled looks of his peers and shrugging defensively. "She would have failed anyway! It turned out that she was legally blind."

As Dr. Pendleton placed a hand to his forehead, Mr. Crimpton settled back in his seat. "Anyway, all of those tactics are only effective to a certain degree. In the end, I know I'm really only prolonging the inevitable," he stated wistfully.

Dr. Pendleton glanced up with a look of hope. "Really?"

Nodding, Mr. Crimpton then appeared to take heart. "Yes, but, like I was saying, taking a leave of absence, that is really a good idea."

Pinching the bridge of his nose, Dr. Pendleton closed his eyes and wilted.

There was a silence, Vanessa sitting on her hands and swinging her legs beneath her chair. "Well, I'm still dodging that pimp, if that's sort of like ditching your boss at work," she announced chipperly. "Not that that scumbag's my boss, but so far so good. In fact, I've been playing hookey so much that I'm contemplating a new line of work."

Dr. Pendleton's head shot up. "Really?" he asked, his brows lifting expectantly. "Do you have some good prospects?"

Vanessa nodded. "Oh yeah," she replied easily. "See, sitting in on these meetings has kind of opened my eyes to the possibilities, you know, broadened my horizons a little. I got to thinking, why be a common every day streetwalker when I could advance my social status? So I'm thinking of becoming a stripper."

She watched Dr. Pendleton sag, smiling as the others shifted uneasily, noting with satisfaction how Chris instantly blushed and looked away.

Father Gilchrist beamed. "Ah, high society awaits such a budding debutante," he proclaimed sardonically. "You must remember to invite us all to your cotillion."

Clearing his throat, Dr. Pendleton was obviously reluctant to pursue this subject, but was just as reluctant to pursue the previous one. "Uh, and how much…progress have you made in that…direction?"

"Oh, a little," she told him casually, which was true. Having been refraining from her previous street hustling, she had made a few random inquiries into the prospect, the results having been decisively counterproductive. The one club owner who had deigned to speak to her and had lewdly undressed her with his eyes—eyes that burned and yet were stone-cold at the same time—had informed her that she was too young to be working legally in a club, a bar, or anywhere. When she had worked up the nerve to ask, point-blank, if he, or anyone in town for that matter, would take a chance on her "under the table," he had requested she define what "under the table" meant to her, then interrupting to explain what "under the table" meant to him and to anyone who would consider hiring her based upon her obvious assets. She had declined by replying that that was the sort of work he could go and do to himself.

Sleazy bastard, she reflected darkly, then dismissing her failure, fairly certain that she wouldn't have been able to go through with it anyway; the insult of knowing that she had, indeed, finally made it onstage and that it was in front of an audience of the ultimate crowd of oglers would have been too much for her to take. The entire affair had already blighted her mood for most of the week, and now that she was feeling slightly better, she wanted to hang onto that edge.

"Anyway, not to get us off topic," she continued, carelessly shrugging. "Yeah, I've been pimp-dodging for a couple of weeks now. How 'bout you?" she asked Mr. McClintock, clasping his thick shoulder. "You been ducking your boss at work?"

Mr. McClintock had been finishing off his cupcake, dabbing unnecessarily at his wide mouth, unable to refrain from smiling a bit. In spite of how brazen her behavior could be considered, he rather liked Vanessa. Something about her nature was so spirited and vivacious. Beyond that, he was still in an exceptionally good mood.

"As a matter of fact, it really is funny that you should say that," he told her, almost mischievously smiling at the others. "Just yesterday, in fact, I was inclined to avoid my editor. And I did so, quite surreptitiously—and serendipitously as well—if I do say so myself."

This was quite true, he reflected brightly. His Monday morning encounter with Mr. Moynihan still regrettably fresh in his mind, he had, nonetheless, failed to undertake any especially noteworthy reviews by Thursday.

He had visited a few of the restaurants on the prepared list, but his dining experiences with them had been quite lackluster, and he had been uninspired to compile anything beyond fundamental reviews, these proving to be so uninteresting that he, in essence, had very little to show for the week. Hence, having heard the approach of the voluminous editor before actually seeing him, he had moved with a swiftness he would not have imagined that he could manage—on tiptoe, no less—to take refuge in a small filing room, noiselessly opening the door, easing his bulk within, and silently closing it. Heart pounding as he listened to the editor bustle explosively past, he stood there, staring at the door, gradually, and then, with growing alarm, becoming aware of the rampantly uneven sound of his respiration. Appropriately startled, his heart began to beat even more violently, as it dawned on him that his sudden velocity had brought on some form of cardiac arrest. He had spun around, in search of a chair in which to collapse, wondering fleetingly if the five Big Macs he had just consumed ostensibly for lunch were, in fact, going to constitute his last meal, his eyes falling upon the couch, which, for whatever reason, had been squeezed into the little room, his heart then shuddering in a different kind of seizure altogether as he beheld the occupants of the couch and realized that *they*, not he, were the source of the frantic breathing.

The girl, he knew, was a receptionist, her pleated skirt hiked upward; the boy, he came to learn, was a Marine, his woolen trousers pulled downward. Mr. McClintock's gasp was just loud enough to drown out their own, the girl's eyes flying open. A scream caught in her throat as she sat up, ruthlessly shoving the boy off her, scrambling to rearrange the direction of her skirt.

As the boy gawked at her, dumbstruck, Mr. McClintock had lumbered over to the girl's rescue, thinking she was being assaulted. Turning, the boy at last perceived this colossal presence, shooting to his feet and, perhaps not knowing what else to do, coming to attention, the girl angrily pushing past him with one hand and tugging fiercely at her panty hose with the other, all while stalking forward on stiletto heels and raking her disheveled hair out of her eyes, shoving past Mr. McClintock and hissing. "Ever hear of knocking, Dumbo?"

Cringing as the girl burst out of the filing room and positively hurled the door closed, Mr. McClintock turned very sheepishly to regard the ramrod figure of the Marine.

Smiling apologetically, he then found that he could not even guess as to what to say, the Marine, baby-faced and towheaded, eyes to the front, saving him the trouble.

"Sir, do you mind if this Private hoists his skivvies and trousers, sir?" he requested with mechanical courtesy.

Startled at the staccato delivery, Mr. McClintock nodded quickly, then blinking in uncertainty when the Marine made no move to do so. Turning a bit more, he then noticed that he was standing on the garments in question, as they had dropped to the boy's ankles when he had leapt to his feet. Wincing, he mumbled an apology and stepped aside, then frowning and glancing down at the Marine's lower body, blinking and staring in fascination at what he was seeing.

"What are you wearing, Private?" he found himself asking in wonder.

The Marine unflinchingly reached down and, grasping each side of his shirt front, pulled the shirttails apart, revealing his unabated stance at attention.

"Sir, that is a prophylactic device known as a condom, sir. It is employed as a method of birth control and as a means of preventing the spread of sexually transmitted diseases, sir. It is often referred to as a Rubber Johnnie, sir."

Mr. McClintock had immediately averted his eyes, his entire head seeming to recede into his shoulders during this starkly uninhibited dissertation, the Marine's forthright frankness very off-putting.

"Er, uh, no, Private," he had amended, stepping back a bit more and reluctantly lowering his gaze to the Marine's lower half again. "I meant, what are *those*?"

He gingerly indicated a pair of white elastic straps that were clipped to the bottom of his shirttails and the tops of his knee-high socks, their tautness forcing the skirt of the shirt to conform tightly over the Marine's midriff and hips.

"Sir, those are called Shirt Stays, Sir. They are devices issued by the USMC Quartermaster to all personnel as optional but highly recommended accessories used to keep this Private's shirt firmly tucked into place, sir," the Marine informed him robotically.

His thick brows lifting, Mr. McClintock was clearly impressed. "Shirt Stays?" he repeated, moving as if to peer more closely at them, but then quickly refraining. "They are affixed to your shirt and to your socks," he mused curiously, seemingly deep in thought. "So they also hold up your socks, and they are not attached in any way to your actual undergarments."

"Sir, no sir," the Marine elaborated. "This Private's shirt is held in place by this Private's Shirt Stays. This Private's skivvies are held in place by a separate piece of elastic. This Private's privates are held in place by this Private's skivvies or, as in this case, by a different kind of elastic, sir."

Mr. McClintock winced. "Yes, I…see that," he said, wishing he did not. He glanced at the Shirt Stays again. "Two in front," he noted.

"Sir, yes, sir, and two in the back, sir." The Marine spun around automatically and candidly illustrated a second pair of Shirt Stays, snapping them sharply for emphasis.

Grimacing in shock, Mr. McClintock was nevertheless still intrigued. "I wonder, Private, do you know where I might be able to get some of these accessories?" he had asked at length. "I'm not in the Service, of course, but…"

"Sir, I believe I can help you, sir. If you go to the Supply Office at Fort Naughattuck, ask for Corporal Dekum and tell him that Private Fulsom sent you, sir. He'll set you up, sir," the Marine told him flatly, then adding. "If he doesn't believe you, then ask for Corporal Dickhead and tell him Private Fucks 'em sent you, sir."

As Mr. McClintock hesitantly registered this advice, the Marine exhaled tautly. "Sir, if you are finished discussing this Private's under-wear, sir, this Private would like to go after that receptionist and fin-ish banging her before he's due back at base, sir," he had outlined conclusively.

Smiling weakly, Mr. McClintock had parted company with him, his instinctual generosity almost prompting him to offer to share a cab out to the base, a notion that he then quietly dismissed as somehow awkwardly inappropriate.

At Fort Naughattack, he had been politely and readily received by the sentries and directed to the Supply Office, where a short, young Marine had at first incredulously and then laughingly acquiesced to Mr. McClintock's request. Bantering in friendly, albeit colorful lan-guage, he had disappeared behind his counter and returned with a dozen of the elastic devices. He had then directed Mr. McClintock into a rear corner of the building and helped him out of his jacket, the corpulent food reviewer surprised at the corporal's obvious intent, the corporal surprised at his surprise. "Sir, we're all Devil Dogs here, sir. No call to be shy, sir," he had insisted.

Before he knew it, Mr. McClintock had removed his enormous pair of pants, and the Corporal had set about affixing not four, but ten of the Shirt Stays, letting them down to their fullest extent. As he stood back, Mr. McClintock was able to view himself in a full-length mirror. He looked—and felt—as if someone had pitched a massive tent over his upper body. The corporal nodded in satisfaction, observing that he resembled a hot air balloon.

This remark aside, Mr. McClintock had replaced his trousers and had then taken a few tentative steps. The spring of the taut elastic made him feel as if he had been outfitted with puppet strings, and yet, from the tips of his toes to the broad shoulder seams of his shirt, he felt very well fortified. He had walked about in shirtsleeves for a moment, sitting down and watching his reflection. With such neat, smooth, and trim, well, perhaps not trim, but with such uniformity, and no chance of bulging or recalcitrant shirttails or a constant, billowing need to tuck his shirt in, he might very well be comfortable enough to take his jacket off at work. Moreover, his socks, the nylon elastic of which had always crumpled and sagged against his elephantine calves, were not going anywhere. The corporal had given him several extra sets, informing him that if they wore out, they were easily replaced. "Sir, you can substitute 'em with those elastic things they sell at the store for clipping picnic tablecloths or bedsheets in place, sir."

Thanking the corporal profusely, he had reached for his wallet, the corporal instantly waylaying his intention. For whatever reason, the story of how Mr. McClintock happened to have come there that day had been reward enough.

He smiled now at the recollection, shifting in his seats and enjoying the stayed conformity of his shirt. He knew they were meticulous, if not fastidious, accessories, almost fussily effeminate. In fact, he had been reminded, upon seeing them, of the rather skimpy garter belts that one always saw prostitutes portrayed as wearing. It had been for this reason that he had been so taken aback to see a U.S. Marine wearing such a thing, although he had been just as startled to have seen enough to know that the receptionist had not been. He stole a curious glance at Vanessa, then dismissing the thought altogether. What mattered was the serendipity of the incident—the double serendipity, he reflected—for, as he was leaving the Supply Office, he had been assailed with a singularly appealing aroma, the new spring in his steps accompanying him toward what turned out to be the Base Commissary.

By the time he had left the Base, Thursday's workday had ended, and he was able to submit his weekly review, complete and punctual, with a fair degree of pride, for he had found that point of interest he had been seeking; and now, he could relax for the entire weekend. Yes, indeed, serendipity.

"I see…," Dr. Pendleton was saying, nodding in a subdued way and then nearly shrugging. "Has…anyone else had an experience this week, in which they, uh…hid from their boss or, in any other way, avoided their…agendas?"

When no one replied, Chris sat up a bit, ferreting out the last of the frosting from the cupcake doily. "I used to skip a few classes in high school," he offered, wiping at his mouth and only making things worse.

Vanessa sneered. *Yeah, pigpen, we can tell—basic hygiene.*

"I guess you can't really dodge your boss, can you, Reverend?" Mr. Crimpton remarked wryly. "Not if He sees all and hears all, anyway."

Father Gilchrist sniffed. "If, indeed," he replied enigmatically, his visage then sharpening. "At St. Leonard's Parish, I *am* the boss, and I openly encourage my subordinates to avoid *me*. In fact, I oftentimes facilitate this by avoiding *them* as much as possible!"

As Dr. Pendleton tried to think of some response, Judge Talbott spoke up in curiosity. "St. Leonard's Parish, is that the name of your church, Father?" she inquired politely. "I've never heard of St. Leonard before. What was he famous for?"

"Oh, not a great deal, although some people may be acquainted with his good deeds," Father Gilchrist replied breezily, before his features crumpled darkly at all of them. "St. Leonard was the patron saint of prisoners and of the insane." He glowered at their ensuing discomfiture, just as briskly smiling again. "Ah, but we digress! What was the topic at hand—ditching one's boss, was it?" He glanced sideways at Mrs. Spindlewood. "And you, dear lady, have you ever avoided Mr. Bergdorf here?"

He smiled tautly at Dr. Pendleton's grimace, as Mrs. Spindlewood blinked up at him. "Oh dear," she warbled. "Have I ever annoyed you, Mr. Bergdorf?"

Dr. Pendleton swallowed a sigh, forcing a smile. "Uh, no, Mrs. Spindlewood, you've never...You're doing just fine," he assured the elderly woman, reluctantly picking up his cup and sipping the tepid water. "And the, uh, coffee is very good too."

When this appeared to reassure her, Dr. Pendleton focused upon the group, Judge Talbott hesitantly raising a hand, her features pensive, but still quite eager. "Dr. Pendleton, you look a bit discouraged," she noted anxiously, gesturing meaningfully. "I want to tell you that even though I took the initiative in making such a big decision, I have to give you and the group credit for inspiring me with the courage to take such a big step."

The doctor maintained a flimsy smile, as Mr. Crimpton nodded. "Yes, I'm grateful too," he affirmed, rubbing his hands together. "Before, it felt like I was completely alone in this, kind of, daily attempt to survive...mainly because I was, but now that I have people to discuss all of these problems with, I feel like...like it's war, now, and that I'm actually winning, for a change."

"I have no doubt that my good fortune is due in part to my being here as well," Mr. McClintock spoke up. "I fear I cannot elaborate, but had I not circumnavigated my editor at precisely that moment, well, suffice it to say that, were this group a restaurant, I would give it an extremely good review."

Vanessa grinned. "Yeah, and look at me. If I hadn't been ditching that pimp, I would never've come here in the first place," she reminded them, nodding with her chin toward Father Gilchrist. "How 'bout you, Padre? At least, this is getting you away from your church for a little while, eh?"

Father Gilchrist, instantly poised to retort, instead paused. "That is true. There are by far worse places I could be trapped for an evening," he allowed, then glancing sideways at Dr. Pendleton. "Although not by much."

"And how about you, Mrs. Spindlewood?" Vanessa prompted. "You like coming here, don't you?"

Mrs. Spindlewood glanced up, smiling vaguely. "Oh my, yes," she chirped. "I like it much better than the spark plug factory."

As they all considered this, Chris squirmed in his seat, not knowing how to begin to explain what he was running away from, but wanting to add some sort of input with all of the others. "Yeah, and I…really like coming here too," was all he could think to say, the other members nodding approvingly to him, causing him to smile and blush, their acceptance of him feeling so good.

His own smile growing weaker with each statement, Dr. Pendleton could scarcely clear his throat. Was it possible that they actually thought that this was what he wanted to hear? He was uncertain if he should permit them to enjoy their enthusiasm a while longer before explaining to them that they had all succeeded, with flying colors, in completely running away from their problems. Could it be that they did not see this or, worse still, that they *did* and were crediting him with having encouraged them to do the exact opposite of what the entire purpose of the group was? If so, where had he gone wrong?

He thought of Dr. Whittaker's admonition that group therapy could take a while to evolve and, in doing so, recalled the other points he had been looking forward to covering that night, and he focused upon them, still able to summon up a bit of confidence for each one.

"Uh, yes, I'm glad you've been able to cope with your various challenges," he began slowly. "You've definitely made progress, uh, of a sort…" He paused, inhaling deeply. "Uh, I was just thinking that at our last meeting's Show' N' Tell segment, I had also brought along something to share."

"Oh?" said Father Gilchrist. "Why didn't you, then? We had plenty of time."

Dr. Pendleton evaded this by stooping to reach into his attaché case, removing a small picture frame that contained a formal-appearing document. He glanced at it with self-conscious pride, actually blushing a bit, the group observing it with interest.

"This is my certification for being a psychologist," he explained, smiling almost shyly at the group. "I wanted to share it with all of you because even though it's only a material item, it has a very special meaning to me."

He moved to hand it to Mrs. Spindlewood. "If you'd like to pass—"

"Oh, thank you, Mr. Bergdorf," she smiled, taking the frame and balancing it on her lap, placing her purse and cupcake on top of it.

Dr. Pendleton blinked. "Uh, no," he explained, gently retrieving it. "I was going to ask you to pass it along."

He extended it to Father Gilchrist, who reluctantly accepted it, gazing at it appraisingly. "Hmm, this is rather handsome."

Dr. Pendleton's smile blossomed. "Thank you. I always thought the calligraphy was very artistically done."

Father Gilchrist pursed his lips. "I was referring to the frame," he said sourly, about to pass it to Vanessa and then peering more closely at it, looking dryly up at the doctor. "Practicing without a license, eh?"

Starting, Dr. Pendleton blanched. "That...that *is* my license."

"Yes, but it appears to have long-since expired," the old priest informed him tautly, shoving the frame toward Vanessa.

Dr. Pendleton grimaced and flushed. "Well, yes, but that's not my most up-to-date documentation...it's my previous one. I took it from my office wall in a hurry earlier this week. But the point is the actual idea behind the document is symbolic of what ended up being my choice of career," he explained earnestly, watching as the frame was passed around the circle. "You see, previously, I only undertook sessions on a one-on-one basis. But the institution of group therapy, in specific, ours, here, tonight, is an extracurricular way for me to branch out, to extend my practice even more so, to get more out of my time and more out of that certificate."

He paused as Mr. Crimpton glanced up from the frame. "Well, we'll all try to do our best to make sure your time is well-spent," he told him candidly, the others nodding in agreement.

Smiling, Dr. Pendleton nodded back. "I appreciate your sentiment, Mr. Crimpton," he replied gratefully, stepping forward as

Chris was handed the frame, gently taking it from him, lest the kid accidentally drop it.

"But please, bear something in mind," he resumed, holding the frame atop his podium and gesturing assertively to all of them, speaking purposefully. "It is essential that you all know that, as a group, this time is *our* time, together, and that, as I've tried to emphasize before, I am not so much here to help all of you, as I am here to help all of you to help each other, to help yourselves."

He nodded once to reenforce this declaration, blushing when he received an instantaneous plaudit, the members heartily clapping, Vanessa cheering raucously, Chris stomping his boots and shouting a punk rock accolade, waving his fists and Mohawk wildly. Even Mrs. Spindlewood and Father Gilchrist applauded, one obliviously, one sarcastically. It was a highly moving, if somewhat offbeat and perhaps even slightly mad, ovation.

Overwhelmed, Dr. Pendleton beamed at them, setting aside his certificate and holding up his small hands, waving modestly.

"Thank you, thank you, folks," he nodded, very much encouraged. "Although you really should be applauding yourselves, uh, which is why…" He paused, smiling as mysteriously as he could, "I have a surprise for all of you."

This statement, so unexpected, served to intrigue the group, and he felt himself become caught up in the moment. "Uh, as you may know, a lot of other anonymous groups have various group activities that they do, in conjunction with their regular meetings," he began.

"Oh! Are we going to have our potluck?" Judge Talbott asked brightly.

Mr. McClintock lifted his eyebrows hopefully.

"Uh, no, I have something even more elaborate in mind," Dr. Pendleton told them, anxiety intermingling with his eagerness. "Uh, now, what some groups do is organize what are called 'retreats,' which are group outings to, say, the beach or to go hiking or such. And so what I have done is made special reservations for all of us to spend next weekend at Fenderman Lodge!"

When the group only stared wordlessly back at him, he faltered and hastily continued. "Uh, Fenderman Lodge is a beautiful…uh, lodge on a lake about a hundred and fifty miles north of here. The Fenderman family once lived there. But it's a time-share property now, and like I've said, I've made all the arrangements. And, uh, the whole place, all three acres, is ours for the whole weekend..." He smiled again, awaiting their reaction hopefully.

"Do you mean we'd be, like, going on a field trip together?" Chris asked, Vanessa rolling her eyes as Dr. Pendleton nodded affirmatively.

"Would there be...very much hiking involved?" Mr. McClintock inquired meekly.

Dr. Pendleton blinked. "Well, no, not really... There's a driveway leading up to the lodge, but it's not really on a hilltop or anything." He paused, smiling nostalgically. "I used to go up there when I was a kid with my family. There's a field and a little pine forest off to one side, and of course, you can go swimming or fishing, and there's even an area where you can have a campfire or a barbecue or a singalong or whatever we wanted to do."

"My, doesn't it sound rustic and folksy?" Father Gilchrist observed.

Judge Talbott's hand shot up. "Are there any bears up there?" she asked anxiously.

"What about poison ivy or mosquitoes?" Mr. Crimpton spoke up, his features pinching in concern. "Or pollen. I have a lot of allergies."

Vanessa cut off each of them with a skeptical question of her own. "How much is this going to cost each of us?" she demanded.

Taken aback, Dr. Pendleton shook his head. "Uh, well, as I've said, I went ahead and rented the place for the whole weekend. So it's all paid for, and I also intend to arrange for our transportation there...and back..."

Mr. McClintock lifted a hand hopefully. "And provisions?"

"Uh, yes, there was an option to arrange with the time-share so that we'll have a full pantry, and the kitchen will be stocked with all we should need," he explained simply. "If we needed anything else, we could drive in to Larkesville. That's the nearest town..."

"Ah, Larkesville, of course!" approved Father Gilchrist. "An oasis of civilization."

Vanessa was shaking her head in disbelief. "A free, all-expenses paid two-day vacation in the country?" she summarized frankly. "Fuckin' A. Hell yeah. I'm going, sign me up, Doc. I'm there!"

Startled, Dr. Pendleton reached for a piece of paper, as Chris waved one arm energetically alongside of him.

"Me too, Dr. Pendleton! I wanna go too," he declared excitedly, blushing and grinning when, before she could stop herself, Vanessa gave him a charged gesture of approval.

"It sounds like it might be…restful," Mr. McClintock posed doubtfully, his countenance then brightening. "And a barbecue would be most enjoyable."

"If there's a campfire, we could all make s'mores," Judge Talbott surmised, her angst abating at the idea, the food reviewer nodding eagerly.

"I guess it wouldn't kill me to get away for the weekend," Mr. Crimpton allowed.

His enthusiasm revived, Dr. Pendleton attached the paper to his clipboard, passing it and a pen to Chris and smiling at the group. "I really do think that we'll all have a fun time, not only doing whatever we wish to do, even if it is just relaxing and talking, but also continuing our meetings, sort of like mixing business with pleasure."

"Or rum and coke," Vanessa added playfully.

"Or dynamite and Plasticine," smiled Father Gilchrist.

Dr. Pendleton blinked, then turning as Chris held up the now-smudged piece of paper. "Um, what did you want me to write on this?"

"Oh, uh, yes, if you'd like to put your names and phone numbers on this list," he explained, folding his arms behind his back. "Uh, one week from today, I'll give you the details about where we'll meet Saturday morning, uh, time and place and all. But for now, just in case there's any change in plans, uh, I'll be able to get a hold of you."

He nodded as the clipboard was passed around, a clamor of anticipation quelling in his stomach as he took pleasure in the response with which his surprise had been met, until Father Gilchrist was handed the clipboard and pen, which he immediately capped.

"And suppose, Dr. Pendleton, that any of us do not wish to partake in this extemporaneous sojourn of yours?" he challenged officiously. "I presume that we are permitted to decline?"

Dr. Pendleton blinked back at him. "You mean you don't want to come with us, Father Gilchrist?" he asked, his slightly hurt tone lost on the elderly priest.

"Go tramping off into the wilderness with seven strangers who just this evening were given carte blanche to indulge their innate degrees of madness?" he charged bitterly. "Why, it's the stuff of which horror films are made!"

Judge Talbott glanced uneasily around the room, Chris doing the same.

"Oh, come on," scoffed Vanessa. "If you come with us, we promise to let you spoil the whole trip. Who else can we count on to complain the whole time?"

Father Gilchrist gave her a frigid smile. "Ah, sweet temptation," he purred, then abruptly shaking his head. "I'm afraid it's quite impossible. The weekend will be far too busy. I have to give mass on Sunday and, come to think of it, on Saturday as well." He spread his hands helplessly.

Dr. Pendleton nodded and then frowned "But...Catholic mass is only on Sundays."

The priest glared. "The Saturday masses are for our Jewish parishioners," he snapped.

Staring at him, Dr. Pendleton then grimaced, taking the clipboard away from this perfectly impossible priest, exasperated at the sheer outrageousness of the man's rationale. "May I at least have your number for our list?" he asked wearily.

"It's in the book," Father Gilchrist replied. "Under 'Revelations.'"

Sighing, Dr. Pendleton turned to Mrs. Spindlewood. "Mrs. Spindlewood, do you mind if I have your telephone number?"

Mrs. Spindlewood gazed up at him. "Certainly, Mr. Bergdorf. It's Glen Haven One-Two-Three-Six-Four."

Hesitating, Dr. Pendleton thanked her and wrote it down anyway.

*****

Vanessa had lowered her window all the way down on her ride back to the hotel, her mood all the more enhanced by the in-rushing breeze. She knew it would be short-lived, for she still had the entire weekend to pass, but she allowed her spirits to soar all the same, content with the contemplation of the next weekend, as well as the tail end of that night's meeting.

She had been stocking up on some doughnuts for dinner and next morning's breakfast, when Chris had come up from behind, stooping awkwardly to reclaim his bag and skateboard, blushing when she glanced down at him. "Hey, Mad Max! How's it hanging?"

Standing upright, he had shifted uncomfortably. "Hey," he managed to return, then adding lamely, "Wow, I can hardly wait for next weekend."

"Fuck yeah, man!" she grinned up at him. "I'll take any excuse to get my ass out of this shit town!"

"Good night, Trudy. Good night, Herbert," Mrs. Spindlewood tottered by.

"Good night, Mrs. Spindlewood," they had both recited, Vanessa now blushing herself as she glanced at Chris again and shrugged casually.

"So what're your big plans for *this* weekend?" she asked disinterestedly, noticing how he seemed to perk up at her modestly conversational demeanor.

"Oh, me and my girlfriend are going to a wedding reception," he told her openly, shrugging into his backpack. "No big deal, but it could be fun… How about you?"

"Girlfriend, eh?" she had repeated, impressed by this and also interested, though only because she was surprised that anyone would be with him. "Well, you have fun with that," she had said dismissively, turning back to the doughnuts and then, seized by an impulse, calling after him. "Hey, killer!"

He paused to look blankly back at her, Vanessa slinging her bag over one shoulder and moving toward him, smiling mischievously.

"You forgot something," she declared, glad to see that he was gaping at her as slack-jawed as always, as it enabled her to push a jelly doughnut roughly but playfully into his mouth. She then stood on tiptoe and lightly grazed the top of his Mohawk with one hand before walking away.

"Don't party too hearty, Wild Thing," she had warned, grinning over one shoulder, pleased to see him still standing there, motionlessly gawking after her, the doughnut neatly half wedged in his mouth. That had decided it, she finally had to concede; like it or not, he was cute.

She smirked now as she reflected on it, leaning back, one arm resting on the window frame, the breeze streaking through her fingers. She turned to Dr. Pendleton, who had been as quietly attentive to the road as usual, his small mouth still clenched in a slight grimace.

"Are you really gonna get us out of this place for a whole weekend, Doc?" she asked him, still amazed at this seemingly unbelievable idea.

Starting back into the moment, he glanced over at her and smiled. "Oh yes, yes. That's the idea," he assured her. "I think it will be a nice change of pace."

She shook her head. "Man, when I think of how, when I was growing up in the sticks, all I wanted to do was come to the city, and now, I can't wait to get the hell out of the city and go back to the country, even if it's just for a little while."

Dr. Pendleton nodded, shifting gears. "Yes, well, I think it might be good for some of the group to get some perspective about their jobs by being away from them, uh, for a short time..." He paused, realizing the connotations of this statement, wondering fleetingly how to change the subject.

Vanessa had been thinking the same, but upon seeing the hotel in the next block, she turned suddenly to the doctor. "Doc, I want to tell you something."

She told him everything, every last detail, every word feeling more liberating as she spoke it. When she was finished, because she had no interest in *discussing* it, she had quickly climbed out of the car, Dr. Pendleton stammering, "You mean the whole thing was just an act?"

Leaning back in, she smiled. "What better way to practice being an actress?" she returned. "See? I warned you I was pretty fucked up."

She had then kissed him on the cheek, half-theatrically, half-affectionately, thanking him and then leaving him in befuddled darkness. She was nonetheless grinning as she mounted the steps of the Hotel Rochester. As much as she may have shocked him, she was positive that she had just made his night.

*****

"Naturally, I fully understand your misgivings, Dr. Pendleton. Yes, thank you, waiter, the marmalade is excellent." Dr. Whittaker spread a bit more of this condiment on an English muffin, wielding the knife with a surgeon's finesse. "Nonetheless, I feel that you are making excellent progress with your group."

Dr. Pendleton took a small bite of his toast, nodding appreciatively, amazed how, even seated at a sidewalk cafe, with the bustle of traffic and pedestrians surrounding them, just being in the presence of the older doctor seemed to create an insulated realm of secure refinement. He watched as Dr. Whittaker extracted a bite of the muffin and savored it without displacing a crumb in his goatee, chewing delicately before continuing.

"I am somewhat surprised to learn of the rather sudden organization of your proposed retreat. While I don't disapprove, not at all, in fact, I do wonder at your choice of timing. Do you feel for certain that after what will have been only six sessions together, your plans are not slightly premature?"

He gazed at Dr. Pendleton expectantly, the latter swallowing his toast harshly, nodding, and clearing his throat. "I, uh, know it must seem like that, Dr. Whittaker," he agreed, linking his fingers together and leaning forward earnestly. "This may seem a little far-fetched, but I actually planned it that way, for a reason. The idea came to me from an experience I had on the bus recently, something that happens to people every day, hundreds of times. A complete stranger began to speak to me, conversationally at first. But then, she began to confide more personal, sensitive details about her life, the sort that you wouldn't think a person would tell to someone whom they'd never met before. But then it hit me—that was just it, that was the point. She told me those things *because* I was a stranger. For whatever reason, we all know that it's sometimes easier to open up to a stranger than it is to, say, someone you've known for twenty years. There are many reasons why this is, but the point is that it's true. And that's what seems to make up the gist of these anonymous groups, the idea of talking, privately, to people without any preconceived notions about you. But unlike the lady on the bus, who, true to form, I never saw again, even in an anonymous group, you'll eventually get to know any consistent members, and some attachments will naturally form. Now, that's a good thing, of course, in terms of, say, sponsors or such. But the thing is, once that happens, you'll end up losing that initial sort of spontaneous freedom—and willingness—to talk openly with a stranger, because, at that point, they're no longer strangers."

"My idea"—Dr. Pendleton continued, his features becoming eager and animated—"is to try to get the best of both worlds. My group is still in a formative stage, it's true. But in spite of some shyness, they are becoming bolder in their sharing, partly because they're getting to know each other better, but moreover because there's still so very much that is new and unknown. What makes this opportunity so unique is that it's a new group that all of the members joined at the same time. As hasty as it may seem, I believe that if we have this retreat now, while that novelty is still so fresh, if we put them in an intensely removed but private, informal, and pleasant setting, we can get the very best out of that sort of 'interaction-between-strangers phenomenon' while at the same time solidifying their trust and confidence in each other as a basis for future sessions and also individual friendships, uh, down the road."

He cleared his throat, avoiding Dr. Whittaker's gaze as he toyed with his toast and concluded. "That's why I thought we should go ahead and have the retreat so soon."

Taking another bite of toast, he glanced up when Dr. Whittaker next spoke, the older man regarding him with his wintry brows lifted in elegantly impressed arches. "An excellent school of thought, Dr.

Pendleton," he responded, nodding affirmingly. "A bit daring, but most definitely worth implementing. Well done."

Dr. Pendleton felt his chest swell a bit at this praise, sitting up as the waiter approached with Dr. Whittaker's eggs Benedict and his own order of bran flakes.

Chapter 7

THE FIFTH MEETING HELD TWO precedents—one at its beginning, and one at its close.

"Has anyone seen Mrs. Spindlewood?" Dr. Pendleton asked when the members had become situated, and yet there was no sign of the old woman.

"I didn't see her at the bus stop," Mr. Crimpton volunteered.

"I'll go check," Vanessa announced, clattering over chairs to the entrance.

Watching her go, Dr. Pendleton then accepted the snack that Judge Talbott was distributing. "Oh, thank you, Judge," he nodded, peering at the Saran-wrapped item uncertainly. "Uh… What is this?"

Judge Talbott smiled shyly. "Oh, I couldn't wait until Saturday," she confessed. "I went ahead and made some s'mores ahead of time."

"Ah," Dr. Pendleton nodded, a trace of excitement alighting within him at the mention of the upcoming retreat and the anticipation that it seemed to be creating.

"Nope, she wasn't out there," Vanessa reported, resuming her seat and chomping on her gum. *Well, that sucked*, she reflected poutingly. She loved watching the prim old lady sit through the sessions, her thoughts clearly elsewhere, not to mention the incompatibility of everything she said. Obviously, she was a little out of it, but who wasn't? Wasn't that why they all came here?

The meetings wouldn't be the same without her.

She accepted her s'more from the judge, smiling in a silly exaggerated way, scarcely able to sit still in her seat; she had had such a rocking weekend. She unwrapped the snack and glanced over at Chris, expecting to see him mauling his, surprised when she saw that he was merely toying with it in his lap, his slumped, almost horizontal posture already extended, the mane of his Mohawk tilted gloomily downward, in keeping with the expression on his face.

Staring at him curiously, she tried once more to figure him out; when he wasn't acting like a total little boy, he just sort of moped around butthurt all the time. Maybe his weekend—with his girlfriend—had bombed. Who knew? She had given him the chance on Friday, dropping the hint in case he might want to go out and do something, but he had plans, so that was that. Too bad for him, because her weekend was the best. She plucked her gum out of her mouth and went to stick it beneath her chair, then stopping, realizing that if these were Dr. Pendleton's chairs, then no way. She wadded it into the corner of the Saran wrap and bit into her s'more, relishing its room-temperature gooiness.

"Well, perhaps she's running late," Dr. Pendleton had concluded, then gesturing broadly. "In the meantime, I suppose we can commence."

Alongside Vanessa, Mr. McClintock had also not yet unwrapped his s'more, nor had he helped himself to any doughnuts. His suit was immaculate, as always, his appearance tautly unrumpled. The only sagging, wrinkled distinction about his person was his face, his features set in a tragically dazed trance, interrupted only by a vague smile or response and those only of the most perfunctory, superficial sort.

"...so glad that you're all looking forward to the retreat," Dr. Pendleton was saying. "As am I, I can assure you."

Chris met the doctor's gaze each time with a mild smile, slipping back into his brooding reverie when the coast was clear. He knew that his shoulder blades were almost touching the seat of his chair, so pronounced was his slouch, and that if he did not sit up soon, he would slide right down to the floor onto his ass. Then, everyone would laugh at him, and he would have the satisfaction of knowing that he had fulfilled another cycle of his purpose in life, being a fool for the benefit of those around him—being the personification of a joke.

"Naturally, though, we mustn't let our excitement get the better of us," Dr. Pendleton continued. "We still have two meetings before our little getaway."

Mr. Crimpton massaged his brow, trying to banish his headache. He had very nearly skipped the meeting that night, only the thought of his barren apartment and TV dinner coercing him to attend. He should be grateful, he supposed; by the time the tow trucks had arrived and the road flares had all died down and the traffic cop had run out of inane questions, his entire shift was finished. He was not grateful, though. Minor fender bender that it had been, it had jangled his nerves into a state of near hysteria. He felt as if his nervous system were a delicate, intricate complex balance of networks and strings, like a fragile, priceless harpsichord from the Renaissance—a beautiful, delicate harpsichord, streamlined and set on casters and then shoved off a cliff to erupt into a thunderous, discordant snarl of twanging, sparking, snapping wires and twisted, splintered debris.

"So in terms of the issues at hand," Dr. Pendleton was proposing, peering hopefully around the room. "Uh, who would like to get the ball rolling?" he asked, instantly wincing, waiting for Father Gilchrist to pounce.

Father Gilchrist did not pounce. He was not even listening, his countenance even more fierce than usual as he glowered at the floor. He had long since resolved not to set foot in that hospital if he could help it, and now, he would avoid that infernal nursery school as well. *That nun,* he thought bitterly. *Scatterbrained dolt.* It was her fault that he had been forced to go traipsing in there in the first place. If she had only returned those keys to their hook like any intelligent, sensible idiot would do; what in blazes was she doing, getting into the sacristy, anyway?

Taking nips, perhaps? Oh no, not Sister Angelica, the Singing Nun, reincarnate. He could see her smiling in delight as she watched the child and could hear its timorous fledgling voice reciting the old nursery rhyme, childishly hollow and cracking. It had stopped him in his tracks.

One glance at the priest prompted Dr. Pendleton to take whatever clemency he could get, and he started on the other side of the room.

"Uh, Claude, how was your weekend?" he asked pleasantly.

Chris had been staring at his padlock buckle, fingering it listlessly, realizing belatedly that he was being addressed. He sat up awkwardly, his various chains and accessories rattling against the seat, his face immediately flushing.

"Um, it was okay," he lied, shrugging apathetically, finding that he did not really care how convincing he was. He simply did not feel like putting on a facade of good humor, although he had never really done so at these meetings, having never had the need. He was just tired, dispirited.

The weekend, having had so much potential to be a good time, had been anything but enjoyable. The newlyweds may well have had ancestral ties to the old country, but those ties had been Americanized, to wit, cauterized. Only the oldest relatives had shared in Chris's disappointment as they had sat, bewildered, beholding the ultracontemporary wedding party pitching and weaving to the latest pop music, a nonstop succession of boy bands, rap, and new age dance beats.

Candy had been in her element, provocatively dressed to kill, insisting that he get up and dance with her, instantly dropping the proposal when he had shown the slightest hesitation. She had flung herself out onto the dance floor and wound her way flirtatiously around every other guy there, including the groom, at first occasionally glancing tauntingly at Chris and then ignoring him altogether as she directed her focus on the tall, well-built hipster-looking kid—a kid who had come with them to the reception, on the bus, though it had seemed no big deal at the time, because he had been with a girl, himself, and they had arrived as two couples. Glancing around the darkened patio, he had located the other girl, off to one side and, for all intents and purposes, attentively kissing the bride.

Faced with that conclusion and not wanting to draw another one, he had reluctantly waded out into the dancers, the dread he experienced almost leaving a bad taste in his mouth. He was very let down that there was not a concertina in sight and that there would clearly be none of the Bohemian music he had hoped to hear; but he would at least have thought there might be something akin to punk rock, which by now would have been more suited to his mood anyway; and to be forced into dancing to the lineup, which had been given to this party's DJ to play, was almost too revolting to manage.

However, and all the more upsettingly, he did have a great deal more than the dance music in mind. He had sidled his way toward his girlfriend, inescapably aware that he was the only punk rocker there, and had gradually ingratiated himself between her and the other guy. She had grudgingly inclined her movements toward him, inasmuch as this form of dancing involved couples only in the loosest of terms. When she finally looked at him, there was a sort of wildness in her eyes, which he had instantly taken to be anger, startled when she suddenly grabbed him and began pivoting roughly against him, spinning around and cutting loose in a fiery display of seductive, suggestive movements. Dumbstruck, he had readily responded to her unexpected, captivating attention, partly because he assumed that this was her typically over-the-top way of saying, "You're on," signifying that she was ready to make her impression on the crowd, and partly because he found that all at once, he genuinely, desperately, wanted to please her, to be worthy of her, to make her proud of him, not only as a showpiece but also as a partner. Partly also, he was forced to admit, because the other guy was watching them.

Hence, the Stud Stomper and his girl had danced, taking up twice as much space as the other couples, definitely the center of attention, Chris's contributions becoming wilder and more extroverted as he felt himself slipping into his element.

Incredibly, even the music was helping, the song having been one of those modern varieties that attempts to incorporate older, traditional qualities into a newer, sleeker format, usually failing but, if nothing else, at least conveying a semblance of the bygone style.

He had actually begun taking liberties with her, grasping her and flinging her around in an almost violent way, these motions gratified by her encouragement of them, her own movements becoming more frenzied and feverish. He was shocked and thrilled by the fact that she honestly seemed supremely pleased with what he was doing; he had never felt closer to her, never so united, for once truly like a couple, a team.

This time, when one of his boots came down on her foot, her reflexes were much swifter than his; and she jerked backward to free it a full second before he had the sense to lift up his own. Her forcefulness was so intense that she tumbled over backward, her miniskirt upturning in such a way that Chris and several other dancers, including the one guy, were unable to see her underwear, because she was not wearing any.

Gawking stupidly, Chris had clambered forward to help her, Candy viciously pushing him away and using the other guy to climb back to her feet. Face to face, most definitely the center of attention, she had shoved him away from her, yanked him back to her by one of his chains, only to shove him away yet again. She had then approached him with one punishing hand uplifted; and he had stood there, prepared for the slap, as she cuffed him abusively on the side of his head, the way one might swat a dog, then pointing severely off the dance floor to the chair he had previously been occupying, the way one might command a dog. Head hanging low, Chris the Clodhopper had shuffled away, turning to gaze pitiably back at her, as she extended an index finger and stabbed downward with it, the way one might order a dog to sit.

He had done just that, hunching meekly in the chair, Candy instantly grabbing at the other guy and resuming her dancing, sending him gleefully malicious looks as her movements and, gradually, his became more intimate. Chris had sat and watched, not really having much choice, his ears burning at the sting of the laughter he had incited, cheeks searing in humiliation. Had he been sitting next to it, he would have burrowed his head into the wedding cake—one part a desire to hide his face in shame and one part self-inflicted penance for being born so clumsy, for being born so fucking stupid, for being born at all.

Three full hours later, he had still been sitting there, by which time the music was fading and the older folks were long gone. He finally had gotten up, reluctantly seeking out Candy, dreading her scorn. His footsteps took him gradually behind a gazebo; and, somehow, as he was making his way around to its far side, he already knew, for he had known all along, hadn't he? There was no secret, could be no scandal, because that was the very nature of an open relationship, right?

When he came upon them, he found them upright, and there was a flash of hope until he realized that they might just as well have been lying down. Pausing only long enough to sneer at him, Candy had informed him that she had other plans for the evening from that point onward and that he might as well go home. When there was an ongoing moment of silence, it occurred to Chris in his dazed, bloodshot perception of what he was seeing that they, the other guy much more so than Candy, were waiting for him to say something.

When he said nothing at all, just nodded slightly, he could see a rapid morphing of reaction on the guy's face, from expectancy to surprise to the slightest hint of shame to a nostril-flared, incredulous disgust and finally an unmistakable look of territorial conquest as he resumed his thrusting. They had both continued to meet his gaze, undaunted, as they flexed with each other; and it was Chris who looked away first, turning to straggle mutely off into the night.

"Kinda quiet. But um, yeah, it was pretty cool, I guess," he told the doctor impassively.

Dr. Pendleton nodded pleasantly. "Excellent, very good… Uh, Judge Talbott, you seem in good spirits. How have you been doing?"

Smiling nervously, Judge Talbott smoothed her skirt. "Oh, I've been fine. I've really been enjoying my vacation time. I went down to the courthouse yesterday and today to lend a hand to some of my colleagues, and I'll probably go back tomorrow. There are one or two big cases coming up, which will need all the help they can get."

Blinking, Dr. Pendleton frowned. "I'm sorry, you, uh…you've been going to the courthouse…now, during your vacation time?" he confirmed doubtfully.

Judge Talbott nodded. "Oh yes, they can always use extra help—the other public defenders, a lot of whom are good friends of mine. The cases they're handling are private, of course, but there's always lots of basic, material research that needs to be done. So I was lending them a hand with that," she explained congenially.

She had also been sitting in the galleries of some of the court-rooms, watching the other judges preside, finding herself spellbound with how swiftly and smoothly they operated.

They were very much like her television judges, as were their courtrooms; there were abusive spouses, hit-and-run victims, teen-aged mothers, recovering alcoholics, shoplifters, transients, weeping parents, angry merchants, and stoic police officers—the real-life drama was all there to be seen, and the judges were all so strong, so incredibly strong to be able to wade through it all and make insight-ful, decisive rulings. Her own robe and gavel were only a few corri-dors away, but she could not imagine donning them and, stepping in for any of these judges, could not see herself doing what they did. Yet this was what was expected of her, and in a few weeks' time, she would have to take her place at the bench.

That meant that she had only those few weeks to get whatever she could out of attending these meetings. She smiled shyly at the other members, hoping that they would not let her down.

Clearing his throat, Dr. Pendleton considered her explanation, nodding slowly. It might just do the woman some good to stay some-what immersed in the legal system, especially with regard to what she had told them so far about her career as a judge.

"Uh, good, Judge Talbott," he told her encouragingly. "That's clearly a good usage of your time—it illustrates your devotion to the legal system, in general..." He paused. "And how about you, Mr. Crimpton?"

Air Traffic Controllers. Everyone was always going on and on about how stressful, how nerve-wracking, it was to be an air traffic controller. Mr. Crimpton grit his teeth. Sure, maybe it was a tough job, but at least, they got to sit in a nice, air-conditioned tower. It wasn't like they were actually up there in the clouds, riding shotgun in one of those jumbo jets, now was it?

It changed the whole scenario when you had to be stuck right there in the death trap, hurtling toward oblivion with a clipboard in one hand. He rubbed his forehead, wishing he had bought a second package of aspirin, having emptied his previous one back at the acci-dent scene. He sneered; it had taken him nearly ten minutes to pry open that damned little tin box; he was in worse shape by the time he had forced its lid open, the castanet rattle of the pills tap-dancing tauntingly on his shrieking synapses.

"Uh, Mr. Crimpton?" Dr. Pendleton repeated hesitantly.

He rubbed his quivering hands together, inhaling tautly. When he was in high school, he had partaken of marijuana a few times, having never had the stomach for alcohol. He had been impressed, even a bit frightened, by its incredible potency; but he definitely recalled its calming, soothing properties. Although he had no idea how to begin to get a hold of any of that stuff now, if he had any, he would not hesitate to use it. He glanced past the judge at Chris, wondering fleetingly if he…no. No, whatever that kid was on would most likely push him over the edge.

"Uh, Mr. Crimpton?" called Dr. Pendleton, waving uncertainly.

"Yes?" he asked sharply, causing the doctor to start slightly himself.

"Er, I was, uh, asking how you were doing," Dr. Pendleton stammered.

Mr. Crimpton stared at him in consternation, very tempted to answer his question honestly. He hoped to God that this retreat thing would help him to relax; he had his doubts about going anywhere with this bunch; but at this point, he was willing to try anything, even spending a weekend with these nuts. He sat up in his chair, exhaling as steadily as he could, glancing wearily at the others and then back at the doctor.

"Oh, fine, thanks…just…more of the same…"

Nodding and smiling belatedly, Dr. Pendleton gladly moved onward. "Uh, Mr. McClintock, how have you been doing?" he asked invitingly. "Did you have a pleasant weekend?"

Mr. McClintock did not hear him, as he was internally listening, once again, to an exchange that had taken place earlier that day and that had been reverberating in his mind ever since.

It had finally happened, just as he had feared. When he had reported to work on Monday, he had kept his ears open and moved about discreetly, in case there should be any problem regarding his latest column. When Monday had passed quietly into Tuesday and all was still calm, he had actually begun to relax, contemplating that the serendipity of the column had apparently been a success after all.

Hence, he was taken thoroughly off guard when Mr. Moynihan had caught up with him in his office, of all places, bursting into the room during the lunch hour, a copy of the Sunday edition in one hand, his face set in a virulence that corrupted into a Mardi-Gras-mask leer of discovery when he beheld Mr. McClintock sitting at his desk, happily eating from the bucket of KFC.

"*Ah!*" he had exhaled in acidic pleasure. "There he is, that tireless champion of epicurean sophistication, our very own topflight cordon bleu gourmand—and busily at work, no less! Subjecting his oh-so-discerning palette to today's specialty! Ah, extra crispy, under-glass, always a favorite!"

Swallowing slowly, Mr. McClintock had regarded his editor speechlessly, the rumbling of his stomach countered with a growing uneasiness.

Unfolding the newspaper with the sharp thrust that an undertaker might use with a funeral shroud, Mr. Moynihan turned his almost crazed smile toward a particular section, reading aloud from Mr. McClintock's column.

"'For these reasons, while the aforementioned restaurants are noteworthy'—ah, 'noteworthy,' such *high* praise—'my personal recommendation for this week is the Enlisted Personnel Commissary at Fort Naughattuck Marine Corps Base?'"

Mr. McClintock swallowed again, dabbing at his spotless lips with a napkin. "Uh, yes, well, you see, I was—"

"A *Marine Corps Commissary?*" Mr. Moynihan shrieked, dashing the newspaper into a waste paper can, Mr. McClintock gasping in shock as the smaller man turned to face him, his livid features flushing into a dangerous hue. "A *mess hall?* You give honorable mention to five-star restaurants and then recommend fine-dining in a jarhead cafeteria, *are you out of your goddamned mind?*"

"Well, the atmosphere was a bit stark, I'll concede," Mr. McClintock began to recount earnestly. "But the soldiers were all quite cordial, and there was an overall...bonhomme to the ambiance, a sort of warm camaraderie—"

215

"*A bonhomme to the ambiance?*" Mr. Moynihan screeched, his sheering voice like dagger strokes in the confines of the little office. "Oh well, now, I guess I hadn't considered that! I guess I overlooked the potential of a government-issue slop house as an establishment of such culinary promise! Why, it could be fun for the whole family! Hey, honey, let's get the kids, hop into the old station wagon, and drive on down to Paris Island for some top-notch grub dished up with leatherneck pride! Not to mention how conducive a mess hall would be to a romantic dinner for two! What better way to say 'I love you' than over a candlelit dinner of MREs and canned spam?"

Mr. McClintock had cleared his throat uncomfortably, lightly encircling the bucket of fried chicken with his plump hands. "Well, naturally, the food, itself, is of course the principal issue," he had stated basically. "For instance, I found that the chipped beef on toast was exceptionally well-rendered—"

"Chipped beef on toast?" Mr. Moynihan stared at him with a murderous intensity. "Chipped beef on toast? Could you, by any chance, be referring to that time-honored entree joyously renowned as *shit on a shingle?*" He pounded the desk with both fists, Mr. McClintock jumping, several pieces of chicken pivoting above the bucket.

"Why not extend your reviews to an ongoing sampling of high school cafeterias, McClintock?" Mr. Moynihan growled. "Why not visit the nearest penitentiary? I hear their metal trays come from the same government contractors as the Gyrenes', and SOS is always on the menu! What's next on your incredibly refined list of upscale eats, the local Automat? Better yet, why not start here in our own break room? You can review all of our vending machines! Lorna Doone, Fritos, and a Coke, the new Food of the Gods!"

Mr. McClintock opened his mouth to respond, unable to think of what he should say, his mouth then grimacing closed as Mr. Moynihan plunged ahead.

"I hope you enjoyed that scrumptious little repast, McClintock, because your last review was just that!" the enraged editor grated, the drop in volume by no means diminishing the vehemence, particularly when this previous statement was considered. Mr. McClintock blinked momentarily, then inhaling sharply, his eyes widening at the implications, Mr. Moynihan nodding in confirmation. "That's right, McClintock. It's over. We've got to face facts, and the fact is that you are too damned fat to say no to anything anyone serves you!"

"But, Mr. Moynihan," he had protested desperately, his mind flooding with excuses, all of which he fleetingly considered and then dismissed, instead going for the basic, simple truth. "Fundamentally speaking... Good food is good food..."

Mr. Moynihan smiled and nodded tautly. "Good food is good food, eh? Good food is good food?" His face then metamorphosed into a deranged convulsion of almost bloodthirsty ferocity. "You have all the taste and refinement of an industrial garbage disposal!" he screamed. "You're fired, do ya' read me, Per-cee-val? *Fired!* You've eaten your last meal, and now, the axe must fall! I don't care if you go off on a cross-country tour of greasy spoons and truck stops or if you take a sabbatical and write a book on Gourmet Dumpster Diving, but as far as this newspaper is concerned, your meal ticket is hereby revoked! You're either going to have to find some other gravy train or else remember your way back to the elephant's graveyard, because it's time to clean out your desk, *if possible*, without eating it! Ya get me, *Mr.* McClintock, paragon of fine dining. It's time for you to say grace, because *this—*"

He grabbed the bucket of chicken away from the mortified food reviewer and dropped it neatly into the waste paper can. "Has been your Last Supper! Bon appétit!" He pinged a flower vase atop a filing cabinet with one finger and then lifted his hand to signal an imaginary waiter. "Check, please!"

The door slamming in his ears, Mr. McClintock had sat there in stunned silence for almost an hour before rising—putting his jacket back on—and quietly leaving his office for the very last time, meekly returning a moment later to retrieve the cold chicken.

The rest of it, he had left, his office having only been a small, token part of the job, the essence of the position having been the conversion of an alcove, a booth, or even a counter stool into his actual office, in which his real work was undertaken.

"Uh, Mr. McClintock?" Dr. Pendleton repeated.

Feeling Vanessa gently elbow him, he glanced at her and then up at the doctor. "Oh yes, ah, my weekend?" he asked, smiling weakly. "Uh, it was fine, yes." This was true; he had sampled a newly opened Chinese buffet on Saturday and had liked it so much that he had returned on Sunday.

"Excellent, very good," Dr. Pendleton nodded, his expression then brightening as he moved on to Vanessa, not only because the girl was obviously in a very buoyant frame of mind but also owing to what she had told him when they had parted company on Friday. He had sat there in shock until a massive moving van nearly rear-ended him, its blaring horn jarring him back into focus.

As he regarded her now, he felt a surge of pride, even if he could not really discern for what reason. If what she had so abruptly told him was true, and he was fairly sure that it was, then he could not credit her group participation for any sort of decision to change careers, because the career in question had not been a real one in the first place.

He supposed that he was simply pleased that she had felt comfortable—and trusting enough—to confide in him. That could, in turn, be attributed to her time with the group, and that felt good. There was, of course, the lingering question of why, if she was not, in fact, embroiled in such a seamy lifestyle, she felt the need to attend their meetings; but he was certain that whatever her reasons might be, she would no doubt share them before long. "Uh, Vanessa, how about you?" he asked conversationally. "Did you have a nice weekend?"

Vanessa grinned back at him, the answer to his question obvious, although she was not going to answer it completely, not until she knew for certain. "Ya can't win" could also be translated as "Don't jinx it before it has the chance to happen," and she knew better than to do that. As high as her hopes were, there was no way she was going to blow it. Keeping it to herself was easy, what was more, because just the thought, the very idea of telling the group with certainty, concrete, real-deal certainty, no second-guessing, no last-minute letdowns, was enough of a stomach-tingling thrill of anticipation to induce her to keep it to herself. She could envision their reaction, knowing that, unlike *any* group of people in her past, they would be genuinely proud of her, their excitement, enthusiasm, and praise would be for real; and she could scarcely wait to be overwhelmed by it, because, for all the misery that this city had heaped on the disaster that was already her life, she honestly felt that she deserved such recognition.

Hence, she decided to keep it to herself, savoring the suspense, the tantalizing rush of expectancy.

"Oh, it was okay," she told him, trying not to laugh at the ridiculousness of such an understatement, grinning and chomping her gum, kicking her legs spastically. She saw Chris steal a forlorn look over at her, and she jerked her chin back at him, smiling, wondering what his problem was when he looked glumly away, Dr. Pendleton distracting her with his very undistracting, bland platitudes.

"Uh, well, good. That's good to hear," he replied, surprised at the brevity of her response, merely nodding, not wanting to rush her if she was only just beginning to feel secure with them. He cleared his throat and maintained his smile as he hesitantly focused upon Father Gilchrist. "And, uh, how about you, Father Gilchrist?" he inquired pleasantly.

Father Gilchrist was staring intently at the wall, his features less angry now, simply pensive and very tired. He had been unable to banish the tenuous, scrawny voice of that little urchin from his thoughts, the verse of that ignorant nursery rhyme rebounding in his mind. Why hadn't that young imbecile taken the confession today? He knew how much Father Gilchrist hated it. What kind of replacement was he going to make? A more important question would be, *who cared?*

His lips twisted as he reflected on his time in the oppressive little box. That was the whole reason behind his having bought a watch with a luminous dial; he was not about to spend one second longer than was necessary in that earthbound oaken purgatory.

The more one sat in that thing, alone, in the dark, in the silence, the more one was left to their own thoughts, their own flaws and demons. The only respite was no respite at all, when some miscreant blundered inside, interrupting the unwelcome introspect by droning, ad nauseam, about their humdrum lives, confessing their misdeeds, and expecting forgiveness. A priest would be able to relate to anyone who had ever been trapped in an elevator or stuck at the top of a Ferris wheel.

Two minutes, two blasted minutes, to go until he was home free and then, lo and behold, he heard that infernal door creak open and had to stifle a curse. Not even able to fidget or kick as an outlet for his anger, he had listened to the usual opener and had then growled an encouragement to hear the rest.

It was a new voice; he knew that much from the start, having developed an ear. It wasn't the Stutterer; now, there was a personal favorite—a half hour, guaranteed. It wasn't the Bronx Squawker, who could just as discreetly have confessed from out in the street. It wasn't the Pause-and-Hum, with the drumming fingers; he had actually banged a fist on his side of the partition once with that guy.

It wasn't the Drive-Thru Confessor, who had her beads out and going even while she was confessing, as if to get a jump-start on her penance so she could go out and sin again without too much inconvenience, nor was it the Playboy, an adenoidal athletic oaf who left the confessional reeking of sweat and testosterone.

No, this was a new voice, a man's, younger; it was, nonetheless, familiar, but unplacable. He caught a glimpse of something dully shiny through the screen, but gave it little thought, because, again, who cared?

Nevertheless, as he sat there listening to the voice, he found himself actually listening to it, his scowl abstractly changing into a frown.

Spousal abuse? He had heard it before, of course, all too often. Usually, it was minor and tearful, and just the one time, little consolation that that was. But three times? What kind of cretin was this? Two minutes before closing, and *this* had to show up, to *him*?

Yes, yes, of course, it was an accident; naturally, it had never happened before and certainly would never happen again—three times later—and he hadn't meant to do it, had been under so much stress lately, had been in a bad frame of mind, and at least the kids, (kids?) hadn't been watching, in fact, he had made sure they were in the other room—since when can you preplan an "accident"? He was very sorry and admitted that he was wrong, and you know what was really great, she forgave him.

She forgave you, eh? Well, Father Gilchrist isn't going to forgive you, you little swine. True, he had controlled his outrage and leveled his tone and volume as he prescribed a penance and strongly urged counseling and all that crap. In the end, he was simply glad when the man left the box, finding that his departure did nothing to ease the stifling, stagnant, rampant disgust with which he had been inundated, a loathsome poignancy that had originated within himself, but was being directed right back at himself. Perhaps, it was a reaction to the utter powerlessness that he always felt when he let someone slip away red-handed. Yet there was nothing else he could possibly do. Bound by secrecy, the only priests who took the law into their own hands were the ones who broke it.

Over the years, he had been tempted to go to the police, many times. He never had, and today could be no different—but if ever he had come closer… The walk to the sacristy in the open air of the church had been no less suffocating, nor was his mood much improved when he found the key missing. *The key.* Once, the key to every lock in the church had been kept on his person, but now, they needed to be available. Oh yes, everyone needed access, starting with Father Ralph. (*Father Ralph!*) *Oh, by the by, lad, could I trouble you to ask if, by some chance, you've seen the— Oh? Sister Angelica has it? Splendid! How abundantly, beauticiously splendid!*

Off to next door, into the dreaded hospital. At least he only had to endure its stink down one hallway and into the nursery, and there she was, Julie Andrews, herself, her ubiquitous guitar in hand. If ever, *ever*, he were to hear this pop-art Pollyanna and her brood of squawling imps, Michael would no doubt keep right on rowing, posthaste.

Today, however, the guitar was poised, but silent, Sister Angelica transfixed as the clever little brat recited that damnable nursery rhyme. His blood had run cold as he heard it, easily for the first time in sixty years, the blasted thing. What was she doing, anyway, having them read *Mother Goose*? Why not pass around the Wall Street Journal and Hustler and just be done with it?

When that tiny, patchy voice had finished its hinge-like recitation, there had been a clatter of applause, one aspect of it ploddingly louder than that of the small, grubby hands; and even while Father Gilchrist stood there in stunned silence, thinking that no other voice could possibly render him so speechless, another voice, *that* voice, did.

His larger hands clapping, he stepped forward from one corner of the room, cheering loudly and then picking up, of all the little gnomes in that place, that exact, self-same babe, cuddling it affectionately and thanking Sister Angelica, who chattered blithely, obliviously in response, patting the child on the head.

It was him; the voice was his, as were the confessions. The shiny glint he had seen through the screen had been a badge; and as the young policeman, at best, a rookie, carried his kid out of the nursery, he had met Father Gilchrist's gaze, grinning and nodding unseeingly, not a second thought, not a blink as he passed him, jostling him slightly with one shoulder.

Not a second thought, not a blink. Free of sin, and on the go. He had stood as if immovable from the spot, staring into dead air, Sister Angelica addressing him cheerfully, then politely, and then with concern; he heard her, but was much too intent upon the spectacle he had just witnessed…just experienced. She had been insistent though, and he had, by God, let her have it. "*What?*"

Dr. Pendleton shrank backward, almost knocking over his crate, Chris sitting bolt upright in his seat. Judge Talbott and Mr. Crimpton both gasped, Vanessa's eyes widened, and even Mr. McClintock's ruminations penetrated with a jolt.

Swallowing harshly, Dr. Pendleton actually wished he had a cup of Mrs. Spindlewood's coffee to gulp, even though it probably would have been spilled just now.

"Uh, I was asking how your weekend went," he repeated shakily.

Father Gilchrist stared at him and then through him, his thoughts immediately slipping back to that episode.

So how do you like that? If you snap, if you give into your own logic, your own decency and actually call the police, the cop you get might just be the guy you're trying to turn in—What a beautifully paradoxical joke. Why, it was a laugh riot. When he wasn't at home, beating on the missus, he was out and about with a badge to serve and protect. To serve and protect. Kind of like a priest, right, except with more stopping power. *By God*, what could he have been, twenty-two, twenty-three? How old could *she* possibly be then? And she forgave him! In this day and age when women were finally starting to realize that they could fight back, she forgave him.

She forgave him, and, for that matter, for all intents and purposes, so had he. He felt his chest swell painfully and his cheeks billowed as he exhaled in a muffled, strangled ghost of a whimper. So had he.

He swallowed the outcry and half of his face with it as he focused instead on his rage. Maybe he had given him the green light of absolution, but just let that little bastard set foot in his confessional again with such a tale of woe. He'd unleash the fire and brimstone like a punishing volcano. He'd flay that punk with a razor-sharp invective, the likes of which no priest had ever before uttered. By the time he was finished, that rookie would be damned glad that he was armed during that session, grinning little cock-swinging prick; there would be a puddle left on the seat of that confessional when all was said and done.

But then, that was just it; it all was brought into the little box, and it all had to stay in the little box, and although he would recognize that voice forever more and while it was for damn sure that that little swine would remember his voice on into the afterlife, that would be the extent of it.

There could be no overt acknowledgement, no carryover, no knowing interaction, and no justice. That rookie—rookie, what kind of cop could the boy possibly make—would know that he had the law on his side and was thus quite safe. Talk about a double standard, and it was the standard that he, as a priest, was forced to wave; and, well now, that was pretty typically standard, wasn't it?

Hence, if they encountered one another in that repellant nursery again, he knew what he could expect, knew the type. Grins all around, handshake, and how do you do, a blissful ignorance of the unspeakable because of the inability to speak of it. Oh yes, he knew the two-faced type. Why, with qualities like those, surely he would be their next chief.

And what could he, in turn, expect from the priest? What he damn well knew he could expect, quid pro quo, of course. With his hands tied and his mouth gagged, Father Gilchrist, in the glowing presence of Sister Angelica, would be obliged to paste on his biggest, brightest, prettiest smile, with Mr. Potato Head perfection.

He sneered venomously; those idiot Beatles had it wrong. It was not Eleanor Rigby, but Father Mackenzie who wore a face kept in a glass by the door. How he had hated that song when it was first unleashed, and how he had grown to despise it, all these years later, now that it was finally coming true. He wondered mirthlessly who then, within his sphere, would be personified by the woman character in the song—certainly not Sister Angelica. If the Trying Nun ever heard the sound of *that* music, she would no doubt think it was a happy little ditty suitable for her pint-sized troubadours. And now, on top of that asinine song, he had that infernal nursery rhyme likewise contaminating his already poisoned thoughts about that hypocritical little son-of-a—

"Father Gilchrist?" Dr. Pendleton repeated, a trace of alarm sounding in his voice. Had the aged priest finally worked himself up into a vinegar-induced stroke? To judge by the shriveling contortions of his face, he looked as though he had suddenly been possessed. He blinked in a millisecond of paradoxical uncertainty. Who did you call when a priest became possessed?

Father Gilchrist blinked, frowning as he sat up a bit, inhaling sharply, becoming aware that everyone was staring at him in concern. Harrumphing, he swallowed and started to apologize. Apologize? *Ha*!

"What was that you said?" he asked gruffly, every bit back in control.

Dr. Pendleton glanced briefly at the others and then slowly continued. "Uh… I was asking, uh, how your weekend was…," he reiterated; it seemed like such an inane question now.

"My weekend?" snarled the old priest. Yes, yes, perhaps it was. "My weekend was lousy, as per usual," he replied concisely, folding his arms crossly.

Shrinking, Dr. Pendleton rubbed his hands together. "Oh, I... I'm sorry to hear that," he offered, reluctantly adding. "Uh, what was so, uh, lousy about it?"

Father Gilchrist positively glowered. "Its existence," he growled, then gesturing dismissively. "Don't waste your ministrations on me, please. Why don't you ask Mrs. Spindlewood how she enjoyed her weekend instead?"

Dr. Pendleton blinked. "But... Mrs. Spindlewood isn't here."

The irate priest scowled. "Well, what difference does that make?" he countered archly. "She was never here in the first place. I'm sure that wherever she is right now, she isn't even there, so it scarcely matters. In fact, I wish I could join her."

Grimacing, Dr. Pendleton thought of a retort he could make, but which, of course, he could not make—did not dare. Instead, he found himself glancing briefly at Mrs. Spindlewood's chair, then grimacing all over again, sighing, and turning to address the group, discovering that he had no idea as to what to say.

*****

Ultimately, the meeting was rather quiet, the doctor eventually focusing more and more upon their upcoming retreat, sharing a few anecdotes about his experiences there as a kid, to which the members responded with polite interest. He was able to sense their own detachment and eventually offered to close early if they wished, anxiously making certain that they were all still interested in having a retreat, gratified by their immediate reassurance. Much relieved, he reminded them that they did still have one more session before their weekend together and that he hoped he could count on seeing them there.

The meeting had dispersed, Father Gilchrist the first one out the door, Mr. Crimpton right behind, shakily igniting a cigarette before he had even gotten outside. Judge Talbott bade everyone good night, Mr. McClintock slowly ambling away, dwelling on the irony that he had also lost his appetite that day, although he did take his s'more with him.

Vanessa had started on a new wad of gum as she sat watching everyone leave, her gaze inevitably settling on Chris.

She observed him as he pulled himself to his feet, slunk over to the side table and squatted down to shove something into his backpack, her eyes darting to the crescent of pink skin that showed between the bottom of his T-shirt and the waistband of his underwear. *Boxers*, she confirmed triumphantly. *I knew it.* She then scoffed at herself for staring. He already had a girlfriend; and, much more to the point, the last, the absolutely last thing she needed right now was an attraction, much less a full-on crush, especially on such a dorky, punk-ass, ass-backward dufus like him.

What she did need, she was finally ready and willing to admit to herself, was a friend, boy or girl. She did not know one other kid in this city, aside from him; and, beyond that, exasperating as he was, she actually had started to like him. He probably had a whole circle of punk-ass retard friends, but there was no harm in trying, was there? Who knew, maybe his girlfriend was cool.

She waited until he had said good night to Dr. Pendleton and came straggling toward the door before calling out to him, pondering again what could have gotten him so down and then realizing that this was a perfect way to open up a conversation with him.

"Hey, Clod, come here a sec," she waved, grimacing a bit at his look of wariness as he hesitated and then moved toward her. When he simply stood there alongside her, uncertainly gripping his skateboard, she had sat up and pushed a chair out for him, wondering if she was going to have to do everything for him, pausing and then telling him to sit down, more or less confirming the thought with a hint of impatience. He did so, gaping at her silently.

She stared back at him for a fraction of a second, confused, almost mystified over what was up with this kid, thinking that it was entirely possibly that she had misjudged him.

"Look, um, Chris," she began, some of her own confidence fading as she pushed on anyway. "I dunno... I was just wondering what was wrong. You seem really...sad today."

Chris blinked at her, oddly enough seeming to relax a bit. "Oh, nuthin," he murmured quietly, looking at the floor. "I just...my weekend kinda sucked."

Vanessa considered this, then switching to her usual directness. "You doing anything tomorrow?" she asked him bluntly.

Lifting his gaze again, Chris blankly thought about the question. "Um, no."

"Good," she replied swiftly, sitting up in her chair. "You wanna get together and do something? Take a walk, grab some coffee, I dunno, just sit and talk, whatever...just as friends," she added as a casual disclaimer.

She watched, surprised as his expression seemed to brighten. He shifted in his chair, regarding her earnestly through the drooping fringe of his Mohawk. "Yeah?" he seemed to ask in response, blushing and then swallowing. "Yeah, um, that'd be great..." He paused, biting his lip. "Do you want to?"

Vanessa felt herself smile and frown simultaneously. Did she want to? It was her idea, wasn't it? Curbing any sarcasm, she merely nodded. "Yeah, definitely." She chomped her gum and gave him a puzzled smile.

*****

It had occurred to Dr. Pendleton that he might have the opportunity to discuss Vanessa's disclosure during their ride to the hotel, but she had automatically turned on the radio, chuckling lightly when she once more adjusted the tuner away from the easy-listening station to something newer, bolder, and much louder. At first, he had been a bit uneasy, thinking that something was bothering her, inasmuch as that was something that kids did when they were upset and unwilling to talk.

One glance at her, though, and he could see that she was, instead, in an even more uplifted mood, her window lowered, hair blowing, a grin on her face. Her spirits helped to elevate his own, for he had been on the verge of second-guessing the evening's meeting. A good deal of the members had seemed so out of sorts. Then again, that was how some of them usually were; that was why they attended after all. Besides, the retreat would definitely help to put all of them in a good frame of mind, he reflected confidently. Nonetheless, it was perplexing; over half of tonight's box of doughnuts had gone untouched.

Chapter 8

THEY MET JUST AFTER NOON the next day, in front of the union hall, the only common ground they knew. It seemed strange to see it in the daytime, as it was to see each other in such an unfamiliar setting. Apart from that, though, the awkwardness that they had both anticipated was rapidly dissolved.

There was a brief moment of uneasiness when, after exchanging greetings, they had stood there uncertainly looking at each other, Vanessa waiting for him to take the lead as she knew nothing of this area and then realizing that he was either expecting her to do the same or at least to tell him to lead the way. It was odd for someone who looked as fierce and domineering as he did in general to behave so submissively, not that she could not see past his getup; but he was a boy, after all; and so damn many of them insisted on being cock of the walk. Still, she was beginning to see that he was accustomed to being the follower; and so, why not, she had no compunctions about seizing the initiative; after all, that was *her* way.

Once she had given him a few hints, he had responded instantly, and they went to a coffee shop a few blocks away, where they both bought sodas, next walking to a nearby park and wandering along its pathway for a while before settling down on a battle-scarred bench facing a deserted playground.

Their conversation was light, but steady; they discussed everything save for her occupation, his girlfriend, and the anonymous group, the three topics that, of course, were foremost on their minds. Nonetheless, their exchanges were sincere and outgoing, and trivial as the subjects might have been, the interaction was enjoyable and engaging, carrying with it the promise of greater depth as common traits and experiences and feelings were discovered, be it a favorite song, an infamous teacher, a morbid fear, or an avowed devotion.

They spoke more freely, leaving the bench for an empty swing set, where they at first gave into the childlike urge to soar and then gradually permitted gravity to slow them until they sat dangling, side by side, slackly gripping the thick chains, alternately talking and falling into modes of dreamy silence, staring at the listlessly stirring leaves that clustered around the roots of the nearby trees, eventually blown against an adjacent chain-link fence.

In time, a school adjoining the park let out, and the playground began to fill with small children, who, far from being daunted by the presence of two such unlikely playmates in their midst, either regarded them with resentment or ignored them altogether, the discordant shriek of their voices finally making conversation impossible.

Vanessa stood up, suggesting they move on, Chris agreeing and then suddenly taking flight again, kicking his long legs sharply, going as high as the swing set would allow them to go and then, as the kids watched in awe, no less so Vanessa, launching himself off its forward thrust and sailing recklessly to the ground, his thick boots slamming into the grass as he ran jarringly ahead a few paces, slowing his momentum and turning back to grin at Vanessa, then slipping on a wet patch and going down in a pile of leaves.

Embarrassed, especially with all of the kids laughing at him, he had blushed up at her as she came running after him, likewise laughing, though not unkindly, for, in fact, she was rather impressed; it was a very punk rock thing to do. Pulling himself to his feet, shaking off the leaves, he had laughed too; and they had left the park, caught up in the autumn breeze, their faces flushed and glowing, their steps light; it had not mattered that they had no place in particular in mind to go.

They walked a bit more; and since they were in his neighborhood at this point and would not be bothering his family as they were all out for the day, they ended up at his apartment, up in his room, Vanessa bursting with excitement and gratitude because it had been so long since she had been in another kid's room—that special private domain where they could just sit, hang out, and chill.

Chris was excited too in that, for the most part, it had been an equally long time since he had done the same, particularly here in *his* room, the special sanctuary that was still the center of his world. Candy did not really count, and he didn't have many other friends to speak of.

He had thought again of Vanessa's unhesitant usage of the word the previous day, still taken aback by it, and by the fact that he had been so surprised by it. Had it really been that long since he had known the thrill of making a new friend? He would have thought that the loneliness he had lived with these past few years would have never let him forget what he was missing, as it was a constant reminder. Just the same, though, to judge by the contrast of what he was feeling now, he was genuinely dumbfounded by this strange but obviously very special change of fortune. Perhaps, it was simply that he could not believe that anyone would actually want to penetrate his solitude, particularly Vanessa, whom he had been certain did not like him at all.

They had continued to talk about trivialities, Vanessa repeatedly surprised by the shyness that he effaced and, even more so, the almost constant, puppylike meekness he displayed. Even when he was speaking about something with earnest animation, when the topic shifted, he would retreat again until, it seemed, she gave him the go-ahead by coaxing him out once more.

Perplexed by it, while it was no longer irritating, but in fact was becoming rather endearing, she was all the more curious about it and began to glance around his room for any hints, surprised that she had not set about doing so the instant she was inside of it, for she had daydreamed about being invited to it, wondering what it would be like. It was messy, of course, but was not the total pigpen that she had expected. Her gaze took in some of the old memorabilia on the walls and shelves, most of it contrasting with the punk rock posters and typical adolescent decor, although in some bizarre and imbalanced way, it all seemed to work, to make sense, all jumbled together.

How or why, she could not guess, she had reflected flippantly, because anyone would be stumped by the almost schizophrenic combination. There could be only one common denominator, though, only one key to the puzzle, and she confronted him then.

"So, Clod… Chris… Clod… Clod*hopper*," she addressed him with a crooked smile, leaning back on his bed, arms thrust casually behind her. "What's the deal? I mean you got the clothes, the studs, chains, and spikes. You got the Mohawk and the combat boots. You got at least one piercing—that I can see, anyway—but I mean I don't get it. We both know that you're not really a punk rocker."

Chris, having been following her outline uncertainly, then blushed, his jawline tightening as he fingered the single gold earring in his right ear. "Yes, I am," he told her quietly, somehow managing to meet her eyes.

"But you're not," she insisted, not unkindly but with emphasis. "I mean it doesn't really matter to me. But, in all honesty, I mean come on, you know you're not."

"What makes you so sure?" he asked her evenly, the slightest defiance in his voice.

She laughed shortly, pushing herself backward until she was resting against the wall, her legs outstretched in front of her. "What makes me so sure?" she repeated confidently. "Well, I mean look at you. You're shy. You're nice. You look like you shower every day. You smell pretty good. You're not drunk off your ass, breaking bottles or crashing parties. You don't look like you do drugs. You're still living at home with your parents. You don't have any gang tats. So I *don't* think you're running with anyone. I mean you may ride a skateboard and listen to a few punk groups and make a mess when you eat and maybe you don't look like one of those made-to-order punks from some do-it-yourself store in the mall. But God, Chris, you're too damned nice and shy to be a punk rocker—I've never even heard you cuss before!" She shook her head, smiling one-sidedly. "I'm sorry, but I just don't see punk rocker comin' from you."

There was a silence in the room as she watched the near-quarter profile of his face, Chris still sitting hunched on the edge of his bed, eyes cast downward. For an uneasy moment, she thought he was angry and was going to ask her to leave, but he only sat there quietly, before turning and regarding her solemnly.

"Yeah, but who says you gotta be all those things to be a punk rocker?" he asked.

Vanessa met his eyes, then blinking as she considered this. Who did, in fact, make up the rules? A few responses occurred to her, but seemed insubstantial in light of whatever he might be about to tell her, and she dismissed them, instead replying, "What do you mean?"

Swallowing, Chris turned more toward her. "I mean why does it have to be that way?" he asked, blushing but determined. "How come someone can't dress the way they want to and be the way that feels the most…right to them without having to fit into some pattern or something? Why does it have to be a certain way?"

Her brows lifting, Vanessa felt her smile return, as she burst into laughter again. "Look, Chris, honey, I got no problem with someone expressing themselves and being themselves," she told him emphatically. "I'm all about 'be yourself' and fuck the trends and fashions and conformity, hell yeah, don't get me wrong. All I'm saying is that if…if you choose to be a punk rocker, then…there's just a lot of stuff that usually goes along with it, okay, and it's stuff that I just don't see in you." She shrugged loosely, not wanting to upset him, but unable to drop it.

To her surprise, Chris was nodding rapidly as she spoke, a glimmer of confidence beginning to surface, maybe because they were on his turf or maybe because of how strongly he felt about this subject. "Yeah, but what if you don't choose it?" he asked her pointedly.

When she made no reply, only stared at him in confusion, but more so in wonder, he swallowed and, clenching his jaw, continued with a growing intensity. "What if it chooses you?" he worked up the nerve to pose. "What if you woke up one day and shaved your hair into a Mohawk because something was pushing you to do it. And when you looked in the mirror, you didn't scream but instead just stared at yourself and tried to figure out why it felt so natural, so real, why the wildness and craziness of it just felt so…right? Next thing you know, you dye it some insane color and start wearing old ripped clothes and dog collars and padlocks and boots."

Cheeks burning now, he continued anyway, the words tumbling out of his mouth, as if, perhaps, for the first time. "That's what happened about a year ago. It wasn't a fad or a phase or any of the crap people would call it. Everyone made fun of me. My parents were pissed off. Everyone kept telling me how stupid I looked and how wrong it was and how I should just grow up and get over it. But the more…shit people gave me, the more everyone rode me, the more right it felt, even though I knew, *I knew*, just like everyone else, how fucking weird it was. It got to the point where I started to hate it, because I didn't understand it either, but I couldn't stop, because it just…it was me."

He grimaced at how shallow his words probably sounded, sighing and looking imploringly at Vanessa. "It was like…do you know how when you're getting undressed, how each thing you take off gets you closer and closer to being…you know, naked and how even if you're alone but you're still kinda embarrassed, even then, as you're taking your clothes off, each thing you take off makes you feel more and more…natural?" He paused, biting his lip, his gaze having slipped self-consciously away, now meeting hers again. "It was like that, except the opposite. All the punk stuff I put on, each piece, each part, felt more and more natural, until I…until…this is it." He gestured at himself.

"As far as the music and the lifestyle goes…yeah, maybe I started to adopt some of the stuff," he conceded hesitantly, his features flexing earnestly. "I mean I didn't know what else to do. I figured I was supposed to do it, to make whatever…changes were happening to me complete. I'd always kinda liked all of it, from off to the side, and I'd always liked a lot of the groups. And so that made it easier, but the problem is that I like a whole bunch of other stuff too. And there's a lot of other things that also come naturally to me, things that have just as strong a hold on me as being a punk rocker does, even though they're things that are the complete opposite of that whole way of life."

He stopped, Vanessa watching in amazement as he fought to organize his thoughts. "Everyone, including myself a lot of the time, wants me to be a certain way. But other people, kind of like you were saying, they want me—expect me—to be a different way. And I've tried so hard to be one or the other, according to wherever I was or whoever I was with. And no matter what, I usually end up flat on my ass. But I started wondering why I couldn't just be both at the same time, all the time, because both ways, put together, is...is *me*. It's the way I am, and there's nothing I can do to change that, and I'm tired of trying! If I am a poser, it's not because I'm trying to be something that I'm not, but because I'm trying not to be what I am."

When he fell into another dejected silence, Vanessa hesitated and then asked quietly, "Well...okay...but why can't you be...both then?" grimacing as she realized that she, herself, had just done an about-face, Chris glancing over at her with a bewildered look, causing her to giggle. "I mean granted I get what you're saying, I think, and it's pretty intense, but...apart from the contradiction of being a nice, shy punk rocker...what exactly is the problem?"

Chris grinned loosely himself, shrugging. "Well, it's not so much that it's the main problem of my life in general," he clarified. "I mean I know that even if I was all one way or the other, I would still be a major screw-up loser. That's not going to change, because of the way I am on...both sides...or all sides or just all over... But then, being the way I am doesn't make it any easier either."

He shrugged again. "The problem with this whole punk rock side of me is mainly just with my music and dancing and the lifestyle in general. The reasons why I can't be a punk rocker *and* be this other way are all there, and they all make sense. But here I am, anyway, and the only time I feel like I'm honestly being myself is when I am being both at the same time." He sat up a bit. "And it's been that way for a long time now. No one really understands. I don't either, but I know what feels natural, and to me...that's gotta be the truth."

Frowning, Vanessa sat up as well, scooting forward to the edge of the bed, trying to make sense of what he was telling her, wanting to comprehend. "Okay, well, what do you mean?" she asked at length, sitting alongside of him once more. "What about the music and dancing? What is all of this other stuff that also comes so natural but isn't really punk? I mean what's the contradiction then?"

Smiling ruefully, Chris stared at the floor, before gazing slowly over at her. "Do you really want to know?" he responded, his smile growing in spite of his shyness.

Her mouth falling open, Vanessa exhaled in a scornful burst, actually punching him in one arm. "Yeah, I really want to know, you dummy!" she exclaimed. "I'm the one who asked, ain't I?"

Grinning, he hesitated, in spite of her encouraging look, self-consciously hedging, clearly scared of whatever he thought her reaction most likely would be to what he was about to reveal to her. Not only was Vanessa excited, but also she sensed that whatever it was, there was something very secret and sensitive about it, something private and possibly even shameful, to judge by his discomfiture.

"Please, Chris," she felt the need to tell him. "I won't laugh or make fun of you. I totally promise. We're like friends now, right? You can tell me anything."

Staring at her with his wide, trusting eyes, he nodded, reassured and about to launch into an explanation, balked, and instead seized upon an easier way to express himself. Vanessa watched intently as he reached over into the milk crate of albums, flipping through a couple and slowly withdrawing the one that would best reflect his situation.

Holding the album face down in his lap, he explained to her that while the music on the album was very special in its own right, it was actually the image depicted on the album cover that so perfectly illustrated his paradoxical, innate, fantasy come true. Her eyes locked on his, she then lowered them to the album cover as he extended it to her, instantly astounded and mystified by what she had been handed. The artist was unmistakable, the album entitled *Weird Al' Yankovik's Polka Party*. Its cover photograph consisted of the singer, himself, bearing an accordion and bedecked in traditional Bavarian garb, surrounded by a roomful of hardcore punks who appeared to be thrashing and moshing in wild, reckless, and above all appreciative abandon to this definitively unpunk music.

Her utter bewilderment straining behind her taut, accepting expression, she inhaled quietly and met his gaze once more as he also took a deep breath and plunged into his story.

She listened to him; she stared at the album cover and listened as he told her everything as best as he could about his favorite music; his preferences; his propensity to dance to the most unlikely songs;

the thrill that he got when he could cut loose to it; and the excitement at the few and incredibly rare opportunities wherein the two worlds intertwined and how, for just an instant, he could relish the fact that everything was in harmony with him and he could feel just like everyone else, like when you were watching a movie that everyone was enjoying except you, until a scene comes along and creates such a paradox; perhaps, the characters in the movie turn on their TV, and it happens to be tuned into a program that is discordantly unrelated to the movie, a program that you, however, loved or if, maybe, the characters went to a movie within their movie and it was some film that was completely out of place but that had always been a favorite of yours; as you sit and enjoy the combination of these incompatible realities, *so does the audience*; and the contradiction ceases to matter, if only for a second or two, because they actually work together; and for that one fleeting moment, you and everyone else are genuinely united in their appreciation. Of course, those occasions were flukes, at best, very rare; and he was left to keeping his desires to himself, unwilling, if not unable, to express them to a world that could not possibly accept them, leaving him with only the notion of how screwed-up he must be as a sliver of an excuse for being the way that he was.

Vanessa listened, and as she did, she saw him as if for the first time. True, none of her previous conclusions were disspelled, but she realized as she steadily met his eager, shining eyes that there was so much more to him.

When he had finished, he leaned forward, arms resting on his legs, lowering his head as if awaiting sentence. "So do you think I'm a complete freak job or what?"

She waited until he glanced over to her before balancing the album on her knees and uniting her fingers over it, sitting up slightly, almost primly.

"Yes," she told him flatly, watching as he sank a bit and then instantly continuing. "Yes, you are without a doubt, a bona fide freak job. A wild party animal punk rocker who gets off on polkas? That is some of the craziest shit I have ever heard in my life!"

She gestured broadly as he reddened and began to crumble. "Yes, you are a major league freak job, and you know what? Fuck 'em. Fuck 'em all. You're right, and they're wrong."

Jolting sharply, Chris stared over at her. "What?"

"Chris, what you just told me is so fucking amazing that it…it just blows my mind!" she proclaimed, almost becoming tongue-tied.

Chris gawked at her, baffled. "But…you just said I was a freak job!"

"You *are* a freak job, you dork!" she shrieked, shoving at his shoulder and laughing. "And so am I! I'm also a first-class bitch, but that's beside the point!" she added, slapping at his arm as if he might dare to pursue the topic. "We're all freak jobs, one way or another. Everybody is!" she declared expansively. "The only difference is that only a few of us ever have the guts to go along with it. Or some of us go with it without even knowing that we're doing it!"

She looked at his confused, trusting face and longed to reach out and touch it as she continued forcefully. "It's not a bad thing, Chris. Trust me! Look at our therapy group, for God's sake! If ever there was a classic bunch of wing nuts! And you know what makes 'em like that—you know what makes 'em so special and why I keep coming back week after week to see 'em? They're *real!* They're real, and they're themselves, and even though a lot of the talking is bull-shit, they're real people, not like most of the phony-ass fools you see everywhere else, and that's what makes them so cool!"

"Look at Dr. Pendleton," she insisted, not sure if he was getting her point, his gaping features blank but attentive. "He is so incredibly and devastatingly uncool that he's the coolest! He fucking rocks out! And you're the same way, can't you see that? You're Chris, Chris the fuckin' Clodhopper, Polka-Punk Rocker dude, and…and that… that is supremely awesome!"

Folding her arms, she sat back and peered with satisfaction at him, pleased with her dissertation, watching as he stared back at her in a dazed, almost stupefied way. She knew she had made her point and rather carelessly pushed forward, curious about something she had just remembered. "There's just one thing that I don't get," she told him, almost slyly, Chris looking at her uncertainly. "'Stud

Stomper'? What's up with that, Clod? That actually does sound kind of phony."

Chris's features shifted from being awestruck into a twisting grimace. "Oh that," he murmured, the grimace spreading into a mirthless grin. "My, um, girlfriend thought of that." He grunted depreciatively.

Vanessa sort of gasped in slow motion, clamping her mouth shut.

"Oops," she allowed a moment later, then snorting in laughter as Chris blushed and did the same. They shared in the humor of her remark for a few moments before lapsing into a comfortable silence.

"Sorry about that," she said at length, glancing once more at the album cover and then handing it back, Chris pausing to look at it, a light smile on his face.

"Don't worry about it," he told her, replacing the album, his grimace reinstated. "She made it up because she thought it sounded cool, and I just went along with it. It does sound phony, though, and I don't really like it that much."

Vanessa shrugged. "Well, what about Clodhopper then?"

Chris flushed deeply as he explained the origin of that designation, his hue deepening when she laughed approvingly.

"Yeah, well, see, at least that's real," she assured him. "I mean you are a pretty big klutz, so it does fit. But, see, it's real, and real is cool."

He shrugged and nodded. "I guess," he conceded. "It's just kind of embarrassing. That's all. I really hate being so clumsy, on top of everything else."

She waved dismissively. "There's worse things to be," she informed him flatly, then shrugging herself. "Besides, there's something about clumsiness that's definitely very punk rock."

As Chris considered this new rationale, she scanned his room again, looking for a specific photograph. Not seeing one, she decided simply to ask, curious, but seeking to sound indifferent. "So… Stud Stomper, what about this girlfriend of yours?" she asked lightly. "When do we all get to meet her? How come you haven't brought her to any of the meetings—or does she actually have it all together enough that she doesn't need to sit and rave and eat doughnuts?" She smiled playfully.

Instantly grimacing again, Chris shook his head. "She…I." He stopped, not knowing how to begin, the telephone's distant ring interrupting the effort.

"Saved by the bell," Vanessa scoffed inwardly; her uncle used to say that whether a bell sounded or not, to get out of answering any of her more serious questions.

Sighing in frustration, Chris stood up, mumbling. "I'll be right back," before tromping down the hallway. Vanessa watched him go, surprised that he did not have a phone in his room; she hadn't had one either.

She glanced around his room again, still grateful for the fact that she was actually there, enjoying just looking at all the different facets of this kid's life, contrasting them with all the preconceived notions she had developed from just staring at him at the meetings. She could admit when she was wrong, all the more readily in that what she was discovering was so strange and special. To think that she had been treating him so meanly, and all along, she could have completely lost out on the chance to share in any of this experience—could have blown it so easily.

Chris returned at that point, looking glum, his mood clearly changed. He sat back down on his bed again and blushed at her. "Um, that was her on the phone," he murmured.

Vanessa stared at him. "Who?"

Blinking, Chris stared back. "My girlfriend."

Pausing, Vanessa regarded him for a moment and then grabbed her bag, pressing it brusquely to her chest. "Oh no!" she exclaimed in mock horror. "We've been caught! What will she do to us? Oh, the scandal, the notoriety!"

Startled, Chris then laughed at her dramatics, Vanessa shrugging caustically at him. "So? Girlfriends do that sometimes, you know?"

Nodding, Chris shrugged as well. "Yeah, I guess. I dunno why, but she wants to come over in a little bit," he said wearily.

Swallowing her disappointment, Vanessa gestured openly. "Well, gee, I wonder why?" she teased him. "Could it be, maybe, because she wants to see you?"

Chris was about to answer her honestly, when Vanessa next stood up, pulling at the straps on her bag, distracting him. "Are you…do you have to go now?"

Surprised, her heart swelling at his words, Vanessa forced a stoic nod and a smile. "Well, yeah, lover boy," she responded rhetorically. "Your girlfriend's coming over, right? You two are probably going to want some private time together."

When Chris did not respond to this, in fact, seeming to be thinking it over, she shrugged once more, impressed with her acting skills, because she did not even remotely want to leave. Her show of casual apathy did prompt her to employ one more device to prolong her stay, something she had been hoping to share with him anyway. "And, anyway, I should go and get ready for tomorrow," she added logically.

Gaping up at her, Chris instantly, endearingly, took the bait. "What are you gonna do tomorrow?" he asked her.

Smiling down at him affectionately, Vanessa allowed some of her excitement into her voice. "Well, I wasn't going to tell any of you until I knew for sure," she began, shaking back her unruly hair and then raking her fingers through it, settling her gaze on Chris, her eyes shining happily "I've got to tell someone, though, because I'm just… so nervous and excited that I feel like screaming."

Chris sat up, nodding quickly. "Oh, is this why you were so excited at the meeting last night?" he asked her eagerly.

Even in her enthusiasm, Vanessa was sidetracked by the idea that he had noticed this, her insides swelling a bit more at the notion. "Yes, it was," she replied, quickly yanking open her bag and pulling out a spiral notebook, opening it to withdraw a folded-up page from a newspaper, handing it to him. "Punk rocker that you are, I'm sure you read the *Village Vice* now and then," she explained. "Well, that was in Saturday's edition of it!"

Biting his lip, Chris read over the piece of newsprint. "Casting calls for the Templeton Theater of the Performing Arts, repertory positions for the Spring Season available. Auditions to commence Thursday at nine." He glanced uncertainly up at her. "Is this…are you, like, gonna try out to be an actress?"

Vanessa sat down again, nodding energetically. "Exactly, Chris. That's why I came to this city," she told him candidly, taking the ad and gesturing with it. "I've been waiting for an opportunity just like this! It's the theater, which means it's stage acting, and even though what I really want to do is film work, it's still a start! I'm so excited, but I'm also so…Agh!" She made her hands into fists and slammed them on her knees, her hair tossing wildly before her eyes again, causing her to laugh self-depreciatively. "I…want this so much Chris, I…I can't even explain it."

Regarding her in awe, Chris could only manage a "wow," his expression enough to convey his impression, Vanessa beaming at him as she forced back her hair.

"So anyway, yeah, that's tomorrow. And so, who knows, it could be just the beginning. I'm going to try to put together some kind of head shot and maybe a few character shots, like," she paused, shoving her notebook into her bag and fishing out a pair of sunglasses. "You know, like this…"

She put them on and made a ridiculously melodramatic face, Chris laughing with her as she yanked them off and shook her head. "Yeah, right. That's what I'll look like if I get famous and turn into some rich-bitch snob, which I won't," she added, her features becoming grave as she stared down at the floor. "I've been through way too much shit in my life to ever turn into that."

There was a silence, Chris waiting for her to elaborate, hoping that she would, Vanessa instead standing up again and gathering up her bag, prompting him reluctantly to get up as well. He saw her to the door of the apartment, then downstairs and out to the lobby, and finally down to the corner, touching her with his unwillingness to part company, for she felt the same way.

To remedy it as well as to test it and moreover because she really did want to make him feel better in an oddly protective instinct to comfort, she suggested that—if he wanted—they could maybe meet again on Friday at noon, hang out, and then go to the meeting that night together.

She beheld his face brighten immensely at the idea, and her heart ached at how clearly uplifted he was by the plan, because it was *she* who wanted to see him again, and to have that desire reflected back at her, it almost hurt.

Vanessa went on her way, shooting Chris one last sly smile over her shoulder, winking and waving, leaving Chris to wave back until she was out of sight, cheeks glowing, mood soaring. Even as he plodded back upstairs to the prospect of seeing his girlfriend, his smile was reenforced.

*****

Candy arrived later that afternoon, allowing him to lead her into his room, where she remained standing, keeping her jacket on and announcing that she could not stay for very long.

Chris sat on his bed, waiting for her to speak, and then guessed that she was expecting him to ask the obvious, inquiring what it was that she had planned for the evening so that he could then hint at being brought along and, after having been granted her permission, would then have had to go along with whatever she wanted to do.

The routine was standard at first; she was going to go to the movies, the deviation arising when she added that she was going with Brad, who was waiting for her. Downstairs. In his car.

Not knowing who Brad was, but having a good idea, Chris wordlessly listened as she continued, her gaze focusing on the various aspects of his room, the disdain in her voice as she spoke. "Anyway, Chris, I came by here because there's something we really need to talk about," she declared, Chris's stomach abruptly solidifying, his features motionless.

"I really think we should just—" She stopped short. "What are those?"

Blinking, Chris gaped up at her. "What are what?"

She scooped up the pair of sunglasses Vanessa had been joking with earlier from a fold in his bedspread.

"Since when are you cross-dressing?" she asked him mockingly, examining the glasses, pulling at the earpieces, about to try them on herself.

Blushing, Chris replied dismissively, "Oh, those aren't mine."

She gazed sharply at him, a gleam in her eyes. "Whose are they then?" she inquired instantly.

Chris shrugged, a bit of uneasiness encroaching upon him. "Just a friend's."

Her eyebrows lifted. "A girl?" she asked doubtfully.

Shifting a bit, Chris sat up. "Yeah," he answered evenly, his tone of indifference made unconvincing by his increased flush.

Her smile was immediate and wicked. "*Really?*" she asked, now sitting down on the bed beside him, her eyes boring into his. "Who is she?

Swallowing, Chris tried not to squirm. "She's just this girl I know."

"How did you meet her?" she pressed, her smile frozen, poised to strike.

Chris cleared his throat, ironically thinking of Dr. Pendleton. He had tried to tell her about the group a few weeks ago, having been so excited about it. Vanessa's question about why he had not been bringing Candy to the meetings had been an interesting one, in spite of the obvious answer. It was the idea of bringing her that was intriguing, in the abstract, because upon consideration, the image of her being at the meetings with him was more than just unseemly—it was wrong. His special haven, spoiled by her presence there, no way could he handle that, nor would he have had to, because she would never have gone with him in the first place. The moment she had discerned that he was not talking about a party scene or a rave or a night club, she had lost interest in what he was saying, just as she always did whenever he attempted to discuss anything special to him. So he had not bothered to finish telling her about it.

"Well, I was telling you about this anonymous group I've been—"

"What does she look like?" she cut him off, her eyes blazing. "Is she pretty?"

His blush deepening, Chris grimaced and looked away. "I don't know. I guess…"

"Is she coming over here tonight?" she challenged him.

"No, she was already here, today, earlier," he responded, his intention being to account for the glasses, the connotations dawning on him too late.

"*Really?*" She drew the word out, twirling the glasses by one earpiece.

"It's not what you're thinking," the cliché required him to say.

"How often do you see her?" Candy asked next, dropping the glasses on his bed and fixing her gaze upon him once more, Chris squirming as he sighed and tried to answer.

"Have you been hooking up with her?" she wanted to know, her eyes afire, her tongue dancing against her lower teeth. It was an over-all ambiguous phrase, but Chris knew how she meant it, the look on her face, the wild angle of her smile identical to that of a fellow guy in a locker room, as if she were not only asking him if he had scored in that jocular, predatory fashion, but also actually hoping, excitedly hoping for his sake, that he had made a conquest; and for one bizarre moment, Chris found that he was hoping that, as imbalanced and awful and wrong as that would be, it actually was her mind-set, if for no other reason than it would be preferable to the alternative.

Such was not the case, though; and he knew it, the ludicrousness of the situation nonetheless maintained when she insistently reminded him as to who she was. "Come on, Chris, you can tell me. I'm your girlfriend, remember?"

Staring at her in bewilderment, Chris closed his eyes and sighed. "Tell you what?"

"Are you fucking her?" she demanded simply.

"What? *No!*" Chris's eyes flew open, along with his mouth as he gaped at her in shock.

She shot to her feet, her features triumphant, her smile gone. "You are, aren't you?" she exclaimed, folding her arms and staring down at him in a sort of repulsed awe. "You're fucking her."

Chris slowly shook his head, beet red now. "No, I'm not," he told her, his jaw tensed, his own eyes flashing now, his features wounded.

"Then what was she doing up here?" she countered with high school logic, looking skeptically over his bed.

Nostrils flaring, Chris clenched his teeth. "She's just a friend," he grated defensively. Then, shrugging, he added darkly, "Isn't 'Brad' waiting for you?"

"Screw Brad," she retorted instantly, Chris's eyebrows shooting upward as a thousand comebacks leapt into his throat, only to be stifled.

"I want to know how long you've been fucking her," she stated simplistically.

Chris sighed through his teeth, shaking his head. "This is such bullshit," he said quietly, then gazing up at her. "I swear to you that I haven't been fucking anyone." He paused and then had to add, "And even if I was, what difference would it make anyway?"

She cocked her head to one side, refolding her arms. "And what is *that* supposed to mean?"

His face seared with a painful and tired confusion, Chris shrugged his shoulders. "You're the one who said we had to have an open relationship," he replied in defeat. "You said you wanted it, and I agreed, and obviously, you meant it because..."

He shook his head again, not wanting to finish. "So like I said, what difference does it make?"

Her mouth having gasped open into a frozen, outraged smile, Candy closed her eyes and then clamped her lips together, exhaling and then nodding tautly, sweetly. "Okay, Chris," she told him, adjusting her purse strap. "Whatever."

She smiled drillingly at him for a few seconds more, her eyes narrowing before she turned and strolled casually out of his room, Chris staring after her, his features drawn and sad, as if he had just been struck.

*****

Chris most likely would have continued to be upset by the entire exchange, but for once, he had more than his usual diversions to take his mind off of things, that being the pleasure with which he reflected on his day with Vanessa. By contrast, it now seemed magical—magical, but not unreal—because with it had come the promise of their time together on Friday. Caught between these two positive considerations, the episode with Candy seemed quick to fade.

When he went to bed that night, he was able to dwell on the simple pleasure of just spending time with another person, laughing and talking, this thought enhanced by the amazing, uplifting way she had listened to his problems and had not only understood them but also disspelled them outrightly, lending him the courage to question the doubts he had always had about himself, all this made more vivid by the fact that, for the second time, she had referred to herself as a friend, as his friend.

He knew how pathetic it would sound if he ever had to explain to someone just what that meant to him; it felt that way even to himself. Yet it was true; the idea that someone would say this to him, especially someone like Vanessa, was astonishing to him, and he permitted himself to celebrate this.

His thoughts on into Thursday were directed toward his anticipation of the following afternoon, his mood flying high, even his interactions with his family unanimously spirited. He was so looking forward to seeing Vanessa again that as he sat in his bedroom that night, preparing to go to bed, listening to some old polka tunes as if in her honor, he did not even notice when Candy had passed through his door until he looked up and saw her standing there. As he gawked up at her, instinctually lowering the volume of the record player, she smiled quietly down at him, her hands tucked girlishly behind her back.

She was dressed in her party clothes, a black T-shirt and a pleated schoolgirl's skirt, her hair done up in its neatly disarranged style, and her face made up expertly. She regarded him for a moment, closing the door behind her and then locking it without taking her eyes off him in a way that made him swallow.

"Hey, Chris," she said softly, stepping forward and sitting down beside him on the bed.

"Hey," he responded hesitantly, mouth still slack. "What are you doing here?"

Her face creased as if she were pained by the question. "I wanted to see you again…because of last night," she told him frankly. "I would have stayed longer, but I couldn't."

"Oh yeah," Chris grimaced. "Brad. Is he waiting downstairs again?"

She shook her head. "Never mind about him, Chris. I came back tonight because I didn't like the way we left things last night." She paused, glancing over at the record player and then at Chris, smiling openly. "So what are you doing right now?"

Chris shrugged, shifting. "Nothing really, just…listening to some tunes."

"You don't have any plans for tonight?" she asked him pointedly.

He shook his head uncertainly. "No, why? Was there something—"

"Good," she interrupted, setting her purse to one side, jutting her chin toward the record player. "Shut that off for a while. And yes, there is something."

Confused, Chris obeyed, lifting the needle and then turning back to face her, frowning warily. "Look, if you came to ask me more stuff about yesterday, I swear to you—"

She shook her head impatiently, moving closer to him. "No, Chris. Forget about all of that," she told him flatly, her eyes once again boring into his. "I came back here because I wanted to give you something." She moved even closer.

"What—" Chris asked her, bewildered and then astonished when she grabbed him and forced her mouth over his, her tongue plunging between his lips and swirling fiercely and then gradually more slowly as he felt himself submit to her, his shocked eyes drifting closed as he hesitantly embraced her, his unasked question evaporating into a soft, exhaled moan.

His eyes then shot open again when, as soon as she heard this, her right hand flew probingly between his legs, her left shoving him roughly backward on his bed and then darting over to his bedside lamp, turning it off and slamming them into darkness.

There was a frenzied struggle, Chris clambering to sit upright, Candy encouraging him by panting, "Come on, Stud Stomper. I know you've been waiting for this for a long time," her quick hands yanking at his shirt fiercely as he fumbled for the lamp, bumping the record player and dislodging the needle so that it crashed back down onto the record, the Pennsylvania Polka hammering merrily forth as he managed to turn on the light.

He sat up, breathing heavily as Candy, her hair now genuinely disarranged and her makeup no longer quite so flawless, blinked and shielded her eyes against the sudden brightness, sighing scornfully as she moved to reassert herself on top of him.

"Come on, Chris. You don't need to bother with any of that!" she snapped misapprehendingly. "I'm on the pill for fuck's sake!"

Chris shook his head, sitting up even more so as she pressed closer to him.

"No!" he told her adamantly, gesturing stayingly. "That's not… really…what I want…to…" He trailed off, his heart pounding violently in his chest.

Candy looked up at him in startled surprise, her own mouth falling open a bit as she stared, her features then shifting to a millisecond of knowing reproach before she smiled twistedly, her eyes attaining a seductive gleam.

"Oh, I get it," she told him, sitting up herself and then scooting down the length of his tensed form, her smile becoming even more wicked. "You bad boy, you wanna be selfish and have all the fun… Okay, Stud Stomper, but just remember," she added, her fingers darting to his waistband, reaching to pry open the top button of his jeans, her eyes locked on his. "I get the next turn!" Her advance paused over his padlock, hovering appraisingly and then moving to grasp it.

"No!" Chris repeated, his voice cracking now as he yanked his legs out from under her and swung around upright to sit on the edge of the bed, fumbling with his buttons, Candy having been so caught off guard by his actions that she ended up tumbling to the floor, her hair splaying haphazardly in her face. She swiped it away and stared at Chris in angry confusion.

"What the fuck's the matter with you?" she demanded, struggling to her feet, her breathing still harshly audible as she stood over him watching his clumsy efforts to rebutton his jeans in disbelief.

"Nothing!" he responded instantly, not sure of what to say because he was still trying to figure out for himself what had just happened. "I…just don't want to do…that."

She glowered at him noncomprehendingly, stepping toward him. "Oh yeah? What's this then?" she challenged, reaching down and grabbing at him.

Chris recoiled as if her touch was ice-cold, jarring backward on his bed. "Nothing," he repeated, so red in the face that his cheeks felt as if they were afire.

Hands on her hips, she glared down at him. "I don't get you," she declared in disgust. "Why would you *not* want—" She broke off, eyes suddenly blazing. "Oh my *god*, it's *her*, isn't it?" she stated emptily "Isn't it?"

"Who?" Chris retorted stupidly, although he knew exactly who she meant.

"Her, that little bitch you've been fucking on the side!" she charged viciously.

"No!" Chris answered automatically, his voice cracking again, as if to give him away.

"I can't believe this!" she continued furiously. "How long have you been seeing this bitch?"

"I keep telling you I haven't been seeing anyone!" Chris insisted, ironically drawing energy from her anger.

"Oh give me a break!" she sneered venomously. "We've been going out for six months, now, *six* months, and in all that time, we've never fucked even once!"

Chris gasped. "Well, it's not like I didn't want to!"

Incensed, she shoved at him. "Well then why the fuck did you stop me just a minute ago?" she nearly screamed.

"I…I don't know," he stammered as she angrily shoved him again.

"It's her then. It's got to be her!" she concluded vehemently.

Chris sat up, his features becoming taut. "No, that's not it at all!" he shot back with some conviction. "She doesn't have anything to do with this."

"Oh really?" she countered bitterly. "Is that so? If that's true, then why are you acting this way, huh? What other reason could it possibly be?"

Chris felt his loins solidify as he stared up at her, his eyes hardening slightly; he very nearly answered her question, Candy mistaking his hesitation for confirmation.

"I knew it!" she nearly spat, her eyes taking on an almost demonic gleam.

"I can't fucking believe it! Six months! Six months, I've been dragging around your ass, putting up with your bullshit!" She paused, glaring maniacally at the record player. "Turn that fucking jack-in-the-box cheesedick ice cream truck crap off!" She kicked at the record player, sending the needle skip-scratching to the end of the album, Chris diving to pull up the stylus arm, his features pained as he examined it.

"Six months I've been tied up with you and all your fucking freak show bullshit," she charged, scowling hatefully around the room, her face contorted as if in revulsion at everything she saw. "All this old bullshit that no one gives a *fuck* about anymore, all your retard ideas and fucking...bullshit!"

She broke off, gesturing wildly, unable to express her utter contempt for what she could not begin to comprehend.

"Six months of having to deal with all this shit from you—" She inhaled deeply, her eyes suddenly rimmed with tears, her fingers dabbing at them. "And now I find out that you've been cheating on me!"

Having been enduring her tirade against everything he loved, Chris had resigned himself to gaping up at her until she was done, his jaw now dropping as her words registered.

"*What?*" he gasped, stupefied. "*Me?* Cheating on *you? How?* Even if I was seeing someone else—which I'm *not*—how is that cheating on you? You're the one who wanted an open relationship?"

She gasped herself, her mouth falling open as if he had just struck her, so stunned in fact that she struck him, slapping him soundly across the face. "Don't you fucking *dare* try to turn this around on me!" she almost shrieked. "I suppose you're going to try to say that

I've been cheating on you! You agreed to have an open relationship, asshole, and you know it!"

Refraining from rubbing his stinging cheek, Chris stared up at her. "Then how could anything I do be cheating on you?"

"Because!" she shouted back, slapping him again, her tears evaporated by the heat of her rage. "You did it behind my back! That's how! We're supposed to tell each other what we're doing! I've always told you who I was doing, didn't I? I've always told you every last detail, every single time! I didn't keep anything from you!"

His cheek now singhed, Chris had to rub it as he glanced evenly up at her. "Yeah," he replied dryly. "Yeah, you've always told me everything. You didn't hold back any details. I was always so grateful for that." He nodded with slow, deliberate emphasis.

"See?" she charged obliviously. "That's how you cheated on me! You've been fucking this little...little *slut* behind my back, thinking that I'd never find out!"

Chris stared at her in such hardened disbelief that his features seemed almost chiseled. "She is not a slut, and I have *not* been fucking her," he replied tersely. "Not her or anybody."

She laughed scoffingly. "If that's true, then we've gone full circle," she sneered. "You have to be fucking her, or else how could you say 'no' to me?" She put her hands on her hips and assumed her most effective pose, glaring triumphantly down at him.

He stared up at her speechlessly, the answer to her question hanging pervasively in the air, obvious, and yet unreachably beyond her comprehension, for to be faced with it would be inconceivable to her. Perhaps she even caught a glimpse of it in Chris's silence and, in doing so, instantly banished it as unthinkable, impossible—unimaginable.

"Whatever," she concluded brusquely, snatching up her purse. "I came over here yesterday to dump your worthless ass, and I came back here tonight to give you one last chance." She shook her head at him in disgust. "But you blew it, though, you dickless wannabe straightedge house-punk prick loser. Have fun fucking your little bitch, but remember something, Chris..."

Her eyes blazed as she witheringly met his gaze, leaning in slightly, her voice lowering intensely. "You will never *ever* do better than me," she told him savagely. "Not even close."

Chris felt his innards roiling as he watched her, jaws clenched, breathing through his nose. She stepped away from him, standing upright, a horrible smile twisting onto her lips as she then grasped the hem of her skirt and yanked it crudely upward, exposing her bare self to him. "And you will never, ever, *ever* get a chance to hit this."

She watched in triumph as Chris's Adam's apple betrayed him, moving toward the door and then turning and maintaining her smile a few seconds more. "Oh, and by the way, Brad is waiting downstairs. I told him this would only last for fifteen minutes or so. Guess I overestimated *that* too."

With this parting sentiment, she strolled out of his room, Chris able to hear her cheerful, "Good night Mr. and Mrs. Galveston," as she left the apartment. He sat there for several minutes, staring into the darkness of the hallway, not even blinking.

Later, as he mutely straightened up his room and lay down in his bed for the night, he turned on his stereo and put in a compact disk of heavy, hardcore punk music, expecting its harsh, reverberating anger to compliment the rage and sorrow and humiliation that he was prepared to undergo as he lay there, staring up at his ceiling. He listened to its pulsations and choked shrieking for a little while before turning it off and just lying there in silence, as neither fury nor tears encroached upon him, these and all other emotions swallowed up when he was instead overcome with an immense, engulfing relief.

*****

Vanessa smiled at the barista until she passed, her smile then vanishing into a scowl as she sipped from her cup of coffee. The sign proclaimed "Free Refills," and she was damn well going to take as many as she wanted, never mind that she'd been there since six when they opened. She took her paper cup with her each time she went to the restroom, just in case they tried to take it and throw it away while she was gone.

She was too angry to give them much thought as she sat there, reading the newspaper unseeingly, images of the last day and a half clouding in front of her eyes, obscuring the lines of print. She continually squeezed her eyes shut, more than ready to cry, to explode into tears, but she was simply too upset. All she could do was look from the paper to the clock and wish that Chris would hurry up and get there.

Chris—even now the thought of their lazy, meandering day together could give her a tiny boost of consolation, and she clung to whatever it might yield. She had enjoyed herself so much and had been savoring the anticipation of seeing him again, permitting it to tease at her, knowing it was to be fulfilled but entertaining a giddy excitement about it anyway; now, however, that anticipation was a virtual desperation just to see him, someone whom she knew and could talk to and just hold onto…

The tears almost came to her, but she attacked them with an internal flamethrower of virulent wrath, her focus once again settling on the day before. When she had parted company with Chris, she had almost skipped to the bus stop, feeling girlish, carefree, and inconquerable. Back at the Hotel Rochester—*that dump*—she had gone through her meager personal items and had begun to compile a resumé for herself with a brand new folder she had stolen from a stationary store, its sleek, unwrinkled crispness and fresh, papery smell only furthering her excitement as she had neatly arranged a strip of photo-booth head shots she had improvised at a video game arcade on her way back to the hotel. They were the best she could manage, and beyond being functional as pictures of her, she had thought it a rather creative idea as she secured them in place with a paper clip.

Then, in her best handwriting, she had listed all of her background and experience, giving her words little flourishes and seraphs, very pleased with how both formal and yet highly personalized it looked when she was finished. She had considered asking the desk clerk—*that cockroach*—if there was a typewriter she could borrow, but had decided to do it her own way, liking it better. Her list of achievements was not long or impressive, but she embellished where she could and was more than prepared to rely upon her skills as an actress, because, after all, that was what they wanted.

She had then gone to bed, her stomach quivering nervously, and sleep not even a remote possibility, but she forced herself anyway. She had opened the curtains, having left them shut up until now to discourage any pervs from getting a free show, knowing that the morning sunlight would awaken her early enough to get a jump on the day, for she could not risk sleeping in and could not count on getting a wakeup call. A wakeup call in that *hole*, yeah, right.

She awoke, just as she had planned, put on her best outfit, and made herself up to look presentably professional. With her hopes and dreams and plans still soaring, she had gone racing through the steaming, foggy morning streets, amazed how, at that hour, even the ugliness of the city seemed diminished, everything covered in a moistly speckled layer of dew, the air chilled and fresh. She had taken the trouble to ask a cashier—in the stationary store, no less—where exactly the Templeton Theater of the Performing Arts was and so knew precisely which bus to take, awestruck when she was deposited in front of a palatial building of gray stone and arched windows.

Quickly mounting its broad steps and passing under its monumental edifice, she had found herself in a massive lobby, its imposing size subverted by the torrential crowd of people, which she joined, the crackle and dyn of their voices ascending into a vaulted, domed skylight and then rebounding back down to them.

For a moment, she wondered why all these people were here, if there was some early morning production they were all waiting to see, thinking that surely they could not all be there for the same reason as she. Having foreseen a fair degree of competition, she had taken comfort in knowing that her age gave her an advantage, for anyone else seventeen or younger would be in school, suggesting that all of the kids in evidence there must be on a field trip or something.

Her puzzlement was disspelled when a harried-looking man with a clipboard harangued the crowd into silence, explaining that anyone wishing to audition that morning must first sign up with him and then wait to be called, the crowd instantly surrounding him with renewed force. Startled, dismayed, but undaunted, Vanessa plunged in with them, determined to put her name on that list, even when it took her an hour to accomplish this.

At that point began the waiting. Seeing no place to sit, all the marble benches and folding chairs religiously claimed, she had resolved to stand, her staunch vigil buckling two hours later when she was still waiting; and she found a spot against the wall and slumped to the floor.

The actual process of waiting was no treat either. There was an unspoken hostility in the air, as if the entryway were one, huge shark tank, in which they all were poised, hoping to be selected but sizing each other up in the meantime, scouting the competition, sniffing for blood. She defiantly met any gaze directed at her, becoming self-conscious just the same. Although she had spent most of her time in the city under a roof in her own room, in a clean bed, she was constantly wary of how she might be appraised, fearful that in some small way, something was showing, and the people she encountered would see the streets on her, the transiency. She did everything she could to scrub any trace of it away, but her fears lingered just the same.

Three hours after she had battled to get her name on that list, she was called forward into a large airy room, where she blinked against the sunlight that shone dazzlingly through a row of windows, which made up one entire side of the room. Her footfalls echoing sharply on the gleaming hardwood floor, she was led by the harried man to stand before a long table at which sat a row of middle-aged men and women, well-dressed and refined, none of them giving her the barest of glances as she stood there, her heart pounding in her ears, her stomach shrunken in excitement and dread.

The man handed her resumé to a woman seated at one end of the table, whose bushy red hair, red blazer, and red nails gave her an air of viciousness.

She flipped open the resumé, peered briefly at it, and then leveled her steely, unimpressed gaze at Vanessa, whose heart then froze.

"Have you ever performed in repertory theater before?" she inquired bluntly.

Vanessa forced herself to maintain eye contact. "No."

"Are you Equity?" the woman asked.

Swallowing, Vanessa shook her head. "No," she replied, her face then pinching in a distracted frown as she noticed that the woman was chomping mechanically on a piece of gum. She stared at those grimly flexing red lips as the woman slid her resumé over to the next person, who appeared to look over it before passing it to the next person, until it had made its way down to the man at the opposite end of the table, who accepted it and closed it, placing it atop one of several stacks of folders.

"Thank you," the woman said at Vanessa, the harassed man ushering her back out of the room and into the entryway again, already calling the next name.

She had found herself standing out on the front steps of the building in a daze, the chill air gradually snapping her back into focus, her thoughts centering around the one-minute interview she had just waited four hours to attend, and then fogging over again, because the interview had been just that, a surreal disembodiment from time and space. As she stood there before that theater, she felt as if she had just been raped, raped, and then halfway through the assault rejected as not good enough, just not really worth the hassle.

She had passed the rest of the day in a sort-of dream state, aware of what had happened, but unable to face it. Her instincts of logic and resolve also surfaced, reminding her of what she had hammered into her mind all weeklong; today would be only a chance, it might be the first of a hundred attempts, there would be plenty of others, and there was no reason to assume that she would not get a call from today's audition.

She ignored these thoughts as well, knowing that if she were to acknowledge this logic, she would have to counter it with still more logic, one factor of which was that her time at the Rochester Hotel was dwindling fast; and once it had elapsed, she straight-up had no place to go.

It was with this thought in mind that she returned to the hotel that night, and as she climbed the stairs and straggled down the hall to her room, she was able to reflect that she should be thankful that she, at least, had about a week more to stay there, and she would have continued to dwell on that fact until such gratitude kicked in and heightened her mood, if she had not entered her room only to find it occupied by the pimp.

He had been waiting behind the door so that when she turned away from locking it, he was abruptly there, looming large over her, his eyes alight, mouth a twisted rictus of triumph. He was dressed exactly as he had been the last night she had seen him, all in black, his long flowing coat lending to his sinister appearance.

She scarcely had the chance to gasp as he backhanded her, sending her sprawling backward, her bag flying away from her as she tumbled onto the bed, its archaic springs lurching beneath her, the entire frame shuddering and nearly retracting itself back up into the wall. She braced herself, trying to hold still until the bed had steadied itself, all the while keeping her eyes on her assailant, daring to lift one hand to her mouth, finding that it was bleeding in one corner. The outrage that this incited in her, the degradation, and the sting of the blow all faded from her attention as she beheld him step closer and stand over her, smiling vindictively.

"I told you I'd find you, little bitch," he informed her, folding his arms and sneering in smug superiority. "It was just a matter of time."

Her skin crawled at the sound of his voice, and she forced the stammer out of her own as she sat up slightly and swallowed.

"How did you know I was staying here?" she asked evenly, not caring, simply trying to buy some time, although time to do what, she didn't know. Her eyes darted around her room, and she saw that all her belongings, sparse that they were, had been dumped on the floor and kicked all over the room. Struck by this abusive, humiliating sight, this gut-wrenching trespass into the only place in this entire unforgiving city that she had been able to call her own, she pondered fleetingly how long he had been up there waiting for her, his reply to her spoken question settling both.

"Oh, Freddie and me, we go back a ways," he told her with a jeeringly casual air. "I been searching every shithole and dive in this city for you. And when I asked him if he had a fine and fiery little cunt stayin' here, he was real quick to describe you, and that's when I knew that today was my lucky day." He paused, the diamond stud in his teeth gleaming hideously at her.

"Twenty bucks is a lot to pay for a house key," he continued, shaking his head in mock regret and then shrugging. "But what the hell? You'll make it up to me five times over your first night out."

Vanessa met his icy gaze, her face twisting in fear and rage. The desk clerk. That little piece of shit let him up here, told him where to find her, and then let him come up here to wait for her. He had been grinning at her, nodding as she walked by, no more than five minutes ago—grinning, because he knew. She felt her insides recoiling loathingly as she contemplated that, her fury distracted as the pimp stepped even closer, his smile taking on an even uglier, more lascivious intensity.

"First, though, I'm gonna have to test the merchandise," he informed her, his rock-hard eyes still managing to gleam in anticipation. "Sure hope you're thirsty." He maintained Vanessa's gaze as she stared at him, baffled.

She smelled it first; then instantly seeing what he meant, her eyes widened in repugnance at the one splash of color amidst the blackness of his clothes. Its exposure was made all the more obscene as he strode forward with a serpentine slowness, because his entire manner was one of business as usual, a definite pride in his shocking and vulgar casualness, the nonchalance of his swagger contradicted only by its aroused, predatorial quivering as he came nearer.

As reserved as he presented himself, the pimp was reveling in this moment, some cheap sense of power clearly surging through him. Vanessa stared in nauseated contempt at it, at this entire menacing creature standing over her, her thoughts converging chaotically in her mind, her heart rampaging as she recalled how she had felt earlier, just after the auditions; and she glibly reflected that she would now have the chance to contrast those feelings with the real thing.

Pausing in his advance, the pimp crouched slightly, reaching into one of his boots and producing the inevitable stiletto, its blade so crudely sharpened as to appear to have teeth.

"You hold back on me, or you give me more than I'm expecting"—he told her, making the blade dance in the light of a wall fixture—"I'll cut you deep."

She continued to stare up at him, unblinkingly, her teeth clenched; she felt her bladder tremble, threatening to spill itself, this one urge somehow jarring her back to a semblance of alertness. She had been conscious of everything up until now, every detail. In fact, she had been struck with how ridiculous this thing that approached her was. Clad in leather, tooth appropriately diamond-studded, stiletto in hand, and hair slicked back and greasy, he was like a cartoon character; this thought had struck her when she had first seen him on the street that night.

A magazine cutout of what he thought a pimp should look like—she imagined him posing before a mirror, making sure that he looked the part; she almost laughed in a disjointed, hysterical way. For some reason, she thought of Chris, of his own struggle to find his identity; and she wondered in fleeting, abstract curiosity if it was the same for this creature, if it was the same for all of them. She might well have conceded had it not been for Chris's explication, words that set him and anyone like him galaxies apart from any lowlife pimp; Chris's identity chose him; he did not choose it. There in lay the difference between truth to one's self and some ludicrous, shallow adaptation to a conformed stereotype.

All of this streaked through her mind in a second and just as quickly vanished, leaving her only with the thought of Chris, his gentle, docile countenance in her mind's eye giving her a modicum of comfort, this only to be erased by a wistful realization that after all of those years of fighting off the assholes in high school, she had been saving herself for this?

"Open wide, little bitch," he instructed her, his voice wheedling as he lolled his tongue lewdly, the entire room now seeming to reek of that vile, sordid odor.

Not a chance, she remembered thinking, her wits now fully restored as she locked her eyes with his, if only to avoid looking at that sickening thing. She knew what she had to do, knew it was her only chance, trying to gauge if he would really be stupid enough to fall for it, unable to conceive how he could be, but forced to hope that he was, to pray that such would be the case, since the only other alternative was death, because there was just no fucking way.

"Come and get it, pig," she told him tauntingly, bracing herself and rolling over the head of the bed as tautly as she could, making her movement as swiftly constricted as she was able, for fear of upsetting the temperamental bed frame, its mechanisms wobbling threateningly beneath her and then groaning precariously as the pimp leapt after her, landing precisely where she had willed him to crash, his attention solely on subduing her, his intent blinding him to all other possibilities; in short, he was stupid enough to fall for it, Vanessa thrusting herself out of the way, this time as forcefully and as recklessly as she could manage, tumbling to the floor as the ancient Murphy bed emitted a screeching protest, its mechanisms buckling and the entire frame lurching upward, the pimp's face contorting from an odious determination, to a horrified gasp as the bed flung itself up and into its alcove, swallowing up the pimp like some immense rattrap, hurling him against the wall and out of sight.

Her own features erupting into a gleeful, noncomprehending awe at her success, Vanessa shot to her feet and grabbed the pull chain affixed to the bed, certain that the pimp, pinioned between the wall and that lumpy mattress, screaming muffled, incensed curses, would surely dislodge the bed with the sheer force of his rage alone.

Pausing uncertainly, knowing she had mere seconds, she wrapped the chain around the adjacent wall lamp, hooking its handle around one of its brass sconces, not trusting the flimsy design to hold for very long. She stood back and watched as the bed began to flex wildly in the alcove, the pimp apparently squirming into a position in which he could force his weight against his jaw-bridge-like prison. Each shove that he gave, however, was reciprocated by the frame's springs, the awkward angle of Vanessa's impromptu restraint, while threatening to pull the fixture out of the wall, preventing the bed from lowering, the springs simply slamming the bed's frame and its captive right back against the wall, again and again as the pimp, every inch a trapped animal, howled in rage and refused to accept his predicament.

Vanessa tore herself away from this spectacle, grabbing her bag and stuffing everything she could into it, skipping over nonessentials, pausing to wonder in grimacing exasperation what among her scanty belongings was *not* essential, the rhythmic desperation of the pimp's efforts to escape strafing her nerves and prompting her to abandon half of it, her thoughts centered around the frantic need to *get the hell out of there.*

She came across the pimp's stiletto, gasping and shrinking away from it, then snatching it up, shoving it into her bag as well, standing up, and staring wildly at the floor, making sure she had everything she needed, her mind racing, trying to think.

The fearsome clambering of the pimp had not abated, nor had his maniacal and yet indiscernible diatribe of threats, a new noise somehow combating with all of this racket as her next-door neighbor began pounding on the wall.

"Awright, you lovebirds!" a cranky voice bellowed. "Knock off the Kama Sutra crap. I'm tryin' to get some sleep!"

Vanessa danced in a panic for a moment or two, her vision almost going cross-eyed as the debris on the floor began to blur, her hands wringing frenetically until she swiped at the air in dismissal. *Fuck it.*

She stepped over to the bed frame and harshly kicked it. "Did you hear what that guy said, asshole?" she yelled with spirit, stunned at her audacity to remain in the room another second. "You'd better find yourself a gloryhole in there, scumbag, 'cause I'm checking out now! I've got your knife here, chief. And if you *ever* come near me again, I swear to God, I'll cut off your dick and shove it so far up your ass, you'll have to jack off with your fucking tonsils, you got me, you lowlife piece of shit pimp pig!"

She kicked the bed frame again, the response a murderous howl of rage, the entire structure jolting so violently that the fixture was yanked out of the wall, exposing its wires with an outburst of sparks, Vanessa stifling a shriek and turning to bolt through the door, slamming it behind her and almost colliding with the woman from across the hall, who gaped at her in bewilderment, drawing her robe against her slight frame and pointing at the room, her query poised on her lips.

"So sorry about the noise," Vanessa apologized, smoothing down her hair in a ludicrous attempt at normalcy. "Our Magic Fingers machine is on the fritz."

With this imparted, she turned and dashed to the staircase, taking the steps two and even three at a time, slowing down only when she reached the first flight, effecting a casual air as she strolled through the lobby, ignoring the desk clerk's look of astonishment, and then turning toward him as if on a sudden afterthought.

"Oh, I meant to tell you," she announced, approaching the desk, the clerk staring at her in confused reproach. "There's a really big cockroach trapped up in my room. You might want to mention it to the chambermaid. Oh!" She pointed to an overflowing glass ashtray situated on the countertop. "I didn't know that you smoked! By all means, have one!"

She grabbed the ashtray and flung its contents into his face and then hurled it at him point-blank, her face taut and fierce as it slammed into his forehead with an ugly sound, causing a sizable gash of red, the clerk bleating angrily, his hands flying to the wound, staring in rage at the blood on his fingers, Vanessa's eyes blazing into his as she spun around and slammed open the front door, bolting down the steps and not looking back at the Hotel Rochester.

She walked for hours into the night, her stomach a coil of bilious, unspent rage, her thoughts a wild jumble of manic triumph, determination, despair, and defeat. She wandered around from one neighborhood to the next, banishing anyone who came near her with a hellish look.

Passing a twenty-four-hour bowling alley, she sat inconspicuously at one of its snack bar tables for a while, trying to write in her journal but instead only staring at the page until she began to sense the wariness of the few employees on hand, standing up and leaving before they had a chance to ask her to do the same.

She had walked at least one more hour, scarcely able to retrace the route across town, her stomach pulsing in weary recognition when she finally located the building.

Bypassing the front entrance, she circled around to the alleyway in the rear, pausing for almost a full minute before crouching down and curling up inside of a surprisingly clean box, closing the flaps down around her head and lying there, the buzz and glow of a phosphorescent lamp overhead the only material intrusions on her refuge.

She rested there in a sort of exhausted delirium, and only after the last of her keyed-up defenses had surrendered to fatigue was she able to drift off into a fitful sleep, huddled in her cardboard shelter in the doorway of the rear entrance of the union hall, as close as she could possibly get to the comfort and security she had known within its walls.

Vanessa awoke to the sound of a garbage truck, and her wits instantly about her, as if she had not slept at all, she stoically climbed out of the box and faced the explosion that was the streets.

Once she had her bearings, she made her way to the coffee shop, pausing only to pick up enough cans and bottles along the way to redeem for the price of some coffee, having to stand in line, even at that hour, with an assortment of scowling street people with ragged garbage bags and shopping carts brimming with recyclables.

With a handful of nickels and dimes, she walked to the coffee shop, stopping to examine herself in store windows along the way, endlessly straightening her clothes, wondering if anyone, if everyone, could see her destitution, could smell it on her.

In the bathroom of the coffee shop, she had freshened up as best as she could, staring resentfully at the cut on her lip and the slight bruise. She considered obscuring them with a little makeup, but decided not to bother, giving up and settling herself at one of the deserted tables arranged near the bank of windows at the front of the coffee shop, periodically raking through her bag as she continually remembered one item or another that she had left behind, their respective values now seeming anything but expendable, in hindsight, especially as she envisioned them being thrown away—or worse, being pocketed by the sleazebags and wing nuts in that hotel.

Tearing through the *Village Vice*, she had even begun to rip away at the regular newspaper, boring as it was, when Chris appeared alongside of her.

Starting, she glanced up into his goofy, grinning, beautiful face and wanted to hug him, so relieved was she to see him. His features instantly shifted to an expression of gaping concern as he looked at her, pointing wordlessly at her face and then allowing her to take him by one arm and lead him away, Vanessa pausing only to bring her cup to the counter.

"Can I have one for the road?" she requested loudly.

The barista gave her a look. "You can only have refills on what you drink here."

Vanessa stared right back. "Oh well, I guess we'll have to stick around then," she concluded flatly.

Reluctantly, the barista refilled the cup and handed it to her, Vanessa then grabbing a to-go lid and jamming it into place. "On second thought, I think we're outta here."

As Chris grimaced in confusion, Vanessa led him out the door, the sunlight pounding at her along with the deafening throb of the city outside, her spirits already elevated, her heart uplifted just from having Chris finally there with her.

Reinvigorated, she turned to a bedraggled homeless man panhandling in front of the shop, making sure the barista could see her.

"Here's your coffee, Mr. Bergdorf," she announced, handing it to him.

She took Chris's arm, prepared to stroll away, glancing back in surprise when the homeless man called after her.

"What is this stuff?" he demanded, scowling.

Glaring depreciatively back, she scoffed at him. "Tequila," she replied sarcastically, grabbing Chris and pulling him along, not even sure where she was taking him, just glad, so very glad, that he was finally, *finally*, there.

They walked around aimlessly for a few minutes, Chris at last asking her what was wrong, what had happened, Vanessa stopping and staring at him and then wordlessly reaching out and touching his face lightly as if to reassure herself that he was actually standing in front of her. He blinked back, confused, but not resisting her actions. Just as abruptly, she dropped her arm and explained that she needed to go someplace where they could talk. Biting his lip, Chris could only think of one place nearby, Vanessa instantly assenting.

They went back to his apartment, his family gone for the day as before; she had been wanting to meet them, eager to compare them with Chris, but not today; and she was glad the place was empty.

As she sat in his room again, she leaned back on his bed and simply breathed, flooded with both the relief of being away from the noise of the outside world and the gratitude she felt just to be there again. It felt like a sanctuary for her, one in which she had been made to feel very welcome, this quality all the more pronounced because it was Chris's sanctuary, and everything about it bespoke of him. It even smelled like him. She lay there, closed her eyes, and breathed, as Chris hastily fumbled in the kitchen for something to eat.

When he returned with some slices of buttered toast and a can of root beer, Vanessa sat up, receiving them appreciatively, forcing herself to eat the toast slowly, even as each bite seemed to glow delectably in her mouth. She was not about to let on how hungry she was, still tucking and pulling at her clothes, and sniffing discreetly at herself, determined to seem as fresh and presentable and stable as she could.

The concern was now rampant in Chris's eyes as he fidgeted next to her, waiting for her to tell him anything at all, Vanessa longing to hug him for it. She would never forgive herself for so misjudging him, she reflected, as she briefly told him what happened.

Chris listened with wide-eyed attentiveness, his mouth at first a taut line of worry gradually gaping open as he took in her hasty breakdown of events. He was very sympathetic about her horrible experience at the auditions, but his mouth then clamped shut, his jaws clenching, when she related what else had happened that night. His face darkened slightly, his eyes growing hurt and angry.

"Are you sure you're okay?" he asked her again, reaching out as if to touch her bruised lip and then refraining with a blush, Vanessa nodding reassuringly.

"Yeah, I'm fine," she said somberly, then managing a wry smile as she dug into her bag and showed Chris the wicked-looking stiletto. "Like I said, I got his toy away from him."

He stared at the knife in her hand with a hard expression, Vanessa watching in touched fascination as he looked directly ahead at the wall, his jaw flexing tensely. "He'd...he'd better not ever try to hurt you again," he said in a low voice.

Vanessa regarded him in wonder, her heart swelling even as a crooked smile sprung onto her face. "Why?" she could not resist blurting out. "What would you do about it?"

Chris's jaw tightened even more, each hand a fist atop his knees as he paused, and a tiny blush crept into his cheeks. "Well...I don't know," he had to admit, some of his ferocity waning. "But all I know is he'd better not. That's all."

A laugh and a sob collided in Vanessa's throat as she gazed at his profile, shaking her head and emitting a muffled sound of strangled emotion, her face melting into a grin as she reached over and lightly ruffled his Mohawk from front to back.

"Thanks, Chris," she told him, forcing a light tone of voice. "You're my hero."

Chris's blush immediately claimed his entire face upon hearing this, Vanessa laughing and leaning back a bit, her stomach warm and full with the delicious toast, her mood a thousand times improved. She gestured carelessly at him, her smile genuinely bright.

"Okay, enough of my drama," she declared scornfully. "How's it hanging with you, Clodhopper—Chris or, as your girlfriend would call you, oh yeah, how did things go with her after I left on Wednesday? You guys end up doing anything fun?" She looked at him casually, watching as he shifted and grimaced deeply, blushing again.

"Oh, um, no," he finally said, the grimace twisting into a humorless smile. "No, um, in fact, we're pretty much not together anymore."

Vanessa felt her heartbeat increase, and she blushed a bit herself, a pang of guilt at her reaction surfacing as she frowned at him, glad that she could at least sound disappointed. "What? You two broke up?" she asked, her surprise definitely genuine. "My god, what the hell happened? Did she do something to make you want to break up with her?"

Biting his lip, Chris tilted his head slightly. "Yeah, she did actually," he responded truthfully, then glancing at Vanessa and shrugging. "But she's actually the one who broke up with me."

Gasping, Vanessa stared at him. "She broke up with you?" she repeated incredulously. "God, Chris, I'm sorry. Should I even ask? I mean if it's private or…"

Chris shook his head, opened his mouth, and then sighed. He then began to tell her about his relationship with Candy, beginning with how they met and concluding with the previous night, his only modifications being the parts in which Vanessa was indirectly involved, not wanting her to feel in any way to blame.

Vanessa, of course, saw right through this, but merely listened, stunned by what she was hearing. Parts of her wanted to grab him and scream at him for letting himself be turned into such a punching bag, but she liked him too much now for such a reaction not to be outweighed by a heart-bursting desire to comfort him upon learning of the whole unbelievable time they had spent together. She had not even remotely imagined that he was caught up in such a thing. Anyone could see that he had problems, but this was majorly fucked. Rubbing her lips together, she tried to think of what to say.

"What I don't get is why, if she wanted to break up with me on Wednesday, she came back on Thursday and wanted to…you know, have sex with me," he was saying, his gaze settled on the floor. "She could have gone out and had sex with anyone—in fact, she did!" He shook his head. "I just…I don't get it."

Vanessa stared at him. "Because, Chris"—she explained pointedly—"she smelled competition. She was all set to dump you, but she hadn't expected there to be anything to get in her way. I mean she was all set, had someone lined up and everything, but…" She shook her head impatiently. "Let's face it, she sensed a challenge."

Chris frowned. "Yes, but we were together for six months," he reiterated. "She had all that time to…you know, tell me she was ready. I wanted to do it, but I figured I should wait for her to… you know…let me know. I mean it's what couples do, right? I didn't think too much about it until this whole 'open relationship' thing…" He sighed quietly, his gaze slipping to the floor again, then meeting Vanessa's once more. "I mean I can understand why she got mad an' stuff, when I didn't want to. But then, if she wanted to do it with me so much, how come she went ahead and dumped me anyway? I…I just don't get it…"

Her eyes fixed on him, Vanessa swallowed her exasperation, focusing instead upon his utter cluelessness. Now, she knew beyond a doubt why she had thought of him as a weak crybaby. He was a baby; he was lost and ignorant and helpless, profoundly vulnerable. She was amazed, but now, instead of contemptuous disgust, she was overwhelmed with an almost maternal desire to comfort and protect him; she had felt stirrings of this inclination before, and now, they were immutable. Nonetheless, she had no intention of sugarcoating anything for him, not when it came to something like this.

"She got mad at you and dumped you because you rejected her, Chris," she told him simply. "It had nothing to do with having sex with you. It was all about controlling you and using you and… basically keeping the upper hand. If you *had* slept with her—and she was positive you would—she would have left anyway. Who knows, she still might have gone ahead and dumped you. What she couldn't believe is that you wouldn't do it, that you said 'no' to her. That must have blown her mind."

She exhaled slowly, raking a finger through her hair. "It's all pretty simple and straightforward, Chris," she concluded flatly. "It's how people play the game, how they play each other…"

Pausing, she studied his pensive features closely and posed the question that she was hesitant to ask but that she could not possibly leave unasked.

"What doesn't make sense or, at least, what isn't exactly clear is why you did end up rejecting her…" She paused again. "I mean it isn't like there's someone else you're seeing or anything," she pointed out carefully. "So…why would you say no to her?"

She watched as Chris's frown dissipated into a look of uncertainty. He blinked and shifted slightly, biting his lip and glancing at her for a split second, his frown returning as if he were struggling to decide whether or not to tell her something, Vanessa sitting still, every muscle tensed, her stomach rolling, and her heart pounding as she awaited his response.

Chris swallowed dryly and finally sighed, gesturing somewhat hopelessly with his hands. "I just..." He stopped. "Like I said, we were together for six months, and I'd always wanted to. But last night, when she was...all over me...I just..." He shook his head, his features pulling together in an expression of bewildered disgust. "She...I just didn't want to, you know, not...not with her. All of a sudden, she was just not... It was like I didn't even want her to touch me... And then, when she got mad, all I could think was how she kept getting uglier and uglier and how I realized that that was exactly the way she always was... I was so glad when she left. I mean I thought I would feel like shit... I even tried to feel all broken up an' stuff, but I just couldn't... I was just glad that it was finally over..."

Vanessa was nodding slowly. "Well, okay. That makes sense," she replied evenly, her voice thick with the logic of it. "You rejected her because you were straight up not attracted to her anymore." She nodded once more, as if to emphasize this to herself.

Nodding as well, Chris turned closer to her, his eyes brighter now, his voice more assertive as he gained confidence in explaining his feelings to her, Vanessa's brows lifting encouragingly. "Yes, but it's also so much more than that!" he told her earnestly. "The main thing is—and I know it'll sound stupid and old-fashioned, but you know, whatever—I just can't... Sex is supposed to be something special and really meaningful and important, and I just can't... I can't do that with someone if I don't really care about them. And I mean, like, love them, you know? I just can't be with someone like that if I don't love them."

He stared at her almost imploringly before his blushing caught up with him, and he was forced to look away, Vanessa regarding him in awe as he worked up the courage to conclude his point. "I mean back in high school, I had a few, like, crush girlfriend flings an' stuff. And like, at the time, that felt like love. But with Candy, I mean she was my first real, like, relationship. And I wanted to do it right, you know. And so the whole time, I thought I loved her. I thought I *had* to love her to be able to put up with all of that. But last night, I realized that... I just...didn't..."

As his words sort of fizzled out, he dipped his focus toward the floor again, Vanessa swallowing harshly as she listened to him, her entire chest swelling. She felt her head begin to shake as she opened her mouth to respond, inhaling deeply and trying to steady her stampeding thoughts and emotions, virtually unable to believe what he had just said to her. After all she had been through, growing up and in high school and especially ever since coming to this city, right up to and including last night, she would have bet money if not her soul that she would never meet anyone who could have feelings like that. As much as she had begun to like Chris, she would not have considered it possible that even he might think that way; he was a boy, after all, and while he was not a typical boy, he was still a typical boy. They were all the same.

And now, here he was, saying these unbelievable words, with nothing to gain by them, because it wasn't even a line! Somewhere in this city was a raving mad jilted chick who would definitely bear that out, so he was dead serious, and she could only stare at him and try to fathom how to convey that she felt exactly the same way without completely flipping out and blowing her cool, because, after all, she wanted to have a bit of the upper hand too since, as shy and passive as he was, she was going to need it if they were going to get anywhere.

"Believe me, Chris," she began slowly, looking steadily into his eyes. "I know exactly what you mean, and I know exactly how you feel. It's…incredible to hear someone else say it, but that is totally how I feel too." She paused, wishing she had the words or, better still, the telepathy to express this minor miracle, which had just emerged between them, so that he could also be astonished at the astounding, beautiful phenomenon of this unity of devout, heartfelt beliefs, in the end simply repeating his own words back to him. "I am exactly like you. I would never have sex with anyone if I didn't love them, no matter what the rest of the world thinks. Fuck 'em! I would have to love someone first, before I could sleep with them."

Chris listened to her with rapt attention, eyes unblinking, a tiny gap in his lips, his breathing inaudible, a slight blush warming his cheeks as she spoke her reassuring words, not only completely validating his beliefs but also expressing them as her own. His face reflected his relief and amazement and then his slight, blinking confusion, a frown developing, his mouth gaping more widely as his uncertainty mounted.

"Um, I'm really glad you agree with me, an' stuff, but…" His frown became more pronounced as he appeared to be puzzling over something. "But I mean how is that possible?"

Vanessa, still caught up in what they were sharing, blinked at him and then frowned herself. "How is what possible?" she asked blankly.

Chris flushed a bit more, shifting on his bed. "Well, I mean, like, how is it possible for you to feel that way since you're…you know…" He hesitated, avoiding her gaze.

Baffled and faced with a sudden increasingly bad feeling, she stared at him sharply. "Since I'm *what*?" she demanded incredulously.

Spreading his hands, Chris met her eyes again and then almost casually shrugged. "Well, like, you know, because you're a hooker."

Vanessa gaped at him. The disbelief she had felt when he was expressing his feelings a moment ago had seemed insurmountable, and yet it had now been surpassed by the unreal words he had just spoken to her. She slowly cocked her head to one side as if she had misheard him, which she *surely* must have. "*What?*"

Chris actually inconceivably shrugged again. "Because you're a hooker."

When she was incapable of responding, he blushed again and quickly continued, gesturing openly. "I mean dealing with so many different people, how would it be possible—"

"Is that what you really think I am?" she nearly screamed, her eyes blazing as he shrank away from her in shock, grimacing and gulping.

"Well, like, I mean…yeah!" he stammered in startled matter-of-factness.

Her mouth moving almost catatonically, Vanessa actually braced her temples with her fingertips, her fury almost incapacitating. "How could you just sit there and say something like that to me?" she charged in a virtually strangled voice.

Bewildered, Chris shook his head and stared at her. "Be… because you are one!" he felt forced to answer, clearly perceiving no other possible response.

Gasping in speechless outrage, Vanessa reached out and slapped him across one cheek, Chris gawking at her in flabbergasted, wounded awe.

"What did you do that for?" he burst out, his entire head turning red, one hand flying to his cheek as she shot to her feet.

"You actually think that I'm some fucking prostitute, don't you?" she accused him, already knowing his response, knowing what it would have to be, and above all knowing why. None of this irrefutable, ludicrously undeniable logic could induce her to face the facts, though; indeed, its concrete, airtight soundness only incensed her to even wilder, almost crazed, anger, because, somehow, through it all, she had thought he had known, that he had to have known, could not *not* have known the truth. These mere thoughts, just thinking about this unthinkable alternative, the one now unfolding in front of her, pushed her further over the edge. "You actually think I'm some filthy, cheap streetwalker!"

Finally realizing that he must have gotten something very very wrong, Chris could only stare up at her, dumbfounded, clinging to the only side of the story that he knew. "But that's what you told us you were," he insisted as straightforwardly as he dared. "You told all of us that that's what you do."

She glowered fiercely down at him, thinking of Dr. Pendleton, of his shock. The logic attempted to ensnare her, but she wrathfully rebuked it. Chris should have known. The others were all grown-ups; they would fall for anything; but Chris was a kid too, an outcast, living in a fantasy world, just like her. He should have known. How could he not have known? It hurt so much to think that he thought she was—

"So you think I'm a hooker," she summarized swiftly, folding her arms in anger. "You think I'm a dirty, scrounging, cock-sucking slut—"

"I never said you were a slut!" Chris broke in assertively, his mind reeling back to his argument with Candy in which he had denied

273

that very accusation, defending Vanessa against such an attack. He fleetingly wished he had some way of proving that to her, as a way of defending himself now.

Vanessa stepped over a pair of raggedy tennis shoes and stood over Chris, jabbing a finger at him almost punishingly. "You'd better get this straight, punk ass, I am *not* a prostitute!" she exclaimed, glaring into his eyes, glad to see him cringe. "You may have thought that, but *you* were totally wrong, got it?"

Genuinely hurt now, Chris could only shake his head. "If you're not a prostitute, then why would you tell all of us that you *were* one?" he insisted desperately. "You kept mentioning it over and over again at the meetings! You told everyone you—"

"*It was an act!*" Vanessa was screaming now, waving her hands violently to keep from reaching out and choking him. "It was all just an act, okay? I made it all up, all of it, so…just get over it!" she ordered him lamely.

Chris stared at her incredulously, his mind spinning. "Why… why would you make up a story to tell everyone there?" he asked in complete bewilderment. "And why would you make up something like *that*?"

Exhaling furiously, Vanessa turned away from him and peered lividly out his window at the maple trees arranged in a parking lot.

"Because…," she began, not knowing how to answer, not even sure if she could. "Because…"

"Look," Chris said, his tone conveying that he was about to use more of his indisputable logic, Vanessa shutting her eyes in advance. "If you're not a prostitute, then who really hit you?" He focused on her steadily, almost challengingly.

Her innards having been tensed, she felt them convulse upon hearing this, her eyes shooting open as she spun around to face him. Seeing the expression on his face, she felt her anger only become further incited as she stepped toward him again.

"A pimp did this to me, Chris," she informed him in a low voice. "A filthy piece of shit pig of a pimp, just like I told you or did you think I made up all of that too?" She folded her arms, glaring as Chris shook his head.

"No, I don't think you made up any of that," he replied evenly, blushing but holding her gaze steadily. "But if you're not really a prostitute, then why would a pimp hit you?"

He stared at her expectantly, Vanessa's mouth falling open as if she were regarding a complete idiot. "Because back when I *was* hustling on the street, he wanted me to work for him and was pissed off when I said 'no' and ditched his ass," she stated emphatically.

Chris shook his head again. "Okay, but I thought you said you weren't a prostitute."

She glared at him. "I'm *not* a prostitute!" she shot back.

"But you just said that you were one!" Chris insisted dizzily.

"I was!" she nearly snarled, throwing up her hands. "But, I wasn't...really... I wasn't, and I'm not. I'm *not*, okay?" She moved closer to him, attempting not to scream. "I am not a prostitute! And if you thought I was, how come you're hanging out with me, huh? How come we got together on Wednesday and went out and did stuff, if that's really what you thought?"

"Because you wanted to," Chris blurted out unthinkingly. "It was even your idea!"

He shrank at the fire in her eyes, Vanessa willing herself not to slap him again. "Oh, my idea, huh? My idea?" She smiled in maniacal sarcasm. "Obviously, a ploy! Some new hooker marketing strategy!"

"No, that's not what I meant!" Chris interjected, a tiny bit of anger daring to show.

"Let me ask you this, then," she challenged sweetly, hands on her hips. "Why would you want to hang out with a hooker anyway, huh? Are you so fucking hard up for friends that you need to take whatever you can get? Are you that desperate?"

"Yes. I am—," Chris responded instantly, so intent on the second part of her question that he overlooked the first part, not having the chance to stammer some explanation as Vanessa, gasping, abruptly slapped him again.

So much for restraint, she reflected briefly, dismissing the thought as she glowered down at him, too outraged by his response to care. Chris rubbed his cheek ruefully and gaped back at her in disbelief.

Were all girls insane? "You know, you're acting just like she did," he heard himself say, too amazed at the similarities to keep the thought to himself.

His statement was so out of context that she could only stare at him in exasperated distraction. "Who?" she countered impatiently.

"Candy," he replied tersely. "You're standing there yelling at me and hitting me and being mean and completely unreasonable, just like—"

This time, she slapped him so hard that his head shot back. "Don't you *dare* compare me to your wing nut ex-girlfriend!" she shrieked, her rage now refortified and nearly exceeding its previous intensity. "I may have issues, but I am not a complete whack job!"

Chris glared up at her, rubbing his cheek with the back of one hand and sitting up angrily. "You'd better stop hitting me...or else..." He trailed off broodingly, clueless as to how to give an ultimatum.

Vanessa's eyebrows pivoted almost comically upward as she nevertheless heard one anyway. "*Or else?*" she echoed scornfully. "Or else *what?* Or else you're going to start hitting back? Let's go, bitch. Bring it on!" She waved her arms at him provokingly, almost dancing as she assumed a stance in front of him. "Did you forget who you were dealing with? I took down a pimp last night! If I can do that, it's for goddamn sure I can stomp your candy ass!" She extended one foot and prodded Chris in the chest with it, shoving him back slightly, Chris making no move to defend himself, merely glaring up at her, his eyes smoldering, mouth clamped shut, jaws clenched so tightly that they were shiny, his slender body tensed. The mane of his Mohawk bristled as he breathed harshly through his nose, resembling an angry young colt.

Seeing this, Vanessa refused to be intimidated, raking back her hair and charging forward with her tirade. "Look, I just want you to get this straight," she told him in a brittle tone. "When you look at me, you are not looking at a prostitute, okay? When you see me, you are *not* seeing some dirty, STD crack whore, got it?"

Chris's look of braced fury shifted painfully into an expression of anguished capitulation. "Vanessa, I *never* ever thought that you were anything like that," he insisted almost pleadingly.

Folding her arms tautly, Vanessa glowered at him. "But you *did* think that I was a prostitute," she countered automatically.

"But that's what you *told* us!" Chris protested miserably, never learning.

Vanessa clawed the air in front of her and groaned up at the ceiling. Stamping one foot, she fixed her wild-eyed gaze on Chris one more time. "Forget what I said at the meetings!" she told him, her own voice becoming slightly beseeching. "All right? Forget all of it! I am *not* a hooker, and I never was one. Even during the time that I *was* one, I still wasn't one."

Chris shook his head. "Here we go again," he mumbled disconsolately.

Stung, Vanessa stared at him a second and then reached down and grabbed her bag. "No, here I go again," she said bluntly, heading briskly to the door.

"Vanessa, wait! Please don't go!" he cried out, his tone desperate as he clambered to his feet. "I'm sorry I made you so mad. I didn't mean to. I just… I don't understand what you're saying… I'm so confused. I… I don't know what to believe."

He paused, watching as Vanessa stopped in front of the door to fuss with her bag straps, studiously ignoring him as she listened to every word, tensed, hopeful, desperate herself. "I want you to know that what really matters is that even if you are a prostitute, I don't care! It doesn't matter to me if you are one," he declared earnestly. "I really honestly don't care."

She turned to face him, tilting her head and smiling tightly. "Gee, Chris, thanks," she replied with poisoned sweetness. "That's so decent of you!"

The smile then vanished into a mask of rage as she dropped her bag and stabbed a finger at him once again. "This is the breakdown, Fuck Face, so listen up! I have never once sold my ass and never will! I am also not in any way comparable to a psychobitch who fucks everyone *except* her own boyfriend, and yes, it was my idea to hang out together. You know why? I'll tell you why because I felt sorry for your lame ass and thought that you could use the company! I also thought that we had a lot of shit in common, and on top of that, I was actually starting to like you. Now, however, I don't give a flying fuck what you think about me, or my life, or *anything*! And as far as not knowing what to believe goes…" She paused, assessing his gawking, stricken face, noting the severe redness of his one cheek and deciding to up the ante but also give him a break.

"Believe this," she concluded, backhanding him this time, but across his other cheek. She then grabbed up her bag, tore open his door, and stomped down the dark hallway, head held high.

Deeply hurt, more by her parting words than her parting shot, Chris nonetheless moved to chase after her, stumbling to avoid the miscellaneous clutter on his floor as he bolted through his doorway. "Vanessa, wait, please—"

He was cut short as one of the elastic loops of his bondage pants caught on the doorknob, and he was flung facedown on the floor, his crashing impact almost mockingly echoed by the slamming of the apartment's front door.

As he lay there, belly down, one leg dangling upward from the doorknob, the silence of the apartment seemed to descend upon him like an avalanche, his young face drawn and wounded as he contemplated the way Vanessa had left, her words sizzling in his mind, particularly her having admitted to liking him, since he very much liked her too and had begun to realize that beyond this he was attracted to her, that the idea of spending time with her excited him and made him happy, and that he had chased after her so desperately because he had wanted to tell her all of this, then and there, to look into her eyes and allow all of his true feelings to come tumbling clumsily and stupidly out of his mouth, to let her know.

All of this, however, faded inconsequentially as he considered not that he may have lost some potential new relationship, but that he had just lost a friend.

*****

Vanessa tore down the sidewalk, stalking at a hurried pace, glancing over her shoulder as if daring Chris to show up following her and then becoming angrier when he did not. *Fuck him then.*

Fuck everything. She glowered at every face she passed, ignored any semblance of her reflection, and simply blazed forward, not even knowing where she was going. She was so filled with rage that the city around her seemed muted, only her pounding thoughts audible and those screaming endlessly at her. The tears were not far off now, and she knew that if she were to stop her aimless progress, if she were forced to stand still, she would explode into hysterical crying.

Refusing to submit, though, she merely kept her anger stoked, feeling it surge with each stabbing step she took. She found herself reverting to a practice she used to employ when she was little and someone had hurt her—she would superimpose faces on the sidewalk right before bringing her foot down on them. Childish, of course, but it had always worked, and she set about using the method now, stomping on the pimp for an entire block, hoping that he ended up having to spend the night in that bed, and next stomping on the desk clerk, his betrayal reigniting a whole new burst of anger. She had had almost one more week to stay there, and because of him, not only had she lost out on that shelter and the money that had bought it, but also she now straight-up had no place to live.

That was a matter she had no desire to consider and gladly shifted to stomping on the woman from the auditions and then abandoning her and facing the issue that she most wanted to ignore, stamping furiously on Chris, actually slowing her pace so that she could grind at his face with more precision.

Why had he thought that about her—*never mind* that she had told him every chance she got and had practically rubbed his face in it. Never mind all that, how could he not have known that it was all bullshit? How could he be that stupid? *Dorky-ass wannabe punk.* She had been so tempted to tear into his entire explication of his split-punk persona, to rip him to pieces with it, ridiculing its insane, laughable contradictions. She could not have, though, not only because it would have destroyed him, would have completely shredded his feelings, but also because she genuinely liked the idea and respected it and was still touched that he took the chance on sharing it with her.

His feelings? What about hers? Didn't her feelings matter? Self-proclaimed bitch that she was, she did have feelings. She ground at his goofy, dufussy face with her heel, her heart thundering in rage. Why did he have to be so gullible, so naive, so ignorant and dumb and inexperienced and trusting and innocent, and all of those other things that made him so incredibly attractive to her? Bristling at the paradox of her angry logic as it thwarted her mind and then her heart, she almost relented, almost let the tears win.

She would not, though; she vowed, harshly resisting them. She ceased stomping on his face, however, her anger nonetheless still rampant. The fact, the very idea, that she was absolutely to blame for this entire misunderstanding did nothing to improve her mood, because she wanted it to be Chris's fault and was determined that it remain that way.

As her fury almost mindlessly progressed, she found herself wondering what she was so upset about, this introspect only making her more angry, because if she had overreacted, if it turned out that she had blown up and behaved like a total psycho and ditched Chris for no reason, she was going to be *pissed!*

Of course, she did have good reason; he had thought she was a hooker. He had believed her outrageous, obviously exaggerated, outlandishly over-the-top remarks; had taken her at face value, the fool; had trusted that she was telling the truth; had trusted her; had believed her; and had believed that she was an honest person.

She almost shrieked out loud—almost, but did not—for if she unclenched her teeth now, she would start crying and would probably never be able to stop. These past few days, her time in this city, her whole life, what was the fucking point? The one, the one truly special thing she had was that group, and the most important part of that had turned out to be Chris, and now, she had blown it with him. Or he had blown it with her. Whatever, the point was, what was the point? The point was that there was no point, only that Chris saw her as either a prostitute or a liar, and although he insisted that it didn't matter to him, it absolutely mattered to her. If she *were* one, if she had actually managed not to screw that up too, *then* it wouldn't matter, and it would be great if he didn't care. But she wasn't one, and he should care—and didn't—and although she was to blame, it was all his fault, so fuck him, fuck her, fuck everything. *Fuck!*

Chapter 9

"I REALLY APPRECIATE THAT, DR. Whittaker," Dr. Pendleton declared, resting his hands upon his desktop, glad that they had met in his office, since he seemed to see so little of it these days. "I only need to check in at the front desk, and they'll take it from there?"

Dr. Whittaker nodded from the adjacent chair. "Indeed. They seldom use those vans on the weekends. I am certain it will be no trouble," he replied lightly, inhaling from his pipe and settling back slightly, peering out the office window at the city skyline. "It's a large vehicle. It should comfortably seat at least eight people. I'm sure it will suffice nicely."

Dr. Pendleton nodded again, smiling and continuously glancing around his office, studying the row of framed certificates and documents on the far wall, Dr. Whittaker following his gaze and smiling himself.

"I meant to tell you, Dr. Pendleton, the review board will be convening again tomorrow morning—a few of our colleagues had conflicting schedules, and so they elected for a Saturday meeting. They are already ninety percent in favor of approving your petition. All that remains now is for me to 'plead your case,' so to speak, and I might tell you that as impressed as I am with your progress, premature as it may seem, I am quite confident that the operative word, shall we say, will be 'congratulations.'"

His eyebrows lifting intently, Dr. Pendleton regarded the older man anxiously. "Oh, do you really think so, Dr. Whittaker?" he asked eagerly.

Smiling and puffing, Dr. Whittaker nodded. "Yes, I think that the time is at hand. Again, mind you, we won't know until tomorrow." He sat up a bit, pointing the stem of his pipe at the other doctor. "I tell you what, I own a small cabin about sixty miles east of Fenderman Lodge. I was thinking of heading up there tomorrow for a little relaxation of my own. I can drop by the lodge on my way there and give you the good news in person."

Nodding rapidly, Dr. Pendleton fidgeted with his small fingers, his excitement apparent. "Oh, that would be wonderful, doctor, if you're sure it's no trouble."

Dr. Whittaker flexed one hand dismissively. "Not in the least," he replied congenially. "Oh, by the way, have you informed your group about it yet? I know you've been anxious to share it with them for some time now."

Dr. Pendleton smiled, shaking his head. "No, I've been waiting for any indication from the review board," he stated earnestly. "I was thinking of telling them tonight, since our retreat is tomorrow. And now that you've given me such, uh, encouraging news, I think I probably will."

"Splendid," nodded Dr. Whittaker, drawing from his pipe again. "Yes, your retreat. Are the members of your group still as enthusiastic about their visit to the countryside?" He lifted his wintry brows expectantly.

"Oh yes," Dr. Pendleton nodded, his features glowing. "They're all really excited about it, as am I." He beamed at Dr. Whittaker. "In fact, we can hardly wait."

*****

Later that evening, Dr. Pendleton stood behind his packing crate, staring rather wordlessly around the room with an almost tongue-tied grimace.

The meeting had begun, typically enough, Chris waiting anxiously at the front door, his obvious eagerness to attend the meeting further elevating the doctor's good mood, though he was a bit surprised when he unlocked the doors and entered the union hall, and Chris remained outside.

He had been about to arrange the coffee and doughnuts when Mr. Crimpton stalked into the room, appearing even more frazzled than usual, actually stumbling into a few of the chairs before collapsing into one of them and holding onto its seat as if expecting something to dislodge him from it.

Blinking in concern, Dr. Pendleton glanced toward the door as Judge Talbott and Mr. McClintock entered, the former carrying a basket filled with little bundles, the latter heading directly for the box of doughnuts.

"I made us all some cookies," the judge announced, extending a baggie to the doctor. "Chocolate chip and oatmeal raisin."

"Oh, that was very nice of you," Dr. Pendleton noted, as Father Gilchrist stormed into the room, greeting the smaller man with a frightful glare.

"Uh, hello, Father Gilchrist. How are you?" he asked, somewhat unnecessarily.

Father Gilchrist gave him a shriveling look. "Such keen powers of perception," he marveled sneeringly. "You must have been the head of your class."

Dr. Pendleton flushed as Vanessa came crashing through the entryway, Chris rushing along behind her. "Vanessa, please, I really want to talk to you!"

Vanessa smiled at him venomously. "Sure thing, sailor! Ten bucks an hour, up front."

She plopped down in her usual seat, Chris staring at her, crestfallen, before reluctantly clomping over to his own seat by the podium, he, his backpack, and his skateboard, sitting down with a clatter, his gaze locked on Vanessa, hers stoically directed elsewhere.

"Uh, welcome back, everyone," Dr. Pendleton began, a bit weakly, forcing a smile as he took in all of them. "It's good to see all of you again."

He paused as his perusal ended with the priest, whose expression had grown even more vitriolic. Faltering slightly, he cleared his throat. "Uh, tonight, because it's our last meeting before the retreat," he continued, drawing energy from this notion. "I had a very special piece of news that I had wanted to—"

He was distracted as Judge Talbott extended a baggie of cookies to Chris, who did not accept them and did not notice until the judge began to wave it hopefully, whispering, "Psst, psst, Claude!"

"Uh, Claude," he interceded reluctantly. "Don't you want any cookies?"

Chris started slightly, glancing up at him and then whipping his head around to face the judge, bright red as he sheepishly took the little bag.

Vanessa glowered at him, folding her arms. *What a dork.*

"Take one and pass it on," Judge Talbott requested of Mr. Crimpton, in what she probably thought was a discreet voice, handing him the basket.

"Uh, as I was saying, I had something along the lines of good news." Dr. Pendleton resumed.

Mr. Crimpton received the basket with a pained expression. If the woman wanted to pass him something, why couldn't it be a bottle? He rubbed his pounding forehead and almost tossed the basket to Mr. McClintock, not bothering to take any cookies. Better yet, if she insisted on bringing in all these baked goodies, why not show up with some of those special, "Magic Brownies" or whatever the hell kids called them. That would definitely jumpstart this crowd. He closed his eyes and pinched the bridge of his nose, his nerves jangling and reeling.

All these years, he had resisted the temptation—in fact, there was a time when he was quite disdainful of such diversions—but he had thought that just this one time might be justifiable.

And it was. It was Friday, after all, and the day had seemed bad enough in its similarity to administering driving tests on a roller coaster, only to turn worse still when he returned to the office to find that, yes, of course, his request to take a leave of absence would be approved, just as soon as this year's examiner's reviews were all done; surely, he wouldn't mind waiting for just another week or two.

By the time he got to that bar, his nerves were shot. One glass, one little glass of bourbon on ice, and he had been buzzed, pleasantly relaxed, content to stare off into space and simply exist, this reverie lasting for almost two hours. It had apparently put him in a convivial mood, for when the patron on the next stool mentioned to the bartender that he was headed over into this part of town, he had conversationally noted the coincidence, the man mistaking his meaning and clasping a jolly hand on his shoulder, insisting that he accept a lift.

He next found himself seated in an immense Cadillac, impressed with the stranger's generosity until the drive commenced. There next ensued fifteen minutes of sheer horror as Mr. Crimpton came to realize that the man not only was a horrendously poor driver but also was drunk.

By the time they had plowed past every stop sign and blazed through every red light along the way, his entire system was shunted back into sobriety as if the inebriation had been wrung out of every pore. The instant he recognized the neighborhood and could find his voice, he had almost leapt from the car a good six blocks away from the meeting, the drunk waving and roaring off with the door still hanging open. He was positive that if he had not been strafed to the point of virtual petrification, he would have wet himself again; and as he staggered to the union hall, gasping at the cool night air, he made a vow to himself worthy of a prohibition teetotaler.

Now, however, as he sat there, struggling to stabilize his nerves, he would have tossed back any manner of rotgut put in his hands.

"Uh, this news is not one hundred percent, uh, carved in stone," Dr. Pendleton had been saying, gaining a bit of confidence. "But I'm told that it's virtually been decided."

Mr. McClintock was attempting to follow the doctor's sporadic words, but was more focused on extracting a bag of cookies from the basket and passing it along to Vanessa without upsetting his plate, on which he had heaped a dozen doughnuts, his concern that their precarious balance would be displaced stayed by the velocity with which he intended to devour them. After only a few days of unemployment, he had quickly regained his appetite, finding that it was even more insatiable than ever.

With the loss of his expense account and, of course, his salary, he would very possibly be faced with the loss of his residence and of his future in general. These worrisomely stressful concerns, rather than killing his desire to eat, instead only stimulated it. In fact, in some bizarre way, the food actually tasted even better now, although, he supposed, this could be due in part to a subconscious intent to savor what he could, while he could.

He put these thoughts aside and directed his attention to the doughnuts, admiring the diversity of tonight's batch. There had even been a thick, grapefruit-sized cream puff of some sort, plump with a fruit filling, which he had somewhat guiltily taken and which now rested alluringly off to one side of the more conventional doughnuts, as he had made up his mind to save that for dessert, eyeing it with anticipation as he sampled a glazed old-fashioned.

"Uh, it may not seem all that significant to you," Dr. Pendleton was explaining, clasping the sides of his podium. "But I can assure you that, uh, to me, it's—"

He paused as Chris, having been increasingly squirming in his seat instead of slouching in his usual torpor, suddenly stood up, hunching over and scooping up his things, and then, in the huddled posture of someone getting up in the middle of a movie, crossed diagonally over to a seat nearby Vanessa, inconspicuously clomping and clambering as he sat down, his face scarlet.

"Uh," Dr. Pendleton blinked. "Uh, as I say, this, uh, bit of news is…"

Vanessa, having been pawing through the cookies in search of the largest bag, had glanced up at Chris's abrupt shift from his seat of the last three weeks, her mouth a perfect "O" of disgust as she tilted her head back and looked to the ceiling for commiseration. Boys were so stupidly obvious. It was almost funny. It *was* funny. Yet she showed no sign of this as she observed Chris take his new seat and then pretend to be absorbed in whatever Dr. Pendleton was babbling, sitting up straight like a good little boy who would never dream of disrupting class. *Pathetic.* She shook her head, digging through the cookies. *What a dork.*

Father Gilchrist glared sourly down at the two of them. Upon first seeing Vanessa earlier, he had stared sharply at her bruised lip, his already foul mood jolted by the contemplation of how she had incurred such a disfigurement. His thoughts had immediately turned to the interval in his confessional earlier that week, and he had almost tasted bile as he contrasted the implications.

In her line of work, he knew, she could have received such abuse in any number of circumstances; but the fundamentals were the same; and although there was little or perhaps nothing he could do for her, and while she had more probably than not created those same circumstances for herself, he was nevertheless disturbed by what he saw. It was absolutely nothing new, but he rankled at the idea of anything happening to the child. He had been on the verge of asking directly how she had become bruised, when he noticed that Chris possessed the same exact wound.

Frowning, he had wondered if it might, instead, be some new and suitably twisted form of adolescent tribalism. Perhaps piercings, tattoos, and branding had become passé; and now, arm-to-arm rites of passage were in vogue. He had found himself scowling, his perusal of the punk rocker reminding him of his experience on the bus ride to the meeting that evening. *Little punks, all the same.* Yes, it was probably some delightful new variety of self-mutilation, he concluded. Either that, he sniffed, or they had had a lover's spat and had done it to each other.

"Uh, I've actually been looking forward to sharing this with you for a while now," Dr. Pendleton elaborated earnestly. "I was just waiting for the right—"

Vanessa abruptly stood up, grabbing her bag and the basket of cookies, Chris gaping up at her, about to bite into his first as she moved to walk away and then paused, grabbing the cookie away from Chris's mouth and tossing it into the little bag in his lap, which she then snatched away as well, placing it in the basket and almost flouncing across the floor, taking Chris's previous seat, then taking his former bag, taking out that precise cookie, and taking a huge bite out of it, chomping daintily.

Father Gilchrist glared triumphantly. Yes, he had thought as much.

As Chris gawked at her with a hurt look, Vanessa once again ignoring him, Dr. Pendleton cleared his throat, glancing from one to the other uncertainly. "Uh…"

Judge Talbott was regarding Vanessa in timid surprise. "I... I'm glad you like the cookies, dear. But...well, I was hoping we could all share them...," she hinted.

Squirrel-cheeked, Vanessa turned toward her, swallowing brusquely. "Oh my, I'm so sorry. Where *are* my manners!" She then shoved the basket toward the startled judge with a crazed smile. "Here! Would you like some?" she offered generously.

Blanching, Judge Talbott shrank a bit and then, perhaps not knowing what else to do, timorously helped herself to a baggie.

"Okay," she nodded in a tiny voice.

Dr. Pendleton cleared his throat. "Uh...where was I?"

"You were telling us about some news that you wanted to tell us about because it was news that you wanted to tell us," said Mr. Crimpton into his hands, withdrawing them from his bloodshot eyes as he darted them toward the doctor. "Again."

Wilting, Dr. Pendleton opened his mouth to continue, ducking instinctually when Vanessa suddenly tossed the basket of cookies to Father Gilchrist. "Here you go, Padre," she told him around a mouthful. "Didn't mean to skip ya."

Father Gilchrist caught the basket with surprising swiftness, giving Vanessa a scorching look. "Thank you, Little Red Riding Hood," he snapped, thrusting the basket onto the empty seat next to him and then clamping his arms back in their usual defiant stance, turning his glare on Dr. Pendleton. "Oh, pray, do continue with tonight's scintillating dissertation," he requested caustically. "I believe the subject was clinical tautology."

Grimacing at the sarcasm, Dr. Pendleton cleared his throat. "Uh—"

Vanessa, swallowing her cookie roughly, sat up slightly, a realization penetrating her angry thoughts as she stared at the basket in the vacant seat.

"Where's Mrs. Spindlewood?" she demanded of Dr. Pendleton, her tone almost accusing as she frowned up at him, the doctor cringing severely at the ferocity of her expression, flushing deeply.

"Uh, well, I...don't know where she is," he admitted at length.

"Maybe she's running late again," Judge Talbott suggested.

"She might have stopped off for a bite to eat somewhere and just lost track of the time," Mr. McClintock proposed over a chocolate with confetti sprinkles. "That happens to me occasionally."

"Does it, indeed?" Father Gilchrist remarked airily. "I should think that the reason for her absence is quite apparent. Unlike the rest of us, the dear old lady no doubt finally came to what's left of her senses and decided to stop coming back here."

Dr. Pendleton shifted, glancing down at his shoes, as Chris raised his hand. "Maybe she's still at work," he guessed, wanting to help.

"I thought she thought this place *is* her work," Mr. Crimpton said to his hands.

"No, she's not still at work!" Vanessa pronounced contemptuously, deigning to give Chris a seething look, thrilling to see him squirm, and then glaring back at Dr. Pendleton. "Have you tried calling her?"

Dr. Pendleton regarded her hesitantly, only then noticing her bruise, frowning in distraction. "Vanessa, how did you hurt your lip?" he inquired with concern.

"Have you tried calling her?" Vanessa repeated scathingly, the doctor almost ducking at her intensity. "This is the second meeting that she's missed! Something might have happened to her!" Her anger seemed to become interposed with a sense of urgency.

"Oh, I'm sure that's not the case," Judge Talbott spoke up, her small features almost instantly consumed with a look of doubt. "Even for her age, she seems very energetic."

"What has age got to do with anything?" Father Gilchrist suddenly snapped.

"That crazy old broad will bury us all," Mr. Crimpton informed them all through his hands, sitting bolt upright when a baggie of cookies struck his temple.

"Don't you *dare* make fun of her, you four-eyed, John Q mental case!" Vanessa yelled at him, Judge Talbott shrinking between them.

"Vanessa, please calm down!" Dr. Pendleton exclaimed, aghast.

"I wasn't making fun of her!" Mr. Crimpton shot back, one hand clutching at his heart, the cookies having shattered his nerves all over again. "We should all be so lucky to live to be that old and yet be that clueless! Frankly, I don't know how she managed to find her way back to this place as consistently as she did!"

"Just because a person has attained a certain age does not mean that they are automatically struck with senility!" Father Gilchrist informed him heatedly, his apparent defense of Mrs. Spindlewood proving itself to be nothing of the kind. "There are countless people less than half my age who exhibit all manner of dementia and incompetence! In fact, numerous such examples come to mind right now!" He glowered around the room with unmistakable intent.

"Were you going to eat these?" Mr. McClintock asked Mr. Crimpton, politely holding up the baggie of cookies.

"You've got her phone number!" Vanessa was insisting of the doctor. "Why don't we just call her? It's worth a try, isn't it?"

Hesitating, Dr. Pendleton caught the look of pained concern in Vanessa's eyes and slowly felt himself begin to nod. "Uh, all right Vanessa," he conceded, stooping for his attaché case as she quickly glanced at the others.

"Does anyone have a cell phone?" she asked impatiently.

"I do!" Chris announced, his voice excited as he eagerly reached into his backpack and withdrew a compact model, holding it up with a smile.

Vanessa stared at him for a withering split second and then gazed at all of the others. "Like I said, does anyone have a cell phone?" she repeated meaningfully.

As Chris slumped in his seat and appeared ready to cry, Mr. Crimpton shook his head. "Don't look at me. I lock mine in a desk drawer every day so that no one can find me," he stated candidly.

"Nor can I oblige," Father Gilchrist announced haughtily. "Oh, the Archdiocese issued me one, but in a moment of geriatric ineptitude, I accidentally tossed it in the baptismal font." He nodded in reflection. "Very odd too. It possessed the most peculiar aversion to Holy Water. It reacted as if it were drowning."

"I have a paging device," Mr. McClintock volunteered, then frowning in realization. "Oh dear, only I left it at home."

"Her number should be in this folder," Dr. Pendleton declared, rifling through several sheets of paper and a flurry of green flyers.

"Oh!" Judge Talbott suddenly sat up, her eyes wide in recollection. She reached beneath her chair and pulled her purse up onto her lap. "I have one!" She began to dig through her purse, beaming in triumph as her hand closed around it, and she pulled out a Rice Krispies Treat. Blinking, she rummaged a bit more, finally extracting a sleek, brand new model, giving it to Vanessa, who passed it to Dr. Pendleton, who stared at it a moment, hesitantly opened it, fumbled with one button, and inadvertently photographed himself.

Startled by the flash, he almost dropped it, Vanessa standing up and grabbing it away from him, staring intently at the list of telephone numbers.

"Glen Haven One-Two-Three-Six-Four?" she read in confusion. "What the hell is that?"

Dr. Pendleton cleared his throat. "Uh, well, it's a telephone prefix. Uh…it means, uh…" He paused, taking the telephone from her and trying to make out the tiny letters on its small buttons. "Uh, let me see. A-B-C is, uh, one. And, uh, D-E-F is two…"

"Let me know when we get to colors," requested Father Gilchrist. "I'll help pass out the crayons."

"It's sort of like when you dial P-O-P-C-O-R-N," Judge Talbott explained to Vanessa. "You know, for when you want to find out what time the movie starts."

"That's not for movie times!" Mr. Crimpton snapped. "P-O-P-C-O-R-N is for the weather."

Mr. McClintock glanced up. Movie popcorn was so good.

"Uh, here, let me get my glasses," Dr. Pendleton eventually surrendered, all of the buttons beginning to blur before his eyes.

"Oh, for God's sake!" Father Gilchrist barked, standing up and snatching the telephone away from the doctor. "Give me this infernal contrivance!" He peered at it, then sneering at the shorter man. "What a flattering snapshot. It conveys your singular befuddlement to perfection!"

He swiped the paper away from Vanessa, glaring at the number and then discarding it. "Since I am the only one suitably ancient enough to recall prehistoric telephone prefixes, it will have to fall to me to undertake the task!" He directed this observation at Mr. Crimpton, who stared haplessly back. *Wasn't the point of coming to these meetings to feel better, not worse?*

The number dialed, Father Gilchrist thrust the telephone at Vanessa, resuming his seat as she took the phone and walked into the rear most section of the room, one hand over her free ear.

Clearing his throat, Dr. Pendleton realized that he *still* had not managed to announce his good news, the moment seeming to have passed. Besides, he had wanted to tell all of them; and as he waited for Vanessa to rejoin them, another thought occurred to him, one of a much lighter and pleasant nature, made all the more so by the fact that it had to do with the upcoming retreat, the discussion of which might put the group in a somewhat less agitated mood. Swallowing, he certainly hoped so.

"Uh, on a quick, incidental note," he began, conjuring up a smile. "Uh, I just now remembered that I had purchased a brand new photo album the other day and three disposable cameras. I thought we would bring them along to our retreat, tomorrow, uh, so that we can take some photographs of, uh, all the fun we're going to have."

He paused, letting this sink in, watching as it sort of just sunk.

"Uh, anyway," he hurried onward. "On the front of the photo album is this really rather, uh…well, here, why don't I just show you." Pausing, he reached into his attaché case and withdrew a new conventional-style album, the brown leatherette cover of which was outlined with a formally decorative filigree design, the center a large gold-embossed rectangle, its interior blank.

"It came with a special gold pen that you can use to label the pictures, but also you can use it to create a title for the album," he explained, clearly pleased with the idea. "At first, I thought that we could all think up a name for our retreat, but then it occurred to me that, better still, we could come up with a name for our entire group!" He nodded, smiling brightly. "I mean other anonymous self-help groups have names. So uh, it only seems right that, uh, we should have a name for our group too."

He paused again, glancing hopefully from face to face. "So, uh, yes, if, uh…if we all wanted to…put on our thinking caps, we could maybe, uh, come up with a few ideas." He swallowed dryly.

There was only silence until Father Gilchrist spoke up with frozen-featured disbelief. "You want for us to come up with names to call *this* group?" he asked pointedly, Dr. Pendleton nodding eagerly.

He leaned back in his chair and lifted his eyebrows. "Now that is indeed a gold-etched invitation," he proclaimed.

Dr. Pendleton cleared his throat, uneasily sensing that he had just triggered an avalanche, his small form braced against whatever the old priest was about to say.

"*Fuck!*" Cringing, he spun around as Vanessa came raging back, almost tossing the telephone at the judge as she crashed down into her seat and glared.

No one seemed willing to ask, the silence extending until Chris finally gave in, his voice hollow and unsure. "So, wha'd she say?"

Arms folded, legs crossed, one foot kicking furiously, Vanessa slowly turned her head to give him a Medusa-like stare, Chris instantly dropping his head in shame.

"Uh, were you able to get through to Mrs. Spindlewood, Vanessa?" Dr. Pendleton asked quietly.

"No," she replied shortly, her gaze slipping to the floor. "All I got was a stupid recording. I even redialed three times."

Mr. Crimpton shrugged. "Well, maybe her number's disconnected."

"Yes, well, we already knew that," Father Gilchrist remarked sagely.

"Well, I'm sure that wherever she is, she's perfectly fine," Dr. Pendleton told her kindly, very much wanting to allay her fears. "She was very excited about going on the retreat, uh, it seemed… I'm sure she'll be waiting at the rendezvous spot."

Vanessa gave him a deprecating look. "How is she supposed to know where that is?" she returned flatly. "You haven't told any of us yet."

Dr. Pendleton blinked at her. He hadn't thought of that.

"Yeah, where are we supposed to meet you?" Mr. Crimpton inquired, rather crossly, not even certain that he still wanted to go.

"Uh, at eleven in the morning in the parking lot of County General Hospital," he explained falteringly. "It, uh, seemed like a fairly centrally located spot to meet…"

It's where we'll all end up sooner or later, Mr. Crimpton mused darkly.

"Well, it's definitely centrally located for me," Father Gilchrist noted with approval. "If I start walking now. Of course, its proximity is made all the more convenient by the fact that I have no intention of going."

Dr. Pendleton cleared his throat. "Well, I really hope that you might, uh, sleep on it first. You might change your mind," he added with little conviction.

Father Gilchrist sniffed. *It would serve you right if I did.*

"Do we have to come up with a group name tonight?" Judge Talbott asked. "Or can we think about it a little while. I have a few ideas, but…"

"I've got a few of my own," Mr. Crimpton thought, then realizing he had spoken aloud.

"Oh, as have *I*," purred Father Gilchrist diabolically.

"I got an idea for, um, what to call it!" Chris spoke up, waving his hand, blushing as various wary gazes turned his way, gulping when his mind went blank. He turned a deeper crimson and squirmed. "Um… I kinda just forgot what I was gonna say." He sank dejectedly in his seat. He really had had a good idea.

"Uh, if it's not too much trouble," Vanessa interjected with renewed anger. "We were kinda talking about something else first!"

When Dr. Pendleton blinked blankly, she exhaled furiously. "Mrs. Spindlewood, remember? Don't any of you nutjobs know where she lives?"

She paused, glaring at the other members. "Don't any of you care if something might've happened to her?"

"Well, now, of course we do, Vanessa," Dr. Pendleton responded quickly, glad when at least a few of the others nodded. "Unfortunately, with her telephone number being invalid, we're rather at a loss as to what to do next… I don't know her address. It hadn't occurred to me to ask." He paused, frowning thoughtfully. "I suppose all of this is in keeping with the idea of an anonymous group."

"Such brilliance," intoned Father Gilchrist, next focusing on Vanessa. "In any event, asking her for her address would most likely have been a futile gesture. To do so, one would have had to assume that the dear woman actually knows where she lives."

Vanessa's eyes blazed as she glared at him. "You're a mean, hateful old bastard, did you know that?" she informed him hotly, virtually everyone in the room gasping, save for the old priest, who flushed but refused to give her the satisfaction of outrage, instead holding her gaze as he leaned forward in his seat.

"How did you guess?" he growled back.

Turning away from him, Vanessa jabbed a finger at Mr. Crimpton, causing him to jump. "You work at the DMV!" she denounced exactingly. "You should know how we could find out somebody's address!"

Mr. Crimpton stared at her in stunned incredulity. "I don't have access to those kinds of records!" he retorted, exasperated. "Even if I did, there's no guarantee that old woman has a driver's license." He suddenly winced ulcerously. "At least, I hope to *God* she doesn't have one!"

"What about State IDs or passports or all of that crap?" Vanessa pressed, now turning to Judge Talbott. "You were a public pretender! Can't you think of something? What about… I don' know, birth certificates?"

"Well," the Judge replied doubtfully, shrinking as she was put on the spot. "Uh, her birth certificate might tell us which hospital she was born in…"

"So would the midwife who attended her," Father Gilchrist helped. "Or perhaps even the stork."

Mr. McClintock snorted, almost losing a mouthful of scone.

"What is she's like, visiting at her grandkids' or something?" Chris suggested.

"Why, in that case, her address is simple," Father Gilchrist concluded. "You would simply go over the hills and through the woods, except in reverse."

"Father Gilchrist, please," Dr. Pendleton beseeched him.

"Can't you think of *anything*?" Vanessa charged Mr. Crimpton.

He gazed back at her in disbelief. How the hell did he get shouldered with this mess? Didn't he have enough problems without having to conjure up the whereabouts of some doddering old biddybat who obviously...

Sighing and grimacing, he shook his head as the thought surfaced, worthless as it no doubt was. "Look, kid, all I can tell you is I've always seen her get off that bus out front at a stop at a place called Saxbury Commons—"

He broke off as Vanessa stood up and began stuffing baggies of cookies into her bag, Judge Talbott pausing and then mutely helping her.

"It's all industrial though!" Mr. Crimpton insisted. "There's nothing out there but warehouses and factories—almost all of it's been condemned!"

"Well now," nodded Father Gilchrist. "That sounds like the right place!"

"Vanessa, I...," Dr. Pendleton began, cringing at the girl's fiercely taut actions, wondering again what had happened to her lip. "Will you...won't you at least stay for the rest of the meeting?"

Vanessa hoisted her bag over one shoulder, turning to give the doctor a scathing look. "Why?" she demanded belligerently, Dr. Pendleton cringing. "So I can sit around here bullshitting about what to call this group?" She laughed abruptly. "I can save you the trouble, Doc. I've got the perfect name for us. I mean it's gotta be just right, right? When you're dealing with a group of people as royally fucked in the head as we are, you can't just settle for any old calling card, no!"

She had walked into the center of the group, gesturing widely, the members staring at her, transfixed. "And let's face it, when it comes to screw-ups, nutjobs, has-beens, and losers, our group wins the prize. I mean we're fucking classic!" She waved one arm broadly at each member, as if introducing them to Dr. Pendleton, who could only watch in speechless dismay.

"We got a judge who can't make up her mind about *jack*," she proclaimed, Judge Talbott blinking sadly at her. "We got a DMV driving examiner who's scared to drive," she continued, Mr. Crimpton glaring mutely.

"We've got a food critic who obviously can't criticize anything." Mr. McClintock glanced up from an apple fritter, deflating a bit.

"And then we've got the Insane Clown Pussy," she decreed, Chris gawking at her in dumbfounded chagrin. "The only punk rocker in the world who wouldn't know GG Allin from Kenny G."

"We got a little old lady who doesn't know which way is up," she went on, pointing to the empty chair and then indicating Father Gilchrist with a grandiose flourish. "And we got a priest who clearly doesn't believe in God anymore."

As Father Gilchrist gazed searingly at her, she stepped to the center of the room again, extending her arms outward in front of Dr. Pendleton.

"And then you got me, Miss Teenage Prostitute, too scared of tweakers, pervs, and pimps to hack it and too much of a prude to spread her legs anyway," she concluded simply, letting her arms fall to her sides.

"There you go, Doc. That's roll call. You wanted a bunch of whack jobs to help out, and you fuckin' hit the jackpot. And you don't even have to worry about the anonymous part. It comes with the territory when you're a reject *and* a nobody! A bunch of anonymous mis-fits? It's a no-brainer, Doc." She waved emptily around her. "Mis-fits Anonymous—that's who we are."

The room was silent as Dr. Pendleton regarded this assessment with a look of squashed defeat, the other members staring wordlessly at Vanessa as she spun around and began to stride toward the door, her eyes downcast but still angrily determined. She moved to step past Chris, who reached out and grabbed her arm, gazing up at her imploringly, half-rising out of his seat to dissuade her.

"Wait, Vanessa, please. I really need to talk to you!" he told her, his expression desperate as she vindictively yanked her arm away from him.

"Go fuck yourself, Chris," she said wearily, without even stopping to look at him. "At least that way, you'll be guaranteed some action."

Chris sank forlornly back into his chair, glancing up hopefully when Vanessa abruptly wheeled around and came marching back toward him, eagerly moving to stand up as she passed a glance over his for once unsmudged, crumb-free features.

"Here, you missed a spot," she informed him helpfully, then plucking the long-anticipated cream puff away from a startled Mr. McClintock and shoving it in Chris's earnest and then dumbstruck face, smearing it around for good measure and then wiping her hand on his shirtfront before spinning away and stomping toward the entrance, leaving Chris motionless and stunned, the other members watching in shock.

"Uh, Vanessa!" Dr. Pendleton called after her worriedly. "Aren't you at least going to wait for me after the meeting like usual?"

His unanswered appeal yielded several baffled looks from the others, Dr. Pendleton blanching and shifting. "Uh, I always give her a ride after each meeting," he explained haltingly to the many uplifted eyebrows. "Uh, strictly professional," he clarified, somehow making things worse. "Uh, that is to say, we go straight to her hotel," he assured them, sealing his fate.

As he flinched and floundered at their gaping scrutiny, the slamming of the door brought everyone's attention back to Chris. Instead of crumpling back into his chair, the crestfallen punk rocker merely stood there, shoulders slack, his proud Mohawk drooping downward, his spattered focus on his boots, his neck, ears, and what little of his face showed bright red. The cloying remnants of the cream puff seemed to permeate his humiliated state, and he slowly wiped at his eyes, his sorry gaze lifting to that of Mr. McClintock, who seemed just as upset. Chris then gawked shamefully at the rest of the group, sighed in almost exhausted determination, and then turned to sprint ploddingly out the door.

Dr. Pendleton watched him go in discouraged uncertainty, then shrinking a bit as the others once again turned their bewildered attention to him.

*****

Chris clambered out onto the sidewalk just in time to see the bus sail away from the curb, Vanessa undoubtedly onboard. He instinctually set out to chase after it, almost tripping as reality and doubt and trepidation pivoted him up onto the toes of his boots and stopped him in his tracks; and he stood and watched the bus recede into the night, those three inhibitors giving way to an intense, smoldering self-loathing as he slumped there, powerlessly, helplessly watching, just like always. The bits of pastry still clinging to his face helped contribute to this choking sense of failure, and he swiped at them bitterly, instantly coating his hands and fingers, moving to fling them clear and then, instead, slowly, miserably beginning to eat the mess, the thick, delicious sweetness of it only adding to his shame.

*****

"Uh, no, you see, the fact is…she's not really a, uh, prostitute at all," Dr. Pendleton was explaining pointedly. "I was hoping she would explain it to all of you herself, but I…" He paused, actually loosening his tie a bit. "Well, I guess, in a way, she, uh…sort of just did…"

"So you have not been making midnight assignations up on Lover's Lane," Father Gilchrist concluded rhetorically. "Yes, that would, come to think of it, strain one's imagination."

"I knew she was too young to be involved in that sort of thing," Mr. Crimpton declared. "She's a little smart-ass, all right. But jeez, that is good to hear."

"Yes, but why didn't she tell us before?" Judge Talbott insisted, relieved but still confused. "We're supposed to share our problems so we can help each other, aren't we?"

"Well, I think the problem wasn't that she wasn't," Dr. Pendleton attempted to explain. "Er, it was that she wasn't able to be what she was, uh, n't."

"I would like to know why, if she is indeed not a Junior League call girl, she would concoct such a story in the first place," Father Gilchrist declared.

"Perhaps what began as a minor fabrication simply became too elaborate for her to reverse," Mr. McClintock suggested, fidgeting with his empty plate.

Dr. Pendleton nodded eagerly. "Uh, yes, that's actually very close to the gist of the situation," he confirmed. "Again, I really do wish she had explained this more succinctly herself. But, suffice it to say, that, where as she was, she actually wasn't." Catching Father Gilchrist's look, he hastily concluded. "Uh, in short, very simply, she never was, and is not now, a prostitute."

As the others nodded slowly, Chris, having wandered back inside in time to hear almost all of the exchange, stared up at Dr. Pendleton. He found that he wanted to share in their discovery and amazement, to participate in this revelation, and to join in the pleasant and relieved surprise, he wanted to, very much, but he could not, for as he stood there, stomach twisting, tensed features still smeared and sticky, he had to accept that he already knew all of this, already knew it, because she had told him herself. She had told him, and he hadn't believed her and then, on top of that, had told her that he didn't care. Now, as he gazed mutely at the group, his face tautening in sorrow, feeling his loins squirm inside of him, as much as he wanted to say, "*She's not?*" the words came out as a flat, knowing statement. "No, she's not."

He slumped quietly in his chair, the others regarding him with curiosity as well as concern, Father Gilchrist diverting their attention with a sharp inquiry.

"While I am delighted to know that she opted to begin and simultaneously end her would-be career with the most symbolic Dear Johns Letter of all time and barring the fact that you seem to have known her true situation all along and opted to keep it to yourself"—he noted to Dr. Pendleton, cutting off his gasping protest—"I have been wondering for quite some time how it was possible for a judge to sit here night after night, listening to these scandalous remarks, mistruths that they might have been, without ever once taking any action against them, much less even comment upon their obviously illicit nature."

Judge Talbott had glanced up at him, caught off guard and meekly taking in the priest's forthright words, Mr. Crimpton frowning alongside her.

"Yeah, I was wondering about that too," he confessed, regarding the little judge uncertainly. "I mean prostitution is illegal, isn't it?"

Dr. Pendleton, posed to intercede, did not, however, instead finding himself glancing at her as well, as he had also pondered that self-same question.

Seeming to grow smaller beneath their inquisitive gazes, Judge Talbott pursed her lips and swallowed discreetly, determined to hold her ground.

"Well," she began, her timidity giving way to a sort of innocent rightness. "I know it's illegal of course, but I didn't think I *could* say anything against it."

When no one appeared to comprehend, she hastened to continue. "I mean we've all come here to discuss our problems with each other, to confide in one another, and to help each other, right?" She glanced up at Dr. Pendleton. "You wanted us to establish our own private place where we could feel comfortable about sharing things, especially personal things, didn't you? So I couldn't say anything to make her feel bad or unsafe, and I certainly couldn't do anything to get her in trouble... I mean isn't that like what they call the doctor–client confidentiality?" she asked him, then glancing earnestly at each of the others. "And if we really are supposed to be an anonymous group, well, then, I couldn't say anything, could I?" she finished simplistically. "I mean I just thought that that was how these groups worked."

She smiled at them all and looked shyly down into her lap, Mr. McClintock beaming at her and nodding, Mr. Crimpton blinking and submitting. That worked for him, he supposed. He guessed. Who knew anymore? He massaged his headache.

Even in his remorseful state, Chris was very touched with the woman's sweet, unassuming outlook, until his mind bleakly forced him to contrast it with his own, and he slunk even deeper in his seat.

Dr. Pendleton regarded her in awe, profoundly impressed with her incredible open-mindedness, not to mention her unhesitant placement of the group's integrity ahead of the law. If and when she ever became capable of making a decision, this woman would make a scrupulously good judge.

Only Father Gilchrist's features had shifted from skeptical anticipation to frigid outrage. He had well-expected some sort of nonjudgmental response from this judge; and, of course, that was precisely what she had rendered, no surprises there. He had not, however, foreseen the almost childlike, laughable scope of her tolerance. Tolerance? Such liberty, such lassitude, such a ridiculous, blank-check open-season, anything-goes frame of mind, was not even a *frame* of mind, such open-mindedness becoming open-mindlessness when any semblance of boundary ceased to exist.

He was about to exorcise the demons of his day by lashing out at her, attacking her skylark attitude as comparable to criminal negligence, to moral irresponsibility, to anarchy! Any courtroom over which this moppet presided would scarcely be better than his own confessional.

His fiery countenance convulsed and then froze, this thought striking him as if with the Centurion's spear, for, as hopelessly ineffective as the judge's ministrations would most likely be, any rendered by him within his own narrow hemisphere would be that much more disempowered and empty. His eyes widened as he gazed at the woman, seeing instead the cop, seeing Vanessa's bruised lip, seeing Sister Angelica, seeing those kids on the bus from earlier, seeing the little girl warbling that insipid, damnable nursery rhyme, her tiny, tremulous voice like that of Mrs. Spindlewood, who, seventy years her senior, at the very least, was her equal in innocence and acceptance. He closed his eyes against this torrent of unwanted introspect, willing his heart to stabilize, clenching his teeth to swallow his pain and rage. In the midst of this inner struggle, his mind randomly conjured up the old woman's first name; and he opened his eyes again, blinking at the coincidence, very nearly snorting in laughter.

Well, well, that infernal Beatles' song had been borne out yet again, he reflected bitterly; its parallel with their reality once more proving abstractly precognitive. He actually took a moment to recall the lyrics, his slight surge of mirth abating as he reflected on their connotation, particularly toward the end of the song. No, no, even he would hope against that eventuality.

He was distracted as Chris suddenly stood up, all eyes turning toward him, the young punk rocker stepping awkwardly toward the door and then stopping, returning to his chair, pausing, and gyrating hesitantly, his clumsy boots the only audible sound as he glanced at all of them with a brief, hangdog look, pausing yet again and then diving downward to retrieve his backpack and skateboard, standing upright and staring at them all again, his mouth, for once, clamped shut. His gaze met Dr. Pendleton's, and he seemed to be on the verge of speaking, then flushing and turning sharply away, slinking hurriedly out the door, Mr. McClintock grimacing worriedly in his wake.

"Uh, good night, Claude," Dr. Pendleton called haltingly, Judge Talbott hastily waving. Mr. Crimpton looked from the empty doorway to them and then at the floor. That kid wasn't the only one who was on something.

Father Gilchrist watched Chris go, nothing at all mysterious about his behavior to the old priest. His thoughts reverted to Vanessa again, and her harsh words resurfaced in his mind. Her delineation of their pathetic group—Mis-fits Anonymous indeed—had been quite cutting and intemperate and true. He closed his eyes again, attempted to douse his inner fires with his usual recourse of vinegar and then gave up, too tired to permit this day to continue. He began to gather up his hat and coat as Dr. Pendleton, perhaps sensing that his group was dwindling in size and in efficacy, had attempted to segue the judge's statement into a discourse of her own issues revolving around her profession.

"Uh, you were telling us that even though you're on vacation, you were lending a hand at the courthouse," he was saying pleasantly. "I think that that's an excellent idea, especially when you consider that, after your vacation is over, uh, you will have to, well, assume the responsibilities of a judge," he added, gently but pointedly.

"Yes, I know," Judge Talbott admitted, smiling shyly, her features then brightening. "But I've been thinking of ways to help make the transition easier, because, yes, you're right, Doctor, I have to face that responsibility. And I intend to."

Impressed with her uncharacteristic assertiveness, Dr. Pendleton nodded encouragingly. "Oh, that's very good to hear," he replied. "Have you come up with anything yet?"

"Well," beamed the judge, gaining confidence. "Theoretically, if I continue up the judicial career ladder, I would eventually attain a judgeship in which the proceedings will be trial by jury, and I wouldn't have to worry about making the wrong decision, because it would be the jury who would be doing the deciding. I would simply have to preside over the trial," she nodded simply at the notion of the scenario.

Dr. Pendleton blinked, while Father Gilchrist drew his lips tautly together, forcing himself to remain silent, his automatic appraisal of the judge's solution so vitriolic as to sting his larynx.

"Uh, yes, that would…spare you from having to make any, uh, decisions, per se," Dr. Pendleton conceded slowly, looking to Mr. Crimpton as if for help, the man appearing to require some sort of help himself. Mr. McClintock's focus seemed to be elsewhere, and he was too afraid even to look over at Father Gilchrist.

He cleared his throat. "Uh, but for now, of course, you're going to have to deal with cases wherein you'll have to, uh, render a verdict, all on your own, based upon your own insight and judgment," he proposed gradually.

"Yes, that's true," Judge Talbott agreed, undaunted, in fact, exhibiting even more confidence. "And I had an idea regarding that too. When a verdict can't be reached at the end of the day, a case can be granted a continuance. If that happens, if it is a very difficult case, with really complex details, it occurred to me that if I was completely unable to make up my mind, maybe I could explain all the facts to all of you at our meetings. And then, we could all deliberate together on what would be the best course of action."

She nodded concisely, Dr. Pendleton's smile becoming pained.

"Are you *mad?*" Father Gilchrist's voice crackled in the silent room, Dr. Pendleton whirling around to gape at him. Mr. Crimpton and Mr. McClintock both jolted back to focus, Judge Talbott freezing in her seat, looking up at the priest in fright as he stood over her, one arm poised in sliding into a sleeve of his raincoat. He jerked it into place and fixed the tiny woman with an almost inquisitorial look.

"You, *an appointed judge*, would presume to preside over a case and then, at the hour of judgment, flash a 'to be continued' sign, instruct the litigants to tune in tomorrow, and *then*, as they await the outcome of this judicial cliffhanger, would race over here to consult the dubious wisdom of our motley group and its milquetoast mastermind by converting this haphazard array of carnival sideshows into your own personalized star chamber?" he shouted, his eyes blazing beneath his wispy, fierce brows.

Judge Talbott shrank. "Well, I...," she gasped.

"Now, Father Gilchrist...," interjected Dr. Pendleton.

"I did my best to maintain composure while you offered your maudlin, kindergarten exposé on the virtues of the sanctity of our happy little group's anonymity—*as if* anyone would be interested in the morbid details of our tawdry lives—and you may be grateful for the fact that certain circumstances on which I am unable to elaborate force me into walking that particular plank with you!"

"However," he continued imperiously, his voice mellifluously malevolent. "If it is my understanding that you intend to administer justice by turning this laughing stock of a therapy group into some extraneous Court of Appeals, I must not only applaud your high ambition but also seek to spurn you onward to even greater channels of deliberation. Why, there will be no need to settle for us when you can be dispensing verdicts with tea leaves and Ouija boards, after which you can apply your profoundly Learned Hand to tarot cards and crystal balls! Why, soon enough, I'm sure you'll be able to refine your methods to the flip of a coin! And, mark my words, with such a keenly discerning sense of right and wrong, why, before long, you and your Nestle Toll-House, Raggedy Anne Jurisprudence will ascend through the judicial strata until you have attained the highest position in the land!" He stomped one foot, gesturing boldly. "Hear ye, hear ye! All rise, the Supreme Court is now in session, the Right Honorable Chief Justice Edith Bunker presiding!" He clapped his hands righteously.

"Father Gilchrist!" Dr. Pendleton exclaimed, flushing as he glanced worriedly at Judge Talbott.

Judge Talbott, now appearing half her size and petrified as well, opened her mouth to form some manner of response, her lips trembling. Her wide eyes then gave way to tears as she grasped for her purse and frantically searched for a handkerchief, withdrawing a baggie of cookies instead.

"Father Gilchrist!" Dr. Pendleton exclaimed again, gulping as the sniffling judge's tears became more pronounced. "I insist that you apologize to Judge Talbott!"

He shrank back a step as Father Gilchrist moved toward his podium, his aged visage becoming a parody of outraged righteousness. "Oh, you do, *do you?*" he countered bombastically, actually tossing his head back theatrically as he boomed, "*Never!*"

Judge Talbott found a handkerchief and began to sob into it, Mr. Crimpton's hands crumpling into his lap as he stared at her in strained sympathy, Mr. McClintock looking on in worry.

Dr. Pendleton tentatively approached his packing crate again, forcing himself to meet the priest's daunting gaze. "Well, uh, in that case, then, I, uh…" He cleared his throat and nodded with finality. "Uh, in that case, I'll have to ask you to leave…"

Father Gilchrist received this decree with a deadly look in his eyes, advancing one more step toward the podium, Dr. Pendleton gulping but holding his ground.

"No words spoken by Romeo to Juliet were half so sweet," he grated, slamming his hat atop his head and storming away from the smaller man. "I must be going anyway," he added, glaring at Mr. Crimpton. "It's time for me to take my Geritol. Then, I must rush off and write the words to a sermon that no one will hear!"

He stomped away, Mr. Crimpton staring after him in exasperated silence, as Dr. Pendleton, clearing his throat again and glancing at the now-wailing judge, raised one hand. "Uh, hope to see you tomorrow," he called lamely after him.

Mr. McClintock heaved himself up out of his chairs and hastened over to the judge's side, Mr. Crimpton reluctantly turning to her as well.

"There, there, Judge Talbott," the affable ex-food critic soothed her, removing a pristinely starched handkerchief from his top pocket

307

and handing it to her. "You mustn't let Father Gilchrist upset you. I'm sure he didn't mean any of those things."

"Yes, don't pay any attention to him," Mr. Crimpton attempted as well. "Just remember what that girl said earlier..."

Judge Talbott, sniffling into the fresh handkerchief, shuddered as she eyed the driving examiner uncertainly. "What did she say?"

Mr. Crimpton stared at her. "That he's just a mean old bastard," he told her, shrugging simplistically, then recalling all the other remarks that Vanessa had made, and grimacing crookedly, Dr. Pendleton doing the same.

"I didn't mean to make him angry," Judge Talbott said contritely. "I was just explaining some ideas I had for dealing with some of the problems I'll have with my job."

"Of course, you were," Mr. McClintock nodded understandingly. "We've all had to think of ways to deal with our jobs. Sometimes, those ideas can be veritable lifesavers."

Mr. Crimpton frowned. His lifesaving ideas entailed jumping out of the car before it burst into flames or collided with a noise barrier. He opted to keep this to himself though.

Judge Talbott blinked trustingly at Mr. McClintock, her tears abating. "Have any of your ideas helped you with the problems at your job?" she asked hopefully.

Mr. McClintock paused, his fleshy features becoming sheepish. "Uh, well, no," he confessed. "In fact, I was fired earlier this week."

Gasping, Judge Talbott seemed on the verge of sympathizing with him, when the implications of his statement struck her, causing her face to freeze and then crumple into a fresh bout of tears, Mr. McClintock flinching in dismay as she grabbed her purse and raced girlishly toward the entrance, all three men gaping at her when she spun around and stifled her tears with the handkerchief to speak.

"Good night. I'll see you all tomorrow for the retreat," she sniffled. "I'm really looking forward to it!"

She then turned and dashed sobbing into the night, Dr. Pendleton wincing and then slowly, pointlessly returning to his podium, Mr. Crimpton standing and reaching for a cigarette, regarding Mr. McClintock appraisingly. Getting fired, he had always considered it a source of angst, but never as a way out. The severance pay, alone, would be—

"Uh, I hope you don't have to leave now too, Mr. Crimpton," Dr. Pendleton said halfheartedly, glancing over at the side table. "There are still plenty of doughnuts left…"

It was Mr. McClintock who ambled over to investigate this, Mr. Crimpton shaking his head in sardonic patience.

"No thanks. I've had enough heartburn for one evening." He waved tersely and headed for the door.

"There really are only a few left," Mr. McClintock informed Dr. Pendleton. "I would be more than happy to take them off your hands."

Grimacing, Dr. Pendleton nodded, Mr. McClintock innocently tucking the pink box beneath one arm, bidding him a good night and strolling away.

Clearing his throat, Dr. Pendleton contemplated the circle of empty chairs. "Well, I'll, uh, see you all tomorrow morning," he stated quietly. "Be sure and dress casually."

*****

The remainder of that evening, in spite of the disintegrated close of the meeting, progressed routinely for most of the members. Mr. McClintock, employing a technique that he had come to master over the years as a method of exercise, that of walking and eating simultaneously, finished the last of the doughnuts and was prepared to go home. Had his steps not taken him past a sight that he had not seen in an almost nostalgically long time, he would have, his evening instead finding him at a Wienerschnitzel Restaurant.

Mr. Crimpton, not even wanting to ride on the bus until he had cleared his mind and taken in some of the bracing night air, had smoked three cigarettes and, incomprehensibly, had ended up in another bar. While its Friday night revelry further shattered his nerves, he resolved to stay there long enough to discern what had gone wrong earlier that day, if he could have had the relaxation of that shot and somehow held onto it. The answer not only presented itself when he partook of three shots this time but also seemed to ascend within him as a revelation imbuing him with pride and strength when he stood up from the bar stool, paid his bill, and left, feeling staunchly fortified but also well within the responsible, upright, perfectly acceptable limits personified by the words "in moderation." What was more, he stoically avoided speaking to anyone, intent on having nothing to do with potentially drunk drivers. Instead, he used his sudden clarity of mind to take the logical, rational action of hailing a cab. As he was thusly conveyed home, he reflected upon the degree to which his reenforced common sense had prevailed, for, while the cabbie was, indeed, sober, this proved in no way to be a guarantee of his skills as a driver.

Judge Talbott, after composing herself as best she could, drove back to her apartment, fed her cats, and launched herself into the baking project she had so excitedly planned for the retreat the next day, her heart heavy but her mind intent upon the comfort and distraction of her kitchen. She was going to bring along the ingredients to make more s'mores at the lodge and was focusing now on a snack for the road, some of her tension exacted as she attacked a mound of dough with her rolling pin. Then, using a cookie cutter and a paring knife, she began to make ginger bread men—and ladies—in the guises of each member of the group, adding extra features to personalize them, resisting the temptation to give Father Gilchrist's cookie two horns and a spiked tail, a little shocked at her irreverence, but still shaken by his harsh words.

When they had finished baking and had cooled, she decorated them with multicolored icings and then made up some popcorn and sat down to watch one of her favorite movies, *Twelve Angry Men*, eventually shutting it off and going to bed. It reminded her too much of their therapy group.

Chris, having been consumed with the unstoppable intention of going after Vanessa, soon realized that, for all of his knowledge of the city, he did not know where Saxbury Commons was and had boarded the wrong bus, virtually out of the city limits and at the end of the line before he thought to ask the driver. By the time he had returned to his neighborhood, hopelessness had set in again, and he had trudged reluctantly home.

All throughout dinner, his increasingly stricken face was tilted toward his untouched plate while his parents debated about what needed to be done that weekend, more back-to-school shopping or the newest exhibit at the zoo, his brothers chiming in with their viewpoints, his grandparents confusing the issue with an insistence on the attendance of a potluck at their senior center. Not even his grandfather's usual histrionics could lift his spirits as he wordlessly left the table and plodded off to his room.

Once inside of it, his sanctuary offered him little solace, its many personal, colorful adornments instead seeming empty and meaningless. He sat down on his bed, kicked off his boots, and merely stared for what might have been hours, his gaze fixed and unblinking, mouth and jaws clamped tightly, his breathing becoming more and more audible to himself as its rhythm quickened.

At length, he switched on his stereo and began to play the same punk rock that he had turned on earlier that week, rolling over on his bed to face the wall, having shut off his light and raised the volume to an especially loud extreme, not so much to take comfort in its grinding discord and tribal screeching as to drown out any sounds that might be overheard as he lay in his bed and sobbed.

Chapter 10

EVEN WHEN THE DRIVER CONFIRMED that she would be passing Saxbury Commons, Vanessa was still very much aware that she had no idea what to do once she got there. Night had fallen, and yet the area into which the bus was taking her was increasingly darker, the stop in question illuminated by a single streetlight and little else. As the taillights receded, Vanessa gazed around at the gloom of old brick warehouses, dilapidated loading docks, and fenced-off demolition sites.

It was almost unthinkable that anyone could live out here, she had reflected, particularly someone as old and frail as the subject of her search. Nonetheless, she set out walking, trying to envision which way a fragile, wispy old lady would go, choosing a fairly uncluttered sidewalk, and proceeding with her senses poised, alert to anyone who might try to sneak up on her, seeing no one, not even the occasional car. She rounded the corner of an abandoned factory and then saw a tall, narrow tenement building, its few lighted windows standing out in stark contrast to the immense, formidable storage company alongside of it.

As it was the only manner of residential structure to be seen, Vanessa hurried over to it, mounting its stoop and pausing at its heavy door, staring at a battle-scarred intercom system, unsure as to which number to summon. She then noticed that the door was ajar, its locking mechanism broken; and she heaved it open, stepping quietly inside, glancing about its murky entryway, her gaze falling upon a panel of battered mailboxes.

Rushing over to it, she scanned over the row of label slots for each one, most of which were blank, the last one bearing a slip of paper so faded that its lettering was almost indiscernible. Nevertheless, she felt a surge of gratified excitement when she made out the name: E. Spindlewood.

Noting the apartment number, she darted over to the adjacent elevator, tapping sharply on its call button and waiting impatiently. Hearing nothing activated behind its scuffed, defaced door, she turned her back on it, located the stairwell, and began to climb the steps with anxious determination.

The stairwell, while not inundated with graffiti, had not been spared various spray-painted excerpts, most of them typically and probably thankfully cryptic, Vanessa ignoring all of it as she dashed upward, finally reaching the eighth and topmost floor, breathless but not stopping as she hastened into the hallway, glimpsed the number she wanted, and moved quickly toward it.

There was no doorbell, and she was forced to knock, doing so as respectfully loudly as she could, glancing over at the opposite door in the musty hallway, wary that someone might question what she was doing there.

It took three sequences of knocking, each one more angst-pro-voking than the previous, before Vanessa's heart leapt at the sound of some kind of life behind the sturdy old door. She heard a dead-bolt disengage, as well as a chain lock, the tarnished doorknob rattling and then twisting, the door creaking open without reser-vation, revealing Mrs. Spindlewood herself, her grayish white hair unpinned and let down to her thin shoulders, her frail body clad in a threadbare but neatly kept pink robe and a frilly, white night-gown, her tiny feet tucked into matching pink, well-worn house slippers.

She smiled vaguely at Vanessa, her milky eyes regarding her unseeingly. "Hello, Trudy," she greeted her absently, stepping away from the door.

Vanessa, her features brightening as she beheld the phantas-mal old woman, hesitated and then ventured into the dim entryway of the apartment, pausing before closing the door behind her, then instinctually locking it again, slipping the chain into its hasp as if to compensate for her intrusion, but also as if to safeguard her presence there from the rest of the building and the world in general.

She then followed the soft, padding tread of Mrs. Spindlewood to the apartment's interior, stopping in the doorway, immobilized by what lay before her. All during her improvised journey out there and even previously during a few of the meetings, she had fleetingly entertained what the old woman's residence would look like, speculating over a dusty hideaway with potted plants and a plethora of mewling cats, the whole place reeking of a feline odor, or some cluttered stale series of rooms filled with stacks of newspapers, milk bottles, and other meticulously accumulated junk or even some pseudocontemporary setup, with a row of mugging grandchildren on a mantelpiece and scrawled crayon renderings proudly arranged with refrigerator magnets—any number of stereotypical notions of the dwelling place of a little old lady occurring to her, none of them seeming quite right, though an actual depiction of what it might then entail likewise eluding her.

None of her predictions had prepared her for what she was to find, though; in fact, it took her more than a few minutes to register what she was seeing as she trailed the elderly woman into her domain, and even then, her gradual comprehension only slowly began to develop. Shortly, however, she understood everything.

She stood in the doorway of a small kitchen and dining room, a yellowish tint cast upon the room from a dusty ceiling fixture. A dark green Formica-topped dinette table was flanked by matching chrome chairs, beyond which the countertop of black Formica was neatly arranged with a gleaming toaster, a bread box, and a large solid Mix Master, the sink of worn porcelain. A small gas stove sat alongside a squat, steadily humming Westinghouse refrigerator, the adjacent cupboards a dull-white color, the two windows outfitted with simple lace curtains, behind which the roll-paper window shades had been drawn for the night. The room smelled faintly of a mixture of cooking and the gas that the stovetop had yielded over the years, this dual aroma, in turn, surpassed by an even more pervasive scent, something that Vanessa had sensed before but that she was unable to place.

When she wordlessly followed Mrs. Spindlewood's tread over the dull linoleum, she passed into a small parlor, its arrangement no less striking. It was furnished with a small brown easy chair and a matching sofa, a narrow coffee table, bare save for a lace setting, a narrow floor lamp with a faded shade, a small bookcase, and an immense oak-encased radio and turntable. A massive radiator stood beneath one of the three windows, the curtains of which matched those of the kitchen. A small expanse of hardwood floor shone from around the frayed edges of a thick, dark rug, while the walls, bare save for a few simple watercolors in flimsy frames, had been outfitted with shelves, most of which were empty, a few housing small porcelain figurines and a flower vase. This room too was yellowish and murky, the aroma from the kitchen likewise present there as Vanessa gazed about uncertainly.

She watched as Mrs. Spindlewood moved, ostensibly, toward the easy chair, instead settling down onto the couch, her small hands resting in her lap as she stared vacantly forward, her gaze seeming to rest on an archaic television set, its wood-encased screen as blank as her expression. Hesitantly, Vanessa approached her, slowly sitting down alongside of her, allowing her bag to slip to the floor. She gripped her knees together, hunched slightly as she stared at the much older woman's profile, realizing that her line of vision was directed at some undefinable point on the lightly cracked plaster of the wall, otherwise discerning nothing from her placid, staid countenance.

"Mrs. Spindlewood," she said at last, her voice dry but firm. "We've all been really worried about you. We haven't seen you at the meetings in over a week now. I was afraid maybe something had happened to you..." She paused, swallowing. "Have you been doing all right?"

Mrs. Spindlewood continued to stare forward as she replied. "Oh, I'm fine, Trudy. How have things been down at the office?" she asked absently.

Vanessa peered at her closely, wishing she could read the old woman's thoughts. "Uh, they've been...about the same," she answered honestly. "Though not exactly the same without you there."

She paused again, considering a different approach. "Mr. Bergdorf has been worried about you," she mentioned pointedly. "He's been wondering why you haven't been coming to...the office the past few days."

As she watched, Mrs. Spindlewood blinked once or twice, her pale features then shifting ever so slightly to a look of puzzlement as she turned a bit in Vanessa's direction.

"It's odd," she responded slowly, her glazed expression mildly ponderous. "They told me they didn't need me to come in anymore. They told me that Mr. Bergdorf wasn't there and that I should go home and wait for the Service to call me, to tell me when to come back."

She trailed off, her focus gradually shifting back to its previous stance, her features resettling into complacency. Vanessa regarded her in confusion, not knowing what to make of her explanation. Obviously, everyone had known from the very beginning that the elderly woman was a little off, but she had seemed to maintain this apparent imbalance with routine ease. In fact, she had struck Vanessa as being the one member of their group most able to keep it together.

Now, however, the extent of the woman's incoherence seemed much more pronounced, not only because Vanessa was visiting her for the first time in her own incredibly surreal environment, for the girl had yet to grasp just what it was about the place that was so unsettlingly astounding, but also because, beyond that, just from the woman's few simple words, she was instinctually certain that something else altogether was very wrong, although she could not guess as to how to go about pinpointing it.

Not willing to give up, she sat up on the couch, speaking more firmly than before. "Yes, but we tried to call you earlier, Mrs. Spindlewood," she told her earnestly. "You gave Dr.... Mr. Bergdorf your number and we tried calling you, but..."

She paused, glancing around the room, noticing a wall-mounted telephone arranged near the arched doorway of the parlor. She stood up and walked quickly over to it, the formalities that would be customary when visiting an older, grandmotherly type giving way as her sense of protectiveness began to assert itself in her need to understand what was going on there.

She lifted the receiver, surprised with how heavy it was, holding it expectantly to one ear, taken off guard when she heard a dial tone, distracted all over again by the telephone number, neatly printed in the center of the rotary dial by the same hand that had produced the label on the mailbox downstairs. Gramercy Six-Seven-One-Two-Eight.

Remembering enough of the confusion from earlier to know that this was not the number she had called, she hung up the receiver, her perplexed frown settling on a small shelf off to one side of the arch, her eyes drawn to a silver-framed photograph that rested there on a rumpled doily. She leaned in to peer at its depiction, a simple studio shot, black and white, posed but natural, of a young man and woman sitting shoulder to shoulder, smiling brightly. The man, his severe haircut and sharply rugged features making him strikingly handsome, looked to be in his early to midtwenties.

The woman, appearing a bit younger, wore her hair neatly up and was very pretty in a shy, demure way. To complement the man's plain, trim suit, she wore an equally reserved dress with a wide collar and brooch, both of which Vanessa had seen before, her heart quickening as she gazed from the pert little face in the photograph to Mrs. Spindlewood, the decades of contrast unable to obscure the fact that they were one and the same person.

Regarding her closely, Vanessa returned to the couch, Mrs. Spindlewood gradually looking up at her, smiling vaguely.

"Hello, Trudy," she warbled. "It's nice of you to come by. Edward will be glad to see you. He'll be home in a little while."

Vanessa eased herself down alongside the frail woman once again, her throat having gone dry. "Who's Edward, Mrs. Spindlewood?" she inquired slowly.

"He'll be home in a little while," Mrs. Spindlewood repeated, her vacant smile still lingering. "He'll be glad you came by to visit."

Her eyes shooting back to the gilt-edged frame, Vanessa bit her lip in contemplative discovery. It had never even occurred to her that Mrs. Spindlewood was married. She lowered her gaze to the old woman's tiny, withered hands. Sure enough, she wore a simple gold ring, twisted neatly at the top to hold a small diamond. She marveled at the idea of there being an adorable, spritely little old man to accompany Mrs. Spindlewood, then instantly wondering if he would be as glad to see her as his wife suggested, dressed as she was, showing up unannounced in their home. She somehow doubted it, especially when, the more she considered it, there seemed to be something wrong with the entire notion.

As she pondered this, she realized that the elderly woman had spoken to her and had to ask her to repeat herself.

"I said, how is Herbert?" she reiterated. "He's such a nice boy."

Caught off guard, Vanessa blushed and nodded quickly. "Oh yeah, Herbert," she replied, somewhat flatly. "Yeah, he's fine. Herbert is just great…" Her thoughts thrown off-track, she contemplated "Herbert," her chest swelling a bit in mixed emotion as she envisioned him, realizing that because she had so fiercely ignored him all night, she had not noticed that his lip was also cut and bruised, obviously from her having backhanded him, and had not noticed, of course, until she had grabbed that creampuff and— A surge of shame rocked through her, and she screwed her lips together, closing her eyes. *Chris.*

"Edward always liked Herbert," Mrs. Spindlewood was saying absently. "He thinks that you two make such a nice couple. We were both so happy to hear that you've gotten engaged."

Vanessa's eyes flew open, and she faced Mrs. Spindlewood, her heart convulsing sharply. She blinked at her rapidly, a stinging sensation overtaking her eyes as she inhaled deeply and then exhaled slowly, the action banishing the unneeded, unwanted, barrage of feelings and giving her the stability, which, in turn, melded with a defeated sense of exhaustion.

"Mrs. Spindlewood," she said to the old woman's profile, her voice tired and direct. "Would you…you and Edward mind if I spent the night tonight?" she asked, somewhat rhetorically, her instincts telling her that she probably did not even have to bother asking.

Mrs. Spindlewood was silent for a moment before blinking and turning slightly toward her. "Of course you can, Trudy. Edward won't mind. I'll tell him that you and I are having a pajama party." She smiled faintly, her eyes continually haunted. "We'll make some taffy and read magazines and listen to records and fix each other's hair, just like when we were girls…" She very slowly began to rise to her feet.

Vanessa stared mutely up at her as the aged woman gazed down toward her, extending one fragile hand. Swallowing harshly, she stood up and took her hand, allowing herself to be led to a set of doors on the far side of the parlor, one closed, the other wide open.

They passed through the open doorway, Mrs. Spindlewood reaching for a light switch, yet another opaque, yellow glow illuminating the room before them, Vanessa staring into the murkiness and then swallowing again, her heartbeat steadily intensifying, seeming to be the only sound in the room save for the old woman's softly padding feet.

It was a bedroom, and as she gazed around in awe, she felt her overwhelming certainty that something was very wrong become intertwined with that faint, stale aroma, which was almost overpowering in this room. It was simple and modestly furnished—a queen-sized bed was arranged in the center, its maple headboard against one wall, a hope chest settled at its foot. A large, thick dresser was situated next to a closet door, a low-set vanity off to one side of the bed, its narrow surface neatly arrayed with a hairbrush and comb set, as well as a powder puff and a number of small, brittle, plastic articles.

The bed was flanked with two nightstands, the one on the far side bearing an empty flower vase, the nearer one a picture frame, the image of which was tilted away from Vanessa's view as she stood there, her hand slipping away from Mrs. Spindlewood's and falling to her side. The shades and curtains were also drawn, the latter a frilly pink, as was the heavy bedspread that neatly engulfed the bed, its wide pillows exposed at the top, the edges of the slipcovers likewise a faded pink.

Mrs. Spindlewood had grasped the hairbrush from the vanity and toddled over to the bed, settling down on its edge, Vanessa speechlessly joining her, sinking onto the plush mattress. She looked down at the large, silver-backed brush in the old woman's hand and then at her profile, her gaze having slipped back into its previous reverie. Not knowing what else to do, she took the brush and hesitantly, gently applied it to Mrs. Spindlewood's lifeless, almost snow-white, beautiful hair, beginning on one side and slowly, carefully making her way around the back, Mrs. Spindlewood motionless, perhaps even unaware. The notion of touching the woman, of arranging her hair, was so awkward as to be virtually irreverent; but Vanessa continued, inasmuch as it seemed to be what was expected.

As she shifted to focus on the back, she caught a glimpse of the picture frame, noting that it held another black-and-white picture, this one of the man she had seen in the other photograph, by himself, a simple studio headshot, the same rugged distinction, in a smiling yet more serious pose.

Staring at it, she paused in her actions and glanced quickly around the room for any other photographs, anything more recent, or recent in any sense of the word, tilting her head to see past the doorway, frowning toward that other photograph, blinking as the only real conclusion finally began to dawn upon her, a sinking unbearable dread washing over her as the question arose to her lips and died there. She lowered her head, herself now fixating unseeingly on the floor, images foggily clouding her mind as her throat constricted and her heart and stomach clenched. She sat there for a timeless duration, her ears dully listening to the silence, to the nothing.

The quietus was dispelled when she felt the hairbrush slip from her fingers, and she stirred slightly, fearing that she had dropped it, looking up sharply, and seeing her reflection in the tarnished mirror of the vanity as Mrs. Spindlewood slowly brought the brush to her hair now. Vanessa sat, mutely transfixed on her image in the mirror as she watched the aged, fragile movements of the woman's arm, seeing the blank tranquility of her features, the vacant, lost hollowness of her eyes as she focused on her task. Her feeble brush strokes scarcely permeated Vanessa's hair, reminding her of the dreamy-eyed attentions a little girl would administer to a favorite doll; and as Vanessa sat there, observing each frail motion, her body tensed and her hands clasped against her thighs, she had to fight to withstand the unendurable urge to get up and run away, to run far away from this place and all of its inescapable, painfully overwhelming conclusions and consequences.

She could not do this, of course, and could instead only sit there and permit the old woman to brush her hair as she gazed in burning anguish at her reflection, her breathing tremulous and sharp, her eyes red and smoldering, as she remembered when her mother used to brush her hair for her, years ago, the last person to do so, up until now.

At length, Mrs. Spindlewood stopped, pausing for a moment of vague contemplation, then slowly standing, Vanessa blinking rapidly, swallowing and standing as well, backing toward the doorway as she watched the old woman replace the hairbrush and then slip out of her bathrobe, folding it neatly and placing it atop the hope chest. Even more ephemerally delicate in just the worn nightgown, she folded back the bedspread and top sheet and then moved toward Vanessa, perhaps not seeing her as she turned off the light.

Even through the ensuing gloom, she could follow the ghostly, tottering figure as she made her way back to the bed, slowly eased herself into it, and pulled the covers into place, settling her head back against the engulfing pillow and turning slightly toward the other pillow, her voice little more than a whisper.

"Good night, Edward."

Vanessa stood in the doorway for several minutes, her skin prickling electrically, her heart pounding, her eyes, having been diverted by the surreal intensity of what they had just witnessed, now stinging again as she abruptly forced herself to turn away, only finding herself in the waxen lighting of the parlor again.

Exhaling shakily through her nose, she clenched her teeth and then noticed the second door again, grateful for at least the notion of a distraction, stepping briskly toward it, turning its knob, and pushing it quietly open. There was the slightest resistance by the doorframe suggesting that it had not been opened in some time, Vanessa briefly wondering if she were about to discover something still more soul-shattering, instead finding, with the flick of the light switch, that the room was completely empty, its hardwood floors showing dully in the meager light. Its musty interior was not suffused with the prominent odor, its air merely dank and dead and strikingly cold.

She peered into its barren depths for a moment, then submitting to a chilling impetus to extinguish the light and close the door, once again facing the parlor, unsure as to why the empty, unused room so repelled her, forced to incorporate that question with all of the others, each of which was predicated upon the horrible conclusion that she had been forced to accept only a few minutes earlier.

Standing before the photograph again, she peered at the incredibly young Mrs. Spindlewood and her equally and apparently eternally unaged husband, whom she now knew would not object to her being there, would not be home soon, would not be home ever. The truth was so obvious as to be devoid of any mystery at all; the pervasive scent that haunted the apartment like a subtle, invisible cloud was not from cooking or the age of the building or the activities of the apartment; it was the smell of stale, musty despair, of dust motes and defeat, sun-faded hopes, and peeling dreams; it was the clinging, powdery, old womanish smell of Mrs. Spindlewood, herself, as she passed her days there. At some point, this tiny apartment had known happiness, perhaps quite briefly, before it was introduced to tragedy and then stalemate. At some point, tears had flown here, had flooded the place before something snapped altogether in the mind of a heartbroken widow, stopping time for her, reducing her to a sentinel, a shrine-keeper. Vanessa was far too young to recognize the exact nuances of the apartment's decor, but she perceived the anachronistic, phantasmal timelessness and could only guess as to how long this anomaly had elapsed into the future. How long could it have been going on—thirty years? Forty? Perhaps more.

Her head spinning, her gaze fell upon her bag, sharply and reassuringly out of place where she had left it on the floor, its discordant presence giving her comfort and spurning her to action, as she did not dare to stand motionless for too long, knowing what would happen if she were forced to dwell upon the enormity of it all anymore.

Scooping up her bag, she raced to the telephone, hastily searching for the business card Dr. Pendleton had asked her to take one night when dropping her off at the hotel. To bring him up to date on the situation would be helpful enough for all of them, but she also knew that just speaking to someone would help her to get a grip. Finding the card, she lifted up the receiver, a bit daunted by the rotary dial and then forgetting about the entire matter as her gaze travelled to the wall above the telephone. She gaped up at a dish-cloth-like calendar, a sort that she had never seen before, its novelty lost as her eyes rested upon its year. *1957.*

Her features became blank as she contemplated that year, the connotations descending upon her like sprinkles of rain and then bitter, stinging hail. Denial in the face of such facts was implausible, even when the facts were unthinkable. She replaced the receiver and backed away from the telephone, clenching her jaws painfully.

1957. That was over fifty years ago—a death sentence of fifty lifelessly dead years, alone. A small cry escaped from between her teeth, and she thought desperately of Chris, of calling him, instead a glimmer of hope surfacing with this idea and then dying as she realized that she did not have his number. She whimpered again, her arms folded to her chest in a semblance of stoicism as she shifted and trembled, trying to reassure herself that she would not have known what to say to him, that he might not have wanted to speak to her anyway, this train of thought yielding no reassurance whatsoever.

She turned her back on the telephone, peering wildly around the apartment for any manner of distraction, any sort of diversion she could turn to in order to allay her claustrophobic, stifling frame of mind. Everywhere she looked, however, every direction in which she focused, every single thing on which she rested her eyes, was landlocked in another era, encapsulated in this surreal time warp, leaving her with nothing to which she could relate, nothing from her own reality, which, pathetic though it was, was at least familiar.

Turning, she almost ran down the short corridor and peered through an adjacent doorway into a bathroom, taking in its pedestal basin and its throne-like toilet and claw-footed tub, the shower curtain a pale pink, its metal hoop neatly arranged with stockings dangling to drip dry, the shelves of the room lined with small Bakelite toiletries and simple little old lady nuances, the powdery smell of old flesh overwhelming in the little room, the tiled floor and faded walls, like the rest of the apartment, clean, tidy, and scrubbed but irreversibly chipped, worn, and stained.

Spinning away from it, she pulled open a door opposite it, revealing a closet, her eyes falling on Mrs. Spindlewood's worn overcoat and felt hat, her little black purse and tiny gloves tucked on a shelf alongside the door.

Almost slamming it in choking frustration, she glanced at the only other door that to the outside world, the door that she had so attentively locked behind her to keep that self-same world at bay. Once again, she considered wrestling those locks open and running out of the building, away from the sorrow and melancholy of this tomb-like haven.

She did not—though, could not—for she would never abandon Mrs. Spindlewood now, but the very thought of that vulnerable old lady was still too much for her to bear in the face of what she had learned; and yet everywhere she looked, her mind was inundated with nothing but the presence of her tragic and arrested existence.

She raced into the kitchen again, still seeking something, anything from which to draw comfort, to bridge the immeasurable gap between this reality and that of her and the rest of the world. She actually yanked open the refrigerator, its archaic outfittings and its metal ice-cube trays prevailing against the stark selection of food stuffs—a few bottles of milk, some butter, and a few eggs.

Pulling open the nearest cupboard, she stared up at the boxes of farina and tapioca and cream of wheat and oatmeal in despair, turning to the next and gaping in dismay at the cans of Campbell Soup and Dinty Moore Beef Stew and canned vegetables and a plethora of other little old lady staples, knowing without knowing but positive that while the labels had changed and the quality had deteriorated over the years, these were undoubtedly the same exact items she would have found in there decades before. In time, she was slamming the doors shut as she moved from one to the next, the action feeling good, her exasperation giving her strength as she dealt with this ludicrous, imbalanced situation. In an abstract way, she told herself flippantly, it was almost funny—

In the last cupboard, she found the anachronism within the anachronism that she had so desperately sought, that link to the present, to the reality that she despised but at least knew. On the otherwise empty shelf, arranged all in a row with almost childlike care, as if for safekeeping, were the Rice Krispies Treat, the baggie of Chex party mix, and the chocolate cupcake given to her by Judge Talbott, each one untouched and still neatly wrapped.

She stood there, staring at them, envisioning the old woman carefully placing them in the cupboard after each meeting, meetings that she would not even have been attending had it not been for...

Backing away from the cupboard, unable to rest her gaze upon anything else, not for another second, she retreated to the bathroom, closing the door and squeezing her eyes shut against her surroundings, her mind instantly flooding with images of the young woman in the photograph, of Edward, and then of the Mrs. Spindlewood she knew, of the Herbert and Trudy the old woman had known, of Herbert as she knew him, of Chris; she thought of her predicament, of the past few days, of Chris, of her life, of its promise and of its disaster, and of Chris who she had treated so badly and so hatefully and who she now was gut-wrenchingly and screamingly against her will forced to admit that she loved; and upon surrendering to this unbidden but inescapable truth, she gave up altogether, sinking to the floor of Mrs. Spindlewood's pretty pink bathroom, drawing her knees up to her chest as she huddled against the bathtub, inhaling in one agonized gasp and then just letting go, at long last giving into the tears.

Chapter 11

Goosey Goosey Gander
Whither dost thou wander?
Upstairs and downstairs
And in my lady's chamber.
There I met an old man
Who wouldn't say his prayers;
I took him by the left leg
And threw him down the stairs.

IN SPITE OF HIS DETERMINATION to be finished with the day, Father Gilchrist had found that the day was not willing to be finished with him. He had stalked to the bus stop, summoning up a snort of cynical, begrudging gratitude when the bus arrived scarcely a minute later. Nonetheless, once on board, he purposefully glared at each passenger as he made his way down the aisle, keeping his raincoat securely buttoned, not about to invite a repetition of his earlier experience on the way to the meeting.

He had been sitting in the rear, amidst a crowd of unruly kids and a few dazed inebriates, all of whom he had succeeded in ignoring by dwelling upon his own perpetually vexing burdens. It was a common practice of his and most likely would have sufficed in maintaining his disassociation with his surroundings, had it not been for one especially piercing exchange a few seats away between a couple of teenaged boys, who, having exhausted the topic of sex, had begun to ridicule theology, in general, their voices high and unchecked, their comments appropriately offensive.

It had been nothing he had not heard a thousand times before; yet it managed to penetrate his isolation; and he found himself glaring up at them, more out of annoyance than any sense of affront, one of the boys glancing back and noticing him, his vulpine little face lighting up as he nudged his cohort, the other turning around to see what was so amusing.

They had both laughed mockingly as they appraised the old priest, his clergical collar having been showing then. He had sat up as if in challenge, giving them his most fearsome scowl, startled and very much riled when it only inspired them to another bout of sophomoric snickering.

"Whassa matter, Pope John?" one of them had sneered. "Don't like what we got to say? We're just expressing our points of view," he enunciated sarcastically.

Father Gilchrist met his gaze, steely eyed. "You boys should know better," he told them evenly. "Religion and politics, any place but a bar or on a bus."

The other boy merely scoffed, grinning wickedly. "Aw, he's just pissed off 'cause he can't get laid," he denounced knowingly. "Ain't that right, priest? Once you sign up, you can't get any!"

At this remark, all of the adjacent kids began to howl at the sheer outrageous irreverence of the remark, Father Gilchrist flushing an angry shade of mottled red.

"Keep a civil tongue in your head, boy!" he shot back, his grated teeth showing.

The other boy stopped laughing long enough to gesture crudely. "Naw, they can still get some!" he corrected his accomplice. "Except their bitches are choir boys!"

This conclusion evoked an uproar of laughter from the others, the two boys almost grappling with each other in their unconstrained glee, as if the unchecked recklessness of their words was so daring as to be amazing even to them.

Enraged, the mockery of the laughter scorching his ears, Father Gilchrist grasped the nearest handrail and stood up from his seat, his face contorted in fury.

Seeing this, the two boys gasped in excited mirth, high on the reaction they had provoked in the old priest, reveling in the obvious approval of the other passengers.

"Uh-oh, here he comes!" one exclaimed to the other, pushing him in mock fear.

"Watch your ass, man! He's on the prowl!" They both began to roar again.

Stunned, Father Gilchrist paused, halfway in the aisle, holding tightly to the rail, incensed with degraded wrath at their inconceivable disrespect, all of his acerbic, bitter resolve unable to stay his reaction to their taunts.

"You shut your filthy mouths, you ignorant little shits!" he thundered volcanically.

The mere intensity of his stentorian voice was enough to silence the surrounding hecklers, the two boys growing still, their faces shifting into expressions of undaunted, confrontational hostility, as they perceived, like so many of their kind, any encroachment on their fun as a direct challenge to their youthful invincibility.

"Fuck you, priest," one of them retorted heatedly. "You know you'd love to come over here and rape me right now, fuckin' perv."

The silence of the bus now on his side, Father Gilchrist withstood this indigestibly, intolerable assessment for barely a moment before swinging away from his seat and storming down the aisle toward them, a terrible, imposing, punishing figure in black seeming to be descending upon them, the boys, taken completely off guard by this unprecedented calling of their bluff, scrambling to their feet and darting toward the rear exit just as the bus was about to pull away from a stop, a ripple of laughter choked by their anger at having to retreat thereby revealing their false bravado as just that, one of them managing a hateful, Parthian shot, his mouth twisting cruelly as he glared at the charging priest. "Child molester."

He had then darted after his comrade, who had exited into a newspaper stand, both of them tumbling over onto the sidewalk, Father Gilchrist's pursuit cut short by the closing doors. He angrily lunged past a startled young couple seated nearby, yanking open their window to its fullest extent and leaning precariously out of it, determined against all odds that he should have the last word, whatever it might be.

"Who'd want to molest you anyway?" he heard himself bellow, even in the twilight darkness able to make out their shocked faces as they glanced up after him from where they had fallen. "I've seen better-looking gargoyles in Notre Dame!"

With this imparted, he stood upright, realizing that he had momentarily sunk to their level and relishing how good it felt, his heart pounding harshly, his breathing intensely invigorating. As he turned and faced the remaining hecklers, he was met with looks of silenced resentment and mouths braced to resume the assault.

Glowering redoubtably back, he reached past the young couple and yanked viciously at the pull cord, waiting until the bus glided to its next stop. Then, moving without seeming to will himself to do so, he stood up formally straight and tall in the aisle, peering solemnly down at all the revelers; and then, his face locked in an immutably righteous glare, he administered the sign of the cross over them, slowly and deliberately, using his middle finger.

Now, as he rode the bus back toward the church, glad that it was mostly empty, he reflected with a hint of guilt upon his behavior earlier, rankled slightly by it—the guilt, that is, not his behavior. He would do that again in a heartbeat, he vowed vindictively, then bitterly considering that he might have to do just that. He had to ride on these damned busses, and the chances were likely that he would encounter those kids again.

Scowling, he angrily disregarded the thought, concluding that it was *they* who would encounter *him* again. *Bugger them, the little swine, making comments, like those. There was a time when...*

He exhaled tautly. "There was a time when" had long since expired. It was all up for grabs now, and he knew it. What was odd was how their remarks, unoriginal as they were, had been so upsetting. There was a time—again?—but, no, there really was a time when he would have been suffused with indignation at much less and would have leapt to the defense of the church. Now, however, he was actually more inclined to agree with some of what they had said, yet he had been infuriated all the same.

The obvious conclusion was that it had turned into a personal attack, and he had been induced to defend his character, even though he had heard such remarks about the priesthood a hundred times before, sometimes from his own parishioners. What priest had not? Still, if he had not been protecting himself or the church, what had he been taking a stand against? What could provoke a priest with a dead soul to jump up and behave like a crusading mad man? He had certainly done a number for PR, he reflected wryly, his actions continuing to chafe him, confound him, and, moreover, to imbue him with a retrospective, unaccountable sense of liberating empowerment.

He was able to put aside all this speculation upon returning to the church, his mood instantly souring as he customarily entered through the side entrance, stopping in the corridor to glare at the side table, sighting the daily mail.

Scowling, he was debating whether or not to sort through it or outrightly discard it, when Father Ralph came bounding into the room, clad in a gray running suit, pausing to jog in place.

"Hello, Father Alistair," he greeted him cordially, still breathing heavily from his sprint around the neighborhood. "I don't think anything came for you today."

"Oh?" Father Gilchrist replied casually, now making it a point to look through the bundle of envelopes.

"You missed a good dinner again tonight, Father," the younger priest continued, perspiration beading his forehead. "Mrs. Tucker's mad at you for not putting in an appearance."

Father Gilchrist turned his glare at him. "And how could I be expected to be here for her marginal repast when I was out participating in my beloved group therapy?" he inquired crossly.

Father Ralph lifted his brows. "Oh yeah. How was your meeting tonight?" he asked with interest, stepping up his pace, the older priest appraising his actions dourly.

"No less of a waste of time than usual," he replied briskly. "The ride on the bus, however, was definitely resplendent with spiritual discourse and enlightenment," he added in fairness.

Nodding, Father Ralph swiped at his forehead with one sleeve, his mane of red hair seeming charged with energy as it bounced with each step. "Mrs. Tucker left a plate for you in the fridge," he mentioned between breaths. "All you have to do is heat it up."

"Oh?" Father Gilchrist returned evenly. "Is it more fish sticks for Friday, in which case all I have to do is throw it away?"

He set the mail back on the table, his eyes then falling upon a small wicker basket that appeared to be filled with condoms. He picked it up in disbelief as Father Ralph abruptly ceased his jogging and rested his hands on his knees, exhaling forcefully.

"And what, pray tell, are these?" he asked the younger priest sharply.

Cheeks billowing, Father Ralph glanced at the basket and then up at him. "Oh, come now, Father Alistair, I think you know what those are," he grinned slyly.

Father Gilchrist bristled at the impudence, pursing his lips astringently. "I meant, *would you believe*, what are they doing in here?" he insisted acidically.

Father Ralph actually shrugged. "Sister Angelica brought them by," he explained simplistically. "Some youth outreach group gave them to her downtown."

"Ah, Sister Angelica, of course." He nodded caustically. "And since when has the church begun to administer birth control methods? Was there something in the Pope's latest encyclical that I missed?"

Smiling broadly, Father Ralph cocked his head to one side. "What can I tell you, Father, it's a whole new church," he responded easily, nodding and turning to head upstairs.

"Oh! Oh, indeed," Father Gilchrist returned the nod. "Well, how splendid! She can distribute them to the members of her preschool! Or, for that matter, we can keep them on hand here. Halloween is only a month away. We can pass them out to the trick-or-treaters."

Father Ralph only grinned. "Well, I'm gonna grab a shower, Father. Oh, and you've got lockdown tonight, okay? I've got to go over to the Am Vets Hall to run Bingo Night."

"A marathon jog around the block, and now, you're prepared to sacrifice yourself to the tempestuous mobs of Bingo Night." Father Gilchrist marveled. "Father Ralph, how *do* you do it?"

Father Ralph continued to grin, shrugging again. "What can I say, Father? I'm a Cathaholic." He nodded and charged up the stairs.

Father Gilchrist gaped in mock awe after him. "Oh! Oh my, well, now, yes, indeedy, you just go on and win one for the Gipper!" he called after him, his features then constricting as he dropped the basket unceremoniously back atop the table. "Young putz."

Scowling, he headed for the kitchen, mumbling irritably. *Cathaholic indeed. Now, who belonged in an anonymous group?* And as for "lockdown," he had half a mind to go and bolt the church doors shut right now. It was not as if anyone would mind, after all, save for the derelicts who came in to shoot up or get warm. Apart from them, no one came near. He snorted; there was that damned song again.

He dismissed the matter. *Let Donald, the sexton, deal with it. Or not. Who cared?* He yanked open the refrigerator, grimacing at the plate of leftovers that greeted him, together with a note instructing him on how to reheat the food in the microwave.

No, it was not fish sticks, he surmised, pulling back the Saran wrap and peering disdainfully at the skimpy portion of cod cakes, which he then dumped in the garbage anyway, making certain it was noticeably on top, then placing the note neatly above it again.

He then set about making a sandwich in a sort of bacheloresque defiance, already entertaining Mrs. Tucker's outrage when she discovered the little surprise he had left for her.

"All the missions you've done, Father, all the hunger you've seen, and here you are, throwing food away!" she would shriek for the umpteenth time. "Don't you know there are children starving all over the world?"

To which Father Gilchrist would reply that if faced with these leftovers, they were probably better off.

Reaching for a jar of mayonnaise, he noticed the bottle of scotch shoved onto the first shelf and pulled it out in exasperation. Who in God's name would refrigerate scotch? He set it on the counter and continued to make his sandwich and then abruptly remembered that it was his scotch—which he kept in the sacristy for those few Sundays when he could use the extra boost.

Sighing in anger, he took his sandwich and the bottle and marched upstairs to his quarters, intending to tuck the bottle someplace where that meddling old harpy wouldn't find it.

His quarters consisted of a small sitting room outfitted with a recliner and a bookcase, a private bathroom, and his bed off in one corner. In spite of the rectory's distinguished classical design, his room had attained a sort of sullen, shabby fustiness, which suited him just fine, as it was *his* sanctuary—his sanctum sanctorum, from the sanitarium that was the world. The church had once been that place of refuge for him, but now, he could only find it in the solitude of his quarters.

He sat in the recliner and munched disinterestedly on the sandwich, the Dijon mustard not sour enough to be very good. He ended up setting most of it aside, staring off into space for a few minutes, attempting to banish the contemplations of the day, as was his usual habit at this time. He had intended to prepare for bed but instead merely sat, eventually glancing over at a wall clock, his gaze settling upon the scotch.

Studying it for a moment, he next took a tumbler from a nearby dry decanter and poured himself a glass. Partaking of drink was not something he did much anymore, considering it too much of a bother. Tonight, however, owing to the mood he was in, he felt very much entitled. It was Friday, fish or no fish; and, after all, he reflected, thinking of Dr. Pendleton, it was not like he had anything to do the next day.

Dr. Pendleton. He grimaced and downed the much too cold whiskey, pouring himself another. *Well-meaning, boob.* He almost smiled as he recalled the flustered little doctor finally standing up to him, asking him to leave. *Good for him, the sap.* If he had had to deal with himself in a similar scenario, he would have thrown himself out long ago.

He savored the scotch for a moment as it occurred to him that what had happened tonight had been just that—he had been asked to leave. That meant, in effect, that he did not have to return. He could tell that to Deacon Richard; and if he didn't like it, well, that was a pity, wasn't it? *Let him attend those ridiculous sessions; he'd turn atheist after the first meeting, the little twit.*

He downed the glass and took another, glad for the bracing bite of the scotch as it glowed its way down his throat. Perhaps there was something to chilling it after all. Either way, he was beginning to feel better. Well, not better, just more alive again.

More alive and less dead. He contemplated the idea of not going back to the meetings, surprised when the notion, while not in the least disappointing, did not seem to offer much appeal. That was truly puzzling, for surely, after only three weeks, he could not possibly have formed any attachments—that could not feasibly occur even after three years. Perhaps it had simply become routine or, more to the point, a break from *this* routine, at least some brief respite from the interminable cycle of pointless tedium that was his life here.

He chuckled. If that were true, then he really was getting something out of those meetings. He could have laughed. *Deacon Richard, perhaps you are not as moronic as I took you to be. A toast to you, you progressive-minded pipsqueak.* Bask in these congratulations, as they will be short-lived, for inasmuch as he had been miraculously cured of his incurably rotten disposition, he obviously did not need to go back. He did not have to do anything that he did not want to do, and no one could make him. His darling support group would surely support him there; faced with the prospect of never seeing him again, they would all join hands and unanimously attest to his successful rehabilitation, supporting the notion on down the line; they would jump at the chance.

Yes, they would not give him a second thought, and that would be that. He poured himself a bit more scotch, savoring the flavor more and more with each swallow. They would surely not miss him, least of all that simpering judge. He grimaced as he recalled his tirade, refusing to feel remorseful about it. The last thing this nightmare world needed was someone like that interpreting the law, especially when they had wife-beating cops enforcing it.

He sank in his chair slightly, pursing his lips in suppressed rage, forcibly shifting his thoughts elsewhere, scarcely succeeding when he next envisioned Vanessa, her bruised, angry face clear and cutting in his mind's eye.

So the little jezebel was purely metaphorical in her demeanor. He was glad for that; it was true. Even he could manage to be grateful for that. Still, in all, though, someone had hit her. It most likely could not have been Clod or Chris or whatever that gawping adolescent's name was; punching bags, after all, very rarely hit back, unlike some *other* little punks running around out there.

Swallowing still more, loving that flavor, he contemplated those hoodlums on the bus once again, seeing their twisted, contemptuous faces, hearing their hateful words. If one priest did it, they all did, right? Wasn't that the prevailing theory? There were so many responses that he could have given their reprehensible statements, so many proper replies that would have benefitted the other people on the bus, those incidental witnesses of this spur-of-the-moment showdown between…well, now, between what, exactly? Good and bad? Hardly. Bad and bad? No. Bad and worse? Warmer. Right and wrong? Nope, ice cold again.

Ice-cold scotch was not really all that bad. It saved you the trouble of fumbling with the damned ice cube trays and that awful watered-down spinelessness that you got if you nursed it too long and the ice melted. No, this was really quite good—so good, in fact, that…

Now, where were we… Oh *that*… How about between screw you and up yours? How about between who gives a damn? That seemed suitable enough. He frowned slightly, blinking against the effects of what had only been a moderate amount of the liquor and then sitting up and pouring himself still more. Weren't those self-same effects the whole point?

He stared at the faded carpet underfoot, trying to retrace his thoughts back to that grand realization he had derived earlier, reen-visioning Vanessa in that effort and focusing upon her once more, having been taken aback by her diatribe earlier that evening, but equally impressed with her synopsis of their merry group, leastwise until she had gotten to him. *That had been a tad presumptuous, the little vixen.* He wondered momentarily if she had succeeded in finding that waiflike old woman, seemingly a fool's errand, at night, with almost no clue as to how to proceed.

Oh well, follow the call of the banshee, that would be his candid advice, if that insipid song was correct.

He shifted a bit at his own callousness, for, truth be told, Mrs. Spindlewood had been the one member with whom he had the most in common—how comforting, considering how loopy the old woman was. Yet age created comrades or, at least, commiserators, and he had not been completely jaded to that fact. How could he be? Soon enough, he would no doubt be in similar straits all around, wandering about the church in a fog.

No, if her time had come, if that asinine song were to be reflected in this reality, she would probably be better off in the end. He poured himself another shot, trying to recall the entire song, his thoughts then jumping back to that infernal nursery rhyme instead, almost all his anger instantly restoked. He sat up in his chair even more so, scowling balefully around his room, his features twisting righteously.

"And 'there you met an old man who wouldn't say his prayers'?" he demanded of the emptiness. "Is that so, you crooning little troll? I'll show you an old man who wouldn't say his prayers!"

He downed what was left of his glass and immediately replenished it, his teeth clenched as his breathing quickened. Once more, he glowered around his room, his refuge, nodding slowly and judiciously.

This was his church now. This was his place of worship, and its covenants were quite simple. *Dr. Pendleton advocated a retreat? Well, it didn't get any better than this.* Here, he could go about his business as he pleased, and why not, Father Ralph and Sister Angelica were both cheerfully manning the helm.

Here, he had come to take heart in fulfilling the role of a mean old man as it was meant to be done. Here, he could turn up the heat in the summer if he felt like it; he could pad around in his house slippers and pajamas and glare at everything he saw from his window and grumble and complain. He could take a shamelessly selfish pride in his few material acquisitions that he had kept hidden on a top shelf of the closet in a locked deposit box. Won't they be disappointed when that day finally comes and they can eagerly break it open, only to discover that it contained a handful of old baseball cards, a few old coins, a pocket watch, the few letters and photographs that he had not burned over the years, and countless other trifling mementoes from eons before. *No, no stocks or bonds or cold cash or pornography or whatever else you dimwits thought I was hoarding in there.*

Here, he enjoyed having a snack in his chair and staying up until all hours, reading some arid mystery novel or occasionally turning on the radio, listening to it for as long as he could and then shutting it off when he could stand no more. He enjoyed shuffling into the bathroom and fussing with the medicine cabinet, brushing his teeth with a scowl, and gargling with especially acidic mouthwash. He liked catching a glimpse of his fearsome visage in the mirror; in fact, it was his ambition to make it quiver and break someday; he could use seven years *better* luck.

He thrived in the moldy, fusty, musty, dusty stale atmosphere, all the more so because of Mrs. Tucker's ardent, rampant disapproval. He kept all the windows closed and the doors shut tight partially out of spite alone. He loved the solitary, curmudgeonly reality of this place, wherein he did not have to act a certain way, smile and grandstand, appeasing everyone he encountered. He did not have to represent anyone but himself, and then, he turned off the lights and crawled into bed. He had stopped saying his prayers three months ago. One night, he had been on his knees, mouthing the recitations of the past sixty-odd years' worth of nights, and the next, he had just skipped it. He could not be bothered anymore.

To be sure, he went through the liturgies of the mass, said all the words, and went through the motions; but that was all for show anyway, wasn't it? Here, however, he could turn his back on everything in the cosmos and drift off to sleep with a defiant, recalcitrant frown on his face.

No, Dr. Pendleton, *this* was a retreat, a true haven of rest and peace of mind; and this would be his, from this point onward until the end, until the bitter end when *Death and the Maiden* or, in his case, a preschool Banshee and Mrs. Spindlewood, came to deliver him; and then they could have it back. Father Ralph would read him his last rites—last rites—they would shove a stake through his heart rather than take any chances on his coming back; and then, he would donate his body to the Conqueror Worm; and that would be the blessed end of that.

No, he did not require Dr. Pendleton's Travelling Salvation Show, thank you so very much, nor did he seek the company of his

Pickwick Society of bewildered group members, his fellow anonymous mis-fits, not now, nor in the future. He did not need to go back there, and he would not go back there, and nobody could make him, nor could anyone make him give up his sanctuary, nor could anyone make him say his prayers. No one. Not some vicious little cretins on the bus, not some domestic-disturbing cop, not some crooning three-year-old, not Mrs. Tucker and her flipping fish, not the would-be parishioners of this decaying cathedral, not the legions of ghosts that haunted its corners and rafters, nor the thousands more drifting aimlessly through the icy corridors of that charnel house next door, not Father Ralph, raging Cathaholic, not Sister Angelica and her guitar and condoms, not Deacon Richard—nor Abbot Bud, Bishop Joey, or Cardinal St. Louis, nor even Pope John Paul, George, or Ringo, not Jesus, Mary, nor Joseph, not even God Almighty on high. No one could make him say his prayers ever again, no one could make him go back to that certifiable therapy group, and no one could make him leave his sanctuary, not now, not ever. *Never!*

He blinked in uncertainty toward the door, frowning and then glaring as the knocking repeated, a thin, whining voice calling to him. "Please, Father Gilchrist, could you step out here for a minute?"

Father Gilchrist downed the rest of his glass. Never! "Come in!" he snapped.

"I tried, Father, but the door was locked," the voice explained.

Scowling, Father Gilchrist climbed unsteadily to his feet. *Tried, eh, before I even said to come in. What nerve!*

He moved to the door on tiptoe, quietly, gently unlocked it, and then yanked it violently open. "*Whadda you want?*" he roared.

A small, mouselike man in a brown topcoat shrank back in horror, whipping a cap off his head so quickly that wisps of his thinning hair stood upright in its wake.

"I'm so sorry to bother you, Father Gilchrist," he stammered fearfully. "It's just that I was lookin' to lock up the church for the night and…well, it's the usual problem, sir. They won't clear out. Now, I've no intention of askin' you to deal with it, sir. In fact, this time, I was thinking of calling the cops."

338

Father Gilchrist steadied himself against the doorframe with his free hand, focusing on the little man, Donald, their idiot sexton, and then reflecting upon what he had just been told.

"If you didn't intend to ask me to deal with it, then why are we having this little chat?" he demanded, lucid enough to be irate.

Donald cringed backward another step, wringing his cap. "Well, I came to ask you if you thought I should call the police," he clarified anxiously.

Smiling unsmilingly, Father Gilchrist lifted his index finger away from the rim of the glass and waggled it at him. "I do so admire your assertiveness," he declared chidingly.

Blinking, Donald watched as Father Gilchrist drank from the empty glass, then frowning at it suspiciously.

"Uh...well then, should I go ahead and call the police?" he asked nervously, already poised to scurry away, frozen in place by the old priest's sharp response.

"No!" he told him flatly, Donald watching in baffled worry as he stepped back into his room and returned with the bottle of scotch, closing the door firmly behind him and shaking his head at the smaller man.

"No, don't call the police, Donald. There's no telling who would show up, and I've no wish to spend the night in jail."

He refilled his glass, Donald peering at it with a pained look and then up at Father Gilchrist. "But why would you go to jail, sir?" he asked in confusion.

"Why, because I might kill 'em, Donald, my lad," Father Gilchrist replied, about to take a sip and then pausing. "Care for a drink, would you?"

"Uh, no, sir," Donald replied instantly. "I've been sober now for seven years, thanks to God and AA." He nodded affirmatively, staring at the glass.

Father Gilchrist's brows lifted slowly. "AA?" he repeated. "Alcoholics Anonymous?"

"The same, sir," Donald nodded again, summoning up a bit of pride.

"Well, now, it truly is a small world, Donald," Father Gilchrist proclaimed, shifting the bottle and glass to one hand and patting the startled little man on the back. "I happen to belong to an anonymous group that actually *drives* a person to drink," he confided jovially. "Seven years sober, eh? Well now, I'll drink to that."

He did so, Donald shifting uncomfortably and wiping his brow with his cap, thrusting it back atop his head. "Uh, yes, sir. Thank you, sir. Uh, what about the church, sir?" he reminded Father Gilchrist, the aged priest's visage darkening.

"I will deal with that, Donald," he said tersely. "I'm just in the mood."

With the little sexton following anxiously, he charged down the stairs at a pace that he had not risked in ten years, pivoting sharply in the hallway; pausing; and then, on a whim, picking up the basket of condoms. Who knew, this could be a chance to get rid of them. He then marched toward the side door and into the church.

Striding up the transept, he stepped up on the platform before the altar, setting his bottle, glass, and the basket aside and then turning to peer into the candlelit, incense-infused gloom.

In addition to the few meager electric lights, the murkiness was illuminated by a series of candles that Donald had yet to extinguish, his rounds having been interrupted by... Glaring about, Father Gilchrist took in three disheveled old men clustered together in the fourth row, and some manner of bag lady seated by herself across the aisle in the fifth. She was discreetly drinking something from an orange juice container, the three men much more overtly passing a bottle, their husky whispers peppered with a snaggle-toothed cackle from time to time.

As Donald watched, cap in hand from the doorway, Father Gilchrist glowered about, his scowl now adequately reenforced, his breathing steadied, as he inhaled deeply and then paused, turning to pour himself another shot, downing it quickly, and then swaying to face front again.

Focusing his thoughts, he paused again, trying to recall what— ah, yes, he was to expel these intruders from their refuge, back into the night as had been done many times before so that he might return to his sanctuary and continue his own evening's introspect.

The insight stuck him sharply, and he blinked as if in slow motion as he considered it. *Sanctuary.* This was theirs, just as his quarters were his. Certainly not in the historical, religious sense— *ha!*—but this place comprised their own style of retreat, he reflected with interest, watching them pass their bottle; even their methods of worship were the same, sit, gripe, and, as with tonight, drink. *Fascinating.* He poured himself still another shot, drowning it and facing these ragtag late-night parishioners.

If they had come to worship in their sanctuary, who was he to stop them? In fact, as a clergyman, he owed it to them to address their spiritual needs, did he not? It all seemed so clear. Yes! If they had come for a midnight mass, then, by God, they were going to get one.

"Bums! Winos! Degenerates!" he called out majestically. "Lend me your ears!"

His voice bounded off the walls as he lifted his arms theatrically, the street people gaping up at him in inebriated curiosity, actually pausing in their partaking.

"We are gathered here together in the House of the Lord on this beautiful, rotten evening to share in the bounties of worship," Father Gilchrist proclaimed in his best Sunday sermon voice, the scotch imbuing it with a sharp, resonant intensity, Donald staring at him in mounting astonishment.

"For, surely as I stand before you, I can discern that you are truly filled with the Spirit, and I must confess that I too am likewise fortified." He smiled profoundly and then blinked. "Did I say 'confess'?" he asked them rhetorically, glancing over at the shadowy confessional.

"Well now, there's a thought! How to proceed without a mirror? Extemporize, I'll wager!" He nodded swiftly, joining his hands together in a formal pose. "Bless myself, Father, for I have sinned. It has been at least a few eons since my last confession, and I confess that whereas I may well have sinned—and who hasn't—I confess that I profess to have nothing *to* confess!"

The street people now watching in bleary-eyed awe, Donald clasping his hands to his mouth, Father Gilchrist replenished his glass to the brim, sipped contentedly, and then swung his focus once more to the task at hand, his mind once again chancing upon the accursed nursery rhyme amidst a miasma of thoughts and distractions; and he seized it, determined to exorcise it once and for all.

"So! You think that you behold an old man who wouldn't say his prayers, eh? Grabbed him by his leg and threw him downstairs? Well, now, you have indeed dragged me downstairs, haven't you?" he challenged them with an almost crazed look. "As far as the question of prayer goes, well, I'll show you who won't say his prayers! Prepare yourselves, keep those beads close at hand, stand by with the fatted calf, for I now offer up to the Powers That Be, the Last Prayer, and Testament of Father Alistair Gilchrist."

Silence now reigned in the church, the street people entranced, Donald mortified as the aged priest swallowed from his glass, clasped his hands together, and bowed his head.

"Our Father, who art in Heaven," he began, his voice crackling through the gloom, his face shooting up to address the rafters. "It was a dark and stormy night, but the State of the Union would not go undelivered. The church bells chimed. It's the twelfth of never, and all's hell! Truly, the theory of evolution has prevailed, for we have evolved from not merely the winter, but from all sour seasons of our discontent, and paradoxically so because it comes at a time when we have everything we've ever wanted!

"The frigid tedium of the Cold War had finally melted at long last to be replenished with the red hot new deal we've all been waiting for! Come one, come all, to the great conflagration! See it live and in person, in the front row, on the front—standing room only, folks!— or watch it from the comforts of your own home, a pay-per-view Armageddon for the masses! They're not selling war bonds this time around, but junk bonds will more than suffice to remind our boys in the field that while they're out there defending the homeland, their minds sharply trained with the best, most highly advanced tactics our video games can provide, all of us safe back here are most definitely keeping the home fires burning! The great society for which they are fighting continues to flourish and prosper! Western civilization perseveres, and America prevails! We can still pledge allegiance, even if not under God—and let's face it, folks, remove In God We Trust from the dollar bill. And lo and behold, Alakazam, you *still* have that dollar bill, the True Deity of the Times, and not just the Times, but the Herald, the Tribune, and the Journal as well!

"Mass media rallies together to promote mass appeal and ultimately mass hysteria with Punch and Judy Perfection! Television, radio, and motion pictures strive to uphold the gospel by debunking all graven images and uniting behind one nationally worshipped American Idolatry. Oh! But where are my manners! And now, a word from our sponsor! Hurry on down to 7-Eleven, where you'll enjoy all seven deadly sins in convenient, one-stop shopping! Small, Medium, Large, or Big Gulp. Super-Sized Sodom and Gomorra! And not to worry, there's something for everybody, even the most pious puritan! Get your Ten Commandments fresh from Taiwan, wallet-sized, earring, keychain, or jumbo extra large! Move over, fuzzy dice, time for something holier. And don't forget your patented Jesus fish! Display your zealous faith for all the world to see, right there between Save the Whales and How's My Driving? And if 7-Eleven is out of stock, have no fear, 9/11 will surely have a surplus! Open twenty-four hours, there's one near you! No assembly required. You'll find one in each specially marked box of Lucky Charms together with a plethora of Orange men, Blue Bloods, Greenbacks, Yellow Journalism, Purple Hearts, and Pink Triangles, which brings us to a point—somewhere, over the rainbow, way back when girls became boys and boys became girls, and they all marched out of the closet ready and willing to engage in mortal combat with the Abominable Dr. Phelps. All was well and good as they took to the streets, screaming for acceptance and never dreaming that they would achieve something far more conventional, a bountiful helping of apathy, for, truth be told, from Castro Street to Fire Island, *nobody cares anymore*!

"But ya know what I find truly queer? That curious breed that traded the closet for the cloister. And now, Holy Hannah, we've got catamites in the choir loft and pederasts in the pulpit. And next thing you know, the Vatican has to have a garage sale!"

Father Gilchrist inhaled, downed another shot, and lifted his arms up, bringing them down in a slow flurry of waggling fingers.

"And the walls came a tumblin' down! Not to worry, though, folks. While Father Flanagan passes the hat, secular society continues to progress, staking its claim in the backs of its children, for they are the future, and the future deserves only the best! The one-room school house has evolved into a state-of-the-art shooting range, a good GPA, and a pulse-guaranteeing elevation to the next level of higher learning, scholastically centered around binging and hazing, after which if you graduate summa cum spring break, you are propelled into the academic elite, Ivy League Strata of Ticky-Tacky Tech. And then, you have arrived, the Ivory Towers are traded for multinational corporate castles. Doctors, lawyers, and Indian chiefs or braves or pirates or Mets or Celtics or Hawks or Doves—the stage is set for the professional fleecing of the Great Unwashed. Conrad Hilton hospitals with HMO hospitality complement the working stiff clinics. Drive-thru abortions with return-to-sender embryos, who's the sinner and who's the winner? Damned if I know, and damned if I don't, but the world continues to rotate.

"The boys in blue protect your homes even while some of them assault their own. Drug dealers are suing the pharmaceutical companies for unfair competition. Prostitutes are filing for bankruptcy, blaming their woes on the dating game and the Internet, whose spidery webs have infiltrated even the most isolated and impoverished slums, providing an endless supply of pornography to the poor and the underprivileged who, otherwise, would have to go without.

"Not to worry, dear friends, for I see your faces growing long. Take heart in knowing that the hallmarks of the faith are still being upheld! Even in the face of sterilizing the separation of church and state to the point of godlessness, we can still rely upon the masses to stoically and reverently maintain all of our time-honored holidays!

"Every spring, we can feel the Spirit move us as we watch Jesus trade his crown of thorns for an Easter bonnet and sail down Fifth Avenue, arm-in-arm with Bugs Bunny, handing out Cadbury eggs to the faithful. Ash Wednesday is ardently observed with barbecuers throughout the land. Palm Sunday is still favored by fortune-tellers and pickpockets. And let's face it, folks, every Friday is Good. Oh, and before you Passover Lent, let me hasten to remind you that, owing to the humble and abiding inspiration of Mardi Gras, many has been the Virgin who gave it up for Lent.

"And, of course, lest we forget that apex of worshipful holidays, December the twenty-fifth! Doth thou ask how the Grinch stole x-mas? Seems someone beat him to it! 'X' marks the spot, as they say, a chalk outline of a cross turned sideways, but still to be seen in store windows up to and including that hallowed day, to advertise half-off sales and last-minute shopping, prominently stamped between the legs of Abercrombie and Fitch.

"No, the covenants are being kept, mark my words. And yet, still, as society howls upon the precipice of the Great Abyss, even in our complacency, we are unsatisfied. We've been as *Mad as Hell* for decades now, and yet we still take it anyway, and why?

"Fools speculate. Philosophers ponder. America wants to know. In the end, they always come racing back to the church for the answer, and as I stand before you tonight as an embodiment of the same, prepared yet again to answer that eternal question—'When God finally closes the door on this dreamy little sphere, will the light stay on?'—I can only comfort you with the sum total of wisdom accrued from all my years in the Clergy, *I don't know.*"

He smiled in bittersweet contemplation, shrugging very slowly, tilting his head to one side, and extending his arms outward, assuming an exaggerated pose identical to that of the massive figure on the crucifix mounted high on the wall behind him.

"I suppose that it is ultimately up to us," he informed his stupefied listeners. "And seeing that responsibility thrust into the hands of men, it is hardly any wonder that—" He turned his head to take in the figure behind him, his smile vanishing as he lowered his arms and stared solemnly up at it. "Jesus wept."

He slowly faced front again, his venomous, caustic, beaming countenance once more aglow as he glanced at the mostly empty pews. "Have no fear, though, brothers and sisters," he assured them, his voice taking on an ominous purr. "Whether as living, breathing, destroying entities or as ghostly disciples of Ozymandias, the legacy of our civilization will endure for all eternity to witness, God help it."

Exhaling briskly, he clasped his hands together. "This has been the Last Prayer and Testament of Father Alistair Gilchrist, who very shortly will lay himself down to sleep, brought to you live and in stereo, in the Name of The Sex, The Drugs, and The Rock' n' Roll."

"Amen." He finished making the sign of the cross and drained his glass.

Donald the sexton slowly revived from his petrified advertence, the street people, as if inspired by the priest's final gesture, stirring and passing the bottle again, the bag lady upending her orange juice container, these actions converging to prompt Father Gilchrist to blink and focus, his clouded features sharpening as if in sudden recollection.

"Oh my Lord, how silly of me!" he proclaimed, instantly refilling his glass and holding up the bottle. "I forgot all about the sacrament! Can't close a proper service without a sacrament, now can we?" He cleared his throat gutturally and waved the bottle at his ragged spectators. "Step right up folks, come and get your sacrament! Come one, come all, belly up to the bar for your sacrament!"

As Donald watched in utter horror, the three grizzled men and the wizened bag lady stood up with zombielike alacrity, eagerly staggering down the aisle toward him, Father Gilchrist smiling in blitzed beneficence, his posture reeling as he turned to glance over the altar for a means of dispensing the "sacrament," even in his state able to be surprised when he found a small tray of sacrament glasses alongside of him. This made perfect sense, though; that was, after all, *not* where they were supposed to be.

No matter, he needed them all the same—so small, though. He'd have to give them all doubles. In the few moments it took him to fill all the tiny glasses, the four worshipful street people had lined up before the altar, looking up at him with the hopeful earnestness of Pavlov's dogs.

Brandishing the tray, he beamed down at them, crossing the glasses formally.

"As ye partake of this scotch, ye partake of the Spirit that guides us all." He decreed, pausing to add, "Well, tonight, anyway."

He next fingered a tiny glass and held it over the nearest begrimed face, emptying the liquor into the gaping, toothless mouth and moving onto the next, at which point Donald, quivering in disbelief, his ashen features aghast, was able to watch no more, turning and scuttling away.

When he had offered each of them a sacrament and then downed one himself, Father Gilchrist began to administer a second round, the incoherently astounded vagrants eagerly partaking as they gaped up at their benefactor in drunken reverence.

"Yes, indeedy, get your ice-cold sacrament!" he reiterated, allowing his voice to reverberate throughout the church again. "Hurry, today, while supplies last! You'll—"

"*For Christ's sake, will you shut up already?*"

The voice ricocheted through the darkness, assailing Father Gilchrist with the force of a whiplash. Thunderstruck, he stood upright in the pronounced, ramrod outrage of the intoxicated individual who has just been incomprehensibly slandered.

"Who *dares* to tell me to silence my words?" he demanded of the candlelit gloom in a righteous snarl, his mouth an invisible line of defiance as he peered about, almost positive that the scotch had conjured up some sort of delusion, unless he had succeeded in working himself up into a stroke—or unless his time had finally come...

"I did!" the voice shot back instantly, possessing a hostile defiance of its own. "Now, shut the fuck up. You're throwing off my rhythm!"

His features withering in rage, Father Gilchrist shoved the tray at the nearest vagrant and stepped down from the platform, stalking down the center aisle in the direction from which the voice seemed to have originated. His heart pounding in a galvanized rush of strident, retributional adrenaline, he peered fixedly to either side as he passed each row of empty pews, until he came across the figures in the darkened corner of the last pew to his right, the glow of the nearby candles scarcely penetrating its shadows but nonetheless enabling him to see precisely that which he beheld, the two figures unaware of his approach, owing to their horizontal position.

For all his years of wading through one moral indignation after another, with all of his marked cynicism, the old priest was still appalled by what he saw, even in that altered state. "You would dare to engage in these carnal acts in the House of God?" he inquired scathingly, his voice sizzling at the offending party. "This is St. Leonard's Church, not our Lady of Sorrows Motel 6!"

The voice, belonging to the figure whose back was to him, gave off a grunt of surprise at his sudden proximity, responding over one shoulder.

"What the fuck do you care, stumblebum?" he countered impatiently. "You weren't exactly singin' a hymn a few minutes ago! Now shut the fuck up before someone hears us, and they throw us all out of here!"

"Yeah!" a female voice emphasized from beneath their coupling.

Bristling in fury, Father Gilchrist stepped forward and grabbed the back of the figure's coat, yanking him out of the pew with as much strength as he had, the figure shouting in anger, spinning around with fists raised as he confronted the aged priest, his grimy young features alighting in astonishment as he saw him in the faint light.

"Someone *has* heard you!" Father Gilchrist grated, watching disdainfully as the younger man, obviously a street kid, hastily grappled with his pants and zipper.

"What the fuck, man?" he sputtered in shock, his equally grungy girlfriend having emitted a squeal as she hastened to cover herself as well.

"Who is it, baby, some kinda perv?" she exclaimed in revulsion.

"Are you, like, the priest here?" the kid demanded in dumbfounded disbelief.

"As a matter of fact, like, I am," Father Gilchrist growled.

The kid gawked at him, as the girl, squeaking in horror, began to gather up her jacket in a panic, her boyfriend waving a hand back at her. "Cool it, babe," he told her sharply, then regarding Father Gilchrist closely, his mouth gaping at an almost twisted angle of lip-curled delinquency. "What the fuck kind of priest are you, man?" he asked reproachfully. "What kind of priest would stand up there and say all that shit? Are you fuckin' tweakin'?"

Father Gilchrist stared at him in almost sober intensity. "The kind of priest who is precariously balanced in the twilight zone between lucid survival and homicidal psychosis," he replied tersely, his eyes boring stonily into the boy's. "Now, if you two mudlarks don't mind, I'm sure you can find someplace close by where you can finish up your cohabitation. If memory serves, there's a perfectly charming bench in the entryway of the Methodone Clinic two blocks up."

"Come on, Bruiser. Let's go," the girl insisted, gathering up their backpacks.

"Hang back, babe, park your ass," the boy, Bruiser, told her commandingly, the girl tossing down the bags and plunking down on the pew, folding her arms in a huff as her boyfriend focused on Father Gilchrist again, a jeering smile now on his lean features.

"You got some serious issues, man," he informed him pointedly. "I was too busy tryin' to score to pay much attention. But fuck, man, you got some nerve yellin' at us!" He gave a barking laugh, jutting his chin toward the frigidly glowering priest. "If lightnin's gonna be strikin' anyone, it's you that's gonna get burned!"

As Father Gilchrist withstood this audacity, his thoughts reverting to the two punks from the bus earlier, their laughter and smugness now revisited in the street hoodlum before him, Bruiser continued to chortle, turning to face his girlfriend. "You might as well open up again, babe," he informed her lewdly, actually reaching to do the same as he turned to resume his position atop her. "Compared to this psycho, we're a couple a' fuckin' Sunday school kids!"

His laughter grew more mocking, the girl tentatively joining in, stealing a glance at Father Gilchrist, who regarded them in wide-eyed frenzied wrath.

If being faced with this churlish adolescent scorn coupled with this shameless temerity that would rankle even Satan himself and then having it compounded with the knowledge that most people witnessing the spectacle would probably side with the kid over him was unfathomably intolerable to him, then the notion that these two urchins actually did appear to be on the verge of going right on with their mating ritual, their blasphemy having been sanctioned *by his*, was enough to incite him to even greater heights of utter, choking, outrage.

Glancing about almost apoplectically, he noticed the long, tapering brass handle of one of the church's candlesnuffers, dangling from one of the higher candle fixtures—where it did not belong—no doubt where Donald had abandoned it when his rounds had been interrupted by tonight's visitors.

Father Gilchrist grabbed it, unhooked its goose-necked bell piece from where it had been resting, swiveling the device in his hands and approaching the kid from behind as with a fishing gaff, extending it between Bruiser's legs and pulling it upward, the young punk crying out in surprise when he glanced down to see his person get snuffed, the girl gasping in shock.

"What the f—," he got out, almost tripping forward when, arms flailing, he was forced to walk backward, Father Gilchrist tugging roughly on the snuffer and pulling him away from the pew and down the aisle as if yanking on the leash of a stubborn pit bull.

"Since you are so intent on participating in our midnight mass," he decreed in acidic formality, "I insist that you come and partake in the offering of the sacrament."

He continued to lead Bruiser down the aisle like a stage manager and a vaudeville flop, the enraged street punk unable to do anything but follow with backward, faltering steps, the length of the snuffer and its awkward pinioning of his self making it impossible to do otherwise, his girlfriend darting after him, her protests intermingling with his obscene objections.

Reaching the altar, Father Gilchrist gracefully retracted the snuffer from its compromising hold, placing it to one side as he beheld that all the sacrament glasses and his bottle as well were empty, his four bedraggled disciples staring up at him in woebegone expectation, their eyes clearly pleading their desire to receive more of the Spirit.

Grimacing for he had wanted to do the same, he glanced over the altar for anything comparable as Bruiser, now free, had spun around in breathless rage, nursing himself and scowling murderously at the old priest, who turned away from the altar just in time to come face to face with him, the much older man gazing impassively into that blazing, angry young face, feeling the hot breath shuddering from out of those twisted lips, his eyes flaming wildly as his girlfriend danced nervously behind him, anxious to be gone but clearly excited to see whatever might next develop.

Seeing Bruiser's lips poise to launch into some torrent of precursory cursing, Father Gilchrist waylaid this prelude to violence by speaking first himself. "It's customary to kneel whilst receiving the sacrament, my son," he informed him, madly pedantic.

Bruiser's eyes widened in a dumbstruck, almost laughing reaction. "Fuck you, man!" he exclaimed. "I ain't kneelin' in front of you! I don't believe in—"

His eyes bulged as Father Gilchrist's knee interjected, Bruiser inhaling with frozen-featured awe as he immediately crumpled to his knees before the aged clergyman, who smiled and briskly moved his hand in the sign of the cross above his stricken face, then flexing his fingers in virtual prestidigitation, producing an item that he held up for all to see.

It was flat and rounded and was definitely the size of a Sacrament wafer; and as such, the condom fit perfectly on Bruiser's pierced tongue when Father Gilchrist plunged it grandiosely into his mouth and then rather unceremoniously clamped the kid's mouth shut, one hand on his greasy forehead, the other beneath his stubbly chin, Bruiser jerking and thrashing, his hands still clutched to his crotch, his girlfriend gasping and racing forward to assist.

"As ye partake of this latex," Father Gilchrist intoned over him. "Ye partake of the flesh or, in your case, the sins of the flesh."

He released Bruiser, who tumbled backward into the arms of his girlfriend, one hand at last clasping his throat, the look on his face unmistakable as he coughed, gulped, and realized what, in his vehement struggling, he had forced himself to do.

"Fuck!" he croaked in disbelief. "Man, I fuckin' swallowed that thing!'

Father Gilchrist regarded him blankly. "That's the general idea of partaking in the sacrament," he explained dryly, turning to look over the altar, his desire to locate some of the regular wine that they used in the church services only mildly distracted by the puzzling array of other articles that had been set there, none of which belonged there. So why then…? No matter; it was hardly a surprise.

"Baby, it's okay!" the girl was reassuring her fallen boyfriend, rubbing his stringy hair soothingly. "You used to swallow those all the time back when you were dealing, remember?"

"Yeah, but I always unwrapped 'em first!" Bruiser snarled back.

The sacristy. There would definitely be some Mogen David in there—*Mogen David, for a Catholic mass.* He smiled wryly. *Well, Jesus was a Jew,* he reflected, wondering if perchance the key was where it was supposed to be. He did not see himself stalking over to Bingo Night or bursting into St. Mary's Convent to track down its whereabouts, not that that wouldn't be amusing.

He heard a savagely abrupt explosion behind him and turned to see Bruiser once more on his feet, the neck of what remained of the scotch bottle in his hand. His face once more blazing in almost primitive ferocity, his girlfriend watching in a mixture of horror and wild anticipation, he waved its wicked edge at him menacingly.

"You wanna get religious, priest?" he jeered invitingly. "Let's stop fuckin' around and go balls to the walls then, huh? I'm talkin' serious Old Testament shit!"

As the four street people began to shuffle hastily away, the church service definitely concluded for them, Father Gilchrist regarded the enraged punk thoughtfully, as if genuinely contemplating his idea.

"An eye for an eye and a tooth for a tooth, is it?" he confirmed at length, his pensive features then slowly twisting into a countenance of drunken, maddened, unrestrained recklessness. "A midnight stroll through the Valley of the Shadow of Death?" He nodded, his smile becoming deadly. "Be it so. Since we've seen enough of *Thy* rod for one night, it is time for *my Staff* to do a little comforting!"

He grabbed up the candle snuffer again and, glancing over at the altar, seized the handle of the church's thurible, yanking it up by its chain and whipping it upward, its gilded, jagged ornamentation creating an ironically un-Godly noise as he began to spin the incense receptacle overhead like a battle mace, his teeth clenched as he stepped down off the platform.

The girl, having screamed at the approach of this deranged, avenging figure, grabbed her boyfriend's sleeve, begging him to flee with her, Bruiser, his jaw slack as he gaped in speechlessness, shaking his head and tossing the bottle aside, turning to join her.

"Man, you are one major-league fucked up psycho priest!" he shouted in retreat, his awe still rampant. "You ain't gotta worry about goin' down when you kick it, man, 'cause you are already the priest from hell!"

With that, he clasped his girlfriend, the two of them racing down the aisle and catching up with the rest of the disbanding flock, grabbing their bags and dashing for the doors.

"Must you leave so soon?" Father Gilchrist roared after them. "I was just about to deliver the benediction!" He shrugged, gradually allowing the thurible to cease its orbit.

"Ah, well, no matter! Godspeed to you all! Be sure and return for our Sunday matinee. I intend to give a stand-up routine on the Day of Judgment, and there'll be an All-You-Can-Eat Sacrament Bar followed by a Roman Orgy, after which Sister Angelica will fiddle on her guitar as we set the church on fire!"

He watched as they fled into the night, shuffling forward and letting his improvised weapons clatter into one pew as he slowly set about locking the doors. That had been the whole point of coming down here in the first place, hadn't it? Now that it was finally accomplished, he could get back to the comfort of his quarters—his sanctuary.

Yes, his sanctuary. He found himself sitting down in one of the rear pews and staring up toward the front of the church. So this was the view, eh? This is what they saw, if and when they came to see it. He sat there for some time, gazing in intoxicated introspect, the notion of returning to his sanctuary arising in his thoughts occasionally and then becoming more remote.

Eventually, he pulled himself to his feet and began to make his way back up the aisle. Quite a little mess to clean up, he noted gravely; he would have to attend to it at once. First, though, there was the question of that wine in the sacristy.

Chapter **12**

THE VAN HAD BEEN QUITE easy to acquire, just as Dr. Whittaker had promised, this fact somewhat consoling as Dr. Pendleton stood alongside of it now, having parked it near the outer edge of the hospital parking lot. He had been so eager to take possession of it that he had not noticed until he had moved to open its sliding door that the van was rather boldly marked on both sides with unmistakably large stenciled letters—Hollingsworth Institution for the Mentally Ill.

Blinking at this in dismay, he had slid the door open, his intention of creating a welcoming effect for his group now bolstered with an impetus to obscure the words that would otherwise greet them. Apart from that unexpected detail, the van rode nicely and offered three rows of seats in addition to the driver's section, providing plenty of room for the members to enjoy a comfortable ride out to the retreat.

In spite of some lingering uncertainties linked to the prior evening's meeting, as well as a few, new, slightly unsettling bits of insight he had just this morning come to learn, he was still excited about taking the trip or, at least, about the *prospect* of taking it, having to remind himself of the folly of placing too much emphasis on anticipation, especially when dealing with such people as—

With surprising punctuality, a handful of members began to arrive, and he felt himself smile at their approach, his excitement refusing to be so logically restrained. As Judge Talbott parked a light-green Pinto nearby, Mr. Crimpton came stalking diagonally across the parking lot, hands thrust in his Windbreaker, a trail of cigarette smoke following him. He stopped in his tracks to glower as Chris came hurtling past him from the opposite direction, mounted precariously on his skateboard, grinning at Dr. Pendleton as he sailed by, only to stop several yards away, his boots plodding loudly against the asphalt.

A taxicab pulled up alongside the adjacent sidewalk, its shocks sagging deeply as Mr. McClintock heaved himself out of the back, the car then lurching back to its usual center of balance, the driver shaking his head as he accepted his fare and sped away, Mr. McClintock ambling forward with a small suitcase.

Mr. Crimpton carried a small duffel bag, which he rested on the pavement as he scrutinized the face of the departing cabbie, giving the entire conveyance a pained look and then staring as Judge Talbott almost backed into a light post. Noting the make of her car, he blanched and swiftly dropped his cigarette, grinding it out and fingering his temples, his headache—a hangover variety, no less—sharpening. He truly wondered if he would be able to make it through this morning's ride, never mind the weekend.

Dr. Pendleton beamed at their approach, his smile only faltering when he noticed that they were all dressed exactly as they usually appeared. He, himself, was wearing a plaid shirt and outdoors man jacket, khaki pants and hiking boots, and a slightly large fishing cap atop his head; and as he viewed their rather unsuitable attire, he nonetheless was the one made to feel out of place.

"Good morning, everyone," he greeted them, all the same, watching as Judge Talbott hurried forward, wheeling a small airline-style suitcase behind her, Chris bearing only his backpack and skateboard, the young punk rocker smiling shyly at him, his face flushed in the morning chill.

"Hey, Dr. Pendleton," he nodded cheerfully. "You look great. Are you goin' on a Safari or somethin'?"

Blinking, Dr. Pendleton blushed himself, as Mr. Crimpton pointed at the Pinto. "Is *that* your car?" he asked Judge Talbott incredulously.

The tiny woman nodded. "Yes," she affirmed proudly. "It was a graduation present."

"Good morning!" Mr. McClintock called, huffing from his short walk, crisp and wrinkle-free as always, his mood jovial. How he loved IHOP. He motioned to his suitcase. "Is there perhaps a cargo area?" he inquired.

Nodding, Dr. Pendleton stepped around to the rear of the van, once again faced with the blatant stenciling, prompting him to pull open the doors as quickly as he could, moving swiftly enough, for Mr. McClintock's next question was only an innocuous inquiry if they would be stopping for brunch along the way.

Chris distracted him from his other side, his features a few shades more pink as he asked. "Um, Dr. Pendleton, have you seen Vanessa yet?"

Turning to acknowledge the boy, he glanced past him in time to see Vanessa come racing across the street toward them, waving and shouting, and then rushing back several paces to assist Mrs. Spindlewood, who was outfitted with her hat, gloves, and overcoat, one hand weighed down by a small, outdated, striped suitcase.

Vanessa helped her to the opposite curb, the old woman's gaze as vacant and unflustered as her toddling steps, Vanessa gently taking the suitcase from her and then darting toward the surprised members, Chris, poised to approach the girl, his visage brightening, eyes shining anxiously, gaping as she bypassed him and threw herself into Dr. Pendleton's startled arms.

As he did his best to embrace her, the others voicing their concerns, Vanessa merely clung to him for a moment, eyes closed as she thrust her chin onto his shoulder, Chris looking on in a poignant mixture of concern and disappointment, much too good-hearted to be jealous, but so very much wishing that it could have been him.

"Uh, good morning, Vanessa," Dr. Pendleton stammered lamely, glad when the girl finally pulled away so that he could address her properly. "Is…everything all right?" he asked her pointedly, nodding past her at the approaching elderly woman. "I see you found Mrs. Spindlewood."

Vanessa nodded quickly, her relief at seeing the doctor and at finding that they had not left without them immense. She had to swallow abruptly and inhale deeply as she met his gaze, staring fleetingly at the others as she spoke.

"Yes, I did. And she's fine, but…" She broke off and seemed about to pull into the doctor's arms again, instead squeezing her lips shut and shaking her head, Dr. Pendleton only then noticing how red and exhausted her eyes were. Exhaling tautly, her composure forcibly renewed, she turned toward Mrs. Spindlewood as she drew nearer.

"Here we are, Mrs. Spindlewood," she called assertively. "See, they did wait for us."

"Good morning, Mr. Bergdorf," the elderly woman chirped, greeting the others as she perceived them, Vanessa absently shoving her suitcase toward the nearest person, this happening to be Chris, who eagerly took it, mistaking the gesture as one of trust or, at least, resumed communication or, if nothing else, acknowledgment that he still existed.

"Uh, good morning, Mrs. Spindlewood," Dr. Pendleton's smile was genuine as he looked down at her. "It's so nice to see you again, and I'm so glad that you've decided to join our little road trip today."

"Oh yes, I'm quite looking forward to it," she returned pleasantly. "I haven't been to Roanoke to see my sister in years."

Dr. Pendleton's smile faded slightly, Mr. Crimpton frowning and stepping forward. "Roanoke? I thought we were only going upstate."

"Come on, Mrs. Spindlewood. Let me help you on board," Vanessa interrupted them, climbing into the van and situating Mrs. Spindlewood in the seat behind the driver, where she sat placidly, her purse in her lap, Vanessa hopping back out and lowering her voice as she spoke.

"Doc, I have got *so* much to tell you," she stated grimly.

As the others waited in concerned uncertainty, Dr. Pendleton cleared his throat, stealing a glance at the sedate form of the woman and then adopting a quieter tone himself. "Uh, yes…so have I…," he confided.

Vanessa, poised to speak, aware of but ignoring Chris's eager, gawking proximity, stared at the doctor instead, something in the weary hollows and creases of his kindly face bespeaking of the knowledge, perhaps even the answers to her questions, and thereby staying her words.

As she had lay all night on Mrs. Spindlewood's lumpy, dusty couch, she had finally fallen into a troubled sleep, which hinged upon her being able to speak to him the next day. When she had awakened, early that morning, instantly alert but completely unaware of her bizarre surroundings, the little old lady was standing over her, her light touch on Vanessa's arm starting her out of her slumber, immediately summoning up the recollection of all which the night before had entailed.

Sitting at the Formica table in the dining area, the hazy stream of sunlight illuminating the unreal spectacle of Mrs. Spindlewood, awake and dressed for the day in her frumpy, adorable clothes, a worn but frilly apron in place as she prepared their breakfast of farina and milk, Vanessa had remained silent, feeling like an invisible intruder, an interloper, as if seeing something on a stage or a TV screen, for she knew that, from the old woman's perspective, one moment Vanessa was there and the next, she was not, her disjointed grasp of her routine so ingrained that, where as her presence there was an anomaly, it did not consistently penetrate the cycle.

Eventually, though, the single meal became a breakfast for two, after which Vanessa had gently insisted that Mrs. Spindlewood pack a suitcase to accompany her on the trip with the others, the old woman vaguely mentioning a desire to visit a relative from whom she had not heard in a while, Vanessa seizing upon this as the point of her trip. She harbored no illusions that any such relations were still living, but saw no harm in letting her believe that such was their purpose. She had even set about helping her pack, choking back tears as she saw the priceless, dainty little sundries in the bureau drawers and the medicine cabinet, little old lady articles from decades past, tiny, neat, precious things that went into the ancient suitcase, the stale mothball odor inoffensive and fitting as she packed her nightgown and robe, copiously modest slips and stockings, dowdy panties, and brassieres, each item carefully folded and layered, the only factor not in evidence being the omnipresent fussiness of an old woman as she prepared for a trip, for Mrs. Spindlewood's every movement was one of calm, slow practiced patience.

When it seemed as if she had the task well in hand, Vanessa had asked to take a quick shower, scrubbing at herself vindictively as she strove to wash away the taint of the past two days, feeling naked, genuinely *naked*, in the old woman's bathroom, as well as unclean and unworthy of its trickling comfort, these emotions causing her to wash with a renewed frenzy, as if in an ardent desire to make herself feel decent and respectable and just *not dirty*.

Her energies were also concentrated for fear of what Mrs. Spindlewood might be doing, having been left on her own, her mind envisioning the old lady becoming disoriented and commencing to unpack her suitcase or, beyond that, going ahead and leaving without her. She had anxiously finished her shower, drying off on a towel she had taken from the Hotel Rochester and quickly dawning her last set of clean clothes; their jumbled placement in her backpack with her soiled clothes had given them a slight mustiness, but she had been in too much of a hurry to worry about it, hastily pulling open the door and finding Mrs. Spindlewood seated in a chair, suitcase alongside her, hands in her lap, ready to go. She might well have been expecting a bus or a train to pull into her apartment, so relaxed and complacent was her posture as she gazed vacantly up into Vanessa's relieved features. "Hello, Trudy."

Her hair still wet, she had bundled her onto a cross-town bus, amazed at how much deference the old woman was shown and grateful too, as it lent speed to their rush to get to the meeting place on time. Even now, as she stood, braced before Dr. Pendleton, she could feel droplets of moisture work their way out of her hair and down the back of her neck.

"What?" she asked him flatly, staring unblinkingly into his eyes. "What did you find out?"

Dr. Pendleton cleared his throat again, taking another look at the oblivious old woman and then stepping away from the van anyway, the others surrounding him in a huddle of concern, this encroaching on his nerves as he nonetheless began to speak.

"Uh, well, after last night's meeting, I got to thinking about your concerns for her well-being, uh, and your concerns about how, uh, concerned all of us were or should have been. And...well, anyway, I did a little checking…," he explained, trying to meet Vanessa's almost manic gaze. "I called the phone company to ask about the number Mrs. Spindlewood gave us, and they told me that not only has that entire area prefix been discontinued for years, but also it wasn't residential. It was for businesses and offices."

"Well, that makes sense," Vanessa confirmed. "Her phone number at home is completely different from the one she gave us."

Dr. Pendleton blinked. "Well, yes, I realized that she must have thought I was asking for the number of the employment agency that sent her to…well, that she *thinks* sent her to our…" He cleared his throat. "At any rate, I called a business directory and finally the Chamber of Commerce, and they went down a list and eventually came across the name of the Temp Service Mrs. Spindlewood mentioned."

Pausing, he smiled. "So that was helpful—and, I've got to say, I was really impressed with how many of these places were open on a Saturday morning."

"What's so impressive about that?" Mr. Crimpton asked sharply, lighting a cigarette. If the DMV ever started that, it would finish him.

The doctor glanced at him uncertainly, Vanessa commanding his attention once more. "What did you find out, Doc?"

"Well," he continued, the worried girl watching his grimace develop closely. "The fact is that particular Temp Service went out of business over forty years ago," he explained, instantly met with confused looks.

"Well, who does she work for then?" Chris spoke up, mouth agape.

"Or for whom does she *think* she works?" Mr. McClintock amended gently.

"Uh, that's probably a better way of putting it," Dr. Pendleton allowed hesitantly, rubbing his palms against his pant legs, finding it increasingly difficult to meet Vanessa's eyes. "Uh, there really isn't an easy way to…account for all of this, so I'll just have to come out and tell you."

He paused, chuckling nervously. "It's really rather, uh, remarkable…" His smile melting at their expressions, he quickly proceeded.

"I thought about it for a while, and then, it occurred to me to try a hunch, and I consulted the phonebook. There were at least two columns, but I was lucky again, because within half a dozen tries, I spoke to a woman who verified that her late father was a Mr. Bergdorf who managed an office here in the city. She had never heard of that particular Temp Service, but she was able to give me the name and number of the company office he directed."

Mr. Crimpton shrugged, exhaling away from the group. "Let me guess, it was long-gone too, right?" he surmised cynically.

"Uh, well, no, actually. It's still a functioning, active business," Dr. Pendleton clarified.

"So Mrs. Spindlewood works for them then?" Judge Talbott concluded hopefully.

Dr. Pendleton shifted. "Well, no"—he replied hesitantly and then obliged to add—"but also yes..." He cleared his throat. "Uh, it's sort of...both..."

As the others stared at him in bewilderment, he hastily continued, moving his small hands calmingly. "The main thing to consider is that, obviously, she's all right," he pointed out, once more glancing at the quiet, unaware figure and nodding to Vanessa, who was still watching him imploringly, causing him to exhale and drop his hands.

"I called the office and spoke to their personnel manager," he told them, his grimace now reinstated. "It's ironic, because the manager had just been going through Mrs. Spindlewood's file earlier this week, ironic because no one had looked at it in decades up until then... The manager was able to give me the whole story. It seems that back in the fifties, the Temp Service sent her to that office, uh, the Tyson-Hendricks Company—it's an accounting firm—to do basic secretarial work. Everything was fine except what no one knew is that the directors of the Temp Service were involved in fraud and money laundering and even embezzlement from their own workers. They were your basic white-collar crooks, and when it looked like they might be investigated, they changed their pay structure so that their employees—including Mrs. Spindlewood—would receive their paychecks directly from the companies who contracted their Temp Workers, thinking it would help cover their tracks.

"It didn't, though, and they were indicted, and the Temp Service was closed. But somehow, Mrs. Spindlewood was never told. And because she was being paid automatically from the Tyson-Hendricks office, she just sort of...continued to report to work, even though she didn't really, technically work there."

Mr. Crimpton held up a hand to interject. "Her service went under, and she didn't know?" he asked incredulously. "How could that possibly have escaped even *her* attention?"

"I don't know," Dr. Pendleton conceded, noticing Vanessa turn her eyes downward in a look of dark contemplation. "I...what I do know is that apparently, somehow, for the next forty-some-odd years, she kept right on reporting for work, even long after Mr. Bergdorf had retired and passed on. She was there for so many years and through so many changes and mergers and downsizings and employee turn-overs that no one consistently knew who she was or why she was there, but because she was such a fixture in the building, it seemed obvious to all of the newcomers that she belonged there. She was also never given any sort of employee reviews because her record was not in the files for regular personnel. In fact, the manager told me that it hadn't been until this past week that they even knew she was attached to their office at all.

"It seems they share the floor with Pullman and Shaw, a publishing firm, and each office had come to assume that she belonged to the other. In fact, she was seen in so many different parts of that office building, wandering about, appearing to be running errands, that, overall, no one knew *who* she worked for."

As the members stared at him in disbelief, Vanessa's eyes had shot back up to meet his. "Doc, what is it that happened earlier this week that caused them to notice her all of a sudden?" she asked pointedly.

Dr. Pendleton cleared his throat. "Well, uh, it seems that where the two office spaces join, there's a little, unused storage room. And, just by a fluke, someone in Tyson and someone in Pullman began to debate about which office was entitled to use it, and when they went inside, they found Mrs. Spindlewood sitting in a chair, staring off into space...sort of...the way she does in our, uh, group sessions."

He flushed, shifting his feet. "Anyway, they began to speak to her, directly, for the first time. And, because of her answers and…disposition and such, it wasn't long before they were able to discern the discrepancy, uh, from all those years ago, uh. At which point, they… well, it's not that they fired her, since she didn't actually, uh, work there in the first place."

The silence that greeted his conclusion was nothing short of profound, Mr. Crimpton inhaling his cigarette into one, long cylindrical ember. "Are you trying to tell us that she got up and went to work in an office building where she didn't even really have a job and then just sat in a closet, staring at the wall for close to fifty years?" he demanded, stealing a glance over at her.

Dr. Pendleton nodded and then shook his head. "Uh, well, no. I'm sure she, uh, did other things too, made coffee, did a little filing, or the like." He cleared his throat awkwardly, attempting to retain some credibility in his explanation. "Uh, the point is, something obviously transpired in coincidental, uh, simultaneousness with this affair involving the Temp Service and the office, something most likely of a private nature, which was so overwhelming as to supersede any vocational matters. It's my professional opinion that Mrs. Spindlewood incurred some sort of personal shock, one that affected her both emotionally and mentally," he informed them gravely.

They all turned to gaze over at Mrs. Spindlewood now, the elderly lady smiling vaguely back, Mr. Crimpton breaking the silence, addressing the doctor in sardonic awe. "Ya think so?"

Dr. Pendleton flinched, Vanessa nodding vigorously, her eyes wide. "Yes, yes, that's just it! That's what happened!" she insisted, grabbing his sleeve for emphasis. "Did the manager say anything about what they thought might have gone wrong with her?"

"Uh, well, no," Dr. Pendleton admitted, now wondering what Vanessa might have learned since their last encounter. "No one in the office knew the slightest thing about her, except that she seemed a bit odd. Apart from that, no one really paid any attention to her."

"Was there no one else still working there from…well, from the time that Mrs. Spindlewood seems to remember?" Judge Talbott inquired, meekly doubtful.

Dr. Pendleton shook his head. "No, as I say, Mr. Bergdorf was long dead. And the others—Mr. Dembrough, Mr. Conklin, Mr. Rasmussen, uh, Odessa, the cleaning woman, Herbert, the office boy, and even another secretary named Trudy—all of them have been gone for ages now." He grimaced sadly.

The others considered this glum and strangely disembodying detail, Vanessa's gaze slipping to the ground again. She knew beyond any doubt what had happened now, her almost frenzied need to share her discovery with the others suddenly stifled in the wake of what the doctor had learned himself, particularly this latter insight, which lent to the inescapable notion that everyone Mrs. Spindlewood had ever known, beginning with her husband, was dead and gone.

Her heart stilled solemnly as the urge to disclose what she knew dimmed, replaced by a tired, sorry resignation. Nonetheless, she met the doctor's gaze once more, her eyes watery but resolute as she spoke.

"Doc, is it possible that you could, you know, have some kind of personal shock, like you were saying. But, um, instead of going completely psycho, you might just kinda, I don't know, go into a fog the rest of your life?" she asked him hesitantly. "I mean you can still do all of your everyday stuff, ya know, cook, clean, maybe even go to work 'n' stuff, you can manage just fine. But, in your head, you're sort of just...stuck in time, like from the point before all of the bad stuff went down?"

Studying her closely, Dr. Pendleton nodded. "Conventionally speaking, Vanessa, anything is possible," he told her slowly. "Clinically speaking, it is actually quite probable that such a scenario could exist, even for a period of decades. A person could be in an altered state and yet also continue to undertake basic, daily tasks. In fact, the regimentation of these basic day-to-day activities can actually serve as an ultimate sort of coping mechanism. It becomes a cycle of pseudonormalcy that helps the individual to elude whatever trauma has unbalanced them, and if unaddressed, it becomes that person's reality, virtually indistinguishable from the world and time and place as we know it."

As he was explaining this, he noticed Vanessa's breathing quicken, her eyes becoming more pained. The others regarded her as well, Chris's mouth closing, his features taut with anxious concern.

"Uh, did you detect something…suggestive of that when you found Mrs. Spindlewood?" Dr. Pendleton asked at length.

"Yeah," Vanessa swallowed as her voice cracked. "Her apartment."

Dr. Pendleton frowned, Mr. Crimpton gesturing openly. "Okay, well, now, wait a sec," he interposed. "We all knew there was something wrong with her up top. I mean that much was a given. But even though she should be attending therapy meetings, even though she was there with us, she wasn't actually there, am I right? If she really is that far gone, how come you didn't pick up on it 'til just now?"

Flushing, Dr. Pendleton shifted. "Well, as I say, Mr. Crimpton, the nuances of her condition are such that they're not especially pronounced," he insisted, somewhat flustered. "Her routine is so well-defined that she effects a strong degree of self-sufficiency. Her mannerisms did seem a bit…off, I agree, and it did occur to me that she was very forgetful, but as far as any problems revolving around her private life went, I thought I should give her the benefit of the doubt and let her share with us when she was ready."

Mr. Crimpton's response—or retort—was waylaid as Vanessa cut in, waving her hands sharply. "She is completely, totally fine taking care of herself, okay? That is not *even* a problem. I know because I've spent a lot more time with her than any of you," she declared flatly, a flash of her usual spirit charging her words before dwindling and dying as she focused on Dr. Pendleton again. "It's just… Her apartment… If you all could just see it… It's—"

She broke off and placed the back of her hand to her mouth, as if to bite it rather than give into any manner of breakdown. As much as she hated drama queen scenes, however, she could scarcely hold back her tears, even after last night's gut-wrenching tidal wave, her chest and stomach still wracked and sore from crying.

Dr. Pendleton held her gaze, the obvious question poised on his lips, his instincts dissuading him instead to put the matter aside until it could be discussed more carefully and discreetly. He cleared his throat. "Well, whatever we may have learned about our fellow… uh, our lady…our fellow lady member, what is quite apparent is that she is well and in good form, eager to participate in our outing. And the fact that she is safe and sound and with us again is a very good indication that...that she'll continue to be fine and well-cared for..."

He smiled at Vanessa in hopeful confirmation, the girl dropping her hand and returning the gesture shakily but forcefully. "Damn straight, Doc," she replied, nodding somberly, almost defiantly. "We're gonna take real good care of her from now on."

Dr. Pendleton nodded back, hesitantly putting one arm around her shoulder and patting her comfortingly, turning to address the others. "Well, now, we do still have our retreat ahead of us!" he announced enthusiastically. "Shall we, uh, commence our adventure?"

The members answered with varying degrees of eagerness, Chris hurrying to stow Mrs. Spindlewood's suitcase in the back of the van and then, when Dr. Pendleton hastily insisted on closing the rear doors himself, quickly and then nonchalantly placing himself near Vanessa, determined that he should just happen to end up sitting next to her. Vanessa, rolling her eyes at such pathetic—and infu-riatingly cute—obviousness, had every intention of sitting next to Mrs. Spindlewood during the trip and would have done so had Mr. McClintock not demonstrated thoughtful but ill-timed gallantry by insisting that she go ahead of him.

She was not above refusing, but stopped herself when she real-ized that the amiable man was much too large to ride in the rear seats, and rather than embarrass him or jostle the old lady around by rear-ranging her, she had forced a smile and made her way to the farthest seat in the back row, knowing that Judge Talbott was right behind her.

She expected the little woman to settle in next to her, annoyed but glad (*glad?*) when she didn't, instead sliding into the center row and fussing with her tote bag.

Sure enough, here came Chris, clambering toward her, his Mohawk scraping the roof of the van as he hunched over and gaped innocently at her, his crimson features betraying the coincidence he was clumsily trying to imply when he casually asked, "Um, is it okay if I sit here?"

Gazing up at him with a blank face and fiery eyes, Vanessa regarded him for the first time that morning, her heart swelling as she trounced his informal air with utterly dismissive indifference.

"I don't care," she replied, allowing herself a tiny smirk of triumph as she watched him eagerly swing into the seat, her eyes taking in his lithe form and his punk attire as he did so, distracted only for a second before she sat up sharply.

"But you see this line?" she demanded, pointing at an almost indiscernible crease running down the width of the bench seat, the sudden harshness of her voice startling him. "This is the border, got it? This half is a dork-free zone, so you just keep your dorky ass over there on the dork side, understand?" She glared at him petulantly, Chris jumping at her ferocity, gawking at her as he nodded rapidly.

"I made cookies for everyone for the trip!" Judge Talbott was announcing cheerfully, pulling a tinfoil bundle out of her tote bag. "They're ginger bread men—and ladies—and I made them personalized for each member of our group!"

She began to unwrap them as Mr. McClintock hefted himself into the seat alongside of her, Vanessa rolling her eyes as she beheld that not only would she have been able to sit next to Mrs. Spindlewood, but also she was now irreversibly trapped in the rear of the van—with Chris.

"Oh, that was very thoughtful," Dr. Pendleton beamed as he closed the sliding door, glad to see Mr. Crimpton already seated in the driver-side seat, the latter having automatically positioned himself there, just as routinely battling open an aspirin tin and dry-swallowing a couple of the tiny pills, just as reflexively cursing his actions and fidgeting nervously in his seat.

Dr. Pendleton scurried to take his place behind the wheel, his excitement revived and surpassing his previous restraint.

"Okay, is everybody ready?" he called out, glancing back at the members of his group as he started the engine of the van, its roaring power further invigorating him.

"Almost everybody," Mr. Crimpton told him crisply, glaring sharply at the doctor's uncertain expression. "Your seatbelt, Doctor," he indicated impatiently.

Blinking, Dr. Pendleton sheepishly pulled the harness over one shoulder. "Almost forgot about that," he chuckled, snapping it in place.

Mr. Crimpton nodded briskly. "Now check your mirrors, signal, and pull slowly away from the curb," he instructed him tacitly.

Pausing, Dr. Pendleton blinked again, then hesitantly doing as he was told or, as he was planning to do, anyway, focusing on finding the driveway of the parking lot.

"Here, Vanessa, here's yours," Judge Talbott was saying as she distributed the cookies. "Claude, here's yours. Mr. McClintock, this is for you."

She handed him a gingerbread man clad in an icing tie and jacket, at least three times larger than any of the others, Mr. McClintock receiving it with wincing relish.

Vanessa stared at her red-dressed gingerbread girl, wishing it did not look so slutty, then glancing over at Chris's cookie, which had been given an iced green Mohawk. He was grinning at it, Vanessa forced to grin as well, inasmuch as it really was sweet and cool. She reached over and gently took it from him, the two of them sharing in impressed smiles, Vanessa then pleasantly biting the entire head off his and handing it back to him, regarding him apathetically as she chomped on it, Chris gaping at his headless cookie, crestfallen, his mouth clamping shut as he then slumped broodingly over into the far corner of his side of the seat, sadly munching on it.

"Now, get ready to merge with the flow of the traffic," Mr. Crimpton was murmuring mechanically, checking all the angles of vision that his position afforded him.

"Uh, Mr. Crimpton," Dr. Pendleton began quietly, easing the van into the street and through the intersection. "Really, you needn't feel like—"

"Dr. Pendleton, that was a yellow light!" Mr. Crimpton grated, tensing.

"Here's your cookie, Dr. Pendleton," Judge Talbott proclaimed, extending it to him, the doctor glancing at it and then appraising its personalized design more closely. True, cookies were a tannish brown themselves, but still, no icing at all?

"Dr. Pendleton, look out!" Mr. Crimpton exclaimed, the doctor grimacing and braking as he jerked the wheel, averting the path of a delivery van, cringing as the driver leaned on his horn.

Mr. Crimpton, both hands braced against the dashboard, gave him a blistering look, Dr. Pendleton shrinking and then thankfully accepting both the cookies the judge shoved at him before hastily retreating to her seat.

"Uh, sorry about that," he told the distraught driving examiner, shrugging as casually as he dared, moving to hand Mr. Crimpton his cookie.

"*Both hands on the wheel!*" the latter admonished in choked panic, the van jolting again as Dr. Pendleton complied, if only to calm the man. Mr. Crimpton eventually reached over for his cookie, leaving the doctor to wonder how he could sample his and keep his hands at ten and two.

As Mrs. Spindlewood gratefully received her cookie, clutching it in her lap, the judge glanced up from the tinfoil bundle. "Oh! I made one for Father Gilchrist too!" she announced, glancing at the others. "I guess he really didn't want to come along with us."

"I hope we didn't leave without him," Mr. McClintock remarked.

Dr. Pendleton, about to speak over one shoulder, instead gazed up at the rearview mirror. "Oh well, don't worry," he called back to them, aware that Mr. Crimpton was steadily watching his actions. Grasping the wheel firmly, he addressed the windshield loudly. "I was planning on swinging by St. Leonard's Church to make sure he hadn't changed his mind."

As the others nodded, Judge Talbott carefully rewrapped the lone gingerbread man. "I hope he does decide to join us," she said sincerely, having managed to put most of the previous night's upset aside. "I don't know what we'll do with his cookie if he doesn't."

Vanessa swallowed the rest of hers and smiled at the Judge. "We can always stick a bunch of pins in it," she proposed sweetly.

Judge Talbott gasped, shaking her head and then smiling shyly into one hand.

*****

"Honestly, sir, I can't imagine where he's got to."

The voice, unappreciably whining and familiar, came from at least a thousand miles away, just barely penetrating the darkness.

He slowly, dreadingly embraced consciousness, reality, life, and identity once more, opening his eyes and seeing nothing.

Frowning with difficulty, for even mere thinking was agonizing, Father Gilchrist shut his eyes with the sole intention of opening them again, this time for real. He did so, puzzled when the result was the same. Had he gone blind overnight? He was a bit too old to make a very good almsman. *Overnight...perhaps it was still night.*

"Naturally, you have tried his private quarters?"

No, nighttime was never absolutely dark. Had he perchance awakened in his coffin, an unwitting recipient of a premature burial? If so, had it been an accident? Or perhaps he had revived to find himself in the Great Abyss. Were these to be his new quarters for all eternity? He would have thought that he at least merited a nightlight. "Quarters." That last voice was familiar too. Fellow lost souls possibly? Where in the hell—literally or metaphorically—was he? And why were his legs so painfully cramped?

"Yes, indeed, sir. They was the first place I looked."

Light. There was a hairline crack of light, at least a mile down, but he could make it out clearly enough. If he had some rope, he could—something just moved down there, just now, edging against that chasm of hope. Some kind of netherworldly entity, a serpent, preventing anyone from escaping into the light? He leaned forward and squinted, realizing that it was one of his shoes.

"Well, Father Ralph insists that he saw him just before goin' off to oversee Bingo Night, and Sister Angelica swears she hadn't seen him all day."

Father Ralph and Sister Angelica? Yes, he was damned all right, he reflected, sitting up and becoming reacquainted with his familiar purgatory, the varnished wooden penalty box of the confessional in which he had...spent the night?

He blinked and frowned more deeply, ignoring the pain. How on earth could he have—? Scotch. It had something to do with scotch, didn't it?

"Well, like I say, sir, last I seen 'im was last night, just after I got interrupted cleanin' all of the sacrament pieces."

Scotch, yes. What in blazes were they going on about? And if that was not Father Ralph and Sister Angelica bantering out there, then who was it? His ringing ears could not discern.

"I tell you, Deacon Richard, sir, he was in a right state! You'd not have believed it with your own eyes!"

Deacon Richard? Father Gilchrist squeezed his eyes shut and tried to will himself back to the netherworld, sighing in defeat when he was unsuccessful and then sitting stock still, listening and focusing, trying to recall.

"Yes, but what precisely did he do, Donald?"

Ah, Donald, of course. Yes, Donald, what precisely did I do? Tell His Nibs so that I can likewise remember, because I have this curious gap in my recollections, the vacancy being filled with a hemorrhaging intensity. So, please, Donald, by all means, tell us, won't you, you servile dolt.

Donald told him, Father Gilchrist listening in shock, sudden recall, a shade of guilt, a smattering of glee, an abiding, growing righteousness, and, ultimately, anger.

"I tell you, sir, you'd simply not believe it, if I wasn't here to tell the tale."

Yes, but you are here, and you did tell the tale, you little Judas. Father Gilchrist clenched his teeth and resisted the urge to burst out of his stuffy hiding place and collar the little sexton, denouncing his treachery on the spot. Instead, he strained his ears, judging that the two of them must be up near the altar, the crunch of broken glass audibly underfoot. He was anxious to hear whatever the Archdiocese official might have to say, his innards already roiling in defiance.

Ambiguity, by its very nature, is imprecise; and Father Gilchrist cursed its inexactitude now as Deacon Richard offered his pragmatic, prosaic, oh so typical response.

"Well, now, Donald, I suppose that Father Gilchrist and I will simply have to have a good long talk."

A good long talk with that blockhead? He would just as soon stay in the confessional; last night was by no means the first time he had passed out in one of them. At least one aspect of the noncommittal reply was not in the least bit ambiguous, that being, of course, a talk with Deacon Richard on any subject under the heavens would be perfectly horrific and was an event to be avoided at all costs.

Very carefully, he eased open the door to the confessional and peered past it, wincing against even the dim light of the church interior. He beheld both men from the back as they surveyed the altar and slowly stepped out of the booth. Moving in comically theatrical stealth, he tiptoed as best he could on his aching, half-asleep legs, grateful that the enormity of the challenge of his escape had at least temporarily banished the thumbscrews in his mind. He made his way alongside the wall, hastily, almost laughably genuflecting at the few stations of the cross he passed as he hurried along his way, seeing the glimpses of daylight beyond the columns of the entryway, which meant that the outer doors were wide open; all he had to do was get to them before—

"Father Gilchrist! Sir, look, there he goes now!"

Judas! Just you wait, Donald O'Flaherty. I'll replace every last one of those tapers with April Fool's Day candles! You'll think you were caught in a flipping time warp!

"Father Gilchrist, good morning, sir. I'd like a word, if you don't mind."

Good morning, sir, is it? Oh, he's a pip, that one is.

Caught but uncaptured, Father Gilchrist spun around, his frosty eyebrows shooting innocently upward. "Whom?" he called out stiltedly. "Father Gilchrist, did you say? Oh, I'm afraid he's just now stepped out! But wait, though, I'll go and try to catch him!"

With that, he turned and bolted out of the church as fast as he could drive his decrepit body to propel him, dashing between the columns and out the front doors to freedom, having to stop at the topmost step and shield his eyes against the blinding intensity of the morning sunlight, almost staggering against it, then forcing himself down the marble steps, only half able to see. Surely, this must be something akin to an escape from damnation, for he truly felt like a bat out of—well, that might be going a bit too far.

Reaching the bottom of the steps, he squinted around the stone expanse of the walkway, feeling oddly out of place without his hat and coat, rather like a fugitive! A renegade priest in search of some path of flight, but to where, *where*?

Even now he could hear Deacon Richard's unflappably calm voice calling after him from the top of the steps. What did the desperado do when there was no horse awaiting him at the hitching post? What did the fleeing outlaw do when there was no getaway car on hand?

He blinked and gasped as he saw the beige van glide up in front of the church. A mirage, perhaps? A fictitious, apparitional conveyance from *the Hollingsworth Institution for the Mentally Ill*?

He cocked his head sideways. No, that was too appropriately unreal to be unreal. He darted toward it, thanking God for small curses, for surely his chariot awaited him. *Roll up, Father Gilchrist, roll up, for the Magical Mystery Tour is coming to take you away, ha-ha, ho-ho, hee-hee*!

Stealing a look over his shoulder, he caught a glimpse of Deacon Richard, who was now descending the steps with measured, disciplined movements, calling patiently after him. Even his methods of pursuit were conservative and practical, he reflected in a flash of disgust; praise be on High that it was not Father Ralph bounding after him.

Nonetheless unwilling to play the hare to his tortoise, he ran wildly up to the van, wrenching open its side door to a chorus of gasps, including his own as he found himself face to face with Mrs. Spindlewood.

"Good morning, Mr. Dembrough," she greeted him with a hazy smile.

Well, well, for whom the bell did *not* toll. "Good morning, dear lady!" he returned wheezily, climbing briskly into the seat beside her and slamming the door. "And to you all! Well, let's go!"

Dr. Pendleton, his mouth stuffed with gingerbread, swallowed harshly, blushing. "Oh, Father Gilchrist!" he nodded, smiling quickly. "We came by to see if you'd changed your mind."

Father Gilchrist tilted his head in mad sarcasm. "*Did you?*" he marveled.

"Er, Father, there appears to be some gentleman trying to catch up with you," Mr. McClintock told him hesitantly.

"We really shouldn't be parked here, even with the engine idling," Mr. Crimpton was saying pointedly. "The curb is clearly red, you know."

"Don't be ridiculous!" Father Gilchrist scolded him. "God parks here all the time!" Seeing a figure peripherally approaching the vehicle, he steadily ignored it. "On second thought, he's right! We musn't tarry! Onward, now, to the call of the open road!"

"Uh, Father Gilchrist," Dr. Pendleton frowned uncertainly, blinking against the pervasive scotch fumes that the winded old priest was expelling. "Is it, uh, possible that that man has something he needs to tell you?" he asked, somewhat unnecessarily, for Deacon Richard was now rapping on the window, clearly calling the priest's name.

"*Hmmm?*" Father Gilchrist responded, all innocence, then feigning an appraising glance at his pursuer and convulsing profoundly.

"Why, don't be a fool!" he exclaimed, looking back at the startled doctor in terror. "Can't you see for yourself? That isn't really a man! It's an Evil Pod Creature, from the third planet of Neptune! It's come to steal my soul!"

Judge Talbott gasped, all of them turning to gape at the placid, bemused face of this perfectly ordinary-looking man.

"But—" Dr. Pendleton was cut off as Father Gilchrist waved his hands wildly.

"Drive, man, drive!" he shouted in frenzy. "That cross it's wearing is actually a death ray! Hurry, before it mutates back into its alien form and vaporizes the lot of us!"

This notion secured more gasps, Dr. Pendleton not knowing what else to do except throw the van into gear and accelerate away from the curb, tires squealing.

"Yield to oncoming traffic," Mr. Crimpton directed. "Yield to... Yield! *Yield!*"

Wincing, Dr. Pendleton cut off an SUV and then tried to placate the virtually hyperventilating driving examiner with a pronounced checking of his mirrors, grimacing when this action reflected to him the reaction of the driver of the SUV, his hand gesture unmistakable.

Having shut his eyes until they had lurched away, knowing that his nemesis's hand had just reached for the door latch, Father

Gilchrist sat up and glanced about, realizing that he had escaped. Overjoyed, he then exercised the very height of audacity, turning and waving merrily back at Deacon Richard, who stood on the curb, arms akimbo, his complacent features at long last registering a mildly perturbed look.

Ha! You tried and you failed, kemo-sabi! Run, run, fast as you can, you can't catch me, I'm the—

"Here's a gingerbread man I made for you, Father," Judge Talbott offered shyly, Father Gilchrist turning, his eyebrows arching intently as he beheld the miniature version of himself.

"Well, saints preserve us, Your Honor! He looks just like me!" he declared, heartily, taking the gingerbread man and admiring it, then gazing at the blushing judge with twinkling eyes, waggling a finger. "But you forgot the little horns and pointy tail!"

*****

In time, they were outside of the city limits, the van gliding smoothly on a highway that led them into stretches of pastureland and relatively unpopulated countryside. The initial elation that usually accompanies any manner of road trip was no different for them, a pleasant, excited quiet settling over the group as they took in the scenery with dreamy composure, only occasional banter arising as the miles began to drift behind them, the unwillingness to converse eventually superseded by the need, as Father Gilchrist was discreetly and then more openly brought up to date on Mrs. Spindlewood's situation, the elderly lady transfixed by the view from her window, only withdrawing from her reverie to answer questions directly put to her, those being of the most pedestrian sort, the discussion then tactfully but directly ensuing around her.

Father Gilchrist was sympathetic, but also unsurprised. "Well, as tragically absurd as that is, in a world such as this, such anomalies probably exist to an exponentially discouraging degree," he told them wearily, his headache beginning to regain some of the footing it had lost to the thrill of his exodus. "I know a man who worked at a job for almost fifty years, who knew precisely what he was doing, and yet who is not much better off. So I suppose ignorance or, in our lady's case, unawareness can be bliss." He shrugged his eyebrows and continued before anyone could question his comparison, shooting a look toward Dr. Pendleton. "Of course, on that note, I find myself pondering if this decisively severe scenario could actually have escaped the attention of our vigilant overseer," he declared, laconically rhetorical. "Small wonder."

Dr. Pendleton flinched, unable to comment as he focused on his driving, if only to placate Mr. Crimpton, who had relaxed as much as he was able, still sitting in ramrod advertence but now only occasionally offering his reflexive instructions. Participating in any conversation was clearly not within his desire or possibly even his ability; and Dr. Pendleton was also hesitant to do so, only intermittently joining in with a question, grateful that his group was actively discussing the welfare of one of their own, for that was the whole point and one of the best ways that he could augment that was by merely listening.

"Yeah, well, we all missed it," Vanessa spoke up in his defense. "If I hadn't spent the night at her place, I would never have known how…" She swallowed and shook her head.

Frowning thoughtfully at her, Father Gilchrist considered her brief description of an apartment in which time had stood still, the girl about to elaborate and then, just as now, stopping herself. It was enough, though, to inspire one's imagination, he reflected, for, while he was not about to risk upsetting the girl by saying so, to him, such accommodations sounded quite appealing. A realm belonging to yesteryear of a half-century past spared the intrusion of "progress"? He glanced at the oblivious, fragile old woman beside him. *Ah, Mrs. Spindlewood, sweet enigma. Where others have tried, you have succeeded. I am asked to take pity, but instead I envy you.*

"It does make one appreciate one's own circumstances," Mr. McClintock offered generously. For an entire week now, he had been in something of a dream state of his own, attempting to focus upon his actually very precarious situation and then, ultimately, reverting to the only cycle he knew, the diversion and appreciation of food, food that he was no longer being paid to appreciate, which he might eventually no longer be able to afford. Still, though, to find one's self unemployed at Mrs. Spindlewood's age, that was truly daunting. "I'm of course concerned about the uncertainties of my own future, but one has to sympathize with the...well, with the extremes of her predicament."

There was a brief silence, Dr. Pendleton suddenly recalling this rather crucial point that had more or less been lost in the shuffle last night as Mr. McClintock had strolled away with the doughnuts. "Uh, yes, Mr. McClintock," he called, glancing in the rearview mirror. "I've been meaning to ask you all along...did you mention that you have lost your job with the newspaper?"

As the others gaped in surprise, Mr. McClintock only smiled and spread his hands self-effacingly. "Well, yes, I'm afraid so—" he began, forcing a dismissive chuckle.

"You got canned?" Vanessa demanded, leaning forward and touching the man's broad shoulder, staring at him imploringly, Mr. McClintock exhaling quietly and turning to smile toward her, patting her hand with his pudgy fingers, as Judge Talbott's eyes widened in guilty recollection.

"Oh! You told us that last night, Mr. McClintock. I... I guess I was a little...distracted," she confessed sadly. "I'm so sorry!"

"Oh, really, it..." Mr. McClintock merely shook his head. "Certainly it's disappointing, but...well, as we've seen, there are much worse eventualities."

"You can say that again," Mr. Crimpton startled them all by speaking up brusquely. "There are plenty of things worse than losing your job!"

Impressed, Dr. Pendleton cleared his throat. "That's true, Mr. Crimpton, and—"

"Watch the road," Mr. Crimpton grated. "And get ready to change lanes."

Dr. Pendleton blinked and then did so—he was going to anyway.

"Well, there is some truth to that," Father Gilchrist mused, picking up the train of thought. "I'll assuredly know soon enough, and while it is not really standard procedure for a priest to be fired, I may just well have set the precedent."

No one knew what to say to this, for Father Gilchrist's change of heart in the matter of joining them had seemed more like that of a murderer fleeing the scene of a crime.

"I got fired once," Chris volunteered, most likely trying to be helpful, glancing earnestly at the others. "I was working for the Dixie-Belle Ice Cream Parlour, and I put a whole bunch of ice cream birthday cakes in a stand-up freezer, but it was actually a heating unit. And when I opened it later, they all had melted and went all over the floor, and I slipped and the unit tipped over, and they all fell on me and made a huge mess all over the kitchen, and I got fired." He nodded with a lopsided smile. "Yeah, um, they told me not to ever come back there again, not even as a customer."

This account likewise produced a prolonged silence, Chris glancing about hopefully and then stealing a glance at Vanessa, instantly looking away from her indisputable appraisal. *What a dork.*

"Well, for what it may be worth, it seems that our retreat has come just in time," Dr. Pendleton observed. "Relaxation and reflection will be our main objectives."

Father Gilchrist curbed his tongue. "Ah, yes, the retreat. We are all agog with anticipation!" He smiled at his elderly seatmate. "You're excited, aren't you, Mrs. Spindlewood?"

"Oh yes," she replied instantly. "I have a cousin who lives in Hackensack."

Pausing, he nodded politely. "Yes, and well that we all should be excited," he continued blithely. "Especially in spite of this dreadful premonition that I had of a doctor who professed to be taking his therapy group to a beautiful resort but who instead abducts them, delivering them to a secret asylum hidden in the hills where he forces them to submit to insane medical research experiments!"

The uncomfortable shifting that this statement created prompted Dr. Pendleton to force a choked laugh. "What...what could have given you such an outlandish idea, Father Gilchrist?" he chortled.

The old priest only smiled. "Oh, it was just a recurring thought, *stenciled* in my mind," he replied.

Frowning, Dr. Pendleton then started in realization, inadvertently jerking the wheel, Mr. Crimpton glowering over at him.

"Would you *please* try to stay in your own lane?" he growled.

Mr. McClintock sat up in his seat, glad that the discourse had focused away from himself and hoping to keep it that way. "One would hope that she would have some sort of pension coming to her," he remarked pointedly. "Even allowing for the illicit actions of the Temp Service."

Judge Talbott nodded, paused, and then slowly shook her head. "I'd like to think so, but the entire process of Social Security and Medicare and everything is so involved and difficult to access, and that's for someone of sound mind and a normal work history," she explained regretfully, almost whispering the last detail.

Vanessa gazed sharply at them. "Wait a minute, what are you talking about?" she asked reluctantly. "What do you mean?"

Father Gilchrist met her eyes. "Well, surely you realize that the discovery of that discrepancy by her pseudoemployers will preclude any further salary for her," he explained candidly. "In fact, allowing for how greedy people can be, I shouldn't be surprised if they attempt to sue for recompensation, especially when they consider that they've been paying her, by the month, for decades, to wander aimlessly around a building, making coffee for dead people and sitting in a chair in an unused room."

Vanessa looked at him in panic. No, surely she had *not* realized that.

"Wait, but what about her apartment?" she demanded. "How is she going to be able to live, to pay rent, or buy groceries or anything?"

Father Gilchrist regarded her as compassionately as he could manage. "My girl, I honestly don't know," he told her quietly. "If she has any manner of life savings or such, she should be fine. Otherwise, frankly speaking, I cannot guess."

Staring at him in livid silence, Vanessa thought of the threadbare apartment, the nearly empty refrigerator, the meager store of her cupboards. The cycle's balance had been perfectly maintained, no less, but certainly no more.

"That apartment..." she began yet one more time. "If she loses that apartment, she'll..." Shaking her head, she gazed at each of them pleadingly. "If you could only see it...all the stuff in it." She didn't have the words and simply gave up, instead telling them, "That apartment is all she's got."

She watched as they nodded solemnly, Judge Talbott turning and touching her arm reassuringly. "Try not to worry, Vanessa," she told her with surprising assertiveness, her eyes steady and serious. "I know the intricacies of the legalities involving someone like her, and I know we'll all be able to help her in one way or another." She smiled kindly, pausing in turning to add. "You already have."

Nodding gratefully, Vanessa nevertheless slumped backward and folded her arms together, focusing on the back of the judge's seat, one foot fidgeting rapidly as she contemplated this new angle. *Just when things couldn't possibly get more fucked.* She had been thinking about that wall calendar, its prominence reflected in all that Dr. Pendleton had learned, establishing that Mrs. Spindlewood had to be, at the very least, in her late seventies.

God, that was old, so old to be traipsing to an office building day after day, and now, she couldn't even do that. She wouldn't last a day on the streets, and if the State shoved her in some nursing home, she wouldn't be much better off.

No, that was not going to happen; she had avoided being pushed into a foster home by the State, and it was for damn sure that she was going to prevent anything like that from happening to Mrs. Spindlewood. No one was going to fuck with her or her apartment because even if it was unreal and maybe even unhealthy, even though it was pretty much a tomb, it was way too late for her to go back, to just give all of that up; it really was all she had, with one exception, that being *her.* She had Vanessa on her side now, and she was prepared to fight for her.

She sensed Chris shifting next to her and glanced up as he gazed hopefully at her, his eyes intently bright. "What was Mrs. Spindlewood's apartment like, Vanessa?" he asked her, eagerly but earnestly curious.

Staring at him, she felt all her anger flare up violently, all her too many aggressions demanding an outlet, as well as a target.

"What the fuck do you care?" she almost snarled at him, watching as his expression collapsed but refusing to feel remorseful, instead sitting up and pointing stabbingly at his position on the seat. "And get your punk ass back into the dork zone!" she ordered him, reaching out and shoving viciously at his temple, forcing him away from her.

Refolding her arms, she turned her back on him and stared out the window with a frozen, tight-lipped smile, her heart pounding stridently as she watched the countryside blaze past, her mind filling with wild, unrestrained thoughts of her future, of her unconquerable intention not only to survive but also to win, in spite of all the obstacles that were poised against her, as well as the unforeseen factor of Mrs. Spindlewood, refusing to be intimidated. Let them try to stop her, let them bring it on… Chris did, she reflected, have a bruised cut on his lip; she had noticed it for sure just now.

Well, so what, so did she, so fuck him. She had already wasted half the night crying over his lame ass; and yet, here he was, all smiles and eager-eyed puppy dog, as if everything was fine when he should be just as pissed off at her, should hate her after yesterday; but he obviously hadn't lost any sleep over their little upset. *Hell, he had said that he didn't care, right? So fuck him, fuckin' loser.* He should be burning mad at her, and he wasn't, and he was just going to have to grow a pair if he wanted her to have anything to do with him, and didn't she have enough to worry about anyway? She could always forgive him later, *if* she felt like it, because she was empowered now, and she could do whatever the fuck she wanted.

Her fearsome reverie was sidetracked by a gradual, displaced sound, an unmistakable one, and she spun around to stare at Chris in surprise. He was sitting uncharacteristically straight upright in his seat, arms limply at his sides, head erect, eyes locked forward. His mouth was clamped shut, jaws tensed, lower lip quivering, his narrow shoulders shaking as he sniffled quietly, his face the reddest she had ever seen it, his tears, in their struggle to be released, inordinately large as they began to stream down his cheeks.

The question lodged in her throat, its answer obvious; she watched him in a pitfall of disbelief, extending one hand toward him as if to test the reality of what she saw, slowly, lightly fingering his cheek, intercepting a hot, glistening tear.

Chris's hand abruptly shot upward, grabbing her wrist and roughly jerking her hand away from his face, Vanessa gasping a shred of an outcry at his unexpected, almost brutal action, rubbing her wrist, the pain not so much physical, but agonizing all the same as she stared at his reasserted, tensed posture, his breathing audible now, his defiance inspired but his defenses weakening, the tears surging within him, refusing to be denied.

Swallowing, Vanessa slowly reached over and took his hand, the hand that had just rejected her, that might as well have just slapped her, enfolding it in her own and squeezing it gently.

Chris abruptly turned to face her, gulping down air, Vanessa seeing into his miserable, tormented eyes and incredibly hurt features, her heart breaking and then melting as she released his hand and moved to grasp his head, Chris instantly surrendering to her, falling into her arms as she pressed his face to her chest and let him cry, biting down mercilessly on her inner cheeks to maintain her own crumbling resolve, determined to remain strong. She knew that everyone was aware of some kind of strife emanating from the rear of the van and could tell by the silence and stoic aversion of all eyes, not resentful of their uninvolvement but grateful for their respect.

Chris clung loosely to her, sobbing torrentially into her chest, into her heart, the intensity of his wailing forcefully silenced and therefore all the more painfully exorcised, his thin shoulders wracked, his slender build convulsing violently as he continued, Vanessa cradling his head, smothering his tears, and bending to encourage him, telling him how sorry she was, absolving him of any blame, guilt, or shame, her words somehow registering to him and giving way to a renewed onslaught of tears, this one Vanessa recognizing as one of relief, the sobs much less painful, slower, eventually subsiding into a steady weeping, Vanessa continuing to embrace his head, gradually moving one arm to encircle his back as well, gently easing him toward her so that he was kneeling on the seat beside her, Chris instantly complying, anxious to move as close to her as he could, even as the tears gradually began to fade. She ushered out the last of them, running one hand to and fro over the crest of his Mohawk, rubbing his shoulders, blowing soothingly on the back of his neck until he grew still, his breathing marked by an occasional, tremulous whimper, Vanessa continuing her tumbling monologue, for his sake as well as for hers, placing his head against her stomach and leaning in to speak directly into his ear, whispering all of the wonderful, special details about Mrs. Spindlewood's apartment, describing everything that she had seen, no matter how tiny or commonplace, and then modifying her tone even more so as she envisioned to him how fantastic it would be if the two of them lived together in such a place.

Even as her own eyes began to sting, she told him of how they would be able to play house in such a magical apartment, how they could bake gingerbread men and sit at the table and drink coffee like grown-ups, and how she would feed him jelly doughnuts and they would talk and he could help her rehearse for a play and she could watch him dance and they would dance together, and time would stand still, and they would never have to leave, except to go to group meetings and Mrs. Spindlewood would live there too, and she would take care of them, and they would take care of her.

Chris listened to every word, pressing firmly against her, shuddering and snuffling from time to time as he stared past her knees into space, asking her questions in a small, ragged voice as he shared in the imagining of this special vision, the lull of her tone and the touch of her fingers caressing the shaved sides of his head combining with the womblike sense of serenity, well-being, and safety he now felt wash over him as he abandoned any reserve or prideful shame, giving into an infantile longing and completely entrusting himself to her protection.

He fell asleep with his head in her lap, and Vanessa sat there in spent silence, waiting to join him, her throat raw, eyes red, body exhausted, her resolve gone, her mind tired, and her heart extraordinarily light.

Chapter 13

FENDERMAN LODGE WAS ALL THAT Dr. Pendleton's enthusiasm had bespoken of it—a modest A-frame structure, augmented with obvious latter-day add-ons, accessed by a long gravel driveway. It possessed a small sundeck in its rear, and a stodgy dock extended from it into the decent-sized lake it adjoined, the peripheral area consisting of sparse red woods and a large, overgrown pasture.

Pulling up to the lodge, Dr. Pendleton had quickly opened the side and rear doors, thankful when Father Gilchrist made no further remarks about the van's stenciling. The group had gratefully piled out, anxious to stretch their legs, for the ride had taken longer than anticipated, even though they had only stopped once, for Mr. McClintock's sake, their schedule having instead been detained by an unusually strict adherence to the speed limit.

Nonetheless, the afternoon was bright and cloudless, and the excitement of arrival comingled with that of discovery as Dr. Pendleton eagerly produced his keys and ushered everyone inside, giving them a tour of the lodge's rustic, but cozy accommodations, the recollections of his boyhood days there obvious in his voice and florid smile as he demonstrated the various, simple amenities, his anticipation of their approval gratified when he led them out onto the deck, the reactions favorable and positive as they took in the view of the lake.

Vanessa had gently roused Chris upon their arrival, the punk rocker sleepily joining her as she hastened to check on Mrs. Spindlewood. At first, she was clearly torn between accompanying her and being with Chris, her uncertainty dispelled when, alternately, each member of the group, for the first time, began to take an active interest in the old woman's well-being and inclusion, and not once as they explored their lodgings was someone not holding her hand or guiding her by the arm, Chris as well and, at one point, both of them, one on each side. Mrs. Spindlewood responded to the kind, inviting words spoken to her with her usual non sequiturs; but it did not matter, for her smile was especially bright as she toddled along, an accepted member of their group, Vanessa's heart bursting, Dr. Pendleton beaming all the while.

Hence, for the most part, the youngest members walked hand in hand from the moment they climbed out of the van. They did not say much to each other, but the older members could virtually see their spirits soaring between them, their youthful faces flushed, smiles bright; no one would have guessed that Chris had cried his heart out only a few hours before, nor did anyone question why he had done so, for it was now clearly unnecessary.

Even when they all trooped back out to the van to retrieve their luggage, the young couple did not separate, each one carrying an item in their outer hands.

"Oh, they're so cute!" Judge Talbott gushed from behind them, her voice conspiratorially low. "They're just like Hansel and Gretel! Or Jack and Jill!"

"Or Mary Quite Contrary and Simple Simon," observed Father Gilchrist, in an only marginally sour tone, not wanting to slight them, but unwilling to entertain any more nursery rhymes. He perceived his returning grouchiness as an indication that he needed, and intended to take, a nap.

In the corridor leading to the few bedrooms afforded by the lodge, Dr. Pendleton addressed all of them earnestly. "Uh, there are three bedrooms altogether, but they're adequately arranged to accommodate all of us," he explained, opening the door of the bedroom farthest down the hall and peering in nostalgically. "Uh, if no one minds, I'd kind of like to take this room. It's where I always stayed when I was a kid." He paused, shrugging self-consciously and then gesturing openly. "Uh, but there are two beds if anyone, you know, wants to be my bunk buddy."

"What an enticing invitation," sniffed Father Gilchrist, pushing open the door nearest him and staring disdainfully at its meager, home-spun furnishings. A bunk bed and a single appeared to be his choices, although there really was no choice to be made, he concluded, automatically lying down on the single, settling himself comfortably.

The three ladies ended up in the identical middle room, Vanessa at last parting company with Chris to investigate, Judge Talbott throwing her hands up in delight upon seeing the bunk beds.

"Oh! It'll be just like a slumber party with my two sisters!" she cried excitedly, Vanessa, never really one for girly girlishness, having to grin at the judge's reaction as she situated Mrs. Spindlewood on the single bed, thinking of the old woman's take on her having asked to stay the previous night, smiling warmly.

"Wait a minute, why should you get the normal bed?" Mr. Crimpton was demanding next door, Father Gilchrist gazing unsympathetically up at him.

"Because I was here first," he replied flatly, not about to budge.

"Yes, but I don't want to have to climb around on some damn bunk beds!" Mr. Crimpton retorted in aggravation, glaring at the offending furniture and then back at the infuriatingly smug priest. "Can't we at least flip a coin for it?"

Father Gilchrist gasped. "For shame! Priests aren't supposed to gamble!" he scolded, then adopting an exaggeratively pathetic tone. "Besides which, would you really force a frail old man up into a bunk bed? Why, I might fall and break a hip!" he crooned.

Mr. Crimpton gaped at the insufferable clergyman, then sitting angrily down on the bottom bunk. "Well, there is no way in *hell* I'm going to be sleeping up there either!" he growled, as Mr. McClintock's massive build filled the doorway, and he peered amicably about the room.

"Well, it looks like we're all going to be bunk-mates!" he declared robustly.

Cringing, Mr. Crimpton shot up off the bottom bunk, gesturing pointedly. "Uh, I'll take the top bunk," he offered quickly. "It's... good for the sinuses."

Mr. McClintock nodded agreeably as Mr. Crimpton shot Father Gilchrist a withering look, the old man winking and then closing his eyes.

*****

Chris had peeked into the bedroom at the end of the hall, nodding shyly to Dr. Pendleton. "Um, is it okay if I stay in here with you, Doctor?" he asked hopefully.

Dr. Pendleton glanced over at him unexpectantly. "Oh, uh, yes, of course, Claude. Come in. You can have that bed in the corner," he offered congenially.

Nodding eagerly, Chris moved over to it, setting his backpack on the neat bedspread and glancing out the window at the lake and wilderness beyond. "Wow, did you use to come here a lot when you were a kid?" he asked the doctor.

"Oh yes, quite a bit," Dr. Pendleton replied, turning away from his suitcase to join the boy at the window. "My dad and I would do a lot of fishing out on that lake…" He hesitated and then tentatively lay a hand on Chris's shoulders, gazing out at the water for a moment and then nodding at him. "Do you ever do much fishing, Claude?"

Chris shook his head, grinning loosely, quickly shifting to place one lanky arm around the doctor's squat shoulders, feeling like he should complete the gesture. "No, I've never gone fishing before, not even once."

Dr. Pendleton nodded, again, gazing back at the lake. "Well, it can be enjoyable and relaxing. I used to think that someday I would be coming up here to go fishing with a son of my own," he confided at length, smiling up at Chris. "In fact, if I had a son, I'll bet he would be right around your age." He patted his shoulder lightly.

Chris smiled back, nodding and then blinking uncertainly. "Why is that?"

Dr. Pendleton paused, blinking right back, now frowning himself. "I... I don't know," he confessed, as they both continued to observe the view from the window.

*****

"Now, uh, everyone, I had wanted to give us all some time to get situated," Dr. Pendleton announced from the corridor, various members emerging from the rooms to join him. "Sometimes, it's nice to rest a bit after a long car ride." He paused. "Uh, is Father Gilchrist in there?"

"Yes, he's resting even as we speak," Mr. Crimpton replied. "Stubborn old goat."

Starting, Dr. Pendleton was approached by Vanessa from his other side. "Is it cool if Chris and me go for a walk and, like, take a look at all the trees and the lake and stuff?" she asked excitedly.

"Oh yes, of course," he beamed at her, then pausing blankly. *Chris?*

"Dr. Pendleton," Mr. McClintock called out politely. "Will we still be having our barbecue?" He smiled hopefully.

"Oh yes, absolutely," he replied affably, looking happily at all of them. "Yes, uh, what I'd like to have us do is all meet back in the main room at around four o'clock. And then we can take it from there."

The others nodded enthusiastically, Judge Talbott eagerly holding up her tote bag. "I brought the goodies to make some more s'mores!" she reminded them brightly, giggling at her little joke and flushing at the group's mild pitter-patter of approval.

*****

Seeing to it that Mrs. Spindlewood was comfortably situated, Judge Talbott assuring her that she would look after the old woman, Vanessa waltzed out of their room, grabbed Chris's hand, and skipped with him through the entryway and out into the open air and sunlight, Chris eagerly allowing himself to be led by her, grinning as she broke away from him only to spin around in a circle, throwing her arms up and shrieking, her excitement thrilling him as he watched, the sun feeling wonderful on them both.

To his joy, they held hands again, circling around the cabin and strolling alongside the lake, Chris observing as Vanessa expertly skipped a few stones across the water, blushing when his attempts immediately sank, her laughter only encouraging his. They explored the forest, their young senses inundated with the ethereal hush and its punctuation with the sporadic sounds of nature, the needles and twigs thick underfoot as they passed.

Eventually, they made their way out into the pasture, where Vanessa again pulled free and began to turn in circles, caught up in the reckless beauty of the moment, Chris joining her this time, his inhibitions evaporating in her presence, as he began to whoop and stomp, free to be unafraid, free from ridicule or recriminations, free simply to be free. His heart soared, liberated by the catharsis they had shared in the van; and his face was radiant as she grabbed him and pushed him and they spun each other around, boisterously, quite roughly, in fact, their wild horseplay only of the most harmless and trusting sort, however unrestrained it may have seemed and felt.

Vanessa's eyes blazed as she inhaled all the fragrances and scents into which they had plunged themselves, dizzy not merely from the frantic circles they had spun, but from the awesome release of burden she was experiencing as well, for, although nothing circumstantially had changed, she was overwhelmed with a sensation that was more than hope, which was something more akin to knowledge, as if she knew that, ultimately, everything would be more than just fine.

As for Chris, the lightness of his spirit was achieving heights he had never before attained, and the jubilation he felt as they romped and danced was almost foreign to him. The latent punk rocker in him had been inspired by Vanessa's abandon and was quickly and unstoppably manifesting itself in a liberating burst of primitive invincibility, an unconquerable force that had somehow been abstractly created by her having conquered him, by the conquest of his heart, and now as this neourban warrior pranced and galloped, Mohawk-thrashing, butt-flap sailing, it was around Vanessa, in a ritualistic dance of sub-mission to the hand that had freed him.

They continued to tussle and pivot, Vanessa grabbing at Chris's vest front, yanking him close to her and then shoving him backward, laughing and darting away from him in a joyful reprisal of her unthinkably mean rejection of him earlier, for this time, her actions were quite clearly intended to make him give chase, which he instantly, doggedly did, charging after her and catching up with her on the gravel driveway where the two of them paused, crouch-ing and panting, giggling in the exuberance of a wild face-off, Vanessa feigning a mad dash in either direction, crowing deliriously when he automatically fell for it each time, eventually standing up straight and walking right up to him, pressing herself against him and just standing there, breathing with him, Chris's arms gently enfolding her.

They stood like that for a while, simply breathing together, Vanessa then abruptly pushing him away and then throwing back her hair and grabbing his hand, resuming their walk, Chris immedi-ately, willingly complying as they headed down the driveway toward the road, for no other reason than that it was there. In all of this time, not a word had passed between them, the intensity of their unspoken emotions engulfing both of them, making the energized silence that they were sharing seem to hum with a soul-rippling potency as they proceeded, Vanessa closing her eyes and tilting her face to the sun and just coasting, letting Chris guide her for a change, Chris's cloddish tread grinding with each step atop the gravel but otherwise light.

He did not know if he were walking with a girlfriend or with a gratefully regained comrade, and he did not think to speculate, for he knew that he was, for once, and if even only for a little while, happy; and, even more so, he knew that he loved the feeling of just holding her hand.

*****

The car, a sleek, early model Mercedes, glided slowly up the driveway, coming to a stop as it pulled alongside of them, Vanessa and Chris gazing expectantly at its driver.

"Are you lost, mister?" Vanessa asked as he lowered his window, both of them impressed with the sleek elegance not only of the car but also of its occupant as he smiled at them.

"I don't believe so," he replied in a sonorous voice, removing a pipe from his mouth. "If memory serves, this road will take me to Fenderman Lodge. My name is Dr. Lionel Whittaker. I'm looking for Dr. Pendleton."

They both nodded eagerly, Vanessa smiling back. "Oh yeah? The Doc's up the road at the lodge now. Straight ahead, can't miss it." She paused, tilting her head. "Are you, like, one of his psychological shrink buddies?" she asked him coyly.

Dr. Whittaker peered up the roadway, his Van Dyke beard seeming to point at them as his smile blossomed. "Oh yes, he and I are, indeed, contemporaries in the field, although my own area of expertise is in psychiatry," he responded pleasantly, reaching to adjust the gear shift. "But, as I am sure that Dr. Pendleton has already told you, he and I are much more than professional colleagues," he added definitively. "Dr. Pendleton is also my patient."

With that, he nodded and continued up the gravel driveway, leaving the two to stare after him in confused silence before wordlessly heading back toward the lodge as well.

*****

"Dr. Whittaker, I'm so glad you could make it!" Dr. Pendleton declared, shaking the older man's hand in the entryway. "I hope it hasn't taken you too far out of your way."

"Not at all," Dr. Whittaker assured him, glancing approvingly around the lodge. "It's true I can only stay for a few moments or so, but I had wanted to confirm the good news in person."

Dr. Pendleton's face lit up eagerly, just as Mrs. Spindlewood tottered by.

"Good morning, Mr. Bergdorf. Good morning, Mr. Kantrowitz," she greeted them cheerfully, settling down on a bench in the entryway.

Blanching, Dr. Pendleton cleared his throat, Dr. Whittaker peering down at her with a warm smile. "And hello to you!" he returned cordially. "Are you enjoying your retreat?"

"Oh yes," Mrs. Spindlewood replied. "I have a niece who lives here in Nantucket." She sat back in the bench as if to await a bus.

"Uh, excuse us, Mrs. Spindlewood," Dr. Pendleton intervened, ushering Dr. Whittaker back out onto the porch, the tall man chuckling and refilling his pipe.

"Uh, you were saying, Doctor?" Dr. Pendleton prompted him anxiously.

Dr. Whittaker struck a match and beamed down at him. "As promised, I am here in person to deliver to you the outcome of this morning's meeting," he stated grandly, lighting the pipe and puffing briskly. "Naturally, the bureaucracy will take a few days to sort itself out, but the wheels are now officially in motion. In short, Dr. Pendleton, the word of the hour is, as I predicted, 'congratulations.'" He extended a hand. "Welcome back."

Dr. Pendleton gaped up at him in excitement, his smile brimming with relief, his eyes shining. "Oh, thank you, Dr. Whittaker, that…that is just terrific!" He continued to pump the older man's hand, his manner almost ecstatic.

*****

Vanessa and Chris were approaching the lodge in time to see Dr. Whittaker depart, hesitantly returning his wave as he passed them. They had walked in a very different kind of silence back up the gravel driveway, their spirits quieted, moods pensive; and while they never once stopped holding hands, there was a limpness to their steps, the uniting of their fingers helping to ease the undefinable anxiety that now had arisen in each of their stomachs.

Entering the lodge, they found Dr. Pendleton standing with his back to the fireplace, eagerly rubbing his hands together, as the others assembled in the sunken living room. They both sat on a couch, Mrs. Spindlewood and Father Gilchrist across from them, Mr. Crimpton and Judge Talbott nearby in a love seat, Mr. McClintock completing their rectangular circle by engulfing an easy chair, his hands clasped over his wide frame.

He was in especially good spirits, the prospect of their forthcoming barbecue filling him with the anticipation that the elite gourmet would insist was one-half of an exceptional meal. That aspect, coupled with the pleasant camaraderie of the others in this beautiful, natural setting would combine, he was certain to make a delightfully memorable repast.

Judge Talbott was similarly looking forward to conversing around the fire as they roasted their s'mores, something she had not done since she was a little girl, when, having been unable to decide whether to join the Camp-Fire Girls or the Brownies, she had been placated with a few family outings up in the hills.

She was wondering now if they would have an actual campfire or if they would use the barbecuer or if they would use the fireplace in here, uncertain which way would be the best, likewise not sure of what to use for skewers. She had seen some shish-kebob sticks in the kitchen, but wouldn't those burn?

Beside her, Mr. Crimpton was bitterly rubbing his eyes. After their endless, laugh-a-minute ride out to this place, all he had wanted to do was take a nap, especially after the scant few hours of sleep that the bourbon and the cabbie's proficiency had permitted him the night before. *Never, ever again.* No sooner had he scaled that damn bunk bed and lay his head down when Dr. Feel-Good started rounding them up for…for whatever. He glowered across the room. *That rotten old priest,* he reflected irritably. *That whole Father Mulcahy bedside manner self-sacrificing Angels of Mercy bit must have slipped his mind. I'll bet his sermons are a real treat.*

Father Gilchrist, appearing no less sourly composed than usual, was far from refreshed, his headache having given way to exhaustion, and that of the sort that rendered sleep a moot point; and where as it had been nice to lay down for a little while, if only out of spite, he did not feel any the better for it. He glanced sideways at Mrs. Spindlewood, who may as well have been sleeping with her eyes open.

As Vanessa and Chris sat, still holding hands, gazing up at the doctor with gravely earnest, hopeful features, their unspoken uncertainties still perplexing them, Dr. Pendleton took a moment to look over this assemblage of the group, *his* group, people with whom he had come so far, here, in this setting, with him, at this crossroads.

He beamed at them, his heart swelling.

Father Gilchrist harrumphed. "Well? Shall we…get the ball rolling?"

Blushing, Dr. Pendleton smiled. "Uh, yes." He cleared his throat. "I want to thank all of you very much for participating in our retreat. It is so significant and special to me that all seven of you could be here." His cheeks glowed as he continued. "Uh, before we get to our evening's activities, I had wanted to share some especially good news with you—I had intended to last night, but…" Pausing, he shook his head. "But here we all are now, and…to tell you the truth, this is an even more appropriate environment to share it in, uh, for me personally, in terms of milestones and such."

He paused as Vanessa slowly raised her hand. "Uh, Doc, before you start, do you mind if I ask you a question?" she inquired hesitantly.

Blinking at her troubled expression, he smiled encouragingly and nodded. "Yes, please go ahead."

Squeezing Chris's hand, she sat up, her gaze steadily meeting his. "Um, who was that guy who was here a little while ago?" she asked pointedly. "That Dr.… Whitmore guy?"

Dr. Pendleton nodded enthusiastically. "Dr. Whittaker, yes. He stopped by to confirm my good news," he explained, glancing at the others. "Dr. Lionel Whittaker, folks, a brilliant psychiatrist and a very close personal colleague of mine. I was hoping you would be able to meet him, but he could only stay a few minutes."

"Yeah, but, Doc," Vanessa continued, looking diffidently at Chris. "I mean I know you're colleagues and everything, but, like, is that all?"

As the others stared blankly from one to the other, Dr. Pendleton blinked, wondering if Dr. Whittaker had said something to the two kids in passing. Not that it mattered if he did, he reflected cheerfully.

"I think I know what's concerning you, Vanessa," he replied lightly, gesturing easily. "If you'll bear with me a moment, I'm sure I can clarify that point. In fact, I'm certain that that matter is actually one point of my good news," he added positively, both kids managing weak smiles in return as they all waited to hear whatever he was about to disclose.

"You see, folks, to put it simply, I've practiced in the field of psychology for quite some time now," he explained concisely. "I've had formal training and several years of experience and also a great love for my work. I've never had any doubts about having selected it for a career choice."

"Now," he continued, warming up to his story, his original glow restored as he gazed out at them. "The fact is that, uh, a little over a year ago, because of some unfortunate events, my actual formal license to practice psychology was put in jeopardy for a time, not revoked, mind you, merely suspended. And I was obliged to, uh, to, in essence, put a hold on my private practice until the matter could be rectified. Now, part of this process, of course, was the attendance of standard, up-to-date psychology seminars and workshops and the like, all very straightforward, as, uh, prescribed by Dr. Whittaker, the gentleman I just mentioned."

He nodded succinctly. "Uh, at any rate, along the way, I proposed an idea that had been broached at one of those workshops, and Dr. Whittaker instantly approved it as an excellent way to supplement the process, uh, that idea being..."

He paused for a dramatic effect, beaming at each of the now confused faces that stared back at him.

"Uh, that idea being the formulation of a sort of informal peer-advocate, self-help counseling group, the purpose of which would be to, uh, create an environment conducive to group therapy, uh, for the...therapeutic purposes that its formulation, in turn, uh, would offer, uh, to me..."

He paused again, his smile faltering slightly at the various expressions he was being served. "Uh, to put it simply, uh, I wanted to create a therapy group, uh, as a means of therapy, uh, for myself," he concluded with a final attempt at positive affirmation.

The looks he was receiving now were less ambiguous, ranging from baffled gaping to open, smoldering skepticism. Grimacing a bit, he cleared his throat, his voice cracking as he quickly sought to reincorporate and then most likely close the matter altogether.

"Uh, so, uh, anyway—my good news that I hinted at before is that, uh, Dr. Whittaker had just informed me that my, uh, case, which was up for review before a panel of experts, uh, was just decided, uh, this morning. And, well, in short, because of the progress I've made, due in no small part to the excellent progress we've all made together as a group, they've decided to reinstate my license in full!"

He nodded enthusiastically, his smile unwilling to flounder as he peered at each of the group members, his smile then gradually floundering anyway. "Uh, so you see, that's the, uh, my good news, because it means that I'll be, uh, able to resume my practice."

There was a deathly dead silence as he hesitantly regarded each of them, Chris and Vanessa frowning in joint confusion, Mr. Crimpton staring incredulously, Judge Talbott and Mr. McClintock competing in looks of bewilderment, Mrs. Spindlewood smiling approvingly.

"Do you mean to suggest"—began Father Gilchrist, gazing at the little doctor in granite-faced awe—"that this ridiculous excuse of a therapy group was little more than a sham, a hoax, a pathetic charade of therapeutic merit, the purpose of which was to augment, in some *inexplicable* way, a process of therapy superimposed over it by an unseen psychiatrist and that the entire time you've been overseeing it in the capacity of a psychologist, you, yourself, have been a mental case undergoing treatment all along. *Is that what you mean to suggest?*"

Shrinking at the priest's increasingly volatile stare, Dr. Pendleton quickly shook his head. "Well, uh, no, that's not…" He paused. "Well, I mean I *personally*—"

"You have presumed to tell each of us how to run our affairs and manage our emotions and overcome our mental idiosyncrasies, when you, yourself, are some kind of a nut?" Father Gilchrist demanded, his voice rising in anger.

"Uh, no. No, not at all," Dr. Pendleton asserted as staunchly as he could. "That's an oversimplification of the—" He paused. "Er, what I mean is, that's not really a—"

"Well, what exactly is the situation?" Mr. Crimpton spoke up, his arms folded tautly, his face agape in a look of aggravated shock. "I mean if a nutjob's psychologist is seeing a specialist himself, doesn't that make him even crazier?"

Dr. Pendleton paused. "Well, no, not necessarily—" He broke off his own chain of thought. This was not going as well as he had hoped.

"Look, folks, I... I think you're missing my point," he tried again, drawing encouragement from Judge Talbott's somewhat hopeful expression. "These are essentially two separate issues. Let's please not lose sight of the exceptional progress that we've made together as a group. I'm merely using the parallel to illustrate the...the intricacies of the interdependence of the overall therapeutic value from which we've all benefited..." He paused again, recalling the equation he had outlined at their fourth meeting and, moreover, the resounding acclaim that it had received. "I'm basically talking about our group equation and taking it one step further," he insisted earnestly. "I helped you to help each other to help yourselves, uh...to help me..." He glanced hopefully from face to face.

The response was less than laudatory, Mr. Crimpton exchanging a flabbergasted look with the others before shrugging at him. "Well, what good does any of that do, when it turns out that you're a nutcase, yourself?" he exclaimed.

Dr. Pendleton shook his head. "Yes, but you didn't know that!" he countered, then becoming flustered. "I mean that you didn't know that I, myself, was seeing a specialist. And it most likely wouldn't have come up at all, except that, well, as I say, I just wanted to share my good news with you." He smiled lamely.

"Well, you're off to one hell of a start!" Mr. Crimpton told him caustically.

Sighing, Dr. Pendleton gestured allayingly. "As I said, you've sort of missed the point—"

"We have definitely overlooked several points, from the appearance of things," Father Gilchrist started in again. "Most prominent of which is the fact that whereas we have been wasting time with a psychologist—and a debunked one at that—you, in turn, have been seeing a *psychiatrist*, which, if the analytical chain of command is any indication, leads me to conclude that whatever delirium may be ailing us, your impediments are of an even greater level of derangement!"

The intensity of this denunciation sent Dr. Pendleton back a step, bumping into the fireplace and starting, turning, and fingering the mantelpiece. He opened his mouth to respond, the incited priest giving him no chance.

"Why, it's all coming clear now. I warned all of you, and now, we have the proof!" he announced, smiling madly at the others. "I wondered why our dear doctor was so anxious to drag us away from civilization, out here to this remote and isolated shack! It was all a ruse, dreamed up by an insidious madman bent on stalking us through the wilderness, knocking us off one by one to satiate his incurable bloodlust!"

Mr. McClintock grimaced profoundly, Judge Talbott gasping.

"Now, Father Gilchrist," Dr. Pendleton attempted to chuckle.

"So what is your choice of implement for this Dismembership Drive?" Father Gilchrist inquired. "A chainsaw? Machete? Hay baler? Cuisinart?"

"Father Gilchrist, please!" Dr. Pendleton interjected, gesturing desperately at the group. "We're greatly exaggerating what was really only a...an incidental point in what is, overall, a very complex... though relatively simple scenario!"

"That doesn't seem like an incidental point to me!" Mr. Crimpton griped pointedly.

"Look, wait a minute!" Vanessa spoke up impatiently, glaring at the others and then staring up at the doctor. "I'm having trouble keeping all of this straight. I mean... Doc, I'm confused. What exactly is the good news in all of this?" she asked him directly, releasing Chris's hand to motion definitively.

Dr. Pendleton regarded her earnestly, grateful for the opportunity to get back on track. "The good news is that my psychologist's license has been renewed," he declared simply.

Vanessa considered this, biting her lip, Chris clearly not knowing what to make of it.

"Well, no news is indeed good news," Father Gilchrist observed, settling back in his seat and steepling his fingers. "Since the bad news you are conversely telling us is that you have been practicing psychology on all of us since the very beginning, *without* a license."

Judge Talbott's eyes grew wider. "But…that's illegal," she stated haltingly.

Mr. McClintock blanched. "Illegal?" he repeated nervously.

"Of course, it's illegal!" snapped Mr. Crimpton. "It's illegal to do anything without a license! I'll bet that's why you're such a terrible driver!" He pinched the bridge of his nose. To think that they had been on the freeway with this man.

Dr. Pendleton's mouth flew open as he tried to discern who to answer first. "Now, wait a minute, please. I assure you I haven't done anything illegal," he stammered. "Our therapy group is not technically a clinical extension of my own practice! It is an informal self-help group patterned after the various mainstream anonymous groups! It is fundamentally based upon principles of peer advocacy! The only real connection that it had to my suspended practice is as an extracurricular pursuit for my own reinstatement process!"

"Yes, you've made it quite clear that we were nothing more than an extra credit project, a weekly homework assignment prescribed by your *psychiatrist* as part of your own therapy," Father Gilchrist summarized pedantically.

His mouth squeezed shut in indignation, Dr. Pendleton vigorously shook his head.

"That is simply not true!" he protested desperately.

Father Gilchrist shot up in his seat, his voice ratcheting sharply into a virtual shout. "You dare to use all of us in some insipid socio-anthropological mental experiment. You stand before us today, purporting to have this 'good news,' freely admitting to this scandalous misplacement of trust, and now, you have the unmitigated temerity to turn right around and deny it?"

Dr. Pendleton's jaw dropped open at this scorching excoriation, Vanessa and Chris both wilting as if feeling his pain, each one too staggered with uncertainty to intervene.

"Don't misunderstand," Father Gilchrist shifted gears, a sure indication of what was to come. "I truly cannot fault your entrepreneurialism, nor does any of this come as a great surprise to me! Why, it all stands to reason! Why else would a psychologist, uncertified and, coincidentally, certifiable, deign to come to the aid of bargain-basement neurotics and delusional delinquents such as we? Why else would a skilled doctor condescend to offer his services, free-of-charge, to the impoverished likes of our reprobate, motley group, if not to further his own means and replenish his own practice?"

He nodded decisively even as Dr. Pendleton adamantly shook his head. "Yes, a highly resourceful plan of action, and lest you think me an ingrate, I will hasten to add that you most generously catered to our needs as well, rewarding our assistance in your clinical apotheosis with an abundance of crackpot analysis stale doughnuts and revolting coffee." He folded his arms in a posture of acerbically mocking admiration, Dr. Pendleton raising an index finger, inhaling.

"Would you like some more coffee, Mr. Bergdorf?" Mrs. Spindlewood suddenly came back to life, moving to stand up.

Vanessa darted to her side, gently staying her as Dr. Pendleton cleared his throat and rallied his thoughts for one final appeal.

"Folks, I… I am a psychologist," he declared simply. "My goal in life is assisting other people, people like you, people like, uh, me…uh, people who need help and guidance and companionship and…and respect and who just need someone to listen. That is why I became a psychologist and that was the main, underlying objective to the creation of our therapy group. And while it has helped me, I'll admit, I, uh, like to think that it's helped all of you too."

He nodded conclusively, shifting his feet slightly.

There was silence, Vanessa glancing up at him from where she knelt alongside of Mrs. Spindlewood, Chris gaping hopefully from face to face.

"Well," Judge Talbott spoke up at length, her voice timorously uncertain. "I guess there's nothing illegal about that," she conceded, distracted by a noise emanating from nearby.

Mr. McClintock tightened his clasped grip over his girth and flushed. He wished he had some of those stale doughnuts now.

Mr. Crimpton shook his aching head, waving a hand up at Dr. Pendleton in frustrated finality. "Okay, so you're saying that, as of now, you are a legal, licensed, bona fide psychologist, is that right?" he clarified bluntly.

"Yes," Dr. Pendleton replied instantly. "Well, I mean, technically…" He paused, flustered. "The actual paperwork is…well, the mail takes, uh, two to three business days. So that would make it, uh…"

As Mr. Crimpton dropped his head into his hands, Chris swallowed and raised his hand. "Um, does all of this mean that we can't call you 'doctor' anymore?" he asked in a small voice, staring up at him with a sad expression, Vanessa moving to sit beside him again, taking his hand as he went on. "What should we call you then?"

"How about 'Sigmund Fraud'?" Dr. Pendleton cringed, his gaze shooting from Chris to Father Gilchrist. "How about 'charlatan' or 'mountebank' or 'quacksalver'? How about the modern abbreviation simply 'quack'?"

The old priest nodded judiciously, pinioning the wincing doctor with a spirit-squelching glare. "Licensed or not, the red tape notwithstanding, we are still left with the glaring inconsistency revolving around your own clandestine visits to some latter-day Carl Jung."

Judge Talbott's brows arched; Mr. McClintock grimaced. They had seemed so close to resolving this upset, after which they would surely be firing up the barbecuer.

Mr. Crimpton's head jerked upright, eyes bloodshot but wide as he stared up at Dr. Pendleton. "That's right!" he charged. "Your psychiatrist, the whole reason for all of this…this…this! Why exactly were you seeing him in the first place? And don't give us any of that doctor–patient privacy malarkey, because this time it's patient–doctor…or doctor–doctor…unless you've been treating yourself." He started suddenly. "Oh my god, you're not one of those, are you? One of those fruit loops with more than one personality? Like that *Three Faces of Eve* dame or *Dr. Jekyll and Mr. Hyde*!" He glanced worriedly around at the others. "Did anyone here actually see this Dr. Wiseacre guy?" he demanded.

"Mr. Crimpton, I assure you, I am not suffering from multiple personality disorder," Dr. Pendleton interjected emphatically.

"Well then what was the problem?" Mr. Crimpton shot back.

"Yes," put in Father Gilchrist. "And exactly how long has it been since you were released from the insane asylum, assuming of course, that you haven't escaped from one," he added dryly.

Dr. Pendleton exhaled, placing one hand on his temple. "All right, in the first place, Father Gilchrist, they're not called 'insane asylums' anymore—"

"Oh dear, there I go again with my *hopelessly* nonclinical terminology!" Father Gilchrist declared apologetically, adopting a thoughtful look. "How about 'nuthouse'? Or perhaps 'funny farm'? 'Laughing academy'? 'Cracker factory'? 'Booby hatch'?"

"All right, Father Gilchrist!" Dr. Pendleton relented, grimacing and glancing at the expectant group, trying to meet each of their wary gazes. "I promise each and every one of you that I have never been in a mental institution," he stated solemnly, then swallowing, clearing his throat, and adding, "Uh, for more than a period of less than two weeks…"

He winced at the inevitable gasp, reopening his eyes and seeing what looked and certainly felt like shattered trust as they all exchanged shocked stares.

"And for what reason were you committed?" Father Gilchrist asked sharply.

Dr. Pendleton sighed. "I wasn't committed," he insisted, gesturing vainly in some hope of salvaging the situation. "I was the one who checked myself in, and it was on an outpatient status. I wasn't on any medication. I was only there for general observation, recuperation, and, basically, just rest."

The members mulled over this, Chris blinking and speaking up hopefully. "So it was just like our retreat then?" he posed earnestly.

"Yeah, but a retreat from what?" asked Mr. Crimpton pointedly.

"Reality, perhaps?" Father Gilchrist suggested with one raised eyebrow. He regarded Dr. Pendleton closely. "What was it, Doctor? Why were you there in the first place?"

Dr. Pendleton cleared his throat. "Uh, well, it was, uh, due to work-related stress," he answered concisely.

"Don't give me that," scoffed Mr. Crimpton. "I've got work-related stress that would drive Joyce Brothers bananas, but I've never even considered checking myself into the loony bin!"

Father Gilchrist snapped his fingers. "I knew I'd forgotten one!"

"The gist of the matter really didn't have anything to do with my own competency," Dr. Pendleton explained almost beseechingly. "It mainly had to do with one of my patients."

Judge Talbott frowned. "But I thought you were the patient."

"I was the patient," Dr. Pendleton clarified. "I meant one of my patients when I was a doctor, uh, before I was a patient."

Mr. McClintock's eyebrows lifted. "Before *you* were a patient?"

"Yes," said Dr. Pendleton, blinking.

"'Yes' *what?*" gasped Mr. Crimpton. "I don't get it."

"You will," drawled Father Gilchrist. "Have patience."

Chris frowned, opening his mouth, Vanessa gently clamping a hand over it.

Mr. Crimpton's hands slammed up into his face, and he groaned into them. He had always wondered what a stroke felt like. He peered over his fingertips at the others and then around the room.

"This is a joke, isn't it?" he asked pleadingly. "I'm actually a victim on *Candid Camera*, right? *America's Funniest Home Videos? Cops?*"

"I would have guessed *The Gong Show*," Father Gilchrist sniffed, focusing on Dr. Pendleton once more. "Pray continue with your riveting *15 Minutes of Fame*."

Dr. Pendleton sighed. "It's really very straightforward," he said haplessly. "I was recuperating from a minor, stress-induced, breakdown, incurred while dealing with one of my patients. It was all an unfortunate accident. During one of our sessions, I happened to mention a recently released form of anxiety suppressant that *might* be worth considering to help him cope with his stress. It was an incidental observation, clearly reenforced with the understanding that it would have to be properly prescribed for him. Now, as it happens, he ended up going ahead and obtaining this drug, on the street so to speak, uh. And he, uh, showed up at our next session, having just swallowed half of the bottle..."

The group regarded him in awe, Father Gilchrist lifting one hand. "And?"

Clearing his throat, Dr. Pendleton shifted a bit, glancing down at his feet. "Uh, well, succinctly, he, uh, was in a very agitated state. And, uh, we were, of course, unable to, uh, really proceed with our, uh, session. And so, uh, as a result, we...ended up having to cancel his, uh...therapy for the day..."

Father Gilchrist's eyes narrowed. "And why was that?" he pressed, the others staring at the doctor in tensed, braced trepidation.

Dr. Pendleton attempted to meet their eyes, failed, shifted, cleared his throat, and then coughed slightly into one hand. "Uh, because he, uh, kind of..." He swallowed. "Jumped out the window."

Vanessa and Chris gasped in unison, Mr. Crimpton's eyes scrunching shut as Judge Talbott's hands shot to her face in horror. Mr. McClintock's mouth fell open aghast. Mrs. Spindlewood only smiled.

Staring in astounded reproach, Father Gilchrist jerked his head to one side. "He did *what?*"

Grimacing, Dr. Pendleton shrugged lightly. "He jumped out the window."

"Well what happened to him?" Vanessa demanded, her features flashing in distress. "Did he die? I mean what floor were you on anyway?"

Dr. Pendleton raised his hands, waving them reassuringly. "Oh no, no, he didn't die. He wasn't even hurt from the fall," he insisted anxiously. "In fact, it was really quite a lucky coincidence, because he fell straight downward into an awning."

Judge Talbott glanced up in relief. "An awning?"

Father Gilchrist was skeptical. "An awning?"

Dr. Pendleton nodded adamantly. "An awning."

Mr. McClintock beamed contentedly. "An awning!"

Chris gawked around in confusion. "What's an awning?" he asked, Vanessa sighing and clamping a hand over his mouth again.

"Oh my god!" Mr. Crimpton startled them all by shouting. "An *awning*?" He stared up at Dr. Pendleton in mortified recognition. "You said over a year ago! A patient—the guy who jumped out of the shrink's window! It was in the paper! He landed on an awning! The shrink—the doctor! That was *you*?"

Dr. Pendleton took a step back, flushing deeply, fingering his collar.

"I thought that sounded ominously familiar," Father Gilchrist grated slowly, giving the doctor a withering appraisal. "I read that article as well."

Mr. McClintock appeared pained. "I feared that it rang a bell," he said apologetically. "Everyone at the *Global Tribune* was talking about it."

Vanessa glanced uncertainly at each of them, shrugging in exasperation. "So? So it was in the paper?" she responded challengingly. "What's the big deal? I mean he survived, right?" She and Chris looked at all of them expectantly.

Father Gilchrist raised one cynical eyebrow toward Dr. Pendleton. "Would you care to enlighten them, or shall I?" he asked darkly.

Judge Talbott blinked, catlike.

Grimacing, Dr. Pendleton gestured halfheartedly. "Well, as I said, he...uh...he broke his fall when he landed on the awning," he repeated reluctantly.

"And *then*?" Father Gilchrist prompted him sharply.

Dr. Pendleton cleared his throat. "And then, uh, he, uh... bounced."

Judge Talbott gasped. "Bounced?"

Mr. McClintock nodded sadly. "Bounced."

"Well, that was actually another bit of good luck," Dr. Pendleton hurried onward. "He bounced off the awning and landed on the convertible top of an El Dorado Cadillac that was driving by!" He nodded placatingly.

Vanessa and Chris nodded hesitantly back, Mr. Crimpton leaning forward in his seat. "*And?*" he prodded the doctor with a manic look.

Exhaling and clearing his throat, Dr. Pendleton alternated his gaze between his listeners and his feet. "And, he, uh, crashed through the convertible top and scared the driver, uh, causing her to lose control of the car…"

One side of Judge Talbott's mouth twisted downward in dread.

"And?" concluded Father Gilchrist, folding his hands in his lap.

Dr. Pendleton coughed into his hand again. "And she went through an intersection diagonally and drove up into a courtyard and, uh, crashed into the base of a, uh, fifty-foot Christmas tree…"

Glimpsing the looks on their faces, he hastily wrapped up the story. "But the driver wasn't hurt and neither was my patient, for that matter. In fact, he walked away from the car without a scratch," he told them, imploringly earnest.

Vanessa and Chris both exhaled in relief, Judge Talbott waving her hand. "So, in the end, he was fine," she double-checked.

"Yes," Dr. Pendleton affirmed, then catching Father Gilchrist's daunting look. He cleared his throat. "Well, uh, almost. He did suffer a few minor abrasions when the, uh, the Christmas tree fell on him," he explained hesitantly, Judge Talbott gaping at him, Chris squirming uncomfortably as Vanessa tilted her head back to stare up at the ceiling.

"But he's fine now," Dr. Pendleton insisted concisely. "He's completely healed, and he's also made remarkable progress toward mental stability. In fact, as far as I know, he'll most likely be released in, oh, another couple of years or so…" He nodded in pronounced emphasis.

There was only silence, until Mr. Crimpton covered his face and leaned back in the love seat groaning. "I can't believe you're the same guy," he murmured in awe, Judge Talbott wilting a bit beside him as he added, "That's the last goddamn flyer I'll ever take off a windshield."

Mr. McClintock grimaced forlornly, sensing that there now might not be a barbecue at all.

"So," Father Gilchrist nodded introspectively, folding his arms. "This is the result that a patient can expect after entrusting himself to your brilliant and velvet-gloved care? The irresistible urge to leap out of a window?"

Dr. Pendleton looked hesitantly over the shambles of his therapy group. "Well, uh, no," he was obliged to reply, trying to will up the words to express what he had so wanted to convey. Where had he gone so terribly wrong? "I... All I had intended to do was to explain about the significant part all of you played in the reissuance of my license," he began glumly. "I never meant to..."

"Yes, your 'good news,'" Father Gilchrist recollected musingly. "Tell me, 'Doctor,' have you anymore delightfully good news to share with us now that you have dragged us all the way out here to participate in this thrilling and inspiring revelation? Perhaps you were next going to unveil something in the nature of a refreshing round of fortified Kool-Aid?" he proposed acidically. "If so, I'll take my glass *now*."

Slumping a bit more, Dr. Pendleton glanced up when Vanessa spread her arms and stared at him blankly. "So, like, now what?" she asked, her voice flat.

Mr. McClintock's brows raised. Perhaps there was still a chance.

"Yeah," Chris spoke up, peering at Dr. Pendleton with a hurt look. "Does this mean we can't have our group anymore?" he asked in a hollow voice.

Dr. Pendleton gaped at him, his expression wounded, and then sickly as Mr. Crimpton gave them a stricken look. "Who'd want to?" he gasped.

The doctor shrank a bit more, looking at his hiking boots.

"Yes, it is a tragedy of almost comically Shakespearean dimensions," Father Gilchrist observed, his tone taking on an edge as he slowly stood up. "The bats have clearly come home to the belfry. The irony is so cutting that it renders one almost bereft of speech."

He tilted his head upright and towered over the doctor, shooting him a monstrous scowl. "Almost. As a dead-in-the-wool man of the cloth, I have seen many inexplicable phenomena and have learned that ours is, indeed, a God with a divine sense of humor. How else, in

His infinite wisdom, could he have designed so intricate, so complex a practical joke as this and with such a terminally unfunny punch line?" He paused, shaking his head. "His wonders to perform."

As the group watched him wearily, he nodded deeply toward Vanessa. "Out of the mouths of babes," he proclaimed, Vanessa staring stonily back. "You were right, Miss. Your intemperate diatribe at last night's lamentable meeting constituted the only truth to be uncovered during our copious strides toward enlightenment, and fittingly enough, it was that one truth that so perfectly encapsulates us all."

"Behold!" he continued, his voice rising steadily. "For we are, indeed, as you so boldly designated us, 'Mis-fits Anonymous.' And our members are legendary. All you lonely people know me, of course. I'm Father MacKenzie, the Irreverent Reverend!"

He turned and gestured with a flourish to the oblivious Mrs. Spindlewood. "And I'm sure you're acquainted with my female counterpart, Mrs. Eleanor Rigby, starring in the role as the *Woman Who Wasn't There*."

He moved to the center of the room, waving his hand grandiosely. "Then we have the nonjudgmental judge," he declared, Judge Talbott sagging meekly in her chair.

"The driving examiner who cannot drive." Mr. Crimpton glowered sullenly up at him through his fingers.

"And the acritical food critic." Mr. McClintock crumpled guiltily.

"Then we have our punk rocker party animal who is curiously housebroken," he went on grandly, Chris gawking at him in awe as he paused before Vanessa. "And lastly, our very own little miracle, the Virgin Mary Magdalene," he pronounced with a bow, Vanessa flushing but saying nothing as he moved away from them.

"If patients are a virtue, then the physician in whose hands these seven basket cases find themselves is truly blessed," he proclaimed, nodding toward the wincing, pain-stricken man behind him, pointing majestically. "And there he is, behold, Fellow Mis-fits, our King, the only man in medical history to take the platonic approach to 'playing doctor.' This fearless defender of our neuroses, this singular genius who has set the most brilliant precedent in the annals of psychotherapy, by perfecting the concept of sympathizing and relating to even the most demented patients, simply by being that much more deranged himself! This pioneer of exploratory research who has managed to bridge the gap of impartiality between doctor and patient by being *both* at the same time, maintaining this delicate equilibrium of balance by being in and of himself *imbalanced!* Here he is, ladies and gentlemen, direct from Bellevue, that dauntless, do-it-yourself pseudopsychologist, whose fortune cookie therapy and finger paint-by-numbers analysis have inspired mental cases across the nation to take charge of their own psyches with the revolutionary cry of 'leggo my Ego,' this healer, whose hands-on approach will surely inspire whole psychewards to join hands in mass defenestration, the man whose astonishing breakthroughs in the field of mental health have helped to put the Id back in Idiotic, I give you our founder, that champion of Psycho-Babbling Bedlamites, who has made it so abundantly clear to us that we are very much in his debt for having opened our eyes to the utter, stark reality of that time-honored adage..." Father Gilchrist focused imperiously upon what was left of Dr. Pendleton. "It is, indeed, true what they say, *Mister* Pendleton, that the Lunatics are running the asylum!"

With these words echoing in their ears, Father Gilchrist took his seat again, folding his arms stolidly. Of all of the silences that they had encountered together in the past, that which now ensued was by far the most profound. The members watched with catatonic expressions as Dr. Pendleton very slowly glanced up at them.

His features appeared squashed flat, resembling a Halloween pumpkin that had been smashed by a horde of brutal trick-or-treaters. His eyes shifted guiltily as his grimace strained to force a dry gulp down his constricted throat, which he next struggled to clear, his small hands weighted limply at his sides as he regarded them motionlessly.

"Uh... I, uh, I can tell that you're all, uh...kind of...or really disappointed in me," he began in a hollow voice, finally managing a blink or two. "I, uh, I'm certainly sorry if you feel like I've let you down... I, uh, just wanted to...to share my, uh..."

He paused, his mouth closing and twisting a bit as he summoned up a semblance of a shrug, forcing one hand upward to gesture absently to one side. "I, uh... I think I'll leave you all, uh, alone for a little while... I hope you'll still enjoy your, uh, stay here..."

Clearing his throat again, he nodded his head in the general direction of an adjacent sliding glass door. "I'll, uh, I'm gonna just..."

He turned and shuffled away, tugging at the door, then pulling more forcefully at it, then pausing to unlock it, opening it, and straggling out of the lodge.

The silence endured for a few stunned moments after he had gone, the members gradually regaining their own ability to move, glancing warily at one another and then almost as quickly avoiding each other's gaze, eventually climbing to their feet, Vanessa and Chris moving morosely away, Father Gilchrist stalking aimlessly off with a scowl, leaving Judge Talbott worriedly clinging to her tote bag.

"Doesn't anyone still want to make s'mores?" she asked in a miniscule voice.

Mr. Crimpton gave her a look of haggard scorn. "You and your snacks!" he snapped bitterly. "You would have been better off baking everyone up a nice fresh batch of straitjackets!"

He stomped away, Judge Talbott wilting and retreating to the kitchen, leaving only Mr. McClintock and Mrs. Spindlewood, the latter as composed as she had been since the start of the disastrous discussion, the former sadly resigned as he peered around at the otherwise empty area.

No, they were most likely not going to be having their barbecue now.

Chapter 14

Dr. Pendleton's faltering steps gradually quickened as he made his way across the wooden deck and onto a nearby path that, if followed assiduously, would lead one around the entire lake. He found himself drawn in that direction, although the serenity of the almost perfectly still water was lost on him as he walked, his focus unshiftingly centered on the ground, his mind a benumbed miasma of what he had just endured or, more to his way of thinking, what he had just caused.

There were no mental floodgates straining to keep a deluge of recriminations and regrets from swamping his already overburdened thoughts, because the sum of all these factors rendered having to face them one by one unnecessary. Failure did not have to be microscopically dissected to discern; it was as fundamentally straightforward as the contemplation of a brick. The bottom line was interchangeably the same, regardless of the tragedies that led one there.

Eventually, he came to the old oak tree with the hollow in its trunk, an anomaly amidst the pines, and left the pathway, knowing that the trail he had so often traversed in his remote past would still be hidden there, his small hiking boots scuffling against the underbrush as he slowly entered into the wilderness.

*****

Mr. Crimpton had moved away from the sunken area, into the adjacent den, where another sofa and recliner were arranged around a television set. Not knowing what else to do, he fell back on his old habits and had begun to ferret out the remote control. You travel for over three hours—with a nut at the wheel, no less—

all so that you can do the same thing you would have done if you had stayed home.

Shaking his head, he gave up his search, realizing as he dubiously appraised the dusty set's rabbit-ear antennae that it might not even have a remote control. Instead, he switched it on manually and stared at the blank screen, waiting for it to warm up and then hoping at least for a surge of static, anything to indicate that it would function at all. Insult to injury, is that what it was to be? Travel over a hundred miles, give into the pathetic decision to watch TV, and then get this slap in the face?

He then scowled, sighing and crouching down to one side to plug in its cord. *Keep it up*, he thought to his inner demons. *Keep it up and see how much fun it will be tormenting a corpse, because if this day gets any better, I'm going to tie this cord around my neck, and then, this Zenith and I are going in for a swim.*

Glaring at the flickering screen, he jumped slightly, Mrs. Spindlewood having appeared on the couch as if she had been sitting there all along, her placid smile intact as she gazed at the blank ripples of snowy lines.

Sighing irately, even though everyone knew ghosts moved around without making a sound, he began to tug at the channel knob, peering at one blurry selection after another, grudgingly asking the old woman if there was anything she wanted to watch.

Listening in disbelief, he was about to tell her that they were most likely not going to find Arthur Godfrey, Milton Berle, or Jack Benny, then dismissing the thought and continuing to pull at the knob, eventually jerking the rabbit ears in an attempt to find anything at all.

In the end, they had two choices, an evangelical station and an infomercial channel. Having already had one sermon that day, thank you very much, he had next sneered at the infomercials, thinking that this was the sort of dreck that was viewed only by people who had truly hit rock bottom, later on reflecting that that was probably why he had settled down to watch it.

*****

Mr. McClintock had reluctantly gone back to the bedroom and munched disconsolately on the remainders of the snacks he had purchased during their stop along the way, tempted to go to the kitchen and explore whatever provisions it might have to offer, but hesitant to do so.

It was not merely the prospect of dining that had whet his appetite; it had been the anticipation of conversation and interaction that had also seemed so appealing. In his capacity as a food critic, he had always dined alone—that was actually one of the basic tenets of reviewing food, a sort of self-imposed singularity of purpose. One was expected to focus upon the food; and while the atmosphere, ambiance, music, and peripheral conversation from other tables could be vicariously taken into account, it had to be done so even while abstaining from it oneself and, even then, only to a certain degree.

That was why, he supposed, having doughnuts and Judge Talbott's snacks during the group sessions had been so enjoyable. At first, it had seemed comparable to munching on popcorn while watching a movie; but, as it became more interactive, it was very similar to dining with other people. Tonight, however, would have been the first time in which they took an actual meal together, and he had been quite looking forward to the experience.

Sighing, he realized that he had dropped a potato chip on the otherwise immaculate carpet and quickly bent to pick it up, a loud elastic *twang* resulting from somewhere on his person, accentuating a sharp, biting sting on his hindquarters, causing him to jerk upright so quickly that his head collided with the frame of the top bunk.

*****

Judge Talbott had stifled her hurt feelings and bustled into the kitchen with renewed resolve. Locating the shish-kebob skewers, she took a handful over to the stove, realizing that it was an electric range and fixing it with a small, wistful grimace.

She considered the fireplace in the other room, but did not want to be faced with any more criticism of her attempts to be generous with everyone.

None of the other public defenders downtown had ever once been unappreciative of the snacks she had brought into share in the lounge. Of course, none of the others ever brought in any snacks either and nor, for that matter, did anyone else in this group, except for Dr. Pendleton.

Her grimace vanished as she thought of him, unsure of what to make of his "good news." If it had been so positive, why was everyone so upset now? She issued a little sigh and wandered over to the window above the sink, peering outside. She had no idea where the fire pit might be and did not really care for the idea of a one-woman campfire anyway. It occurred to her that there was still the question of the barbecuer, and she ventured out onto the deck, her spirits lifting when she saw not only a small, conventional model but also a bag of charcoal and lighter fluid.

She eagerly went about setting up the grill, knowing full well how to do it, from all the years of watching her father battle with his out on their tiny, enclosed patio space in the apartment complex in which she had grown up. She arranged the briquettes neatly, her thoughts scattered between then and now.

It was not really as if the doctor had done anything wrong, per se; he had been very honest in answering all of their questions.

Applying a bit of lighter fluid, she fired up the coals, containing a little shriek of excitement when the flames instantly took, remembering how long it would take her father some nights.

She eagerly removed the ingredients from her tote bag, skewering a marshmallow and a wedge of a Hershey's bar between two graham crackers and plunging it all into the flames, so intent on watching its deliciousness ensue and congeal that she did emit a squawk when the skewer burned through and the s'more tumbled into the fire, disintegrating into gooey ashes.

Stung at this bitter setback, she instantly set about making another with a sort of frazzled determination, this time holding the snack and its skewer over the flames with a sturdy pair of barbecue tongs, smiling boldly as she watched the process again, this time with the assurance of success, her back to the lodge as Father Gilchrist came wandering dourly around the corner, his attention drawn to her endeavors, his frosty eyebrows lifting skeptically.

*****

Vanessa had pulled Chris down the corridor, pausing only to duck into her room for her bag, then yanking him down to the farthest room, stalking inside and staring from one bed to the other, seeing Chris's backpack, and then sitting abruptly down on his bed, Chris instantly sitting alongside of her.

"Here," she said briskly, shoving her bag into his lap and grabbing his away from him, Chris gaping uncertainly.

"What are we going to do?" he asked, gently clasping her bag, Vanessa glancing over at him.

"We're going to look at each other's crap," she told him simply, unzipping his backpack and frowning intently inside of it.

Chris watched her with interest. "Why?" he asked curiously.

Sighing tautly, she shot him another look. "Because it's fun."

Turning back to his bag, she began digging absently through the clothes and various bits of junk Chris had packed, then suddenly rezipping it, and brusquely dumping both of their bags to the floor, Chris blinking at her in surprise.

"No, forget it," she murmured, sighing again and turning to face him. "Don't get me wrong, it's a really cool thing to do, but…"

She stood up, pacing momentarily, closing the door in a way that suggested she would have liked to have slammed it, and then crashing down beside Chris again, letting her hair fall in her face.

"Fuck," she mumbled, sighing yet one more time before sitting up and raking back her hair to stare at Chris. "What do you think about all of that shit that just went down in there?" she asked him, her anger obvious as Chris sighed glumly himself.

"Yeah," he agreed slowly. "That was really pretty bad."

Vanessa shook her head, slamming her hands on her knees, her eyes flashing as she gestured in furiously taut motions.

"Every time. *Every fucking time* I think that it can't possibly suck any more than it already does, that it is as royally fucked up as it can possibly get, something else happens, and it gets even worse!" she declared fiercely, glaring at Chris, who could only nod sadly.

"I mean, first, I show up to this town and sink so low that I decide to try to become a hooker. Then, I find out that I can't even get that right. Then, I lose out on my one chance to get into the theater, get jumped by a pimp, wind up on the street, and that's just with me! Then, we got Mrs. Spindlewood's whole outer-limits trip, not to mention that whole thing about her job and whatever's gonna happen to her now. We got everyone else in the group obviously not doing much better. And now we got all this crap with the Doc!"

She threw her hands up into the air. "And if that ain't enough, now it sounds like we're not even going to have our group anymore, the *one* thing that I had going for me in this fuckin' city!" She turned to Chris again, her eyes red but dry. "The only reason I'm not bawling right now is that I bust a gut crying all last night, *partly* because of you," she pointed out accusingly, letting Chris flinch and then deflating him a bit by adding, "But *mainly* because I was sad for Mrs. Spindlewood and also just for my own sorry ass. I just don't have any tears left."

She fell silent, and the two of them sat like that for a while, Chris wanting to take her hand and instead swallowing. "I'm sorry I was part of what made you cry," he said quietly. "I cried all last night too."

Vanessa looked over at him sharply, her features then softening as she regarded his profile. She dipped her hand into his and waited for him to face her.

"Chris, whatever it is that we're gonna have goin' on between us, the only way it's gonna happen is if we both get it straight up front—we gotta be completely honest with each other, no lying, no holding anything back." She paused gravely. "Okay?"

Chris met her gaze with earnest intensity, the inverted crescent of his gaping mouth small and solemn. "Okay," he answered softly, nodding slowly. "I promise. And I wasn't lying just now."

Vanessa stared at him with a tiny, sad smile, extending her free hand and lightly touching his face. "I know you weren't," she told him honestly, sighing quietly and glancing toward the floor.

Chris swallowed again, wanting to say so much more, his emotions and words clumsily tripping over each other as he tried to focus, instead looking down at the floor as well, his gaze falling upon their two bags. He had liked the idea of learning about her by carefully sharing in the contents of her bag, and he had liked the idea of her looking at his things, asking questions and commenting as she touched each item. There was something interesting and intimate about it, and he was disappointed that she had dismissed the notion, even though he was also upset about all that had just transpired. He sighed again himself, then brightening slightly as he remembered something, a trace of excitement alighting on his face. "Um, I did have one thing that I really wanted to show you," he told her with quiet eagerness, blushing when Vanessa glanced up at him with a hint of curiosity.

"Um." Encouraged, he almost giggled as he stood up and began to tug at the buttons of his studded vest, purposefully keeping it clasped together as he did so, Vanessa regarding him with mounting interest, one hand sweeping her hair back, holding it in place.

"Um," Chris repeated, his flush more pronounced as he shifted shyly and then, seeming to brace himself for any reaction, pulled his vest front open, revealing the T-shirt he wore beneath it, a dark green garment, the chest of which was emblazoned with an embossed golden slogan in graffiti-like style that read, "Polka Power."

Vanessa's depressed features lit up as she gaped at him, bringing her hands together as if to clap and then drawing them to her mouth, a crack of a cackle punctuating the silence in the room as she gasped in astonishment.

"Oh my god, Chris, that is fucking awesome!" she shrieked, Chris beaming in red-faced pride as she laughed in genuine appreciation. "That is so cool!" She shook her head in disbelief. "Where did you get that? How come I've never seen that before at any of the meetings or anything?"

Chris shifted his big feet again, his cheeks now burning as he enjoyed her enthusiasm. "Um, my grandpa got it for me at this Oktoberfest concert a few years ago," he told her, moving as if to rebutton his vest and then leaving it open, glancing down at his shirt front bashfully as he sat down beside her again. "Today's actually the first time I ever wore it anywhere."

Vanessa gazed from the shirt to Chris. "How come?" she asked him incredulously. "When someone gets me a present, I pretty much bust it out the very next day!"

Chris paused, his flush still prominent as he shrugged and squirmed a bit. "Well, just 'cause…well…" He hesitated, rubbing his hands against his jeans, looking at the floor. "Well, you remember when we were talking in my room and I told you all about when I turned punk, but how I also still liked some really unpunk music and you told me that you understood and that you thought it was, you know, kinda cool an' stuff?" he asked, slowly glancing over at her, her rapid nodding encouraging him. He shrugged again and continued. "Well, it's just that you…kinda gave me the courage to put it on."

He gave her a small, simple smile, Vanessa's heart glowing at his words. She smiled back, taking his hand in both of hers and looking at it, exploring his fingers and touching his palm, her smile then wilting as she glanced up at him again, exhaling slowly.

"I…" She hesitated, her voice cracking; and she swallowed fiercely, meeting his eyes again, her smile now gone. "I was so mean to you yesterday, Chris, never even mind today." She shook her head when Chris moved to respond, actually reaching out and pressing her fingers to his lips, pausing as she wished she could keep them there and then slowly withdrawing them.

"I was just so mad about how our conversation went! When you were telling me your whole thing about how you couldn't sleep with anyone unless you loved them, and I was trying to tell you that I felt exactly the same way. I truly, sincerely meant that, even though it seemed like I was just saying it to agree with you, especially since you thought I was a prostitute. That's what made me so fucking furious that, for the first time, *ever*, I had met someone who felt the same way I did. And because of all my bullshit, instead of *me* being the one to say, 'Yeah, right. I'll bet you're just saying that to get some,' I ended up being the one who looked like they were lying!"

She sat up, Chris meeting her gaze unblinkingly as she continued, her voice weary but intense. "So here it goes," she proclaimed flatly. "The real truth is that the reason I sucked so badly at being a prostitute was because I felt that way and not just then, but always, even back in school. All the guys there were such assholes that all they saw when they looked at a girl was a fuckin' bull's-eye."

"We were all just a score to them, literally, because that's all it was to them, just a competition! One by one, I had to watch all my friends get fucked and then get fucked over, and I made up my mind I was *never* going to give any of those pricks the satisfaction. And the more I refused, the more pissed off they got. And the more pissed off those pigs got, the better I felt about what I was doing. Turned me into a megabitch, and if I hadn't skipped town when I did, it probably would've turned me into a gangbang and a body bag. But fuck them, 'cause I got out and here I am now."

She glared at him with a fiery triumph, her expression softening as she watched Chris gulp and shift. "But like I said, the truth is that is how I feel, and because of that, I have never been with anyone in that way...ever."

She swallowed quietly herself, forcing her eyes to meet Chris's gaze, in spite of how small she now felt, seeing the gradual comprehension of exactly what she had been telling him register in his eyes as he looked away, blinking down at the floor and then swinging his focus back up to her once more.

"Okay," he told her quietly, inhaling and continuing slowly. "Well, um, there's a couple things I should tell you." He paused, squirming and then exhaling. "Remember when I was telling you about the couple of girlfriends I thought I was in love with in school and then about Candy and how, even though in that relationship, in the whole six months we were together, even though I wanted to and thought that we would, at some point have, you know, sex, um, that we never did?"

He hesitated, Vanessa nodding in silence. "Well, the other girlfriends were just, you know, high-school dating and stupid little dramas and stuff. And so what I'm trying to tell you is that I've never been with anyone before either...ever..."

Biting his lip, he regarded her earnestly, Vanessa looking into his eyes and then taking his hand again, staring at it, and then meeting his gaze once more, trying to contain her amazed happiness at what he had just told her, knowing that no boy on earth would ever confess such a thing, unless it was an obvious line or unless it was a fact. And even without Chris's pledge of honesty from a few moments before, she would still have known that he was telling her the truth.

At length, they glanced away from each other, Vanessa exhaling forcefully to maintain her look of composure, squeezing his hand lightly. "So… I guess that means…you and I are both…"

She didn't really want to say the word and didn't have to, Chris nodding with a meek, resigned smile. "Yeah, I guess so…" he confirmed.

Vanessa chuckled, a nervous, weak sound, patting his hand as they both stared at the far wall. "Wow," she observed eventually. "We really are a couple of screw-ups."

They both laughed at this assessment, the tension between them broken, though not expelled. Vanessa's eyes rested on Dr. Pendleton's suitcase on the floor next to the other bed, taking in its solid, stodgy, functional blandly brown shape, her thoughts shifting as she stared at it, a bit of her former depression returning to darken her mood.

"So what do you think about everything that just happened?" she asked him again, her tone grim as she turned to study Chris's face.

He only shook his head, his voice also glum as his Mohawk hung low. "I dunno."

"Yeah, me either," she agreed, sighing. "I mean it's not like he deliberately lied to us or anything, and I really don't feel like he was using us and maybe he screwed-up, and we all should be pissed off at him, but I just don't feel like it!" She shook her own head, glancing at Chris again. "I mean you're not really mad at him either, are you?"

"Oh no, I love Dr. Pendleton!" he declared in an almost hurt voice, looking at Vanessa with unself-conscious emphasis.

"Well, so do I!" she responded insistently, touched by Chris's unhesitant assertion, impressed that any boy could be that open with his feelings, her own loyalty to the doctor only strengthened by his simple but strong take on the matter.

They sat in silence again, staring at Dr. Pendleton's suitcase, a light smile crossing Vanessa's face. "Isn't it funny how you can start to feel that way about someone even though you've only known them for a couple of weeks?" she mused quietly. "One day, you're total strangers, and the next day you meet, a week later you're talking—still don't know 'em that well. But a week or so after that, and suddenly, there it is…"

She trailed off, her throat all at once dry as she turned toward Chris, who was shifting and blushing more than usual, the thought occurring to her with the clarity of a bullet.

"Chris," she said slowly, watching his profile. "You said you had a couple of things to tell me… What was the other thing?"

Chris continued to fidget, his gaze fixed on the far wall. "Um, yeah, well…do you remember when I told you about how that last night, Candy was really coming on to me, for the first time in all of those six months, and how I could have finally been with her and done anything that I wanted, but then how I didn't, how I just couldn't you know…be with her, how it seemed really just…wrong?"

Vanessa nodded, frowning. "Yeah, of course," she replied evenly. "You told me—it's what we've just been talking about. You couldn't be with her because you realized that you didn't really love her." She nodded succinctly, waiting for him to agree.

"Yeah," Chris nodded, blinking in his steadfast focus on the wall. "Um, well, the reason why I realized that I didn't love her, and never really had, was, I mean obviously 'cause of the stuff that she did, but the main reason why I just couldn't be with her was that…"

He paused, swallowing almost guiltily and finally turning to meet Vanessa's anxious gaze. "The whole time she was there, I just kept thinking about you."

Vanessa's breathing seemed to cease as she witnessed his clumsy exhibition of what was in his heart. "She was my girlfriend, and I could have had her, and by thinking of you, I was almost technically cheating on her," he explained awkwardly, then shaking his head. "But what it really felt like was…that if I went ahead and did anything with her, ever, it would have really been like I was cheating… on you…"

He became silent, only able to gaze haplessly at her, Vanessa staring wordlessly back and then slowly reaching out her hand, studying her own fingers as they lightly traced his lips in almost surreal motions, neither of them breathing, Vanessa watching as he closed his eyes and inhaled tremulously, then slowly withdrawing her hand, and waiting for him to open his eyes and regard her once more.

She inhaled deeply herself, smelling his scent, his proximity, staring intently at him as her heart pounded relentlessly, one tenuous, eternal second elapsing during which she staid her frustration and resigned herself once more to be the one to seize the initiative and lead the way for him, knowing that if she waited for him to do so, the moment might pass. She summoned up her resolve to be the strong one for both of them, all prepared to leap into the advance as he leaned forward, engulfing her lips in his own.

*****

Even in the now rapidly fading sunlight, Dr. Pendleton was able to find his way along the winding foot trail, his progress hampered by the underbrush as he was met with images from his past, recollections of the many times before when he had passed beneath these trees. He was unable to entertain them, though, his nostalgia spoiled by the upset that he was, in essence, fleeing, but that he was also bringing with him every step of the way.

In time, he reached a clearing, making his way through a waist-deep pasture of grass, entering into a smaller section of trees, and then stepping through some foliage out onto the pavement of the road that would lead him into Larkesville, the sparse twinkling of lights ahead of him outlining the rows of houses and small businesses arranged on its outskirts.

He knew precisely where the old drugstore would be, his intention being to escape there for a little while, in hopes that the memories that it would hold for him would succeed in helping him put aside the events of the past hour or so.

What he had not known, having never really noticed it before, was that the course to the drugstore and its soda fountain took him past a small, quiet barroom, his surprise at his own actions genuine as he found himself turning and passing through its doors.

*****

Mr. McClintock had been left a bit dazed by the slight blow to his head and had eventually slid out of his jacket and lay down, feeling the bunk-bed frame strain beneath his weight as he rested his head on the pillow, his stomach still grumbling in disappointment even as the rest of his body gratefully gave over to the notion of resting for a while, his dreams sufficiently abundant with a variety of excellent refreshments from which he could choose.

*****

The streamlined pressure cooker—junk that it probably was— did, at least, look to have potential, the glossy-plastic couple who were so exuberant in their endorsements clearly having won over their paid audience of amazed spectators.

Mr. Crimpton, however, was not especially impressed with it, nor had he been with the fully disassemblable, stow-and-go canoe, the faux pearl necklace and earring set, the Hello Kitty throw pillows, or the Barry Goldwater Commemorative Silver Dollar.

In fact, he was scarcely paying attention to any of the infomercials, the television little more than the pretense of a distraction, his thoughts elsewhere. One glance at Mrs. Spindlewood was enough to confirm that the same could be said for her as well.

He had attempted to focus his aggravation on Dr. Pendleton, realizing in time that it was an empty pursuit. All that resulted was the conclusion that their group leader was just as screwed-up as they were, something that he had more or less been telling them all along, in his insistence that he was, himself, on their level, and considered himself to be a member of the group.

No, his real exasperation lay in the fact that they all were pretty much back to square one, having not budged all that far from it in the first place. He had no idea how these other people were going to deal with their own paradoxes, Vanessa's outburst last night and the priest's confirmation of it just today, so clearly illustrating their laughable circumstances; and truthfully, in spite of the rankling self-ishness that he sensed as a result of it, he could not let himself worry about it.

The driving review, which had been haunting him for over a month now was soon to be a reality, was next week, in fact; and in the shape he was in at the moment, the only way he could successfully handle it would be to drive the test car off a cliff and settle the matter once and for all.

The infomercial switched its focus once more, now advertis-ing a deluxe set of microbrews, twenty-four bottles of excellent beers from all over the country. Mr. Crimpton viewed the commercial with a guarded look, the slightest hint of yearning permeating his jittery nerves, creating yet another form of anxiety.

*****

"Perseverance is an upstanding quality," Father Gilchrist remarked, startling Judge Talbott as he approached from behind, arms behind his back as he surveyed her undertaking. "I admire your tenacity."

"Oh!" Judge Talbott jumped, smiling nervously up at him, almost dropping her second attempt, pulling it away from the flames and then realizing that she had brought no paper plates or napkins with her. Fumbling with the tongs, she managed to tear one of the cardboard flaps from the box of graham crackers and placed the ooz-ing s'more atop it, hesitantly offering it to the priest. "Would you like one?"

Staring at it with instinctual distaste, Father Gilchrist accepted it with a tart smile, watching as the judge instantly busied herself with putting together another. He settled down on a nearby wobbly picnic table, holding the snack on its improvised dish and observing her actions in silence. In only a few minutes, hers was finished, and she carefully arranged it on another flap before glancing about for any other diversion at all and then reluctantly sitting across from Father Gilchrist, her gaze demurely focused on her s'more.

Disguising his sigh as a quiet exhalation, he looked at his own, taking a bite from it, surprised at just how good it was and at how hungry he was. Apart from the gingerbread cookie, he had not eaten since…last night, he supposed, the sandwich he had made in place of Mrs. Tucker's codfish cakes, and only half of it, at that. The rest of it must still be on his side table, in his quarters, at the church, which was now far, far away. He dismissed the thought and chewed at the rest of his s'more, keeping his fingers as unsticky as possible.

"That was really rather good," he told her frankly.

Judge Talbott's eyes shot up to meet his, and she smiled shyly, flushing. "Oh good, I'm glad," she replied, having yet to sample hers. "Would you like another one?"

Before he could answer, she was on her feet, eagerly putting together a second one for him, Father Gilchrist watching her actions, his sigh now less disguised. He sat in silence for a moment, glancing up as the first traces of twilight fast began to dim the sky, the faint chirping of crickets gradually asserting itself, preparing to take back the night.

"To say that I owe you an apology would be something of an understatement," he told her at last, Judge Talbott's focus on her task instantly doubled. "My assessment of your judicial ideas was the product of an excessively foul mood brought on by an insufferably trying day, not that such is in any way a justification or even a barely passable excuse. It is neither, of course, and suffice it to say, I do apologize for having so wrongfully and insensitively upset you."

The original piece of cardboard she had given him was within easy reach on the tabletop before him, but Judge Talbott instead wrested off yet another flap, only then stepping toward him and handing him the snack, quietly resuming her seat.

She stared at the flames in the barbecuer as they began to wane, finally forcing herself to acknowledge the old man, smiling shyly at his inscrutable features.

"You don't have to say you're sorry, Father Gilchrist," she told him in a soft voice, offering the meekest of shrugs. "I was really upset, but the truth is, I thought a lot about what you said, and… well, you're right." She nodded with growing emphasis even as his frown became more pronounced. "I can't possibly expect to be an affective judge if I can't oversee the issues brought into my courtroom all by myself. It's so obvious that I feel really silly even saying it. You were right. What kind of a judge can't make up her own mind about what's right and wrong? You don't have to apologize because you actually helped me to make what will probably be the most important decision of my entire life."

Father Gilchrist's second s'more remained untouched as he stared at her. "Which would be what?" he inquired, rather bluntly, his voice edged with coiled doubt.

Sighing quietly herself, she shook her head and continued to smile at him. "I decided that it's my best judgment not to be a judge at all," she replied simply.

His lips twisting, Father Gilchrist united his fingers and peered at her, keeping his voice calm and even. "You've decided not to be a judge?" he reiterated. "I see. And what then will you do for a living, may I ask?"

Judge Talbott shrugged once more, watching the flames give way to smoldering coals. "I'll go back to being a public defender, I guess," she replied easily. "I was very good at it, and I really enjoyed the work. And, even though, in the career sense, it would be unheard of to take such a backward step, it really is all I can think to do."

Father Gilchrist considered this darkly, about to unleash a fraction of his take on her decision, when his indignation was further confounded as she continued, turning her gaze back to his again.

"I know that you understand that kind of work because it's almost identical to what you do," she told him.

Restraining his initial response to any such notion, he maintained his composure and merely stared at her. "Oh? And in what way?"

"Well, just fundamentally," she explained simply. "We both are responsible for helping clients to prepare their defenses before they go up in front of a judge. I would be in the courtroom, and you would be in your confessional booth, but it's really very similar. We offer advice, council, penance, and possible penalties. We both try to comfort the person who's done something wrong, to reassure them that someone is still on their side, that they still have some hope for forgiveness."

Listening to this childlike comparison in silence, Father Gilchrist swallowed his inherently angry reaction, because, of course, she was right. He had been thinking the same thing just last night, had he not? In fact, that was part of what had unleashed his wrath on the poor woman. This, however, did little to ease his anger now, especially in lieu of what she was telling him.

"And are you saying that you actually *wish* to resume this previous position?" he summarized flatly.

"Well, it is what I know best," she elaborated, nodding openly. "It is so much easier, by comparison, so much more clear-cut. You're on a very definite side, and you know precisely how to handle each case, and what's more—and here is where I don't envy prosecuting attorneys at all—when you are offering the defense, it's with the presumption of innocence or even with the open acknowledgement of guilt.

"Either way, you feel like you are addressing the humanity of that person, that you're giving them a second chance to do good or to face responsibility or just to show them that you see in them the potential for…well, for redemption, for salvation."

She paused, gesturing earnestly. "You see, Father, the two jobs are really very similar. I know you've got to be able to appreciate that." She peered at him expectantly.

While Father Gilchrist did not in the least appreciate it, he certainly could not disagree. "I take your point, of course," he allowed grudgingly, attempting to steer them back toward a more practical line of thought. "But what of your actual career? You have said yourself that to reverse your progress would be an unprecedented action."

Judge Talbott smiled down at her s'more. "I don't think I have any other choice," she confessed quietly, then meeting his gaze again. "I mean if we continue to consider the comparison between us, imagine if you were approached one day and given such a huge promotion."

Father Gilchrist's incredulousness would not be stifled. "To the Archdiocese?" he shot back in outrage, the image of Deacon Richard's meticulous, mincing pursuit of him earlier filling his thoughts, replaced with the notion of being elevated into a position in which he would be dealing with an entire staff of Deacon Richards. *Monsignor Gilchrist, indeed!* "I would sooner be named Mother Superior and have to go in drag for the rest of my days!"

"No, no, that's not what I meant, Father!" Judge Talbott amended, giggling shyly at his outlandish irreverence, growing still as she carefully regarded him again.

"I meant what if you were promoted from a priest to...well, to being a judge...in the religious sense of the word?"

Grimacing, Father Gilchrist sighed. "My dear lady, that is not precisely how the Catholic chain of command works," he informed her pedantically.

Smiling and nodding, Judge Talbott rested her hands in her lap. "Yes, I know. But to use our comparison, just...conversationally... what would you do?"

He stared at her in the encroaching dimness, the crickets more actively calling now as he attempted to dismiss this ridiculous conjecture, unable to do so as echoes of his explosive, off-the-cuff sermon from the night before resurfaced to haunt him. He had felt a sense of just that sort of empowerment as he had ranted his shocking but very profoundly truthful words.

He had, all-in-all, passed judgment on the entire world, not as a God, of course, but as a man—as a petty, bitter, disappointed, soured, mean old man. He winced as he thought of his incredibly unconventional Sacramental offering, gritting his teeth as he recalled his tussle with the two street kids, drawing a hint of vindication from that, for their actions were not—in anyway—upstanding. *Angels with dirty vices, indeed.* But to be the judge, to have to deal with all that had bent his shoulders and smothered his compassion and poisoned his heart-sick soul over the course of all of these painful years, as an actual deity? *Thank you, no.* At least as a man, he had the solace of a grave to anticipate, where as a God, Nietzsche's neo-kraut philosophy notwithstanding, a god might well have to go on dealing with the insanity of life without the promise of death, forever and ever, Amen. *No, thank you.*

"I must confess that I would be an extremely unsuitable candidate for the job," he told her flatly, then grimacing at the knowing, conclusive look on her face. "But your comparison is very much in the abstract!" he continued forcefully. "It seems wholly premature to stunt the furtherance of your career by falling back upon previous accomplishments for comfort and complacency's sake!"

Starting a bit at the urgency of his words, Judge Talbott sat up slightly, spreading her hands uncertainly. "Well, as I said, I have given it a lot of thought, and I did have every intention of discussing it with Dr. Pendleton and the group. But of course…"

Seeing his scowl begin to emerge, she hastily continued. "That may have to wait, for now, I suppose." She nodded euphemistically. "Anyway, in the meantime, I'm really glad that I've had the opportunity to talk it over with you, Father. After all, I really do respect your opinion."

He regarded her in speechlessness, very much tempted to ask why. His eyes fell on the luminous dial of his wristwatch, its shimmery presence reflecting the nightfall. He watched as the minute hand crept to six o'clock, rather facetiously enacting something he had not done in close to thirty years.

"And God said, 'Let there be light,'" he stated simply, just on the off-chance that it might work.

And it did. At six o'clock, somewhere within the lackluster lodge, an automatic timer, pragmatically set for that hour, activated the few buzzing outdoor lights with which the deck had been outfitted, bathing them in a phosphorescent glow.

Judge Talbott gasped in delight, glancing about as if she had just witnessed a miracle. "How did you do that?" she asked him in wonder.

He could only smile sadly at her, his features crumpling, not unkindly, but in definite, slightly hurt resignation.

*****

Even in spite of their lack of experience, both Vanessa and Chris knew of the difference between making love and basic sex, but what they could not have known when they gave themselves to each other that day was that that which they were to share was something that very, very few people, older or younger, for all of their interaction, could ever know; and had they been aware of this, it would have saddened them to think that something so beautiful could not be known to everyone.

The converse would be argued, naturally, that their unconventional abstinence until the right moment had, in turn, alienated them from a plethora of experience; but such discourse would not get very far, because of the one aspect that had created the right moment, that being the love that they wordlessly confessed to each other, in a way that rendered the scale of extremes contrasting making love and having sex irrelevant, for what happened between them was so immeasurable as to transcend by far any such science.

When Chris had appeased Vanessa by at last swallowing his inhibitions and embracing her, she had gladly and instinctually taken over, her role as the leader always at hand, even as it was then gradually and strangely challenged by his growing assertiveness until finally, in a sort of bewildered, frightened relief, she submitted to him, allowing him to lead, tentatively entrusting him with the control that she, the angry, independent survivor, had never before relinquished to anyone. She did so now, daring to place it in his hands and then watch in powerlessness to see what he would do with it, stunned to the point of tears when he took it and bore it with strength and tenderness, with a virtual reverence.

As she lay atop the bed and let him take her, when she was able to force her eyes to remain open, to cherish her sight as well as her other senses, she watched his face in a way she had never beheld that of another person's before, his eyes too only intermittently able to stay open, his features taut and lean, the crest of his Mohawk silhouetted against the ceiling, giving him the appearance of a conquering warrior, only contributing to the already wild intensity of their actions. She could see his face clearly for only a while, as their first kiss had occurred just as the sun had been setting, the room then slowly sinking into shadows so that by the time they had finished, night had since fallen.

In the ensuing darkness, the invisibility of their interaction merely heightened their other senses and, consequently, their sensations. Apart from their ragged, united breathing, the sound of the crickets was uninterrupted, save for in one respect, that being Chris's almost hypnotized repeating of her name, rhythmic and slow, as if some manner of incantation, Vanessa's self-consciousness giving way to an almost ashamed joy at hearing him speak it to her, for whereas she had always disliked the name, it now had an almost musical quality as it issued with growing urgency from his lips. She had tried, so hard, to reciprocate, to give back, to let him know how magical his name was to her, but could not keep up, her voice lost to the panting exhalations that overtook both of them.

For all his longing, for all the passionate desire he felt for her and dared to believe that she felt for him, Chris was astoundingly gentle with her, his natural virginal uncertainty and innate clumsiness far from detracting from their bonding, only enhancing it, by making it more endearing, more special, more real; and when they finally climaxed, when Vanessa thought she might faint because of the waves of unendurable pleasure that she had withstood only to be sent soaring upward into a staggering, pulsing ecstasy, between her plaintive gasps, she heard from Chris a single, tremulous whimper, the sound, while desperate and pleading, not in the least bit enfeebling the assertion of his semblance of young manhood, instead only serving to remind her that he was just as exposed, just as vulnerable, just as dwarfed, and in awe of what they were sharing and was just as grateful to give into this inexplicable momentum of surrendering power and to accept the bliss with which it was superimposed.

He collapsed beside her in exhausted, heaving respiration; and they lay together in the utter silence of the room until sleep finally overtook them, neither of them moving, just laying together, breathing.

They were both still fully clothed; Chris had paused to shrug out of his vest, but Vanessa had wordlessly stopped him, Chris staring at her in earnest uncertainty, realizing that the urgency that was

431

consuming him was shared by her. Touched and inspired by this, he had moved to rejoin her, to proceed, pausing and then glancing down at the padlock and chain that dangled across his waist, fingering the lock, and then groping awkwardly for its key, his face awash in a humiliated red, his features then becoming mutely blank as Vanessa extended one hand, looking at him searchingly; and he slowly gave the key to her, placing it in her palm, gaping down at her as she unlocked the padlock for him, refastening the two lengths of chain at the back of his waist, their eyes meeting again with this action complete, an unspoken comprehension passing between them as Chris swallowed and moved to embrace her again, Vanessa receiving him willingly.

The fact that they did not undress for this, their very first time, did not fully explore each other's bodies, the fact that they were not now eagerly preparing to undertake the act again, the fact that they were not even speaking as they lay together, only lent to the notion that while their previous wait was now over, the consummation of their love was only just beginning, the revival of still more patient, slow-paced anticipation promising the gradual, amazing enlightenment of discovery that they would come to learn from each other in the times ahead. With this unspoken but mutual understanding between them, their clothing permitted them the best of both worlds, for, whereas their mating was now complete, they still had a universe of exploration to savor, the quiet prolongation of which could only heighten and extend its beauty.

Hence, they did not set about anxiously repeating their experience, nor did they discuss what they had shared, nor did they even question it; they merely lay there in stunned, overwhelmed silence, the pure joy and innocence of their actions safeguarded by that one element that they had brought into their union with them.

The silence that they shared before they fell asleep in each other's arms was unbroken save for a single exchange. Vanessa, on the verge of giving way to sleep, refused to submit, seeking out and finding his hand in the dark, her voice small and tenuous in the imposing stillness as she spoke.

"Tell me what I need to hear, Chris."

The pause that ensued was not one of hesitation, Chris moving to place himself in her arms and lift his lips next to her ear as he gladly returned her control to her, entrusting his own heart into her hands as well, drawing himself up close to her in willing, almost worshipful submission, whispering simply and truthfully, "I love you, Vanessa," Vanessa then exhaling in trembling relief, at last surrendering to her dreams.

*****

Father Gilchrist had eventually made a convincing display of fatigue, yawning and slowly standing, thanking Judge Talbott for her snacks, and declaring himself in need of some rest, the small woman nodding understandingly and bidding him good night, then resuming her preparation of several s'mores, retrieving a plate from the kitchen with the notion of reheating them in the microwave oven for anyone who might wish to have any later. Her mood was greatly elevated due to her talk with the old priest, her astonishment that he, of all people, could make her feel better contributing all the more to her smile.

Discussing her decision with him had been helpful, and the issue did not rest as heavily in her mind now. It would still be quite an undertaking, especially since it was such a colossal step backward; but sometimes, facts had to be faced. Such was the very nature of the courtroom, and despite the irony of her one and only ruling as a judge having been *not* to be a judge, she was willing to accept it, due to the second even greater irony—what choice did she have?

His facade intact until he reentered the building, Father Gilchrist resumed his scowl and latent mumbling, heading down the hall and to his accommodations for the night. He could not stand the idea that the judge was basing her decision upon his temperamental words, but had been unable to discern how to undo the damage he had inflicted, inasmuch as he had meant every syllable. With her sweetness and straightforward integrity, she would clearly make an excellent judge; but for those same exact reasons, what kind of a judge could she *possibly* make?

It was a conundrum that, if considered, could only revitalize his headache, and he gratefully dismissed it. Let Dr. Panacea try to deal with it, the pathetic little quack; as for him, he was going to bed. If he, himself, were unfortunate enough to survive the night, he could assist in dealing with it tomorrow. Maybe.

Throwing open the door, he stared at the sight of Mr. McClintock's slumbering form, his massive girth engulfing the entire bottom bunk as he slept, his necktie rising and falling neatly with his breathing.

Glowering, he settled down on his bed, not even removing his jacket, resigned to sleep a second night in his clerical raiment. If the whale had swallowed Jonah, then it was quite obvious who had swallowed the whale, he reflected, quite uncharitably, tugging fussily at his pillow. Now, if only oblivion would kindly swallow all of them up in turn.

*****

Mr. Crimpton had glanced up to see the sullen old priest stalk by, rolling his eyes and focusing on the television again, the ultra-retro fourteen-piece fondue set now being offered yielding little interest to him.

He had watched the old man and the judge talking a moment or so earlier when he had ventured out for a pointless cigarette, realizing then that he was now down to three.

That was typical, he had reflected, pausing in the kitchen on his way back inside, hesitantly looking in the refrigerator.

Sure enough, a six pack of beer sat right in front, the bottles gleaming and tempting. He had stared at them, sensing a longing interest even while inundated with the repugnance that he felt for the stuff. Who could *conceivably* like the flavor? It was almost worse than bourbon.

This contrast gave him no comfort—quite the opposite in fact. Yet he was reaching out for a bottle, craving the prospect of relaxation that it might just yield, when he heard the judge reentering through the side door and quickly ducked out of the kitchen.

Stomping wearily back to the den, he noticed that Mrs. Spindlewood was gone. Gone? Oh, she was gone all right.

Plunging back down into the recliner, he had stared miserably at the television, wishing that he was not so…thirsty?

Hadn't yesterday been enough of a lesson? Didn't he have enough problems, did he have to be a drunk as well? All he needed was to wind up joining Alcoholics Anonymous and then discover that its group leader was actually a brewmaster or the shareholder in a vineyard or, better still, a bartender who didn't bother with doughnuts and instead brought in shot glasses and whisky to the meetings.

The old hands-on approach, right? He sighed and watched as the infomercial station now exhibited an incredible audacity by pausing for a commercial, a raucous advertisement for a new video game that placed the player in the driver's seat of a race car that was then enabled to plow through the city streets, wreaking havoc, running down pedestrians, sideswiping other cars, and ultimately crashing into the side of a building and erupting into flames.

Mr. Crimpton watched it in slack-jawed disbelief. *Keep it up*, he thought furiously, *just keep it up. I hear the water is fine tonight.* He glanced bitterly toward the kitchen, taking an abstract consolation in the fact that he did not really even want a beer. No, indeed, he did not. Beer wouldn't be strong enough.

*****

"No, actually, I think that I'll have something a bit stronger," Dr. Pendleton had told the bartender, a tall, rangy man with a handlebar moustache and a dubious expression. The doctor sat on a stool in the dim, mostly deserted bar, avoiding his murky reflection in the mirror behind the bartender. "Do you have any sherry?"

The bartender's bushy brows lifted, his look of doubt only intensifying. "Uh, no, we generally don't like our patrons losing control," he replied evenly, turning to reach for a bottle beneath the bar. "How about some brandy? That's close."

Dr. Pendleton nodded, resting his elbows on the bar and watching as a tumbler was filled. Sherry had seemed like something Dr.

Whittaker might drink; but, no, brandy was even more likely. Of course, he was no Dr. Whittaker. Dr. Whittaker would not have walked out on his own therapy group and gone to a bar. Moreover, Dr. Whittaker would most likely never have become embroiled in such a mess as to be inclined to escape in the first place.

He sipped the brandy, wincing a bit, the bartender observing him with an unimpressed gaze. He did not drink often, almost never, in fact; but now seemed like an ideal time.

Everyone had their own outlets for relaxing, and whereas this was not really his, it would have to do. In any event, he only wanted something of a bracer, something to stimulate his relaxation. Odd, though, stimulation and relaxation were, after all, opposites.

No matter, he merely wanted to settle his nerves a bit and then head up to Farmington's Drug Store, which would be bright and airy, where they would have a variety of Soda Fountain treats from which to choose, where all of the fixtures and furnishing were chrome-plated and gleamingly unchanging; and he could enjoy a bit of the nostalgia that he had hoped to relive but that had thus far been denied him.

"Do you want another?" the bartender asked him abruptly, startling him as he noticed his tumbler was empty, not realizing he had drained it so quickly.

"Uh...yes, I suppose," he ventured, the bartender already having the bottle in his hand, replenishing his glass.

From somewhere in the gloom, someone started up a jukebox; and shortly, the haunting strains of "Memories Are Made of This" could be heard, prompting Dr. Pendleton to smile warmly.

"I always liked Perry Como," he confided to the bartender.

"Yeah? That's Dean Martin," the bartender informed him, moving away.

Blinking, Dr. Pendleton then nodded, resuming his smile. He downed his drink and decided to stay, just to listen to the entire song.

*****

Judge Talbott had smothered the coals in the barbecuer by replacing its lid, then glancing around the glow of the outdoor lighting, strolling to the far side of the deck, and peering out at the shimmering lake. Most everyone had simply gone off to bed, she supposed, wondering briefly where the two kids had gone and, for that matter, where Dr. Pendleton was. Obviously, he must have wanted to take a walk, she decided, hoping that he knew the area as well as he seemed, as, being so far away from any other residences, the descent of night upon the lodge had been surprisingly absolute in its darkness.

Shivering a little, she ventured back indoors, catching a glimpse of Mr. Crimpton grumbling, apparently to the television set, reluctant to join him, but glad that she was not the only night owl. *Night Owl?* It was only early evening, she reflected, heading for the room she would be sharing with the other ladies. Amazing how it suddenly seemed like midnight.

She quietly eased open the door, seeing the frail form of Mrs. Spindlewood neatly attired in her nightgown and tucked into bed. She smiled at the image, carefully turning a nightstand lamp toward the wall before switching it on and settling onto the lower bunk, observing the peacefully sleeping old woman, scarcely able to discern her shuddery breathing. There was something sad in her aura, and the judge found herself looking away, digging into her purse for the new murder mystery she had purchased the other day, figuring that now was just as any a good time to begin it.

It had taken her nearly an hour to decide on it, and she had lost even more time in the dusty old used bookstore, listening to an argument between two boys over a series called *Choose Your Own Adventure Books.* When they had at last made their purchases and gone, she had picked up one of these paperbacks, reading several of its concise pages, intrigued with the concept of being given choices on virtually every page, then shocked when, after having boldly made three of what she thought were very sound and wise decisions, her character rounded a corner and faced certain doom.

She had put the book aside, disturbed with the abruptness of its basic similarity to life, for it only reenforced the notion that even if someone had the gumption to make the choices and even if those were definitively the right ones, there was no guarantee that…that there was any guarantee at all.

She already knew this, of course; but, somehow, to have a children's book revitalize it for her in such a way was even more disconcerting. Sighing now as she recalled it, she wondered how she had managed to get as far as she had in life. Glancing over at the window, she thought again of Dr. Pendleton, hoping that he was all right.

*****

"Yes, perhaps just… 'one more for the road,'" Dr. Pendleton told the bartender, his smile very warm now as he took a cue from the song that had just now ended; whoever was selecting those old numbers had excellent taste in music. The bartender, however, did not appear to be amused at the little witticism, but refilled the tumbler anyway, regarding his customer reluctantly.

"So what brings you to Larkesville?" he asked, wiping at the bar with a damp towel.

Dr. Pendleton sampled his third glass of brandy, appreciating its flavor and then glancing up at the bartender.

"Hmmm? Oh yes, uh, Larkesville…" He sat up, clearing his throat.

"I came to Larkesville on a retreat with my group," he explained succinctly.

The bartender frowned. "You came in here alone, buddy," he told him flatly.

Blinking, Dr. Pendleton inhaled and shook his head. "Oh no, no. I mean I'm staying at Fenderman Lodge, uh, with my group. We've all come here together for a retreat."

He nodded concisely, then considering an interesting point. "And now I have retreated from my retreat."

This struck him as somewhat humorous, a sentiment unshared by the bartender, who merely watched as he moved to lean back on his stool and almost kept on going. Sitting up abruptly, he blinked again. *Odd, the stools at Farmington's Drug Store all had backrests, even though the barroom stools were clearly the seats that could use such added support.*

"Easy there, pal," the bartender said dryly. "One retreat at a time."

"Excuse me," Dr. Pendleton murmured, recentering himself. "My...equilibrium is not all that it should be today."

"Yeah, well," the bartender nodded, shrugging stiffly. "You just let me know, and I'll go and adjust the gravity in here."

With that, he moved away, Dr. Pendleton grimacing and having some more of his brandy, catching a glimpse of himself in the mirror behind the bar but not feeling the need to look away.

He very nearly raised his glass and tilted it in salute, instead signaling for the bartender again.

"Can you tell me if Farmington's Drug Store still stays open late on Saturday nights?" he inquired with a hopeful smile.

The bartender shook his head. "They're not open, period. Farmington's has been closed for almost five years now," he said bluntly.

Actually gasping upon hearing this, Dr. Pendleton sagged on his barstool, then staring sadly at the waiting bartender. "Really? Did they relocate to a new spot?" he asked halfheartedly, for even then it would not be the same.

"No, old man Farmington bought the farm," he explained matter-of-factly. "They turned the whole place into a pool hall."

Stung, Dr. Pendleton stared forlornly at his glass, slowly emptying it.

"You wanna settle up?" the bartender nodded to him, then gesturing loosely. "Or will you be having *two* more for the road?"

Dr. Pendleton did not, in fact, want another, which was strange, he was later to reflect, because that was precisely what he requested.

*****

Vanessa awoke, sometime later, peering intently into the darkness, and then feeling Chris's sleeping form nestled against hers and then remembering, her heart jumping happily.

She sat up, Chris stirring gradually and then sitting up too, both of them slowly moving to sit on the side of the bed in sleepy silence. Eventually, Chris fumbled for the switch of a small table lamp, its glow unintrusively dim, yet illuminating the room and instantly solidifying the reality of what had taken place there, each of them awkwardly turning away to adjust their clothing, an unnecessary modesty, for they were never again to feel the slightest bit self-conscious in each other's presence, their embarrassment only due to the incredible newness of what they were now free to share. As Vanessa watched, motionless, Chris refastened the two lengths of chain in front of his self, securely closing the padlock and removing its key, which he once again gave to Vanessa, this time laying it in her palm and gently enfolding her fingers over it, his eyes holding her gaze as he wordlessly entrusted it to her, the previous import of this action now solidly consummated as Vanessa accepted his key and all that accompanied it, Chris lowering his head in a tamed submission to her once more, both of them sitting in a charged but meditative silence in the dim bedroom. This room, itself, had lent to the wonder of their experience, for, if their union had taken place in the privacy of some personal space of either of them, while this would not have diminished the enormity, it would have influenced it to some degree. Here, however, in a neutral space, unknown to both of them, their relating to each other was all the more profound for the way in which they were obliged to look to the only semblance of familiarity that such a place had to offer, that being each other.

When they left that room, it was with something akin to trepidation, neither of them quite knowing why they should feel this way, Vanessa taking Chris's hand, drawing as much comfort from it as she hoped she was giving back. It was as if they were now facing a whole new reality not only between one another but also between themselves and the world, and it was with pounding hearts that they opened the unlocked door and ventured out into the hallway beyond.

Nothing happened, of course, and they fell to giggling nervously at each other, Vanessa turning to Chris and backing him against the doorframe, grasping his vest front and smiling at his

T-shirt, leaning her head against his chest and smelling him, listening to his heart race.

Chris reached up and stroked her hair as he had been longing to do for almost three weeks. Sometimes, he was amazed at his own stupidity. How could it be that he had been so attracted to her all along and yet he had not even seemed to know it? How could it possibly work that way?

He did not try to understand it, gave up on guessing and second-guessing, and merely buried his lips in her soft, fragrant smell. God, how he had loved her scent from the very beginning, it having been so much at odds with the image she had tried to project, so fresh and clean and vibrant.

And now it was done, and he did not feel like any more of a man than before; he felt every bit like himself, but with one immense exception; he was, for the first time in his entire life, so excruciatingly glad to be himself, because for whatever crazy reason, Vanessa had chosen him; and if he had been anyone else, he might not have been the one; and the fact that he was the one made his loins tingle and his stomach quiver; it made him want to jump and shout; it made his heart ache for her, even while she stood before him, stoking his excitement, quickening his pulse.

Vanessa eventually lifted her head up to peer at him, toying with his vest-front again and surprising him by blushing.

"I never finished what I was trying to tell you in there, Chris," she began, looking away and inhaling as she then met his gaze again. "I wanted to tell you how sorry I am for everything I've done to you, for hitting you yesterday and for yelling at you and acting just like your ex and, God, for just being such a bitch to you."

Chris was shaking his head, almost in confusion, for what she was mentioning seemed to have taken place years ago, seemed almost not to have happened at all. He opened his mouth to intervene, to stop her tumbling words, words that hurt him because he could see that they were hurting her to speak them, Vanessa's fingers pressing gently to his lips. "You're not a b—"

"Don't interrupt," she insisted, resigned to her task. "I'm sorry I've been so unbelievably mean to you since we first met." She paused, inhaling deeply as she very nearly burst into tears, savagely forcing herself to continue, changing to an equally sincere yet lighter angle. "And I'm sorry I bit the Mohawk head off your gingerbread punk, and I'm sorry I shoved Mr. McClintock's creampuff in your face."

Gaping at her, Chris blinked. "No, you're not," he told her simply and honestly, Vanessa staring back and then snorting in laughter, Chris's lopsided grin self-abasing but genuine as he laughed as well.

Steadying herself, she inhaled deeply and beamed up at him, her eyes moist and bright. "Yeah, you're right. I'm not," she allowed with a touch of her usual spirit, nodding frankly. "I really enjoyed that actually. In fact, I'd like to do that again some time." She smiled crookedly, then shrugging. "But right then, at that point, what I'm trying to say is, you didn't deserve that."

She swallowed, Chris leaning toward her with a confidence he had only just been beginning to feel. "You can smash a hundred creampuffs in my face if you promise to let me kiss you after you're done," he almost whispered to her, Vanessa squeezing her eyes shut and grasping his head, pulling it alongside her own, the two of them standing together like that for a moment.

At length, Vanessa found her voice again, swallowing and speaking softly in his ear. "I know it'll sound like psychobitch bullshit, but there actually is a reason why I treated you so badly," she told him, feeling him tense, about to interject but hesitating; and she knew he was listening intently. "I didn't even realize it myself until the other day. It'll sound completely fucking insane, but I was so mean to you because I wanted you so badly, even just as a friend. And I thought I couldn't have you, figured you wouldn't want to have any kind of connection with me. And the more I wanted to be with you, the meaner I got, 'cause I just...knew that it wasn't gonna happen... I know that's a fucking lame excuse, but if you think about it...it's kind of a good thing... I don't mean a good thing to *do*, I mean a good reason for doing it."

She trailed off, wondering how ludicrous that all sounded, Chris's only response being to draw himself closer to her, as if to comfort her but also as if to enfold himself in the security that her honesty had just now made all the more absolute to him; and sensing

442

this, she fought with all of her years of hardened strength to provide the fortitude for both of them to withstand but also embrace this rush of shared emotions.

Exhaling shakily, she forced herself to continue her ongoing apology, for fear that she would become lost in the depth of the silence that churned so rampantly between them. "So, yeah, I'm sorry for treating you that way, and I'm sorry I called you Insane Clown Pussy and all those other names too."

She felt Chris swallow, blinking when she heard him mumble something in response.

Gently pulling away, she stared at him in surprised wonder. "What?"

Chris stood with his back to the wall and stared shyly at the floor. "I said, I kinda like when you call me some of those names"—he repeated quietly—"like 'Wild Child' and 'Mad Max' and 'Party Animal' and stuff." He looked up at her, shifting awkwardly, a small bashful grin tugging at his mouth. "It makes me feel tough."

Vanessa regarded him as if in awe, then clamping her mouth shut and composing herself. "I thought you already were pretty tough," she retorted, as playfully gruff as she could manage.

"I am," Chris told her, nodding evenly. "Just not as tough as you."

Her lips pressing together tautly, she swallowed again, exhaling harshly through her nose, so determined not to give into her tears. She summoned up her most steadfast resolve and forced a crooked grin, reaching up and fingering the small cut on his lip. "I like your bruise," she said, self-depreciatively shrugging. "It's very punk rock."

He smiled back, holding her gaze. "It matches yours," he replied, lifting his slender fingers and lightly touching her own cut.

"People will say we're such a happy couple," she continued, mock-theatrically.

He nodded, still caressing her cheek. "We remind me so much of that couple from *Fight Club*," he told her, his voice almost dazed.

Vanessa gave him a perplexed grimace. "*Fight Club*?" she repeated incredulously.

"Yeah," he went on, nodding more assertively. "I've been thinking that for a long time, the couple in that movie, you know, who go to all of those meetings and eat doughnuts and like, well...fight sometimes and argue an' stuff."

Vanessa's grimace twisted into a sardonic smile. "Oh great, yeah, that sounds just like us, all right!" she agreed, Chris shrugging a bit sheepishly.

"I dunno," he said at length, his gaze slipping to the floor again. "I actually had thought...somehow...that our group was going to be kind of like that movie."

Her mouth dropping open in gleeful amazement, Vanessa gasped in laughter. "Mis-fits Anonymous like *Fight Club?*" she proposed, tilting her head back in delight and then grabbing his vest again, as she met his somewhat chagrinned eyes. "Oh yeah, right, no shirt, no shoes, you and Father Gilchrist are gonna go the first round!" She grinned wickedly at him, her eyes gleaming, one finger jabbing sharply at his chest. "He is gonna kick your ass!" she informed him triumphantly.

Chris's face melted into a defeated chuckle as he flushed and nodded his head. "Yeah, I know," he conceded self-effacingly, letting his Mohawk hang low.

Vanessa gazed at him, her heart swelling in adoration. Scarcely three weeks ago, she had not known that this person existed, and now... *Now...*

She placed a hand on his cheek. "There's one other thing I forgot to tell you in there, Clodhopper," she now wanted to say, now knowing the words to be true. She lifted his gaze up to meet hers, Chris blinking trustingly at her.

"I love you too," she said simply, thrilling as she saw his features brighten and then seem to glow in the euphoria of this confirmation. He clearly wanted to speak, too slack-jawed to find the words, Vanessa only smiling, her strength returned to her as she reached out and calmed him, rubbing his spiky green mane from front to back, exhaling in weary happiness.

"Yeah, our group is a regular *Fight Club* all right. That's for damned sure. That's what we do best." She paused. "So we're just like that couple, huh?" she stated summarily. "You and me, two screw-up losers trying to survive with Mis-fits Anonymous getting our back, holding hands, and taking on the whole world together, is that it?"

Chris nodded slowly as he looked into her eyes. "Yeah, kinda," he agreed.

Vanessa nodded slowly back. "Cool."

*****

Dr. Pendleton contemplated his reflection in the mirror, very much perplexed. The problem was that he couldn't think of what the problem was. A sip of his fourth—no, fifth—brandy did not seem to assist his thinking any.

The problem was…that there was no problem; that was it! That *was* the problem.

He smiled benevolently at his other self and downed the glassful, excited that he had been able to recall his discovery. Yes, there was no problem! He had started up the therapy group to help people, including himself; and, simply put, they were all winners from that, weren't they?

He had had no intention of discontinuing the group—the very idea was upsetting. To get to know these people who had built up such a level of trust and then send them on their way—most of them with their problems unresolved? He could not possibly do that. It had not been some month-long seminar after all, but an ongoing process that was designed to keep right on going, helping people all the while. The only obstacle to this self-proliferation would be if the members themselves opted to terminate it, which seemed to be the case.

He sighed wistfully, trying a few times to rest his cheek glumly on one fist, his elbow and the bar not cooperating. What had he done so wrong? What kind of good news caused such a catastrophic reaction? He had been a psychologist, had continued to be a psychologist, and now was once again a psychologist, right? Right!

So what was the problem again? Ah, yes, the problem was that there was no problem.

Dr. Whittaker had brought him the news, himself; his license had been renewed. He went to drink from his empty tumbler, the bartender approaching him with a look.

"You want another, or do you prefer yours dry?" he asked briskly.

"My license was renewed!" he informed the bartender with a look of bliss.

The bartender raised his brows. "Is that a fact?" he countered, pausing with the bottle in his hand. "Well, keep it in your wallet, 'cause you've had too many to drive."

Dr. Pendleton chortled coughingly. "N'no, you see, I'm a psychologist," he amended.

Scowling, the bartender leaned one arm on the bar to speak to him eye to eye. "Oh yeah? Well, I don't care if you're Dr. Ruth, just 'cause you're a shrink don't mean you can say, 'Poof,' and hypnotize yourself back into being sober!"

Swallowing a hiccough with a bleary-eyed smile, Dr. Pendleton raised a finger toward the glowering man. "I sense a bit of s'subliminal hot-stility from you, sir," he pronounced sagely. "Do you ever feel like you are somewhat overburdened with the stress of your job?"

His eyes bulging, the bartender lifted his arms, waving his towel at the mostly empty room.

"Well now, I've officially heard it all!" he exclaimed, startling Dr. Pendleton upright. "All these years having to play marriage counselor, matchmaker, AA advisor, debate moderator, referee, and all-around swami to every nutcase that staggers in here looking for a couch trip and now, at long last, in walks a bona fide psychologist looking to hear me out for a change!" He shook his head in disgust. "Where *shall* I begin?"

Dr. Pendleton grimaced his focus upward, having begun to sag again. "I certainly meant no offense," he declared, puffing out an exhalation. "I was merely mentioning the renewal of my psychologist's license."

"Yeah?" the bartender shot back. "Well, you see that frame on the wall?" He pointed in one direction, Dr. Pendleton unwittingly looking in the other. "That's my recently renewed bartender's license! And you know what the only difference between yours and mine is?"

He glared at him heatedly. "Yours lets you peddle bullshit and mine lets me peddle booze!"

Clearing his throat, Dr. Pendleton blinked, then realizing that the man had been shouting something at him. He went to apologize, noticing his empty tumbler and fingering it, his mind then distracting itself all over again. "It really is too bad about Farmington's Drug Store," he said dejectedly. "I had my heart set on one of their grape phosphates."

The bartender put his hands on his hips, shaking his head. "Yeah, well, don't look at me, pal. We don't have any of that kind of foo foo here." He jerked his head to one side. "Your best bet for that is the fern bar up on Ninth."

Blinking wistfully at the bar, Dr. Pendleton nodded. "It doesn't matter," he replied quietly. "I really should be getting back to the group... They'll be wondering where I am... Maybe..." He rested both elbows on the bar and stared at it, crestfallen.

"Yeah, well, remember what I said, pal. You got any car keys, you keep 'em outta sight 'cause I'll take 'em away from you," the bartender told him straightforwardly.

Dr. Pendleton shook his head. "Oh no, you needn't worry. I walked here."

Staring at him incredulously, the bartender shook his head. "All the way from Fenderman Lodge?" he demanded. "That's at least seven miles from here!"

Smiling pleasantly, Dr. Pendleton gestured lightly. "Ah, but I know a shortcut!"

The bartender only scowled. "You know a shortcut, eh? Yeah, well, I hope you know another shortcut, to either the drunk tank or the nuthouse, 'cause either one'll sign you up."

Flinching, Dr. Pendleton shook his head almost pleadingly. "You really mustn't call them 'nuthouses'!" he chastised the bartender. "They are Institutions for Psychologically Maladapted Individuals."

Glaring at him, the bartender tossed aside his towel. "Awright, *Frazier*, I've heard enough toasted shrink speak for one night! I don't know what your problem is, but we've got enough around here already, so settle up and saddle up 'cause there's the shortcut to the door!"

Dr. Pendleton nodded, sort of falling off the stool and onto his feet, reaching for his wallet, slowly withdrawing a bill and handing it to the bartender, lifting one finger demonstratively.

"But that was just it, sir!" he proclaimed insightfully. "The problem was that there is no problem!" He nodded at the profound clarity.

The bartender paused over the drawer of the cash register. "Then why did you come in here in the first place?" he asked grudgingly.

Dr. Pendleton nodded all over again, hiccoughing. "Exactly!"

Sighing, the bartender stepped back to the bar with a few singles. "Yeah, 'exactly,'" he concurred irritably. "Here's your change, Doc."

"Oh no, no, no," Dr. Pendleton beamed at him, gesturing openly. "Please keep that as a 'thank you' for helping me put things in perspective! Consider it a tip!"

The bartender slouched his arms on the bar and merely stared at him. "Sure, thanks," he returned grumpily. "And consider this a tip too—as a bartender, I have to lay off the sauce, but that doesn't mean that a shrink can't go and get his own head examined, ya' read me? At the very least, you should go and join one of those sob-story therapy groups!"

Chapter 15

As Vanessa and Chris made their way down the hall, they moved quietly past the door to her room in case the others had gone to bed, Vanessa then pausing at the ajar door to the first room, peering into it and inducing Chris to stop as well. "Look."

"What is it?" he whispered back as Vanessa led him into the room, pushing the door open so that a narrow chasm of light was cast upon the inert form of Father Gilchrist, lying flat on his bed, his hands clasped across his chest, head resting deeply in the pillow. They paused at the side of his bed and looked down at him, Chris shifting uncomfortably, Vanessa releasing his hand.

"Look at him," she said softly, watching his still frame scarcely move with his shallow breathing, her eyes travelling from his white hair to his polished shoes, his jowls flush against the formal clerical collar, the lapels of his jacket neatly meeting beneath his large, spotted hands. "That's exactly how he'll look when he's in his coffin."

Chris gasped, Vanessa instantly grabbing his hand again. "No, I'm not saying that to be mean, Chris. I swear." She glanced away from the prone figure and met Chris's bewildered eyes in the dim light. "It's just a fact. I've had to see just about everyone I've ever loved laid out like that."

Blinking uncertainly at her, Chris followed her gaze as it returned to the sleeping form before them. "That's why you've got to look at the people you care about, while you can, while they're still around, especially when they don't know you're looking at them, like when they're driving or reading a newspaper or sleeping... That's when you can see them the way they really are, without any words or bullshit getting in the way, you know?"

She silently knelt down, Chris hesitantly joining her, staring anxiously at the old priest, terrified that he would awaken and become enraged at their invasiveness, yet slowly becoming fascinated with what Vanessa was telling him, his youthful face soon gaping in awe.

"Look at him," she repeated, almost inaudibly. "He can be such a bastard. But he's really just a sad, tired, lonely old man." She extended a hand toward his relaxed yet dignified features, his wintry eyebrows unfurrowed and reposed, not daring to lay a hand upon him, merely permitting her fingers to hover above his face. "He's almost as old as Mrs. Spindlewood, and he's been alone almost all of his life too. He has some of the same pain in his face as she does."

They regarded the aged priest a bit longer and then quietly rose to their feet, stealthily backtracking out of the room and closing the door behind them, Vanessa turning to look up at Chris, grateful to see his expression of sad comprehension, knowing that he understood what she had wanted to show him. Instinctually, she wanted to ask, wanted to make sure, her need to know that he knew overriding her fledgling trust, but she forced herself to remain silent as she met his eyes, instead wordlessly reenforcing her meaning by taking his hand yet again and holding it up to demonstrate its intertwining bond with her own, squeezing it forcefully, nodding ever so slightly.

Chris nodded slowly, unflinchingly back, and then kissed her hand gently, and she knew for certain.

United as such, they rounded the corner of the hall and passed the kitchen doorway, startling Mr. McClintock, who had just been headed into the sunken area, one hand clutching a plate bearing a heavily fortified sandwich ringed with a number of s'mores, the other clasping a glass of milk.

"Oh hello, children," he greeted them, flushing awkwardly, Vanessa and Chris at first only able to stare back at him, for he was clad in an immense pair of gray pajamas, the tops of which were so copiously flowing and low-hemmed that they might have been a raincoat fashioned out of a parachute, the bottoms so wide-legged that they resembled a twin set of shower curtains, his improportionately small feet tucked neatly into a tiny pair of house slippers.

His entire tall frame seemed to billow before them, filling the doorway as he gave them an embarrassed smile.

"I...that is, we didn't end up having our barbecue, it would seem. And so I thought I would just have a little...premidnight snack," he explained, pausing and then lifting his thick eyebrows. "Would you like for me to fix you anything to eat?" he offered, his tone affably hopeful.

They both returned his smile, Vanessa shaking her head, Chris politely following suit. "No thank you, Mr. McClintock. We just wanted to come out here and hang out, if that's okay," she told him, grinning as he nodded vigorously and then patting his arm with affection. "Thanks, though. You're really sweet."

"Yeah, thanks, Mr. McClintock," Chris added, his Mohawk bobbing up and down.

They left him to his snack, beaming after them, and wandered out into the spacious, tiled entryway, Chris looking expectantly to Vanessa, who glanced past a corner into the den at Mr. Crimpton, his sphinxlike consternation now centered around what appeared to be an infomercial for some form of solar-powered lawnmower.

Rolling her eyes, she turned to a cabinet arranged to one side of the entryway, opening it to reveal a stereo system and a few shelves of phonograph albums, Chris stepping forward with interest, kneeling and flipping through a few, Vanessa then startling him with a gasp and darting back toward the hallway.

She returned a moment later with his backpack, her face flushed with excitement as she set it down and then moved over to the easy chair in the sunken area, pausing to tug at it and then giving him an impatient look. "Well? Get over here and help me!"

Gawking at her, he quickly helped her to lift the chair up onto the tiled area and pivot it around so that it was facing them, Vanessa then plopping down into it and grabbing his backpack, Chris watching in wonder as she dug into it and pulled out his compact disk player and a small, vinyl case, thrusting them into his hands and grinning up at him expectantly.

When Chris merely stood there, gaping at her, she sighed in mock exasperation, gesturing sharply. "Come on, killer. I know you must have brought along some hardcore tunes with you!" she declared, folding her arms and jutting her chin toward him challengingly. "I wanna see it for myself, here and now. I wanna see this funky-punk polka combo you've got going on and find out if you really are for real!"

Chris's jaw fell open even wider as he began to blush, shifting uncomfortably in front of her. "Oh no, I mean, like...h*ere*? Right now?" He shook his head, grinning shyly.

Vanessa sat up. "Yeah, right here, right now!" she shot back sharply. "We're stuck out here aren't we? What else is there to do? Besides, I've been dying to see this."

Biting his lip, he glanced around the lodge, grimacing weakly, his shoulders slack. "Yeah, but what if everyone else comes out to watch too?" he countered plaintively.

Now gaping back at him, Vanessa lifted her hands openly. "Well, so what if they do?" she scoffed. "That's the whole point, ain't it? And they're all members of the group, right? All they'd do is shrug and say, 'Business as usual in the nuthouse,' and that's it. So what's the problem? You got nothing to be scared of!"

She watched him stare uncertainly back at her and could almost see his heart beating indecisively. She leaned forward, now speaking earnestly. "Look, Chris, all that stuff I told you in your room was true. I wasn't just telling you what you wanted to hear. I did think that it was weird, and I didn't totally understand it—and neither did you—if I'm remembering correctly." She stabbed a finger toward him pointedly. "But I *did* think it was really cool, and now, I actually do understand it!" She nodded smugly, Chris regarding her in wide-eyed amazement. "I mean you don't spend a whole night completely pissed off at someone without thinking about that person, right? Well, I figured it out!"

She shrugged, Chris motionless now, his focus rapt as she looked at him with blazing eyes. "It's all about 'fuck you,' Chris," she explained simply. "I know that you've got to at least know that punk rock, by definition, is all...counterculture and future shock and straight-up, in your face, nonconformity! Well, Clod, that's you. You are all that, but to a way more awesome extreme! Everything you've told me about how all of this makes you feel can only mean that you are a *true*, fucking counterrevolutionary, Anti-Establishment Poster Boy Wild Child! And trust me, if *any*body tries to tell you that you can't be a genuine punk rocker and mosh to polkas because you're only supposed to listen to a certain kind of music or be a certain way, you just ask them who's the real punk and who's the real conformer. And if they still give you shit, then they'll know you're real deal when you give them this right back."

She gestured with her middle fingers now, slowly and meaning-fully. "It's all about 'fuck you,'" she repeated, gradually shaking her head at him. "I'm telling you, Thrasher, it doesn't get any more punk rock than that."

His face lost in astonishment, Chris could only stare at her as she leaned forward and plucked at the hem of his T-shirt apprais-ingly, then sitting back in the chair and letting her hands fall upon its armrests. "You put that shirt on for me today, Chris," she told him simply. "Let's see if it really does go with your outfit."

She regarded him expectantly, and when he hesitated for only one second more, she gave him a scornful look. "Come on, *Stud Stomper*, I wanna see you work it, *now*. So either trot out the clod-hopper or sit your wannabe poser-ass down!"

Chris's mouth clamped shut, his eyes alighting with a gleam of their own, his jaw becoming taut; and she knew she had him. "Come on, Polka Boy! Either rock out or wuss out!"

He turned and stomped over to the stereo, fumbling with a con-verter-cassette and then rifling through the vinyl case, his expression set and determined, almost angry, Vanessa sitting up in excitement.

"All right, Clodhopper," she crowed, clapping boisterously, thrilling as his face became a mottled red of embarrassed pride, overjoyed that she had forced him so squirmingly to assert himself. "Remember, Champ, this is a command performance for your new Queen B. So pick your most favorite song of all and then work that punk ass for me!"

Beaming at his now dangerously flushed features and deadly expression, she sat up so that she was kneeling in the chair, watching in eager suspense as he inserted a disc, jabbed at a few buttons, and jerked the stereo volume up by several settings, then hesitating and moving it back, then flexing his jaw, static sizzling as he yanked it right back to his original choice, pausing one final time, and then pressing the play button.

He clomped back into the center of the entryway, avoiding her anxious gaze, eyes locked on the floor, breathing tensely; and the music suddenly burst forth in an archaic, shuddery series of dazzling accordion riffs, the staccato intensity rebounding back at them from within the vaulted A-frame as Chris abruptly began to dance.

Vanessa's mouth flew open now as she beheld him throw himself into a series of movements so incredibly unforeseeable as to be mind-blowing. His large boots pounded heavily but gracefully against the tiles as his slender body twisted lithely to this unlikely choice of music, his thin arms and legs contorting and weaving fluidly but also spastically, his green Mohawk slicing at the air as his head bobbed backward and forward in violent intensity. His motions, while not seeming merely sporadic but completely unbound, were nevertheless in perfect coordination with the simple but throbbing polka beat.

Each step, each turn, each gyration and pivoting, vicious kick of his legs, was synchronized with the blaring song, his frenzied, rhythmic convulsions somehow impossibly uniting this boxy folk music with the pure anarchy of the mosh pit in a wildly unrestrained exhibition of definitive if discordant harmony.

Vanessa watched in gasps of astounded laughter, her face clutched in her hands as she gaped at this, her unchained warrior, knowing that whereas she had been the one to let him off his leash and goad him into this virtual metamorphosis, all that she was now witnessing had been his alone for her to coax out and discover; and her amazement was marked by both pride and speechless appreciation for her own good fortune.

Elsewhere in the lodge, the sheer explosiveness of the dancing was overheard, Mr. Crimpton's head spinning with whiplash velocity as he was startled out of his chair and came stumbling forward to stare in outraged disbelief. Mr. McClintock had reappeared, pausing in midbite as he looked on in awe.

Back in her bunk bed, Judge Talbott was jarred awake, her murder mystery book tumbling off her chest; and she hastened forth from her room to investigate, while next door, Father Gilchrist's eyes flew open in disoriented uncertainty, his confusion mixed with outrage, as he too climbed to his feet and came striding out into the main area, blinking in the light even as his scowl focused upon the sight before him.

Aware of the gathering audience, Vanessa only felt her pride continue to swell as she cheered Chris on, unable to sit still in the chair as she called to him and unwilling to intervene, for Chris was now out of control.

"Go, Clodhopper! Work that punk ass for me!"

Through it all, the polka still hammering crazily at them, Chris continued to pitch and jump, his movements becoming still more erratic and more interlaced with the melody, his eyes squeezed shut, not in embarrassment, nor in concentration, but in what looked to be a trancelike embodiment of the music he adored as it embraced and absorbed him, ultimately manifesting itself through him in this insanely incongruous amalgamation of bygone dance music and neopunk adrenaline, forming an iconoclastic dynamic of frustrated anachronism, of stylishly storming thrashing and stomping, a rebel yell of defiant rage.

The song soared toward its conclusion with impending momentum, Chris likewise undertaking a feverish upswing of manic, ritualistic devotion, entering into one final sequence of tribal, head-banging ferocity, before the song's finale engulfed him, propelling him across the tile floor and partway up the far wall into a complete backflip, his boot soles slamming down upon the floor with a thunderous grace, his form tensed and still, his landing perfectly coinciding with the ending of the song, punctuating its last note with pistol-shot precision.

There was a stunned silence, Chris's eyes opening as a ragtag but sincere burst of applause ensued, the older members impressed, grudgingly or otherwise, Vanessa leaping from her chair and embracing Chris, who flushed crimson and blushed shyly over her shoulder, panting heavily as Vanessa hugged him close, then brusquely clutching his jaw.

"You rock, Polka Punk," she told him happily, laughing all over again. "You're the genuine article, Clodhopper, just like I thought. You're my champion."

Chris, overwhelmed by the appearance of the others, as well as their response, nonetheless, gaped down at her; and she could sense his longing relief at her approval.

"That was amazing, Claude!" Judge Talbott called, still clapping excitedly.

"Yes, I've not heard the 'Tiger Rag' in close to forty years," Father Gilchrist declared, smiling sourly but not unkindly, Chris glancing at him in grateful surprise at his recognition of his favorite song, impressed that someone, that anyone else, would share this knowledge about that which was so special to him.

"Well, hearing it just now took forty years off my life," Mr. Crimpton had stopped applauding to gripe. "It's fine and all for you kids to be having fun, but isn't it a bit late for you two to be partying?"

Chris wilted a bit guiltily, Vanessa glaring over at him. "Oh, come on," she chided, "Were you really all that into watching them demonstrate the 'Solar Mower 9000'?"

Mr. Crimpton grimaced back, as Father Gilchrist folded his arms. "Well, I was into three-quarters of a coma before *Your Hit Parade* came marching into my brain!" he proclaimed, more to the driving examiner than to Chris, who shifted meekly anyway.

"I suppose I must have dozed off too," Judge Talbott reflected.

"Well, jeez!" Vanessa exclaimed impatiently. "It's Saturday night, and we're on a weekend getaway! And on top of that, it's really not all that late!"

"Well, that doesn't mean you have to raise the roof!" Mr. Crimpton lectured.

"We may have no choice," observed Father Gilchrist archly. "If we wish to make a corresponding boot print on the ceiling to match the one on the wall."

Chris gawked over at the far wall, wincing at the impression he had made on it as Vanessa waved at it dismissively.

"The whole idea to coming out to this place was to relax and have fun, wasn't it?" she challenged them hotly.

"'And have fun'?" Mr. Crimpton echoed, as if it were a foreign concept.

Mr. McClintock stepped forward, his plate down to two remaining s'mores. "It was a very, uh, arresting performance," he offered diplomatically.

Father Gilchrist glanced and then openly stared at him, having not noticed him up until now. *Good God, and if only Groucho Marx could be here to see this, it would settle once and for all his question of elephants and pajamas.*

"Cardiac arrest is more like it," snapped Mr. Crimpton, fingering one temple. "How can you possibly call blaring that gypsy music 'relaxing'?"

Vanessa gasped at him. "If a hardcore *punk* can enjoy listening to polkas, then I'm pretty damn sure all of you can too," she charged flippantly.

"Only when I'm trying to get rid of a migraine," Father Gilchrist told her sweetly.

Judge Talbott blinked. "Has anyone seen Dr. Pendleton?" she inquired suddenly.

"No, but if he were here, I'll bet he'd be fine with us playing some music," Vanessa responded decisively.

"Wait a minute, he's not back yet?" Mr. Crimpton asked warily, his features freezing.

"It wouldn't appear so," Mr. McClintock noted, glancing about the room.

"I was wondering earlier where he had gone," Judge Talbott explained nervously.

"You think he just went off and left us here?" Mr. Crimpton demanded, becoming even more agitated.

"He wouldn't have done that!" Vanessa interjected disparagingly.

"I should hope not," Father Gilchrist declared. "I doubt very much that I will ever find myself in a more ideal setting in which to tell him to go jump in the lake."

"The van's still here," Chris volunteered from a front window, anxious to be helpful.

"You don't think he went swimming, do you?" Judge Talbott asked doubtfully.

"Why would a psychologist go swimming?" Mr. Crimpton scoffed abstractly.

"Obviously to assist salmon to get in touch with their inner spawn," said Father Gilchrist.

"I wonder if he knows how to swim," fretted Judge Talbott.

"Oh, I'm sure he does," spoke up Mr. McClintock. "Don't psychologists *have* to know how to swim?"

"Licensed ones do," sniffed the priest.

"Look, no one knows this area better than the Doc, so I'm sure he's fine," Vanessa spoke up impatiently. "He just went out to clear his mind and think and probably to just get away from all of us for a while—I *wonder* why?" She rolled her eyes. "Anyway, since we came all the way out here, I don't see why we can't just enjoy ourselves. I mean we might as well!"

Judge Talbott nodded, albeit uncertainly. "Well, what did you have in mind?"

Mr. McClintock's ears perked up, a suggestion reoccurring to him.

Vanessa gestured in exasperation toward the stereo. "Let's just cut loose and listen to some more music!" she almost yelled, Chris darting out of her way as she stalked over to the shelf of albums. "There has *got* to be some kind of music here that you'd actually like to listen to!"

Father Gilchrist smiled. "How about a nice funeral dirge?"

Mr. Crimpton, now down to his last cigarette, stared at her with it dangling from his lips. "Who says we want to listen to any music *at all?*" he asked, flabbergasted.

"That does it! Chris!" Vanessa knelt down and began to shove at the albums in anger, Chris hurrying to crouch beside her in uncertainty. "Help me find the oldest most crustiest damn record in here!" she ordered, then seizing one with a faded, dilapidated jacket, yanking out the scarred album, and then pausing before shoving it at

Chris, recalling even in her anger that she didn't know how to work a record player.

"There!" she pronounced to the others, as Chris placed the needle on the decrepit album, a skin-crawling series of skittering scratches sizzling sharply out at them, the older members staring at her in bewilderment as a mournful rendering of Glenn Miller's "Moonlight Serenade" began to waft hazily from the speakers and throughout the lodge.

"How's that?" she challenged them above the slowly meandering melody.

The cigarette quivered in Mr. Crimpton's lips as he glowered, Judge Talbott and Mr. McClintock exchanging hapless glances, Chris visibly impressed with the selection.

"Why, it's lovely," Father Gilchrist commended her. "It puts one in mind of those halcyon, bygone days of Pearl Harbor and the Holocaust."

A virtual standoff ensued as Vanessa positioned herself in front of the stereo and folded her arms in defiance, clearly daring anyone to try and so much as adjust the volume, her wild-eyed vigilance flinching and then dissolving as she glimpsed something behind the others, Chris's mouth falling open.

As the others turned in confusion, Mr. McClintock hastily moving to one side, Mrs. Spindlewood appeared among them, her nightgown giving her obscured steps a ghostly effect as she seemed to float forward, her head uplifted and her face, for the very first time in their company, animated and alert, her eyes bright and searching.

"Edward," her tiny voice seemed to cry out even amidst the deafening music, as she wandered forward, her intensely unseeing gaze tilting around the room and then settling on Father Gilchrist. "Edward," she called again, moving toward him.

As the others watched, speechless, Father Gilchrist glanced from them to the approaching figure, backing against the easy chair as he moved to retreat, his face crumpling pensively.

"Edward," Mrs. Spindlewood declared joyously, reaching out to him.

"I'm not Edward. I'm Mr. Dembrough, don't you remember?" Father Gilchrist informed her desperately, even as she embraced him, placing her head against his chest and closing her eyes, her little face frozen in a dazed smile.

As Father Gilchrist lowered his arms in defeat, his features pinched in painful reluctance, Mrs. Spindlewood feebly clutched one of his hands, lifting it as she wrapped her arm around the back of his jacket, assuming a dance pose, the grimacing priest grudgingly upholding the stance and gradually moving with her as they began a slow, faltering waltz upon the tiled floor to the melancholic strains of the song.

They watched, motionless, as the ramrod form of the old clergyman enabled the frail tottering steps of the little old woman, her hair hanging limply as she held her face to his chest, her expression dreamy and at peace, the hem of her nightgown scarcely fluttering as she moved in the small circles of a box step.

Mr. Crimpton gaped at them, his cigarette almost touching his chin, Judge Talbott's tears slipping down her cheeks to border her quivering smile. Mr. McClintock's plate sat aside, untouched, as he watched in respectful awe.

Vanessa stared at them in wonder, her hands clasped to her mouth as her own tears began to spill over, sniffling as her heart melted in both love and remorse at this tragically beautiful sight, Mrs. Spindlewood's ephemeral China doll features blissfully lost, Father Gilchrist's visage locked in a stoic, statue-like pose of unshiftingly resigned endurance, his mouth an invisible line, his eyes also unseeing as they gazed fixedly beyond their surroundings. Vanessa managed to glance up at Chris, seeing that his eyes too were red-rimmed and moist and loving him all the more for his being a boy who was unwilling, possibly even unable to hide his emotions. She found his hand and was overwhelmed with relief when he immediately enfolded her in his arms from behind, the only sound in the world seeming to be that of the haunting, wailing melody, its brittle, crackling recording indoctrinating the timelessness of the moment with solemn, ethereal reality.

The song ended in a shimmering, evaporating fanfare, Chris quietly lifting the needle as Father Gilchrist guided Mrs. Spindlewood to the adjacent easy chair, gently easing her into it, a muffled noise stifled in his throat as he was forced to bend down on one knee to accommodate her, the old woman showing no sign of abandonment or upset as she reopened her eyes, her smile still weakly radiant, her look one of serenity.

"Oh, Edward," she sighed, already seeing past Father Gilchrist as she resumed her familiar stance, the aged priest climbing unsteadily to his feet and then standing up straight, glaring around at the others, taking in their sorrowful expressions with a scowl.

"Well," he stated briskly, his voice cracking hoarsely, forcing him to harrumph in annoyance, shaking his head sharply, and continuing to glower at the others. "It would seem they were playing our song." He gave Chris a withering look. "So what other bouts of musical mayhem have you in store for us?" he snapped acidically.

Vanessa pulled away from Chris and approached the priest, staring up at him with swollen eyes as she stood before him, her arms shifting tentatively, as if she wanted to hug him but did not dare. "That was so sweet for you to do."

Father Gilchrist regarded her with pursed lips. "Yes, not bad for a rotten, mean old bastard, now, was it?" he mused.

Her smile blossoming as she gasped in affection, Vanessa put her arms around him, kissing him quickly on the cheek.

"Well! Really, I—" he sputtered, his voice catching as she did so, his return of her embrace warm and close as she felt him give into a tired, capitulative sigh.

Judge Talbott continued to sniffle, her hands fretting fussily as she looked about for a box of Kleenex, Mr. McClintock, always prepared, producing a handkerchief from his pajama pocket.

As Vanessa gently pulled away from Father Gilchrist to hug Mrs. Spindlewood, Mr. Crimpton, having lost sight of his cigarette, inadvertently stepped on it in his search, grimacing in aggravation at the smashed result. "Son of a—"

"Here," Father Gilchrist intervened, reaching within his jacket and producing his omnipresent package of cigarettes. "Keep the pack. I'm trying to cut back."

Staring skeptically at him, Mr. Crimpton hesitated. "You sure?"

"Of course," smiled the priest. What use had he for a twenty-year-old package of cigarettes?

"Thanks," Mr. Crimpton murmured, somewhat appreciatively, then pausing in removing one. "Look, folks, I hate to bust up the party, but we still haven't settled what we were talking about a few minutes ago," he pointed out guardedly.

Judge Talbott dabbed at her eyes. "What was that?"

He gestured slackly. "We still don't know where Dr. Pendleton went."

"And how exactly is that a problem?" inquired Father Gilchrist wryly.

"He is out rather late," Mr. McClintock observed, taking up his plate again.

"He couldn't have gone too far," Chris pointed out. "Like I said, the van is still here."

"I'm sure he'll at least be back by morning," Vanessa put in wearily, standing upright from embracing Mrs. Spindlewood.

"By *morning?*" echoed Mr. Crimpton, tugging at the stubborn plastic covering the packet of cigarettes.

"But why would he stay out all night?" Judge Talbott asked, now disconcerted once more.

"Perhaps he's a werewolf," Father Gilchrist hypothesized, Vanessa giving him a look.

Chris glanced out the window. "Yeah, but it's not a full moon tonight," he frowned, Vanessa giving him and then the ceiling a look.

Sighing in exasperation, Mr. Crimpton managed to wrench one of the cigarettes free. "Look, what if he's *not* back by morning?" he demanded. "Or noon or even night? We could be stuck here having this same conversation, this time tomorrow night!"

"Hey, he did say it was for the whole weekend," Vanessa shrugged indifferently.

"Well, do you think we should go looking for him?" Chris asked uncertainly.

"But how can we, if we don't know where he went?" reasoned Mr. McClintock.

"He probably went to have himself committed," Father Gilchrist surmised. "Again."

"We can't even take that heap and go driving around looking for him!" Mr. Crimpton declared despondently. "I mean he took the keys with him, for Christ's sake! That means we really are stranded here!"

"Well, you can always hotwire it if he's not back by tomorrow night, can't you?" asked Vanessa irritably. Man, these people could always keep her in a good mood.

"I'm a driving examiner, not a repo man!" Mr. Crimpton snapped back, his brows then lifting defensively. "Although I'm under just as much pressure!"

"I certainly *hope* he's back by tomorrow night," Judge Talbott stated worriedly. "I promised the other public defenders I would be in early Monday morning to help with an affidavit..." She gasped. "And I have to feed my cats!"

"I should be back at the church by then, at the very latest," Father Gilchrist mused. "It will give me time to rehearse my amnesia routine."

"Well, I *have* to be back by tomorrow night," Chris spoke up earnestly. "I told my mom and dad I'd be back home by dinnertime."

Vanessa took his hand. "Chris, honey, you have so much to learn," she told him sadly.

Mr. McClintock ate one of the s'mores somewhat morosely. He did not have to be anywhere Monday morning.

Mr. Crimpton sighed through his nose. Not being back in time to go to work was not even remotely unappealing to him. Yet being stranded here, with these nuts, did not seem much better. He thought fleetingly of those bottles of beer and then winced, gesturing swipingly at the others.

"All right, so basically, we are probably looking at, at the very least, being stuck out here for another twenty-four hours?" he demanded conclusively.

"Such is eternity," clucked Father Gilchrist.

Vanessa went to roll her eyes, then gasping insightfully. "Holy shit!"

Father Gilchrist turned to her. "Wouldn't that be for me to say?" he inquired with one eyebrow.

The others watched in confusion as she grabbed Chris and pulled him over to the stereo, locating his disk case and quickly flipping through it.

"Chris, you've shown every one that you're a real-deal punk rocker," she told him briskly. "But let's see how much you really kick ass!"

Chris gaped at her as she tore through the plastic sleeves, at last finding a disc that she clutched to her chest, spinning around.

"Yes!" she shrieked, giving him a look of fierce affection as she inserted this other disc into the player, setting it to start and then swiftly pausing it, beaming mischievously at the others.

"Chris, you rock," she told him succinctly, grinning at the older people. "If we're gonna be stuck here another day, then I've got a way to kill at least the next few minutes!"

She nodded boldly, hands on her hips, jerking her chin toward the stereo. "Here's the deal—I guarantee you that if you all just listen to the first part of this song, the words will be so perfect for all of us that I'll bet you'll all dance to it!"

Father Gilchrist laughed abruptly. "What is it, a tarantella?"

"You think we're going to want to dance to a *punk rock* song?" Mr. Crimpton confirmed incredulously.

"Once you hear the words, you'll be obliged," Vanessa told him with a flippant smile. "After all, Stan, my man, you're the one who called it, if we're going to be stuck here twenty-four more hours…"

As Mr. Crimpton grimaced at her familiarity, Chris gestured eagerly, trying to think of what it was that Vanessa had found among his music that could possibly be so compelling.

"What song is it, Vanessa?" he asked her, gaping in suspense.

"Clod, you punk," she told him, smiling crookedly as she gave his face a light, invigorating slap and then pointing at him in charged excitement. "Trust me—this song is going to be the fucking Mis-fits Anonymous anthem!"

With that, she pushed the play button.

There was one braced moment of silence and then a pounding, upbeat rhythm began pulsating from the speakers, booming throughout the lodge, Vanessa's grin crazed now, Chris gasping in delighted recognition as the older members stared in baffled, displaced curiosity, each one tensed and listening expectantly as a flatly dulcet voice launched into the Ramones hit, "I Wanna Be Sedated":

Twenty-Twenty-Twenty-Four Hours to go;
I wanna be sedated.
Nothin' to do, Nowhere to go;
I wanna be sedated.
Just get me to the airport,
Put me on a plane;
Hurry-Hurry-Hurry-Before I go insane!
I can't control my fingers,
I can't control my brain,
Oh, No, Oh, Oh, Oh, Oh!

The brash rhythm reasserted itself in an interlude, picking up more intensity as Vanessa, having been dancing since the onset, gazed at all of them, sweeping her hair back from her face, a few strands remaining wildly out of place as her eyes shone vividly.

"Well?" she shouted challengingly, throwing her arms up into the air. "Try to tell me that *that* is not us!"

When her question was only met with motionless stares, even Chris merely standing there, she waved her arms in frustration.

"*Come on*, you guys!" she screeched. "This song was practically made for this moment! If we're all really as psycho as we're s'pose to be, what've we got to lose? Let's go! How many chances do you get like this where everyone can just say 'fuck it' and go crazy?"

There was one more instant of intolerable indecisiveness, Vanessa resolutely taking control as the song rocketed onward. She turned and jabbed a finger at Chris.

"Clod, get hopping!" she commanded, then taking the others one at a time, determined not merely to bridge the generation gap, but to toss it aside altogether, truly believing that their united, common denominator transcended such restrictions.

"Come on, Judge!" she urged incitingly. "Show us the verdict!"

Judge Talbott stared back in surprise, glancing quickly at the others, wringing her hands. "Well, I guess it does seem appropriate for our situation," she allowed.

Vanessa gently tugged her forward. "Well, let's go then!"

Not knowing what else to do, Judge Talbott flushed and sort of gave herself over to the beat, timidly but with nimble grace, Chris gawking in admiration as he clomped and pivoted alongside her.

"All right, Judge!" Vanessa cheered. "Work it, Aretha, work it!"

As the judge flushed all the more, her momentum increasing, the others watching in disbelief, Mr. Crimpton's scrutiny was distracted as Vanessa grabbed his arm and yanked him almost trippingly forward.

"All right, Mr. C.!" she proclaimed exuberantly. "You've heard the words! You know they're for real, so let's get with it! I wanna be sedated!" She tossed her hair back, wildly thrash dancing in front of him, Mr. Crimpton glaring in outrage, his new cigarette dangling, his nerves stoked to the point of a breakdown. He had no intention of dancing, yet seemed to have no choice either, as Vanessa clutched his hands and dragged him into an imbalanced, stiffly offbeat cadence against his will.

"All right, all right!" he relented, smiling in spite of his exasperation as beside him, Judge Talbott was trying to resurrect what she could remember from her disco years, her moves incompatibly perfect for this song and her smile genuine. Mr. Crimpton reluctantly gave over to a rigid interpretation of the 'Twist,' the two anachronistically complementing each other, Vanessa whooping in approval.

She darted over to Mr. McClintock, who, having been enjoying the spectacle while finishing his last s'more, glanced at her blankly and then in mounting panic as she seized one of his arms and tugged him forward. Surely, she didn't think—

"Okay, Mr. McClintock, now it's your turn!" she informed him, shoving Chris out of the way to give him plenty of room.

"I'm not especially agile…," he had been stammering and then gazing at the expectant, excitedly grinning kids as they pitched and tilted encouragingly.

Simply not able to disappoint them and not knowing what else to do, he began to sway to the beat, his incredible girth rotating in massive gyrations, his pajamas billowing neatly as his tiny feet dared to pivot in a tidy little jig, his movements akin to spinning a Hula-Hoop, not, he suspected, that he could ever get one to encircle himself.

Vanessa almost crumpled in joy at this sight, Chris's young face euphoric as he matched the enormous gourmand's style.

Father Gilchrist took in all of this with a look of utter, almost maddened, awe. If bedlam was the order of the day, clearly they had all arrived.

"It's all on you, now, Padre!" Vanessa announced, startling him as she grabbed his arm and pulled him forward, the old priest resisting as he found himself plunged into the midst of this virtually schizophrenic dance, his features instantly shriveling.

"One dance per night is sufficient for me, thank you!" he told her, his words lost in the chaos, Vanessa refusing to let go, the scowling old clergyman then considering how little he had to lose and how little he cared anymore. Why not make his *Lost Weekend* complete?

Glaring imperiously, he gently retracted his arms and began an improvised dance of his own, managing to be liturgical and spontaneous as he countered her moves with stodgy, stiff-jointed motions, a wisp of a smile haunting his face as Vanessa beamed proudly up at him.

The song thundered onward, the laconic voice continuing to belt out the words that had engendered this particular selection with its perfect appeal for them, the refrain booming overhead of this unlikely spectacle that so flawlessly portrayed its essence.

"I wanna be sedated" is right, Mr. Crimpton reflected in his ongoing disbelief that he was actually dancing, Judge Talbott's face alight as she continued to boogie. Vanessa, having made her way

back to Chris, just as quickly darted away from him, dashing over to Mrs. Spindlewood, the old woman still sitting but participating anyway, her tiny hands clapping on her knees, her little face aglow as she childishly kept time.

Vanessa knelt down before her, wanting to take her by the shoulders and shake her in joy, instead lightly kissing her forehead and stroking her hair, peering lovingly at her before throwing herself back into the mix with an even more heightened ferocity.

She grabbed Chris by his vest front, pressing up close to him and then pushing him away, placing herself before Mr. McClintock, just as his energy was beginning to diminish. He beamed down at her, purposefully willing up one more wobbling rotation, clapping his hands, and then executing a conclusive little quick step, maneuvering his bulk in an impossibly nimble turn, his tremendous form sailing neatly backward into the entryway bench, where he exhaled in heady satisfaction, wondering if he might actually have begun to perspire, distracted as Vanessa almost jumped into his lap, gathering up his rolling corpulence in her arms and hugging him, her head on his shoulder for a blissful moment before she kissed his glowing cheek and leapt back into the dance, clutching at Chris's vest again, thrusting her face up toward his expectantly, Chris leaning into kiss her as she lifted one hand to his forehead and shoved him away, grinning deviously at his chagrin. She then grappled with Father Gilchrist again, the aged priest obliging her with a semblance of a waltz, which she accepted, converting it to a punk rock interpretation, Father Gilchrist patiently indulging her. Wheeling to and fro, she continually shot teasing looks toward Chris, who watched with his mouth clamped in a twisted expression of jealous humility, his shining eyes locked on hers as he contemplated how this was exactly how Candy treated him on the dance floor, with one profound difference, that being that he loved it this time, savoring it as he stomped and thrashed.

"This is it!" Vanessa called out as the song hurtled to its finale, the motley dancers reinvigorated to see it through to its close in style, Mr. Crimpton and his cigarette still twisting with determination as Judge Talbott cheered girlishly to the "Hustle," Mr. McClintock heaving himself upright not wanting to be a killjoy and dancing in place, rotating gelatinously, Mrs. Spindlewood's tiny hands still clapping, her little house slippers still bobbing up and down to the spiraling crescendo, Vanessa taking in everyone in one last ecstatic glance, half-dancing with Father Gilchrist and beckoning with her free hand to Chris, who audaciously resisted, romping freely off on his own with a look of such recalcitrant defiance that Vanessa almost screamed, stabbing commandingly at the floor beside her, Chris then leisurely trotting over to her like a languidly obedient colt, forced to drop his act as Vanessa seized him in a headlock, dancing with him like that as the song swelled and pitched toward it close, the final lyric drawing out in strained intensity, Vanessa freeing Chris so that she could jump into his arms as it ended, her champion gladly catching her as they all froze in a perfect tableau of united, unleashed, beautiful madness, each person then remaining motionless, the magic of what they had shared diverted as, one by one, they took notice of the reappearance of Dr. Pendleton.

He stood in the doorway, gaping at them with an expression of utterly enlightened bliss on his remarkably florid features, his booted feet firmly planted, even as his body swayed slightly. His thinning hair was severely disheveled; and his jacket, slightly stained and layered with cobwebs and pine needles, had been pulled backward to the point where only his arms held it in place.

It had taken him well over an hour to fight his way back to Fenderman Lodge in the dark, but after several wrong turns and an eventual, forthright trailblazing directly through the foliage, he had made it back in time to witness this spectacle. He had heard the music from afar and, staggering through the doorway, had stood, transfixed, his inebriated faculties instantly sharpened with that momentary surge of ultraclarity, which is known only within the deceptive disorientation of an alcoholic haze.

"Choreography!" he managed to exclaim with gratified discovery. "I knew it! Choreography an' orchestration! I... I was tryin' to introduce them into th' group, annow, look! Look! I was... I was right!"

He paused as if to weep in the stupefaction of having been proved so correct, his entire form then faltering slightly, the motion stirring the others from their shocked stances to action, Vanessa racing forward to steady him, Chris about to do the same when the stereo began to bellow forth the next song, the young punk rocker hurrying to silence it.

"Dr. Pendleton, where have you been?" Judge Talbott cried, rushing forward with the others, Father Gilchrist sniffing and then glaring appraisingly.

"It would appear that he's been moonlighting with another anonymous group," he discerned dryly.

"Oh, Doc, you're hammered!" Vanessa said to him worriedly.

"What?" demanded Mr. Crimpton. He had been stuck here, climbing the walls, resisting the urge, *and the whole time…?*

"Um, are you okay, Dr. Pendleton?" Chris asked anxiously, peering at him as he regarded all of them with bleary-eyed insight.

"I want you all to know," he announced at length, speaking between gusty, labored breaths. "That the problem is…that there is no problem."

When, for whatever reason, no one seemed to understand this statement, he cleared his throat and, with tremendous effort, began again. "We all started out as a group of different problems who needed help with different people—an' that hasn't changed."

Mr. McClintock blinked, Judge Talbott frowning.

"I was a psychologist…annow I still am a psychologist," he continued succinctly, nodding and gesturing with emphasis. "An' that hasn't changed."

Father Gilchrist raised an eyebrow. Mr. Crimpton stared in confusion.

"Our group sessions together an' our trip out here this weekend are all part of the idea of helpin' each other through social interaction," Dr. Pendleton explained haltingly, his cheeks billowing as he arranged his thoughts.

He paused, Vanessa looking at him intently. "And that hasn't changed?" she guessed.

"An' that hasn't changed," Dr. Pendleton pounced on it affirmatively, nodding and smiling from face to face. Chris and Vanessa exchanged glances, listening intently with the others, only Mrs. Spindlewood silently agreeable to whatever might be said.

"Our goal, as a group, is not only to overcome our os-bstacles but also by helping each other to persevere in th' future, in achieving even greater accomplishments...an'...an'...accomplishing even greater achievements."

He paused, smiling pleadingly at them as he tried to impart the enormity of this high ideal, moving his small hands in fading desperation as he willed up a final impetus of persuasion.

"An' *that doesn't have to change!*"

He took a few shambling steps forward, the others permitting him to pass even as they observed him in uncertainty, Vanessa still flanking him.

"So...what exactly are you saying, Doc?" she asked him, daring to be hopeful.

"Yes, you're not making a whole lot of sense!" Mr. Crimpton informed him.

"And that hasn't changed," observed Father Gilchrist archly.

They all gazed expectantly at him as his eyes wandered fondly around the interior of the lodge, Vanessa's question eventually registering in his muddled thoughts.

"I'm sayin'," he concluded, honing his words with intoxicated exactness. "That even if you may have lost confidence in me, that does not mean that you should lose your trust in each other. My supervision of the group is secondary to the fact that all of you...all of you, *are* the group, and therein lies your potential."

He trailed off, as the others considered the import and yet possible ramifications of his words, frowning at one another in uncertainty, Dr. Pendleton's gaze settling upon Mrs. Spindlewood, smiling hazily as she glanced up at him.

"Good morning, Mr. Bergdorf," she smiled back. "Would you like some coffee?"

Blinking, he was about to respond but passed out first, the last words he was able to discern amidst the gasping and rushing footsteps as he hit the floor being those of Father Gilchrist answering for him.

"No, I should think that he's had enough."

*****

"This meeting of Mis-fits Anonymous will now come to order."

With some difficulty, Dr. Pendleton lifted his head and opened his eyes, his disorientation not at all abated by the very familiar surroundings and instantly recognizable faces that were peering anxiously toward him.

He had a vague recollection of being roused from a sound sleep to the contemplation of the varnished ceiling in the bedroom and then of being assisted down the hallway, his half-asleep condition obscuring much past that point and up until now, as he glanced up through his headache to see that he was seated at the kitchen table, still clad in his rumpled outdoors man clothes, and that it was now unforgiving daytime.

Seated around the table were the members of the group, who were watching him with concerned looks and eager smiles. Father Gilchrist stood at the opposite end of the table gazing at him expectantly, setting aside the ladle he had used as a gavel only seconds before, as Mrs. Spindlewood shuffled forward, placing a coffee mug in front of him.

"Here's your coffee, Mr. Bergdorf," she told him cheerfully, sitting down alongside of him, Dr. Pendleton staring at the mug as if in confusion.

"Since it is Sunday," Father Gilchrist stated, his features, as well as his voice, blandly wry. "Even though in regard to my church, I am incommunicado—and am probably soon to be *ex*communicado—I have been asked, owing to its special significance, to consecrate today's meeting."

Dr. Pendleton blinked as the others all lowered their heads, Father Gilchrist clasping his hands together and speaking routinely but with deliberate formality.

"We humbly beseech the Powers That Be to imbue our group with the unity and strength to assist one another with shared insight and enlightenment whilst acknowledging our gratitude for having been brought together in the first place. May we always be thankful for the opportunity and potential which our group affords us. Amen."

The group members repeated the word as Father Gilchrist took his seat and reclasped his hands atop the table, gazing at Dr. Pendleton.

"Well, Doctor?" he posed at length. "As our founder, overseer, and our peer, would you like to commence our meeting this morning?"

Dr. Pendleton gaped back at him, staring at the faces of the others, most still smiling in the sunlight that beamed hazily in through the kitchen's windows. He opened his mouth to respond, clearing his throat instead, and shifting uncertainly in his chair.

"Uh," was all he could manage, blinking indecisively.

"No matter," Father Gilchrist told him lightly. "After all, you were dozing during our formulative discussion. Judge Talbott, perhaps you would like to commence with the initiating decrees?" He gestured invitingly, Judge Talbott climbing timidly to her feet.

"Uh," spoke up Dr. Pendleton again, his brow pinching in confusion. "Uh, what exactly are we, uh, doing? 'Initiating decrees'?"

"Of course," Father Gilchrist replied, the others smiling and nodding almost secretively as the old priest leaned forward, speaking clearly and candidly.

"You see," he explained. "Step One is admitting that you have a problem."

Dr. Pendleton blinked.

"Step Two"—continued Father Gilchrist—"is admitting that you are a misfit."

Dr. Pendleton's eyebrows lifted.

"And Step Three"—concluded the priest with grave simplicity—"is admitting that being a misfit is *not* the problem."

As the others nodded in agreement, Dr. Pendleton frowning as he considered these words, Judge Talbott, having been standing nervously all of this time, began to speak.

"My name is Vivian Talbott, and I am a misfit," she recited quickly, her eyes shyly closed. "I have been a misfit for... I don't know how many years."

She plunked back down in her seat, folding her hands in her lap as Mr. Crimpton abruptly stood.

"My name is Stanley F. Crimpton, and I am a misfit," he announced, somewhat reluctantly. "I have been a misfit for at least twenty-two years."

He briskly resumed his seat, Mr. McClintock easing himself upward.

"Uh, my name is Percival McClintock," he declared with a small smile, then nodding meekly. "And I am a misfit. I have been a misfit for perhaps seven years."

As he sat, Father Gilchrist rose, placing his hands behind his back. "My name is Alistair Gilchrist, and I am, indeed, a misfit," he pronounced, almost regally. "I have been a misfit for close to thirty years."

He resumed his seat, Chris moving to stand up and knocking a glass of orange juice into his lap. Gaping down at himself, he blushed in shame at the others and then apologetically toward Dr. Pendleton, forcing himself to speak.

"My name's Christopher Galveston, and I am a total misfit," he told them glumly, then shrugging as he recalled something that had previously seemed important. "Oh, and it's not 'Stud Stomper' anymore, but it still is 'Clodhopper,'" he informed the abundantly smiling faces. "Anyway, I've been a misfit since the day I was born."

He sat down dejectedly, right in the puddle of orange juice, his features then crumpling miserably into an even more disgusted resignation, Dr. Pendleton wincing for him, Vanessa beaming at him in an ironically proud way as she stood.

"My name is Vanessa Fox, and I am a complete misfit," she informed them with a virtual relish. "And I've also changed, from a Lady of the Night, to the Mistress of the Dork."

She paused, directing her majestic smile down at Chris, who returned the look with a sullen resentment, then having to drop it as he hung his head and grinned. Her happiness almost tangible, Vanessa ran her hand over his Mohawk and focused on the group again.

"Anyhow, I have been a misfit since before I can remember."

She sat down in satisfaction, a pause ensuing until she lightly addressed Mrs. Spindlewood, Dr. Pendleton gaping as the old woman rose and smiled dazedly around at all of them.

"My name is Eleanor Spindlewood," she warbled. "And I'm from the Working Girl Temporary Employment Agency. I take shorthand, I'm very good at filing, and I can type forty words a minute."

She gave her little curtsy and sat down, Vanessa hugging her shoulders approvingly as the others exchanged inscrutable looks, a silence then settling over the room.

Dr. Pendleton glanced at the various members uncertainly, it beginning to dawn on him that they were all looking toward him now. He blinked and shifted as Father Gilchrist gestured to him.

"And you, Dr. Pendleton?" he proposed concisely. "As a fellow group member, won't you also offer the initiating decree?"

Staring back at the old priest and then at the lively smiles of Vanessa and Chris, Judge Talbott, and Mr. McClintock both nodding encouragingly and even Mr. Crimpton lifting his brows in anticipation, Mrs. Spindlewood giving him a look of hazy support, Dr. Pendleton blushed slightly as, even in his cloudy, befuddled mind-set, he finally realized what all of the members were doing and, moreover, what the implications of their actions could lead him to conclude. He stood up, his heart pounding, his words stammered as he cleared his throat and addressed his tensed, waiting group.

"Uh, my name is, uh, Charles C. Pendleton, uh, and, uh, I am... I am a, uh, misfit," he declared slowly, clearing his throat again. "Uh, I've, uh, been a misfit for...well, at least for a couple of years now."

He trailed off as his words were enfolded in a burst of applause, at long last a hesitant smile flickering onto his face. He sat down again, it dawning on him as he beheld these smiling, approving people that he suddenly felt a lot better—a great deal better, in fact, than he had in quite some time.

It was a sensation that was only to increase as they went on to undertake the most involved meeting they had thus far experienced together, one of an entirely new and charged dynamic, over which he was encouraged to preside, his mood sailing as he did so, sampling Mrs. Spindlewood's coffee and enjoying it very much, even after removing the teabag and delving eagerly into the matters at hand.

Chapter 16

"HELLO, HELLO! WELCOME BACK, IT's good to see you," Dr. Pendleton nodded to the members, as they entered, beaming from his packing crate, so glad to be standing behind it again.

Nearby, Vanessa was holding Chris back, allowing Mr. McClintock first pick of the doughnuts, Vanessa reveling in Chris's anxious expression as they watched him gratefully load up his plate, the selection of jelly doughnuts dwindling. He bowed thankfully to them, ambling away, Chris moving toward the box, Vanessa then shoving him roughly back. He responded with a mock yet savage growl, Vanessa play-smacking his cheek and stabbing a finger at him, producing an entreating whimper.

"I know it's ladies first and everything," she said suggestively. "But tonight I'm cutting in line!" She watched as his mouth clamped shut, and he stood there, roiling in debased excitement, Vanessa having to resist dropping her act and hugging him.

They played these games constantly, and neither of them ever tired of the pure enjoyment they yielded. Chris watched as she meticulously rooted out all his favorites for herself, flaunting them under his nose and flouncing away. He exhaled tautly through his nostrils, knowing what was in store for him as he hurried after her, sitting in his seat and eagerly staring up at her, his ferocity completely tamed.

Vanessa set her plate down in her seat, ordering him not to touch it as she darted over to help Mrs. Spindlewood get situated, the elderly woman patting her hand appreciatively even while addressing her by the wrong name, Vanessa accepting the misnomer with an unquestioning smile as she carefully arranged her belongings, watching her hobble away, only then returning to Chris, finding him waiting, earnestly, just as she had left him, the doughnuts untouched. She was almost disappointed, because, of course, punishing his misbehavior was even more fun than rewarding his obedience.

Watching them warmly, Dr. Pendleton glanced up as Judge Talbott approached with a tray of candy apples.

"I know it's not quite Halloween yet," she confessed, blushing. "But there are so many snacks to make that I thought I would get a head start."

He thanked her cordially, and she joined Mrs. Spindlewood at the side table as Mr. Crimpton and Father Gilchrist entered, neither smiling, yet neither looking as disconcerted or sour as usual, the doctor addressing them amiably. "Hello. Welcome back."

"And to you, Mr. Kotter," Father Gilchrist returned crisply, seating himself as Mrs. Spindlewood approached with a Styrofoam cup.

"Here's your coffee, Mr. Bergdorf," she announced, then taking her seat.

"Uh, thank you, Mrs. Spindlewood," he told her, peering at it and then tentatively sampling it. It was not bad, he mused, even for being ice cold.

"What do you say, *punk*?" Vanessa was whispering, dangling a jelly doughnut above Chris's mouth, tantalizingly moving it up and down.

"Please," said Chris instantly. "Please— Please— Please!"

She sighed languidly. "Oh, all right," she consented, giving him more than a mouthful, Chris chomping at it messily, causing her to giggle. She had come to love his untidiness; and to contribute to it too, though, as slathered or smudged as Chris might get or, more generally, as intimate as their interaction in public and at the meetings might become, she always drew the line well before they began to annoy people, Chris in complete agreement when, in her own words, she told him, "That shit in public makes people sick, myself included."

As Dr. Pendleton now cleared his throat discreetly, she grew quiet, nudging Chris to do the same, his sticky features agape as they both sat up and paid attention.

"Well, again, it's so nice to see all of you." He beamed at them all, enjoying the thrill that he felt each time they commenced their meetings, especially now that they had agreed to meet only once a week on Tuesday evenings and, as a result, saw less of each other, making the meetings that much more special. It had been a good decision, though, allowing for how busy everyone's schedules were now, and moreover, there was still to be considered all the extracurricular activities that had been proposed.

"Uh, I'm sure we all have a great deal to share since our last meeting," he continued pleasantly, very nearly falling silent and simply gazing at each of them. The words "our last meeting" would forever more be synonymous with their meeting that Sunday morning of the retreat, because, in many ways, while it was actually their very first *real* meeting, it was so groundbreaking as to stand out to him as being the precedent of being that last meeting from which point forward everything had commenced to evolve.

Not to devaluate their first three weeks together, he always hastened to recall, knowing from discussions with the group that they would all agree. No, those first three weeks leading up to the retreat were essential as a prelude, a foundation for that which now existed.

"Uh, I certainly do as well," he went on, nodding and then gesturing to the side table. "Uh, Judge Talbott has brought some candy apples to share with us, and I'm sure she'd be pleased if you felt free to help yourselves."

"Really?" Chris gawked, turning to leap toward the table, Vanessa yanking him back into his seat by the waistband of his underwear, answering his yelp with a simple, firm, "*Later.*"

Grimacing, Dr. Pendleton paused as Mr. McClintock moved quietly over to the table, then nodding to the smiling judge. "Uh, I'm sure we all would like to know how everything has been going for you, uh." He paused, adding almost playfully. "Uh, Your Honor."

Judge Talbott almost giggled as she shrank shyly in her chair, glancing at the others and forcing herself to sit up as she responded, her answer already somewhat apparent.

In many ways, she was still in shock. It was the greatest irony to her that she, a woman who could not seem to make up her mind, had finally reached a decision on her own and had then been completely talked out of it in such a way that reenforced what, at that point, should have been her irreversibly shattered confidence. That morning, when she had begun to outline her reasons for deciding against pursuing a career as a judge, she had been afraid for a moment that they were all going to gang up on her, their reactions instead being measured and earnest, but far from candy-coated. Father Gilchrist had pleaded her case while at the same time prosecuting it, insisting that, candidly speaking, there were few other judges before whom he would want to appear.

"Not to imply that you do not have the gumption to lay down the law," he had amended carefully. "I simply foresee a degree of merciful leniency in your rulings."

"You expressed not only your willingness but also your ability to perceive the potential of redemption in even the most hardened defendant," he continued emphatically. "That would suggest an excellent judgment of character—our group, of course, notwithstanding," he could not refrain from adding. "Judgment of character is a rudimentary element of what it takes to be a judge, overall, and you clearly already possess that."

"Yeah, and you don't automatically have to be a hanging judge or a bleeding heart," Mr. Crimpton had spoken up with surprising forcefulness. "I mean it's all about a happy medium, isn't it? Like the balance of right and wrong and that blind lady... Scales of Justice Statue."

Chris nodded. "The Statue of Liberty," he put in, Vanessa rolling her eyes.

"No, I think he means Libra," Mr. McClintock intervened helpfully. "The horoscopes were right next to my food review column."

"You *have* to be a judge, Judge," Vanessa cut in impatiently. "I mean it's what we all know you as, just like the Doc had to be a Doctor! It's what you two are!"

Judge Talbott and Dr. Pendleton had exchanged a glance, Vanessa gesturing sharply. "If you don't, then someone else will, someone not halfway as nice and cool as you are!" she predicted. "The court could end up with some hard-ass like Judge Judy or that Texas Justice jackass or that one bald guy!"

"Those TV judges aren't real!" scoffed Mr. Crimpton. "And Kojak wasn't a judge. He was a cop!"

"I used to enjoy Perry Mason," Mr. McClintock remarked.

"That's a nice program," Mrs. Spindlewood startled them all by saying.

Judge Talbott had rubbed her small hands together. "When I was a public defender, I used to watch that almost every day. I used to tape it so I could watch it later while I had dinner." She smiled shyly at the confession. "And I would often say to myself when I was on the job, 'What would Perry Mason do?'"

Father Gilchrist lifted an eyebrow. "Now that's a new one to me."

"I know it's just a TV show and that it sounds so silly," she continued, looking haplessly into her lap. "But I really did take a lot of comfort in the idea…"

Dr. Pendleton cleared his throat, speaking up at length. "Well, Judge Talbott, it's only a sort of abstract train of thought, but, if, uh, hypothetically, Perry Mason, as a defense attorney, like you were, had been approached with a judgeship, again, uh, just like you, while he might not have accepted it because…well, because it would have changed the whole program." He paused, clearing his throat again. "Uh, apart from that, the real question would be… What sort of a judge do you think Perry Mason would have made?"

Judge Talbott had gazed in earnest curiosity at the doctor, nodding slowly as he explained the question. "Oh, he would have made an excellent judge," she replied in a virtual reverence.

Dr. Pendleton nodded, pleased with her response, waiting for her to draw a conclusion from this logic.

"Yes, he would have made an outstanding judge," Father Gilchrist had stated. "Pity he had to go on to be *Ironside*," he added, not unsarcastically, then interlacing his fingers and leaning forward, peering at the woman solemnly. "Judge Talbott, since we are once more speaking in the abstract, do you recall our own hypothetical scenario in which I had also been promoted to a, shall we say, spiritual judgeship?" he inquired concisely.

"Oh yes, I remember," she nodded quickly. "That was such a good conversation."

"Indeed," Father Gilchrist returned dubiously. "I should like to explore that notion, and whereas we are told never to bargain with God—as well as not to deal with the devil—" He winked slyly at her, brusquely continuing. "I wonder if you, as a judge, would be amenable to a little arrangement with myself, in my capacity as a Supreme Being?"

As the others stared at him in wordless confusion, Judge Talbott looked at him with an expression of trusting uncertainty.

"What did you have in mind?" she asked.

Father Gilchrist smiled. "Why, something in the nature of one of your very own ideas, as a matter of fact," he explained lightly. "Except, in the inverse. If I may borrow from a contemporary faith, we would be exploring a variation on Mohammed and the mountain." He lifted his frosty eyebrows. "Interested?"

Intrigued, Judge Talbott had found herself slowly nodding.

In the end, the entire group had heartily agreed long before she had, ultimately and ironically making her mind up for her. Caught up in the excitement of the notion and its robust endorsement, she found herself compelled to listen and to agree.

Hence, a week or so later, after she had cancelled her vacation, set her office in order, organized the incoming dockets, and second-guessed herself a thousand times, she had been unable to back out of her side of the bargain. And at eight o'clock in the morning, as she had donned her robe and prepared to enter her courtroom, she whispered a prayer that the others would uphold theirs.

Inhaling deeply, she had pulled open the door, smiling at the grim bailiff who immediately called out, "All rise. Court is now in session. the Honorable Judge Vivian Talbott presiding," his words both frightening and pleasing to the ear, like a musical death sentence.

She had climbed up behind her bench with almost giddy trepidation, feeling dwarfed, perched in the massive chair, her eyes downcast as she looked at her gavel, up at her water glass, then the back of her name plate, and up at the courtroom.

The defendants and plaintiffs were at their separate tables, slowly resuming their seats, revealing the few other litigants and spectators in the gallery, who in turn sat down; and there they were, lined up in the back row, just as promised, all beaming up at her as they took their seats together.

She had stared back in awe, longing to join them; and yet, as soon as the clerk handed her the first docket, the day took on the semblance of the routine with which she was so familiar, with the exception that she was in a different seat, in a different capacity.

She listened as the cases presented themselves to her, the litigants both so eager to please that the interaction was almost conversational; and then, before she knew it, the time to make her first judgment was at hand.

Drawing a blank, she thought wildly of taking the only other refuge available to her at this point, a recess, a mad dash out of the courtroom and back to her office. She did not resort to this, though, instead glancing past the litigants to the back row, drawing so much support from the confident, proud smiles she saw, from their very presence there—with her. She had then looked over the facts before her in the docket, in essence closing her eyes to the litigants in taking into consideration that justice must be blind and that its interpretation must be insightful.

Without seeming to realize it, she had lifted her head and straightforwardly found in favor of the defendant, awarding him the total of $53.81, gently, hesitantly rapping her gavel, her tiny features almost wincing against the consequences.

Nothing happened, of course, except that justice was carried, and the litigants departed, staring at the seven individuals in the back row who were, for whatever reason, applauding and cheering, Judge Talbott blushing and swelling in bashful pride. Dr. Pendleton had even stood up and taken a snapshot with one of the unused cameras he had brought to the retreat, nodding in satisfaction until the bailiff sternly confiscated it, giving it, as it happened, to the judge, who returned it to him later, that photograph of the very instant she had made her first ruling, the moment when she officially became a judge, being the very first image to be placed in the gilt-edged, leatherette group photograph album.

Such was her first case, such was her first day, and the proceedings ensued very much like clockwork, for, true to form, when nine o'clock was at hand, as per their agreement, Mr. Crimpton stood up, waving encouragingly to her and leaving the courtroom to go to work.

In like fashion, for the Star Chamber Cheerleaders, as Father Gilchrist had dubbed them, could convene but once, just long enough to see their judge take flight, every hour, on the hour, throughout the day, one by one, they withdrew with an enthusiastic smile or a wave or a thumbs-up, until only Dr. Pendleton remained, his hour's end finding him standing and watching in almost fatherly pride as Judge Talbott tactfully mediated between a funeral director and an overnight express courier, before quietly, victoriously departing.

Father Gilchrist observed her now, biting his tongue when Dr. Pendleton continued with his clever gambit. "And so what is the, uh, verdict?" he chuckled.

Smiling brightly, Judge Talbott inhaled and nodded. "It's…been fantastic," she told him unabashedly, looking at them all. "Some cases are more difficult than others, but the process in general is going so well." She paused, shaking her head. "I just don't know how to thank all of you…"

The response was a resounding cheer, causing her to blush and laugh, her joy almost tearful. Her parents would have been so proud of her and had it not been for the courage these people had given to her…

"I'm sure we'd all like to thank you too," Dr. Pendleton told her kindly, nodding at her uncertainty. "We all told you that it could be done, but you went up there and showed us how to do it!"

"Here! Here!" Father Gilchrist proclaimed, the others cheering once more.

"And don't forget," Dr. Pendleton continued. "We still want to take you out for a celebration dinner at your favorite restaurant."

"Yes!" spoke up Mr. McClintock, pausing on his way back to his chairs, half of his candy apple still in his hand. "I'm so curious, Judge Talbott, which is your favorite?"

"Oh," Judge Talbott frowned. "You know I still can't make up my mind."

Dr. Pendleton blinked. "Uh…well, you let us know." He nodded to Mr. McClintock, noting a folded newspaper alongside his plate of doughnuts, his eyebrows lifting in interest.

"So, Mr. McClintock, how have things been going for you?" he asked, pausing and smiling with more playfulness. "Anything interesting in the, uh, *paper* today?"

Mr. McClintock glanced from him to the paper, his wide features than taking on a sudden smile.

"Oh yes!" he nodded gradually, modestly fingering the paper. "As a matter of fact, there is."

"Oh no way!" Vanessa exclaimed, pausing to shove her own jelly doughnut in Chris's mouth and then leaping toward the startled man, grabbing up the newspaper and flipping through its pages. "Did you really get it, Mr. McClintock?"

Beaming up at her, he nodded rapidly, blushing as she shrieked happily, the others looking toward him in glad surprise, Dr. Pendleton nodding, sharing in their excitement.

When his turn had come that Sunday morning, there was little to be said, short of a concise and somewhat embarrassing account of how he had lost his job. This had elicited some colorful descriptions of his former employer but little more at first because, basically, his position had been so uniquely *not* in demand that to envision securing a post as a food critic for some other form of media was almost too far-fetched to consider.

Likewise, he had confessed, undertaking some other occupation in the food-service industry might be beyond his capabilities. As accustomed as he had been to dining on fine food, its preparation was a task he could not imagine performing.

"And as for being a waiter or a maître d' or the sort"—he had continued contritely—"I simply don't think I'm…light enough on my feet."

There was some quiet contemplation, Mr. Crimpton absently suggesting looking into writing for some sort of gourmet magazine, Vanessa then frowning and speaking up.

"What about the *Village Vice*?" she suggested, shrugging, Chris gaping in impressed agreement. "That's a newspaper, and I'm pretty sure I've never seen a food review column in there. Maybe you could be their first one."

"The *Village Vice*?" Mr. Crimpton had waylaid Mr. McClintock's response by retorting. "Isn't that that practically X-rated subversive paper all the punks read?"

"An interesting use of the word 'read,'" put in Father Gilchrist dryly. "Never mind the subscribers, I had always concluded that the publishers of that rag were themselves illiterate."

Chris slunk a bit, Vanessa sighing. "It's not *that* bad," she countered disparagingly, nodding to Mr. McClintock. "What have you got to lose?"

"That's true!" declared Judge Talbott. "Nothing ventured, nothing gained."

Taking in all of their input, Mr. McClintock had looked to Dr. Pendleton, who, knowing the sort of paper the *Village Vice* was, meekly shrugged.

"It couldn't hurt to try," he told him with a watery smile.

Feeling that he should at least explore the option, Mr. McClintock had dressed in his best job interview suit and sought out the building in which the *Village Vice* was managed, finding himself in the seedier part of town, seated in a musty brick building, his resumé in his hand, glancing about at his surroundings as inconspicuously as he was able, an unfeasible notion, for every aspect of his person was absolutely at odds with the atmosphere in the office.

The walls and parts of the ceiling were plastered with concert posters, news clippings, and rather avant-garde artwork; the furniture was battered and scarred; and there was a general dark moodiness to the entire place, perfectly engendered by the people who occupied it. They were all quite young and resembled either Chris or Vanessa in many ways, the Mohawks, spikes, studs, piercings, tattoos, chains, fishnet stockings, combat boots, and leather in general making it difficult to discern the actual gender of some of them, much less which of them in fact worked there. Unlike Vanessa and Chris, though, these kids, if they noticed him at all, regarded him with suspicious, almost hostile looks; and he found himself wishing that he had observed more of the customs and behavioral traits and catchphrases of his two youngest group acquaintances so that he might not feel quite so displaced and ill at ease.

Seated across from him behind a cluttered desk was a militantly angry young man dressed all in black, whose spiked black hair made him resemble a battle mace and whose facial piercings were so abundant as to give him a bullet-riddled appearance.

He had skeptically accepted Mr. McClintock's resumé, glancing briefly at it as the older man shifted precariously in the rickety chair and listened to the music emanating from elsewhere in the office, a low guttural voice serenaded by what could have been a band saw.

"So," the angry young man, apparently the editor, had said at length, pushing the resumé back toward him. "You're Percival McClintock from the *Global Tribune*. I think I've seen your column. What was it called?" He gestured apathetically.

"Uh, 'Menu du Jour,'" Mr. McClintock responded with a prompt smile.

"'Menu du Jour,'" the editor repeated slowly, as if confirming something to himself. He leaned back in his chair and placed his heavily tattooed arms behind his head, affecting a more than casual appearance as he peered at him in unimpressed, virtual disdain. "Well, Mis-ter McClintock," he said eventually, his voice even and indifferent. "My name's Cervix. What can we do for you today?"

Momentarily speechless, Mr. McClintock had inhaled deeply and had then candidly told his story.

Cervix listened, his borderline sneer twisting as his expression shifted from boredom to incredulousness to mild interest to rapt focus, until he sat up and leaned forward in earnest amazement, seeming to hang on every word, his abruptly gaping features reminding Mr. McClintock of Chris's wild yet gentle visage, comforting him slightly.

When he had finished his account, he watched as Cervix stared back at him, open-mouthed, then suddenly excusing himself and dashing into another room. Startled, he sat nervously wondering if he had somehow misrepresented himself. His resumé, he knew, was not especially impressive, and the notion of walking into an office and instantly securing a job now seemed even more preposterously outlandish.

The strangled voice of the singer became even less distinguishable as that of the editor and two others became more heated in the next room, their words unintelligible but their tone making him swallow and dab at his dry forehead. He started when Cervix reappeared with two others, equally fearsome, one a girl, the other… Mr. McClintock blinked uncertainly. Their tentative smiles were warm, though, and he smiled amicably back as the younger man took his seat again.

"Look, it's like I said, we've never had anything like this before," he was insisting to the other two. "A food review column in the *Village Vice*? That, on its own, is insane!"

Blanching as the editor continued to speak to them as if he were not there, Mr. McClintock did his best to appear invisible as he listened with faltering hopes.

"But what about the *Global Tribune* connection?" the girl asked uncertainly, even as the third person began to nod with a flourishing grin.

"That's my point!" Cervix declared with almost boyish excitement, the kid in him that had been so stoically disguised earlier now genuinely exhibited, the angry young man vanished. "A topflight columnist from the *Global Tribune* comes to write for us? It's…it's fucking classic! Those fuckers will be crying into their lattés and kicking holes in their SUVs! Think about it! This is like…a golden opportunity!"

"Yeah, but what about the actual food column?" the girl asked pointedly.

"That's easy," Cervix scoffed, turning eagerly to Mr. McClintock, who braced himself, dreading what might be coming.

"Look, um, Percival… Mr. McClintock," he amended quickly, gesturing with what could only be called respect. "Um, we can't afford to pay you anywhere near as much as you used to make, and we can't give you an expense account or anything, like they did at the Tribune, but…well, like I mean we'd do our best to accommodate you."

Mr. McClintock's tensed wince slowly gave way to a puzzled frown. "Uh."

"And we don't really have any office space open for you right now, but..." Cervix shrugged, motioning to his own desk. "But fuck, I mean I could move my shit out of here, and you could use my desk. It wouldn't be any big deal."

Now bewildered, Mr. McClintock held up one hand. "One moment, please," he requested, blinking rapidly. "Do you mean to say that you're considering me for the position?"

Cervix licked his pierced lips, smiling wildly as he stood up to join the other two in grinning contemplation. "Check it out," he marveled, clutching at himself and then folding his arms in abstract approval. "Middle-class, bourgeois, uptight, white bread, wing-tipped, pinstriped ultraconservative executive columnist *working for the Village Vice.*" He shook his head in awe as all three of them regarded him in obvious appreciation.

Mr. McClintock had smiled meekly back. "Are those all reasons why you might hire a prospect?" he asked, hesitantly hopeful.

"No," Cervix told him happily. "Those are all reasons why we would specifically *not* hire someone." He nodded proudly as Mr. McClintock sagged in confusion, crumpling all the more so when he added, "And then there's the whole thing about your size!"

Grimacing profoundly at this forthright candor, he winced glumly as the girl appeared to consider this, the third person nodding vigorously. "Yeah, I mean he'd be unmistakable all over the city. No matter which restaurant he went to, everyone would know he was with us."

Baffled, Mr. McClintock could only gape at the editor as he inhaled in the staunch exhilaration of discovery.

"Fuckin' A, Mr. McClintock, they'd see you coming from a mile away. You would be our A-Number-One Toast-of-the-Town Class Act."

Mr. McClintock shook his head. "Forgive me, but do you mean to say that you want for me to represent your newspaper as a food reviewer?" he inquired directly.

Cervix exhaled through his grin. "Oh man, Mr. Mc, I absolutely do."

"And do you mean to say," he continued with a perplexed frown. "That, far from being a reason to decide against hiring me, one of the reasons why you actually would hire me is due to the fact that I am...well..."

"*Fat?*" the editor concluded, not unkindly, simply without the tact that he just did not possess. He nodded eagerly as Mr. McClintock cringed, sitting down again and staring at the older man earnestly. "Please, Mr. McClintock," he requested almost pleadingly. "Please come and write for us on the *Village Vice*. If you do, I fucking promise you, you will become a subculture *god*. Anything you need or want, if we can pull it for you, it's yours." He paused, swallowing as he regarded him imploringly. "What do you say? Will you give us a chance?"

As questionable as the editor's change in attitude was, Mr. McClintock could tell that he was quite sincere, and inasmuch as it was why he had gone to that office that day, he accepted the offer, the editor grinning with an almost childlike glee, the other two likewise excited, their enthusiasm, while confusing, nonetheless encouraging. When he mentioned that he would most likely not require any office space or even a desk, he had thought that the fierce kid was going to hug him.

The starting salary was, indeed, much less than he had previously been making, but he knew that he would be able to manage, and as far as the issue of an expense account went, Cervix had already foreseen a solution.

"A lot of the restaurants where our readers go are anywhere from low-key Yuppie places to dirt cheap but awesome hole-in-the-walls, a lot of them just getting started," he had explained eagerly. "If we call these places ahead of time, I'll bet they'll jump at the chance to comp you a free meal with all the frills, just for the free advertising. Plus, if you give 'em a good review, word'll spread and pretty soon, places'll be putting you up on the house, balls out as soon as you walk in the door! I'll bet you anything!"

This was not quite the way in which formal food review was undertaken, but Mr. McClintock, having begun to understand that this was something of an unconventional newspaper, had let him make the arrangements and had visited each of the establishments on this new list, finding that the young editor was right.

At each of the restaurants, most of which constituted less than fine dining, the proprietors had been very accommodating; and each meal had been both complimentary and abundantly proportioned. Most importantly, the food had been consistently delicious, a quality that, he found, seemed to increase in direct ratio to how dilapidated the actual dining area was.

He had worked his way through the agenda, enjoying incredibly diversified cuisines, all of which were of the highest caliber; and by the fifth restaurant, he had found himself guiltily asking the manager if he were certain he would not accept payment for such a divine meal, his offer politely but firmly refused. From the beginning, he had taken to leaving at least a gratuity for the service, a practice that he continued to maintain, if only to ease his conscience.

The entire trial yielded immediate and favorable results, the only uneven aspect being the way in which the brazenly nonconformist staff of the *Village Vice* initially viewed their newest coworker, their original skepticism reluctantly giving way to a sort of grudging tolerance, until Cervix both out of curiosity and in a genuine effort to ease this tension secured several back issues of the *Global Tribune*, he and the others taking the time to read the final series of reviews that Mr. McClintock had written for that paper.

In doing so, they came to realize that, in a bizarre, offbeat way, this unlikely man had rebelled against the system as they saw it, not merely by speaking up for the preferred eating places of the common people, but by basically taking an antiestablishment stand against his employers, a stance that, while inspired by his appetite, had cost him his job.

Their view of this sacrifice altered their snide patronization to a form of dumbfounded admiration for this gentle, refined man who now had so gladly descended to their level to join them, and it was not long before he was a highly celebrated figure among them; the girls all made a fuss over him, and the boys all "had his back." Least ways, he thought they were boys.

Moreover, the editor was also proven correct when, before long, he was being stopped in the streets by all manner of people and greeted warmly, oftentimes thanked for having pointed them toward a good place to eat. It had proven to be a thoroughly rewarding decision; and he never once regretted it, although, when his first column was released and he eagerly picked up the edition to see it in print, glancing through some of the newspaper's other features and realizing just how underground the *Village Vice* was, he had swallowed a bit harshly, wondering what the reaction would be amidst his former colleagues back at the *Global Tribune* and if they really would, as Cervix had triumphantly predicted, "collectively shit a brick."

Too excited to locate it, Vanessa instead hugged him, kissing his flushed cheek. "Can I keep this copy?" she pleaded, Mr. McClintock nodding vigorously, causing her to cheer as she flew back to Chris and they both began eagerly tearing through the pages.

"Well, congratulations, Mr. McClintock," Dr. Pendleton told him proudly, the others joining in approvingly, the reinstated food critic beaming shyly.

"Yeah, free food, even at no-name places, that's not a bad setup," Mr. Crimpton nodded. "I don't envy you the heartburn, but that's not a bad setup."

"Are your coworkers nice?" Judge Talbott asked, glancing a bit hesitantly at some of the pages as Vanessa turned them.

"Oh yes," nodded Mr. McClintock, smiling good naturedly. "Yes, they're quite nice, in fact... A little, uh, roughly hewn, I suppose, and slightly...ribald at times...but very friendly."

"Yeah?" Vanessa grinned up at him. "Well, if any of them ever give you any shit about not fitting in with them 'cause you're not punked out, you just tell us, and Chris'll set 'em straight."

Chris nodded a jelly-faced grin at him, Mr. McClintock smiling noncomprehendingly back as Vanessa found the column.

"Here it is!" she pronounced, glancing up enthusiastically. "I'm gonna save all your reviews." She smiled at his blush.

"That's a good idea!" Dr. Pendleton declared. "We can put some in the group album. What is your column called?"

"'The Gobbling Gourmet,'" read Vanessa proudly.

Father Gilchrist raised an eyebrow. "'The Gobbling Gourmet'?" he intoned.

Mr. McClintock shifted. "It's a, uh, working title."

Dr. Pendleton nodded hesitantly. "Yes, well, uh, congratulations again," he told him, clearing his throat and focusing on the two youngest members. "Uh, Vanessa, how is everything going with the two—or, should I say, the *three* of you?" he inquired, smiling toward Mrs. Spindlewood as well.

Vanessa glanced up at him, her features taking on a mix of seriousness and pronounced relief, Chris sitting up beside her, fingering his chin and then swiping at his mouth with the back of his hand.

"Doc, everything's going great," she replied, her smile gradually becoming radiant as if to illustrate how perfectly everything had evolved.

In the short period of time that had elapsed since the retreat, her life had changed more than in all her previous years, having done so in her single-minded focus on someone other than herself.

When the conversation that Sunday had turned to her, she had instantly directed everyone's focus toward Mrs. Spindlewood, who sat obliviously as they tactfully but arduously delved into her situation.

Ultimately, the group's resolution to help each other once again transcended stationary conversation, Judge Talbott spearheading the issue. Rather than risk upsetting Mrs. Spindlewood by asking her too many potentially volatile questions, they had concentrated on learning whatever they could about the old woman on their own, putting Mr. Crimpton on the spot, finally inducing him to agree to use the resources of the DMV to find out what he could.

His reluctance was even greater when, later, he had to inform them that the late Edward Spindlewood must not have been interested in driving, because he could locate no record for him at all.

With any possibility of looking into widow's benefits indefinitely subverted, Judge Talbott had reassured them that there were still other approaches they could make. Obviously, appealing to the company that had been erroneously paying her for all of those years was not even an option, although, the judge told them, it was unlikely that they would try to recover any of the money, inasmuch as it most likely did not exist.

Vanessa had flatly refused to search in her apartment for any kind of paperwork or records and could only just barely be convinced to slip away from the table and look in the old woman's purse.

Reverently, almost crying when she opened it to find the gingerbread cookie, together with the meager assortment of little old lady articles, she found a small bankbook, flipping quickly through it noting that its last entry was, predictably, from 1957.

She returned to the table, halfheartedly mentioning the idea that if a dormant account, even one with, say, only fifty dollars in it, had sat idle for almost fifty years, wouldn't it have accrued massive amounts of interest, suggesting that Mrs. Spindlewood might actually be sitting on a sizable amount of money?

Judge Talbott had tenuously agreed that anything was *possible*, Father Gilchrist instantly quashing the idea, Mr. Crimpton and Dr. Pendleton and even Mr. McClintock concurring—banks automatically absorbed what they perceived to be abandoned accounts; it was what banks did.

They had finally elected a very straightforward approach, Judge Talbott going through the channels of Social Security and helping to expedite the arrangement of a basic assistance pension plan, running into one obstacle, that being the question of whether or not Mrs. Spindlewood was competent to handle her own affairs.

Vanessa had adamantly and then vehemently insisted that such was the case and had then been forced to leave it to the judge, who promised to do what she could.

Within a week, they met again, the judge explaining the situation very clearly—because of Mrs. Spindlewood's good physical health, but because of her balanced yet imbalanced mind-set, they needed legal paperwork to be drawn up and then endorsed by a professional who could assess her capabilities and faculties as being competent.

Even then, it was explained, there was still more to the process. Due to the fact that Mrs. Spindlewood was clinically almost but *not quite* well enough to be assessed and adjudged as being able to manage her affairs independently, the only way in which she could be permitted to remain in her own residence and receive government assistance was if she had a live-in attendant to look after her, to help her maintain her household, and generally just make sure she was all right. Since there did not seem to be any relatives to turn to, the only options were either to designate such a person to the task or permit the State to take over.

Such a person, Judge Talbott explained to Vanessa, had to be honest, trustworthy, and devoted to Mrs. Spindlewood's welfare. Such a person also, by law, had to be at least eighteen years of age. The judge and the doctor having conferred beforehand, they next asked Vanessa if she knew of anyone who was old enough to undertake such a responsibility.

Vanessa promptly replied that she, of course, qualified.

With this matter quietly, discreetly settled, the psychologist endorsed the papers and the judge expedited them, and Vanessa thus became Mrs. Spindlewood's legal caregiver, a position that also allocated a small but completely unexpected stipend of her own.

It was official. Vanessa had jumped at the retreat because it would buy her two days off the street and had spent that weekend thinking about everyone but herself.

When they had returned to the city, both Mrs. Spindlewood and Vanessa were let off at Saxbury Commons, and she had gone with the old woman upstairs.

At first, she slept on the couch, gradually making her way into the empty room, where she slept on the floor and was stoically grateful for it. Later, when the legalities made it clear that she was legitimately residing there, her mind-set did not change; and she very sparingly began outfitting the room with the barest necessities.

She finally brought Chris up to see the place, sharing in his awe of it with an odd sense of pride, as if she had come to regard the apartment as her own, for, in truth, her feelings toward it had become quite militant; and she felt like some sort of an acolyte maintaining a very special shrine, making sure that nothing about it changed or came to harm, herself keeping it as neat and timeless as she had found it.

She had been thrilled to share it with Chris, but as they sat, whispering on the floor of the room that was now hers, dwarfed by their own youth in the enormity of the apartment's essence, she had pointedly told him that there was one action she would never permit them to partake in there, insisting that it just would not be right.

Far from disagreeing, Chris had actually been hurt that she would think that he was so insensitive as not to have realized that himself, and Vanessa had pulled him into her arms, the two of them holding each other in silence as they huddled together in amazement of their good fortune and of the sad, sacred intensity of the apartment's aura.

As for Mrs. Spindlewood herself, she seemed blissfully accepting of these subtle changes in her routine. At first, Vanessa had tiptoed around in keeping with the ghostliness of the place, but in time had realized that the old woman simply had no objections to her being there, in time reacting to the presence of Trudy and oftentimes Herbert in her apartment as if they had always been there.

Chris had discovered a cache of old phonograph albums in her stereo cabinet and would play them, slowly, gently dancing with Mrs. Spindlewood while Vanessa watched with the spellbound attention of a little girl mesmerized by the twirling figures of a music box, the disjointed image of these two unlikely dance partners not only perfectly normal but circumstantially beautiful to her.

Although Mrs. Spindlewood saw them as two office coworkers and they knew her to be a group member, it was not long before an unspoken, mutual adoption occurred, the old woman's grandmotherliness abstractly countered with her proverbial grandchildren being the ones to take her to the park or on walks or to the grocery store, for she viewed herself as being their age and all three of them were as children taking care of each other.

"Yes," Vanessa nodded slowly, folding her arms as she exhaled. "Everything is so totally cool that I'm just waiting for something to come along and fuck it up."

Dr. Pendleton twisted his grimace into a smile, gesturing soothingly. "Well, now, Vanessa, let's just, uh, think positively."

"After all, the transition appears to have gone quite smoothly, uh, wouldn't you say so, Mrs. Spindlewood?" He nodded to her encouragingly. "Is everything going well, do you think?"

Mrs. Spindlewood glanced up at him with her smile. "Oh yes, Mr. Bergdorf," she nodded. "They finally fixed the PBX machine, and now, I'm receiving my paychecks again."

Dr. Pendleton blinked, Father Gilchrist *almost* smiling.

"Congratulations, Vanessa," Judge Talbott whispered to her, patting her arm. "You've made a world of difference in her life, you know."

Vanessa stared at her and for a split second almost began crying. She had thought that this woman was such an airhead, and now, she owed all her current stability and a good portion of her happiness to her intervention.

"Thank you so much, Judge Talbott," she told her solemnly, holding her hand. "You are so...you...you rule." She leaned over and kissed her cheek, the little woman blushing and gushing, fussily patting her hand and sniffling.

"You be sure and get your candy apple now," she insisted divertingly, Vanessa lowering her head in laughter, amazed at how much she now revered the woman.

"Well, now, and how have you two been?" Dr. Pendleton continued with a cordial smile, Vanessa sitting upright and taking Chris's hand, then dropping it in disgust and snatching up a napkin, wiping at her fingers as she glared and then scoffed at Chris's cheerfully smudged face.

"We're good," she replied, now dabbing at Chris's mouth, causing him to recoil and blush, then submitting in chagrin as she attended to him. They both appreciated the doctor's sometimes laughable euphemisms, for, in this case, the subtlety of asking about "you two" afforded them the degree of respect that even the very young desire, especially since, as was in their case, in spite of the colorfulness of each of their personalities, they affected a very private sort of romance.

It was obvious, of course, that they were very much a couple now; but, in spite of the fact that they could not abstain from basic displays of affection, always within the limits of Vanessa's savagely enforced "puke factor," the others were both accepting and reserved in regard to them, no one overtly referring to them as "lovebirds" or asking any forward questions, instead merely acknowledging their union as fact.

"Um, yeah, we're good," Chris confirmed, once he was able to speak, his Mohawk nodding proudly. Good was an understatement to him, for he had never been so happy in his entire life. His heart and his loins were in the safekeeping of the girl he loved, making him free and invincible, and when he sailed down the street on his skateboard, he was flying.

He had been floored when she had shared Mrs. Spindlewood's apartment with him, not even remotely considering the elderly lady a burdensome addition to their equation but willingly embracing her too, participating in the amazement of discovery that accompanied their entering into the mystery that was her life, learning from her unspoken lessons of hardship and profoundly simple wisdom, both Vanessa and himself joined in awe of a love that was so profound that it had stopped time, lost in the hope and desire that their own love could be so true.

He took a heartfelt joy in the fact that he was completely free to be himself in the company of others, especially Vanessa's, and his spirit soared in the liberation of the punk rocker that was in him, the acknowledgment of it by others as being real making up a large part of its manifestation. He reveled in the feeling of wildness that she inspired in him, astounded at how similar many of her actions were to Candy's. In many ways, physically and emotionally, Vanessa was even more ruthless than Candy had ever been; but the real amazement lay in the fact that while their actions were similar, his reactions were absolutely opposed to what they had been, for when Vanessa reigned supreme over him, it was with the power of pure love; and the more relentless her taunts and torments were, the more he *begged her to let him be her slave*.

Staring fondly up at Dr. Pendleton now, he felt his smile widen into a grin, so grateful to the little doctor, so glad that their group was still together, so thankful that he was misfit enough to have joined in the first place.

"Um, and, like, even better," he continued. "I talked to the building manager, um, yesterday. And he said that not only will the apartment be ready pretty soon, but also since he doesn't think anyone else is gonna wanna live there, the rent might be really cheap!"

He nodded happily, both of them glancing around the circle. "Yeah, so, um, we both might be able to live right across the hall from Mrs. Spindlewood's place."

The group nodded appreciably, Dr. Pendleton very much impressed. "Really? That was just a tentative idea a few days ago," he remarked with enthusiasm. "That would be ideal. Are you prepared to move out of your family's apartment?"

Chris nodded lightly. "Yeah, I mean I am almost nineteen, and my little brothers want their own rooms, and my mom and dad are okay with it," he replied easily. "I can get a job doing whatever, and we really should be okay."

He took Vanessa's hand and smiled at her, wanting to kiss her but willing to wait. When the talk at the retreat had gotten around to the two of them, they had responded as a couple even though they had only just united as such. Everything from science to cliché dictated that they should analyze their newfound relationship and take everything quite slowly; and, in many ways, they were doing just that; but their instincts and perhaps something even less tangible led them quietly and inseparably forward; and there had not been very much for the group to discuss. The punk rocker who loved polkas had already been gratified and ratified and could not now be stopped, and the off-putting prostitute who would not put out was not even considered.

Other previously all-consuming concerns were instead put forward, such as Vanessa's interest in acting, a pursuit on which they both could now focus, especially if the question of their sharing a residence were settled. She had eventually met Chris's family, who had instantly liked her and endorsed the idea, and at present, they were merely faced with the everyday questions of the immediate future, financial aid and scholarships, and in time utilities and groceries and all the other grown-up responsibilities that two kids would have to undertake as they commenced to play house for real. It was scary, but in an exciting way, and their hearts pounded at the thought of it, their fears countered with the comfort of being in it together.

"Well, be sure and let us know how it all develops," Dr. Pendleton requested pleasantly, nodding to the group. "Why don't we all have a round of applause for their good luck?"

The kids both blushed as another pitter-patter of clapping ensued, Chris grinning at Vanessa, and Vanessa grinning right back. How she wanted to kiss him, instead plunging an éclair into his mouth, delighting in his sputtering reaction and savoring the excruciating anticipation that they both instilled in each other every day, oftentimes to deliciously intolerable levels.

Dr. Pendleton beamed at them, turning to nod toward Father Gilchrist, who stared blankly back. *What? Was he, Mr. Priest, supposed to lecture Mr. Doctor because Mr. and Mrs. Punx were going to bed down without first becoming a Mr. and Mrs.? Fat chance.* As far as he was concerned, the kids had gotten the Old Maid in this game, and if they were ready and willing to take on that challenge, then they were clearly ready to do as they pleased in their spare time. At least, they were not all lovey-dovey in public like some couples; not even a whole box of Dramamine could keep his lunch down at one of those exhibitions.

"Uh, Father Gilchrist, how have you been?" Dr. Pendleton asked him, drawing confidence from the warmth of the conversation thus far.

"I believe you skipped Mr. Crimpton!" Father Gilchrist rebuffed him severely.

As Dr. Pendleton flinched, Mr. Crimpton's gaze shot upward, his eyes narrowing. That old man had done the same damn thing that Sunday morning when the discussion had turned to him. Now, as before, he did not really have much to say, having been virtually tongue-tied at the retreat.

He had appreciated, genuinely appreciated, the unselfish spirit of fellowship and suggestion that had embodied that discourse and had been glad to take part in it, finding a sort of desperate gratification in helping other people in the face of certain knowledge that he, in turn, could not be helped. It honestly pleased him to know that at least some of these others would make it, would be okay—or, as okay as their individual nuttiness would permit, he had reflected dourly, then returning their looks with an impatient shrug.

What could be done for *him*? He told them about the forthcoming review and his trepidations, even confessed that he had been flirting with drinking as an escape mechanism or at least as a temporary device for relieving the pressure.

"Oh well, that's not always such a good idea," Dr. Pendleton had rather sheepishly stated.

"No, it can make a person's behavior quite erratic," put in Father Gilchrist placidly.

Like he needed *them* to tell him that. No, as far as he could discern, there was nothing that could be done for it. They had all seen what a nervous wreck he had been during the drive up there, and that had just been as a passenger; could they imagine him behind the wheel?

There had been one of their patented group silences, during which Father Gilchrist had lifted his brows speculatively.

"Do you know," he had remarked, ominously conversational. "It's funny you should say that, inasmuch as Dr. Pendleton, owing to his shameless night of debauchery, will not be in any condition to drive us back to civilization."

Dr. Pendleton had shrank as all eyes turned toward him, Mr. Crimpton glaring at him with manic alarm. "*What?*" he choked.

Somehow, Dr. Pendleton managed to take the old priest's cue, nodding even at the expense of his own character. "Yes, I, uh… I was so…overindulgent last night that, uh, even now I feel like my, uh, equilibrium is, uh, still spinning."

"Are you sure that's a result of the *booze*?" Mr. Crimpton had snapped unkindly, turning to scowl at the others. "Okay, well, one of you is going to have to drive us back then!" he concluded with crazed finality. "Because there is no way that I'm doing it! I haven't driven in almost a year!"

Neither Chris nor Vanessa could oblige, neither of them having ever had a license.

"I keep mine in my glove compartment," Judge Talbott said apologetically.

"Well, couldn't you drive without your license?" the DMV employee shot back angrily.

"But isn't that illegal?" the judge pointed out haplessly.

"I have a valid license," Mr. McClintock had not assisted matters by announcing. "However, I fear that I wouldn't be able to… well, the size of the driver's compartment."

Mr. Crimpton glowered at him. "Ya mean you're too fat to fit behind the wheel?" he finished for him forthrightly, Vanessa gasping as Mr. McClintock deflated slightly.

"That leaves only you or Mrs. Spindlewood," Father Gilchrist pronounced with a conciliatory smile. "I say, Mrs. Spindlewood, do you by any chance own a car?"

"No," Mrs. Spindlewood replied with her smile. "But my niece has a new Studebaker. She lives here in Schenectady."

Father Gilchrist beamed in a sincerely unapologetic manner at the infuriated driving examiner as Mr. Crimpton then stabbed a finger toward him. "You! What about you? Priests drive. I know they do! I tested one once! Stupid jackass almost backed us into a swimming pool!"

"Well"—Father Gilchrist surmised—"perhaps he was a Baptist. At any rate," he continued, steepling his fingers. "I do not possess a driver's license, and even if I did—" He broke off, shriveling his fingers arthritically and adopting his hideously sarcastic old man's croon. "They would have long since taken it away from me on account of I'm so old and decrepit and senile. I would surely do us all a mischief!"

He then abruptly dropped the act, regarding Mr. Crimpton smugly. "So you see, it has to be you. Otherwise… I guess we're all stranded here."

Mr. Crimpton had gaped at him, his jaws working in speechless outrage as he finally managed to point a finger at the intolerable old man, shaking his head slowly.

"You're…you're the devil!" he declared, incensed, now nodding madly. "You've already cut a deal with the judge and now you're after me! Alistair Gilchrist, my ass. Alistair Crowley is more like it!"

Father Gilchrist regarded him with supremely cartoon innocence. "Hmmm, could be!"

Mr. Crimpton had shot to his feet, glaring furiously at all of them, slapping almost primevally at his chest as he searched for his cigarettes, biting one out of the package and shaking it at each of them, like a dog wringing a dead fish.

"If you think… If you all think…," he almost screamed through his clenched lips, before quivering in flabbergasted rage, thrusting his hands into his jacket pockets, and stalking away, mumbling a defeated. "I don't believe this!"

*****

Mr. Crimpton had driven them back to the city.

Stopping to stare at the side of the van, he and the others noticing the stenciled wording for the first time, he opened his mouth to speak and then kept on walking instead as if too staggered to voice an opinion that more or less went without saying anyway.

Finding himself behind the wheel, he had sat there in disbelief as, beside him, Dr. Pendleton quietly extended the keys to him, pausing and then clearing his throat.

"Uh, naturally, you know that once you've started it up and removed the emergency brake—"

"*Aw, shuddup!*" Mr. Crimpton had snarled, giving him a baleful look.

Grabbing the keys, he started up the engine and glared back at all of them in the rearview mirror. "I hope all of you have your affairs in order, because, so help me *God*, today could be your last day on earth!" he had screamed.

Father Gilchrist had leaned forward and clasped his shoulder comfortingly. "Relax, my son," he told him soothingly. "That's the whole idea."

Dr. Pendleton blinked back at the old priest as Mr. Crimpton muttered venomously about an "old bastard," putting the van in gear and gunning the engine, and then gunning the engine, and then gunning the engine.

"Uh, you have to let out the—" Dr. Pendleton attempted to help.

"*Quiet!*" Mr. Crimpton roared, letting the engine die, the van sitting in utter silence as he fumblingly lit up a cigarette, puffing at it and roughly rolling down his window, the group members motionlessly watching the back of his head.

"Oh, and thanks for the coffin nails, by the way," he called back disparagingly to Father Gilchrist. "Nice and fresh. Who gave them to you, King Tut?"

"Cleopatra, actually," Father Gilchrist replied. "King Tut was a Marlborough man."

Mr. Crimpton snorted in nervous laughter at this, absently checking and rechecking his mirrors, starting the engine again and placing his hands on the wheel, staring intently through the windshield, his breath hissing through his clamped teeth. Beside him, Dr. Pendleton did not say a word, swallowing quietly as he longed to clear his throat.

All at once, Mr. Crimpton let out the clutch, and the van lurched forward, swinging them in a wide, gravel-crunching arc toward the lodge and then away from it as he shifted again and sent them sailing down the driveway. That was literally downhill, and thankfully the gate had been left open, for it was questionable if Mr. Crimpton could or would have stopped to deal with it, turning the van out onto the highway and among other vehicles, his shoulders hunching as he focused unblinkingly on the roadway, visibly wincing each time a car whizzed past them, keeping the van as close to the shoulder and as removed from the traffic preceding them as he could manage.

The others rode in silence, watching the scenery until finally Mr. Crimpton was able to glare up at them in the rearview mirror.

"Well, don't just sit there!" he yelled, actually spitting his dwindling cigarette out the window. "Talk! Converse! Pretend that this isn't really happening!"

Gaping back at him, the others paused and then began to talk in an awkwardly jumbled manner, Mr. Crimpton instantly shaking his head.

"Not so loud!" he shrieked, inundated with petrified silence once more. "Talk, yes, but just...keep it down so you don't distract my driving!"

He hunched over the wheel again as the others hesitantly resumed their interaction, Dr. Pendleton waiting until a few uneventful miles had passed before quietly clearing his throat. "Uh, you're doing very well, Mr. Crimpton," he said gently.

Mr. Crimpton shot him a glance, surprising him with a rueful smile. "Yeah? Well, don't pass me just yet. My real handicap is parallel parking."

As Dr. Pendleton smiled in bland appreciation at the empty joke, Mr. Crimpton, hands securely at ten and two, stared out at the road, too tense even to light another cigarette. The first ten or so miles had been surreal, and like in a dream, he expected to wake up and then crash at any minute.

Instead, as ten and then twenty miles drifted past, something of a different nature transpired, reflected in the thought that had struck him when they had been idling on the threshold back at the lodge.

He had considered the hundreds of times he had sat beside the prospective driver and reluctantly instructed them as to what to do and had pondered the novelty of the fact that this time, he was the one literally, figuratively, metaphorically, and at long last actually in the driver's seat.

Now, as he clutched the steering wheel, every time he flinched or winced or cringed at the actions of some other fool on the road, he found that he was no longer quite so helpless, no longer powerlessly forced to cower in the impotence of the passenger's seat and hope and pray that the kid or the old lady or the redneck or the frat boy or the nun would react in time, stop in time, or turn in time to avoid certain death.

He did not have to sit there and watch as, having placed his life in the hands of each potential kamikaze, they entered into the demolition derby, which were the public streets. Sure, the emergency brake was right there alongside his white-knuckled fist and, if ever used, was the perfect complement to, say, a ninety-degree spin or a rear-end collision or the celebrated forward flip.

No, that wild card afforded no sense of security compared with the empowerment that he was now feeling reawaken within him— being able to react *and* act, all on his own.

The epiphany was not long in the coming—he was not afraid to drive. In fact, he was the only one he could genuinely *trust* behind the wheel. It was *them*, those lunatics who had invented the need for the concept of defensive driving, those fighter pilots who climbed into the car with him and pleaded for their license to kill. *Endow me with this inalienable right to float through stop signs, or I will crash us into the next bridge abutment we come to.*

As many times as he had flunked them, he had passed them as well, in the deranged notion that he would thereby never have to test them again. Out of sight, out of his mind, if he had thought that such a ploy would work...

Never mind. The fact was he now knew the root of his fears, and although that changed nothing at all as regarded his job, it was enlightening all the same, amazing inasmuch as it was so obvious. He tested the theory by increasing their speed and then pulling one hand away from the wheel and punching in the cigarette lighter, eyeing it warily when it popped out again and then working up the nerve to light another cigarette, taking both hands from the wheel momentarily in order to do so.

A series of horn blasts and the thrust of passing velocity slammed into his budding confidence, shattering it into brittle shards as he dropped the lighter and seized the wheel, gasping and glancing to his left even as the other members were shifting and exclaiming, pointing at the anomaly, a sleek minivan that had previously been behind them and was now audaciously riding alongside of their vehicle, its occupants a group of teenagers gesturing frenetically at them as the driver continued to blare at the horn.

"What the *hell* are they doing?" Mr. Crimpton demanded, his voice almost hysterical.

"They're talking smack about us!" Vanessa yelled from the rear. "Look! It's because of what's written on the side of our van! They think we're a bunch of wing nuts out on a field trip!"

Father Gilchrist shrugged. "Well, after all, when you stop to consider it…"

Mr. Crimpton, his eyes bulging at this idea, glared out his window, seeing the teenagers, indeed, gesticulating in every conceivable way to suggest that they were all mental patients, either on leave or freshly escaped. Dr. Pendleton winced as if in pain. Mr. Crimpton, on the other hand, let his jaw drop as he watched the minivan flank them for a few more daredevil seconds and then shoot ahead of them, in time to avoid colliding with oncoming traffic.

He felt his face virtually petrify, in fury now, as he contemplated the sheer recklessness of their actions, implemented at the risk of a fatal, multivehicle pileup, simply in order to mock them as they passed on the left—illegally. His introspect was of a split-second duration, however, for, seeing a clear stretch of roadway ahead, he gripped the steering wheel, tautly, savagely upshifting.

"Bastards!" he bellowed, going red in the face, Dr. Pendleton jumping beside him, the others gaping up toward him in shock as he gunned the engine and spun the wheel. "You're not supposed to pass over a double-yellow line!" he roared.

"Then why are we doing it?" Dr. Pendleton stammered in horror.

As the tires screeched, the van hurtled forward, Mr. Crimpton plunging them into the opposite lane and flooring the accelerator, bringing them alongside the minivan and hammering psychotically on their horn as the vehicles came nose to nose.

"All right, you loonies! Let's show 'em how crazy we really are!" he screamed, pulling one hand off the wheel and shoving it past Dr. Pendleton's shrinking form in order to stab his middle finger viciously at the opposite driver. "It's called *offensive driving!*"

Seeing this, the others immediately followed suit, the teens in the minivan, for all of their delinquency, transfixed in terror as the passengers of the institution's van bombarded them with a variegated barrage of deranged signals. Father Gilchrist assumed a Nixonian stance, his hands outthrust in a gesture a kid had once made at him when coming out of a KISS concert, while beside him, Mrs. Spindlewood smiled and waved gaily. Judge Talbott, at a loss, stuck out her tongue and waggled her fingers, Mr. McClintock giving them his most critical two thumbs-down. In the rear, Vanessa had thrown one arm around Chris's neck, fearing his meek reservations and shrieking. "Do it, Chris, do it for the group, do it for me, do it for Billy Idol!" as she and then he flung out all four middle fingers and both tongues with obscene intensity, moving from the side to the rear window to prolong their vulgar assault as Mr. Crimpton pulled in front of the minivan in such a way that they were almost forced off the road, the driver hitting his brakes, the teens halted on the shoulder as they plowed onward, Mr. Crimpton assailing the roadway with a few last, spirited horn blasts.

Dr. Pendleton gradually sat back up from his crouch as the van forged bravely ahead, the members cheering resoundingly, rebelliously, Mr. Crimpton grinning madly from ear to ear as he peered triumphantly through the windshield, not bothering to silence them, instead sharing in their euphoria.

He had endlessly lectured his test subjects about road rage and had now experienced his first bout with it. *Damn, that had felt good.*

He smiled wryly in recollection as Dr. Pendleton nodded apologetically toward him. "I'm sorry, Mr. Crimpton. I didn't mean to skip you. Uh, how have things been going with you, uh, particularly as regards your occupation?" he asked tactfully.

"Lousy," he replied promptly, shrugging. "It's the same old thing, no better, always worse. I mean who's kidding who? At least, my nerves are a little less fried."

"No doubt due to your exemplary skills as a stunt-car driver," observed Father Gilchrist.

"For sure!" said Vanessa, laughing sharply. "Those little jerk offs you passed up probably shit their pants when they saw us going by!"

"Yeah," put in Chris, mumbling around a mouthful of éclair. He then swallowed abruptly to add, "You were just like the Road Warrior!"

Dr. Pendleton cleared his throat. "Yes, that was very… well-handled."

Mr. Crimpton grimaced, surprised to feel himself blush a bit. "Yes, well, that was what they call 'temporary insanity' folks," he retorted depreciatively. "It was only a departure from the full-time insanity, which is my job. But, in some weird way, it's helped—only a little, mind you. But hell, I'll take what I can get."

His nerves were little better now, it was true; but if nothing else, his confrontation of what turned out not even to be his actual fears had refortified whatever nerve he had left, giving him courage enough to either leave the insecure security of his job or stick it out the few more years until the earliest of early retirements. He had yet to make up his mind, and while the fact that, any day now, a semitruck or a pimple-faced lead foot might make the decision for him did not help his condition, he was determined to try to see to it that the choice was his and not his circumstances or even his hypertension's to make. He had already succeeded in ruling out any chance of his supervisor's making the choice for him, having passed the Driving Examiner's Review with an appreciably high rating. The entire ordeal had gone miraculously smoothly; the only irritant, in fact, had been the behavior of the examiner who had conducted his review, a shriveled-up sun-bleached shrimp who behaved as if he thought Mr. Crimpton were going to end their lives in a ball of flames at any second, his coiled, nerve-stripped anxiety almost palpable. Now, *there* had been a candidate for a rubber room.

He glanced up at the claptrap applause at his words and nodded, smiling dimly. Their little group was becoming more and more like actual anonymous group meetings, he reflected, taking in the others. *Oh well.*

Nodding concisely, Dr. Pendleton grasped the sides of his podium, gradually turning toward Father Gilchrist, maintaining his smile. "Well, now, Father Gilchrist, uh, perhaps now you would like to tell us how, uh, everything has been going for you as of late," he proposed hopefully.

Father Gilchrist gazed silently back at him, gradually favoring him with a smile. It was true that, at the retreat, when that decisive conversation had turned toward him, he had merely deflected its course elsewhere, not willing or even able to discuss his innate problems with any of them, with anyone, for that matter, moreover, because he was subconsciously beginning to come to terms with them himself, not realizing that he was on the brink of overcoming them.

It was a remarkable catharsis, he was later to consider, made all the more incredible by the fact that it had been happening to him all along, without his having been aware of it.

Mr. Crimpton having made noteworthy—perhaps even illegally—good time in getting them back to the city, Father Gilchrist had requested to be let off in the rear of the church, where he had snuck inside, as usual, via the back door of the rectory. He had crept through the corridor like a guilty teenager who had stayed out too late and had almost made it to the stairs when, with her usual, infernal, bat-like vigilance, Mrs. Tucker had come bustling out of the kitchen to accost him.

"Father Gilchrist!" she had shrilled, hands on her hips. "Where have you been? Everyone has been looking all over the place for you! That nice Deacon Richard was here this morning, yesterday too, wanting to talk to you!" She glared at him reprovingly.

"Why, didn't you all read the note that I left?" Father Gilchrist asked in mock surprise. "I was off making my annual pilgrimage to Mecca!"

Leaving her to gasp in outrage, Father Gilchrist had then plunged up the stairs, finally returning to the stuffy safety of his sanctuary. Beaming around at his realm, his appraisal became vexed as he noticed that the draperies had been pulled aside and the window opened.

Briskly attending to these invasive disruptions to his routine, he had then settled into his chair and exhaled in contentment, glad to be back in his own space. He had been clad in the same clothing for almost three days now, yet he felt fresh and anew, his heart beating robustly as he surveyed his kingdom, his spirits high and light for reasons he could not even discern and that he did not question since—

A knock came at his door, his features collapsing into an avalanche of a scowl as he grit his teeth and completed his thought—since the euphoria would surely be short-lived.

The dousing anger that had struck him became a flash of rage when next the door was pushed open and His Nibs, Himself, entered, smiling with plastic delight upon seeing him, stepping into the room and quietly closing the door behind him. "Ah, Father Gilchrist!"

Father Gilchrist made an exaggerated show of cupping his mouth and calling over to the door a wheedling, "Come in?" then effacing surprise at seeing his visitor standing there.

"Oh, Deacon Richard! What a pleasant surprise!" he intoned, as if caught completely off guard. "How are you? And how is Sister Moore Tyler Mary?"

Deacon Richard stepped forward, his eyes travelling around the room without appearing to shift from his focus on the old priest, his nostrils quivering assessively. "Father Gilchrist, it's very good to see you, sir," he declared formally. "I had hoped to speak to you Saturday morning. But as it happened, I seem to have lost sight of you on the street in front of the church."

Smiling venomously back, Father Gilchrist settled deeper into his easy chair, folding his hands over his chest. "Do you know, I *thought* I saw you racing down the front steps on that same morning," he returned lightly. "I had wanted to speak to you *too*, but you appeared to be in a great hurry, almost as if you were chasing someone, so I thought it best not to detain you."

His smile somehow intensifying, Deacon Richard clasped his hands before his own chest, as if assuming an opposing dueling stance.

"Well, now, as it happens, I was chasing after you, Father Gilchrist," he clarified, pointedly patronizing.

"*Were you?*" Father Gilchrist seemed in awe. "I thought perhaps you were headed next door, to the hospital, to attend their fund-raising event. That's where I was going myself!"

Frowning slightly, Deacon Richard paused. "I wasn't aware of any fund-raising events there," he replied, hesitantly contemplative.

"Oh my, yes, it was all for a very good cause!" Father Gilchrist declared grandiloquently. "Convulsion and seizure research. It's a pity you missed it. It was the charity function of the year! Why, the entire spastic ward was there, and we all did the St. Vitus's dance while Sister Angelica and the nuns sang 'How Do You Solve A Problem Like Chorea?'" He beamed at him cheerfully.

As Deacon Richard's smile hardened slightly, Father Gilchrist gestured lightly, relaxing in his chair. "Well, in any event, it would appear that you have caught me," he allowed conclusively. "So here I sit, your captive—if uncaptivated audience."

Deacon Richard's features remained unchanged. "It happens that on Saturday morning, I received a rather disquieting telephone call from Donald, who informed me—"

"Donald?" Father Gilchrist interrupted, clearly perplexed. "Donald?"

"Donald O'Flaherty," Deacon Richard elaborated, his smile at last flickering slightly. "Your sexton."

"Oh, *him*," Father Gilchrist returned dismissively. "Yes, well, he is a bit addle-minded. He was probably attempting to order a pizza, you see, and dialed your number by mistake."

He stood up suddenly, gesturing lightly. "I do apologize for any inconvenience. Do drop by again some time." He stepped toward the door.

"As I am sure you are aware, Father Gilchrist," Deacon Richard told him, not budging from his spot. "Donald informed me of some really rather extraordinary behavior on the part of none other than yourself. He gave me an incredible account of some sort of improvised church service with markedly unorthodox aspects, conducted by you."

Father Gilchrist sat back down in his chair again, reinterlacing his fingers. "Well, that is hardly astonishing," he remarked evenly. "We are, after all, a Catholic denomination. All our services are *un*Orthodox." He shrugged his shoulders.

Deacon Richard pursed his lips. "I was told of an outright mockery of both the Holy Communion and the Eucharist, as well as the basic tenets of the church, in some sort of extemporaneous mass of sacrilegious import, perpetrated in an obvious state of inebriation."

"Ah!" pounced Father Gilchrist insightfully. "There is your answer! Donald, as you may well know, is a notorious drunkard!"

The younger man frowned. "Donald O'Flaherty is a long-standing member of Alcoholics Anonymous," he responded at length. "He has been sober for over seven years."

"Well, then, that settles it!" Father Gilchrist declared. "Seven years sober! Why, you can't believe a word he was saying! He probably hallucinated the whole affair!"

Unable to conceive the elder priest's abstract sarcasm, Deacon Richard did not even try. "Father Gilchrist, it has been made quite clear to me that it was you who, in a state of incoherent intoxication, implemented these profane actions!" he concluded sharply.

Father Gilchrist glared back at him. "For shame!" he proclaimed indignantly. "You suggest that I undertook these purported actions while drunk beyond all manner of lucid recollection? Why, it's preposterous! I don't remember doing any such thing!" He folded his arms and smiled in defiant triumph up at the younger man.

Deacon Richard's lips twisted gradually, as if he were very slowly swishing mouthwash from one cheek to the other, the motion becoming more pronounced when Father Gilchrist shrugged again and continued.

"Anyway, I hardly think that any such occurrence need be deemed a scandal. I mean, after all, the few people who would be on hand to partake of such a spontaneous service would not even be regular parishioners of this congregation. It would in no way effect the take of the collection plate," he added in mock reassurance.

In the silence that followed, Deacon Richard's expression became quite devoid of any superficiality. "Father Gilchrist, if I may speak candidly, I have since found your obtuse and rather trying sense of humor to be quite offensive and unamusing," he stated evenly.

Father Gilchrist allowed his own smile to fade. "And I have long since found your *face* to be quite offensive," he charged gratingly. "Particularly in lieu of the fact that it is attached to the rest of you! You mention speaking in candor? Pray, let us cease mincing words and do so!"

Standing up a bit taller, Deacon Richard uplifted his head. "In my advisory capacity to the Archdiocese, I have been gratified to learn that my various suggestions and input not only have been favorably received but also have been consistently implemented by His Excellency as well as my other superiors," he explained with an air of accomplishment.

"Oh, I have no doubt!" Father Gilchrist responded, oh so impressed. "You're no doubt a regular cleric in the gray flannel cassock! Let's run it up the steeple and see who genuflects!"

"After all," continued Deacon Richard, unphased. "It was I who first suggested that you, Father Gilchrist, could so richly benefit from seeking professional counseling."

Father Gilchrist raised his eyebrows lightly. "Well, now, that hardly comes as a surprise," he replied easily. "I deduced that it had to be the work of some backbiting little sycophant. It stands to reason that it turns out to be you." He smiled kindly.

Deacon Richard put his hands behind his back. "I could very easily envision myself posing the question of your competence in continuing as the pastor of this church or, indeed, in maintaining the basic functions of an active priest at all," he stated concisely, finally meeting the elder priest's gaze again. "In short, I find myself wondering how my superiors and, of course, how you would respond to the notion of your retirement."

Father Gilchrist climbed to his feet, instantly looking down at the Deacon as he faced him in an uncomfortably close proximity. "I thought you'd never ask," he growled.

Clearly startled, Deacon Richard's features took on a puzzled frown. "Do you mean that you...you would willingly..."

"Step down?" Father Gilchrist finished for him with a chilling smile. "Abdicate my corrupted power so that Father Ralph can ascend to the throne? Deacon Richard, the notion of retiring, of withdrawing, of escaping from all of this theological miasma, is a profoundly euphoric notion, ranking equivalent with the attaining of passage through yon Pearly Gates! The very concept of removing myself from this suffocating gossamer of rubrics and red tape bestills my heart with joy to such a momentous degree that there can only be one clear and clarion, resoundingly concise response to your beatific proposal, that, of course, being." His features collapsed into a horrifyingly pronounced scowl. "*No!*"

Deacon Richard, mortified, felt his jaw drop open. "But...," he began to stammer.

"Whereas the notion of departing from this interminable wonderland of gilded gargoyles and Gothic gloom is without a doubt a hallowed dream to which I cling, it is a dream to which I will aspire when I and *only* I am fully prepared so to do!" he very nearly shouted through his teeth. "And until I deign to deem that crossroads as being at hand, I shall remain here, lashed to the wheel, at my post, the only golden handshake that I shall willingly accept being that of the Almighty, Himself, when Jesus H. Christ on a bicycle comes swinging down from on High to deliver me beyond the sunset, unto that great retirement home in the sky!"

Sputtering in outrage, Deacon Richard actually took a step backward, lifting a quivering finger at him. "You...you blaspheme!" he managed to hiss, shaking his head in a mighty effort to regain his conservative composure. "Father Gilchrist, I am faced with irreversibly grave doubts about your abilities to continue to represent the church! I intend to recommend fully to the Archdiocese that—"

"Oh, shut up, Mel!" Father Gilchrist raged. "Your recommendations to the Archdiocese have already been fulfilled. As far as Friday night's aberration is concerned, it has come and gone! You were not there and have no way of substantiating so much as a syllable of these supposed goings on! That only leaves your meddling suggestion that I should undergo professional counseling, which I have long since undertaken to do, and which I *can* substantiate! Hence, your 'recommendation' has been met. And apart from my graceful largess, full cooperation, and eager compliance *with* said recommendation, you have nothing whatsoever to report to the Arch-Blessed-diocese, *now have you?*"

He glared scorchingly down at the smaller man, Deacon Richard speechlessly staring back, choking in nonresponse, a flush at long, long last drawn over his staid features.

"Now, if you'll excuse me, I have a task that I have put off for far too long now." Father Gilchrist was smiling cheerfully once more. "I must set about mending my socks. In the dark." He stepped past the

Deacon and pulled open his door, adding very meaningfully, "When there's nobody there."

Deacon Richard bristled and then turned his heel, walking stiffly through the doorway. "Good night, Father Gilchrist," he said swiftly, not looking back.

"And a pleasant evening to you as well, Deacon Richard!" Father Gilchrist sang out merrily. "Please do give my best to Morey and Rose Marie!"

He closed the door, paused, and on second thought reopened it to its widest extent and slammed it as hard as he possibly could, brushing his hands together in satisfaction. Deacon Richard was going to be trouble, he knew, but then, pausing again, he smiled as the equation finally became complete—*What did he care?*

In the weeks to come, this overall summation of his mind-set gradually reincorporated all the aspects of his life and contrasted them against the last month or so, and that one telltale question became the nucleus of his own last-hour enlightenment.

At some point during that retreat, the impetus having been building for some time, when Father Gilchrist the priest had retreated for a while from the church, Alistair Gilchrist, the man, regained a few vestiges of his lost sense of compassion.

As far as revelations went, it was scarcely complex, for, in truth, Father Gilchrist, man and priest both yearning for death's release, held no trepidations, no fears or even uncertainties, about what awaited him in the afterlife; in that sense, his convictions were quite sound. He had not stopped saying his prayers because he no longer believed in God, but because he no longer believed in man, because he no longer cared.

His exposure to the inequities and brutality of people in general had rendered his heart hardened and had smothered his soul; and he had gladly, even righteously, turned his back on the whole world, prepared to leave them at the mercy of their self-inflicted suffering.

This dire attitude had only been compounded if not heralded by his own personal evolution into the wickedly mean old man whom he had so willingly become and whom he relished being, at full throttle, when he was alone in his quarters.

His forced attendance of the group therapy, however, and the stifling indignity that went with it had forced him into a position in which he was being openly invited to reveal himself to others in a private setting, not as a priest but as a person.

Well, if they had wanted to play with fire, he was by God going to oblige them; and he had done just that, shamelessly sharpening his claws on Dr. Pendleton and his carnival-like cabal, opening up wide and being himself in the most unrestrained and nastiest way that he could; and when the old dragon had ceased his reign of hellfire and peered disdainfully around at the ashes, he had found himself, as before, surrounded by six—no, seven—strangers who were still at rock bottom with him, staring dazedly back.

This phenomenon had repeated itself, endlessly, until it began to dawn on him that these seven people were very much as he was, save for the fact that they knew no comfort, not like his own dubious form of coping by not coping at all.

They differed in another respect, he was to learn, in that these people—these simple, silly, half-witted absolutely typically representative people—actually did care. They cared about themselves but moreover cared about each other and were willing to help one another claw their way toward the light, not of sanity, but of stability, not of salvation, but of survival.

Even in the face of being unable to overcome their own asinine problems, they had given of themselves to assist the next person and did so with an unselfish, indeed, hopeless lack of expecting anything in return.

It was the soul of Alistair Gilchrist, the mean old man, that had to be revived first, long before the spirit of Father Gilchrist, the priest, could be resurrected; and it would remain to his everlasting wonder that such was precisely what these seven strangers had managed to do.

When his turn to share had come that Sunday, as it did now, he had been unable to express this transformation, because he was still in awe of the fact that it was enveloping him. He almost wished that he could bring himself to tell them, to let them know that they had achieved such an impossible feat; but the mean old man, and a bit of pride—as well as shame—coupled with the remnants of his once ardently guarded principles as to how a priest should appear to be always composed and collected, if only to signify an ability to be of service, on demand, all these factors prevented him from doing so; and he instead endeavored simply to show them in any way that he could, at every opportunity, finding that it was not nearly as difficult as he dreaded it would be.

Indeed, not merely with the group, with whom he was free to be as nice or as horrid as he pleased, but during the course of his days, in general, as a priest, he was finding it easier to implement this uplifting outlook. The basic endeavors were routine enough, but he was soon taking pains to mean the words he offered in the liturgies once again and actually listening to the whispers confided to him in the confessional.

He found himself able to view Father Ralph as the eager, informal, but always respectful young novice that he was and to see Sister Angelica for the genuinely sweet and well-intentioned nun whom she was; he was able to be congenial with Mrs. Tucker, who only needed a compliment now and then to be rendered all smiles and energy; he was even able to treat Donald with cordiality, once the latter finally began to come out of hiding; it was amazing how easy it was to be civil to these insufferable and irritating people.

The beauty of this miraculous change—for it was nothing short of a miracle—lay in the fact that he was free to let the mean old man have full reign now, even while maintaining the dignity of a priest. With age came privilege, and whenever this patronizing consideration was afforded him, he punished the offender by taking them for all they were worth.

If they had expected him to emerge from this internal transition as Father Sunshine, they were to be tragically mistaken, for whereas he was no longer careless, he was care*free* to say or do as he saw fit, the most devilishly, devil-may-care priest who ever undertook the calling, and as his position as pastor became revitalized, he found that a sense of geriatric, reckless abandon had been reborn with him, opening his eyes to the spiritual powers beholden in an old priest who had discovered that he was not only able still to care, but that he could do so in blissfully nonconventional ways, not unlike an avenging superhero.

"Vengeance is Mine, sayeth the Lord," but the Lord helps those who help themselves and Lord knows that sometimes you have to take the Lord into your own hands.

It had been decidedly easy, all accomplished with a few discreet and anonymous telephone calls and had gone like clockwork.

He had watched from behind a potted plant as first the senior nurse, Nurse Wretched, came bustling into the nursery, demanding of Sister Angelica what the emergency was, the nun's bewilderment growing when the chief physician, Dr. Blue Blood came striding pompously in, asking the same question.

Sister Angelica had been at a loss as to how to respond when in rushed the mother, a thin, willowy waif of a woman, faded attractiveness with oh, there it was, a big, beautiful ugly black eye.

Rushing up to her child—the Mother Goose-spouting urchin, no less—the young mother, perceiving that the girl was fine, glanced up in uncertainty at the other adults, asking, surprise surprise, what the problem was.

Even though he was staring at the backs of their heads, Father Gilchrist could see the expressions of the nurse and the doctor grow cold as they surveyed the woman, the nurse politely but doggedly asking the question, leaving it routinely open-ended.

"Oh, this?" the waif had responded in an Oscar-losing performance of sheepish nonchalance. "Oh, I pulled open the freezer door too quickly, and it caught me right across the eye. I'm always so clumsy." She tugged at the long-sleeved concealment that her jacket afforded her thin arms.

Nurse Wretched and Dr. Blue Blood exchanged a look worthy of a ventriloquist act.

Oh, but the coup de grace; enter stage right, the star of the show, the rookie, with, by God an unexpected but very special guest appearance by his partner, a haggard, granite-faced warhorse of a veteran officer—complete with a wedding ring.

The rookie rushes in, asking what's the problem and then seeing his dearly beloved, who gapes back in wedded fright. The rookie's smile becomes as bright and flashing as his own badge, and its greetings all around, taking his position alongside his spouse, one hand on his offspring's head, speaking through his teeth when he finally can.

"Honey, what are you doing here?" the question, so innocuous and simple and belabored with the potential of a plethora of belt-buckled backhands.

"Your wife"—says Dr. Blue Blood, for Nurse Wretched is too consumed with wrathful doubt to speak—"was just telling us about her predisposition to clumsiness."

The rookie frowns slightly and then, figuring it out, laughs loudly, throwing an arm around the wispy, pale creature, who, by God, flinches. "Oh yeah!" he returns easily. "She's clumsy, all right. One of those big, old-fashioned fold-down ironing boards—you know the kind, spring-activated, fits right up into the wall? Yip, came crashing down and bruised my baby bad!"

He kisses the creature, whose smile reveals her loving revulsion, as the rookie laughs again; and they all join in and laugh together, laughing loud and long over this silly, trite little happenstance, laughing at the involuntary contradiction, even though it was perfectly understandable. Father Gilchrist knew that he confused freezer doors with ironing boards all the time! Yes, they laughed and laughed.

Only they didn't. Upon hearing the rookie's words, Nurse Wretched and Dr. Blue Blood and Sister Angelica had all exchanged looks, then turning to gaze at the veteran officer, who stared at his fledgling partner who blinked back at all of these people who now knew; and suddenly swallowing and stealing a quick glimpse of his wife, he also knew what they knew; and at that point, everyone knew the answer to the question of the hour—what's the emergency? Everyone knew as the rookie began to burn on the spot and, for the moment, anyway, silence reigned.

It had occurred to Father Gilchrist as he silently stole away that he might actually have instigated one final prize fight, from which there could only emerge one loser, the winner being the corpse.

He considered this, but had faith to the contrary; he was certain that the secular forces at work could do what he could not, just as he had known what they did not; and he had managed to empower them with this knowledge while maintaining the sanctity of the confessional. He was fairly sure that the rookie would never touch his wife again, perhaps in every sense of the words, but such might just be the solution. The church did not encourage divorces, but Father Gilchrist, the Avenger, did not sanction wife-beating.

He had wondered later, if he were perhaps playing God, but had dismissed the thought as immaterial. After all, Judge Talbott had been the one to place the thought in his head, hadn't she? And now, she was an authority on the Law of the Land, so it had to be okay, then right? If Judge Talbott says so, then it must be okay!

Such imbalanced dogma rampantly appealed to him, as it upheld his blank-check license to keep the faith in his own absurdist fashion, not unlike good old Ebeneezer, for, as had been established, Father Gilchrist could be as nutty as a fruit cake and eat it too; and the liberty to be Reverend Scrooge, in all of its rotten and curmudgeonly glory and humbug, was his to claim, because, after all, God loves the insane.

Father Gilchrist sat up in his chair, his smile growing.

Mistaking the expression as a prelude to an unexpectedly positive response, Dr. Pendleton nodded encouragingly.

"Uh, do I take it things have been going well?"

Blinking, Father Gilchrist focused on him, his smile vanquished by his immediate scowl.

"You may take it with a grain of smelling salts if you wish. It will make no difference," he declared sharply, tilting back his head to glare and then, just for old time's sake, looking at his watch. "Suffice it to say, I have a pulse, which is all one requires these days to be ranked as still among the living, so I suppose in that sense, I have prevailed."

He folded his arms and glowered challengingly around at the others, although, apart from Dr. Pendleton's flinching grimace, each of the other members was smiling insightfully back at him, as if they could see into his heart. He felt his features almost betray him by giving into a returning smile, and he redoubled his defiant posture, frowning back at them.

"Well?" he demanded acidly. "Where is my paltry, pathetic round of applause for that profoundly self-analytical assessment?"

Pursing his lips stiffly, he withstood a boisterous, half-mocking, half-serious, all-affectionate ovation, nodding and almost letting that smile get away, pondering what had become of his stoic self-control. Clearly, he was spending too much time with these reprobate do-gooders.

Dr. Pendleton's confidence restored, he was more than willing to leave it at that, for it was no secret nor mass hallucination that the resentful, spiteful old clergyman was allowing himself to be softened—for their group anyway. The man was undoubtedly still hell on his parishioners, and the doctor did not envy that flock.

"Uh, good," he concluded shortly, eager to move onward, pausing for anyone to ask and then clearing his throat. "Uh, I, myself, am doing well. I'm happy to say—"

He flushed, his heart swelling as the room erupted into a calamitous applause, the members, particularly the youngest ones, wildly unrestrained in their cheering.

Waving modestly, he beamed back at them, hiding his modest pride as he stooped to retrieve his attaché case, withdrawing something from it.

"Thank you, thank you, folks," he nodded, flushing even more so as he fingered the item. "I, uh, have something here that I wanted to share with all of you." He held up a small picture frame. "Can anyone tell me what this is?"

"Oh, splendid, a Rorschach test!" Father Gilchrist exclaimed, studying it closely. "It is a butterfly, with an Oedipus complex, holding a spatula."

Dr. Pendleton paused patiently. "Uh, no, Father Gilchrist. Actually, this, is my new, updated, certified psychologist's license."

The response was thunderous now, Dr. Pendleton unable to resist the urge to hold it up over his head like a champion, for, in many ways, he was.

When he had been faced, befuddled, and still slightly tipsy that Sunday morning, with the question of his own misfitism, he had falteringly acknowledged that he was fairly certain they had all witnessed it the previous afternoon.

As for the solution, he had drawn a blank, until the members gently told him that he had already offered them a true and frank self-assessment when he had returned from his outing. When he reluctantly confessed that he could not remember what he had said to them, they helped him to recall his thought process, all the way back to the barroom.

Instead of speaking, he had listened as they told him that he was, of course, right, that he had overcome his problem with their help by helping them; and he had witnessed the truth of this as he watched them help each other help themselves, then and there.

He nearly wept at this profound realization of the success of his dream, having never imagined that the group, originally designed to be an exercise that, at best, would yield marginally positive results, all-around, had instead proliferated itself into such a completely, unexpectedly real anomaly, staggered at the almost frighteningly haphazard way in which they had all been thrown together.

That these eight people could find themselves tossed into each other's lives, out of all the myriad other possible configurations that chance and fortune could conceive, was a happenstance that would leave the most cynical member stunned in contemplation of the contrary, of how simplistically, fatalistically close they all could have come to missing this crossroads, in which case the bond, the reality that they had all helped to create, would never have been.

"Serendipity," Mr. McClintock had concluded, sharing in their awe.

With the notion that Dr. Pendleton's problem had, in essence, been solved, there came, of course, the matter of the continuation of their group, each of them looking to him to settle the issue, Dr. Pendleton jumping at the chance, affirming that he had had every intention, all along, in seeing the group through to whatever manner of conclusion it outlined for itself, this leaving only the question of the group's ongoing confidence in him as their leader, their interdependability having already been so clearly established.

In the silence that followed, he had focused downward until, at length, Vanessa spoke up for all of them, looking at him gravely. "Well, Doc, I mean here we are, right?" she had pointed out with a simple shrug. "This is it. This is our group. None of us would be here if it hadn't been for you, and none of us wants to go back. We're all with you, Doc. So like, you gotta stick around for us." She had paused, expressing it bluntly. "We need you."

And so it was that group and founder remained united, although, as Dr. Pendleton beamed proudly out at them, touched by their cheers, he could not imagine them needing anything but each other.

Still, as a fellow group member and as a licensed doctor again, he surely needed them; and as such, he thrilled with their enthusiastic, devout acceptance of him; and, at long last, his good news, its belated reception made all the sweeter for that last mile uphill.

"Yes, congratulations," Father Gilchrist allowed. "Although I liked the other frame better."

Only smiling, Dr. Pendleton put his prized certificate aside, glancing at it just once more and then focusing happily on the group again.

"Well, uh, that was my little surprise." He cleared his throat, slipping on his reading glasses and clasping his clipboard. "Uh, and now to the business at hand... I've reviewed all your suggestions from last week's thinking cap assignment, and I must say that some of your ideas for possible future group activities sound like lots of fun. I've put them all on one list so I can read them off to you, and we can discuss them. I also put in an idea of my own, so well, let's see what we've got."

The members settled in their seats as he began to read from the list.

"Uh, there was a suggestion that we return to Fenderman Lodge at some point," he informed them, glancing up expectantly.

"Well, now, I wonder whose suggestion that was?" pondered Father Gilchrist.

Vanessa and Chris nodded energetically at the flinching doctor.

"Hell, yeah, we definitely wanna go back," Vanessa affirmed.

Encouraged, Dr. Pendleton continued. "Uh, here's a suggestion that we all go bowling some night." He nodded musingly.

When no one responded, Mr. Crimpton sighed irately. "Well, we wouldn't have to become a team or enter a tournament or anything," he growled.

"It could be fun," ventured Judge Talbott.

"Uh, here's a suggestion that we sample the new smorgasbord out on Route Twelve," Dr. Pendleton read hesitantly.

Mr. McClintock nodded vigorously. "It's all-you-can-eat for $4.99," he explained enthusiastically. "I'm told it's very popular with truck drivers."

"Yes, I hear that Jimmy Hoffa is a regular there," noted Father Gilchrist.

"What's a smorgasbord?" asked Chris, whipped cream dappling his nose.

Mr. McClintock focused on his doughnuts as Dr. Pendleton continued.

"Here's a suggestion that we all go and visit the Metro Art Museum."

"What a ghastly notion," Father Gilchrist sneered. "You can most assuredly count me out."

Dr. Pendleton blinked at him. "But...that was your suggestion."

Frowning, Father Gilchrist shrugged off his uncertainty. "No, I could not have made such a proposal," he returned dismissively. "It must have been my doppelganger."

Chris gaped at him. "What's a doppelganger?" This was worse than school.

"Actually, it's a psychological term." Dr. Pendleton prepared to warm to the subject, distracted when Vanessa swiped the splotch off Chris's nose with a doughnut she then shoved in his mouth.

"They say that we all have a double," Judge Talbott explained in an awed voice, nodding spookily at each of them. She was so looking forward to Halloween. "And that our doubles are actually evil and are always secretly trying to replace us!"

Mr. Crimpton jutted out his chin. "So that's what happened to Father Gilchrist."

Mr. McClintock's mass convulsed as he swallowed a snort, Vanessa outrightly cackling as the old priest glared at them witheringly, then turning to Dr. Pendleton.

"Actually, that was my idea," he informed him, having just remembered.

Dr. Pendleton regarded him with an impressed look. "Well, I think that it definitely has merit," he commended the aged clergyman. "Appreciating artwork can be very constructively therapeutic."

Father Gilchrist glared. "Who said anything about appreciating it?" he demanded. "It's an exhibition of modern art! I thought we could all go down and make fun of it!"

Dr. Pendleton grimaced, Judge Talbott gasping. "That's horrible!"

His frown becoming bewildered, Father Gilchrist shrugged. "I know! That's why I suggested it!"

Clearing his throat, Dr. Pendleton focused on the list again. "Well, perhaps we'll consider it," he segued lamely. "Uh, next is a suggestion that we go, uh, peewee golfing."

Judge Talbott beamed, Chris nodding his Mohawk happily. "Yeah!"

"What is 'peewee golfing'?" Mr. McClintock raised a thick hand to ask.

"What's peewee golfing?" Vanessa repeated in disbelief. "Come on, you know, it's for kids. It's fun. There's like little buildings and windmills and sh-tuff like that."

"You've never been miniature golfing before?" asked Mr. Crimpton laconically.

"He's never been miniature anything before," Father Gilchrist murmured.

"I'm certainly willing to try anything once," Mr. McClintock spoke up agreeably. Such was the credo of any food critic. "Uh, but, I fear I may be unable to ride in one of those little golf carts."

Vanessa rolled her eyes, Dr. Pendleton attempting to take refuge in the list once again. Finding none, he was forced to continue anyway. "Uh, next is a, uh...well, a...suggestion that we all go and sit in as part of the studio audience for the, uh, Lawrence Welk show," he read haltingly.

As Father Gilchrist lowered his head into one hand, Mr. Crimpton frowned. "Lawrence Welk?" he repeated doubtfully. "The comedian?"

"In a manner of speaking," said the old priest.

"No, I believe that's Lawrence Block," stated Mr. McClintock.

Mrs. Spindlewood was nodding with sudden coherence. "He promised all of us girls in the steno pool that he would get us tickets," she announced proudly.

"Who did?" Mr. Crimpton asked incredulously.

"Mr. Bergdorf," replied Mrs. Spindlewood promptly.

"Is that true, Bergdorf?" growled Father Gilchrist.

Cringing, Dr. Pendleton cleared his throat. "Uh, Mrs. Spindlewood, I, uh, don't think we'll be able to do that," he attempted to explain.

"How come?" Chris asked in disappointment. "It would be so cool."

Dr. Pendleton blinked, Father Gilchrist's eyebrows almost lifting up off his head.

"We're all going to drive up to the Trianon Ballroom in Mr. Bergdorf's Edsel," Mrs. Spindlewood recited dreamily.

Mr. Crimpton snorted at Dr. Pendleton. "You bought an *Edsel?*"

"Why can't we go?" Vanessa demanded defensively, seeing Chris's crestfallen look and leaping fanatically to Mrs. Spindlewood's aid. "We should be able to do anything Mrs. Spindlewood wants to do!"

Shrinking, Dr. Pendleton gestured haplessly. "I... I agree," he assured her truthfully, trying not to become tongue-tied as he began to stammer. "But, in this case, I'm afraid it's impossible! To be in the studio audience for that program... I... It's simply not being broadcast anymore!"

"But they show the reruns on public television," Judge Talbott pointed out, trying, if not succeeding, to be helpful.

"Well, maestro?" challenged Father Gilchrist. "How are you going to oblige us with this whim? Has the Hollingsworth Motor Pool any time machines you can borrow?"

Sighing, Dr. Pendleton pinched the bridge of his nose, motioning stayingly to Vanessa. "I, uh…we'll figure something out. I'm sure," he declared conclusively, glancing desperately at the list and then squinting at it. "Our final suggestion is that we go and see, uh…" He blinked. "'Flogging Molly?'"

Vanessa and Chris held hands, smiling proudly as their joint suggestion was read.

Judge Talbott tilted her head slightly. "Molly *who?*" she asked.

"What the hell is a Flogging Molly?" Mr. Crimpton griped in exasperation.

"It's a girl's seminary school in New Jersey," Father Gilchrist informed him airily.

Mrs. Spindlewood frowned. "I don't think Molly works here anymore," she declared. "I heard she was transferred to the Sheboygan branch."

Dr. Pendleton peered at the list again. "Perhaps I'm reading it wrong."

"No," Vanessa told him, her eyes flashing angrily. "You got it right."

"Isn't a Molly-flog a little water frog you find in a creek?" frowned Judge Talbott.

"That's a *Polliwog*," Mr. Crimpton grated tersely. "A molly is a type of fish!"

"Really?" Mr. McClintock's eyebrows lifted. "How is it prepared?"

"Flogging Molly is a punk rock group!" Vanessa exclaimed. "They're having a concert next month, and Chris and I thought we all could go!"

Father Gilchrist turned to Mrs. Spindlewood. "So! Lawrence Welk, was it?"

"There is no way in hell I'm going to a punk rock concert," Mr. Crimpton stated flatly.

Dr. Pendleton opened his mouth, instantly at a loss for words.

"But it'll be really cool!" Chris explained, nodding earnestly. "There's gonna be a mosh pit and stage diving and, like, lots of punk stuff—"

"And pushing and shoving and trampling and screaming and fighting and drugs and explosions and violence," Mr. Crimpton listed caustically.

"*Exactly*," Vanessa confirmed audaciously.

"I think my coworkers are planning on attending that!" Mr. McClintock proclaimed in excited recollection. "What was the group called again?"

"The Molly McGuires," Father Gilchrist replied informatively.

"Oh," sighed Mrs. Spindlewood. "I love the McGuire Sisters."

"Uh, perhaps we can consider it, I suppose," Dr. Pendleton said weakly.

"There's nothing to consider!" Vanessa told him hotly. "Chris and me already got tickets, and the rest of you can do whatever you want!"

"But, like, please, at least think about coming with us!" Chris pleaded.

"Well, it does sound better than bowling," sniffed Father Gilchrist.

"Now just a minute, *Rev*!" Mr. Crimpton began to snarl.

"Maybe instead of peewee golf, we could all go to the roller-skating rink," Judge Talbott called out diplomatically, smiling shyly. "Remember the Hokey Pokey?"

"You know, *your* idea wasn't so hot either," Mr. Crimpton snapped. "I don't want to go to a museum and look at a bunch of modern art crap!"

Father Gilchrist glowered. "*Neither do I!*"

"Does the roller-skating rink have a snack bar?" asked Mr. McClintock.

"What's the Hokey Pokey?" Chris wanted to know.

"If *any* of you are interested in going to the concert," Vanessa interposed brusquely, "I suggest you get your tickets now, 'cause they're gonna sell out quick!"

"Yes, Mr. Bergdorf," nodded Mrs. Spindlewood sagely. "We had best not wait to get tickets. Remember what happened with the Ed Sullivan show."

"Well, feel free to give mine to someone else," Father Gilchrist told her generously. "I have season tickets to the McCarthy hearings, so I'll be busy that night."

"Uh, folks, folks!" Dr. Pendleton waved his hands desperately. "Let's not all get too upset. We'll have plenty of time to argue—to *discuss* it later." Grimacing, he cleared his throat, gesturing conclusively. "Right now, why don't we all relax and enjoy our orchestration and choreography segment for tonight's meeting."

When this notion secured a few less-than enthused looks, he hurried onward, shaking a finger pointedly at them.

"Now remember, folks, we all agreed after the retreat that we wanted to incorporate it as a regular part of our meetings, and we all agreed that it was a fun and diversified way to ease anxiety and, uh, excess energy and tension." Pausing, he lifted his eyebrows, motioning adamantly. "And we all agreed to agree with whoever's turn it is… that is we agreed not to disagree with whatever… we agreed to enjoy anything that we brought in to share with each other!"

"What, like last week?" gaped Mr. Crimpton. "My head is still pounding."

"Yes, but it was so appropriate for our Mis-fits Anonymous soiree!" Father Gilchrist purred. "What was it they were called?"

Chris blushed and squirmed. "The Mis-fits," he answered sheepishly.

"Uh, Judge Talbott, I believe tonight is your turn," Dr. Pendleton continued. "Uh, Clod— Chris, would you set up the, uh…"

He smiled as Chris leapt up and clomped over to the side table to retrieve a portable stereo, Judge Talbott excitedly removing a cassette tape from her purse.

"Thinking of all those old disco moves back at the lodge reminded me of this song," she explained shyly to all of them. "It was one of my favorites."

Chris inserted the cassette for her, raising the volume and playing it, the group poised in a mixture of anticipation and perhaps dread as a bracing, euphoric song burst forth, a highly energized piece with a compulsory beat.

"Oh my *god*!" shrieked Vanessa. "Is that ABBA?"

"Yes!" Judge Talbott confirmed in pleased surprise, "Take a Chance on Me!"

She moved to begin dancing, bashfully stopping when no one else budged.

"Uh," Dr. Pendleton, still new at this, hastened around the packing crate to join her, Vanessa already jump-starting the group with unconstrained laughter.

"C'mon, Clodhopper!" she commanded with a ridiculous grin. "I gotta see you rock out to this! Move your punk ass!"

Grinning back, Chris immediately jumped into the song, romping playfully around her as Vanessa continued to laugh and cut loose, because it was all for fun.

Delighted, Judge Talbott began to sway to the vibrant music as if entranced, beaming when Dr. Pendleton rather stiffly attempted to follow her lead, his face flushed but smiling.

Sighing tautly, Mr. Crimpton had reluctantly joined in, grateful that the song was at least tolerable and even a bit appealing. Mr. McClintock had gladly stood up and commenced his slow-paced wobbling, bringing his hands together to keep time.

Father Gilchrist, watching in surprise as Mrs. Spindlewood got up and hobbled into the chaos, felt obliged to go after her, thus winding up integrated in the ragtag dance as well.

It was an eclectic, almost epileptic, mixture of disjointed movements, which, thrown all together, equated harmony.

As the Swedish hit evolved in its progressive, intensified stamina, Judge Talbott was thrilled to see that her choice was, likewise, a hit with the group. True, they had all agreed to share in anything, but she could tell that they were actually enjoying it. None of them fostered any delusions about the imperfectly ludicrous spectacle they all made, frenetically, almost convulsively twisting and skipping about, like a deranged kindergarten class reunion, and therein lay the magic—they didn't care. This was their time, their group, their way. The only judgment that mattered was their own.

Reflecting on this, she realized with a smile, that she liked the last sentiment. If only her legal associates could see her now. Her smile flourished as she stepped lively, working her arms. She loved this time of year; soon it would be Halloween, and she would bring everyone in the little trick-or-treat bundles she planned to make. Perhaps, they could all carve Jack-o-lanterns.

Although their suggestions review had dissolved into a virtual shouting match, she knew that an entire series of outings and picnics and retreats and dinners and field trips and get-togethers lay ahead of them, each to be enjoyed in time, even in spite of the quarrels that surely would accompany them. After all, they were dancing together now, weren't they? She took heart and excitement in looking forward to engaging that balance in the future.

Mr. Crimpton actually sensed his mood relaxing slightly as he focused on the surging pulsation of the music. It was not a bad song, he conceded, as he maneuvered his basic twist steps. It was, of course, silly for a bunch of grown-ups to behave in this way, but hell, what better excuse than their shared insanity? When you were crazy and finally faced the fact, you could do whatever the hell you wanted. He felt a smile tugging at his pinched features. If you're crazy and you know it, clap your hands. How was that? If Dr. Pendleton ever got a hold of it, he would probably incorporate it into one of his more profound therapeutic techniques, he thought drily, glancing over at the little psychologist as he clumsily tried to match Vanessa's exaggerated moves, the girl alternately dancing circles around him and clinging to him to keep from collapsing in hilarity, the doctor good-naturedly supporting her, while Chris grinned toothily from the side.

Those kids. Already they had approached him with the request of helping them learn to drive, a task that he would be forced to undertake in his spare time. As daunting as the favor would be to render, he could hardly say no, and perhaps, it would be easier to give lessons to kids who he could curse at or, indeed, with, and with whom, afterward, he could have a few beers. Well, no, perhaps they could; as for him, since he had started driving again, he was dry. If and when his nervous breakdown finally came, it would find him completely sober. Now, if he could only give up smoking.

Mr. McClintock, his handkerchief in hand, just in case he might inadvertently perspire, slowed his rotations a bit, feeling the taut pull of his shirt stays giving his legs the puppet-string sensation, literally putting a light, bouncing spring in each step.

He was pleasantly filled with doughnuts, the candy apple also adding to the dessert that so perfectly complimented the Pakistani restaurant he had reviewed earlier. His palette still tingled in savory recollection of the meal, even as it was already set for the Thai restaurant the *Village Vice* was sending him to tomorrow.

His broad features glowed as he envisioned the reaction of his new colleagues if they could only see him now. Perhaps, he was more "hip" than they had originally thought. He blinked, considering that such was actually true; he *was* more hip now. He was going to have all his trousers let out another inch or so the next chance he got.

It was amazing, he reflected in endless astonishment; whereas his last employer had in essence fired him for getting too big, his job security now seemed to lay in his gaining as much weight as he possibly could. It was the most incredible diet he had ever tried. What was more, even though he did not conduct his work there and had no reason to do so, he knew he could actually be comfortable in removing his jacket in the office of the *Village Vice*, for, if he did, no one, he knew confidently, was going to give him a second thought.

Vanessa, having been shoving Chris away from her and using Dr. Pendleton to make him good and jealous, noticed that Mrs. Spindlewood was on the floor and made it a point to keep her eye on the old woman as she executed some fragile moves to what must seem unimaginably foreign music to her. She was surprised to see the little old lady obviously enjoying it, her frumpy dress and tiny Mary Jane pumps swinging and tottering in beautifully anachronistic bliss, as if she had been magically transported, from some black-and-white dance floor of the past into their midst, the elderly woman's firm and unshakable grasp of her perception of reality so strong that she could just as easily teleport all of them back into her time and space just by being there, in her ghostly, magical way.

She was glad to see that Father Gilchrist was half-waltzing, half-flanking her, his sour smile patronizingly patient but empathetic. Trusting Mrs. Spindlewood to him, she militantly glanced around for Chris, spotting him prancing about in goofy unrestraint and springing toward him, grabbing him roughly, and then merely smiling up into his face, laughing at his smudged surprise, longing to kiss his lips clean and instead attacking him with a napkin. If he were clean-featured, after all, it made it more fun to make him a mess all over again later.

Chris submitted his face only, his lanky body still cavorting and kicking restlessly as she brusquely clasped his chin and then did give into a quick but well worthwhile kiss, pulling abruptly away, reveling in his torment, thrilling in her own. God, how she loved their little games.

She fixed him with a fiery gaze and beckoned for him to come to her, waiting for him to take one step before wadding up the napkin and tossing it in his face, watching him gape as it bounced off his forehead and fell to the floor. She jabbed her finger at it savagely and he scowled, bending to pick it up, Vanessa's foot instantly slamming into his rump. *Ha! What a dork!*

Jumping upright, he turned to grab her for this intolerable action, his mouth clamping shut as he observed her somehow already on the other side of the room, dancing obliviously with Mr. Crimpton, as if she had been with him all night and Chris had never existed. His cheeks burning, he threw himself into the dance again, trying to control his excitement.

God, how he loved it when she drove him crazy like that. She was in especially feisty spirits tonight because she had given him a present earlier, a punk rock album of a band called "The Damned," her reasons for getting it for him in part due to the especially sweetly messy album cover, depicting three leering punks bearing the remains of a cream pie. She had coyly told him that the two of them would have fun making their own version of the cover photograph, an idea that richly appealed to him. This album cover, coupled with that of the "Weird Al" Yankovik album, would come to represent the two of them as a couple, as one. Vanessa had melted Chris's heart yet again, when she had him pull up the "Polka Party" album from his collection, flipping it over to its reverse side, which showed a young punk couple gaping in wonder at a concept foreign to the mosh pit.

"That's us, Chris," she had whispered, watching as his face became radiant with joy at the idea that she not only accepted his musical paradox, but wanted to make it her own as well, to share in it with him.

The painfully slow progression of their relationship continued to yield more discoveries, more pleasures, more insight into each other as they shared their thoughts and ideas, dreams, and desires. The notion of taking an apartment together was, of course, somewhat scary, in an awe-inspiring sort of way; but they knew that this was as it should be; and they looked forward to the gradually unfolding adventure that the prospect would afford them.

Licking his sticky lips, Chris felt his heart leap when Vanessa suddenly flew back toward him, moving enticingly to grab him, this time, his arms moving first. Holding her firmly even as she struggled to free herself, he lowered his Mohawk and nuzzled its bristly crest gently against her face, knowing how she loved its ticklishness.

Lifting his head, he peered expectantly down at her, finding her smiling approvingly up into his face, and he gave himself into her arms, his heart singing in the happiness that he felt every hour, every single day now of his previously pathetic life, so tearfully grateful that he had such a love and such a friend, an all-around playmate with whom to hold hands and confront the future, even if it were riddled with pitfalls and misfortune, for at this moment, it resembled nothing so much as a rainbow-dappled playground of colors and textures stretching endlessly before them, inviting them to explore and enjoy its everlastingly fresh potential.

They held each other and breathed together, standing as one among the chaos of the dancing, their happiness flowing electrically between them, even once they separated and resumed their own untamed steps, recommencing their game of stealth and rejection.

Father Gilchrist had paused in his own dignified and exaggerated motions, to place Mrs. Spindlewood in front of Dr. Pendleton before bowing like a chaperone and withdrawing to sit down, the doctor smiling falteringly and then carefully moving to dance with the hazily smiling old woman, more than willing to slow down a little, the resoundingly vivid rhythm of the song inviting a much more upbeat approach than he could maintain, although he was very impressed and singularly pleased with the gusto of the other members. It was so rewarding to have this feature in their meetings now, not merely as an outlet for aggressions or a method of overcoming shyness or the fear of behaving foolishly or even in an imbalanced way, the bedlam of their dancing most definitely allowing for that, but also as a peace-keeping process, for whereas they had been conversing as dysfunctionally as usual, they were now united in their common bond of musical mayhem. There was certainly something to be said for its therapeutic merit, he knew, even if their grace and agility were not of the most conventional sort. *Yes, indeed, choreography and orchestration.*

Sitting off to the side, Father Gilchrist exhaled slowly, thinking very much the same thing. Arthur Murray would collapse on the spot if he were there to behold this scene, he mused wryly, nonetheless enjoying the view as he rested.

As his mind wandered, he thought of Deacon Richard and his dour expression took on a slight, sour smile, a sudden realization occurring to him. Father Gilchrist's recent reemergence from apathy and his rejoining of the human race were directly due to his having attended these group sessions, an action that never, but *never*, would have transpired if he had not been forced to go in the first place.

In short, Deacon Richard had been right.

That meddlesome little prig and his presumptuous recommendations were directly responsible for his current disposition. His wintry brows lifted as he pursed his lips, introspectively impressed. Even an idiot could hit an occasional bull's eye, he supposed. That might even be worth a special prayer of thanks tonight.

He watched as Vanessa continued to torture Chris, delightedly encouraging his dufousy clodhopping antics, Judge Talbott joyfully gyrating nearby, and Mr. Crimpton stoically twisting and grinding. Mr. McClintock's girth rotated and pivoted atop his small spritely feet as Mrs. Spindlewood continued to toddle happily in front of Dr. Pendleton, who smiled and flushed, trying to keep time with the reverberating nuances of the song's compellingly bounding momentum.

They were a colorful, mismatched bunch, he reflected, in something approaching satisfaction, for how much less colorful and how much more mismatched were they before they had stumbled unwittingly into each other's embrace?

Having been at odds with the rest of the world's own exclusive brand of insanity, these lonely survivors appeared to have found their haven in the company of their fellow mis-fits.

He grimaced. All these lonely people. Where they all came from was anybody's guess. Where did they all belong? That much was obvious. They all belonged here, by themselves with each other; alone together. Father Gilchrist smiled at this notion, gradually chuckling and then laughing, genuinely laughing his first real laugh in a very, very long time.

Epilogue

"AND THAT IS A COPY of a restaurant review written by one of our members," Dr. Pendleton was explaining to Dr. Whittaker, the group photo album laid open upon his lavish, immaculate desk. "His column appears in the…uh, in a local publication, uh, and this is a picture of the clergyman in our group, uh, during one of his sermons."

"Oh?" inquired Dr. Whittaker, glancing up at him over his precise gold-rimmed spectacles. "What was the subject of his sermon during the service?"

"Uh, I'm not entirely certain," Dr. Pendleton hesitantly allowed. "That photograph was taken shortly before he asked us all to leave." He paused, clearing his throat uncomfortably. "Uh, but, of course, it was good to know that he was, uh, back in the pulpit again, uh, so to speak."

He quickly turned the page, wincing slightly. "Oh, and, uh, this is a sort of, uh, satirical version of a, uh, punk rock album cover made by our two youngest members, uh, just, you know, for fun."

"Well, how creative and explorative," Dr. Whittaker surmised graciously. "What medium did they opt to use? Is that plaster of paris?"

"Uh, no, I think it's, uh, whipped cream," Dr. Pendleton quickly closed the album, glancing over at the regal clock mounted on the paneled wall and standing upright, tucking the album under one arm as Dr. Whittaker interlaced his splendid fingers and smiled up at him.

"Well, Dr. Pendleton, as always, I am endlessly impressed with your endeavors with this exceptionally singular therapy group," he pronounced majestically, Dr. Pendleton beaming at this very high praise. "Likewise impressive is your perseverance with what was originally intended to be a purely extracurricular exercise. After all, it has been over two months since you instituted this little group, and yet you continue to pursue it so devoutly!"

Dr. Pendleton shifted, blushing as his gaze slipped to the floor. "Well, I know my whole intention was to get back into private practice, and that has been going quite well, but…" He paused, almost giving into a shrug. "I have found a great deal of fulfillment both from my supervision of this group and from my participation in it."

Dr. Whittaker nodded, beginning to fill his pipe. "Well, Doctor, I heartily applaud your efforts. I think that we might all take a lesson from your exemplary tenacity." He paused to light the pipe, inhaling thoughtfully and then gesturing toward him with its delicate stem. "Do you know the progress you have made with these seven people coupled with the very unique and somewhat unconventional circumstances that accompanied your variegated approach to them, individually and on the whole, and the confidence that they, in turn, placed in you leads me to believe that you may possibly be on the verge of setting any number of precedents in the psychotherapeutic field."

He puffed on the pipe as Dr. Pendleton stared back in surprise at this assessment.

"Well, I don't know about that, Dr. Whittaker," he replied, uncertainly flattered.

Dr. Whittaker gestured lightly. "Only time will tell, Dr. Pendleton," he responded, rising from his throne-like chair. "You could very easily be on the threshold of making psychological history," he declared, smiling broadly down at him and extending a tapered hand. "In any event, I shall continue to take a professional interest in your ongoing progress in the future, as a staunch acquaintance and professional colleague!"

His smile radiant, Dr. Pendleton gratefully shook his hand, inhaling deeply as he picked up his little attaché case and strode toward the door to the office, pausing on his way out, when Dr. Whittaker called after him, having reseated himself, puffing introspectively.

"I was just curious, Dr. Pendleton," he explained at length. "The name. I like to think that I would have undertaken this project with the same style and alacrity that you have exhibited, save for in one respect, that being the name... 'Mis-fits Anonymous.'"

He paused, stroking his Van Dyke beard thoughtfully. "It is rather a candid and somewhat extreme designation, don't you think? I, myself, most likely would have elected for something a bit more... streamlined and refined, I think." He nodded musingly. "Are you quite certain about the name?"

Dr. Pendleton glanced from the older man to the photo album he held, its gilt-edged front having finally been embossed with the gold letters identifying their group. His eyes then travelled pleasantly around Dr. Whittaker's sumptuous office, taking in its subtle hues and tones, the doctor's trim spectacles, his elegant fingers, his sterling sophistication, his gaze then dropping toward the floor, resting on his battered brown attaché case and his stodgy brown penny loafers, his stubby fingers poised upon the sleek doorknob, his focus then meeting Dr. Whittaker's once more, as he slowly began to nod.

"Oh yes, Doctor. I'm sure," he stated firmly, smiling and flushing in modest pride. "That name fits us perfectly. In fact, I can't think of anything more suitable."

Nodding cordially, he withdrew from the office and headed down the hallway, his pace quickening a bit as his features displayed a hint of anticipation.

There was a meeting scheduled for that evening; it was only a few hours away, and he didn't want to be late. He still had to pick up the doughnuts on the way.

About the Author

In addition to writing this book, Mr. E. likewise experienced it. A Mis-Fit, himself, he sees this work as an opportunity to showcase that the fundamental means of survival rests in balancing ones' imbalances with the purest and most instinctual form of commiseration, humor, and that by way of the Gift of Laughter which we give to each other, we can find the courage to be crazy enough to live in this world and just sane enough to get by, day by day, with, one hopes, a smile...

CPSIA information can be obtained
at www.ICGtesting.com
Printed in the USA
LVHW030332151019
634227LV00001B/14/P